The Red Sphinx

ALEXANDRE DUMAS

The Red Sphinx

{or}

The Comte de Moret

A Sequel to *The Three Musketeers*

EDITED AND TRANSLATED
BY LAWRENCE ELLSWORTH

PEGASUS BOOKS
NEW YORK LONDON

THE RED SPHINX

Pegasus Books Ltd
148 West 37th Street, 13th Fl.
New York, NY 10018

The Red Sphinx, by Alexandre Dumas, Translated by Lawrence Ellsworth
Translation and Original Material Copyright 2017 © by Lawrence Schick
Front cover art: detail of "The Duel After the Masquerade" (1859) by Jean-Léon Gérôme
Back cover art © 2017 by Lee Moyer, after a 1900 phototypogravure by Maurice Leloir

First Pegasus Books hardcover edition January 2017

Interior design by Sabrina Plomitallo-González, Pegasus Books

ISBN: 978-1-68177-297-4

10 9 8 7 6 5 4 3 2 1

Printed in the United States of America
Distributed by W. W. Norton & Company, Inc.

Other Titles of Interest from Pegasus Books

By Alexandre Dumas

THE LAST CAVALIER

By Lawrence Ellsworth

THE BIG BOOK OF SWASHBUCKLING ADVENTURE

Dedications

Alexandre Dumas:

To Monsieur Dmitri Pavlovitch Narischkine

Lawrence Ellsworth:

Dedicated to my son, Wyatt—and about time, too

CONTENTS

INTRODUCTION

Everyone has heard of the great French writer Alexandre Dumas, and of his most famous creations, *The Count of Monte Cristo* and *The Three Musketeers*. You've most likely read *The Three Musketeers* or at least seen one of its many film or TV adaptations, and are therefore familiar with the dashing d'Artagnan and his friends Athos, Porthos, and Aramis. You're probably aware that the novel spawned a series of sequels, culminating in the most famous, *The Man in the Iron Mask*, likewise filmed many times over.

So why, until now, have you never heard of *The Red Sphinx*—especially if, as advertised, it qualifies as "a sequel to *The Three Musketeers*"?

Let me tell you a story.

Our tale's protagonist is a man of endless energy and talent, a bigger-than-life personality whose work was an international sensation, who lived large and loved without limit, earning fortune after fortune and squandering it all, on theaters and publishing houses, on mansions and mistresses, reveling in drama, haute cuisine, and revolutionary politics.

His name, of course, was Alexandre Dumas.

The young Dumas began his writing career in the late 1820s as a poet and playwright; his first melodrama, in 1829, was a hit big enough to enable him to write full time, and throughout the 1830s he turned out play after play, each more shocking and lurid than the one before. At first he gave his dramas contemporary settings, but then he turned to historical sources, and late in the decade he began turning his stories into prose. At that time, periodicals publishing serial fiction were just coming into vogue, and the episodic format was perfect for Dumas, trained by writing for the theater to create vivid scenes punctuated by pithy dialogue.

After a few modest successes with prose serials, in 1844 he knocked it out of the park with *The Three Musketeers,* followed the next year by *The Count of Monte Cristo.* Both books were worldwide sensations, and for the next fifteen years he could do no wrong; he wrote novel after successful novel, including such famous tales as *The Corsican Brothers, The Women's War, The Queen's Necklace, The Black Tulip,* the *Valois* trilogy, and a story called *The Dove,* about the half-brother of King Louis XIII, the Comte de Moret. These books were translated into over a dozen languages and were bestsellers in every publishing market, including Great Britain and, especially, the United States.

But Dumas was a social animal who couldn't resist involving himself in politics, and his sharp and impulsive wit made him many enemies. In 1851 his patron, King Louis-Philippe, was ousted by Louis-Napoléon Bonaparte; the new President of France was no friend to Dumas, and the author thought it wise to leave the country for other climes. He moved to Belgium, then Russia, and finally Italy, where he involved himself in the tumult of Italian independence. He never stopped writing, but his output dwindled, and even in France his sales declined to a trickle. In his home country, the great social lion had become . . . unfashionable.

In 1864, he returned to Paris, determined to recoup his reputation and fortunes. He'd been writing books about his travels in Russia and Italy, but thought he should return to historical adventure tales, the source of his greatest successes. In 1865, Jules Noriac, editor of the weekly paper *Les Nouvelles,* obliged by asking Dumas if he would write a serial revisiting the setting of his earliest success, *The Three Musketeers.* Dumas, who had not lost his fascination with the reign of Louis XIII and his prime minister, Cardinal Richelieu, was quick to accept. The result was a new serial titled *Le Comte de Moret,* a swashbuckling tale of King Louis, his adventurous half-brother Moret, Moret's love Isabelle de Lautrec, and the great statesman Cardinal Richelieu.

Especially Cardinal Richelieu; the novel is as much about Richelieu as it is about the Comte de Moret, and eventually it came to be known better as *The Red Sphinx*. The focus on the Cardinal explains why Dumas refused to include appearances by d'Artagnan and his three Musketeer friends, as they would surely have walked away with the story. Besides, Dumas had already written over a million words about d'Artagnan and company. Why repeat himself?

So Dumas returned to the court of Louis XIII and got down to business. Writing rapidly, for six months he spun out a tale of adventure, politics, and romance in the classic manner—but the decades had taken their toll, the writer was ailing, and *Les Nouvelles* stuttered and then stopped. And so, at that point, did the story: after writing nine-tenths of the novel, Dumas never completed it.

One would think that in such dire need, and after so much good work, surely Dumas could have mustered the effort to finish the novel so it could find book publication, like so many novels before it. But he just never found an ending for it.

It's speculation on this editor's part, but I think I know one compelling reason why. To my mind it's because it's a problem Dumas had already solved when he wrote his novella *The Dove* fifteen years earlier. In that self-contained, standalone tale, he'd already presented his ending to the story of Richelieu, the Comte de Moret, and his lady love Isabelle de Lautrec. *The Dove,* though little known because its shortness made it inconvenient for book publication, gave the question of the fate of Moret and Isabelle a thoroughly satisfying conclusion.

So he'd been there and done that. Why repeat himself?

In this edition, for the first time, the reader can find Alexandre Dumas's late, great novel *The Red Sphinx* completed by the inclusion of *The Dove.* I think you'll like it.

PART I
The Red Sphinx

I

The Inn of the Painted Beard

Toward the end of the year of our Lord 1628, the traveler who came, for business or pleasure, to spend a few days in the capital of what was poetically called the Realm of the Lilies could depend on hospitality, with or without a letter of introduction, at the Inn of the Painted Beard. There in the Rue de l'Homme-Armé, in the house of Maître Soleil, he was sure to find good cheer, good food, and a good room.

Though next door to a wretched cabaret on the corner that had, since some time in the Middle Ages, given the lane its name thanks to its sign depicting an armed man, there was no mistaking the Painted Beard. That inn, to which we now introduce our readers, was far more prominent, and attracted travelers by a sign so majestic that, once seen, none would go farther.

There, squeaking in the tiniest breeze on a rod tipped with a gilded crescent, was a tinplate sign that depicted a Grand Turk sporting a beard of the brightest hue, justifying the strange name of the Inn of the Painted Beard.

Add to this the rebus adorning the front of the house above the entrance:

Which meant, taking into account both sign and rebus:

AT THE PAINTED BEARD

SOLEIL HOSTS BOTH YOU AND YOUR HORSE

The Painted Beard would vie, if it could, for seniority with the Armed Man Cabaret—but in the interest of honesty, we must admit the latter was there first.

Barely two years earlier, the inn's former owner, Claude-Cyprien Mélangeoie, had sold his establishment to Master Blaise-Guillaume Soleil for the sum of a thousand *pistoles*. And the moment the contract was settled, this new owner had called in the painters and the decorators, despite the exterior rights of the nesting swallows and the interior rights of the secret spiders. He refurbished the façade, renovated the guest chambers, and finally, to the surprise of his astonished neighbors, who wondered where Maître Soleil could have found the money for it, emblazoned that rebus we've had the honor to present to our readers.

Shaking their heads from right to left, the old women of Rue Sainte-Croix-de-la-Bretonnerie and of Rue des Blancs-Manteaux had predicted, in accord with the sibylline qualities of their advanced age, that these embellishments would be unlucky for the inn, whose customs and appearance had been established for centuries. But despite these old ladies, and to the astonishment of those who took them for oracles, their predictions of disaster were false. On the contrary, the establishment thrived, thanks to an entirely new clientele which, though without meaning to disrespect the old ways, nonetheless increased and even doubled the trade of the Inn of the Painted Beard. Meanwhile, the swallows quietly built new nests in the corners of the windows, and the spiders no less quietly wove new webs in the corners of the chambers.

Gradually, light was cast on this great mystery: the rumor went around that Madame Marthe-Pélagie Soleil—alert, charming, self-possessed, still young and pretty at barely thirty years old—was the foster sister of one of the great ladies of the Court, whose funds—or the funds of another, even more powerful lady—had been advanced to help establish Maître Soleil. Furthermore, it was this foster sister who sent the Inn of the Painted Beard its new clientele: noble foreigners who now frequented the streets of the glassmakers' quarter around Rue Sainte-Avoye, previously almost deserted.

What was truth and what was invention in these rumors? This story will tell us.

We start by recounting what took place in the common room of the Inn of the Painted Beard on December 5, 1628—that is, four days after the return of Cardinal Richelieu from the famous siege of La Rochelle, which provided one of the episodes of our novel *The Three Musketeers*. It was four o'clock in the afternoon, which, given the height of the houses and the way they leaned toward each other, meant that twilight was already falling in the Rue de l'Homme-Armé.

At that time, the common room was occupied by only one person, a regular of the house—but this person occupied as much space as four ordinary drinkers.

He had already emptied one mug of wine and was halfway through a second, lying across three chairs and shredding with his spurs the wicker seat of the fourth, while with the point of his dagger he carved a miniature hopscotch pattern into the table. His rapier, whose pommel was never far from his hand, extended along his thigh and between his crossed legs.

His face was just visible, thanks to the last ray of light that filtered through the narrow mullioned window and found its way under his broad hat. He was in his late thirties, with the dark hair, eyebrows, and mustache of the sun-touched men of the South. There was steel in his eye and scorn on his lips, which curled like those of a tiger to reveal bright white teeth. His straight nose and prominent chin indicated a strong will. His animal jaw reflected a reckless courage that wasn't a matter of choice, but rather the heritage of the carnivore. Finally his face, rather handsome, displayed a brutal and frightening candor that was immune to lies, tricks, or treason, and was no stranger to anger or violence.

His costume was that of the petty gentility of the time: half civil, half military, doublet open to show the sleeves, shirt puffing out over the belt, with broad knee-breeches and tall boots from the knees down. All clean and, though not luxurious, worn with ease and—almost—elegance.

Two or three times the host, Maître Soleil, passed through the common room. Doubtless in hopes of avoiding an outburst of anger or violence, he didn't complain about the double devastation in which the man seemed so absorbed. On the contrary, he smiled as agreeably as he could—easy for this host, whose face was as placid as that of the drinker was mobile and irritable.

However, appearing for his third or fourth time, Maître Soleil could no longer refrain from addressing his customer. "Well, my gentleman," he said in a benevolent tone, "it seems to me that lately your business has suffered; if that goes on, this merry fellow, as you call him"—he pointed at the regular's sword—"risks rusting in his sheath."

"Indeed," replied the drinker in a mocking tone, "and that worries you because of the ten or twelve bottles I owe you for?"

"Jesus above, Monsieur! I swear you could owe me for fifty bottles, or even a hundred, and I wouldn't lose sleep over it! I know you well! For eighteen months you've frequented my inn, and I wouldn't think of worrying about you. But you know, in every trade there are ups and downs, and the return of His Eminence the cardinal-duke means that, for a few weeks at least, all swords must remain in their sheaths. I say for a few weeks, because no such limit lasts long in Paris, and soon he and the king will set out again to carry the war beyond the mountains. Once more it will be as it was during the siege of La Rochelle: to the devil with the edicts! And gold will once more fill your purse."

"Well, that's where you're wrong, Maître Soleil. Because yesterday and today I plied my honorable trade as usual, though each time as the day faded, Phoebe declined to bless me. But as for the cash that so concerns you, you see, or rather you hear"—the drinker jingled his pouch—"there are still a few coins in my purse, if the sound is to be believed. So if I don't pay my bill right here and now, it's only because I hope to have it settled by the first gentleman who comes to engage my services. And perhaps," he continued, turning from Maître Soleil and peering out the stained glass of the window, "perhaps my new employer will be that one there coming from the Rue Sainte-Croix-de-la-Bretonnerie, nose in the air, like a man looking for the sign of the Painted Beard. In fact, he's seen it, and couldn't be happier. Eclipse yourself, Maître Soleil, as it's clear this gentleman wants to speak with me. Back to your kitchen, and leave men of the sword to their business! But first light the lamps—within a few minutes this place will be dark as a tomb, and I like to see the faces of those I do business with."

The drinker was not mistaken, because just as his host, hastening to obey him, disappeared through the kitchen door, a figure, silhouetted by the last light of the day, appeared in the street doorway.

The newcomer, before venturing into the doubtful twilight of the common room of the Inn of the Painted Beard, peered cautiously into its depths; then, seeing that the room was occupied by only one individual, and that this individual was probably the one he sought, he drew his cloak up to his eyes and approached him.

If the cloaked man feared to be recognized, his caution was rewarded, for just then Maître Soleil, glowing like the star that bore his name, reentered the room with a lit candle in each hand, which he set in two tinplate sconces on the wall.

The stranger watched with an impatience he didn't try to conceal.

Obviously he preferred the room's former twilight, a gloom that would further thicken as night fell. However, he said nothing, satisfied to watch the activities of Maître Soleil over the edge of his cloak. It was only after the kitchen door had closed again behind the host that he addressed the other occupant, saying, "Are you the one called Étienne Latil, formerly with the Duc d'Épernon, later a captain in Flanders?"

The drinker, who was lifting his mug to his mouth as the question was asked, looked as if the tone of the question didn't quite satisfy him. He turned and said, "If I did answer to that name, what would that be to you?"

And he finished lifting the mug to his mouth.

The cloaked man gave the drinker as long as he liked to tend to his mug. When the empty mug was back on the table, the man said, somewhat sharply, "I have the honor to ask if you are the Chevalier Étienne Latil."

"Ah! Now that's better," the drinker said, nodding approval.

"Do me the honor to answer."

"Very well. Yes, Monsieur, I am Étienne Latil in person. What can I do for you?"

"I have a proposition for you."

"A proposition!"

"Yes, a good one; excellent, even."

"Pardon me—I acknowledge the names Étienne and Latil apply to me; but before we go further, permit my caution to echo yours: whom do I have the honor to address?"

"My name isn't important unless my words suit your ears."

"You're wrong, Monsieur, if you think I'll sing to that song. I may be a younger son, but I am nonetheless noble, and whoever referred you to me must have mentioned that I work for neither peasants nor the common bourgeoisie. If you want me on behalf of some carpenter, or some merchant neighbor of yours, count me out. I don't involve myself in such affairs."

"Well, I don't wish to tell you my name, Monsieur Latil, but I have no problem with revealing my title. Here's the ring I use as a seal, and if you can recognize a blazon, this should acquaint you with my rank."

And drawing a ring from his finger, he passed it to the bravo, who took it to the window to examine in the last light of the day.

"Ah-ha," he said, "an onyx, engraved in the style of Florence. You are Italian, and a marquis, Monsieur. The vine and three pearls indicate wealth. The gem alone, mounting aside, is worth forty *pistoles*."

"Enough to warrant a talk?" asked the stranger, replacing the ring on a hand long, white, and fine. A second, gloved hand, appeared and re-gloved the first.

"Quite enough, and it proves your bona fides, Monsieur le Marquis—but as down payment on the bargain we're sure to conclude, it would be gallant of you to pay the price of the ten or twelve bottles I owe to this cabaret. I don't make a condition of this, but I'm an orderly man, and if I had an accident during our enterprise I'd hate to leave a debt behind me, no matter how small."

"That's no problem."

"And it would top off your gallantry if, as the two mugs in front of me are empty, you could summon two more to replace them," said the drinker. "My throat is dry and I feel a need to moisten it—arid words just scorch the mouth as they leave it."

"Maître Soleil!" called the stranger, as he wrapped himself even further in his cloak.

Maître Soleil appeared as if he'd been right behind the door, ready to obey whatever commands were given him.

"This gentleman's bill, and two mugs of wine—your best."

The landlord of the Painted Beard disappeared as quickly as if he were an Olympic Circus clown dropping through a trap door, and reappeared almost at once with two mugs, one of which he deposited in front of the stranger, the other before Étienne Latil.

"*Voilà*," he said. "As for the bill, it is one *pistole*, five *sous*, and two *deniers*."

"Here's a gold crown worth two and a half *pistoles*," said the stranger, tossing a coin on the table. As the landlord reached for his pouch to make change, the stranger said, "Don't bother. Keep the balance on behalf of monsieur, here."

"No mistaking it," murmured the bravo. "His words betray the merchant from a league away. These Florentines are all tradesmen, and even their dukes are moneylenders as bad as the Jews of Frankfurt or the Lombards of Milan. However, as our host said, times are hard, and one can't always choose one's clients."

Meanwhile, Maître Soleil was withdrawing behind bow after bow. He'd found that lords were rarely eager to pay debts, so he regarded his new guest with profound admiration.

II

What Came of the Proposition
the Stranger Made to Étienne Latil

The stranger followed Maître Soleil with his eyes until the door had once more closed behind him. When he was quite sure that he was alone with Étienne Latil, he said, "And now, since you know you're not dealing with a baker, are you inclined, my dear Monsieur, to help a generous cavalier rid himself of a rival?"

"I am often made such offers, and I rarely refuse. But before going further, I think I should acquaint you with my fees."

"I know them: ten *pistoles* to act as second in an ordinary duel, twenty-five to act as direct challenger, under whatever pretext, if your employer doesn't fight—and one hundred *pistoles* to pick a fight that results in an immediate meeting with the designated target, who is to be killed on the spot."

"Killed on the spot," repeated the sell-sword. "If he doesn't die, I return the money, regardless of wounds inflicted or received."

"I know that. I also know that you are not only an expert swordsman, but a man of honor."

Étienne Latil inclined his head slightly, as if accepting only what was due. Indeed, he was a man of honor—in his way.

"Thus," continued the stranger, "I know I can count on you."

"Slowly; don't rush it. As an Italian, you must know the proverb, *chi va piano, va sano*—what goes slowly, goes well. Before proceeding, I need to know the nature of the business, the target in question, and which category of service you require. And the cash must be paid up front. I've been in this game too long to be taken advantage of."

"Here are one hundred *pistoles*." The stranger dropped a purse on the table. "You may count them, if you wish to be sure."

Despite the temptation, the sell-sword didn't touch the purse—he barely glanced at it. "It seems you'll want the deluxe service," he said with a hint of sarcasm and a slight curl of the lip. "An immediate meeting."

"To end in death," the stranger answered, unable to keep a slight tremor from his voice.

"Then you need only state the name, rank, and habits of your rival. It's my practice to act honestly in these affairs, so I need to be thoroughly acquainted with the person I'm to face. As you may or may not know, everything depends on the manner in which one first crosses steel. You don't engage a rustic from the provinces the way you do a Parisian coxcomb, or a guardsman of the king or of monsieur the cardinal. If you don't tell me everything, or if I'm misinformed, and I end up engaging the target improperly, it might be your rival who kills me—and that would suit neither of us. Furthermore, the risks are not just in the meeting, particularly if one challenges a person of high rank. If the affair causes a big stink, the least I can expect is to spend several months in prison. Such places are dank and unhealthy, good drink is costly there, and as a result you will incur additional expenses. All these considerations must be taken into account. But unless you'd prefer me as a second," the sell-sword concluded with some disdain, "running the same risks I do, there's a price to be paid—is there not?"

"That cannot be. In this case, for me to challenge is impossible—though, by my faith as a gentleman, I regret it."

This answer, made in a tone both firm and calm, displaying neither weakness nor bluster, made Latil begin to suspect that he'd been mistaken, that he was dealing with a man who really had no recourse but to employ someone else's sword, and that only serious considerations kept his own in its sheath. His opinion improved even more when the stranger nonchalantly added, "As to the question of an additional twenty, thirty, or even fifty *pistoles*, you can expect me to do what is right without argument."

"Then let's get to it," said Étienne Latil. "Who is your enemy, and how shall I come at him? But first of all, his name."

"His name matters little," replied the man in the cloak. "This evening we'll go together to the Rue de la Cerisaie. I'll show you the door of the house he'll emerge from around two hours after midnight. You will wait there and, as no one but he will come out in the early hours of the morning, a mistake is impossible. Besides, I'll tell you how to recognize him."

The sell-sword shook his head, and then—reluctantly—pushed the purse of gold across the table. "Not good enough," he sighed. "I said it once, and I repeat it now: I have to know who I'm dealing with."

"Truly," the stranger said impatiently, "you have too many scruples, my dear Monsieur Latil. Your adversary isn't known to be in Paris—he hasn't been here in years, and is believed by everyone to still be in Italy. Besides, you'll have him on the ground before he ever gets a look at your face, and to be completely safe you could wear a mask."

"You know, Monsieur," said Latil, resting his elbows on the table and his head on his hands, "your affair begins to sound like an assassination."

The stranger was silent. Latil once more shook his head and slid the purse across the table. "In that case, I'm not the man for you. That kind of work doesn't suit me."

"Was it while you served the Duc d'Épernon that you learned all these scruples, my pretty friend?" asked the stranger.

"No," replied Latil, "it was because of my scruples that I left his service."

"Oh, I see. You couldn't abide working beside the infamous Simon."

This Simon was one of the old duke's notorious torturers. "Simon," Latil said with scorn, "was a man of the whip. I am a man of the sword."

"All right," said the stranger, "I see that in this case the sum should be doubled. Perhaps two hundred *pistoles* will assuage your scruples."

"You're missing the point. I don't work from ambush. You'll find people who do that sort of thing over toward Saint-Pierre-aux-Bœufs, where the cutthroats congregate. You must recognize, above all, that I do my work in my fashion, not yours—and that how I manage it is solely my affair, so long as I remove your rival. That's what you want, isn't it—to have him removed from your path? As long as he's no longer in your way, you're satisfied."

"I can't have it done your way."

"*Ventrebleu*! I am disgusted. Perhaps the Latils of Compignac don't date back to the Crusades like the Rohans or the Montmorency family, but we're honest nobility, and though I may be the cadet of the family, I'm as noble as my elder brother."

"I can't do it your way, I tell you."

"Am I to just assassinate a man in such a fashion? I could never hold my head up in good company again!"

"It's not assassination."

"Oh? The cardinal might not see it your way."

As answer, the stranger drew two rolls of coins from his pouch, one hundred *pistoles* in each, and placed them on the table next to the purse—but in doing so, his cloak fell open, and Latil could see the stranger was a hunchback.

"Three hundred *pistoles*," said the gentleman hunchback. "Does that calm your scruples and put an end to your objections?"

Latil shook his head and sighed. "You're very persuasive, Monsieur, and it's hard to resist you. Indeed, I'd have to have a heart like a rock to disappoint a lord in such a predicament, so let's try to find a compromise. This is certainly plenty; I couldn't ask for more."

"I don't know what else I could offer," replied the stranger, "other than two more rolls like these two. But," the stranger added, "I must warn you, that's all I have. Take it or leave it."

"Ah! Tempter!" murmured Latil, swayed by the purse and four rolls of gold. "You'll have me betray my principles and forego my practices."

"Then let's go," said the gentleman. "We can finish our discussion on the way."

"What can I do? You're so persuasive, no one could resist. So, then: we go to the Rue de la Cerisaie, correct?"

"Yes."

"Tonight?"

"If possible."

"You'll have to be clear; I can't afford a mistake."

"Just so. Moreover, now that you're being reasonable, and at my side, bought and paid for. . . ."

"Almost: I haven't yet put the money in my pouch."

"What, more trouble?"

"No, I'm just stating some exceptions. *Exceptis excipiendis,* as we said at the College of Libourne. . . ."

"State your exceptions."

"First: the target is neither the king nor the cardinal."

"No; their enemy, if anything."

"No ally of the king?"

"Hardly. Though, I must say, a favorite of the queen."

"No retainer of old Cardinal Bérulle?"

"No, he's a man of only twenty-three."

"Ah . . . then he's in love with Her Majesty."

"Possibly. Is that all your exceptions?"

"My God, yes!" Latil began transferring the gold from the table to his pouch. "Our poor queen. Nothing but bad luck for her since they killed her Duke of Buckingham. . . ."

"So, then," interrupted the gentleman hunchback, doubtless hoping to put an end to Latil's vacillations and get him moving, "you're the man to kill the Comte de Moret."

Latil froze. "The Comte de Moret?"

"The Comte de Moret," repeated the stranger. "He wasn't among your exceptions, I think?"

"Antoine de Bourbon?" Latil said, placing his hands on the table.

"Yes, Antoine de Bourbon."

"The son of our good King Henri?"

"The bastard son, you should say."

"Royal bastards are often the true sons of kings, born as they are by love rather than duty." He shook his head. "Take back your gold, Monsieur. I won't raise my hand against a Son of France."

"The child of Jacqueline de Bueil is not of the royal house."

"He's still a son of Henri IV." Rising, Latil crossed his arms and fixed his eyes on the stranger. "Do you know, Monsieur, that I was there when his father was killed?"

"You?"

"On the running-board of the carriage, as page to the Duc d'Épernon. The assassin had to shove me aside to get to the king. Thanks to me, perhaps, he failed to get away. I'm the one who grabbed him by the lapel and held him, held him . . ."

Latil showed his hands, patterned with scars. "Here are the marks from his knife. The blood of our great king mixed with my own. And I'm the one you try to hire to assassinate his son! I'm no Jacques Clément nor Ravaillac, no king-slayer—but you, Monsieur, are a miserable wretch. Take back your gold before I nail you to the wall like a venomous snake!"

"Silence, lackey," said the stranger, recoiling a step, "or I'll make you silent."

"You call me lackey? You, an assassin? I'm no policeman, and it's not my business to keep you from hiring someone else who might actually do it, but I'll thwart both your plot and your ugly self. *En garde,* you wretch!"

And with these words, Latil drew his rapier and lunged.

But the stranger, though backing away, was by no means in retreat. Latil's thrust, strong and skilled, and intended to nail its target to the wall like a butterfly, just missed its mark. The stranger was on his guard, and replied with such a series of thrusts and rapid feints that the sell-sword had to draw on all his skill, caution, and coolness. Latil even, as though delighted to unexpectedly meet a skill that could rival his own, seemed to want to prolong the fight for the sheer love of the art. He fenced with his opponent as if in an academy of arms, prolonging the bout until his opponent's fatigue or some error would give him the opportunity to employ one of those final thrusts, attacks he knew so well and could use to such advantage.

However, the irascible hunchback, less patient than Latil and tired of making no headway—in fact, feeling more pressed than he liked, and seeing himself cut off from the door, cried out suddenly, "To me, friends! Help, I'm being assassinated!"

The gentleman hunchback had barely made his cry when three men, who were waiting for him outside the door to the street, rushed into the common room and attacked the unfortunate Latil. Turning to face them, he had no defense against the boot put in his back by his first adversary. Meanwhile, one of his attackers thrust from the other side. Suddenly he took two sword wounds, one running him through from chest to back, the other from back to chest.

Latil fell in a heap to the floor.

III

In Which the Gentleman Hunchback Realizes His Error in Desiring the Death of the Comte de Moret

After the execution there was silence for a few moments, as rapiers were wiped quietly and carefully and returned to their sheaths.

But then, thanks to the noise that preceded the silence—the cries of Latil and the clashing of swords—Maître Soleil and his cooks rushed in through the kitchen door, while a few curious heads appeared in the door to the street.

All gazed in amazement at the man stretched out on the floor, and at the blood, streaming in all directions, that flowed from the four wounds he'd taken.

Into this silence, a voice said, "Someone should call the Watch."

But from among the three friends who had come to the rescue of the gentleman hunchback, the one who had attacked poor Latil from behind cried, "Stop! Nobody move! We can explain everything. You see how things are—you're all witnesses that all we've done is help our friend, the Marquis de Pisany, defend himself against that infamous cutthroat, Latil, who'd lured him into a trap. Don't worry, you see before you nobles of high name, and friends of the cardinal."

Though the commoners then took their hats in their hands, it was with skepticism that they nonetheless eyed those who tried to reassure them. This was a serious incident, though perhaps less rare then than now.

The speaker realized he still needed to convince his audience. Indicating one of his companions, he said, "First of all, you see before you Monsieur Vincent Voiture, poet, wit-about-Court, and one of the first of those invited when Monsieur Conrart founded the French Academy. He is also the Receiver of Ambassadors for 'Monsieur,' the king's brother."

A small man, alert, elegant, with a ruddy face, dressed all in black and angling his sword straight out behind him, acknowledged these titles, to the respect and admiration of the audience.

"Then," the speaker said, "we have here Monsieur Charles, Comte de Brancas, son of the Duc de Villars and Knight of Honor to Her Majesty the queen mother. Finally, there is me," he continued, raising his voice and lifting his head like a horse shaking its mane. "I am Sieur Pierre de Bellegarde, Marquis de Montbrun, Seigneur de Souscarrières, son of the Duc de Bellegarde, Grand Equerry of France, Officer of the Crown, close friend of the late King Henri IV, and loyal servant of King Louis XIII, our glorious monarch. If these guarantees aren't good enough for you, you'll have to appeal to Our Eternal Father.

"Now," he continued, "those who must wash the floor and bury the body deserve recompense. Here's your pay." And taking the purse from the table, the Sieur Pierre de Bellegarde, Marquis de Montbrun, Seigneur de Souscarrières, threw it at the feet of the host of the Inn of the Painted Beard. As it spilled forth a score of golden coins, Souscarrières slipped Pisany's four rolls of *pistoles* into his purse. This prestidigitation escaped the notice of the Marquis de Pisany, who, eager to avoid compromise in the affair, had slipped out the door and taken to his heels—an easy matter for one with such long legs.

The innkeeper and his cooks were amazed at hearing such high names and pompous titles, and even more so by the sound of gold ringing on the floor. Heads bared, they bowed awkwardly, and two of their number hastened to take the candles from the wall to light the way of the fine gentlemen who had condescended to murder a man in their house. Madame Soleil, a thrifty housewife, was quick to gather the scattered coins into her purse—and did so, we hasten to add, with no thought of keeping a few from her husband, as they managed their affairs together.

Whereupon Souscarrières, with a dignity of bearing to match the pomp of his speech, donned his cloak, straightened his mustache, cocked his hat over his left ear, stepped forth, and departed with an air of majesty.

The others departed more modestly, though still with enough haughtiness to impress the masses.

While the three set out to catch up with the Marquis de Pisany, let's give our readers some essential details about these characters who've stepped onto our stage.

As Souscarrières said, the main actor in our recent drama was the Marquis de Pisany, son of the Marquise de Rambouillet. To name the Marquise de Rambouillet is to name the woman who set the tone and customs of French high society in the seventeenth century for some fifty years.

The Marquis de Pisany came into the world as beautiful and straight as the other five children of the marquise, and doubtless like them would have been numbered among the "White Pillars of Rambouillet," as this lovely family was called, had not his nurse dislocated his spine. This accident made him the man we have seen, a person so cruelly deformed that he'd never been able to find back-and-breast armor that fitted his double hump, though he'd engaged the finest armorers of France and Italy. This deformity had gradually twisted him, a gentleman of breeding, courage, and wit, into one of the most abominable beings in creation, a kind of demon who sought to destroy everything that was young and handsome. Disappointment, particularly in affairs of the heart, could send him into fits of rage in which he could commit the most heinous crimes. It was most unbecoming to a gentleman of his name and rank.

Our second actor was Vincent Voiture, son of a wine merchant, and a great piquet player, who had given his name to the *"carre de Voiture,"* that is, seventy points scored by four counters in a square.

As Souscarrières said, Vincent Voiture, a famous man of letters in the seventeenth century, was not only Receiver of Ambassadors for His Royal Highness, the king's brother Gaston d'Orléans, but was also one of the premier wits of the era. He was small but well made, dressed elegantly, was always amiable but never naïve, and was so addicted to gaming that if he played for no more than five minutes, he got so excited that he was obliged to change his shirt. He was a favorite of the princesses and ladies of the Court, who all knew him: protégé of Queen Anne of Austria; confidant of Madame la Princesse, the wife of that Duc de Condé who belied his family of heroes by his cowardice and greed; friend of the Marquise de Rambouillet, the lovely Julie d'Angennes, and Madame de Saintot, who all regarded him as the Frenchman whose mind and spirit were most pleasing to women. Brave as well, if there was an affair at hand, his sword didn't long stay hanging at his side. He'd been involved in three celebrated duels: one in daytime, another under the moon, the third by torchlight. The Marquis de Pisany often relied on him in his wicked adventures.

The third was, as Souscarrières proclaimed, the young Comte de Brancas, Knight of Honor to Queen Mother Marie de Médicis. Except for La Fontaine, there was possibly no man in the seventeenth century more absentminded than he. Once, while riding home at night, horse thieves stopped him by grabbing his horse's bridle. "Hey, you stable hands," he said, "let go of my horse!" But he realized the true situation when a pistol was put to his throat.

On his wedding day, he told the fellow with whom he sometimes shared a bed—as was usual at the time between roommates—to keep it ready for him, as he would spend that night at home.

"What are you thinking, Monsieur le Comte?" objected his roommate. "You're getting married this morning."

"Why, by my faith, that's true! I'd forgotten."

The fourth and final actor was Souscarrières, about whom we'll add nothing to what we've already said, as the story will soon provide us an opportunity of making his full acquaintance. We've already provided a sample of his manner of speech, which hopefully will give you a glimpse of his unusual character.

These three, as we've said, exited in triumph from the Inn of the Painted Beard and crossed the barricade that closed both ends of the Rue de l'Homme-Armé: two by jumping over, and one by ducking under. They were pursuing the Marquis de Pisany, and had every hope of catching up to him on his way to the Hotel de Rambouillet in the Rue Saint-Thomas-du-Louvre, where in our time the Vaudeville Theater stands.

In fact, they did catch up with him, but only at the corner of Rue Froidmanteau and Rue des Orties, about a hundred paces from the Hotel de Rambouillet.

Hearing the sound of their approach, the marquis turned and recognized them. He was glad to give his long legs a rest and catch his breath as he waited for his friends.

The three newcomers, like the Curiatti of myth, had been left behind, not due to their wounds, but because of their lengths of leg. Souscarrières, who was quite athletic despite being no more than five foot six, was in the lead, followed by the Comte de Brancas, who had already forgotten what had happened and was wondering why they were running this race. Last came the petite Voiture, who though no more than thirty was already tending toward obesity; wiping his forehead, he kept up with Souscarrières and Brancas only by great effort.

Souscarrières stopped when he reached Pisany, who was seated on a borne, a corner barricade. With arms crossed, eyes dark, and expression grim, he looked like one of those fantastic sculptures that fifteenth-century architects had set staring down from roof-corners. "So, Pisany," Souscarrières said, "are you so consumed by rage that you must continually drag us into your evil affairs? Now a man has been killed. True, it was no great loss—he was a known ruffian, and I can testify it was self-defense, so you should escape prosecution. But if I hadn't shown up and thrust from one side just as you thrust from the other, you'd have been gigged like a frog."

"Oh?" Pisany replied. "And would that be such a tragedy?"

"What do you mean, such a tragedy?"

"Who says I'm not trying to get myself killed? Indeed, what a fine life I have: mocked by men, misjudged by women—wouldn't it be just as well if I were dead, or even better, had never been born?" He ground his teeth and shook his fist in the air.

"All right, my dear Marquis, so you want to get yourself killed. But then why call out for us just as Étienne Latil's sword was about to grant your wish?"

"Because before I die, I want my revenge."

"The devil! He wants revenge, and he has a friend in Souscarrières, but he takes his business to a petty cutthroat in the Rue de l'Homme-Armé."

"I went to find a cutthroat because a cutthroat could do the work I needed done. If a Souscarrières could have done it, then I could have done it, and I wouldn't have needed anyone else. I would have called out my man and killed him myself. To see a detested rival lying at one's feet, writhing in the agonies of death, is too great a pleasure not to take it when one can."

"So why didn't you do it yourself?"

"Don't ask me to tell you, because I can't."

"What? *Mordieu*! A friend's secret is a sacred trust. So you want a man dead—strike him down and kill him."

"Listen, wretch!" Pisany cried, carried away by passion. "Can one fight a duel with a prince of the blood? Can a prince of the blood stoop to fight a simple gentleman? No! When you want to be rid of such a one, he must be murdered."

"And then what?" said Souscarrières.

"After he was dead, I'd be executed. So? What is my life but horror?"

"Oh, right!" Souscarrières struck his forehead. "And that would be my fate as well?"

"It's possible," Pisany said, shrugging dejectedly.

"My poor Pisany. This man you're jealous of, could he be . . . ?"

"Go on, finish it."

". . . But no, it can't be. He hasn't been back from Italy more than a week."

"It doesn't take a week to go from the Hotel de Montmorency to the Rue de la Cerisaie."

"So, it must be . . ." Souscarrières hesitated a moment, then burst out, "It must be the Comte de Moret!"

The marquis's only response was a terrible blasphemy.

"Ah! But who, then, are you in love with, my dear Pisany?" Souscarrières asked.

"You know who lives there." Pisany scowled. "Is that so . . . so laughable?"

"Madame de Maugiron, the sister of Marion Delorme?"

"The sister of Marion Delorme. Yes."

"Who lives in the same house as her other sister, Madame de la Montagne?"

"Yes, a hundred times yes!"

"Well, my dear Marquis, if your reason for wanting to kill the poor Comte de Moret is that he's the lover of Madame de Maugiron, then thank God you didn't get your way, because a noble gentleman like you would have suffered eternal remorse for having committed a pointless crime."

"How so?" Pisany asked, standing bolt upright.

"Because the Comte de Moret is not Madame de Maugiron's lover."

"Then whose lover is he?"

"Her sister, Madame de la Montagne."

"Impossible."

"Marquis, I swear it."

"The Comte de Moret is Madame de la Montagne's lover? You swear this?"

"Faith of a gentleman."

"But the other night, when I visited Madame de Maugiron . . ."

"The night before last?"

"Yes."

"At eleven in the evening?"

"How do you know that?"

"I just know. As I know that Madame de Maugiron is not the Comte de Moret's mistress."

"You're wrong, I tell you."

"Here we go again."

"I'd seen her that day, and she'd said that if I came by, I should find her alone. Once past her servant, I came to the door of her bedroom and, within the bedroom, I heard a man's voice."

"I don't say you didn't hear a man's voice. I only say it wasn't the voice of the Comte de Moret."

"Oh! You're torturing me!"

"You didn't actually see the count, did you?"

"Yes, I saw him."

"How so?"

"Later I was hiding in the doorway of the Hotel Lesdisguières, across the street from Madame de Maugiron's house."

"And?"

"And I saw him come out. As clearly as I see you."

"Except you didn't see him leave Madame de Maugiron. You saw him leave Madame de la Montagne."

"But then, but then," cried Pisany, "who was the man I heard in Madame de Maugiron's bedroom?"

"Bah, Marquis—be a philosopher!"

"A philosopher?"

"Yes, why worry about it?"

"What do you mean, why worry about it? If the man isn't a Son of France, I mean to kill him."

"Kill him! Ah!" said Souscarrières with an accent that plunged the marquis into a world of strange doubts.

"That's right," the marquis said, "kill him."

"Really? No matter who he was?" said Souscarrières, in a manner increasingly arrogant.

"Yes. Yes. A hundred times yes!"

"Well, then," Souscarrières said, "kill me, my dear Marquis—because I was the man."

"You villain!" Pisany said through his teeth. He drew his sword. "Defend yourself!"

"No need to ask me twice, my dear Marquis," said Souscarrières, sword in hand and falling on guard. "At your service!"

They fell to, and despite Voiture's cries and Brancas's incomprehension, the Marquis de Pisany and the Seigneur de Souscarrières began a furious combat, all the more terrible as there was no more light than that of a cloud-veiled moon. Each combatant, as much from pride as the will to live, displayed all his fencing skill. Souscarrières, who excelled at athletics, was clearly the stronger and more skillful. But Pisany's long legs, employed to their full, gave him an advantage in sudden attacks and quick retreats. Finally, after about twenty seconds, the Marquis de Pisany uttered a groan that barely escaped his teeth, raised his arms, and dropped his sword. He turned and leaned against the wall, sighed, and collapsed.

Souscarrières lowered his sword and said, "You are witnesses that he challenged me first?"

"Yes, alas!" Brancas and Voiture responded.

"And you can attest that everything followed the rules of honor?"

"We can attest to that."

"Very well! Now, as I prefer this sinner's health over his death, carry Monsieur de Pisany to the house of madame his mother and then send for Bouvard, the king's surgeon."

"The very thing! We'll do it," said Voiture. "Help me, Brancas. Fortunately, we're barely fifty paces from the Hotel de Rambouillet."

"Ah!" said Brancas. "What a shame! And the party had begun so well."

While Brancas and Voiture carried the Marquis de Pisany as carefully as they could to his mother's house, Souscarrières disappeared around the corner of the Rue des Orties. "These damned hunchbacks," he said. "I don't know why they infuriate me so. This makes three I've had to dispose of by running them through."

IV

The Hotel de Rambouillet

The Hotel de Rambouillet was located between the church of Saint-Thomas-du-Louvre, which was built in the late twelfth century to commemorate Saint Thomas the Martyr, and the Hospital of the Three Hundred, founded during the reign of Louis IX upon his return from Egypt, to house those three hundred gentlemen whose eyes had been gouged out by the Saracens.

The Marquise de Rambouillet, who had built the hotel—we'll tell how later—was born in 1588, that is, the year the Duc de Guise and his brother were murdered at Blois by order of Henri III. She was the daughter of Jean de Vivonne (the elder Marquis de Pisany) and Julie Savelli, a Roman lady of a family so illustrious that it sired two popes, Honoré III and Honoré IV, and a saint of the church, Saint Lucina.

At the age of twelve, she married the Marquis de Rambouillet of the house of Angennes, another illustrious family, renowned for both the famous Cardinal de Rambouillet, and that Marquis de Rambouillet who was Viceroy of Poland before Henri III assumed that title.

The Rambouillet family was known for both wit and propriety. A parable of the grandfather of the Marquis de Rambouillet bears witness to the one, as an anecdote about his father illustrates the other.

The grandfather, Jacques de Rambouillet, had married a woman of questionable character. One day he was arguing with her in a dispute that was becoming an actual fight, when he stopped suddenly, lowered his voice, and, speaking as calmly as can be, said, "Madame, pull on my beard."

"Why?" she asked in amazement.

"Just pull on it. I'll tell you afterwards."

The Marquis de Rambouillet's grandmother grabbed her husband's beard and pulled on it.

"Harder," he said to her.

"But I'll hurt you!"

"Don't worry."

"That's what you want?"

"Yes, but much harder. Harder still. Now, with all your might. There! That didn't hurt me. Now it's my turn."

He yanked on a lock of her hair. She shrieked.

"You see, Madame," he said calmly, "I'm stronger than you. Argue with me if it pleases you. But don't try to fight me."

In that way this new Xanthippe was warned that, though her husband might be as wise as Socrates, he was not as patient.

The Marquis de Rambouillet's father was, as we've said, appointed Viceroy of Poland while that country awaited the arrival of Henri III. While performing this duty, he had saved a hundred thousand crowns in cash, which he presented to the king.

"Do you mock me, Monsieur de Rambouillet?" said Henri III. "A hundred thousand crowns isn't much to a king."

"Take them, Sire," said Monsieur de Rambouillet. "If you don't need them on this day, you'll need them on another." He made the king accept them—and later Henri wasn't sorry he had.

At the battle of Jarnac, where the Prince de Condé was so brutally murdered, this same Monsieur de Rambouillet had worked wonders, so much so that the Duc d'Anjou had sent his brother, King Charles IX, a letter in which he gave Rambouillet credit for the victory. The family displayed that letter in a golden frame.

In 1606, that is to say after six years of marriage, Monsieur de Rambouillet found himself in financial difficulty and sold the Hotel de Pisany to Pierre Forget-Dufresne for 34,500 *livres*. In 1624,

Forget-Dufresne turned around and sold it, at a great profit, to the cardinal-minister. By the time of our story, Richelieu was busy building on that site what would later become the Palais Cardinal. While waiting for this palace of marvels to be made habitable, Richelieu had two country houses, one at Chaillot, the other at Rueil, as well as a town house in the Place Royale, next door to that of the celebrated courtesan Marion Delorme.

Meanwhile, for thirty years Paris expanded, building daily. You could say that it was Henri IV who laid the groundwork for what would become modern Paris. At the end of the reign of Henri III, Paris had covered an area of 1,414 acres. During the reign of Henri IV, the Tournelles park, the suitable parts of the Marais, and the neighborhood around the Temple were all built up with new houses. The Rue Dauphine and the Place Royale were constructed, the suburbs of Saint-Antoine, Montmartre, Saint-Martin, Saint-Denis, and Saint-Honoré were increased by half, and the new Faubourg Saint-Germain became the seventeenth quarter. Paris grew to enclose over 1,660 acres.

In 1604, the Pont Neuf, begun by Henri III in 1578, was finally completed. In 1606, the Hotel de Ville (City Hall), begun by François I in 1533, was likewise completed. In 1613 were built the Saint-Gervais gate and the aqueduct of Arcueil. From 1614 to 1616, the houses and bridges of the new Île Saint-Louis were constructed. The equestrian statue of Henri IV was placed on the Pont Neuf, and the foundations of the Palais du Luxembourg were laid. Marie de Médicis, during her regency, established the long ranks of trees along the Cours-la-Reine.

In a new burst of building, from 1624 to 1628, Paris grew even further. The western walls were extended to contain the Palais des Tuileries, the neighborhood of Butte-des-Moulins, and that of Ville-Neuve. The new walls began at the Seine at the Porte de la Conférence, at the far end of the Tuileries gardens, ran to the Rue

Saint-Honoré, with its new Porte Saint-Honoré, to Rue Galion, where they built the Porte Montmartre, and joined the old walls at the corner of the Rue Neuve-Saint-Denis, at the gate of the same name.

The Marquise de Rambouillet, after the sale of the Hotel de Pisany, resided in her father's small house in Rue Saint-Thomas-du-Louvre, but this dwelling was too cramped for the lady, her six children, and numerous domestics. It was then that she decided to build the famous Hotel de Rambouillet, so celebrated thereafter. However, dissatisfied with the plans submitted by the architects, which she felt didn't make good use of the available area, she decided to draw up the plans herself. For a long while she labored uselessly at this endeavor, until one day she cried, like Archimedes, "Eureka!" She took pen and paper and quickly sketched both the interior and exterior of the mansion, all with such excellent taste that it impressed Queen Regent Marie de Médicis, then employed in building the Luxembourg. She, who had seen in her youth in Florence the most beautiful palaces in the world, and who had brought to this new Athens the leading architects of the time, sent them to ask for advice from Madame de Rambouillet and to use her mansion as an example.

The eldest child of the Marquise de Rambouillet was the beautiful Julie-Lucine d'Angennes, more celebrated even than her mother. Since the days of Helen, that adulterous wife of Menelaus who drew Europe into war with Asia, no woman's beauty had been more highly praised, in every key and with every instrument. No one whose heart she stole ever recovered it. The wound inflicted by the surpassingly lovely eyes of Julie d'Angennes, the famous Madame de Montausier, was mortal, or at least incurable. Ninon de Lenclos may have had her "martyrs," but Julie's admirers were known as "the perishing."

Born in 1600, she was now aged twenty-eight, and though her first youth was past, she had arrived at the full bloom of her beauty.

Though Madame de Rambouillet had four other daughters, her eldest eclipsed them all, and today the younger are nearly forgotten. Three of them took the veil: Madame d'Hyères, Madame de Saint-Étienne, and Madame de Pisany. The youngest, Claire-Angélique d'Angennes, was the first wife of Monsieur de Grignan.

In our previous chapters, we made the acquaintance of her eldest son, the Marquis de Pisany. Madame had had a second son who died at the age of eight when his nurse, who'd visited a plague victim at the hospital, had recklessly kissed the child upon her return. Within two days, the plague had taken them both.

The early fame of the Hotel de Rambouillet was due to the passion the beautiful Julie inspired in every man of breeding, and to the curious devotion of the family servants. The Marquis de Pisany's tutor was Chavaroche, who had been Voiture's opponent in one of those three duels we mentioned, fighting him by torchlight and giving him a flesh wound in the thigh. Chavaroche was, always had been, and always would be one of the lovely Julie's "perishing" admirers. When Julie, after being married for twelve years, finally decided at the age of thirty-nine to fulfill her husband Monsieur de Montausier's desire for a child, she had a very difficult labor. Because they knew he'd be willing to go, they sent Chavaroche to the Abbey of Saint-Germain for the Girdle of Saint Marguerite, a holy relic known to help with childbirth. Chavaroche went at once, but as it was three in the morning, he found the monks in their beds and was obliged, despite his impatience, to wait nearly half an hour.

"By my faith!" he cried. "The nerve of these monks, sleeping while Madame de Montausier is in labor!"

And after that, Chavaroche spoke naught but ill of the monks of the Abbey of Saint-Germain.

One degree of domestic rank below Chavaroche, we find Louis de Neuf-Germain, with his long sword slapping his leg and his goatee almost brushing his chest, and who bore the title Poet-at-Large

to Monsieur, the king's brother. He had an easy facility for dog-
gerel. One day, Madame de Rambouillet had asked him to impro-
vise something for Monsieur d'Avaux, brother of the President of
Mesme, the ambassador extraordinary who had signed the Peace
of the North. Neuf-Germain rattled off an entire ode on d'Avaux's
name, with rhymes on *da* and *vaux*. Here is the first stanza:

> Jove, one day in heaven, had a
> Job for Mercury, his bravo,
> To have the gods sing a cantata
> In praise and honor of great Devaux

Those who wish to read his other works will find them collected by
Voiture.

Neuf-Germain had a mistress in the Rue des Gravilliers, the last
street in Paris where a gallant was likely to find a mistress. A certain
rogue, who insisted he had a prior claim to the damsel, encountered Neuf-Germain and they quarreled in the street. The rogue
grabbed Neuf-Germain by his goatee and yanked so hard, it came
off in his hand. Neuf-Germain, who always wore a sword and had
given the Marquis de Pisany his first lessons in arms, drew and
struck his attacker a blow that made him drop his handful of beard.
The rogue, wounded, fled screaming, pursued by half the watching
mob, while Neuf-Germain gleefully slashed the air with his rapier,
mocking the rogue and loudly calling for him to return.

After Neuf-Germain left, a cobbler who knew that the victor
belonged to the Hotel de Rambouillet, the reputation of which had
reached even the lowest commoners, noticed that the goatee torn
from his chin was still on the battlefield. He picked it up to the last
hair, folded it carefully in white paper, and proceeded to the Hotel
de Rambouillet.

The household was at dinner when the Marquis de Rambouillet

was told that a cobbler from the Rue des Gravilliers wished to speak with him. This was such unexpected news that Rambouillet was curious as to what this cobbler had to say. "Let him enter," he said.

It was done. The cobbler came in, bowed humbly, and approached Rambouillet. "Monsieur le Marquis," he said, "I am pleased to present the beard of Monsieur de Neuf-Germain, which he had the misfortune to lose in front of my door."

Without really knowing what that meant, Monsieur de Rambouillet took from his pouch one of those new crowns struck with the image of Louis XIII, called a *louis d'argent,* and gave it to the cobbler. The man retired completely satisfied, not for having received a crown, but for having had the honor of seeing at table, eating like mere mortals, Monsieur de Rambouillet and his family.

Rambouillet and family were still looking uncomprehendingly at this handful of beard when Neuf-Germain came in with his stubbly chin, surprised that despite his quick return to the mansion, his beard had arrived before him.

One floor down we meet Silésie the equerry, or rather the *quinola,* as a sub-equerry was known at the time. Everyone at the Hotel de Rambouillet had his quirks and caprices, but Silésie was a madman of a different stripe. Madame de Rambouillet called Neuf-Germain their indoor madman and Silésie their outdoor madman, as he lived with his wife and children outside the main house, albeit only a few steps away.

One morning, everyone who lived in the same house as Silésie came to complain to the marquis, saying that since the weather had grown hot, it was impossible to sleep under the same roof as his equerry.

Monsieur de Rambouillet called Silésie before him. "What were you doing last night," he asked, "that all the neighbors complain about not being able to sleep for a moment?"

"With respect, Monsieur le Marquis," replied Silésie, "I was killing my fleas."

"And how can you make so much noise killing fleas?"

"Because I kill them with a hammer."

"A hammer? Explain that, Silésie!"

"Monsieur le Marquis is aware that no animal's life is harder to take than that of a flea."

"That's true."

"Well, to make sure mine don't escape, once I catch them, I carry them to the staircase and crush them with a large hammer."

And Silésie continued to kill his fleas in this fashion, until one night, when he was probably half asleep, he missed the first step and tumbled from the top of the stairs to the bottom. When they found him, he had a broken neck.

After Silésie comes Maître Claude the silversmith, a sort of comic buffoon. He was crazy about executions, and despite the cruelty of the spectacle, he never missed one. But once three or four were held in quick succession, and yet Maître Claude never left the house.

Worried, the marquise asked him the cause of this aberration. "Ah, Madame la Marquise," replied Maître Claude, shaking his head with an air of melancholy, "I can no longer take pleasure in criminals' death throes."

"And why is that?" she asked her servant.

"Because since the beginning of the year, the executioners have been strangling the condemned before hanging them. Can you believe it? If, someday, they return to hanging them outright, on that day I'll return to the execution ground."

One night, he went to see the fireworks in honor of Saint-Jean, but as they launched the first rockets, he found himself behind a very tall onlooker whose large head blocked his view. He thought, rather than bother anyone, he would go up to Montmartre, only to find when he arrived breathless at the top of the hill and turned toward the Hotel de Ville that the fireworks were over. Thus instead of seeing poorly, Maître Claude saw nothing at all.

So instead he went to Saint-Denis to see the treasures, and greatly enjoyed himself. Upon his return, when questioned by the marquise, he said, "Ah, Madame, what beautiful things they have, these rascals of churchmen!"

And he began to list the bejeweled crosses, the surplices studded with pearls, the golden monstrance and silver candlesticks. "But there was one thing most important of all," he added.

"What thing do you think the most important, Maître Claude?"

"Ah, Madame, they have our neighbor's arm."

"Which neighbor?" asked Madame de Rambouillet, who wondered who among their neighbors could spare a limb to donate to the treasure-trove of Saint-Denis.

"Why, *pardieu,* the arm of our neighbor Saint Thomas, Madame; his church is so close we can practically touch it."

There were also two other servants at the Hotel de Rambouillet who were a credit to the collection: the secretary Adriani and the embroiderer Dubois. The first published a volume of poetry dedicated to Monsieur de Schomberg. The second, who felt called to the vocation, became a Capuchin monk. But the calling didn't last, and he left his monastery before the end of his novitiate. Not daring to reapply for a place with Madame de Rambouillet, he became supervisor of the actors at the Hotel de Bourgogne. "Because that way," as he said, "if Madame de Rambouillet ever chanced to go to the theater, I might see her."

Indeed, the Marquis and Marquise de Rambouillet were worshiped by their servants. One evening, the lawyer Patru, so influential on the modes of polite speech at the Académie Française, was dining at the Hotel de Nemours with the Abbé de Saint-Spire. One of the two mentioned the Marquise de Rambouillet. The sommelier, Audry, who was crossing the room after telling the waiters which wine to serve, heard the marquise's name and stopped. When the two guests continued to talk about her, the sommelier sent all the other servants from the room.

"Why the devil did you do that?" Patru asked.

"Ah, Messieurs!" the sommelier said. "I was with Madame de Rambouillet for twelve years. If you have the honor to be friends of the marquise, no one shall serve you but me."

And despite the dignity of his position, he placed a waiter's towel over his arm, stood behind the guests, and served them until the end of the meal.

Now that we have made the acquaintance of the masters and servants of the Hotel de Rambouillet, we will bring our readers inside the mansion on a night when it was host to the leading celebrities of the age.

V

What Occurred in the Hotel de Rambouillet as Souscarrières Was Disposing of His Third Hunchback

On the evening of December 5, 1628, which we began at the Inn of the Painted Beard in the first chapter of this book, all the literary luminaries of the era, those whose society was ridiculed by Molière as they ridiculed him in return, were gathered in the marquise's mansion. That night they were not ordinary visitors to the marquise's salon, but specially invited guests, each having received a note from Madame de Rambouillet announcing a special soirée.

The guests had rushed to attend.

This event took place during that happy era when women were beginning to have an influence on society. Poetry was in its infancy, born in the previous century with Marot, Garnier, and Ronsard, and was just then prattling out its first tragedies, pastorals, and comedies by way of Hardy, Desmarests, and Raissiguier. Dramatic literature would follow, thanks to Rotrou, Corneille, Molière, and Racine, elevating France above all other nations, while perfecting that beautiful language created by Rabelais, purified by Boileau, and distilled by Voltaire. Due to its clarity, French would become the diplomatic language of all civilized nations. In language, clarity is integrity.

William Shakespeare, the great genius of the sixteenth century—or rather, of all centuries—had been dead only twelve years, and was as yet known only to the English. Make no mistake, the European popularity of Elizabeth's great poet is a modern phenomenon; none of the fine minds gathered at Madame de Rambouillet's had even heard the name of the man who, a century later, Voltaire would call a barbarian. Moreover, at a time when the theater was dominated by plays such as *The Deliverance of Andromeda, The Conquest of the Boar of Calydon,* and *The Death of Bradamante,* works like *Hamlet, Macbeth, Othello, Julius Caesar, Richard III,* and *Romeo and Juliet* would have seemed harsh to the delicate French palate.

No, due to the influence of the queen and of the Catholic League of the Guises, it was Spain who set the fashion in literature, through Lope de Vega, Alarcón, and Tirso de Molina; Calderón had not yet appeared.

To end this long digression, which began of its own accord due to the force of circumstance, we'll repeat our own words: this event took place during a happy era, and we would add that an invitation from Madame de Rambouillet made it doubly special. All knew the marquise's grand passion for surprising her guests.

For example, consider the day she'd presented the Bishop of Lisieux, Philippe de Cospéan, with a quite unexpected surprise. In the park at Rambouillet was a large, round boulder from which a fountain sprang. Veiled by a curtain of trees, it was dedicated to the memory of Rabelais, who had worked sometimes in his study and sometimes in his dining room. One bright morning, the marquise led the Bishop of Lisieux toward the fountain. The prelate squinted as he approached, trying to make out something that shone through the branches. Soon he could clearly distinguish seven or eight young women dressed as nymphs—that is to say, barely dressed at all. Leading them was Mademoiselle de Rambouillet attired as Diana: quiver on her shoulder, bow in her hand, and circlet on her brow. Beyond her, all the demoiselles of the household posed prettily on the great rock, presenting, according to Tallemant des Réaux, the loveliest tableau in the world. A bishop of our day might be scandalized by such a spectacle, but Monseigneur de Lisieux, on the contrary, was quite charmed. He never saw the marquise thereafter without asking for news of the rocks of Rambouillet.

In a similar circumstance, Actaeon was transformed into a stag and torn apart by dogs, but the marquise held that this case was entirely different, as the good bishop was so ugly that, while the nymphs might make an impression on him, he was unlikely to impress the nymphs, other than to make them flee at his approach. Besides, the Bishop of Lisieux was well aware of how ugly he was, going so far as to joke with the Bishop of Riez that he was far from being an Adonis.

"That's why I owe you my thanks," replied the Bishop of Riez, "because before you became my colleague, I was the ugliest bishop in France."

It may be that Madame de Rambouillet's male guests, who outnumbered the females, rushed to the mansion in hopes that the marquise was staging a surprise like the one she'd prepared for Monseigneur de Lisieux. Certainly the exquisites invited that evening had elevated hopes, and were ready for whatever the evening might reveal.

Their conversation turned on all matters of love and poetry, but most particularly on the recent piece performed by the actors of the Hotel de Bourgogne, which the exquisites had begun to patronize since the team of Bellerose, la Villiers, Mondory, la Beaupré, and his wife, Mademoiselle Vaillot, had taken over direction of the theater.

Madame de Rambouillet had made plays fashionable by staging *Frédégonde* and Hardy's *Chaste Love* in her home. After that, it was decided that decent women, who until then had avoided it, could go to the Hotel de Bourgogne. The play under discussion that evening was a piece titled *The Hypochondriac,* the debut work of a young protégé of the marquise named Jean Rotrou. Though of middling rank, thanks to the support of the Rambouillets he had enjoyed enough success for Cardinal Richelieu to hire him into his household at the Place Royale. There he joined the company of Richelieu's famous "collaborators": Mairet, L'Estoile, and Colletet, as well as the even more celebrated Desmarests and Bois-Robert.

As they were discussing the merits of Rotrou's questionable comedy, which Scudéry and Chapelain were chopping into mincemeat, a handsome young man in an elegant suit came in. With the air of a complete cavalier, he crossed the salon to pay his respects to the ladies in order of precedence, starting with Madame la Princesse, who in her quality as wife of Monsieur de Condé, first prince of the blood, was entitled to preeminence. After her he addressed the marquise, then the lovely Julie.

He was followed by a companion, two or three years older and dressed all in black, who advanced into the midst of this learned and imposing company a step behind his friend.

"Here he is now," said the marquise, indicating the first of the two men, "the conqueror himself. It must be fine to ride to the Capitoline at such a young age—and without, I hope, someone behind you in the chariot saying, 'Caesar, remember you are mortal.'"

"On the contrary, Madame la Marquise," replied Rotrou, for that's who it was. "No critic could ever complain of my poor work more than I do myself. I swear I'm only here because I received a direct order from the Comte de Soissons to leave off work on my *The Dead Lover*, as if it were actually dead, in order to begin on the comedy I'm working on now."

"So, what is the subject of this comedy, my fine cavalier?" asked Mademoiselle Paulet.

"A ring that no one would wish to put on his finger once he's seen you, adorable Lioness: the Ring of Forgetfulness."

A nod greeted this flattery from the one to whom it was addressed. Meanwhile, the young man dressed in black stayed as far in the background as he could. But as he was totally unknown to everybody, and as everyone to be presented to the marquise either had a name already or was on his way to making one, all eyes were fixed upon him nonetheless.

"And how do you have time to write a new comedy, Monsieur Rotrou," asked the lovely Julie, "now that you've accepted the honor of working with the cardinal's company?"

"Monsieur le Cardinal had so much to do at the siege of La Rochelle that we were left to ourselves," replied Rotrou, "so I took the opportunity to do some work on my own."

Meanwhile, the young man dressed in black continued to attract all the attention that was not devoted to Rotrou.

"He's not a man of the sword," said Mademoiselle de Scudéry to her brother.

"No, he has an air more like that of a law clerk," he replied.

The young man in black overheard this exchange, and acknowledged it with a good-natured smile. Rotrou heard it as well. "But yes!" he said. "In fact he is a law clerk—and a law clerk, I assure you, who will one day outdo us all."

Now it was the turn of the men in the company to smile, half in disbelief and half in disdain. But Rotrou's extravagant prediction only made the women all the more curious.

Despite his youth, the man in black had an austere look to him. He had a broad brow already lined with the wrinkles of thought, beneath which were eyes flickering with flame. The rest of his face was more commonplace, with a large nose above thick lips, partly concealed by a burgeoning mustache.

Rotrou decided it was time to satisfy the company's curiosity. "Madame la Marquise, allow me to introduce my dear compatriot Pierre Corneille, son of the Advocate General of Rouen—and soon to be a son of genius."

The name was completely unknown.

"Corneille," repeated Scudéry. "The name of a bird of ill omen."

"Yes . . . to his rivals," Rotrou said.

"*Ab ilice cornix*," Chapelain whispered to the Bishop of Grasse. "The raven cries from the oak."

"Corneille," the marquise repeated in her turn, but with more warmth.

"Ah!" Rotrou said to Madame de Rambouillet. "You're trying to remember on what title page or frontispiece you've read that name. On none, Madame, as yet. It appears only at the head of a comedy he brought with him yesterday from Rouen. Tomorrow I'll take him to the Hotel de Bourgogne and present him to Mondory—and a month from now, we'll be applauding him."

The young man lifted his eyes to heaven, as if to say, "May God grant it be so!"

The female guests approached the two friends with more curiosity. Madame la Princesse was in the lead, seeing in every poet a potential rhapsodist on her beauty, which was beginning to fade. While the men, especially the poets, stayed firmly in their places, she eagerly took a seat in the group forming around Rotrou and his companion. "So, Monsieur Corneille," she said, "what is the title of this comedy of yours?"

Corneille turned curiously toward the source of this haughty voice. As he did so, Rotrou whispered a word in his ear. "It's called *Mélite*," Corneille said, "unless Your Highness would care to grace it with a better name."

"*Mélite*," repeated the princess. "*Mélite*. No, we'll leave it as is. *Mélite* is charming—and if the story is as well . . ."

"What's charming about it is that it's not a story," Rotrou said, "but rather a history."

"A history? How so?" asked Mademoiselle Paulet. "Do you mean it's a true tale?"

"Come now," Rotrou said to his companion, "tell the ladies the story, you rascal."

Corneille blushed to the ears. No one could seem less of a rascal than he did.

"The question is whether the story can safely be told at all," said Madame de Combalet, covering her face with her fan in case Corneille's story should be indelicate.

"Instead of just telling the story," Corneille said timidly, "I'd rather recite some verses."

"Bah," said Rotrou, "you're embarrassed over nothing. I can recount the plot in two sentences. But there's no merit in that, since the story is true, and as my friend is the hero he gets no credit for inventing it. Imagine, Madame, that this libertine had a friend. . . ."

"Rotrou, Rotrou!" interrupted Corneille.

"Ignoring the interruption, I continue," said Rotrou. "Imagine that this libertine had a friend who introduced him into a decent household in Rouen, in which the friend was engaged to the family's charming daughter. What do you think Monsieur Corneille did? He, the best man, no less, waited until the wedding was over, and then—well . . . You understand, don't you?"

"Monsieur Rotrou!" said Madame de Combalet, drawing her Carmelite's veil over her eyes.

"And then—what?" said Mademoiselle de Scudéry with a roguish air. "Others may understand you, Monsieur Rotrou, but I certainly do not."

"I hope they do, beautiful Sappho" (for so Mademoiselle de Scudéry was called in that company of exquisites). "Ask Mademoiselle Paulet and Monseigneur the Bishop of Grasse, since they understood it—didn't they?"

Mademoiselle Paulet gave Rotrou a provocative little tap on the fingers with her fan, and said, "Go on, you villain. The sooner you finish, the better."

"Then I will follow Horace's maxim of *ad eventum festina* and hasten on," Rotrou said. "Well, Monsieur Corneille, in his capacity as a poet, followed the advice of the friend of Maecenas: there's no point in putting things off. He found the lady alone, demolished her Edifice of Fidelity, and in the ruins of his friend's happiness built a temple to his own joy, a joy so powerful that a stream of poetry gushed from his heart, that same stream from which the Nine Muses drink."

"The Stream of Hippocrene gushing from the heart of a law clerk?" said Madame la Princesse. "That's not to be believed."

"Unless proven otherwise, Madame la Princesse. And that proof my friend Corneille will give you."

"Then this Mélite is a very lucky lady," said Mademoiselle Paulet. "If Monsieur Corneille's comedy is as successful as you predict, Monsieur Rotrou, she'll be immortalized."

"Yes," Mademoiselle de Scudéry said drily, "but I doubt that this immortality, even if it lasts as long as that of the Cumaean Sibyl, will result in bringing her a husband."

"Oh? And do you find it such a great misfortune to remain unmarried?" said Mademoiselle de Paulet. "As long as one is pretty, of course. But ask Madame de Combalet if being married is such divine joy!"

Madame de Combalet's only reply was to sigh, raise her eyes to heaven, and shake her head sadly.

"This is all very well," said Madame la Princesse, "but Monsieur Corneille has offered to recite us some verses from his comedy."

"And he's quite ready to do so," said Rotrou. "Asking for verses from a poet is like asking for water from a spring. Come now, friend Corneille!"

Corneille blushed, stammered a bit, put his hand to his forehead, and then, in a voice that seemed made more for tragedy than for comedy, recited the following verses:

> "I admit, my friend, my disorder is so incurable
> That only one remedy offers me relief;
> And after the disdain Mélite has treated me with,
> It would be only just to quit her for another.
> But in spite of all her cruelty, she rules with
> Such powerful sway o'er my heart, that I dare to murmur
> Only in her absence. In vain, I make every effort to
> Surmount this passion, and make a thousand
> Resolutions when she is not present; then, I no sooner

See her again, when a single glance rivets my
Fetters stronger, and throws such a pleasing and delightful
Veil o'er my reason, that I pursue my disorder,
And fly from every remedy I proposed. But this
Flattering hope, this pleasing delusion only rekindles
Up my flame, and confirms me the more her slave."*

*Adapted from the anonymous 1776 English translation.

These verses were greeted two or three times by approving murmurs, indicating that the muse of poetry did not reside only in Paris, but sometimes visited the provinces, and that not all the wits of France were to be found at the Hotel de Rambouillet or the Place Royale. At the final verse, ". . . And confirms me the more her slave," general applause broke out. Madame de Rambouillet was the first to clap, which was the signal for the others to follow. Only a few of the men protested by their silence, among them the younger Montausier brother, who couldn't abide this sort of poetry.

But the poet heard only the approval and, intoxicated by the applause from the assembled wits of Paris, bowed and said, "Next comes the sonnet to Mélite. Should I go on?"

"Yes, yes," cried Madame la Princesse, Madame de Rambouillet, the beautiful Julie, and Mademoiselle Paulet all together, along with all those who echoed the tastes of the mistress of the house.

Corneille continued:

"What beauty with Mélite can compare,
What more than my passion can prove,
So matchless her charms, I declare,
Can be equaled by nought but my love.

"Though new beauties appear to my eyes,
Though her coldness embitters my heart,
Too cruel, she hears not my sighs,
Too lovely, she fixes the dart.

"But no wonder she's deaf to my flame,
To the pow'r of the god I submit,
Since love's whole pow'r I must feel,
But she only beauty and wit."*

*Adapted from the anonymous 1776 English translation.

The sonnet exceeds all other forms of poetry in exciting admiration—though Boileau, who wouldn't be born for another eight years, hadn't yet said "A faultless sonnet is still just a long poem." And this sonnet was hailed as faultless, particularly by the women, who applauded loud and long. Even Mademoiselle de Scudéry deigned to bring her hands together.

Rotrou, his loyal heart overflowing, enjoyed his friend's triumph more than any.

"In truth, Monsieur Rotrou, you were right!" said Madame la Princesse. "Your friend is a young man who must be championed."

"If you think so, Madame, do you suppose that, through Monsieur le Prince, you might find him a position?" asked Rotrou, lowering his voice so as to be heard by Madame de Condé alone. "Because he has no fortune, and, as you can see, it would be a shame if, for lack of a few coins, a career of genius should die unborn."

"Ah, well, Monsieur le Prince! There's no use trying to talk to him about poetry. The other day, he found me dining with Monsieur Chapelain. Later he asked, 'Who was that little black bird dining with you?' When I told him it was Monsieur Chapelain, he said, 'Ah. And who is this Monsieur Chapelain?' 'The creator of La Pucelle.'

'Oh, he's a sculptor, then.' Hopeless. But I will speak to Madame de Combalet, who will speak to the cardinal. Do you think he would agree to work on His Eminence's tragedies?"

"He would agree to anything that would enable him to stay in Paris. If he was capable of *Mélite* as a law clerk, imagine what he could do in this world where you are the queen and the marquise is prime minister."

"It's a good play, this *Mélite,* whether or not it succeeds. We will see to it that something is arranged."

And she held out her lovely, near-royal hand to Rotrou, who took it in his own and looked at it, as if considering its beauty.

"Well, what are you thinking?" asked Madame la Princesse.

"I look on this hand, and wonder if it can really feed two poets. Alas, no—it's too small a thing."

"Fortunately," Madame de Condé said, "God gave me two of them: one for you, and one for him you ask about."

"Corneille, Corneille," Rotrou called, "come here! Madame la Princesse, in honor of the sonnet to Mélite, permits you to kiss her hand."

Corneille nearly fainted. To be applauded by Madame de Rambouillet and to kiss the hand of Madame la Princesse, all on the evening of his debut in Paris—never in his most ambitious dreams had he aspired to even one of these favors.

But who, really, was honored here? Was it Corneille and Rotrou, who kissed the hands of the wife of the first prince of the blood? Or was it Madame de Condé, whose hands were kissed by the future authors of *Wenceslas* and *The Cid*? Posterity says that the one honored was Madame la Princesse.

Meanwhile, Maître Claude, white wand in hand like Polonius in *Hamlet,* came whispering to the Marquise de Rambouillet. She listened, gave him some quiet orders and directions, and then lifted her head to make an announcement. "Noble lords and dear ladies, my precious and excellent friends, had I invited you to spend the evening with me just to hear the verses of Monsieur Corneille, you would have no reason to complain. But I've gathered you tonight for a purpose less ethereal and more material. I have often spoken of the superiority of the sorbets and ice creams of Italy to those of France. After long search, I've found a glacier of sorbet that comes straight from Naples, and at last I can have you taste it. Don't follow me because you love me—follow me because you love sorbet! Monsieur Corneille, give me your arm."

"And here's my arm, Monsieur Rotrou," said Madame la Princesse, who that evening was determined to follow the example of the marquise in everything.

Corneille, trembling and awkward, the man of genius just arrived from the provinces, held out his arm to the marquise, while Rotrou, gallantly and like a complete cavalier, extended his to Madame de Condé. The Comte de Salles, the younger of the Montausier brothers, volunteered to escort the beautiful Julie, while the Marquis de Montausier led in Mademoiselle Paulet. Gombauld escorted Mademoiselle de Scudéry, and the others arranged themselves as seemed best.

Madame de Combalet, the severity of her Carmelite habit mitigated by a corsage of violets and rosebuds, accepted no man's arm, but followed immediately behind Madame la Princesse. Beside her was Madame de Saint-Étienne, the marquise's second daughter, who also aspired to a life of religion. However, there was a difference between her and Madame de Combalet, in that every day she took a step further into that life, while Madame de Combalet took another step out.

Up to that point, there'd been no surprises for Madame de Rambouillet's guests, but then the marquise, in her quality as guide, walked past the princess to a spot on the wall that wasn't known to have a door. There she tapped the wall with her fan.

Instantly, the wall opened as if by magic, and they stood on the threshold of a beautiful room decorated with furniture of blue velvet trimmed with gold and silver. The wall hangings, like the furniture, were blue velvet with similar trim. In the middle of this room was a table laden with flowers, fruits, cakes, and ice cream, presided over by two little cherubs, who were none other than the younger sisters of Julie d'Angennes and Madame de Saint-Étienne.

The company gave a unanimous cry of admiration; all had thought that beyond that wall was the neighboring garden of the Three Hundred, but here was a chamber so marvelously furnished and wondrously painted that it seemed as if the architect must be a fairy and the decorator a magician.

While everyone raved about the tasteful opulence of the chamber, which was to become famous as the Blue Room, Chapelain took pencil and paper into one corner of the salon, sat, and sketched out the first three stanzas of his *Ode to Zirphée*, a work that was to be nearly as celebrated as his *La Pucelle*.

The guests had seen what Chapelain was up to, so there was a profound silence when he who was considered the first poet of his time stood up, extended a hand, placed one foot forward, and with eyes alight pronounced the following verses:

> "Urgande once knew well
> The favor of Amadis and his noble band.
> By her charms she broke the laws
> Of time, that heaven shall take all it gives.
> I had to show your eyes what she did by charm:
> Keep Artemisia with the art that Urgande
> Had used to keep Amadis.
>
> "By the power of this art,
> I built this lodge to keep
> Time and fate at bay,

To outstrip the corruption of change—
For what passes in this paradise passes not at all.
Where rushing time hides its terrible face,
Old age trespasses not.

"This incomparable beauty
That a hundred evils could not bring to surrender,
Enchanted by this building,
Baffled by its defenses,
Shining from her throne with a divine radiance
That then, over mortals, spreads out
Without cloud, eclipse, or end."

Cries of enthusiasm and three rounds of applause greeted this improvisation—when suddenly, in the middle of the cheers, Voiture rushed into the room. Pale and covered in blood, he cried, "A doctor! A doctor! The Marquis de Pisany had a fight with Souscarrières and is badly wounded!"

And right behind him the Marquis de Pisany, unconscious and pale as death, was carried into the salon in the arms of Brancas and Chavaroche. "My son!" "My brother!" "The marquis!" The cries went up, and, forgetting the pleasures of the Blue Room, everyone rushed to the side of the wounded man.

Even as the unconscious Marquis de Pisany was borne into the Hotel de Rambouillet, back at the Inn of the Painted Beard an unexpected event, one that would greatly complicate things, threw everything there into disarray.

Lying atop the table where previously he had set his mugs of beer, believed dead and just awaiting his shroud, was Étienne Latil—who sighed, opened his eyes, and said, in a low but perfectly intelligible voice, these two words: "I'm thirsty."

VI

Marina and Jacquelino

A few minutes before Latil uttered the two words that so often signify the return of the wounded to life—and which, in any case, were entirely typical of our swordsman—a young man presented himself at the Inn of the Painted Beard and asked if room number thirteen was occupied by a peasant woman from Pau named Marina. He added that she would be easily recognized by her beautiful hair, her lovely dark eyes, and by her red bonnet, of the style worn in the rugged mountains of Coarraze where Henri IV had, bareheaded and barefoot, so often climbed as a child.

Madame Soleil took her time in replying, admiring her inquirer's youthful good looks while favoring him with her most charming smile. Finally she admitted, with a knowing look, that a young woman called Marina was in the room referred to, and had been waiting for half an hour or so.

And Madame Soleil, with the sort of graceful gesture that women of thirty to thirty-five like to make before handsome lads of twenty to twenty-two—with this graceful gesture Madame Soleil indicated the stairs, at the top of which the young man would find room number thirteen.

The young man was, as we've said, a handsome lad of twenty to twenty-two, of medium height but a good figure, every move of which showed elegance and strength. He had the blue eyes of the Northerner, sheltered by the dark eyebrows and hair of the South. His complexion, tanned by the sun, was slightly pale from fatigue. A thin mustache and a nascent goatee enhanced a pair of fine, smiling lips that, when opened, revealed a double row of white teeth that any lady of the Court might envy.

His costume, that of a Basque peasant, was both comfortable and elegant. It began at the top with a red, or rather oxblood, beret, decorated with a black tassel and two drooping feathers that framed his face charmingly. Below, he wore a doublet of the same color as the beret, trimmed with black lace, with the left sleeve open and hanging loose so that it could, in this period of assaults by day and ambushes by night, serve as a quick defense against the slash of a dagger or sword. This doublet was buttoned from top to bottom, as was no longer the fashion in Paris, where one now wore the doublet partly unbuttoned to show off one's lace-trimmed shirt beneath. Below the waist the young man wore a sort of buff gray trousers, and a pair of high-heeled shoes rather than boots. A dagger was thrust through the leather belt at his waist, from which a long rapier hung down along his legs. These were the arms of a gentleman, not exactly compatible with the costume of a peasant.

He arrived at the door, made sure the room was in fact number thirteen, and then carefully knocked in a deliberate pattern: two quick taps, a pause, two more taps, and then finally a fifth.

At the fifth knock the door opened, indicating that the visitor was expected.

The person who opened the door was a woman of twenty-eight to thirty, a lush flower at the peak of her beauty. Her eyes, which the young man had mentioned downstairs, sparkled like two black diamonds under the velvet shadow of her long eyelashes. Her hair was so dark and lustrous that no comparison with India ink or a raven's wing could do it justice. Her pale cheeks were flushed with the heat that speaks of sudden passion rather than enduring regard. Her neck, draped in strings of coral, descended to a generous bosom that trembled provocatively with each breath. Though her contours, sculpturally speaking, were more those of Niobe than of Diana, she was nonetheless rather petite, slim of waist above the flare of her rather Spanish hips. Her skirt, which was on the short side, was striped red and white, and displayed a lower leg rather more aristocratic than her costume would indicate, and feet that seemed almost too small to support the bounties above.

It was wrong to say that the door opened, as in fact it was only half opened until the young man said *Marina,* spoken more as a password than a name. The reply was *Jacquelino,* at which the door opened completely. The guardian stood aside to let the man enter, after which the door was shut and bolted. She turned quickly and surveyed him, as if to make sure of whom she was dealing with.

They regarded each other with equal curiosity—Jacquelino, arms crossed, head high, smile on his lips; Marina, head forward, her figure relaxed yet slightly coiled, in a manner reminiscent of a panther ready to spring.

"*Ventre-saint-gris!*" the young man said suddenly. "I had no idea I had such a delicious cousin!"

"Neither did I, upon my soul, 'cousin,'" the young woman replied.

"And, by my faith," Jacquelino continued, "relatives like we are, who've never even met before, should certainly get acquainted with a kiss."

"That seems to me a very appropriate welcome between . . . cousins," said Marina, offering her cheeks, which were colored with a glow that an observer might take for the flush of desire rather than the blush of modesty.

And they kissed.

"Ah! By the merry soul of my father," said the young man, in a good-natured tone that seemed natural to him, "it's the finest thing in the world, I think, to embrace a beautiful woman—especially as what follows may be a finer thing yet." And he spread his arms again to put the idea into action.

"Gently, cousin," said the young woman, stopping him short. "Not that I don't think that's a fine idea, but time is short. And that's your fault. Why did you keep me waiting for half an hour?"

"*Pardieu*! What a question! Because I thought I would be met by some fat German nanny or some dried-up Spanish duenna, not, God knows, a cousin as fair and succulent as the one I actually found waiting."

"I accept that excuse, but right now I have to be able to report to the one who sent me that I saw you, and that you're ready to obey her orders in all respects—as befits a noble cavalier when addressed by a great princess."

The young man dropped to one knee. "I await these orders humbly and eagerly."

"Oh! You can't kneel to me, Monseigneur!" Marina cried, lifting him to his feet. "What are you thinking?"

Then she added, with a sly smile, "What a shame you're so charming."

"Come," said the young man, taking the hands of his supposed cousin between his own and seating her beside him, "tell me whether my return is regarded with at least some satisfaction."

"More than that," she said, "with joy."

"And she's not unhappy to grant me this audience?"

"More than happy."

"And the message I carry will be greeted with sympathy?"

"With enthusiasm."

"And yet it's eight days since I arrived, and I've been waiting two days since our first contact!"

"You're charming, my cousin, but charm can't mint days. How long has it been since we returned from La Rochelle? Two and a half days."

"That's true."

"And of those two and a half days, how were the first two spent?"

"On the holiday fêtes, as I know—I watched them."

"From where?"

"From the street, like a mere mortal."

"What did you think of them?"

"They were superb."

"He has some imagination, doesn't he, our dear cardinal? His Majesty Louis XIII, dressed as Jupiter!"

"And as *Jupiter Stator*."

"*Stator* or otherwise, who cares?"

"Some care, my fair cousin. Such symbols matter."

"How so?"

"Do you know the significance of *Jupiter Stator*?"

"Not in the least."

"It means 'Jupiter comes'—or rather, where he comes *to*."

"And where does Jupiter come to?"

"To the foot of the Alps, of course."

"Ah, of course. So the lightning in his hand was meant to threaten both Austria and Spain?"

"Well . . . lightning made only of wood."

"And with no thunder."

"None at all, especially as the lightning of war is made from money, and neither king nor cardinal are well off at the moment. So, dear cousin, *Jupiter Stator*, after threatening both East and West, must set his lightning down without launching it."

"Oh! Say that tonight to our two poor queens, and you will make both of them very happy."

"I have better than that to tell them. I have a letter for Their Majesties from the Duke of Savoy, who swears that the French army will never pass over the Alps."

"Yes, well. Assuming that this time he keeps his word. Which isn't his way, as you may know."

"But this time he has every incentive to keep it."

"We chatter, cousin, a useless expense of time we can't afford to lose."

"It's your own fault, cousin." The young man smiled warmly, showing his teeth. "You're the one who didn't want to put the time to better use."

"So, because I'm devoted to my mistress, this is how I'm repaid? With reproaches? *Mon Dieu*! Men are so unjust!"

"I'm listening, cousin." The young man adopted the most serious expression he could manage.

"Well, then: Their Majesties expect to receive you this evening, around eleven o'clock."

"What, tonight? I have the honor to be received by Their Majesties tonight?"

"This very evening."

"I thought there was to be a ballet at Court tonight!"

"There is—but the queen, upon hearing of your arrival, immediately complained of fatigue and an unbearable headache. She said only sleep could give her relief. Bouvard was called, and recognized the symptoms as those of chronic migraine. For Bouvard may be the king's doctor, but he belongs to us, body and soul. He recommended rest and absolute repose—and thus the queen awaits you."

"But how shall I get into the Louvre? I don't imagine my name's been left at the gate."

"Don't worry, everything is taken care of. Tonight, dressed as a cavalier, take a stroll down Rue des Fossés-Saint-Germain. A page in buff and blue, the livery of Madame la Princesse, will be waiting for you at the corner of the Rue des Poulies. Give him the password and he'll conduct you to the corridor that leads to the queen's chambers, where he'll turn you over to her maid of honor. If possible, you'll be admitted immediately to Her Majesty's presence. If not, you'll wait in a nearby chamber until the time is right."

"And why can't you keep me company in the meantime, dear cousin? That would be infinitely more enjoyable."

"Because now that my duties are completed, I have business awaiting me elsewhere."

"You have the air of one who combines her business with pleasure."

"What would you have, cousin? We live only once."

At that moment they heard the chime of the clock from the Blancs-Manteaux convent. "Nine o'clock!" Marina cried. "Kiss me quick, cousin, and hurry me out. I barely have time to report to the Louvre and say that my cousin is a charming fellow who brings . . . what is it you bring the queen?"

"My life! Is that enough?"

"It's too much! Don't offer something that, once lent, can't be returned. *Au revoir,* cousin."

"Wait a moment." The young man stopped her. "What's the password I must give the page?"

"Of course, I forgot. You say *Casale,* and he'll answer *Mantua.*"

And the young woman presented her face for a kiss, not on the cheek this time, but on the lips. He kissed her—twice.

Then she rushed down the stairs like a woman who would stop for nothing.

Jacquelino stood for a moment, smiling, then picked up his beret, which had fallen at the beginning of the conversation, and adjusted it carefully on his head—presumably to give the messenger from the Louvre enough time to get away and vanish. Then he slowly descended the stairs, singing a song of Ronsard's:

> "It seems to me the day drags on
> Longer than a year goes on . . .
> Sadly, when I did my best
> To see the beauty of the lass
> Who holds my heart, at this pass
> Nothing I see, and nowhere I rest."

⁓

He was on the third verse of the song and the last step of the stairs when he glanced into the ground-floor common room and saw, by the glow from a wall sconce, a man lying on a table, pale, bloody, and apparently dying. At his side stood a monk who appeared to be listening to a last confession. Curious folk peered in at the doors and windows but dared not enter, restrained by the presence of the monk and the solemnity of the man's final act.

At this sight he ceased his song, and as the innkeeper was at hand, said, "Hey! Maître Soleil!"

Soleil approached, hat in hand. "What can I do for you, my handsome young man?"

"Why the devil is this man lying on a table with a monk beside him?"

"He's making his confession."

"*Pardieu*! I can see that! But who is he? And what does he have to confess?"

"Who is he?" The innkeeper sighed. "He's a brave and honest fellow named Étienne Latil, and my best client. Why confess? Because he probably has no more than a few hours to live. He was calling for a priest, so when my wife saw this worthy friar coming out of the Blancs-Manteaux, she begged him to come."

"And how does your honest man come to be dying?"

"Oh, Monsieur! Anyone else would already be dead ten times over. He took two terrible sword wounds through the chest, one from the front and one from the back."

"So he had a fight with two men?"

"Four, Monsieur, four!"

"A sudden quarrel?"

"A deliberate murder!"

"A murder?"

"Yes—to keep him from talking!"

"And if he'd talked, what would he have said?"

"That they'd offered him a thousand crowns to assassinate the Comte de Moret, and he'd refused."

The young man started at the name, fixed his attention on the innkeeper, and said, "Assassinate the Comte de Moret! Are you sure of this, my good man?"

"I got it from his own mouth. It was the first thing he said after asking for drink."

"The Comte de Moret," repeated the young man. "Antoine de Bourbon?"

"Antoine de Bourbon, yes."

"The son of King Henri IV?"

"And of Madame Jacqueline de Bueil, Comtesse de Moret."

"It's strange," murmured the young man.

"Strange or not, that's what he said."

After a moment's silence, to the astonishment of Maître Soleil, the young man pushed his way through the crowd of cooks and maids blocking the door, despite cries of "Hey! Where do you think you're going?" He entered the room occupied by the Capuchin and Étienne Latil and, approaching the table, dropped a heavy purse next to the wounded man.

"Étienne Latil," he said, "this is to pay for your treatment. If you recover, when you can be moved, have yourself brought to the hotel of the Duc de Montmorency, in Rue des Blancs-Manteaux. If you die, die in the knowledge that masses will be sung for your soul."

At the approach of the young man, the wounded man had risen on one elbow and, as if at the sight of a ghost, appeared struck dumb, eyes wide and mouth gaping.

But when the young man turned and walked away, the wounded man murmured, "The Comte de Moret!" and fell back on the table.

As for the friar, at the first entrance of the false Jacquelino into the room, he had stepped back and pulled his hood over his face, as if afraid of being recognized.

VII

Stairs and Corridors

Upon leaving the Inn of the Painted Beard, the Comte de Moret, for it was indeed he, went down the Rue de l'Homme-Armé, turned right on the Rue des Blancs-Manteaux, and knocked on the door of the Hotel de Montmorency. This was the town mansion of the Duc de Montmorency, Henri, the second of the name, and it had two doors, one on the Rue des Blancs-Manteaux and the other on the Rue Sainte-Avoye.

Clearly, the son of Henri IV was known to the household, for as soon as he was recognized, a young page of fifteen grabbed a four-branched candlestick, lit the tapers, and went on before him. The prince followed the page.

The Comte de Moret's rooms were on the first floor. In the outer room, the page lit the candelabras, then said to the prince, "I'm at His Highness's command."

"Has your master assigned you any duties this evening, Galaor?" asked the Comte de Moret.

"No, Monseigneur—I'm free."

"Will you go with me, then?"

"With pleasure, Monseigneur!"

"In that case, dress warmly and bring a good cloak. It's a cold night!"

"I'm ready!" said the young page. His master frequently employed him as a street runner, so he was an old hand at such matters. "Will I be guarding your horse?"

"Better: you'll be an honor guard at the Louvre. But not a word, Galaor, even to your master."

"Say no more, Monseigneur," said the lad, smiling and placing a finger to his lips. He moved toward the door.

"Wait," said the Comte de Moret. "I have further instructions."

The page bowed.

"Get a horse ready to go, and put loaded pistols in both holsters."

"Just one horse?"

"Yes, just one—you'll ride behind me. A second horse would attract attention."

"Just as Monseigneur orders."

Ten o'clock sounded. The count listened, counting each bronze beat. "Ten o'clock," he said. "Go, and have everything ready within a quarter of an hour."

The page bowed and went out, proud of being in the confidence of the count.

As to the latter, he went to his wardrobe and dressed in the outfit of a cavalier, simple but elegant, with a red doublet and blue breeches, both of velvet. His fine cambric shirt was trimmed with magnificent Brussels lace, showing through his doublet's slashed sleeves at cuffs and wrist. He drew on tall knee boots and donned a gray felt hat decorated with feathers that echoed the colors of his clothes, red and blue, pinned in place with a diamond brooch. Then he draped a rich baldric over his shoulder, and hung from it a red-hilted sword, a weapon both handsome and practical.

Finally, with that vanity natural to youth, he spent a few minutes on his appearance, making sure his naturally curly hair framed his face correctly, and that his fashionably long love-lock—which he wore because his mustache and goatee refused to grow as thick as he would have liked—fell properly to the left. He took a purse from a drawer to replace the one he'd left with Latil, and then, as if that reminded him, murmured, "But who the devil would want me killed?"

He reflected for a moment, but as he could think of no satisfactory answer to his question, with the insouciance of youth he set the matter aside. He patted himself to make sure he hadn't forgotten anything, glanced once more at the mirror, then went down the stairs singing the last verse of the song he'd begun at the Inn of the Painted Beard.

> "Song, go where I'm thinking of,
> Into the chamber of my love,
> There to kiss those fingers
> That brought to me such healing.
> Promise them all the feeling
> That in my heart still lingers."

At the street door, the count found the page waiting for him with a horse. He leaped into the saddle with the lightness and elegance of a consummate horseman. At his invitation, Galaor climbed up behind. After making sure the page was well seated, the count set his horse at a trot down Rue Maubué, took the Rue Troussevache to the Rue Saint-Honoré, and finally reached the Rue des Poulies.

At the corner of the Rue des Poulies and the Rue des Fossés-Saint-Germain, beneath a lamp-lit Madonna, a young lad sat on a borne. Seeing a cavalier with a page on his crupper, and thinking it was probably the gentleman he was waiting for, he rose and opened his cloak. Beneath it he wore a jacket of buff and blue: the livery of Madame la Princesse.

The count recognized the page as the one he was to meet. He set Galaor on the ground, dismounted, and approached the lad.

The page got down from his borne and waited respectfully.

"Casale," the count said.

"Mantua," the page replied.

The count gestured to Galaor to stay back, came near his guide, and said, "So I'm to follow you, my pretty lad?"

"Yes, Monsieur le Comte, if you would," the page replied, in a voice so musical, the prince immediately suspected he was dealing with a woman.

"Well, then," he said, abandoning the tone a man takes with a boy, "please be so kind as to show me the way."

The count's altered tone didn't escape the notice of the person he addressed. The page gave him a sidelong glance, tried and failed to stifle a laugh, then gestured in the direction they were to go and marched on before him.

At the drawbridge, the page whispered a password to the sentry, and they crossed over to the gate of the Louvre. Passing into the courtyard, they headed for the northeast corner.

Arriving at the inner gate, the page removed his cloak, displaying his livery of buff and blue, and said, in as masculine a voice as possible, "Household of Madame la Princesse."

But in doing so, the page's face was exposed to the light from the gate lantern. The rays glanced from golden hair that fell to rounded shoulders, glinted from blue eyes full of mischief and merriment, and glowed on a mouth both full and fine, as ready to bite as to kiss. And the Comte de Moret recognized Marie de Rohan-Montbazon, Duchesse de Chevreuse.

He caught up with her at the turn of the stairs, saying, "Dear Marie, did my friend the duke send you to make me jealous of him?"

"No, my dear Count," she said, "especially since he knows you're making a fool of yourself over Madame de la Montagne."

"Good answer," laughed the prince. "I see that as well as the most beautiful, you're still the wittiest creature in the world."

"If the end result of my journey from Holland is to hear compliments from you, Monseigneur," she said with a bow, "then the trip was worth it."

"Indeed! But I thought you'd been exiled after that little intrigue in the garden at Amiens."

"Oh, that! In recognition that I and Her Majesty were both

quite innocent—and at the insistence of the queen—the cardinal has deigned to forgive me."

"Unconditionally?"

"Well, I did have to take an oath to forego meddling in intrigue."

"And how are you keeping that oath?"

"Scrupulously, as you see."

"Does your conscience have nothing to say to you?"

"Why should it? I have a papal dispensation."

The count laughed.

"And besides," she continued, "is it intrigue to conduct a brother-in-law to meet his sister-in-law?"

"Dear Marie," said the count, taking her hand and kissing it with the passion he had inherited from his royal father, as we already saw with his "cousin" at the Inn of the Painted Beard. "Dear Marie, will you surprise me by revealing that your room is on the way to the queen's chamber?"

"Ah, you truly are the only genuine son of Henri IV! All the others are just . . . bastards."

"Even my brother, Louis XIII?" laughed the count.

"Especially your brother, Louis XIII—whom God preserve! How can he have so little of your blood in his veins?"

"We don't have the same mother, Duchess."

"And maybe not the same father, either."

"Ah, Marie!" the Comte de Moret cried. "You're too adorable not to be kissed!"

"Are you crazy? Trying to kiss a page on the staircase? It will be the ruin of your reputation—especially for one who just came from Italy."

"We can't have that," said the count. "And that's it—there goes my mood." He dropped the duchess's hand.

"Well!" she said. "The queen sends one of her loveliest women to meet him at the Inn of the Painted Beard, and he complains!"

"My cousin Marina?"

"Your 'cousin Marina,' who else?"

"Ah! *Ventre-saint-gris*! Who was that little enchantress?"

"What! You don't know?"

"No!"

"You don't know Fargis?"

"Fargis, the wife of our ambassador to Spain?"

"Exactly. She was given a position near the queen after that affair in the Amiens garden got the rest of us exiled."

"Well, well!" the Comte de Moret laughed. "I see the queen is well guarded, with the Duchesse de Chevreuse at the head of her bed and Madame de Fargis at the foot. My poor brother Louis! You must admit, Duchess, he has no luck at all."

"You're so delightfully impertinent, Monseigneur, that it's a good thing we've arrived."

"We're there?"

The duchess took a key from her pouch and opened the door of a dark corridor. "Here is your path, Monseigneur," she said.

"You're not going to take me all the way?"

"No, you're going by yourself."

"Am I? Well, I swore an oath I'd do this. Now a trap door will open beneath my feet, and it'll be good night to Antoine de Bourbon. Not that I have much to lose, since the women treat me so badly."

"Ingrate. If you knew who waited for you at the other end of this corridor. . . ."

"What! Does another woman await me at the end of the passage?"

"Yes, the third one this evening. Any more complaints?"

"No, no complaints from me! *Au revoir*, Duchess."

"Watch out for that trap door."

"I'll risk it."

The duchess shut the door, and the count found himself in complete darkness.

He hesitated for a moment. He had no idea where he was. He considered turning back, but the sound of the key turning in the lock forestalled that idea.

Finally, after hesitating a few more seconds, he decided to press on. "*Ventre-saint-gris!*" he said. "After all, the lovely duchess says I'm the true son of Henri IV, and it's no lie."

Arms extended in the dark, he advanced slowly toward the far end of the corridor. In complete darkness, even the bravest man will hesitate.

He'd gone scarcely twenty paces when he heard the rustling of a dress and the intake of a breath.

He stopped. The rustling and breathing stopped as well.

He was trying to decide what to say to the source of this charming sound, when a soft and trembling voice asked, "Is that you, Monseigneur?"

The voice was no more than two steps away. "Yes," said the count.

He stepped forward, and an outstretched hand found his own. But she instantly withdrew it, and he heard a faint cry, as melodious as a sylph's sigh or the sound of a wind-brushed harp.

The count started at the sound. He felt a new and unknown sensation.

It was delicious.

"Where are you?" he murmured.

"H-here," the voice stammered.

"I was told I would find a hand to guide me on my way. Are you . . . refusing it?"

The timid presence hesitated a moment, then said, "Here it is."

The count took the hand between his own and tried to bring it to his lips, but stopped as the voice cried, in alarm and appeal, "Monseigneur!"

"Your pardon, Mademoiselle," the count said, as respectfully as if speaking to the queen.

He lowered her hand, already halfway to his lips, and both fell silent. He yet kept her hand in his, and she didn't try to remove it, standing as still as if she'd lost the power, or the will, to move.

Her hand, resting in his, was as still as she was. But that didn't keep the count from realizing that it—that she—was small, fine, elegant, aristocratic, and, above all, virginal.

He stood, motionless and silent, holding her hand, entirely forgetting what had brought him there.

"Are you coming, Monseigneur?" the sweet voice asked.

"Where do you want me to go?" asked the count, somewhat at random.

"But . . . the queen is waiting for you. The queen."

"Oh, yes! I'd forgotten." He sighed. "Let's go."

He resumed his walk in the dark, a Theseus in a labyrinth simpler but darker than that of Crete, guided not by Ariadne's thread, but by Ariadne herself.

After a few steps, his Ariadne turned to the right. "We're here," she said.

"Alas!" murmured the count.

And in fact they had stopped before a large glass door that looked into the queen's antechamber.

Due to Her Majesty's indisposition, all the lights were out except for one lamp hanging from the ceiling. Through the glass, the lamp glinted like starlight.

By this dim glow the count tried to see his guide, but could distinguish no more than her outlines.

The girl stopped. "Monseigneur," she said, "now that there's enough light to see by, please follow me." And she removed her hand from his, despite his slight effort to retain it. She opened the door and entered the queen's antechamber. The count followed her.

Both tiptoed quietly across the chamber to the door on the opposite side, which opened into the queen's bedchamber. Suddenly they were stopped by an approaching sound: the noise of people coming up the grand staircase that led to the queen's suite.

"*Mon Dieu!*" murmured the girl. "Is it the king, leaving the ballet to check on Her Majesty—to see if she's really sick?"

"They're coming this way," said the prince.

"Wait here," said the girl. "I'll go see!"

She sprang to the staircase door, glanced through it, and dashed back to the count. "It's him!" she cried. "Quick, into this closet!"

And, opening a door hidden behind a tapestry, she pushed the count through it and went in after him.

Just in time. As the closet door closed, the staircase door opened and, preceded by two pages carrying torches, and followed by his two favorites, Baradas and Saint-Simon, behind whom came his valet, Beringhen, in walked King Louis XIII. Signaling his entourage to wait, he went on into the queen's chamber.

VIII

His Majesty King Louis XIII

We hope our readers will forgive us, but we believe it is time to present King Louis XIII to them, and to devote a chapter to his strange personality.

King Louis XIII was born Thursday, September 27, 1601, and was thus twenty-seven years and three months of age at the time of our story. A sad and drooping figure with a dark complexion and a black mustache, he didn't exhibit a single trait that recalled Henri IV in either appearance or character. He was so cheerless, so prematurely old, that he didn't even seem French. Spanish rumor held that he was the son of Virginio Orsini, Duke of Bracciano, a cousin of Marie de Médicis. Indeed, on her departure for France, Marie de Médicis, already twenty-seven, had received some advice from her uncle, the former Cardinal Ferdinand—the same Ferdinand who had poisoned his brother Francis and his sister-in-law Bianca Capello in order to ascend the throne of Tuscany.

Ferdinand's advice: "My dear niece, you go to marry a king who divorced his first wife because she was childless. You will be one month on the journey, with three handsome lads in your company: Virginio Orsini, who is already your paramour; Paolo Orsini; and finally, Concino Concini. By the time you arrive in France, make sure you are in such a condition as to prevent repudiation."

The Spanish asserted that Marie de Médicis had followed her uncle's advice to the letter. The trip from Genoa to Marseilles alone had taken ten days. Henri IV, though not particularly eager to see his "fat banker," as he called her, thought the journey strangely prolonged. The poet Malherbe sought a reason for this delay and, right or wrong, thought he'd found one: Neptune was so fond of the bride of the King of France that he was loath to give her up.

> Ten days at sea spent on pleasure?
> Such a thought would betray her.
> The Sea-King, fond of such treasure,
> Was just trying to delay her.

In Rubens's painting of Queen Marie's arrival, which hangs in the Louvre, her ship is surrounded by Neptune's Nereids. Perhaps this mythic excuse for her delay wasn't very credible—but Henri's former wife, Queen Margot, had never found his excuses very credible either.

Nine months later, Grand Duke Ferdinand was reassured to hear of the birth of the Dauphin Louis, immediately dubbed "the Just" because he was born under the sign of Libra.

From childhood, Louis XIII displayed the melancholy that was the hallmark of the house of Orsini. From birth, he had the tastes of a decadent Italian. A passable composer and musician, and an adequate painter, he was always cut out to be more of an artisan than a king, despite his reverence for the idea of royalty. Never physically strong, and subjected as a child to the abominable medical practices of the time, as a young man he was so sickly that three or four times he was almost given up for dead.

His first doctor, Héroard, kept a journal for twenty-eight years with daily records of everything he ate and everything he did. Héroard reports that even as a child, Louis was hard of heart, even cruel, with little feeling for others. He was whipped twice by the royal hand of Henri IV: once because he'd conceived such hatred for a certain gentleman that he demanded to be given a pistol to kill him with; the second time, because he'd used a mallet to crush a sparrow's head.

Once, just once, he displayed the determination of one who deserved to be a king. On the day of his coronation, as he was given the scepter of the Kings of France, a weighty object of gold and silver encrusted with jewels, his hand began to tremble. Seeing this, Monsieur de Condé, who in his capacity as first prince of the blood was near the king, reached out to help support the scepter.

Louis frowned and turned away. "No," he said. "I intend to bear it alone."

As a child, his chief amusements were coloring printed engravings, making houses of cards, and hunting small birds with his pet shrikes. "In everything he did," said L'Estoile, "he acted the child."

His two favorite pursuits were always music and hunting. In Héroard's journal, largely overlooked by the historians, we find the curious activities that defined his days:

> At noon, he played with his dogs, Patelot and Grisette, in the gallery. At one o'clock he returned to his room and went into the corner with Igret, his nurse, to play his lute—because he loved making music, and singing to himself, above all else.

Sometimes, for fun, he wrote poems about trifles, in the form of proverbs or maxims, and when that was his mood he wanted others to be in the same frame of mind. One day he told Doctor Héroard, "Turn this prose into verses: 'I want those who love me to love me long, while those who love me little should leave me, and soon.'"

And the good doctor, a better courtier than poet, replied with the following couplet:

> "Let those who love me linger near,
> While those who don't should disappear."

❦

Like all those of melancholy disposition, Louis XIII was a habitual liar. He always smiled his warmest upon those he was about to ruin. It was on Monday, the second of March, in the year 1613, that he first used that favorite phrase of François I, "I swear by my honor as a gentleman."

That same year, etiquette called for Louis to start being treated as an adult monarch, beginning with the practice of a nobleman presenting the young king his shirt every morning. The first to do this was Courtauvaux, one of his earliest companions. (The reader may remember that a later successor, Chalais, was accused of intending to poison the king while passing him his shirt.)

It was at around the same time that Luynes was first brought to the king by Concino Concini, who'd been elevated by the queen to the rank of Maréchal d'Ancre. Previously, the only servant Louis had had to keep his birds was a simple peasant from Saint-Germain named Pierrot. Luynes was named chief falconer, and thereafter Pierrot, who before had mostly obeyed only himself, was forced to recognize the authority of Luynes. The new chief falconer designated all the hawks, falcons, and shrikes as the king's "Cabinet of Birds." Louis was delighted by this whimsy, and from then on kept Luynes near him from morning till night—even, according to Héroard, calling out for him while asleep.

If Luynes wasn't always able to amuse him, at least he managed to distract him by encouraging the young king's taste for hunting—within the limits allowed such royal children. We've already seen Louis chasing birds around his apartment with his pet shrike. Luynes took him hunting rabbits with small greyhounds in the dry moats around the Louvre, and hawking at the Plaine Grenelle. It was there on January 1, 1617 (all dates are important in the life of a king like Louis XIII) that he took his first heron, and on April 18, at Vaugirard, he brought down his first partridge.

This led, eventually, to the Louvre's Pont Dormant, where he hunted man for the first time, and slew Concino Concini.

Let us consult the page of Héroard's journal for Monday, April 24, 1617, when Louis XIII first hunted man rather than sparrow, rabbit, heron, or partridge. Its account is curious, for the philosopher as well as the historian.

Here it is, verbatim:

Monday, April 24, 1617

His Majesty awoke at half past seven; his pulse was full and steady, face slightly flushed, complexion good, piss yellow. Did his business, combed, dressed, prayed to God; breakfast at half past eight: bread, jelly, a little clear wine, watered.

Between ten and eleven o'clock in the morning, the Maréchal d'Ancre was killed on the bridge of the Louvre.

Dined at noon: a dozen asparagus tips in salad, ten spoonfuls of chicken soup, a boiled capon served on asparagus, boiled veal, two roast pigeon wings, two slices of roast grouse with bread and jelly, five figs, fourteen dried cherries, more bread, some full-bodied claret, all tempered with a teaspoon of fennel.

Then there is a gap. Given the significance of the day's events, the young patient feels a need to escape his doctor for a while. He climbs up onto a pool table to address his courtiers. He receives members of Parliament. He makes pronouncements like a king. But at six, his appetite returns and he falls back into the clutches of his doctor.

Six-thirty, supper: a dozen asparagus tips in salad, bread, a boiled capon served on asparagus, mushrooms in butter on toast, two roast squab wings, bread and jelly, the juice of two oranges, five sweet figs, candied beans, dried cherries, a little more bread, some full-bodied claret, all tempered with a teaspoon of fennel.

Played until half past seven.

Did his business: soft, yellow, copious.

Played until half past nine.

Drank tea, undressed, went to bed. Pulse steady, complexion good. Prayed to God; asleep by ten; slept until seven.

Very reassuring, isn't it, this account of the royal child's day? You might be afraid that the murder of his mother's lover, the man who was most likely the father of his brother Gaston, who bore the title Constable of France—in short, the second man in the kingdom after himself—would cause him to lose his appetite for food and for fun. With blood on his hands for the first time, it might even make him hesitate to pray. But no. It's true, lunch was delayed an hour, but he couldn't very well eat lunch at the same time he was peering through the window of the Louvre to watch Vitry assassinate the Maréchal d'Ancre.

He even found time to play, from seven to seven-thirty, and again from nine to nine-thirty—which was contrary to his habits, and in the twenty-eight years that Doctor Héroard chronicled in his journal, occurred just this once.

Moreover, he went to bed with a good complexion and a steady pulse. He prayed to God at ten o'clock, then slept until seven in the morning: nine hours' rest.

Poor child!

When he awoke, he was king in fact as well as in name. After the manly activities of the day before, his good night's sleep gave him the strength to behave like a king. The queen mother was not only disgraced, but exiled to Blois. She was forbidden to see her daughters the princesses, or her beloved son Gaston. Her ministers were dismissed, and only the Bishop of Luçon, later to become the great cardinal, was permitted to follow her into exile, where he would try to fill the place in her heart left empty by the murdered Concini.

But if he was king, Louis XIII was not yet a man. Married for two years to the Infanta of Spain, Anne of Austria, he was her husband in name only. Monsieur Durand, the Minister of War Finance, wrote court ballets for Louis in which he appeared as a Demon of Fire who sang tender verses to the queen, gallantry that amounted to no more than:

> Beautiful sun, for you I would
> Suffer your fires forever,
> Just look where you lead me,
> And know your power,
> In making me what I am.

But though he dressed in ballet clothing like one aflame, when he went to bed and removed his clothes, the flames went with them.

As the simulated passions of *The Deliverance of Renaud* had led nowhere, they tried again with *The Adventures of Tancrède in the Enchanted Forest*. In this ballet, the choreography of Monsieur de Porchère depicted a boy-king who was curious to know what happened between a husband and bride on their wedding night. Monsieur d'Elbeuf and Mademoiselle de Vendôme even gave the king a personal, private reprise of the action of the play on their own wedding night. No good: the king spent two hours in their nuptial chamber, sitting on the edge of the bed, and then retired quietly to his own chamber, still a boy.

Finally, it was Luynes who, tired of being harassed by the Spanish Ambassador and the papal nuncio, undertook to force the consummation of the king's marriage, despite the risk to his favor and position.

The big day was set for January 25, 1619. We turn once more to Doctor Héroard's journal for the entry of that date.

On January 25, 1619, the king, unaware of what awaited him at the end of the day, arose in excellent health and good countenance, and was even relatively cheerful. After breakfasting at 9:15, he heard mass at the Chapelle de la Tour, presided over the King's Council, dined at noon, made a visit to the queen, went to the Tuileries by the river gallery, returned the same way at half past four to meet the Council once more, went to Monsieur de Luynes's rooms to practice ballet, supped at eight, visited the queen again, leaving her at ten o'clock, returned to his apartments, and went to bed—but he had barely settled in before Luynes entered his room and urged him to get up.

The king looked at Luynes, as astonished as if the man had proposed a trip to China. But Luynes insisted, saying that Europe was beginning to worry about seeing the throne of France without an heir, and it would be a shame for him if his sister, Madame Christine, who had just married Prince Victor-Amadeus of Piedmont, son of the Duke of Savoy, should have a child before the queen had a dauphin. But as these reasons, which appealed only to the head, didn't seem to move the king, Luynes simply picked him up and carried him to where he didn't want to go.

If you doubt this little detail because you hear it from a novelist instead of from the historians, read the dispatch of January 30, 1619 of the papal nuncio, in which you will find a sentence that seems conclusive: *Luynes took the king against his will and led him almost by force into the queen's bed.*

But if this didn't lose Luynes his favor—on the contrary, he won the title of Constable of France—he gained little else for his pains. The dauphin, in his race to appear before the first-born of the Princess of Piedmont, failed to win the day, as he wasn't born until nineteen years later, in 1638—while Luynes, who should have had the pleasure of seeing the tree he'd planted bear fruit, died in 1621 of spotted fever. His death left the way open for the return to Paris of Marie de Médicis, and with the end of her exile she brought Richelieu back to the King's Council. A year later, he was a cardinal; and the year after that, prime minister.

Thereafter it was Richelieu who ruled, and who, by opposing the policies of Austria and Spain, fell out with both Anne of Austria and Marie de Médicis. From that moment, he earned their hatred and became the object of their plots. Marie de Médicis, like the king, had a cleric presiding over her council, and as with the king, he was a cardinal: Bérulle. But Cardinal Richelieu was a man of genius, while Cardinal Bérulle was a fool. Meanwhile, Monsieur, the king's brother, for whom Richelieu had arranged a marriage, used the immense fortune he'd gained from Mademoiselle de Montpensier to conspire against the cardinal. A secret council was organized around Doctor Bouvard, who'd replaced the brave Doctor Héroard as the king's physician.

Monsieur would be successor to Louis XIII should Louis die without an heir, and through Bouvard he had his finger on the pulse of the patient—for Bouvard, a man devoted to the Spanish cause, and who lived for the Church, was the evil genius of the two queens. Everyone knew that this melancholy king, consumed by ennui, wrought by care, who felt loved by none and hated by all, whom the doctors plagued with the lethal medicine of the time, purging relentlessly and bleeding repeatedly, might vanish from one moment to the next, disappearing into the black humors that defined his life.

If the king died, Richelieu would be at the mercy of his enemies and, within twenty-four hours of the death of the king, would be hanged. The Comte de Chalais was disinclined to wait for this event, however, and offered to kill the cardinal. Marie de Médicis seconded the motion, Madame de Conti bought the daggers, but sweet Anne of Austria voiced an objection of only three words: "He's a priest."

Thus the king, who since the assassination of Henri IV had hated his mother, since the conspiracy of Chalais had suspected his brother, since the love affair with Buckingham and, especially, since the scandal of the garden of Amiens despised the queen—the king, who abhorred his wife as he loathed all women, lacking the virtues of the Bourbons but with only half the vices of the Valois, became increasingly cold and aloof from his family. He knew that his projected war in Italy, or rather the cardinal's projected war, was anathema to Marie de Médicis, Gaston d'Orléans, and particularly Anne of Austria, because it was really a war against Ferdinand II and Philip IV, and the queen was half-Austrian and half-Spanish.

So when, under the pretext of a violent headache, the queen declined to attend the ballet being danced that evening in honor of the capture of La Rochelle—that is, in honor of the victory of her husband over her lover—Louis XIII suddenly suspected her of conspiring. Throughout the evening he'd had his eye not on the dancers, but on the queen mother and Gaston d'Orléans, meanwhile sharing in a low voice with the cardinal, who stood beside him in his box, comments that had nothing to do with the choreography. When the ballet ended, instead of returning to his chambers, Louis had the idea of paying a surprise visit to the queen, to see her situation for himself. And that's why we've seen him arrive so unexpectedly, preceded by two pages, accompanied by his two favorites, and followed by Beringhen, appearing in the hall just as the Comte de Moret and his guide disappeared into the closet.

Five minutes after entering the queen's chambers, Louis XIII left them. Here's what happened during those five minutes.

Royal etiquette decreed that, when the king slept under the same roof as the queen, it was forbidden to bar the doors of the queen's chambers. The king thus had no difficulty in passing through the three doors that separated the gallery from the queen's bedroom.

Upon entering her bedroom, he took a quick look around, peering into all the darkest shadows and farthest corners.

Everything was in perfect order. The queen was sleeping with a calm that spoke only of chastity, breathing smoothly and deeply as Louis XIII, more jealous of his power as king than of his rights as a husband, left the doorway and approached the bed.

But queens are light sleepers, and though thick Flanders carpets muffled the footsteps of her august husband, her breathing fluttered and paused, and a hand of wonderful whiteness and elegance drew aside the bed-curtain. A head, hair adorably disarranged, rose from the pillow, and two large astonished eyes fixed for a moment on the unexpected visitor, as a voice, trembling with surprise, exclaimed, "What, is it you, Sire?"

"Myself, Madame," the king coldly replied, while taking his hat in his hand, as every gentleman must before a lady.

"And by what happy chance do you favor me with a visit?" continued the queen.

"I heard that you were unwell, Madame. Concerned for your health, I wanted to come myself to say that, unless you take the trouble to visit me, I will probably not have the pleasure of seeing you tomorrow or the day after."

"Your Majesty goes hunting?" asked the queen.

"No, Madame; Bouvard felt that after all these festivals, which are fatiguing for me, I should be purged and bled. So tomorrow, and the day after, I shall bleed. Good night, Madame, and excuse me for having awakened you. By the way, who is serving you tonight, Madame de Fargis or Madame de Chevreuse?"

"Neither, sire—it is Mademoiselle Isabelle de Lautrec."

"Ah! Very good," said the king, as if the name were reassuring. "But where is she?"

"In the next room, where she sleeps fully clothed on a couch. Does Your Majesty wish me to call her?"

"No, thank you. *Au revoir,* Madame."

"*Au revoir,* Sire." And Anne, with a sigh of regret—feigned or real, but, under the circumstances, we suspect feigned—released the curtain of the bed and dropped her head to the pillow.

As for Louis XIII, he resumed his hat, gave the room a final look, which showed he was still suspicious, and went out, muttering, "It seems this time the cardinal was mistaken."

He entered the antechamber where his retinue awaited him. "The queen is indeed very ill," he said. "Follow me, Messieurs!" And in the same order they had come, the procession resumed its march toward the chambers of the king.

What Passed in Queen Anne of Austria's Bed-chamber After the Departure of King Louis

No sooner was the sound of footsteps fading down the hall, along with the last reflections of the flickering torches, when the door of the closet in which the Comte de Moret had taken refuge was gently opened by his guide, and the head of the young lady peeked from the opening.

Then, seeing that all had returned to silence and darkness, she ventured out and looked down the gallery, where the last rays of the pages' torches were disappearing.

Finding that the danger passed, she returned to the closet and said to the count, light as a bird, "Come out, Monseigneur."

Then, remaining always at a distance where the young man could not quite see her face clearly, she opened one after another the three doors which the king had closed behind him.

The young man followed her, speechless, breathless, bewildered. In the narrow, dark closet, the girl had had no choice but to squeeze up against him, and, although protected by the powerful hand of chastity, she couldn't prevent the count from becoming drunk on her breath, absorbing through every pore the sensuous scent that emanates from the body of a young woman, the very fragrance of nubile youth.

Before opening the last door, hearing his footsteps approaching, she extended her hand toward the count and said, in a voice not entirely steady, "Monseigneur, be so kind as to wait here. When she wants to receive you, Her Majesty will call." And she went in to the queen.

This time, Anne of Austria was neither sleeping nor pretending to sleep. "Is that you, dear Isabelle?" she asked, drawing aside the curtain more quickly and rising more eagerly than she had for the king.

"Yes, Madame, it's me," the young woman replied, standing so her head was in shadow and the queen couldn't see the flush that lit up her face.

"You know the king just left?"

"I saw him, Madame."

"He doubtless suspects."

"Perhaps, but he can't be sure."

"The count is here?"

"In the next chamber."

"Light a taper and give me a hand mirror."

Isabelle obeyed, giving the mirror to the queen, and holding the candle to illuminate it.

Anne of Austria was pretty rather than beautiful. Her features were very small, the nose undistinguished, but her skin was clear and she had the glorious blond hair of the Flemish dynasty she shared with Charles V and Philip II. A thorough coquette, she was well aware of its effect on men, even her brother-in-law Monsieur, so she took the trouble to arrange a few locks that had become ruffled, straightened the folds of her long silk robe, and raised herself to pose on one elbow. Returning the mirror to her maid of honor with a smile of thanks, she indicated that she was ready.

Isabelle put the mirror and the candle on the vanity, bowed respectfully, and retired through the door where the queen had told the king her maid of honor was asleep on a couch.

The bedchamber remained lit by the double glow of the candle and a small lamp, both placed so as to shed their rays on the side of the bed where Anne of Austria had spoken to the king, and now waited to give audience to the Comte de Moret.

However, left alone, the queen, before calling him, seemed to be awaiting someone or something. Several times she turned toward the rear of the room, gesturing and muttering impatiently.

Finally, almost together, two doors opened at the back of the room. From one came a young man of twenty, with a lively face, black hair, and hard eyes, which softened into insincerity. He was splendidly attired in white satin, with a red cloak embroidered with gold. He wore the Order of Saint-Esprit at his neck, as shown in contemporary portraits of him, and held a white felt hat decorated with two feathers the color of his cloak.

This young man was Gaston d'Orléans, usually referred to as Monsieur, and according to the scandal-mongers of the Louvre was the particular favorite of his mother because he was the son of the handsome Concino Concini. And anyone who sees the image of the one next to the other, as we did the other day at the Museum of Blois, where hang the portraits of the Maréchal d'Ancre and the second son of Marie de Médicis, would note the extraordinary resemblance between the two that gives credence to that grave accusation.

We said that since the Chalais affair, the king had held Monsieur in contempt. Indeed, Louis XIII did have a kind of conscience—he was sensitive to what was then called the honor of the crown, and is now called the honor of France. His egotism and vanity had, in Richelieu's hands, been molded from vices into a sort of virtue. But Gaston, both disingenuous and cowardly, had been deeply implicated in the conspiracy of Nantes. He had wanted to enter the King's Council; and to keep the peace, Richelieu had consented; but when Monsieur wanted to bring with him his adviser, the corrupt Ornano, Richelieu had refused. The young prince had shouted, sworn, stormed, and declared that the Council could either accept Ornano voluntarily or by force. Richelieu, who couldn't arrest Gaston, instead arrested Ornano. At that, Gaston had burst through the door of the Council, and in a haughty voice demanded to know who had dared to arrest his adviser.

"It was I," Richelieu calmly responded.

And that would have been the end of it, leaving Gaston seething in quiet shame, if Madame de Chevreuse, at the urging of Spain, had not herself urged Chalais on. Chalais went to Monsieur and offered to rid him of the cardinal. This is what he proposed, or rather whispered, to Gaston: he would go with his followers to dine with Richelieu at his château of Fleury, and there at his table, betray his hospitality by having his men-at-arms assassinate the defenseless priest. For sixty years, Spain had extended its hideous yellow-stained hand in this way to remove anyone great enough to oppose it. In politics, removal means death. Thus she had removed Coligny, William of Nassau, Henri III, Henri IV—and now it was Richelieu's turn. It was a process as crude as it was effective.

But this time, it failed.

After that incident, Richelieu, like Hercules in the Augean stables, began cleaning the Court of its treacherous princes. The Vendômes, two bastards of Henri IV, were arrested. The Comte de Soissons fled, Madame de Chevreuse was exiled, and the Duc de Longueville was disgraced. As for Monsieur, he signed a confession in which he denounced and renounced his friends. He was then married and enriched, but dishonored.

Chalais bore the shame of the conspiracy alone, and it cost him his head.

And yet Monsieur, already so deep in dishonor, was then only twenty years old.

Entering by the other door, at almost the same time as Monsieur, was a woman of fifty-five or fifty-six, royally dressed, wearing a small gold crown atop her head, a long ermine-trimmed purple robe, and a dress of white satin with gold embroidery. The ensemble was new, but neither beautiful nor distinguished. Her corpulent bulk showed why Henri IV had called her his "fat banker." Marie de Médicis, resentful and discontented, delighted in intrigue. Though she was the mental inferior of Catherine de Médicis, she eclipsed her in debauchery. If we are to believe all that was said, only one of her children belonged to Henri IV: Henriette, later Queen of England.

But of all her children, she loved none but Gaston. She was willing to advance his interest even if it meant the death of her eldest son, an event she already welcomed as inevitable. As with Catherine de Médicis and her son Henri III, her obsession was to see Gaston on the throne. But Louis XIII hated her as much as she hated him for a more serious charge than that. It was said that she as good as placed the knife in the hands of the assassin Ravaillac, who killed Henri IV. A confession taken from Ravaillac on the wheel had been said to implicate both her and the Duc d'Épernon—but a fire at the Palace of Justice had removed all trace of this confession.

The day before, mother and son had been summoned by Anne of Austria, who informed them that the Comte de Moret, who had arrived in Paris a week earlier, had letters for them from the Duke of Savoy. They came to the queen, as we have seen, by two different doors, which led to their own apartments. If caught, they planned to plead concern for the indisposition of Her Majesty, learned of only at the ballet, an illness that so worried them that they came directly, without even changing their clothes. As for the Comte de Moret, in the event of surprise, he was to hide somewhere. A young man of twenty-two is always easy to hide; Anne of Austria had experience with that sort of conjuring trick.

Meanwhile, the Comte de Moret waited in the next room where he, to the bottom of his heart, thanked God for the delay. How could he appear before the queen troubled and trembling after parting from his unknown guide? The ten-minute reprieve was barely enough to enable him to calm the beating of his heart and steady his voice. From this agitation he passed into a reverie, more sweet than any he'd known before.

All at once, the voice of Anne of Austria made him start and break out of his reverie. "Count," she asked, "are you there?"

"Yes, Madame," replied the count, "here and awaiting the orders of Your Majesty."

"Come in, then, for we are eager to receive you."

X

Letters Read Aloud and Letters Read Alone

The Comte de Moret shook his young and graceful head, as if to dispel his dreams, and, pushing open the door before him, stood on the threshold of Anne of Austria's bedchamber.

We must admit that his first glance, despite the high-ranking people present, was to look for his charming guide, who had left him without ever revealing her face. But though his eyes sought the most obscure corners of the room, eventually he had to give up and set his gaze and mind on the group within the light.

This group, as we've said, consisted of the queen mother, the reigning queen, and the Duc d'Orléans.

The queen mother was standing beside the bed; Anne of Austria was upon it; and Gaston was sitting beside his sister-in-law.

The count bowed deeply, advanced toward the bed, and fell on one knee before Anne of Austria, who presented her hand to kiss. Then, stooping to the floor, the young prince touched his lips to the hem of Marie de Médicis's robe, and finally, still on one knee, turned to Gaston to kiss his hand—but Monsieur lifted him up and said, "Come into my arms, my brother!"

The Comte de Moret, who as a true son of Henri IV had a frank and honest heart, could not believe all that was said of Gaston. He'd been in England during the Chalais conspiracy, and afterward had known Madame de Chevreuse there, who'd been careful in what she'd said about the affair. He'd been in Italy during the siege of La Rochelle, when Gaston had pretended illness to avoid going to the front. And, having avoided the enticements of the Court, he had taken no part in those intrigues which had furthered the jealousies of Marie de Médicis against her husband's other children.

He thus went joyfully into Gaston's embrace, honoring his brother with the warmth of his heart.

Then, saluting the queen, he said, "Your Majesty should know, given the joy I feel at admission to the royal presence on his behalf, that I am profoundly grateful to the Duke of Savoy."

The queen smiled. "Indeed," she said, "it is for us to be thankful for your kind help to two poor disgraced princesses, one rebuffed from the love of her husband, the other from the affection of her son, beside a brother who's been refused his brother's embrace—because you bear, as you say, letters that must bring us consolation."

The Comte de Moret took three sealed envelopes from his doublet. "This, Madame," he said, handing a letter to the queen, "is a letter addressed to you from Don Gonzalès de Cordova, Governor of Milan and representative in Italy of His Majesty Philip IV, your august brother. He begs you to use all the influence you have to keep Monsieur de Fargis as ambassador to Madrid."

"My influence!" repeated the queen. "I might have influence over a king who was a man, but who could have influence over a king who is a ghost but a necromancer such as the cardinal-duke?"

The count bowed, then turned to the queen mother and presented her with a second letter. "As to this note, Madame, all I know is that it's very important, and in the personal handwriting of the Duke of Savoy. Everything within it is secret, and it was to be given to Your Majesty in person."

The queen mother took the letter eagerly, opened it, and, as she could not read it where she was, approached the candle and the lamp on the vanity.

"And finally," continued the Comte de Moret, presenting the third letter to Gaston, "here is a note addressed to Your Highness from Madame Christine, your august sister, who is more beautiful and charming than August itself."

As each read the letter addressed to him or her, the count took advantage of the time to sweep his gaze once more into every corner of the room—but it held only the two queens, Gaston, and himself.

Marie de Médicis returned to her daughter-in-law's bedside and said, addressing the count, "Monsieur, when we deal with a man of your rank who makes himself available to a disgraced prince and two such oppressed women, it's best to keep no secrets from him. Better to accept his word of honor that, as an ally or a neutral, he will religiously keep any secret entrusted to him."

"Your Majesty," said the Comte de Moret, bowing and pressing his hand to his chest, "you have my word of honor to remain silent, whether as neutral or ally. But my silence should not be regarded as a commitment of devotion."

The two queens exchanged a look. "You have reservations, then?" Marie de Médicis asked with her voice, as Anne of Austria and Gaston asked with their eyes.

"I have two, Madame," replied the count in a soft but firm voice. "To my regret, I must remind you that I am the son of King Henri IV. I cannot draw my sword against the Protestants or against the king my brother. Likewise I cannot refuse to draw steel upon any foreign enemy against whom the King of France makes war, if the King of France calls for this honor."

"Neither the king nor the Protestants are our enemies, Prince," said the queen mother, emphasizing the word *prince*. "Our enemy, our sole enemy, our mortal enemy, who has sworn our destruction, is the cardinal."

"I have no affection for the cardinal, Madame, but I have the honor to point out that it's difficult for a gentleman to make war on a priest. However, on the other hand, if it pleases God to send him adversity, I shall regard it as punishment for his improper conduct toward you. Is that enough for Your Majesty to trust me?"

"I believe you already know, Monsieur, what Don Gonzalès de Cordova wrote to my daughter-in-law. Gaston will tell you what his sister Christine wrote to him. Gaston?"

The Duc d'Orléans held out his letter to the Comte de Moret, inviting him to read it. The count took it and did so.

The Princess Christine wrote to her brother reasons why it was best to give her father-in-law, Charles-Emmanuel of Savoy, possession of Mantua and Montferrat rather than allowing the Duc de Nevers the legacy of the Gonzaga, as the duke was no friend to Louis XIII—while the heir to the Duke of Savoy, her husband Victor-Amadeus, was brother-in-law to the King of France.

The Comte de Moret returned the letter to Gaston with a friendly salute. "What do you think, brother?" asked the latter.

"I am no politician," replied the Comte de Moret, smiling; "but as regards the family, it certainly sounds reasonable."

"And now, for my turn," said Marie de Médicis, presenting to the Comte de Moret her letter from the Duke of Savoy. "It's only right that you know the contents of what you were carrying."

The count took the sheet and read the following: "Do everything possible to prevent the war in Italy—but if, despite the efforts of our friends, war is declared, be confident that Susa Pass will be defended vigorously." That was, ostensibly at least, all the letter contained.

The young man bowed before Marie de Médicis with every mark of profound respect. "Now," said the queen mother, "it remains for us to thank our young and able messenger for his skill and dedication, and promise that if we succeed in our projects, his fortune will follow ours."

"A thousand thanks to Your Majesty's good intentions, but as soon as devotion sees the hope of reward, it is tainted by calculation and ambition. My own fortune is sufficient to my needs, and I ask little personal glory to justify my birth."

"Then," said Marie de Médicis, while her daughter-in-law presented her hand for the Comte de Moret to kiss, "any such obligations are ours alone. Gaston, give your brother your love. But quickly: when midnight strikes, he must be out of the Louvre."

The count sighed and took one last look around. He'd hoped that the same guide who'd brought him here would lead him to the exit.

With a sigh of regret, he gave up that hope. He saluted the two queens, and then, somewhat agitated, followed the Duc d'Orléans.

Gaston led him to his own apartments, where he opened a door to a secret staircase. "Now, my brother," he said, "receive my thanks once more, and believe in my sincere gratitude."

The count bowed. "Is there a password?" he asked. "Something I need to say to escape?"

"None. Just knock on the window of the Swiss Guards and say 'Household of the Duc d'Orléans, night service,' and they'll let you pass."

The count took one last look behind him, sent his most tender sigh toward his unknown guide, then went down two flights, knocked on the window of the Swiss Guards, spoke the necessary words, and immediately found himself in the courtyard. Then, as one needed a password to enter the Louvre but none to leave it, he crossed the drawbridge and found himself again at the corner of the Rue des Fossés-Saint-Germain and the Rue des Poulies. There waiting for him were his page and his horse, or rather the page and the horse of the Duc de Montmorency.

"Ah," he whispered, "I'll wager she's less than eighteen and ravishingly beautiful. *Ventre-saint-gris*! I think I must conspire against the cardinal if that's the only way to see her again."

Meanwhile, Gaston d'Orléans, after making sure the Comte de Moret had made it safely into the courtyard, returned to his chambers, locked himself in his bedroom, closed the curtains to ensure that no prying eyes could see him, and, taking the letter from his sister Christine from his pocket, held it with trembling hand over the flame of a candle.

Slowly, under the influence of the heat, in between the lines written in black, new lines appeared—written in the same hand, but traced in secret ink, now appearing in yellow and red.

These newly revealed lines read: "Continue your apparent courtship of Marie de Gonzague, but secretly reassure the queen. It is only upon our older brother's death that Anne of Austria can assume the crown—and if she does not, my dear Gaston, then with the support of Madame de Fargis and Madame de Chevreuse, she must find a way to be, if not queen, then regent."

"Oh," murmured Gaston, "don't worry, my dear little sister, I'll be on guard." And, opening a desk, he locked the letter in a secret drawer.

As for the queen mother, as soon as the Duc d'Orléans had departed, she took leave of her daughter-in-law and returned to her apartment, where she undressed, donned her night-clothes, and then dismissed her women.

Left alone, she pulled a bell-sash hidden by curtains. Within moments, a man of forty-five to fifty, with a yellow face and black hair, eyebrows, and mustache, answered the bell, entering through a door hidden by the tapestry.

This man was musician, physician, and astrologer to the queen mother. He was, sad to say, the successor of Henri IV, of Vittorio Orsini, Concino Concini, Bellegarde, Bassompierre, and Cardinal Richelieu: the Provençal Vautier, who had made himself a doctor to manage her body and an astrologer to manage her mind.

Richelieu's fall, if you can call it such, had been succeeded by the rise of Cardinal Bérulle, a fool, and of Vautier, a charlatan—and those who knew what influence he had on the queen mother said that, if anything, his exceeded that of the cardinal.

Vautier came into the antechamber outside the queen's bedroom. "Quick, quick," she said, "bring here, if you have it, the liquid that reveals the invisible writings!"

"Yes, Madame," Vautier said, drawing a flask from his pouch. "Your Majesty's needs are never forgotten! Here it is. Did Your Majesty finally receive the letter she was expecting?"

"Right here," said the queen mother, taking the letter from her bosom. "Just a few insignificant lines from the Duke of Savoy. But it's obvious he has something more important to tell me, or he wouldn't send such a banal letter in care of one of my husband's bastards."

She handed the letter to Vautier, who unfolded and read it. "Indeed," he said, "there must be more to it than that."

The apparent writing, as previously shown, was five or six lines at the top of the page in the hand of Charles-Emmanuel. But given the axiom that one must always read between the lines, it was clearly time to call on the chemical expertise of Vautier.

One thing was certain: if some invisible message was hidden in the letter from the Duke of Savoy, it would be below the last line, on the remaining three-quarters of the page.

Vautier dipped a brush in the liquid he'd prepared and carefully washed the bottom part of the letter. As the brush moistened the white surface, lines immediately began to form here and there, and after five minutes of such treatment, the following advice was distinctly visible:

"Pretend to oppose your son Gaston's fervent courtship of Marie de Gonzague. If an Italian campaign is decided upon despite your opposition, get Gaston command of the army as a pretext for separating him from La Gonzague. The cardinal-duke, whose sole ambition is to be the foremost general of our age, will resign in protest. The king will accept the inevitable!"

Marie de Médicis and her adviser shared a look. "Do you have any better advice to offer me?" asked the queen mother.

"No, Madame," he replied. "I have always found it wise to follow the advice of the Duke of Savoy."

"Then let's follow it," Marie de Médicis said with a sigh. "We can't be in a worse position than we are now. Have you consulted the heavens, Vautier?"

"This evening I spent an hour atop Catherine de Médicis's observatory."

"And what say the stars?"

"They promise Your Majesty complete triumph over your enemies."

"So be it," said Marie de Médicis, and presented the astrologer a hand somewhat distorted by fat, but still attractive, which he kissed respectfully.

And they withdrew into the bedchamber together and closed the door behind them.

Alone in her room, Anne of Austria listened to the receding footsteps of Gaston d'Orléans and of her mother-in-law. When the sound had completely faded, she slowly rose, pushed her petite feet into her Spanish slippers of sky-blue satin embroidered with gold, and sat down next to her vanity. From a drawer she took out a small canvas bag containing iris powder, a perfume she preferred for her clothes above all others, and which her mother-in-law had brought her from Florence. This powder she sprinkled on the blank second page of the letter from Gonzalès de Cordova—just as, by different means, the same result was obtained from the note from Christine to Gaston, and from that of Charles-Emmanuel to the queen mother.

Under the powder, letters soon appeared on the sheet sent from Gonzalès de Cordova to the queen. This message was from King Philip IV himself. She read:

Sister, I know from our good friend Monsieur de Fargis of the plan by which, in the event of the death of King Louis XIII, you promise to marry his brother and heir to the

throne, Gaston d'Orléans. However, it would be even bet-
ter if, at the time of Louis's death, you were with child.

The Queens of France have a great advantage over their
husbands in that they can produce dauphins without them,
an ability their husbands lack.

Ponder this incontestable truth, and as you do not need
my letter to inspire your meditations—burn it.

—Philip

The queen, after reading this letter from her brother the king a second time, no doubt in order to engrave its every word upon her memory, took it by one of its corners, put it to the candle, set it alight, and held it in the air until the fire consumed it, illuminating her beautiful hand and making the tips of her fingernails glow pink. Only then did she drop the letter, which dissolved into thousands of sparks before it struck the floor. But, to reinforce her memory, she then transcribed the entire letter on paper, and locked it in a secret drawer in her desk.

She then returned slowly to her bed and slipped her satin dressing gown from her shoulders to her hips, emerging like Venus in a wave of silver. She lay down slowly and with a sigh dropped her head on her pillow, murmuring, "Oh, Buckingham! Buckingham!"

And thereafter only a few stifled sobs troubled the silence of the royal chamber.

XI

The Red Sphinx

In the gallery of the Louvre there hangs a portrait by the Jansenist painter Philippe de Champaigne depicting Cardinal Richelieu as he truly was, a figure fine, keen, and vigorous.

Unlike the Flemish, his countrymen, or the Spanish, his masters, Philippe de Champaigne was spare in his use of color, avoiding the bright hues seen in the palettes of Rubens and Murillo. In fact, he bathed the somber minister in a flood of half-light, as if emerging from the twilight of politics, he whose motto was *Aquila in Nubibus*—an eagle in the clouds. The image could be more flattering, but that would elevate a lie above the truth.

Study this portrait, all you men of conscience who would, after two and a half centuries, resurrect the illustrious dead and get a sense of this physical and moral genius, a man maligned by his contemporaries, ignored and almost forgotten during the following century, who found the respect he was entitled to by posterity only after two hundred years in the grave.

This portrait has the power to stop one short and almost force contemplation. Is it a man or is it a ghost, that creature in the red robe, white cappa magna, Venetian collar, and red biretta, with the broad forehead, gray hair and mustache, piercing gray eyes, and hands fine, though thin and pale? This figure, burning with eternal fever, seems alive only in the flush of the cheeks. Does it not feel like the more you contemplate this portrait, the less you know if it's a living being or, like Saint Bonaventure, a dead man returned from beyond the grave to write his own memoirs? Does it not seem as if he might suddenly emerge from the canvas, step out of the frame, and walk up to you, causing you to recoil as if from a ghost?

What is clear and undeniable in this painting is that it depicts a man of mind and intelligence, and nothing more. Here is neither heart nor spirit—fortunately for France. In the vacuum of the monarchy between Henri IV and Louis XIV, with a king so weak and diffident and a Court so turbulent and dissolute, among princes so greedy and faithless, to bring order out of chaos required a brain above all.

God created this terrible automaton, placed by Providence exactly between Louis XI and Robespierre, in order to crush the great nobles, as Louis XI had crushed his "grand vassals," and as Robespierre would crush the aristocrats. From time to time, like red-stained comets, there appear these machines of history, these great harvesters that advance of their own accord, cropping the field of state, remorseless, relentless, stopping only when their work of scything is done.

So Richelieu would have appeared to you on that evening of December 5, 1628, when, aware of the hatred that surrounded him, he was nonetheless intent on the great projects he contemplated: exterminating heresy in France, driving the Spanish from Milan, and expelling Austria from Tuscany. He it is who appears before you in his study, trying to speak without betraying himself, to see without revealing, that impenetrable minister whom the great historian Michelet called the Red Sphinx.

He had left the ballet when his intuition told him that the queen's absence had a political cause behind it, which could only mean a threat to him. Something poisonous was brewing in the royal chambers, those few narrow rooms that caused him more toil and trouble than the whole rest of the wide world. He went home sad, tired, almost disgusted, murmuring like Luther, "There are times when our Lord seems to tire of the game and just lays His cards on the table."

He was well aware that what was threatened was not just his power, but his life. His hair shirt was made of the points of daggers. He felt that he was, in 1628, where Henri IV had been in 1606: everyone wanted his death. Worst of all was that even Louis XIII hated him. The king was Richelieu's sole support, but at any moment the cardinal might take the fall for any royal failure. A man of genius, he might have borne this if he'd been healthy and vigorous, like his idiot rival Bérulle; but the ongoing shortage of money, the continual need to invent new resources, the fact that at any given moment there were a dozen Court plots against him, kept him in constant anxiety. That was the source of the fever that reddened his cheeks, while making his forehead and hands as pale as ivory. Add to this endless religious disputes, the rage they inspired in him, and the need to suppress all his bitterness and fury, and he was burning up from within, never more than inches from death.

It was a wonder that he wasn't dead twice over. Fortunately, the king somehow sensed that, if Richelieu were gone, his kingdom was lost. On the other hand, Richelieu knew that if the king died, he had less than twenty-four hours to live: hated by Gaston, by Anne of Austria, by the queen mother, by Monsieur de Soissons from exile, by the two jailed Vendômes—hated by the whole nobility— hated, moreover, by all of Paris for having forbidden public duels, he knew the best he could hope for was to die the same day the king did—in the same hour, if possible.

Only one person was faithful to him in this endless game of seesaw, when good and bad fortune followed each other so rapidly that the same day brought both storm and sun. This was his niece and adopted daughter, Madame de Combalet, whom we've seen at the Hotel de Rambouillet in the Carmelite habit she'd worn since the death of her husband.

The first thing the cardinal did upon entering his house in the Place Royale was to knock on a certain panel. Three doors opened simultaneously: from one appeared Guillemot, his confidential valet;

from another appeared Charpentier, his secretary; from the third came Rossignol, his decoder of dispatches.

"Has my niece returned?"

"This very moment, Monseigneur," replied the valet.

"Tell her I need to spend tonight at work, and ask her if she wants to visit me here or would prefer that I go to her."

The confidential valet closed his door and went to execute his orders.

The cardinal turned to Charpentier. "Have you seen Father Joseph?" he asked.

"He's been here twice tonight," said the secretary, "and says he must speak to Monseigneur this evening."

"If he comes back a third time, bid him enter. Monsieur Cavois commands in the guard chamber?"

"Yes, Monseigneur."

"Tell him not to leave. I may need his services tonight."

The secretary retired.

"And you, Rossignol," asked the cardinal, "did you solve the cipher in the letter I gave you? You know, the one taken from the papers of Senelle, the royal physician, on his return from Lorraine."

"Yes, Monseigneur," the code-master replied in a pronounced southern accent. He was a small man of forty-five to fifty whose habit of stooping made him almost hunchbacked. His most salient feature was a long nose that could have supported three or four pairs of glasses, though he made do with only one. "It couldn't have been simpler. The king is called Céphale, the queen Procris, Your Eminence the Oracle, and Madame de Combalet Venus."

"Good," said the cardinal. "Give me the key to the cipher. I'll read the dispatch myself."

Rossignol bowed and began to withdraw.

"By the way," added the cardinal, "remind me tomorrow to give you a bonus of twenty *pistoles*."

"Monseigneur has no other orders for me?"

"No, return to your office and prepare the cipher key for me. Have it ready when I call for it."

Rossignol backed away, bowing to the ground.

As the door closed behind him, a bell quietly sounded from within the cardinal's desk. He opened a drawer and found the bell still trembling. His immediate response was to press his finger upon a small button that must have communicated with the apartment of Madame de Combalet, for less than a minute later she appeared across the room in yet another doorway.

A great change had taken place in her attire: gone were her veil and bandeau, her scapular and wimple, and now she was dressed only in a sheer tunic confined at the waist by a leather belt. Her beautiful auburn hair, released from restraint, fell in silken curls to her shoulders above a décolletage considerably more generous than a strict Carmelite would have allowed, displaying the curve of her bosom beneath a bouquet of violets and rosebuds—a bouquet indicating both birth and beauty, and one we've previously remarked upon, though at Madame de Rambouillet's it had been on her shoulder.

The deep brown of her blouse highlighted the white satin of her elegant neck and her beautiful hands; and, as its fabric was not imprisoned in the iron corset common at that period, its folds were free to drape her shapely form.

At the sight of this adorable creature, who appeared in a heavenly cloud of perfume, and who was, at twenty-five, in the full flower of her beauty, made even more lovely and graceful by the simplicity of her outfit, the cardinal's furrowed forehead relaxed, his somber face lit up, and he stretched his arms toward her, saying, "Oh! Come to me, Marie."

The young woman needed no encouragement and came to him with a charming smile. She detached her bouquet, brushed it against her lips, and presented it to her uncle.

"Thank you, my lovely child," said the cardinal, who, under the pretext of scenting the bouquet, brought it to his own lips. "Thank you, beloved daughter."

Then, drawing her toward him and kissing her on the forehead as a father would his child, he said, "I love these flowers, as fresh as you, and scented like you. . . ."

"We are yours a hundred times over, dear Uncle. You said you wanted to see me? It would make me happy to know you needed me."

"I always need you, my dear Marie," said the cardinal, regarding his niece with delight, "but tonight I need you more than ever."

"Oh, my good Uncle!" said Madame de Combalet, trying to kiss the cardinal's hands, who resisted by drawing her own hands to his lips. "I see you're worried again tonight." She added, with a sad smile, "By now, I think you'd be accustomed to worries. What do they matter, so long as you succeed?"

"Yes," said the cardinal, "I know. I shouldn't be simultaneously high and low, happy and unhappy, powerful and helpless—but so I am, as you know better than anyone, Marie. Public success brings no private happiness. You love me with all your heart—don't you?"

"With all my heart! With all my soul!"

"After the death of Chalais, you remember, I seemed to have won a major victory: I had the queen, the two Vendômes, and the Comte de Soissons on their knees before me. I pardoned them—and what did they do in return for my pardon? They chose to attack me in my very heart. They know I love nothing in the world so much as you, that your presence is as necessary to me as the air I breathe, as the sun that shines. Yet they condemn you for living with that 'damned priest,' that 'man of blood.' Live with me? Yes, you live with me, and more than that—I live because of you! Yet this life, so devoted on your side, so pure on mine, so that even seeing you as lovely as you are now, within my arms, no idea of sin has crossed my mind—this life, of which we should be proud, they denounce as a disgrace. You were so frightened of them, you renewed your vow to take the veil and enter a convent. I even had to ask the Pope, with whom I was in conflict, for the favor of a brief delay of your retreat. Worried? How should I not be worried? They can kill me, that's nothing—at the siege of La Rochelle I risked my life twenty times over. But if I'm dismissed, exiled, or imprisoned, how am I to live apart from you?"

"My beloved Uncle," said the beautiful Carmelite, bestowing on the cardinal a look that seemed to reflect more than the tenderness of a niece for her uncle, and perhaps even more than the love of a daughter for her father, "when I took that vow, though you'd been as good as it's possible to be, I didn't know you as I know you now—didn't love you as I love you today. I made a vow, but the Pope has waived it; and today, that vow is no more. Today I swear that no matter what, I'll follow you wherever you go: palaces and prisons are all the same to me. Wherever a heart may be, it lives where it loves. Well, my dear Uncle, my heart is with you, for I love you and will always love you."

"Yes, but when they defeat me, will the victors allow you to continue your devotion to me? Look, Marie, what I fear more than dismissal, more than lost power, more than thwarted ambition, is to be separated from you. Oh! If I had to fight only Spain, Austria, and Savoy, that would be nothing. But to have to fight the very people who surround me, those whom I made rich, happy, and powerful! I dare not raise my foot to crush them, vipers and scorpions though they are. This is what wearies me to despair. My foreign enemies, Spinola, Wallenstein, Olivares—who are they? I can deal with them; they're not my true enemies, my true rivals. My real rival is this Vautier, my real enemy is Bérulle—or else some stranger awaiting me in a shadowy alcove, a man whose name I don't know, of whose existence I'm entirely unaware. Me, I write tragedies—yet I know of no play darker than the drama I enact! Thus, even while battling the English fleet, while tearing down the walls of La Rochelle by sheer force of genius—I say it, though I speak of myself—I had to reach beyond our current army to raise twelve thousand more French troops so the Duc de Nevers, legitimate heir to Mantua and Montferrat, can win his inheritance. It would be enough if I just had to fight Philip IV, Ferdinand II, and Charles-Emmanuel, that is to say, Spain, Austria, and Savoy. But this astrologer Vautier 'sees in the stars' that the army will never pass over the mountains, while the pious Bérulle fears that the success of Nevers might imperil the 'understanding' between His Catholic Majesty of Spain and His Most Christian Majesty of France. They send word through the queen mother to Créqui, that same Créqui I made a peer of the realm, a Marshal of France, the Governor of Dauphiné—that Créqui who also hopes to become constable, at the expense of Montmorency, that Créqui whom nothing will sate. And suddenly there is hunger in the army, which causes desertion, and who benefits but Savoy? And who is it who prepares to roll boulders from the mountains of Savoy upon French troops—who but a Queen of France, Marie de Médicis? She who is the daughter of an assassin, and the niece of a defrocked cardinal who poisoned his own brother and sister-in-law.

"But the astrologer Vautier saw it in the stars! Very well, let them try to stop me—or, rather, my army. They hope to undermine me here, to sabotage me and forestall our march. But for the good of France we march to Mantua and Montferrat, small domains perhaps, but in strategic positions. The fortress of Casale is the key to the Alps! In the hands of Savoy, that key would be at the disposal of Austria and Spain.

"Then there's Mantua, the domain of the Gonzaga family, after Venice the last center of the arts in Italy. Mantua, which at once overlooks Tuscany, Venice, and the Papal States. What use to raise the siege of Casale if one fails to save Mantua? I'm negotiating with Gustavus Adolphus, but what use to ally with the Protestants of the north before I have crushed the Protestants of the south? If this southern campaign succeeds, I could concentrate in these hands power both spiritual and temporal, and guide France for the rest of my life. And to think that what stands in my way is a charlatan, Vautier, and an idiot, Bérulle!"

He rose. "And moreover," he added, "to think that I'm balked by this daughter-in-law and this mother-in-law, when I hold proof of the adultery of one and the complicity in the murder of Henri IV of the other. But though the words are nearly bursting from my mouth, I dare not breathe them—because it would mean a stain upon the glory of the crown of France!"

"Uncle!" cried Madame de Combalet, in alarm.

"Oh, I have my witnesses," the cardinal said. "For Queen Anne of Austria, there's Madame de Bellier and 'Patroclus.' For Marie de Médicis there's the Escoman woman. I'll yet find her, maybe in the dungeon of the Daughters of Repentance—and if she's dead, poor martyr, I'll nonetheless have words with her cadaver." He strode back and forth in agitation.

"My dear Uncle," said Madame de Combalet, placing herself in his path. "Don't talk about this tonight. Leave it for tomorrow."

"You're right, Marie," Richelieu said, stopping himself by sheer force of will. "What have you done today? Where have you been?"

"I went to Madame de Rambouillet's."

"What happened there? Anything good? What says the illustrious 'Arthenice'?" asked the cardinal, trying to smile.

"She presented us with a young poet just arrived from Rouen."

"Do they make poets in Rouen? It's only three months since Rotrou arrived, fresh off the boat."

"In fact, it was Rotrou who presented him."

"And what is this poet called?"

"Pierre Corneille."

The cardinal shrugged, as if to say: *an unknown.* "And I suppose he arrives with a tragedy in his pocket?"

"With a comedy, in five acts."

"And the title?"

"*Mélite.*"

"That's not a name from history."

"No, its source is pure fantasy. Rotrou says the work is destined to eclipse all poetry, past, present, and future."

"Sheer impertinence!"

Madame de Combalet delicately changed the subject. "Then Madame de Rambouillet presented us with a real surprise: she'd secretly had constructed, beyond the wall facing the Three Hundred, and unknown to anyone but the masons and carpenters, an addition to her hotel—a beautiful new chamber, all hung in blue velour, gold, and silver. I've never seen anything decorated in such exquisite taste."

"Would you like something like it, Marie? Nothing could be easier—I'll include it in the palace I'm building."

"Thank you, but for me, please remember, all I need is an austere monastic cell—so long as it's near you."

"Is that all the news?"

"Not quite all—though I'm not sure if I should tell you the rest."

"Why is that?"

"Because the rest involves . . . a sword."

"Duels! Always duels!" Richelieu hissed. "What must I do to rid France of this insane obsession with honor?"

"This time it wasn't a duel, just a simple encounter. The Marquis de Pisany was brought to the Hotel de Rambouillet disabled by a wound."

"A dangerous wound?"

"No, because he has the luck to be a hunchback: the blade hit the top of his hump and, unable to penetrate, slid down his side. 'My God,' the surgeon said, 'it slid along the side of his chest and went through his left arm.'"

"Do we know the cause of this fight?"

"I think he mentioned the Comte de Moret."

"The Comte de Moret," Richelieu repeated, frowning. "I think I've heard that name in these last three days. And he gave this pretty sword wound to the Marquis de Pisany?"

"No, it was one of the marquis's friends."

"His name?"

Madame de Combalet hesitated, knowing how much her uncle hated dueling. "My dear Uncle," she said, "you know what I said: this wasn't a duel, or a summons of honor, or even a meeting. The opponents just had a disagreement at the door of the hotel."

"But who was this opponent? His name, Marie."

"A certain Souscarrières."

"Souscarrières!" said Richelieu. "I know that name."

"Perhaps, but I can assure you, my dear Uncle, that he's not to blame."

"Who?"

"Monsieur de Souscarrières."

The cardinal drew a notebook from his pocket and consulted it. He seemed to find what he sought.

"The Marquis de Pisany," continued Madame de Combalet, "drew first and lunged like a madman, according to Voiture and Brancas, who were witnesses."

"Here he is—the very man," murmured the cardinal. And he knocked on a panel.

Charpentier appeared. "Call for Cavois," said the cardinal.

"Uncle! You're not planning to arrest this young man and bring him to trial?" exclaimed Madame de Combalet, clasping her hands.

"On the contrary," the cardinal said, laughing: "I just might make his fortune."

"Oh! Don't mock, Uncle!"

"With you, Marie, I never mock. This Souscarrières has, at this moment, his fortune in his hands. Even better, it's the fortune he needs. It's up to him not to fumble it."

Cavois came in. "Cavois," said the cardinal to the captain of his guards, who was still half asleep, "go to the house at Rue Traversière and Rue Sainte-Anne and seek out a certain cavalier who calls himself Pierre de Bellegarde, Marquis de Montbrun, Sieur de Souscarrières."

"Yes, Monseigneur."

"If you find him at home, tell him that despite the late hour, I would like the pleasure of a brief chat with him."

"And if he refuses to come?"

"Oh, Cavois, I think you can handle a little problem like that. Willing or unwilling, I want to see him. Is that clear?"

"Within the hour he will be at Your Eminence's service," Cavois said, bowing.

At the door, the captain of the guards met a new arrival. He deferred to the newcomer with such respect that he was obviously important.

And in fact, it was none other than that famous Capuchin, du Tremblay, known to all as Father Joseph, or His Gray Eminence.

XII

His Gray Eminence

Father Joseph was so well known as the cardinal's "second soul" that upon seeing him, the minister's confidential servants withdrew at once, so that in Richelieu's chambers the *Éminence grise* had the privilege of respectful space about him.

Madame de Combalet, no less than the others, was subject to the unease inspired by this silent apparition. At the sight of Father Joseph, she presented her forehead to the cardinal for a goodbye kiss. "Please, dear Uncle," she said, "don't work too late."

Then she retired, eager to escape through the door opposite the one through which the monk had entered, keeping half the room between herself and the new arrival as he approached the cardinal.

By the date of our story, the religious orders—except the Oratory of Jesus, founded by Cardinal Bérulle in 1611 and confirmed, after long opposition, by Pope Paul V in 1613—had mostly fallen under the influence of the cardinal-minister. He was recognized as the protector of the Benedictines of Cluny, the Cistercians of Saint-Maur, the Premonstratensians, the Dominicans, the Carmelites, and finally the whole hooded family of the monks of St. Francis: the Miners, Minims, Franciscans, Capuchins, and so on. In recognition of this protection, all these orders, whether preaching, begging, teaching, or spreading propaganda, wherever they traveled, acted as a covert source of intelligence, all the more trustworthy since the main source of information was the confessional.

Chief over all this religious police, zealous in its duty of surveillance, was the Capuchin Father Joseph, experienced in the ways of diplomacy and intrigue. Like those who came after him, such as Sartine,

Lenoir, and Fouché, he had a genius for espionage. Through his influence his brother, Leclerc du Tremblay, had been named Governor of the Bastille, so that a prisoner detected, denounced, and arrested by du Tremblay the Capuchin was shackled, jailed, and guarded by du Tremblay the Governor. And if the unfortunate died in prison, as was so often the case, his confession and last rites were administered by du Tremblay the Capuchin—which kept it all in the family.

Father Joseph's ministry was divided into four divisions, each headed by a Capuchin. He had a secretary named Father Ange Sabini, who acted as Joseph to Father Joseph. When his business required him to travel, he rode on horseback, followed by Father Ange on a second horse. But one day, Father Joseph rode a mare while Father Ange's mount was a stallion, and the two animals formed a conjunction in which their riders found themselves in roles so grotesque that Father Joseph felt his dignity required him to abandon that means of mobility. Thereafter, he rode in a litter or carriage.

However, in the usual course of his duties when he needed to remain incognito, Father Joseph traveled on foot, pulling his cowl down over his eyes so as not to be recognized—easy enough in the Paris of that time, thronged as it was with monks of every order.

That very night, Father Joseph had been out, anonymous and afoot.

The cardinal, sitting keen-eyed at his desk, waited until the first door had closed on his captain and the second on his niece, then turned to Father Joseph. "Well," he said, "so you have something to tell me, my dear du Tremblay?" The cardinal had retained the habit of calling the monk by his family name.

"Yes, Monseigneur," he replied, "and this is the second time I've had the honor of trying to see you!"

"I've heard. It led me to hope you might have learned something about the Comte de Moret—of his return to Paris, and of the reasons for that return."

"I don't know exactly what Your Eminence wants to know, but I think I've picked up the trail."

"Ah-ha! Your white-cloaks have been at work. They've found . . . ?"

"Nothing special. They've learned only that the Comte de Moret was staying at the Hotel de Montmorency with Duke Henri II, and came out at night to visit a lady who lives in the Rue de la Cerisaie opposite the Hotel Lesdiguières."

"Rue de la Cerisaie, opposite the Hotel Lesdiguières . . . but that's the house of the two sisters of Marion Delorme!"

"Yes, Monseigneur, of Madame de la Montagne and Madame de Maugiron, but it's uncertain which of the two is his lover."

"Well, I'll soon know," said the cardinal.

And signaling the Capuchin to pause in his report, he began to write on a slip of paper:

Which of your two sisters is the Comte de Moret's lover?
And who is the other's lover? Is there an unhappy rival?

Then he turned to a panel above the desk, which opened when he pressed a button. This panel communicated with the neighboring house, and when opened revealed a gap the thickness of the wall to another panel on the other side. Between the doors were two door-bells, one left, one right, that activated an invention so new that it was unknown to any but the cardinal.

The cardinal placed the paper in between the doors, rang the bell on the right, and then closed his panel. "Go on," he said to Father Joseph, who had watched without any evidence of surprise.

"I was saying, Monseigneur, that the white-cloaks had done some work for us, but that Providence, which watches over Monseigneur's affairs, had done the most."

"You're sure, du Tremblay, that Providence watches over me in particular?"

"What better occupation, Monseigneur?"

The cardinal, who asked nothing better than to believe it, smiled and said, "Let's hear the report of Providence on Monsieur le Comte de Moret."

"Well, Monseigneur, I'd learned from the white-cloaks, as I'd had the honor to tell Your Eminence, that the Comte de Moret had been in Paris for eight days, that he lodged with Monsieur de Montmorency and had a mistress in the Rue de la Cerisaie, which was little enough."

"I think you are unfair to the good fathers. Who does what he can, does all he must—and there is always Providence, which can do all. Let's hear what Providence has done."

"Only set me face to face with the count himself."

"You've seen him?"

"As certain as I have the honor to see you, Monseigneur."

"And he, he saw you?" asked Richelieu anxiously.

"He saw me, but didn't recognize me."

"Sit down, du Tremblay, and tell me all about it!"

Richelieu was accustomed to offer the Capuchin the false courtesy of a seat, knowing he wouldn't take it. Joseph nodded and continued: "Here's how the thing happened, Monseigneur. I had just left the white-cloaks and was on my way to bring their information to you when I saw people running toward the Rue de l'Homme-Armé."

"Speaking of the Rue de l'Homme-Armé, isn't there an inn there which you've had under your eye? The Inn of the Painted Beard?"

"That's where the crowd was running, Monseigneur."

"And you joined the crowd?"

"Your Eminence knows well I wouldn't fail to do so. It seems a kind of assassination had been performed upon a poor devil named Étienne Latil, a former retainer of Monsieur d'Épernon."

"Of Monsieur d'Épernon? Then remember this Étienne Latil, du Tremblay—he may be useful someday."

"I doubt it, Monseigneur."

"Why is that?"

"I think he's taken a voyage from which no one returns."

"Ah, yes—you said he'd been murdered."

"Exactly, Monseigneur. Believed dead at first, he'd revived and called for a priest . . . and there I was."

"Providence indeed, du Tremblay! And you gave him his confession, I presume?"

"In full."

"And there was something of import in it?"

"Monseigneur shall judge," said the Capuchin, with a laugh, "but only if you absolve me of revealing his confession."

"Very well, very well," said Richelieu, "I absolve you."

"Well, Monseigneur, Étienne Latil was assassinated for refusing to assassinate . . . the Comte de Moret."

"And who would have a motive for killing this young man who, at least till now, has joined neither faction nor cabal?"

"A rival in love."

"You're sure?"

"I believe so."

"But you don't know who killed this man?"

"No, Monseigneur, and neither did he. He knew only that it was a hunchback."

"We have two hunchbacked swordsmen in Paris: the Marquis de Pisany and the Marquis de Fontrailles. It might be Pisany, who himself received a sword-wound last night at nine o'clock, at the gate of the Hotel de Rambouillet, at the hands of his friend, Souscarrières. But Fontrailles should be watched nonetheless."

"I'll have him watched, Monseigneur, but stay a moment—I've something even more extraordinary to tell Your Eminence."

"Speak, speak, du Tremblay. Your story is captivating."

"Well, Monseigneur, here's what's even more extraordinary: while

I was hearing Latil's confession, who should walk into the room but the Comte de Moret himself?"

"What, at the Inn of the Painted Beard?"

"Yes, Monseigneur, at the Inn of the Painted Beard. The Comte de Moret himself came in, dressed as a Basque esquire; he stepped up to the wounded man and laid a purse of gold on the table next to him. 'If you recover,' he said, 'take yourself to the hotel of the Duc de Montmorency. If you die, die in the faith of the Lord, certain that there will be prayers at mass for the salvation of your soul.'"

"The intention is good," Richelieu said, "but nonetheless, let's send my doctor Chicot to have a look at this poor devil. Are you sure the Comte de Moret didn't recognize you?"

"Yes, Monseigneur, quite sure."

"What was he doing, disguised, at that inn?"

"We may yet find out. Your Eminence, would you care to guess who I met at the corner of the Rue du Plâtre and the Rue de l'Homme-Armé?"

"Who?"

"Disguised as a peasant of the Pyrenees. . . ."

"Tell me instantly, du Tremblay! It's getting late, and I don't have time to spare."

"Madame de Fargis."

"Madame de Fargis!" the cardinal exclaimed. "And she was coming from the inn?"

"It seems probable."

"She as a Catalan, he as a Basque. It was a meeting."

"That's what I thought—but there's more than one kind of meeting, Monseigneur. The lady is a libertine, and the young man is the son of Henri IV."

"It was no love rendezvous, du Tremblay. The count comes from Italy, by way of Piedmont. He had, I'd wager my head, letters to the queen—or even queens. He must take care!" Richelieu said, glowering. "I already have two other sons of Henri IV in prison!"

"In short, Monseigneur, that was my evening. I thought it important enough to report it."

"With good reason, du Tremblay. And you say this young man is staying with the Duc de Montmorency?"

"Yes, Monseigneur."

"So he's in it as well? Has Montmorency forgotten that I've already had to behead one of his family? He wants to be constable, like his father and grandfather before him. He already has a rival in Créqui, who thinks he deserves the title because he married a daughter of the Lesdiguières. As if it were so easy to bear the sword of du Guesclin! At least Montmorency is a true knight who values honor. Well, he who wants the constable's sword must go look for it before the walls of Casale. It's been a good evening so far, du Tremblay, and I hope to complete it as well."

"Does Monseigneur have anything else he'd like me to do?"

"Keep an eye, as I've said, on the Inn of the Painted Beard, but discreetly. Don't lose sight of that wounded man until he's either healed or buried. I thought the Comte de Moret was already busy with another woman than Fargis, who's already juggling Cramail and Marillac. But if Providence points to her, du Tremblay, that changes the entire affair. But Providence, as you know, doesn't do everything for us."

"And on this occasion, we should recall the proverb, or rather the maxim, 'Heaven helps those who help themselves.'"

"You are bursting with insight, my dear du Tremblay, and I would have been sad to have missed you. Let me just help the pope by ridding him of the Spanish, whom he fears, and the Austrians, whom he hates, and we'll arrange so that the first red hat that arrives from Rome fits the measurements of your head."

"If it were not for the size of my head, I would beg Monseigneur just to give me one of his old hats as a sign that, whatever favors heaven brings me, I will always be his servant and never his equal." And, crossing his hands on his chest, Father Joseph bowed humbly.

At the door he met Cavois, who stood aside to let him leave, as the others had withdrawn upon his arrival. His Gray Eminence having left, Cavois said to the cardinal, "He is here, Monseigneur."

"Souscarrières?"

"Yes, Monseigneur."

"He was at home, then?"

"No, but his servant told me he'd be in a gambling den he frequents on Rue Villedot, and in fact, there he was."

"Have him enter."

Cavois stood immobile, eyes cast down.

"Well?" asked the cardinal.

"Monseigneur, I wish to ask a favor."

"Do so, Cavois. You know I esteem you and will do what I can."

"I only hoped that, once Monsieur Souscarrières departs, I might be permitted to spend the rest of the night at home. Since our return to Paris, Monseigneur, it's been eight days, or rather eight nights, and I've yet to spend one in my own bed."

"And you're tired from your duties?"

"No, Monseigneur. But Madame Cavois is tired of sleeping . . . alone."

"Madame Cavois is amorous, then?"

"Yes, Monseigneur. But it's her husband she's amorous for."

"She would be a good example for the ladies of the Court. Cavois, you may spend the night with your wife."

"Oh! Thank you, Monseigneur!"

"I authorize you to go and find her."

"Find Madame Cavois?"

"Yes—and bring her here."

"Here, Monseigneur? To what end?"

"I'd like to speak with her."

"Speak? To my wife?" Cavois cried, astonished.

"I have a gift to bestow in recompense for these sleepless nights on my account."

"A gift?" Cavois said, beyond astonished.

"Bring in Monsieur Souscarrières, Cavois, and while I talk with him, go fetch your wife."

"But, Monseigneur," said Cavois, "she'll have gone to bed."

"Get her up."

"She won't want to come."

"Take two guards with you."

Cavois laughed. "Very well, I'll do it, Monseigneur," he said, "but I warn you, Madame Cavois says what she thinks, and plenty of it."

"Good. Candor is all too rare at Court, Cavois."

"So, Monseigneur's order is . . . serious?"

"I've never been more serious, Cavois."

"Then Monseigneur will be obeyed." Cavois, still skeptical, bowed and withdrew.

The cardinal took advantage of his brief solitude to open the panel above his desk. In the same place where he had put his request he found a reply, written with the brevity he required in dispatches:

> *The Comte de Moret is the lover of Madame de la Montagne, the Seigneur de Souscarrières of Madame de Maugiron. The unhappy rival: the Marquis de Pisany.*

"It's astounding," murmured the cardinal as he closed the panel, "how everything tonight seems to tie together. It's almost enough to make one believe, like that fool du Tremblay, that there really is a Providence."

Just then his secretary, Charpentier, assuming the role of a footman or steward, opened the door and announced, "Messire Pierre de Bellegarde, Comte de Montbrun and Seigneur de Souscarrières."

XIII

In Which Madame Cavois Becomes
Partner to Monsieur Michel

As our readers know, the man announced with such a pompous display of titles was none other than our friend Souscarrières, whose portrait we sketched at the beginning of this volume.

Souscarrières entered with such an air of nonchalance, giving His Eminence such a casual greeting, that it was tantamount to effrontery.

The cardinal cast his gaze about, as if searching for someone who might have entered with Souscarrières.

"Pardon, Monseigneur," Souscarrières said, putting one foot gallantly forward and posing with his hat in his right hand, "but is Your Eminence looking for something?"

"I'm looking for those other people who were announced along with you, Monsieur Michel."

"Michel?" repeated Souscarrières, astonished. "Who bears that name?"

"Who? I believe you do, my dear Monsieur."

"Oh! I mustn't let Monseigneur make such a grave error. I'm the acknowledged son of Messire Roger de Saint-Larry, Duc de Bellegarde and Grand Equerry of France. My illustrious father still lives and would be happy to so inform you. I am Seigneur de Souscarrières thanks to an estate which I acquired. I was made a marquis by Madame la Duchesse Nicole de Lorraine upon my marriage with the noble Demoiselle Anne de Rogers."

"My dear Monsieur Michel," replied Richelieu, "allow me to relate your history. I know it better than you do, and will instruct you."

"I'm aware," Souscarrières said, "that great men such as Your Eminence, after days of hard work, sometimes enjoy an hour of amusement. Blessed are those who can provide such a genius with some amusement, even if it's at their own expense."

And Souscarrières, delighted with the compliment he'd concocted, bowed before the cardinal.

"You are wrong from start to finish, Monsieur Michel," the cardinal continued, stubbornly clinging to that name. "I'm not tired, am in no need of amusement, and wouldn't take such at your expense. But as I have a proposal for you, I'd like to demonstrate that I do so because of your personal merit, and not because I'm deceived by your purported names and titles."

The cardinal accompanied this last sentence with one of those wry smiles that, in his moments of good humor, were particular to him.

"Then let Your Eminence speak without any beating around the bush," said Souscarrières.

"Shall I begin then, Monsieur Michel?"

Souscarrières, in no position to resist, just bowed.

"You know the Rue des Bourdonnais, do you not, Monsieur Michel?" asked the cardinal.

"One would have to be from Cathay not to know of it, Monseigneur."

"Well! In your youth there was a notable baker who kept the Inn of the Chimneys there. This worthy man, who was a fine cook and whose fare I sampled many times when I was Bishop of Luçon, was named Michel and had the honor to be your father."

"I thought I'd already mentioned to Your Eminence that I'm the acknowledged son of the Duc de Bellegarde," insisted the Seigneur de Souscarrières, albeit with less confidence.

"Quite so," replied the cardinal. "And I can tell you how this recognition came about. This worthy baker had a wife, very pretty, to whom all the gentry who came to the Inn of the Chimneys paid court. One happy day she gave birth to a son. This son was you, my dear Monsieur Michel, and as you were born during a marriage in which your father—or, if you will, your mother's husband—was still living, you must bear the name of your parents. Remember, my dear Monsieur Michel, that only kings have the right to legitimize the children of adultery."

"The devil!" muttered Souscarrières.

"Let's get to your acknowledgement. A pretty child, you became a handsome young man, excelling at athletics, fleet of foot, playing tennis like d'Alichon, and flashing a sword like Fontenay. Having reached such a degree of perfection, you resolved to turn these talents to making your fortune. To commence your campaign, you crossed over to England, where your success at sports won you five hundred thousand francs. Is that accurate?"

"Yes, Monseigneur, give or take a few *pistoles*."

"It was there that you had, one morning, a visit from a certain Lalande, who was Tennis Master to His Majesty the King. Here's what he said, more or less: '*Pardieu*, Monsieur de Souscarrières!' Ah, pardon me, I forgot—I don't know why you've never liked the name Michel, which is a very pleasant name, but the first time you came into some money, you spent a thousand *pistoles* to buy a crumbling hovel in the country near Grosbois that went by the name of Souscarrières. Thereafter you were no longer Michel but Souscarrières, and eventually the Seigneur de Souscarrières. I apologize for the long digression, but I think it's essential to understanding the story."

Souscarrières bowed.

"So this Lalande said to you, '*Pardieu*, Monsieur de Souscarrières, you've done well: you have spirit, you have heart, you excel at sports, and you're lucky in love. You lack only the advantage of birth. I know one is unable to choose one's father and mother, or we'd all choose for father a Peer of France and for mother a Duchess of the Queen's Circle. But when one is wealthy, there are ways to correct these small aberrations of chance.' I wasn't there, my dear Monsieur Michel, but I imagine that your eyes widened at this

preamble. Lalande continued, 'You have only to choose, you understand, between all the great nobles who made love to madame your
mother, and select the least fastidious. Monsieur de Bellegarde, for
example: his heavenly reward is approaching. Your mother will be
delighted to make you a gentleman; she need only inform Monsieur
le Grand that you're not the baker's son but his, and his conscience
won't allow such a fine youth to call the wrong man his father. Since
his memory is failing, he won't even remember if he was her lover
or not; he'll acknowledge you, and that acknowledgement will be
worth thirty thousand francs.' Isn't that how it went?"

"More or less, Monseigneur. But I must say Your Eminence has
overlooked one thing."

"What's that? Though my memory may be better than Monsieur de Bellegarde's, if it's at fault, I'm ready to acknowledge my
mistake."

"That in addition to the five hundred thousand francs Your Eminence mentioned, I brought back from England the innovation of
the sedan chair, and for the last three years I've sought the French
patent for it."

"You're mistaken, dear Monsieur Michel. I've forgotten neither
that invention nor your application to me for the patent—on the
contrary, that's exactly why I've sent for you. But everything in its
turn. 'A proper order,' says the philosopher, 'is one-half of genius.'
First let's discuss your marriage."

"Couldn't we skip that, Monseigneur?"

"By no means. Where did you get your title of marquis, if not
from the Duchesse Nicole de Lorraine on the occasion of your
wedding? At the time, there were many rumors linking you and the
worthy duchess, rumors you were careful not to deny, and when
she died six months ago, you dressed your five-year-old child in
mourning. But everyone has the right to dress their children as they
will, so I won't admonish you for that."

"Monseigneur is very good," said Souscarrières.

"Anyway, you returned from Lorraine with a young girl you brought away with you, Mademoiselle Anne de Rogers. You claimed she was the daughter of a *grand seigneur*, but in fact she was simply the daughter of the duchess. It was on the occasion of your marriage with her that you were, you say, made Marquis de Montbrun; but for that elevation to be valid, it would have to have been Monsieur Michel who was made marquis and not Monsieur de Bellegarde, for an illegitimate son could not be so recognized. Since you don't have the right to use the name Bellegarde, you couldn't become a marquis of that name, which is not and cannot be yours."

"Monseigneur is very hard on me!"

"On the contrary, dear Monsieur Michel, I'm as sweet as syrup, as you'll see. Madame Michel, who had no idea what circumstance she'd fall into by marrying a man like you—Madame Michel allowed herself to be beguiled by Villaudry. You know Villaudry, the younger son of the man Miossens killed. You caught wind of something going on when you heard she'd given Villaudry a bracelet made from a lock of her hair. You threatened to throw her into the canal of Souscarrières—but you weren't quite sure of her betrayal, and, as you're not a bad man at heart, you waited upon further proof. When you had that proof—a letter written entirely in her hand, which left no doubt as to your dishonor—you followed her into the garden, drew your dagger, and told her to pray to God. She could see that this wasn't like when you'd threatened to throw her into the canal, that this time you were serious. You stabbed twice but fortunately only struck her hand, cutting off two of her fingers. Seeing her blood, you pitied her, spared her life, and sent her back to Lorraine.

"As for Villaudry, because you'd been lenient to your wife, you decided to show him no mercy. You found him at mass at the church of the Minims near the Place Royale and charged in, sword in hand, but he refused to commit sacrilege and kept his own blade in the scabbard. Not that he didn't want to fight you; he even said, 'I'd draw on you if I had a reputation to protect, but as I don't, there's no reason to fight here.' And indeed, he then formally called you out, as if you really were the son of Monsieur de Bellegarde, and met you in the Place Royale, the same place where Bouteville fought Beuvron. You carried off the affair extremely well, accepting all your opponent's requirements, then giving him six wounds with the point of your sword and any number of blows with the flat of your blade.

"But Bouteville, too, had carried off his affair extremely well, which didn't stop me from having him beheaded. I'd have shortened you as well, Monsieur Michel, if you'd really been Pierre de Bellegarde, Marquis de Montbrun, and Seigneur de Souscarrières— because, worse even than Bouteville, you'd drawn your sword in a church, which would have meant cutting off your hands as well as your head. Do you hear me, my dear Monsieur Michel?"

"*Pardieu*! Yes, Monseigneur, I hear you," Souscarrières replied. "And I must say that I've heard conversations much more welcome than this one."

"Then it's just as well you didn't meet your end that time, although this evening you returned to your former ways with the poor Marquis de Pisany. He must have been mad with rage to get in a fight with a buffoon like you."

"I didn't pick a fight with him, Monseigneur; he's the one who attacked me."

"Well, at least this poor marquis wasn't so unlucky as to pick his fight in the Rue de la Cerisaie, where he'd have had to face both you and the Comte de Moret."

"Monseigneur! What do you know . . . ?"

"What I know is that if the point of your sword hadn't struck his hump and slid down, and that if his ribs didn't overlap each other like an iron breastplate, you'd have nailed him like a beetle to the wall. You really have a rotten temper, dear Monsieur Michel."

"I swear, Monseigneur, I wasn't looking for a fight. Voiture and Brancas will tell you so. I was just overheated from having followed him from the Rue de l'Homme-Armé almost all the way to the Louvre."

At this mention of the Rue de l'Homme-Armé, Richelieu was suddenly all attention.

"He'd had a quarrel in a cabaret," Souscarrières continued, "and was all worked up about it."

"Indeed he had," said Richelieu, following the line the unsuspecting Souscarrières had opened for him, "in the Inn of the Painted Beard."

"Monseigneur!" cried Souscarrières, astonished.

"Where he went," Richelieu continued, at the risk of overplaying his hand, but keen to know everything, "to see if, by means of a certain Étienne Latil, he might be able to rid himself of his rival, the Comte de Moret. Fortunately, instead of finding a cutthroat, he found an honest swashbuckler who refused to dip his hands in royal blood. So you see, my dear Monsieur Michel, that between drawing your sword in a church, dueling with Villaudry, complicity in the murder of Étienne Latil, and having an encounter with the Marquis de Pisany, I could have you beheaded four times over—if only you had two quarters of nobility instead of being a full-blooded commoner."

"Alas, Monseigneur!" said Souscarrières, badly shaken. "But you heard me declare that I owe my life to your magnanimity!"

"And your wits, my dear Monsieur Michel."

"Ah! If only Monseigneur would allow me to use my wits in the service of Your Eminence," Souscarrières cried, throwing himself at the cardinal's feet, "I'd be the happiest of men!"

"God forbid I should refuse—for I have need of men like you."

"Yes, Monseigneur, men of wit and—dare I say it—devotion!"

". . . Whom I will hang on the day their devotion ends."

Souscarrières started. "Oh! But that will be never," he said. "How could I ever forget all I owe to Your Eminence?"

"Hmm. Consider, my dear Monsieur Michel: you hold your fortune in your hands—but I hold the end of the noose in mine."

"If only Your Eminence would deign to tell me how to employ these wits that he's been so good as to recognize."

"As to that . . ."

"I listen with full attention!"

"Well, then . . . suppose I grant you the patent on this invention from England?"

"The patent on sedan chairs?" cried Souscarrières, who was beginning to see, taking shape before him, that fortune which the cardinal said he held in his hands, but which until now had been no more than a dream.

"Half of it," said the cardinal, "only half. I reserve the other half for a boon I wish to grant."

"Monseigneur wishes to reward another's wits as well?" ventured Souscarrières.

"No, something rarer than brains. Devotion."

"Monseigneur is the master. If I'm given half the patent, half is what I'll settle for."

"Indeed. So you'll have half the sedan chairs in Paris; two hundred, let's say."

"Yes, as you say, Monseigneur, two hundred."

"That makes four hundred chair porters. Well, Monsieur Michel, let's suppose these four hundred porters are intelligent, that they note where they take their customers and pay attention to what they say. Suppose further that the head of their company was also intelligent, and that he related to me, and to me alone, all that was seen and heard. Finally, suppose this man took in twelve thousand francs a year— though it could easily be twenty-four thousand—and that, instead of being called merely Michel, he wished to be called Messire Pierre de Bellegarde, Marquis de Montbrun and Seigneur de Souscarrières. I'd say, my dear friend, take as many names as you like—the more, the better! As for the names you've already appropriated, you may have to defend them against those you've claimed them from, but, rest assured, I won't give you the slightest trouble about them."

"You're serious about this, Monseigneur?"

"Quite serious, my dear Monsieur Michel. I'm granting you the patent for half the sedan chairs in circulation in Paris. Tomorrow your partner, who will already have signed for the other half, will bring you a letter for you to sign in your turn. Does that suit you?"

"And what will this letter state about my obligations to you?" Souscarrières asked hesitantly.

"Nothing at all, dear Monsieur Michel. That matter, you understand, is between you and me. Complete confidentiality is essential. *Peste*! If my connection were known, all would be lost. It must not be revealed to Monsieur or the queen. You must always speak of me as a tyrant who persecutes the queen, and say you can't understand how King Louis XIII can live under a yoke as heavy as mine."

"But I could never say such things!" cried Souscarrières.

"Well, if you try hard enough, you might find that you can. So, we're agreed. Your chairs will become all the rage, stifling the competition, and the entire Court will refuse to travel anywhere except by chair—especially if yours have two seats and very thick curtains."

"Does Monseigneur have any specific instructions for me?"

"Indeed! I particularly recommend the ladies to you: Madame la Princesse first of all, then Mademoiselle Marie de Gonzague, Madame de Chevreuse, and Madame de Fargis. Then the men: the Comte de Moret, Monsieur de Montmorency, Monsieur de Chevreuse, and the Comte de Cramail. I leave out the Marquis de Pisany; thanks to you, we don't have to worry about him for a few days."

"Monseigneur shall have nothing to worry about at all. And when should I start this operation?"

"As soon as possible. You should begin within the week, unless you lack the funds to do so."

"No, Monseigneur. Indeed, this is the kind of affair I'll attend to personally."

"In that case, proceed—but if you need to, you can contact me directly."

"You yourself, Monseigneur?"

"Yes. Haven't I an interest in the matter? But pardon me, here's Cavois, who seems to have something to say. He's the one who will bring you the little agreement to sign tomorrow, and as he will be aware of all its conditions—even those between us alone—he's the one who will remind you of them, should you forget. Come in, Cavois, come in. You see monsieur here, do you not?"

"Yes, Monseigneur," Cavois said, obeying the cardinal's order.

"Good. He's my friend—but only among those who come to see me between ten o'clock at night and two in the morning. To me, and to me alone, he'll be known as Monsieur Michel; to everyone else he's Messire Pierre de Bellegarde, Marquis de Montbrun, Seigneur de Souscarrières. Goodbye, dear Monsieur Michel."

Souscarrières bowed to the ground and departed, unable to believe his good luck and wondering if the cardinal was serious, or was merely mocking him. But considering the cardinal's many concerns, he eventually realized that the cardinal didn't have time to make fun of him, and in all probability had been quite serious.

As for the cardinal, convinced that he'd managed to recruit the efforts of a capable ally, his good humor had returned, and it was in his most pleasant voice that he called out, "Madame Cavois! Come in, Madame Cavois!"

XIV

In Which the Cardinal Begins
to See the Chessboard Clearly

The words were barely out of his mouth before the cardinal saw a petite woman enter, aged twenty-five to twenty-six, nimble, dainty, with her nose in the air, and seemingly not at all intimidated by being in his presence. "You called, Monseigneur," she said, speaking first, with a strong Languedoc accent. "Here I am!"

"Good! And yet Cavois said you might not want to come."

"I, not come when you do the honor to call for me? What should I fear? Your Eminence didn't ask me to come alone."

"Madame Cavois!" the captain of the guards growled in warning.

"'Madame Cavois' all you like. Monseigneur called me here for a reason, for this or for that. Does he want to talk to me? Let him talk to me. Does he want me to talk to him? Then I'll talk to him."

"For this and for that, Madame Cavois," said the cardinal, signaling his guard captain not to interfere with the conversation.

"No need to silence him, Monseigneur," said Madame Cavois. "If I tell him to shut up, he'll shut up. Or maybe he wants us to think he's in charge here?"

"Monseigneur, please excuse her! She doesn't know the Court, and . . ."

"Let Monseigneur ask my pardon! Look at you yawning, Cavois. Why, it's Monseigneur who owes me an apology."

"What!" said the cardinal, laughing. "I'm the one who needs to be pardoned?"

"Certainly! Is it Christian to keep people who love each other eternally separated, as you do?"

"Ah! So you love him, then—your husband?"

"How could I not love him? You know how I first knew it, Monseigneur?"

"No, but please tell me, Madame Cavois. It interests me enormously."

"Mireille, Mireille!" said Cavois, trying to call his wife to order.

"Cavois, Cavois!" laughed the cardinal, imitating his guard captain.

"Well, I'm the daughter of a gentleman of quality from Languedoc, you know. While Cavois is the son of a Picardy squire."

Cavois twitched.

"That doesn't mean I look down on you, Louis. My father's name was de Serignan, and in Catalonia he was a brigadier, no less. I was a widow by name of Lacroix, very young, childless, and, I can say without bragging, very pretty."

"You still are, Madame Cavois," said the cardinal.

"Well, I *was* pretty. I was sixteen then, and I'm twenty-six now, with eight children, Monseigneur."

"What, eight children? You've had eight children from your wife, you dog, yet you complain to me when I keep you from sleeping with her?"

"Why, you complained, my dear Cavois!" cried Mireille. "Oh, you little love, let me kiss you!"

And, despite the presence of the cardinal, she threw her arms around her husband's neck and kissed him.

"Madame Cavois!" cried the guard captain, trembling, while the cardinal, his good humor completely restored, choked with laughter.

"To go on, Monseigneur," said Madame Cavois, still carelessly embracing her husband. "He was with Monsieur de Montmorency in those days, so it wasn't surprising that, though he's a Picard, he'd come to Languedoc. Once there, he sees me and falls in love with me, but he isn't very rich, and I'm well off, so the idiot won't declare himself. But he picks a quarrel with somebody, and the day before he's to fight, he goes to a notary and makes a will in my favor, leaving me what? Everything he has, no more and no less—to me, who didn't even know he loved me. So I go to the notary's house to visit his wife, who is a friend of mine, and she says, 'Do you know what? If Monsieur Cavois dies, you inherit all he has.' 'Monsieur Cavois? Who's that?' 'You know, that handsome lad.' And he was good-looking in those days, Monseigneur. He's declined a bit since then, but no matter: I don't love him any the less for it. Isn't that so, Cavois?"

"Monseigneur," Cavois said, beseechingly, "you'll forgive her, won't you?"

"What do you say, Madame Cavois?" said Richelieu. "Shall we put this whiner out the door?"

"Oh, no, Monseigneur! I see him little enough as it is. So, my friend tells me he loves me like crazy, that he's fighting a duel the next day, and that if he's killed he leaves me his entire estate. This moves me, you understand, and I tell my father, my brothers, and my friends all about it. The next morning I ride out to try to stop this encounter between Cavois and his opponent. But I arrive too late! Monsieur, here, who has a deft hand, has already given his opponent two sword wounds. Himself, nothing—he comes through safe and sound. I throw my arms around his neck and say to him, 'If you love me so, you must marry me. You shouldn't suppress such desires.' And he married me."

"His desires weren't long suppressed, it seems," said the cardinal.

"No, but now, Monseigneur, he's no happier than that other rascal. Since he's been in service to Your Eminence, I have to manage all his affairs. On the rare occasions he comes home, he's sluggish and dull. I caress him, call him my little Cavois, my little husband, and make myself as pretty as I can to please him. He never hears any whining, any complaints or reproaches. But I swear, it's as if he's all used up."

"I can see by all this that Master Cavois is more important to you than the rest of the world."

"Oh, yes, Monseigneur!"

"More than the king?"

"I wish the king every prosperity—but if the king dies, I won't die, whereas if my poor Cavois died, the only thing I'd want would be to go with him."

"More than the queen?"

"I respect Her Majesty. However, I find that, for a Queen of France, she doesn't have enough children. If the king had a misfortune we'd all be in trouble, and for that I blame her."

"More than . . . me?"

"I believe even more than you, Monseigneur. You don't do it to hurt me, but he wears himself out for you, and sometimes you take him away with you, even to war, as you did for almost a year at La Rochelle, and that doesn't please me."

"But," said Richelieu, "if the king died, if the queen died, if I died—if everybody died—what would you two do on your own?"

Madame Cavois laughed and gave her husband a sidelong glance. "Well!" she said. "We'd do . . ."

"Yes, what would you do?"

"We'd do what Adam and Eve did, Monseigneur, when they were alone together."

The cardinal laughed with them. "So," he said, "you have eight children in the house?"

"Your pardon, Monseigneur, but there are only six. It pleased the Lord to take two of them."

"Oh. You will make up your loss, I'm sure."

"I hope so—isn't that so, Cavois?"

"Well, then; we must provide for these poor children."

"They're not suffering, Monseigneur, thank the Lord."

"Yes, but if I'm taken by death, they will suffer."

"Heaven preserve us from such a misfortune!" the two spouses cried.

"I hope it will preserve you, and me as well. Meanwhile, we must look to the future. Madame Cavois, I am granting you, in share with Monsieur Michel, called Pierre de Bellegarde, Marquis de Montbrun, and Seigneur de Souscarrières, one-half of the monopoly on all sedan chairs in Paris."

"Oh! Monseigneur!"

"And now, Cavois," continued Richelieu, "go off with your wife, if she's still satisfied with you, or I'll put you under arrest and confine you to her bedroom for a week."

"Oh, Monseigneur!" cried the husband and wife, throwing themselves at his feet and kissing his hands.

The cardinal held his hands out to them. "What the devil are you muttering there, Monseigneur?" asked Madame Cavois, who didn't know Latin.

"The loveliest phrases of the Gospel, which, unfortunately, cardinals are forbidden to preach. Now go!"

And he pushed them out of that study where, in just two hours, so much had happened.

Left alone, the cardinal's expression resumed its usual gravity. "Come," he said, "let's summarize and recapitulate the events of the evening." And, drawing a notebook from his pocket, with a pencil he wrote the following:

The Comte de Moret arrived eight days ago from Savoy. In love with Madame de la Montagne. Rendezvous with La Fargis at the Inn of the Painted Beard. He, disguised as a Basque, she as a Catalan. Charged, in all probability, with letters to the two queens from Charles-Emmanuel. Étienne Latil assassinated for refusing to kill the Comte de Moret. Pisany, rejected by Madame de Maugiron, wounded by Souscarrières. Saved by his hump.

Souscarrières granted patent for sedan chairs and recruited as intelligence chief in secular counterpart to du

Tremblay, chief of religious intelligence.

The queen absent from the ballet due to a migraine.

"And what else? Let's see." He searched his memory. "Ah!" he suddenly said. "There's that letter taken from the bag of the king's doctor, Senelle, and sold to du Tremblay by his valet. Let's see what it says, now that Rossignol has had time to solve the cipher."

And he called, "Rossignol! Rossignol!"

The little man in spectacles reappeared.

"The letter and its code?" asked the cardinal.

"Right here, Monseigneur."

The cardinal took them. "Very good," he said. "Until tomorrow, then—and if I'm pleased with the translation, it's worth forty *pistoles* to you instead of the usual twenty."

"Then I hope Your Eminence will be satisfied."

Rossignol withdrew. The cardinal opened the letter and read it. Here, verbatim, is what it said:

If Jupiter is driven from Olympus, he can take refuge in Crete. Minos will offer him hospitality with great pleasure. But Cephalus's health can't be sustained. In the event of his death, why shouldn't Jupiter marry Procris? The rumor at Court is that Oracle wants to get rid of Procris so as to marry Cephalus to Venus. Meanwhile, if Jupiter continues to woo Hebe in a pretense of passion, Juno must feign disapproval. It's important, even at this late hour, that Oracle be fooled into believing Jupiter is in love with Hebe.

—Minos

"Now," said the cardinal, after reading this, "let's see the cipher."

The cipher, as we've said, accompanied the letter. We reproduce it here for our readers.

CEPHALUS	THE KING
PROCRIS	THE QUEEN
JUPITER	MONSIEUR
JUNO	MARIE DE MÉDICIS
OLYMPUS	THE LOUVRE
ORACLE	THE CARDINAL
VENUS	MADAME DE COMBALET
HEBE	MARIE DE GONZAGUE
MINOS	CHARLES IV, DUC DE LORRAINE
CRETE	LORRAINE

Replacing the real names with their substitutes created the following dispatch, which shows that Rossignol had not exaggerated its importance:

If Monsieur is driven from the Louvre, he can take refuge in Lorraine. The Duc de Lorraine will offer him hospitality with great pleasure. But the king's health can't be sustained. In the event of his death, why shouldn't Monsieur marry the queen? The rumor at Court is that the cardinal wants to get rid of the queen so as to marry the king to Madame de Combalet. Meanwhile, if Monsieur continues to woo Marie de Gonzague in a pretense of passion, Marie de Médicis must feign disapproval. It's important, even at this late hour, that the cardinal be fooled into believing Monsieur is in love with Marie de Gonzague.

—*Charles IV, Duc de Lorraine*

❖

Richelieu read the dispatch one more time, and then said, with the smile of a triumphant player, "So! I begin to see the chessboard more clearly."

XV

The State of Europe in 1628

We've arrived at a point where we believe there would be no harm in helping the reader, like Cardinal Richelieu, to see the chessboard more clearly.

This clarity will be easier for us, after two hundred and thirty-seven years, than for the cardinal, surrounded as he was by a thousand different schemes, conspiracy upon conspiracy, fending off one plot after another, while smoke and mists veiled the far horizon he needed to perceive in order to see past the parochial interests blocking his overall vision.

If this was merely one of those books bought to show off next to a picture album or scrapbook, a book for the coffee table so visitors could admire its engravings, or a book for a little light reading in the dressing room after one has enjoyed some time in the boudoir, we'd pass over the details that some frivolous minds might find boring. But, as we presume to hope that our books will become, if not during our lifetime then after it, part of society's standard library, we ask our readers for permission to pass before them, at the beginning of this chapter, a review of the situation in Europe. This will clarify the coming chapters and, in retrospect, illuminate the previous ones.

During the final years of the reign of Henri IV, and increasing in the early years of Richelieu's ministry, France not only joined the ranks of the great nations, she became the object upon which all eyes were fixed. Already at the head of the other European kingdoms due to her culture and intelligence, she was about to advance to the same rank in material and martial power.

Here, in a nutshell, is the state of the rest of Europe.

We'll start with that great center of religion, influencing at once Austria, Spain, and France—we'll start with Rome.

Ruling over Rome physically and the rest of the Catholic world spiritually is a morose little old man of sixty, born in Florence and glorying in Florentine greed. An Italian first, a prince always, but above all a grasping patriarch, he is forever pondering how to add territory to the Holy See and thus wealth for his many nephews, who include three cardinals—Francis and the two Antonios—as well as a fourth nephew, Thaddeus, general of the Papal troops. Rome has been plundered to feed this nepotism. As Marforio, that Cato, that scourge of the popes, has said, it needed no barbarians to do that, just the Barberini. And indeed, Matteo Barberini, elevated to the papacy as Urban VIII, has reunited the lands of St. Peter under the duchy that bore that saint's name. Under him, Jesuit propaganda, begun by that good nephew of Gregory XV, Monsignor Ludovico, flourishes and spreads. Under the flag of Ignatius Loyola, the Jesuits have become the world's religious police, using propaganda as their weapon of conquest. From Rome marches their army of preachers, as gentle in China as they are severe in Europe.

At the moment, the pope is hoping to contain the Spaniards in their duchy of Milan and keep the Austrians from crossing the Alps, so long as it can be done without personal effort or risk. He presses France to secure Mantua and lift the siege of Casale, but declines to commit one man or a single Roman *baiocco* to the effort. In his spare time, he revises Church hymns and composes Anacreontic poetry. In 1624, Richelieu had taken his measure, seeing past its pope into the hollowness of Rome, whose dithering politics had already drained it of religious prestige and who borrowed what little strength it had first from Austria, and then from Spain.

Spain: since the death of Philip III, Spain has hidden its decline behind big words and grand airs. She has for a king Philip IV, brother of Anne of Austria, a lazy sort of monarch who reigns through his prime minister, Count-Duke Olivares, as Louis XIII rules through the Cardinal-Duc de Richelieu. However, where the French minister is a man of genius, the Spanish minister is a mere reckless autocrat. The Spanish West Indies, from which a river of gold rolled during the reigns of Charles V and Philip II, produces under Philip IV only five hundred thousand crowns a year. Meanwhile, Admiral Piet Hein of the United Provinces has captured galleons in the Gulf of Mexico loaded with ingots worth, it's estimated, over twelve million.

In her last gasp, Spain is so weak that even the Duke of Savoy, the hunchback Charles-Emmanuel, known derisively as the Prince of Marmots, has twice held in his hand the fate of that empire upon which Charles V boasted the sun never set. Spain has nothing left and can no longer even bankroll Ferdinand II, who complains she sends him no money. The holy bonfires of Philip II, the king of flames, had burned the spirit from a people who once abounded with it, and Philip III, in driving out the Moors, had destroyed the fresh stock that could have revived that spirit. She has leagued herself with the bandits who burned Venice; her greatest general, Spinola, is an Italian mercenary; and her most effective ambassador, Rubens, is a Flemish painter.

Germany, since the beginning of the Thirty Years War, that is, since 1618, has been a human slaughterhouse, with butchers retailing death in its east, north, west, and center. Anyone desperate to avoid being killed—or turning monk, the suicide of the Middle Ages—has to find a way to buy passage across the Rhine, the Danube, or the Vistula.

Europe's eastern marches are held by old Bethlen Gábor, who calls himself King of Hungary and who will die having taken part in forty-two battles, after having invented all those tricks of military costume—the bearskins of the Uhlans, the billowing sleeves of the hussars—which our modern troops use to intimidate each other. His army is the school that teaches all Europe the principles of light cavalry. And what does he promise his recruits? No pay, no food, just whatever they can find to eat and whatever they can take to enrich themselves. He gives them war without law, loot without limits.

The northern marches are held by Gustavus Adolphus—good-hearted Gustave who, unlike Bethlen Gábor, catches looters and hangs them. This illustrious captain, student of the Frenchman La Gardie, has through his victories in Poland gained the strongholds of Livonia and Polish Prussia. He is occupied at the moment in making an alliance with the German Protestants against Emperor Ferdinand II, the mortal enemy of the Protestants, who despise his Edict of Restitution—that document which will serve as a model for Louis XIV fifty years later when repealing the Edict of Nantes.

Gustavus Adolphus is the master of his epoch and, in the military arts, the creator of modern warfare. His grand spirit will have no part of the gloom of Coligny, the severity of William the Silent, or the bitter anger of Maurice of Nassau. Unflappable and serene, a smile plays on his lips even in the midst of battle. Six feet tall and broad into the bargain, he rides an enormous horse, and though his obesity is sometimes a problem, it can serve him as well: a bullet that would have killed that lean Genoese Spinola only lodged in Gustave's fat, which closed over it, never to be seen again.

The western marches are held by Holland, which is confused and divided against itself. Holland had two heads, Barneveldt and Maurice, and severed them both. Barneveldt, that gentle spirit, was a friend of freedom, but placed peace above all; leader of the provinces and supporter of decentralization (and, therefore, weakness), ambassador to Elizabeth, Henri IV, and James I, when traveling through Brille, Flushing, and Ramekan, was seized as a heretic and traitor and slain on the scaffold.

It was Maurice of Nassau who'd killed Barneveldt, and though he'd saved Holland ten times over, by this murder he lost his popular support. Prince Maurice wishes to be loved but fears he is hated. One morning, crossing the Gorcum market, he greets the populace with a smile, believing the people will throw their hats in the air and cry happily, "*Vive* Nassau!" But the people are silent, and their hats stay on their heads.

From that moment on, he suffers the death of unpopularity. The ever-vigilant sentinel, the captain without fear, becomes a sleepwalker caught in a trance, a dreamer who cannot wake. Maurice is succeeded by his younger brother, Frederick Henry, who handles his inheritance as if buying and selling in a market of men: investing in only a few, but those few well chosen, well clothed, well fed, and regularly paid. A strategist, he occupies the key roads anchored by the remaining marshes, siting his men scientifically, even if that means placing them in knee-deep water. The brave men put up with it, though the thrifty Dutch government, when it sees its soldiers exposed to guns and musketry, cries, "Careful, there! Each of those men represents a capital expense of three thousand francs!"

But the key battlefield isn't to the east, the north, or the west. It's the center of Germany, occupied by a man of doubtful race, a leader of robbers and bandits whom Schiller will later make out to be a hero. Is he a Slav? Is he a German? His round head and blue eyes proclaim him Slavic; his red-blond hair says he's a German; his olive complexion declares him Bohemian. In fact, this lean, grim captain, who signs himself Wallenstein, was born in the ruins, fires, and massacres of Prague.

He holds to neither faith nor law. But he does have a belief—or, rather, three. He believes his fate is ruled by the stars. He believes in luck. And he believes in money.

Wallenstein has established in Europe the reign of the soldier, just as sin established in the world the reign of death. Enriched by warfare, protected by Holy Roman Emperor Ferdinand II (who will eventually have him assassinated), he is a general wearing the mantle of a prince, though he has neither the serenity of Gustavus nor the agility of Spinola. Bereft of emotion, even anger, he is as insensible to the cries, tears, and complaints of women as he is to the curses, threats, and accusations of men. Worse than that: he treats the world as a contest, and life as a lottery. He lets his soldiers play for any stake: the lives of men, the honor of women, the blood of the people. Now anyone with a whip in his hand may play the prince; anyone with a sword at his side can be a king.

Richelieu has long studied this demon. In his eulogy for Wallenstein, he cites not the crimes he committed, but the crimes whose commitment he enabled; and to characterize his diabolical amorality, he merely repeated the man's own words: "As for all that, so what?"

But the Thirty Years War is not yet through with Germany—far from it. Its first, or Palatine, period ended in 1623 when the Elector Palatine, Frederick V, attempted to assume the crown of Bohemia and was defeated by the Emperor. Now the Danish period is in full swing, as Christian IV, King of Denmark, contends with Wallenstein and Tilly. Not for long: a year from now the war will enter its final, Swedish period.

So much for Germany. Let's move on to England.

Though richer than Spain, England is no less sick. The king is simultaneously at odds with his country and his wife, and quarreling with half of Parliament. Soon he will dissolve his Parliament—though, as with his wife, he'll want it back again.

Charles I had married Princess Henriette of France, that daughter of Henri IV who was probably his only true child. Henriette was a lively and witty brunette, seductive rather than agreeable, pretty rather than beautiful, peevish and obstinate, sensual and flirtatious. She'd had a difficult childhood. Brought to England when only seventeen, she'd been escorted there by Bérulle, who'd recommended that she adopt the repentant Mary Magdalene as her model. Compared to France she thought England morose and uncivilized;

accustomed to our cheerful and boisterous folk, the English seemed grim and austere. She found her husband lukewarm at best. Danish on his mother's side, Charles I had a bit of the arctic in his veins. Marriage to a king, especially one so cold, haughty, and disparaging, seemed a penance.

At least he seemed honest. She tried exerting her power with petty squabbles, but the king always won out. Still unafraid, she became even more difficult, and began to scold.

The king's marriage had opened the door to a Catholic invasion. Bérulle, who'd escorted Henriette to her husband, and who'd advised her to emulate Magdalene's forbearance, knew how much the English had come to hate the "popish" religion. But his new bishop's hat filled him with zeal and ambition, especially after the weak King James had allowed him to confirm eighteen thousand Catholics in London in one day. Bérulle thought to test his new strength by demanding that, since the children of Catholics were allowed to remain in their mothers' care until the age of thirteen, and as the young queen had a Catholic bishop, the bishop and his clergy should be allowed to appear in the streets of London in full regalia. When the king granted this request, the queen took it as a sign of weakness, and as a result Charles I found in his bed, instead of a loving wife and grateful subject, a severe and scolding Catholic who wouldn't submit to the king in the desires of religion—or of the flesh.

It didn't stop there. One beautiful May morning, the young queen, accompanied by her bishop, her almoner, and all her women, crossed the length of London to the gallows at Tyburn where, twenty years earlier during the Gunpowder Conspiracy, Father Garnet and his Jesuits had been hanged. There, before the outraged eyes of London, she prayed for the souls of those notorious assassins who, with thirty-six barrels of powder, had planned to blow up the king, his ministers, and Parliament.

The king was stunned by this public insult to the people and religion of the state. He flew into a violent rage at this commemoration of those who ought to have been forgotten. "Let them be driven away like wild beasts," he decreed, "these priests and women who would pray at the gallows of murderers!"

The queen lamented, the queen cried. Her priests cursed the unbelievers and threatened excommunication. Her women wailed like the daughters of Zion being led into slavery, though really they were only being sent back to France. As they were leaving, the queen, wailing in her grief, ran to the window to call out her farewells. Charles I, entering her room at that moment, asked her to refrain from further scandalizing the morals of the English. The queen only cried all the louder. Charles grabbed her around the waist to pull her away from the window, but the queen clung to the bars. Charles dragged her away by force. The queen swooned, lifting her bleeding hands toward the sky to call the vengeance of God down upon her husband.

God answered on another day when, from another window, this one in Whitehall, King Charles stepped out and walked to the scaffold.

This quarrel between wife and husband, which prefigured the quarrel between France and England, caused all the queens of Christendom to condemn Charles I as a British Bluebeard. Pope Urban VIII was outraged, and told the Spanish ambassador, "If your master doesn't draw his sword in defense of this persecuted princess, he's neither a Catholic nor a gentleman." Meanwhile the young Queen of Spain, Henriette's sister, wrote to Cardinal Richelieu, appealing to his nobility to ask him to come to the aid of the oppressed Queen of England. The queen mother and the Infanta of Brussels both appealed to King Louis. Bérulle added his own voice. As you may readily believe, Louis XIII, ever petty and mean of spirit, regarded King Charles's expulsion of the French from his court as an insult to the French Crown.

Richelieu alone stood firm in opposition. From this act of resolve came the aid the English would send to the Protestants of La Rochelle, the assassination of Buckingham, the broken heart of Anne of Austria, and the universal league of queens and princesses against Richelieu.

Now back to Italy, where we will find, in the political situation of Montferrat and Piedmont, and the conflicting interests of the Duke of Mantua and the Duke of Savoy, the explanation of the letters borne by the Comte de Moret to the queen, the queen mother, and Gaston d'Orléans.

Charles-Emmanuel, the Duke of Savoy, all the more ambitious as his sovereignty was cramped, some years before had violently annexed the Marquisate of Saluzzo. When he couldn't get France under Henri IV to acknowledge the legitimacy of his conquest, he supported Biron's conspiracy with Spain against King Henri— which was not only treason against the king, but against the land and country of France, which Biron intended to dismember. The southern provinces were to go to Philip III of Spain, Savoy was to have Lyonnais, Provence, and Dauphiné, while Biron was to get Burgundy and Franche-Comté, with the hand of a Spanish *infanta* into the bargain.

The conspiracy was discovered, and Biron was shortened by a head.

Henri IV would have left Savoy alone if he hadn't been pushed into war by Austria. The need for money forced him into marriage with Marie de Médicis. Thus funded, he marched on Savoy and defeated the Duke soundly, leaving him the Marquisate of Saluzzo but taking all of Bresse, Bugey, Valromey, the Gex district, both banks of the Rhône from Geneva to Saint-Genix, and finally, Château-Dauphin at the head of the Goito valley.

Outside of Château-Dauphin, Charles-Emmanuel retained the rest of Piedmont. However, instead of being astride the Alps, he was now confined to their eastern slopes, though he remained master of the passes leading from France to Italy.

It was on this occasion that our witty King Henri had referred to Charles-Emmanuel as the Prince of Marmots—and the nickname had stuck.

After that, the Prince of Marmots was an Italian prince, and looked to Italy for further expansion of his state. He made several unsuccessful attempts to do so, until an opportunity presented itself that he regarded as both opportune and predestined.

Francis IV of the Gonzaga, Duke of Mantua and Montferrat, died, leaving the young princess Marie de Gonzague as the only child from his marriage to Margaret of Savoy, daughter of Charles-Emmanuel.

The Duke of Savoy claimed the right of governorship of Montferrat in the name of his granddaughter Marie. He hoped to marry Marie to his eldest son, Victor-Amadeus, and reunite Mantua and Montferrat with Piedmont. But Cardinal Ferdinand Gonzaga, brother of the late duke, rushed up from Rome, seized the regency of Mantua, and confined his niece to Goito Castle to keep her from falling into the hands of her maternal uncle.

Cardinal Ferdinand died in his turn, and Charles-Emmanuel knew a moment of hope, but the third brother, Vincenzo Gonzaga, came and, uncontested, assumed the Mantuan regency.

Charles-Emmanuel had patience. Riddled with infirmity, the new duke couldn't last long. He fell ill, and the Duke of Savoy felt sure that this time Montferrat and Mantua would fall to him.

But he didn't see the storm that was forming against him on the other side of the mountains.

There was in France a certain Louis de Gonzague, Duc de Nevers, the eldest of a cadet branch of the Gonzaga family. His son, Charles de Nevers, was the uncle of those last three sovereigns of Montferrat, so his grandson, the Duc de Rethel, was the cousin of Marie de Gonzague, the heir to Mantua and Montferrat.

Now, the interest of Cardinal Richelieu—and the interest of Cardinal Richelieu was always that of France—was in having a zealous supporter of the *fleurs de lys* amid the powers of Lombardy, which were always ready to declare for Austria and Spain. The Marquis de Saint-Chamont, the French ambassador to Mantua, was sent his instructions, and he passed his master's wishes on to Vincenzo Gonzaga. And Vincenzo Gonzaga, when dying, named Charles, the Duc de Nevers, as his heir.

The Duc de Rethel took possession on behalf of his father, with the title of Vicar General, and Princess Marie was sent to France, where she was placed under the care of Catherine de Gonzague, Dowager Duchesse de Longueville. She was the widow of Henri I d'Orléans-Longueville, the daughter of Louis de Gonzague, and thus Marie's aunt.

One rival to Charles de Nevers was Caesar Gonzaga, the Duke of Guastalla, whose grandfather had been accused of having poisoned the dauphin, the elder brother of Henri II, and of murdering the infamous Pierre-Louis Farnese, Duke of Parma and son of Pope Paul III.

The other rival, as we know, was the Duke of Savoy. The policies of France pushed him closer, moment by moment, to Spain and Austria. On his behalf the Austrians marched into Mantua with an army commanded by Spinola, while Don Gonzalès de Cordova undertook to wrest from the French Nice-de-la-Paille, Montcalvo, the Pont de Sture, and Casale.

The Spaniards took everything except Casale, and within two months the Duke of Savoy found himself master of the valleys of the Po, Tanaro, and Belbo, and all the land in between. This all occurred while the French were occupied with the siege of La Rochelle.

When it was able to do so, France sent a force to aid the Duc de Rethel, sixteen thousand men under the Marquis d'Uxelles. However, due to lack of experience, poor judgment, neglect, and very likely the betrayal of Créqui, they were repulsed by Charles-Emmanuel, much to the aggravation of the cardinal.

But there remained, in the center of Piedmont, a town that continued to hold out under the flag of France: Casale, defended by a brave and loyal commander named the Chevalier de Gurron.

Despite Richelieu's many statements to the effect that France intended to support the rights of Charles de Nevers, the Duke of Savoy had high hopes that this would be a fight that Louis XIII would eventually give up, as he knew Nevers was hated by Queen Mother Marie de Médicis. In his youth, Nevers had refused to marry her on the grounds that the Médicis weren't noble enough to be allied with the Gonzaga, who had been princes when the Médicis were still lowly gentry.

Thus, the cardinal's support of Nevers was another cause of the resentment that surrounded him, and of which we heard him complain bitterly to his niece.

The queen mother hated Cardinal Richelieu for many reasons. The first and most bitter is that he was once her lover, and was her lover no more; she had started out obeying him in all things, and eventually came to oppose him in all things. Where Richelieu wanted to enhance the greatness of France at the expense of Austria, she desired the expansion of Austria and the humiliation of France. And if he wanted to support Charles de Nevers as Duke of Mantua, she, driven by her old grudge, must oppose it.

Queen Anne of Austria hated Cardinal Richelieu because he'd frustrated her love affair with the Duke of Buckingham, exposed the scandalous episode of the gardens of Amiens, exiled her accomplice Madame de Chevreuse, and balked the English to the benefit of France. Worse, she harbored the ugly suspicion, never stated aloud, that the cardinal had somehow induced Felton to bury his knife in Buckingham's chest. And finally, she hated him because he monitored her closely to prevent the advance of any new lovers, and she knew that nothing she did, no matter how hidden, escaped his knowledge.

The Duc d'Orléans hated Cardinal Richelieu because he knew the cardinal recognized his true nature: ambitious, cowardly, and vicious. Gaston eagerly anticipated his brother King Louis's death, and was even willing to hasten the event. He'd been denied entry to the King's Council, his mentor Ornano had been imprisoned, and his friend and accomplice Chalais beheaded for conspiring to kill the king—while Monsieur's reward for the same crime had been to be dishonored, though enriched. Furthermore, though he loved no one but himself, he hoped, upon his brother's death, to marry his queen, although she was seven years his elder—most especially if she was pregnant.

Finally, the king himself hated the cardinal because he felt that Richelieu embodied genius, patriotism, and a genuine love of France, while he reeked of selfishness, indifference, and mediocrity; because he felt he would never really rule while the cardinal lived, and rule only badly if the cardinal died. But one thing always drew him back to the cardinal, though it, too, was a source of resentment. Was it a potion he'd drunk, some magic talisman he wore around his neck, an enchanted ring that had been placed on his finger? No: the magic charm was an ever-full chest of gold, one that was always open for the king. Concini had kept him in misery, Marie de Médicis in poverty; Louis XIII had never had any money until this wizard had touched his wand to the ground, and under the wondering eyes of the king, the golden River of Pactolus sprang forth. Richelieu was careful to ensure that the king always had money to spend, even when he himself had none.

Now, in the hope that everything on the chessboard is as clear to our readers as it was to Richelieu, we will resume our story where we left off.

XVI

Marie de Gonzague

Eight days have passed since the events last told of. To resume our story where we left off, we ask our readers to be so good as to follow us to the Hotel de Longueville, which, backed up against that of the Marquise de Rambouillet, shared with it the block between Rue Saint-Thomas-du-Louvre and the Hospital of the Three Hundred. But the Hotel de Longueville was entered from Rue Saint-Niçaise, opposite the Tuileries, while the marquise's mansion, as we've said, faced Rue Saint-Thomas-du-Louvre.

This mansion had belonged to Prince Henri de Condé—the same who'd mistaken Chapelain for a sculptor—and formerly had been occupied by himself and Madame la Princesse, his wife, whom we met at Madame de Rambouillet's soirée. He abandoned it in 1612, two years after his marriage to Mademoiselle de Montmorency, when he bought the great hotel in Rue Neuve-Saint-Lambert and caused the street to be rebaptized as the Rue de Condé, the name it bears to this day. At the time of our story—that is to say, on December 13, 1628 (events are so critical at this point that it's wise to be specific about dates)—this former mansion of the Prince de Condé was occupied by the Dowager Duchesse de Longueville and her ward, Her Highness Princess Marie, daughter of François de Gonzague (whose estate was causing such tumult not only in Italy but in Austria and Spain) and Margaret of Savoy, the daughter of Charles-Emmanuel.

Marie de Gonzague, born in 1612, had then attained her sixteenth year. All historians of the time agree that she was ravishingly beautiful, and from contemporary chroniclers, whose statements are more trustworthy, we learn that her beauty was the pinnacle of those perfectly shaped, dark-complexioned women born in Mantua—who, like the women of Arles, blossoming in the mists of the surrounding marshes, are blessed with black hair, blue eyes, pearly teeth, eyebrows and eyelashes like velvet, and lips that didn't even need to speak to offer sweet promises.

As fiancée of the Duc de Rethel, son of Charles de Nevers, who was heir to Duke Vincenzo, it goes without saying that her role would be important in the events to follow. Marie de Gonzague, whose beauty was sufficient, like the pole star, to draw the gaze of all the young cavaliers of the Court, caught the attention as well of those men of any age whose interest or ambition was in politics.

It was known that she was under the particular protection of Cardinal Richelieu—which was just one more reason for those who wanted to pay their respects to the cardinal to pay assiduous court to Marie de Gonzague.

It is evidently thanks to the sponsorship of the cardinal—of which the presence of Madame de Combalet is proof—that we see, arriving at the doors of the Hotel de Longueville about seven in the evening, several of the new sedan chairs, the monopoly of which is shared between Souscarrières and Madame de Cavois, and which are suddenly the favored transport of everyone of importance. The passengers are admitted into the front salon, which is hung with tapestries, below a ceiling painted with scenes representing the life of the bastard Dunois, founder of the house of Longueville. Candelabra flicker from mantels and sconces, and an immense chandelier is suspended in the center of the room, beneath which stands Princess Marie.

One of the first to arrive was Monsieur le Prince.

As Monsieur le Prince has a certain part to play in our story, and a major role in the time both before and after it, a part both shady and sad, we ask permission to acquaint the reader with that dubious offspring of the royal house of Condé.

While the first Condés were brave and jovial, this one was somber and aloof. He'd been heard to say "I may be a coward, but I'm not as bad as my cousin Vendôme"—as if that was some consolation, assuming he needed any.

How to explain this difference from his forefathers?

The first Prince de Condé, though he was small and a little hunchbacked, was every woman's darling. Of him it was sung:

> The little prince so fair,
> That laughing, singing lad,
> With lovers everywhere,
> God guard him, though he's bad.

Upon his death, slain at Jarnac by Montesquiou, this charming little Prince de Condé left a son who, along with the young Henri of Navarre, became one of the leaders of the Protestant party.

That man, Henri de Condé the first, was a worthy son of his father, leading a charge at the Battle of Jarnac at the head of five hundred gentlemen, despite having one arm in a sling and a broken leg with its bone jutting from his boot. When, on Saint Bartholomew's Day, Charles IX demanded, "Death or the mass," it was Condé who replied *death*, while Henri of Navarre, more prudent, replied *the mass.*

He was the last great Condé of the early race of that name. However, he didn't die on the battlefield, gloriously covered with wounds and slain by another Montesquiou—he died from being poisoned by his wife.

After an absence of five months, he returned to his Château des Andelys to find his wife, a daughter of the house of La Trémouille, pregnant courtesy of a Gascon page. At the dinner celebrating his return, she served her husband a peach for dessert.

Two hours later, he was dead. The page fled to Spain that same evening.

There was a public outcry, and the poisoner was arrested. Her son of adultery was born in prison, where his mother languished, no one daring to bring her to trial, as she was sure to be found guilty. After eight years, King Henri IV, who didn't want to see the end of the Condés, that lovely branch of the Bourbon tree, ordered her released from jail without trial. The widow was absolved by royal clemency, though convicted in the eye of the public.

Her son was the second Henri, Prince de Condé, the one who mistook Chapelain for a sculptor, and we can relate in just a few words how he came to marry Mademoiselle de Montmorency. It's a curious story that deserves its own parenthesis, despite the risk of making this digression overlong. But there's no harm in learning about history from a novelist, especially those details that historians find unworthy to relate, assuming they even know them.

In 1609, Queen Marie de Médicis put on a court ballet. During rehearsals, King Henri IV sulked because, though the ballet had all the prettiest women of the Court for its dancers, the queen had refused to admit Henri's mistress Jacqueline de Beuil, mother of the Comte de Moret. And since all the dancers on their way to the rehearsal hall in the Louvre were obliged to pass the door of Henri IV, the king, to show his displeasure, had shut that door.

One day, he left it ajar—and through the gap beheld Mademoiselle Charlotte de Montmorency.

"There was nothing under heaven," said Bassompierre in his memoirs, "more beautiful than Mademoiselle de Montmorency, nothing more graceful or perfect."

She was a vision so radiant that the king's bad mood immediately took wing and fluttered off like a butterfly. He rose from his chair and followed her, drawn like Aeneas following cloud-wrapped Venus.

On that day, for the first time, he attended the ballet.

There was one scene in which the ladies dressed as nymphs—and scanty as the costume of a nymph is today, it was scantier in the seventeenth century—and there was a point at which all the nymphs raised their spears, as if to strike at once. At this moment, Mademoiselle de Montmorency turned with hers and almost ran the king through. The king, not anticipating any danger, wasn't wearing a cuirass, and could easily have been stabbed to the heart. Which, he later said, is exactly what happened when he saw the beautiful Charlotte's graceful thrust.

Madame de Rambouillet and Mademoiselle Paulet were both at the ballet that day, and immediately befriended Mademoiselle de Montmorency, though they were five or six years older than her.

From that day on, good King Henri IV completely forgot Jacqueline de Beuil. (He was forgetful that way, as we know.) Thereafter, his only thought was to find a way to possess Mademoiselle de Montmorency. His plan was to find the beautiful Charlotte a complaisant husband who, for a dowry of four or five hundred thousand francs, would look the other way when the king sought to take advantage of his wife's proximity.

He'd done the same thing for the Comtesse de Moret when he'd found her a husband in Monsieur de Césy, whom he'd sent overseas as an ambassador on the night of her wedding.

The king thought he had just the man close at hand. Because if a son of murder and adultery married the daughter of a Constable of France, with the king as his patron, the stain on his birth would disappear.

The man was open to such a negotiation, and all his conditions were agreed to. The constable gave his daughter a dowry of a hundred thousand crowns, King Henri added a half million more, and Henri II de Condé, who the day before had an income of ten thousand, found himself on the morning of his wedding with fifty thousand a year.

Of course, that evening he would have to depart.

Only he didn't.

However, he did stick to his agreement insofar as to spend his wedding night in a room separate from that of his wife. Meanwhile Henri IV, the eager fifty-year-old lover, obtained Charlotte's promise that, to prove she was alone and mistress of herself, she would appear on her balcony between two torches with her hair down on her shoulders.

When he saw her there, the king nearly died from joy.

It would take too long to follow Henri IV through all the turns of his final *amour*, his mad fury when Condé fled with his wife to the Netherlands, his royal mania cut short by the knife of Ravaillac while he was on his way to visit the lovely Mademoiselle Paulet, for what consolation the charming Lioness could provide.

After the king's death, Monsieur de Condé returned to France with his wife, who was still technically Mademoiselle de Montmorency, as the marriage wasn't consummated until during the three years they spent together in the Bastille. It's probable that, given Monsieur de Condé's preference for the schoolboys of Bourges, without those three years in the Bastille neither the Grand Condé nor Madame de Longueville would ever have been born.

Monsieur le Prince was best known for his greed and parsimony. When going to visit his attorneys, he rode through the streets of Paris on an everyday hackney, accompanied by a single valet. La Martelière, a famous lawyer of the time, had, like doctors, those days when he would consult with clients for free. Condé visited him on those days.

Though always badly clothed, on the evening of which we speak he had dressed more carefully than usual, perhaps because he knew his brother-in-law, the Duc de Montmorency, would be paying his respects to Princess Marie, and the duke had said that, should he encounter Condé dressed in a manner unworthy of a prince of the blood, he would pretend not to know him.

Indeed, Henri II, Duc de Montmorency, was the complete oppo-site of Henri II, Prince de Condé. He was the brother of the beautiful Charlotte, and was as elegant as Monsieur de Condé was coarse, as generous as Monsieur de Condé was stingy. One day, upon hearing that a certain gentleman's fortune would be made if he could find twenty thousand crowns to borrow for two years, he said, "Seek no further: they are found." Taking a piece of paper, he wrote on it, *Good for twenty thousand crowns.* "Bring this to my steward tomorrow," he said to the gentleman, "and may you prosper."

And indeed, two years later the gentleman offered to return Mon-sieur de Montmorency his twenty thousand crowns. "Go, go, Mon-sieur," the duke said. "It's enough that you offer them to me; keep them with my good wishes."

He was deeply in love with the queen, as was Roger de Bellegarde, whose throat he almost cut over it. The queen flirted with both, and though Monsieur de Montmorency had thirty years while Monsieur de Bellegarde had sixty, she couldn't decide between them—until Buckingham came to Court and settled the matter. The older gen-tleman made so much noise about the affair that the younger duke coined a couplet that was soon heard in all the alcoves:

> Roger's star shines
> No more at the Louvre;
> Everyone finds
> He's had to move.
> The arrival from Dover
> Has shoved him over.

Kings, when they marry, are no more tolerant than other husbands, so Louis XIII had exiled Monsieur de Montmorency to Chantilly. Restored to favor through the influence of Marie de Médicis, he had returned to spend a month at Court, then left for his governorship of Languedoc. It was there that he heard the news of the duel and execution of his cousin François de Montmorency, Comte de Bouteville.

The queen mother's fondness for Montmorency came from the fact that his wife, Maria Felice Orsini, was the daughter of that Virginio Orsini who'd accompanied Marie de Médicis to France. This made Montmorency her nephew-in-law.

Maria Orsini, who according to the poet Théophile was as white as heavenly snow, was Italian—which is to say, jealous. She tormented her husband, who, as Tallemant des Réaux tells us, couldn't keep from pursuing every woman with the least bit of coquetry to her. The duke and his wife finally reached a compromise whereby he was allowed to act as gallant whenever he pleased—so long as he told her all about it.

One of her friends told her she couldn't understand how she could give her husband such latitude, and then insist on hearing the details. "Well," she replied, "I always wait to ask till we're about to go to bed, and then I get everything I'm owed."

And indeed, it's no surprise that women, especially in this lusty period, would succumb to passion for a handsome prince of thirty-three years of the first family of France: a millionaire, governor of a province, Admiral of France at seventeen, Duke and Peer at eighteen, Chevalier du Saint-Esprit at twenty-five, who counted among his ancestors four constables and six marshals, and whose entourage was composed of a hundred gentlemen and thirty pages.

That evening, the Duc de Montmorency was more handsome than ever. Upon his arrival, all eyes turned his way, and there was general amazement when, after greeting Princess Marie, he respectfully kissed the hand of Madame de Combalet.

Since the death of his cousin Bouteville—a wound felt more deeply in his pride as a Montmorency than in his affection for a relative—this was the first such advance he'd made to the cardinal. But no one was fooled by this demonstration: war with Savoy, Spain, and Austria was imminent, and like Monsieur de Créqui, the Duc de Montmorency was ambitious to bear the sword of the Constable of France, which had been borne with distinction at the king's knee by both his father and grandfather.

He who best understood the duke's ambition, as he'd had similar hopes which had been thoroughly crushed, was Charles de Lorraine, Duc de Guise, son of the Guise known as the Scarface who had perpetrated the Massacre of Saint Bartholomew's Day. The younger Guise was born in 1571, the year before the massacre, and was known more for his love affairs than for his deeds of war—though he'd served valiantly at the siege of La Rochelle, where he'd continued to fight even after his ship was completely afire. He ought to have a fair claim to the constabulary, or at least a prominent position in the army. Indeed, even if he were a simple gentleman like Bassompierre, Bellegarde, Cramail, or even Schomberg, he would have had the precedence, but against the Duc de Montmorency he could never hope for anything better than a secondary position. Given his birth, Montmorency's victory over the Calvinists in destroying the fleet commanded by the Duc de Soubise, from whom he'd also retaken the islands of Oléron and Ré, placed him above all other captains of the time.

There was another rivalry between them: the conquests of love. Although Monsieur de Guise had a broad, flat nose and was short in stature, he had inherited from his father some of the airs of royalty, which made him quite the ladies' man. The women found him guilty of only one great fault, his age—a thing which only Henri IV had briefly made fashionable and converted into an asset. But as we know from the date of his birth, the Duc de Guise was now approaching his sixtieth year, a condition he tried to regard as a new adventure.

One night he was standing in for a counselor—not, however, in his role on the council, but in his bed. The counselor, who was traveling, wasn't expected to return before noon, but arrived unexpectedly at about five in the morning. He had the key to the house, and made his way to the door of his bedchamber, where his wife, fortunately, had thrown the lock. The counselor knocked loudly and called her name. His wife, acting without haste, as that might give rise to suspicion, took a few moments to thrust Monsieur de Guise, naked, into the counselor's wardrobe, picking up the lace collar he'd left on a chair and shoving it into her pocket. Then, rubbing her eyes as if surprised from sleep, she opened the door to the counselor, thinking he would go right to bed, giving her lover a chance to escape.

Upon entering, the counselor drew the curtains to let in the daylight, and the first thing he saw was the rest of the duke's clothes. "So," he asked, frowning, "what clothes are these, my love?"

"Clothes I have on approval from a second-hand merchant, and which I can get for almost nothing if they suit you. But lie down and rest—you must be tired."

"No," the counselor said, "I have an early appointment at the palace, and must go there directly."

Then, taking off his travel-stained garments, he put on those of the duke, which were resplendent. "By my faith," he said, "these fit like they were made for me. Pay your second-hand merchant, my dear, and if he has any more like this, tell him to bring them. I'm off to the palace."

And indeed, taking only the time needed to get some papers from his desk, he threw his cloak over his clothes and left for the palace.

Behind him, his wife closed the bedroom door and opened the closet. "Dear me, Monseigneur," she said, "you must be frozen!"

"Faith, no," replied the duke. "While your husband was donning my clothes, I dressed in his. Don't you think I make a good attorney?" And with these words, he clapped a lawyer's cap on his head and stepped out, dressed in the complete outfit of a counselor.

The counselor's wife laughed, finding it all very amusing. But for the Duc de Guise, the best part of the joke was yet to come. As he had an audience at the Louvre that morning with King Henri IV, he thought it would be funny to go in his counselor's garb.

The king didn't recognize him at first, and when he finally did, he asked, half seriously and half laughing, what was the meaning of his masquerade.

Monsieur de Guise recounted his adventure, and as he told it well, and the king laughed heartily, he decided to press the point. "Sire," said the duke, "if you doubt me, send a guard to the palace to escort the counselor back to the Louvre. You'll see that he's dressed in my clothes."

The king, who never passed up an opportunity for amusement, approved of this joke, and summoned the counselor to appear before him within the hour. The counselor, dumbfounded, with no idea what could have earned him this honor, hastened over to the Louvre.

The king, who was never at a loss when it came to *gouailler* (to use the old Gallic word for shenanigans, a term much in vogue at the time, which we're sorry to see has almost been lost from the language), drew the counselor aside, and while chatting with him about a hundred trivialities, began undoing the man's cloak. The counselor, astonished, didn't dare to protest. Suddenly the king cried, "Hey! *Ventre-saint-gris*! Monsieur Counselor, you're wearing the clothes of Monsieur de Guise!"

"Of who? Monsieur de Guise?" asked the counselor, fearing the king had gone mad. "My wife bought these from a merchant."

"My faith!" said the king. "I didn't think the House of Guise had fallen so low that its head was reduced to selling his old clothes. Thank you, Monsieur Counselor, for showing me something I didn't know." And he sent the proud counselor off, glorying in the knowledge that he wore the clothes of a Prince of Lorraine.

When he arrived at home, the first thing he said to his wife was, "Do you know, my dear, whose clothes I'm wearing?"

"My faith, no!" she replied anxiously.

"Well! These are the clothes of Monseigneur le Duc de Guise," said the counselor, preening.

"Who told you that?" asked his wife in alarm.

"The king himself. And if you can find any more at the same price, buy them."

"Very well, my love," said his wife. "Under those conditions, I believe I may be able to get his entire wardrobe."

Monsieur de Guise was absent-minded, and his woolgathering had once led him into an amorous adventure. One evening he'd lingered over cards at Monsieur de Créqui's until it was too late to send for his carriage. The Hotel de Guise was quite far, so Monsieur de Créqui offered to lend the prince his own horse. Monsieur de Guise mounted the horse, but his mind was astray, so instead of guiding the horse he just gave it its head. At this time of night, the horse was used to taking Monsieur de Créqui to visit his mistress, so it bore Monsieur de Guise there and stopped at her door. Guise didn't recognize the door, but he was amused and amenable: wearing his hooded cloak, he dismounted and knocked.

The door was opened by a pretty maidservant, who slapped the hackney, sending it straight back to the stable where it knew it would find its oats. Then the maid led Monsieur de Guise up a staircase lit just well enough to keep him from breaking his neck, to a room no more well-lit than the stairs. The rider was apparently as expected as his horse, and he fell into a pair of open arms.

No one spoke. Everything happened in the dark. Monsieur de Guise, who was a friend of Monsieur de Créqui, must have known him well enough to imitate his performance, as the lady fell asleep without noticing her mistake. But in the morning she was awakened by Monsieur de Guise as he turned in the bed.

"*Bon Dieu*, my love," she said, "why do you turn so?"

"Because," said Monsieur de Guise, who was as indiscreet as he was absent-minded, "I need to get up so I can go tell all my friends that, instead of spending the night with Monsieur de Créqui, you've spent it with Monsieur de Guise."

Monsieur de Guise offset his faults with the virtue of generosity. One morning the Président de Chevry sent him by way of Raphaël Corbinelli, father of that Jean Corbinelli famous for his friendship with Madame de Sevigné, fifty thousand *livres* that the duke had won the day before at cards. The sum was divided into five sacks, four large bags each containing ten thousand *livres* in silver, and a smaller bag containing ten thousand *livres* in gold.

Corbinelli wanted to count it out for him, but the duke wouldn't allow it. He just saw that one bag was smaller than the others, and without looking inside it, said, "Here, my friend. Take this for your trouble."

Corbinelli went home, opened the bag, and found ten thousand *livres* in gold. He immediately returned to Monsieur de Guise. "Monseigneur," he said, "I think you made a mistake and gave me a bag of gold believing it was a bag of silver."

The duke drew himself up as far as his small stature would allow. "Keep it, keep it, Monsieur," he said. "The princes of my house don't make a practice of taking back what we once have given."

And Corbinelli kept his ten thousand *livres*.

When Monsieur de Montmorency was announced, the Duc de Guise immediately sought out Monsieur de Grammont in order to commence a quarrel as only he could. "Well, my friend," he said, "I must say I have a bone to pick with you."

"It can't be about gaming, Duke," Grammont responded. "Every year, good or bad, you win from me around a hundred thousand *livres*. My wife even offered you ten thousand crowns a year if you'd promise not to play with me."

"Which I refused! No, my faith, there's no question of that."

"What is it, then?"

"What? Why, since I know that after me you're the most talkative of men, last week I told you that I'd won Madame de Sablé's ultimate favors. I assumed you'd tell all of Paris, but you haven't said a word."

Monsieur de Grammont laughed. "I was afraid to get on Monsieur de Montmorency's bad side."

"Oh," said Monsieur de Guise, "I thought it was all over between them."

"You can see by the way they argue that it isn't."

And indeed, the marquise and the duke were arguing.

"Find out what it's about, my dear Comte," said the duke, "and then come and tell me."

The count approached. "Monsieur," said the marquise, "it's intolerable. I've heard that at the last ball at the Louvre, you took advantage of the fact that I was sick and danced with all the most beautiful women of the Court."

"But my dear Marquise," said the duke, "what would you expect me to do?"

"To dance only with the ugly ones, Monsieur!"

The Comte de Grammont, who'd arrived in time to hear this dialogue, reported it to the duke. "My faith, Comte," replied the duke, "this is the moment, I think, to go to Monsieur de Montmorency and share with him what I confided to you."

"By my faith, no!" said the count. "I wouldn't say such a thing to a husband, let alone a lover."

"So," said the duke with a sigh, "I'll go and tell him myself."

But as he took his first step toward Montmorency, both halves of the double door were thrown open and the usher announced, "His Royal Highness Monseigneur Gaston d'Orléans."

All conversation stopped, those who stood remained that way, and everyone sitting arose, including Princesse Marie herself.

"Well," said Madame de Combalet, the confidante of the cardinal, as she rose in her turn, bowing more respectfully than anyone, "now the comedy begins. I mustn't miss a word of what's said in the theater—and if possible, behind the scenes."

XVII

The Commencement of the Comedy

And indeed, it was the first time, publicly and in the midst of a grand soirée, that the Duc d'Orléans had presented himself to Princesse Marie de Gonzague.

It was easy to see he'd paid particular attention to his appearance. His doublet was white velvet laced with gold, as was his cloak, which was lined with scarlet satin. His velvet breeches were the same color as the lining of his cloak. Below he was clad in silk stockings and white satin slippers. He wore, or rather had in his hand, because, against his usual custom, he'd entered the room uncovered, a white felt hat with diamond braid and scarlet feathers. Ribbons in the two colors he'd adopted flowed and curled from every seam.

Monseigneur Gaston wasn't much liked, let alone esteemed. We've mentioned how much damage had been done to his reputation in this brave, elegant, and chivalrous society by his conduct at the trial of Chalais; his entrance was greeted by a general silence.

Hearing the announcement, Princess Marie cast a knowing glance toward the Dowager of Longueville. That day, Madame de Longueville had received a letter from His Royal Highness notifying her of his intended visit and requesting, if possible, a few minutes' conversation with Princess Marie, to whom he had matters of the utmost importance to communicate.

He advanced toward Princess Marie, whistling a little hunting tune, but as everyone knew he never stopped whistling, even before the queen, no one worried about the impropriety—not even Princess Marie, who gracefully offered him her hand.

The prince kissed it, holding it long and firmly against his lips.

Then he bowed courteously to the dowager, bowed slightly less to Madame de Combalet, and, addressing both lords and ladies, said, "My faith, Mesdames and Messieurs, I must recommend this new invention of Monsieur de Souscarrières's. Upon my honor, nothing could be more convenient. Have you tried it, Princess?"

"No, Monseigneur, I've only heard of this vehicle from some who used it to come here tonight."

"It's quite comfortable, and although Monsieur de Richelieu and I aren't great friends, I can only applaud his award of the rights to this invention to Monsieur de Bellegarde. His father, who is Master of the Horse, never in all his life invented anything the like, and I propose to give his son as much income as I can from this service. Imagine, Princess, a sturdy wheelbarrow, lined with velvet, where one sits comfortably, with windows when one wants to see, and curtains when one does not want to be seen. Some carry only one, but others can take two. I was carried by some lads from Auvergne who could walk, trot, or gallop as required, without damaging the car. I tried it slowly within the Louvre, then at a trot once we were outside. Their pace was strong but gentle.

"When the weather is bad, they can come right into a hall at the carriage door, so one can step in without even getting muddy. A marvelous convenience. They put the chair—they call it a chair, you know—right down on the floor, so one needn't step up. I will make it my business, I swear, to ensure that this invention becomes fashionable. I recommend it, Duc," he said, addressing Montmorency with a little bow of his head.

"I've used it today," said the duke, bowing, "and I am entirely of the opinion of Your Highness."

Gaston d'Orléans next turned to the Duc de Guise. "Greetings, cousin. What news from the war?"

"It's you we must ask about that, Monseigneur. The closer one is to the sun, the more its light reveals."

"Yes, when it doesn't blind us. As for me, I find politics quite over-dazzling. If this continues, I may need to ask Princess Marie to lend me a room so I can ask for news from her neighbors the Three Hundred Knights."

"If Your Highness wishes to hear some news, I can give it to him: I've been told that tonight, after she completes her duties to the queen, Mademoiselle Isabelle de Lautrec will bring us a letter she received from the Baron de Lautrec, her father, who as you know is in Mantua with the Duc de Rethel."

"But," asked Monseigneur Gaston, "is this news that can be made public?"

"The baron believes so, Monseigneur, and said as much in his letter."

"In exchange," Gaston said, "I'll give you some hallway gossip, which is the only kind of news that interests me, since I've given up politics."

"Tell us, Monseigneur! Tell us!" said the ladies, laughing.

Madame de Combalet, as was her habit, covered her face with her fan.

"I'll wager," said the Duc de Guise, "you're going to talk about my scoundrel of a son."

"Just so. You know that he now insists on being presented his shirt, like a prince of the blood. Eight or ten people have been foolish enough to do him this honor. But a few days ago he designated the Abbé de Retz, who pretended to be nervous and dropped it into the fire, where it scorched. After that, the abbé picked up his hat, bowed, and left."

"Well done, by my faith, well done," said the Duc de Guise, "and I'll compliment him on it next time I see him."

"If one dared to speak," said Madame de Combalet, "one might say your son's done even worse than that."

"Oh, tell us, tell us, Madame!" said Monsieur de Guise.

"Well, on his last visit to his sister Madame de Saint-Pierre, the abbess in Reims, he dined with her in the parlor, and then went right into the convent like a prince. There he was, sixteen years old, and chasing after the nuns. He caught the most beautiful and, willy-nilly, began to kiss her. 'My brother!' cried Madame de Saint-Pierre, 'My brother! Don't joke like this! These are the Brides of Christ!' 'Good,' replied the villain, 'God is powerful enough to keep me from embracing his brides, if that was His will.' 'I'll complain to the queen!' cried the nun, who was quite pretty. This frightened the abbess. 'Embrace that other one, too,' she said to the prince. 'But, sister, she's very ugly!' he replied. 'All the more reason—it will look like you were acting childish and didn't know any better.' 'Must I, sister?' 'If you don't, the pretty one will complain.' 'Well, then, ugly it is!' And he kissed the ugly one, who was grateful, and kept the pretty one from complaining."

"And how, beautiful widow, do you know of this?" the duke asked Madame de Combalet.

"Madame de Saint-Pierre made her report to my uncle—but my uncle has such a weakness for the House of Guise, he only laughed!"

"When I saw the lad last month," said Monsieur le Prince, "he had a yellow silk stocking as a feather in his hat. What does that folly mean?"

"It means," said Monsieur d'Orléans, "that he was in love with La Villiers of the Hotel de Bourgogne, and she was playing a role in which she wore yellow stockings. He sent Tristan l'Hermite to pay her a compliment on her legs. She pulled off one of her stockings and gave it to Tristan, saying, 'If Monsieur de Joinville wears this as a plume on his hat for three days, he can then come and ask me for whatever he wants.'"

"Well?" asked Madame de Sablé.

"Well, he wore it for three days, and my cousin de Guise, his father, can tell you that on the fourth, he returned to the Hotel de Guise at eleven in the morning."

"A fine life for a future archbishop!" said Madame de Sablé.

"But these days," His Royal Highness continued, "he's in love with Mademoiselle de Pons, a great big blonde. The other day she went for a purgative. He asked for the address of her apothecary and took the same drug, writing her, 'No one can say that if you're being purged, I'm not being purged as well.'"

"Ah!" said the duke. "This *amour* with an actress explains why, the other day, the great ninny invited every trained-dog buffoon in Paris to the Hotel de Guise. Imagine me coming into the mansion and finding the courtyard full of dogs dressed in all sorts of costumes. There were about three hundred, with about thirty clowns standing around, each with his pack. 'What are you up to now, Joinville?' I asked. 'I'm putting on a show, Father,' he replied. Guess why he'd invited all these buffoons? He promised each one a crown if, three days hence, three hundred trained dogs of Paris would jump at once for Mademoiselle de Pons."

"By the way," said Gaston, too impatient to stay with one subject for long, "as his neighbor, dear Dowager, have you heard about poor Pisany? Voiture saw him yesterday and said he's not doing too badly."

"I called this morning, and was told that the doctors were still hovering around him."

"I have fresher news than that," said the Duc de Montmorency. "I left the Comte de Moret at the door of the Hotel de Rambouillet, where he'd decided to go in person."

"What, the Comte de Moret?" said Madame de Combalet. "The man whom Pisany wanted killed?"

"Quite so," said the duke. "It seems it was all a misunderstanding."

At that moment, the door opened and the usher announced, "Monseigneur Antoine de Bourbon, Comte de Moret."

"Stay a moment," said the duke, "here he is. He'll tell you all about it himself, and much better than I would, as I start mumbling every time I have to say more than twenty words."

The Comte de Moret came in, and all eyes turned toward him—especially, we must say, those of the women.

Having not yet been presented to Marie de Gonzague, he waited at the door till Monsieur de Montmorency came to lead him to the princess, which the duke hastened to do with the same elegant grace he did everything.

No less elegant, the young prince bowed to the princess, kissed her hand, gave her the regards of the Duc de Rethel whom he'd seen in passing in Mantua, kissed the hand of Madame de Longueville, and picked up her bouquet, which had fallen from her bodice as she'd stepped aside to make room for Madame de Combalet. He returned it with a charming gesture, bowed profoundly before Monseigneur Gaston, and then took a modest place near the Duc de Montmorency.

"My dear prince," Montmorency said when the ceremony was over, "we were talking about you just before you came in."

"Me? Bah. What could you have to say about me in such celebrated company?"

"You're right, Monseigneur," said a female voice. "A man wants to murder you just because you're a lover of Marion Delorme's sister. Why ever would we care about that?"

"Ah!" said the prince. "There's a voice I know. Is that not my little cousin?"

"Indeed, Master Jacquelino!" replied Madame de Fargis, approaching and holding out her hand.

The Comte de Moret bent over her hand, whispering, "You know I must see you again, simply must speak with you. I'm in love."

"With me?"

"A little—but with another, a lot."

"Impudence! What's her name?"

"I don't know her name."

"Is she pretty, at least?"

"I don't know what she looks like."

"Is she young?"

"She must be."

"And why do you think that?"

"From the voice I heard, the hand I touched, the breath I drank in."

"Ah, my cousin. How can you say things like that?"

"I'm twenty-one. I say what I feel."

"Oh, youth! Youth!" said Madame de Fargis, "Priceless diamond that tarnishes so quickly!"

"My dear Count," interrupted the duke, "You're making all the ladies jealous of your 'cousin,' as I believe you called Madame de Fargis. They want to know why you were visiting a man who tried to have you assassinated."

"First," said the Comte de Moret, with a charming air, "because I'm a cousin of Madame de Rambouillet."

"A cousin? How?" asked Monsieur d'Orléans, who prided himself on his knowledge of noble genealogy. "Please explain, Monsieur de Moret."

"Through my little cousin Fargis, who married Monsieur de Fargis of Angennes, cousin of Madame de Rambouillet."

"And how are you the cousin of Madame de Fargis?"

"That," said the Comte de Moret, "is our secret—isn't that so, Cousin Marina?"

"Yes, Cousin Jacquelino," laughed Madame de Fargis.

"Then, besides being a cousin to Madame de Rambouillet, I'm one of her friends."

"But I've seen you at her house only once or twice," said Madame de Combalet.

"She asked me to stop paying visits."

"Why's that?" asked Madame de Sablé.

"Because Monsieur de Chevreuse was jealous of me."

"Had he the right to be?"

"Hmm. How many of us are there in this salon? Thirty or so. I'd tell each one for a thousand. That makes thirty thousand."

"To dogs, we give our words away," said Monsieur.

"Then he had the right—on behalf of his wife."

A roar of laughter greeted the count's admission.

"But," said Madame de Montbazon, who was afraid she might not get the whole tale to pass on to her stepsister Chevreuse, "that still doesn't tell the story of the assassination."

"Ah! *Ventre-saint-gris*! That's simple enough. Who compromised Madame de la Montagne by saying I was her lover?"

"None other than Madame de Chevreuse," said Madame de Sablé.

"Well, poor Pisany believed it was Madame de Maugiron who was my delight. Certain issues with his shape make him touchy, while certain truths told by his mirror make him positively irascible. Instead of calling me out for a duel, which I would've been happy to grant him, he decided to pay a bravo to pick a quarrel. His luck was out: he tried to hire an honest man, who refused. He tried to kill the bravo, but failed. He tried to kill Souscarrières, and failed. And that's the story."

"But that's not what we want to hear," insisted Monsieur. "Why did you go to visit a man who tried to assassinate you?"

"Because he couldn't come to me. I'm a good soul, Monseigneur. I thought poor Pisany might think I was out to get him, and would have nightmares. So I shook his hand and told him that if, in the future, he believes he has reason to complain of me, he should just call me out for a duel. I'm just a simple gentleman, and have no right to refuse someone who believes his honor offended. Though I'd rather not offend anyone."

As the young man spoke these words so gently and yet, at the same time, so firmly, a murmur of approval answered the frank and honest smile on his lips.

He'd hardly finished speaking when the door opened again and the usher announced, "Mademoiselle Isabelle de Lautrec."

As she entered, they could see behind her the footman, wearing the livery of her château, who'd accompanied her.

At the sight of the young woman, the Comte de Moret felt a strange feeling of attraction and took a step toward her.

She walked, blushing and graceful, to Princess Marie, and bowed respectfully before her. "Madame," she said, "I come from Her Majesty bearing you a letter from my father, with good news for you, and I beg leave with respect to place this letter at your feet."

At the first words spoken by Mademoiselle de Lautrec, the Comte de Moret's heart leaped. He seized Madame de Fargis's hand and, pressing it, he murmured, "It's she! It's she! The one I love!"

XVIII

Isabelle and Marina

As the Comte de Moret had foreseen without truly knowing anything, even a name, but by the wonderful insight of youth that makes a feeling more reliable than the senses, Mademoiselle Isabelle de Lautrec was perfectly lovely, albeit with a beauty different from that of Princess Marie.

Marie de Gonzague was a brunette with blue eyes, while Isabelle de Lautrec was blond with eyes, eyelashes, and eyebrows of black. Her skin was a dazzling white, fine and transparent, with the delicate shading of a rose petal. Her neck had that long lovely curve seen in women painted by Pérugin and in the early work of his pupil Sanzio. Her hands were long, slim, and white, the very model of the hands of Leonardo da Vinci's La Ferronière. Her long flowing dress didn't reveal even the shadow of her feet, but one could guess that if they were in harmony with her hands, they would be slender and delicate.

As Isabelle knelt before the princess, Marie embraced her and kissed her forehead. "God forbid," she said, "I should allow to kneel before me the daughter of one of the best servants of our house. Just give me your good news. Now, daughter of our dear friend, does your father say this is news for me alone, or may I share it with those who love us?"

"As you'll see in the postscript, Madame, His Majesty's Ambassador, Monsieur de La Saludie, has authorized the news to be spread in Italy—and Your Highness may, in turn, let it be known in France."

Princess Marie turned an inquiring look toward Madame de Combalet who, with a slight nod, confirmed what the beautiful messenger had said.

Marie read the letter to herself.

While she was reading it, the young woman turned her eyes to the rest of the assembly. Until then, she'd seen only the princess, the other twenty-five or thirty people in the salon appearing as in a mirage.

When her look reached the Comte de Moret, their eyes met, and along their gaze flashed an electric jolt that went right to both their hearts.

Isabelle paled and leaned against the princess's chair.

The Comte de Moret saw the emotion strike her, and seemed to hear a choir of heavenly angels singing, *Glory to God!*

The usher had named her as a member of the old and illustrious family of Lautrec, whose noble history almost equaled that of the princes.

And she had never been in love. He knew it: he had hoped as much, but now he was sure.

Meanwhile, Princess Marie had finished her letter. "Messieurs," she said, "here is the news from my dear Isabelle's father. On his way to Mantua he met Monsieur de La Saludie, His Majesty's Envoy Extraordinaire to the Italian powers. Monsieur de La Saludie was charged by the cardinal with telling both the Duke of Mantua and the Venetian Senate of our conquest of La Rochelle. He was also responsible for declaring that France was prepared to come to the aid of Casale and to support Charles de Nevers in the possession of his new dominions. Passing through Turin he had seen the Duke of Savoy, Charles-Emmanuel, and had enjoined him, in the name of his son-in-law our king, and on the behalf of the cardinal, to abandon his claim to Montferrat. He was empowered to offer the Duke of Savoy, in return, the city of Trino, with a sovereign income of twelve thousand crowns a year. Monsieur de Bautru has departed for Spain and Monsieur de Charnace for Austria, Germany, and Sweden, with the same message."

"I hope," said Monsieur, "this doesn't mean the cardinal plans to ally us with the Protestants."

"As for me," said Monsieur le Prince, "if that was the only way to keep Wallenstein and his bandits in Germany, I wouldn't be against it."

"That's your Huguenot blood talking," replied Gaston d'Orléans.

"I would think," laughed the prince, "that there's more Huguenot blood in Your Highness's veins than in mine. Between our fathers Henri de Navarre and Henri de Condé, the only difference is that one took the mass to gain a kingdom, and the other didn't."

"Just the same, Messieurs," said the Duc de Montmorency, "this is great news. Do we have any idea who will be given command of the army we send to Italy?"

"Not yet," replied Monsieur, "but it's likely, Monsieur le Duc, that the cardinal, who paid you a million for the office of Admiral so he could conduct the siege of La Rochelle as he saw fit, will spend another million for the right to direct the Italian campaign in person—even two million, if need be."

"But confess, Monseigneur," said Madame de Combalet, "that if he ran the campaign as well as he led the siege of La Rochelle, neither the king nor France would have cause for complaint. Some others might demand a million to undertake the task, and yet not fare as well."

Gaston bit his lip. He hadn't appeared for a moment at the siege of La Rochelle, after having received five hundred thousand crowns for his campaign expenses.

"I hope, Monseigneur," said the Duc de Guise, "that you won't let this opportunity to assert your rights escape you."

"If I go," said Monsieur, "so will you, cousin. I've received quite a bit from the House of Guise through the hands of Mademoiselle de Montpensier, and would be glad for a chance to show I'm not ungrateful. And you, my dear Duke," Gaston said, going up to

Montmorency, "would be particularly welcome, as it would give me an opportunity to correct some injustices. Among your father's trophies of arms is the Sword of the Constable, which I don't think would be too heavy for the son. But remember, my dear Duke, in that event I would be delighted to see at your side, making his debut under such a fine mentor, my dear brother the Comte de Moret."

The Comte de Moret bowed while the duke, flattered in his supreme ambition by Gaston's speech, said, "Those words are not planted in sand, Monseigneur. If the opportunity presents itself, Your Highness will see that I'll remember them."

Just then, the usher came in through a side door and said something to the Dowager Duchesse de Longueville, who immediately left with him by the same door.

The gentlemen all gathered around Monsieur. The chance of a war—all the more likely as everyone knew Savoy had no intention of raising the siege of Casale, and that the Spanish were determined to deny Mantua to the Duc de Nevers—granted Monsieur sudden importance. It was impossible that such an expedition could be undertaken without him, and in that case his high position in the army would give him the disposal of some important commands.

The usher returned after a moment and spoke quietly to Princess Marie, who followed him through the same door Madame de Longueville had used.

Madame de Combalet, who was nearby, heard the name *Vautier* and shuddered. Vautier, the reader will recall, was the secret confidant of the queen mother.

Five minutes later, it was to Monseigneur Gaston that the usher came to ask him to join Madame de Longueville and the Princesse Marie. "Gentlemen," he said, bowing, "remember that I am no one special, that I aspire to nothing in the world other than to be a devoted knight to Princess Marie. And being no one, I can promise nothing to anyone!"

With these words, he put his hat on his head and skipped off, both hands tucked into the top of his breeches, as was his habit.

He was hardly gone before the Comte de Moret, taking advantage of the general astonishment at the successive disappearances of the Duchesse de Longueville, the Princesse Marie, and His Royal Highness Monsieur, went straight across the salon to Isabelle de Lautrec. Bowing before the blushing and tongue-tied young woman, he said, "Mademoiselle, please know that there is in the world a man who, the night he met you without even glimpsing you, vowed to be yours through life and death—and tonight, after seeing you, he renews that oath. This man is the Comte de Moret."

And, without waiting for an answer from the young lady, more blushing and tongue-tied than ever, he bowed respectfully and left.

Passing through a dim-lit corridor leading to an antechamber, itself poorly lit, as was customary at the time, the Comte de Moret felt an arm slipped through his, while a black hood lined with rose satin appeared before his face. He felt a breath like flame from beneath the hood, and a voice in tones of mild reproof said, "And thus is poor Marina sacrificed."

He recognized the voice, and even more he recognized the hot breath of Madame de Fargis, which had once before touched his face at the Inn of the Painted Beard. "The Comte de Moret flees, it's true," he said, leaning toward that breath so avid it seemed to come from the Venus Astarte herself, "but . . ."

"But what?" demanded his interrogator, lifting herself at his side on tiptoe, so that, despite the gloom, the young man could see her eyes glowing within the hood like two black diamonds, above teeth like a string of pearls.

"But," continued the Comte de Moret, "Jacquelino is still here, and if that will satisfy her . . ."

"Then Marina will be content," said the lady magician.

She leaned forward. The young man immediately felt on his lips the sweet taste and the acrid bite of antiquity, which had a word for such a thing and a name for such a feeling—and that word and name was Eros.

Then, dazed by the voluptuous thrill that coursed through his veins and into his heart, Antoine de Bourbon, eyes closed, head thrown back, leaning against the wall with an anguished sigh, heard the lovely Marina, light as the bird of Venus, release his arm, step into a sedan chair, and say, "To the Louvre."

"My faith," said the Comte de Moret, detaching himself from the wall with an effort, "*vive la France pour les amours.* There's no shortage of them! I returned only a fortnight ago, and am already involved with three—though I really love only one of them. But, *ventre-saint-gris*! I'm not the son of Henri IV for nothing! And if I could have six amours instead of three, well, bring on three more fair faces!"

Drunk, dazed, and stumbling, he reached the porch, called his porters, climbed into his chair, and, dreaming of his three amours, was carried to the Hotel de Montmorency.

XIX

In Which Monseigneur Gaston, Like King Charles IX, Puts On His Little Comedy

Having seen the Dowager of Longueville, Princess Marie, and Monseigneur Gaston called by the same usher and leave by the same door, the other guests thought maybe something extraordinary had happened. On the other hand, since eleven o'clock was striking as Monsieur withdrew, it might simply have been an indication that it was time to retire, so after a few minutes the guests began to leave.

Madame de Combalet began to depart with the rest, but the usher, who seemed to be waiting for her in the dim passage we already mentioned, drew her aside and whispered, "Madame the Dowager would be obliged if you would wait to leave until you've seen her." And he opened the door to a little drawing room where she could wait.

Madame de Combalet hadn't been wrong when she thought she'd heard the name *Vautier*. He had indeed been sent to Madame de Longueville to convey the queen mother's disapproval, as he had on the two or three previous visits Gaston d'Orléans had made to Marie de Gonzague. Upon his arrival, Madame de Longueville had called her niece to hear the message from the queen mother.

Princess Marie, who was honest and forthright, proposed at once to call the prince and ask for an explanation. Vautier was about to retire, but the dowager and the princess insisted he remain and repeat his message to the prince.

We've already seen how the prince left the salon. Guided by the usher, he was led to the room where he was awaited. At the sight of Vautier he appeared, or pretended to appear, surprised. Giving him a hard look, he approached and said, "What are you doing here, Monsieur, and who sent you?"

Vautier was well aware that Gaston's anger was feigned, as he'd read the letter from the Duke of Savoy—he just hadn't known until then when the apparent quarrel that would divide mother and son was supposed to begin. "Monseigneur," he said, "I'm only a humble servant of your august mother the queen. I'm forced, therefore, to execute her commands. And I come at her command to beg Madame de Longueville and the Princesse Marie not to encourage a courtship that is contrary to the wishes of the king and of herself."

"You hear, Monseigneur," said Madame de Longueville. "A royal desire so expressed is almost a command. We must wait for Your Highness to inform Her Majesty the Queen as to the purpose of your visits."

"Monsieur Vautier," said the Duc d'Orléans in the superbly haughty tone which he could assume at need, "you are too well aware of this century's key events at the Court of France to be ignorant of the day and year of my birth."

"God forbid, Monseigneur. Your Highness was born on April 25, 1608."

"Well, Monsieur, today is December 13, 1628—which makes my age twenty years, seven months, and nineteen days. I'm no longer of an age to take lessons from women. Moreover, when I was married before, it was against my will. I am wealthy enough now to enrich my wife if she is poor, and of high enough rank to ennoble her if she is common. The State has no say over who a younger son may marry, and this time I intend to marry as I see fit."

"Monseigneur," said both Madame de Longueville and her niece, "you need not insist, out of regard for us, that Monsieur Vautier take such a response to Her Majesty the Queen, your mother."

"If it suits Monsieur Vautier, he can say I told him nothing. When I return to the Louvre, I'm the one who will reply to Madame my mother."

And he motioned for Vautier to leave. Vautier bowed his head and obeyed.

"Monseigneur . . ." said Madame de Longueville.

But Gaston interrupted. "Madame, for several months now, in fact ever since I first saw her, I've loved Princess Marie. The respect I have for her and for you is such that I would probably not have confessed this before my twenty-first birthday, as, being only sixteen, she has time to wait, God willing. But since, on the one hand, I face the ill will of a mother who would keep me from her, while on the other hand is the policy of state that would marry her to a petty Italian prince, I must say to Your Highness: Madame, my rosy-cheeked youth may undermine my attempts at gallantry, but if I was older and paler I could love her no less. It's up to you to consider my offer—because, as you must know, to offer my heart is to offer my hand. So choose, then, between the Duc de Rethel and me, between Mantua and Paris, between a petty Italian prince and the brother of the King of France."

"Oh, Monseigneur!" said Madame de Longueville. "If you were as free to act as a simple gentleman, if you weren't accountable to the queen, the cardinal, the king . . ."

"The king, Madame? I am accountable to the king, it's true. But it's my business to obtain his permission for this marriage, and I'm determined to do so. As to the cardinal and the queen, well, soon they may well be accountable to me."

"How so, Monseigneur?" asked the two ladies.

"My God, do I have to tell you?" said Gaston, all candor and sincerity. "My brother, Louis XIII, has been married for thirteen years and had no children—and considering his health, he never will. And considering his health further, you know that someday he will leave me the throne of France."

"So," said Madame de Longueville, "you think the early death of the king, your brother—is inevitable?"

The Princesse Marie said nothing, but her heart's ambition was in her eyes, and she hung on Monsieur's every word.

"Doctor Bouvard considers him as good as dead, Madame, and is amazed he still lives. And on this point, the auguries agree with the doctor."

"The auguries?" asked Madame de Longueville.

Marie redoubled her attention.

"My mother consulted Fabroni, Italy's premier astrologer, and he said Louis would bid the world adieu before the sun traversed the sign of Cancer in the year 1630. Fabroni gives him eighteen months to live. And I and my retainers heard the same prophecy from a certain Doctor Duval. Unfortunately, Duval has come to a bad end, for the cardinal, who'd heard he'd cast the king's horoscope, had him arrested and secretly condemned to the galleys, invoking the old Roman laws that forbid fortune-telling on the lives of princes. Well, madame my mother is aware of all this. Like the queen and myself, my mother sadly awaits the death of her eldest son. That's why she wants to preserve me, as she did my brother, for a royal wife who'll bring me a crown. But that won't happen. By God, I swear it! I love you, Marie, and unless you absolutely can't stand me, I'll make you my wife."

"But," asked the dowager, "do you have any idea what Cardinal Richelieu might think about this marriage?"

"Don't worry, we have an answer for the cardinal."

"What's that?"

"This, Madame," said the Duc d'Orléans, "is where you can help us out."

"In what way?"

"The Comte de Soissons is tired of exile, isn't he?"

"He's in despair, but can't think how to persuade Monsieur de Richelieu to allow his return."

"What if he married the cardinal's niece?"

"Madame de Combalet?" Both ladies stared at him.

"The cardinal," said Gaston, "wants to join his family to the royal house, no matter what it takes."

The ladies' eyes opened even wider. "Is Monseigneur serious?" asked Madame de Longueville.

"I couldn't be more serious."

"And my daughter, who has such influence over her brother-in-law Soissons—that's what you want me to tell her?"

"That's it, Madame." Then, turning to Princess Marie, "But this effort is all in vain, Madame, if your heart isn't in it."

"Your Highness knows that I'm engaged to the Duc de Rethel," Marie said. "I can't personally break such a bond nor speak against it—but the day that bond is broken and I'm free to speak for myself, I believe Your Highness will have nothing to complain about my answer."

The princess curtsied and began to withdraw, but Gaston grabbed her hand and kissed it passionately. "Ah, Madame!" he said. "You've made me the happiest of men! We'll succeed in the end, and my happiness is assured."

Then, as Princess Marie left by one door, Gaston rushed out the other, with the haste of a man who needs fresh air to cool his passion.

Madame de Longueville, who remembered that she'd asked Madame de Combalet to wait, opened a third door—and almost gasped in astonishment. For the usher had imprudently left the cardinal's niece in the next room to the one where the interview with Gaston had taken place.

"Madame," the dowager said, "insofar as Monseigneur le Cardinal is our friend and protector, and we wish to conceal nothing, I arranged for you to overhear that discussion about the Queen Mother's disapproval of the visits paid us by His Royal Highness Monsieur."

"Thank you, dear Duchesse," said Madame de Combalet, "and I appreciate your thoughtfulness in allowing me to slightly open the door between the rooms so I wouldn't lose a word of the conversation."

"And," the dowager asked with some hesitation, "you heard the parts concerning yourself? As for me, after the pleasure of seeing my niece as Duchesse d'Orléans, nothing could make me happier than to see you enter our family, Madame. My daughter will use all her powers of persuasion on the Comte de Soissons to that end—assuming that's what's desired."

"Thank you, Madame," replied Madame de Combalet, "and I fully appreciate what an honor it would be for me to be the wife of a prince of the blood. But when I donned widow's weeds, I made two vows: first, never to remarry, and second, to devote myself entirely to my uncle. But believe me, Madame, I would dearly regret it if your connection with Monsieur didn't happen because of me."

And bowing respectfully, showing a tiny yet gracious smile, she took her leave of Madame de Longueville, who couldn't believe that any oath, no matter how proudly taken, could keep a lady from becoming the Comtesse de Soissons.

XX

Eve and the Serpent

"To the Louvre!" Madame de Fargis had said. And obeying her order, the porters had carried her chair to the foot of the stairs that led to both the king's and queen's chambers. The door opened to admit her, though it was after ten o'clock at night, when that grand staircase was officially closed.

Madame de Fargis was to serve the queen for the next week, resuming her service that very evening. The queen was very fond of her, and loved her much as she still loved Madame de Chevreuse. But the Duchesse de Chevreuse had been involved in a whole host of indiscretions, and the king and the cardinal had their eyes on her. Her eternal laughter irritated Louis XIII who, even as a child, had never laughed ten times in his life. When Madame de Chevreuse was exiled, her place, as we've said, was taken by Madame de Fargis, who was pretty, bold, passionate, and even less inhibited than La Chevreuse. Her good luck in being placed so near the queen was due partly to the prominence of her husband, Monsieur de Fargis d'Angennes, cousin to Madame de Rambouillet and ambassador to Madrid, and even more so to the three years she'd spent at the Carmelite convent of the Rue Saint-Jacques, where she'd become acquainted with Madame de Combalet, who'd recommended her to the cardinal.

The queen was waiting impatiently. This romantic princess, while still weeping for her lost Buckingham, was nonetheless ready for new emotions and other loves. Her twenty-six-year-old heart, in which her husband had never been tempted to take the slightest place, needed at least the semblance of love. In the absence of real passion, her heart cried out, like an Aeolian harp from the top of a tower, to every other heart that passed.

The future promised no more joy than the past. This morose king, this sad monarch, this husband without desire, was keen to keep her from fulfilling her own desires. What more could she hope for than the happy hour of his death that everyone insisted was imminent? Then she might marry Monsieur, who though seven years her junior would be eager to wed her, for fear that, out of personal ambition or love for another, she might get herself declared regent, and keep him from the throne forever.

If the king did die, she had three possible fates: marry Gaston d'Orléans; assume the regency; or abdicate and return to Spain.

So she waited, sad and dreaming, in a small room next to her bed-chamber where only her most trusted ladies were admitted, her eyes staring past the book she held, a new tragicomedy by Guilhem de Castro called *The Youth of the Cid* given her by Señor Mirabel, the Spanish Ambassador.

When she heard scratching at the door, she knew from the sound that it was Madame de Fargis. Tossing aside the book that, a few years later, was to have such a great influence on her life, she called out a sharp and happy "Enter!"

Encouraged by her call, Madame de Fargis didn't just enter; she actually burst into the room and fell at Anne of Austria's feet, seizing both her beautiful hands and kissing them with a passion that drew a smile from the queen. "Do you know," Anne said, "I sometimes imagine, my beautiful Fargis, that you're secretly a lover disguised as a woman—and one day, when you're completely assured of my friendship, you'll suddenly reveal yourself."

"And if that were so, my beautiful Majesty," she said, teeth shining and lips parted, her burning eyes fixed on Anne of Austria, "would you be so desperate as to accept me?"

"Desperate, yes, because then I'd have to ring the bell and show you to the door—to my great regret, because other than Chevreuse, you're the only one who can distract me."

"My God, virtue like that is perverse and against nature, since it must result in the separation of loving hearts. Indulgent souls, like mine, are more in the spirit of a loving God—not like those prudish hypocrites who take even the tiniest compliment the wrong way."

"Do you know that I haven't seen you for a week, Fargis?"

"That's all? Good God, my sweet Queen, it seems more like a century!"

"And what have you been doing for the last century?"

"Not much good for myself, dear Majesty. I fell in love with an idea."

"With an idea?"

"Yes."

"My God, you say such crazy things, we should clap our hand to your mouth at the first word."

"Your Majesty should try it and see how her hand would be received."

Anne put her own hand to her lips, laughing into the palm that Madame de Fargis, still kneeling before her, had kissed so passionately. She dropped it suddenly. "Don't kiss me so, my sweet, you'll give me a fever. So, who is it you love?"

"A dream."

"A dream? How's that?"

"Yes, it must be a dream, in this age of such men as Vendôme, as Condé, as Grammont, as Courtauvaux and Baradas, to find a young man of twenty-two who's so handsome, noble, and amorous."

"So that's your dream?"

"Yes, but only a dream. For he loves another."

"Truly, Fargis, you're mad, and I don't understand a word you say."

"And I believe, Your Majesty, that you must truly be religious."

"And you're not? Didn't you learn anything from the Carmelites?"

"I did, if only from Madame de Combalet."

"So you say you're in love with a dream?"

"Yes—and my dream is of someone you know."

"Me?"

"When I think that I may be damned for this sin, and it will be all for Your Majesty that I've lost my soul!"

"Oh, my poor Fargis, don't carry on so."

"Didn't Your Majesty find him charming?"

"Who?"

"Our messenger, the Comte de Moret."

"Indeed, he seemed a worthy gentleman, who gave the impression of being a true knight."

"Ah, my dear Queen, if another son of Henri IV I know were at all like him, I believe the throne of France wouldn't lack an heir, as it does now."

"As to an heir," the queen said thoughtfully, "I must show you the letter the count brought me. It was from my brother, Philip IV, and I confess I don't quite understand some of his advice."

"I'm sure I can explain it. You know there are few such things I don't understand."

"Sibyl!" said the queen, who had no doubt her friend was right. She smiled and began to rise.

"Can I save Your Majesty some trouble?" Madame de Fargis asked.

"No, I'm the only one who knows how to open the secret drawer." Anne went to a small vanity, pulled open a drawer, removed a tray, and took from its false bottom a copy of the letter brought by the count. The letter, ostensibly from Don Gonzalès de Cordova, bore instructions, we recall, that it should be read by the queen alone.

With this letter in her hand, she returned to her seat. "Sit here, near me," she said, patting the divan.

"What, on the same seat as you!"

"Yes, we need to speak privately."

Madame de Fargis glanced over the paper the queen was holding. "So," she said, "I'll listen while you interpret. What do these first three or four lines say?"

"Nothing. They just advise me to keep your husband in Spain as long as possible."

"Nothing? Your Majesty calls that nothing? I think it's quite important. Indeed, Monsieur de Fargis must stay in Spain as long as possible. Ten years—twenty years, even! This is good advice indeed. If the rest is as good as the first, then Your Majesty is advised by King Solomon himself. More, more!"

"Can you never be serious, even in the gravest matters?" The queen shrugged, but smiled. "Now, here's the advice from my brother, Philip IV."

"And that's the part Your Majesty doesn't quite understand?"

"The part I don't understand at all, Fargis," said the queen, adopting a perfect air of innocence.

"Let's hear it."

"'My sister,'" the queen read, "'I know from our good friend Monsieur de Fargis of the plan by which, in the event of the death of King Louis XIII, you promise to marry his brother and heir to the throne, Gaston d'Orléans.'"

"A vile plan," interrupted Madame de Fargis, "by which you'd trade bad for worse."

"Wait, there's more." The queen continued: "'However, it would be even better if, at the time of Louis's death, you were with child.'"

"Oh, yes," murmured Madame de Fargis, "that would be better for everyone."

"'The Queens of France,'" Anne of Austria continued, seemingly trying to find the meaning in the words, "'have a great advantage over their husbands in that they can produce dauphins on their own, an ability their husbands lack.'"

"And that's the part Your Majesty doesn't understand?"

"Or, at least, I don't understand how it's possible."

"What a pity," said Madame de Fargis, raising her eyes to heaven, "in matters like these, which involve not only the happiness of a great queen, but the future of a great people—what a pity on top of everything else to have to deal with an honest woman!"

"What do you mean?"

"I mean that if, in the gardens of Amiens, you'd done what I'd have done in your place, in the arms of a man who loved Your Majesty more than life itself, and who gave that life for you—if, instead of calling for Laporte and Putange, you hadn't called at all. . . ."

"Well?"

"Well! Perhaps your brother wouldn't need to give you the advice he does, and a dauphin wouldn't be so hard to find."

"But that would have been a double crime!"

"Does Your Majesty really see crime in an act advised not only by a great king, but by a king renowned for his piety?"

"I would have wronged first my husband, and second the throne of France by placing on it the son of an Englishman."

"That first wrong is, in every country of the world, no more than a venial sin, and Your Majesty has only to look around to see that the majority of her subjects share that opinion. Furthermore, to deceive a husband like King Louis XIII, who's so far from being a husband he's unworthy of the name, is more virtue than vice."

"Fargis!"

"You know, Madame, in your heart of hearts, what you lost by that untimely scream, when by your silence you could have won all."

"Alas!"

"So that addresses the first matter, and your 'Alas!' tells me you agree. But the second matter, that of a foreigner's dauphin, remains—and there I must say Your Majesty and I are in agreement."

"Do you say so?"

"But consider this: suppose, for example, that instead of dealing with an Englishman, who though charming was nonetheless a foreigner—suppose you were dealing with a man no less charming"—Anne gave a sigh—"but a Frenchman, and even better, a Frenchman of royal blood, a true son of Henri IV—unlike King Louis, who seems to me, by his tastes, his habits, and his character, to instead be the son of a certain Virginio Orsini."

"You, Fargis—you believe these slanders?"

"Slanders, perhaps, but they come from Your Majesty's home country. But suppose, in short, that you'd taken the Comte de Moret in place of the Duke of Buckingham. Would the crime be so great? Or, on the contrary, would it be an act of Providence that brought the true blood of Henri IV to the throne of France?"

"But, Fargis, I'm not in love with the Comte de Moret!"

"Well, there, Madame, you'd have to sacrifice, which would atone for the sin—and in this case, your sacrifice would be more to the glory and future of France than to your own interests."

"Fargis! I don't understand how a woman could give herself to a man who isn't her husband and not die of shame the first time she comes face to face with him."

"Oh, Madame, Madame!" said Fargis. "If all women thought as Your Majesty, how many husbands would be in mourning for their wives without knowing why they'd died? Perhaps in the past facing a lover was such a problem, but since the invention of fans, deaths from shame have become far less frequent."

"Fargis, Fargis! You must be the most immoral person in the world. I don't know if even Chevreuse is as perverse as you. And this is the dream lover you speak of?"

"No, not mine. He loves your protégée Isabelle."

"Isabelle de Lautrec, who brought him to me the other night? But where did he see her?"

"He didn't see her. This love came over him while playing blind-man's-buff with her in the dark."

"The poor boy! This isn't going to go his way—I believe there's an agreement between her father and a certain Vicomte de Pontis. Anyway, Fargis, we'll talk more of this later. I want to thank you for the service you've rendered me."

"And which the count could still render you."

"Fargis!"

"Madame?"

Anne spoke as calmly as if they hadn't been discussing great affairs. "Fargis, my dear, just help me to bed. My God, what foolish dreams I'll have after listening to your stories."

And the queen, getting up, walked into her bedchamber, more casual and languid than usual, leaning on the shoulder of her confidante Fargis. The queen had many faults, but no one could say she didn't love her friends.

XXI

In Which the Cardinal Uses, on His Own Behalf, the Invention for Which He'd Granted Souscarrières the Patent

Since he'd been warned by the letter found on Doctor Senelle and deciphered by Rossignol, the cardinal wasn't surprised by the scene between Monsieur, the Dowager of Longueville, the Princesse Marie, and Vautier (as described to him by Madame de Combalet). It accorded perfectly with the plan agreed between his enemies and Marie de Médicis.

Marie de Médicis was, indeed, his most implacable enemy—we've gone into the reasons for her hatred elsewhere—and she was also the enemy he feared most, because of her influence over her son and through her control of Cardinal Bérulle, who sat on the King's Council.

So it was the fatal influence of the queen mother that Richelieu had to remove, an influence that had grown since her return from exile. Louis XIII needed to be purged of his mother far more than he needed to be purged of the black humors feared by Doctor Bouvard.

There was one sure way to do this, but the means was terrible. Richelieu had always shrunk from it in the past, but it seemed that the time had come for heroic measures. It was time to prove to Louis XIII that his mother had been an accomplice in the death of Henri IV. For Louis XIII respected his father King Henri so much that it almost amounted to worship.

When Louis had punished Concini by having him assassinated and then hung from the bridge of the Louvre, it was more for being an accomplice in the king's murder than for being his mother's lover and for plundering the French treasury.

So the cardinal was sure of one thing: the moment Louis XIII was convinced of his mother's complicity in Henri's assassination, that moment would be the beginning of her final exile.

When his office clock sounded half past eleven, Richelieu took two documents from his desk, both already signed and sealed, and called his valet Guillemot. He removed his red robe and lace-edged fur cloak, donned a simple Capuchin robe like Father Joseph's, and sent for a sedan chair. Pulling his hood over his face, he entered the chair and gave orders to be taken to the Inn of the Painted Beard in the Rue de l'Homme-Armé.

From the Place Royale to the Rue de l'Homme-Armé wasn't far. They went by way of Rue Neuve-Sainte-Catherine and the Rue des Francs-Bourgeois, turned left on the Rue du Temple, then right past the convent of the Blancs-Manteaux and onto the Rue de l'Homme-Armé.

The cardinal noticed something that, to his mind, spoke well of Maître Soleil: though midnight was ringing from the belfry of the Blancs-Manteaux, his inn was still well lit, ready to receive travelers, and a lad was posted at the door to welcome potential customers.

The cardinal ordered his porters to wait at the corner of the Rue du Plâtre. He descended from the chair and made his way to the door of the Inn of the Painted Beard, where the lad, taking him for Father Joseph, asked if he wanted to see the penitent Latil.

It was for just that purpose that the cardinal had come.

Latil was the kind of man who, since he hadn't been instantly killed, had immediately begun to recover. He'd taken so many previous sword wounds that new ones just followed the tracks of the old. Though still very weak, he could foresee the day when he could be carried to the Hotel de Montmorency, with what was left of the Comte de Moret's gold still jingling in his purse.

Father Joseph, to whom he'd confessed all unknowing, hadn't returned, but to his amazement he'd been visited by the cardinal's own doctor, who'd been ordered by His Eminence's secretary to take good care of him. Latil had no idea to what he should attribute this good fortune.

No longer laid out on a table in the lower hall, Latil had been carried up to the bed in room number eleven, which was adjacent to number thirteen, the room the beautiful Marina—or Madame de Fargis, if you will—kept on a monthly retainer.

He awoke to the glow of the candle borne before the minister by the lad from the door. The first thing he saw by this candle, which the lad set on a table before withdrawing, was a long gray figure in a hooded robe. Latil thought here was yet another Capuchin monk, possibly even the same one—because it must be admitted, even if it offends our more religious readers, that that confession had been his first acquaintance with that ancient and venerable branch of the tree of Saint Francis.

It occurred to him that perhaps the worthy friar thought he was worse, and might need to be confessed a second time, or was even dead and ready to be buried. "Hold on, Father," he said. "No need to rush. By the grace of God, and thanks to your prayers, there's been a miracle on my behalf. It seems Étienne Latil is going to live on, in his poor honest way, despite marquises and viscounts who, four against one, try to cut his throat."

"I know of your noble conduct, brother, and I congratulate you on your convalescence."

"The devil!" Latil said. "Is that why you got me up at such an hour? Couldn't you wait until daytime to pay me such compliments?"

"No, my brother," said the seeming Capuchin, "for I needed to speak with you urgently and secretly."

"On affairs of State, I suppose?" Latil laughed.

"Exactly. On affairs of State."

"Well," continued Latil, still laughing, "if you need to speak to me despite my two injuries and four wounds, you must be no less than His Gray Eminence!"

"Oh, better than that," said the cardinal, laughing in his turn. "I am His Red Eminence." And he lowered his hood so Latil could see who he was.

"What!" Latil started back in fear. "By my patron saint, stoned before the gates of Jerusalem—it really is you, Monseigneur."

"Yes, and that should tell you the importance of my business, since I come to speak to you by night and alone, despite the risk that entails."

"Monseigneur will find me his obedient servant, so far as my strength allows."

"Good. Now take a moment and collect your memory."

There was a moment of silence during which the cardinal's eyes were fixed on Latil, as if to penetrate the depths of his mind.

"Though young at the time, you must have been devoted to the late king," the cardinal said, "since you refused to kill his son, despite the enormous sum you were offered."

"Yes, Monseigneur—I must say that I've remained loyal to his memory. That was one of the reasons why I left the service of Monsieur d'Épernon."

"I'm told you were on the running board of the king's carriage when he was assassinated. Can you tell me what you remember about the murderer at the time, and afterward? And how did the Duc d'Épernon take this catastrophe?"

"I was at the Louvre beforehand, waiting, with the Duc d'Épernon. The king came down at four o'clock."

"And did you notice," asked the cardinal, "whether he was happy or sad?"

"Very sad, Monseigneur. But is this really the time for me to tell, well, everything?"

"Everything!" said the cardinal. "If you have the strength."

"The king's sadness wasn't just a mood—it was due to all the prophecies. You must know about those, Monseigneur?"

"I wasn't in Paris at the time; I didn't arrive until five years later. So speak to me as if I don't know anything."

"All right, then! I'll tell you everything, Monseigneur, because I feel like your presence gives me strength, and because the cause in which you ask must please the Lord God—who may have permitted the death of my master, the king, but that doesn't mean his death must go unpunished."

"Take courage, my friend," said the cardinal, "for what you do is righteous."

The wounded man continued, making a visible effort to recall his memories despite his loss of blood. "In 1607, several books of astrology appeared at the Frankfurt fair that said the King of France would die in his fifty-ninth year, that is to say, 1610. That same year, a mysterious series of letters stating that the king would be assassinated was found on his altar by a prior of Montargis.

"And one day, the queen mother came to see my duke at his hotel. They locked themselves inside his study, but, being a curious page, I sneaked into a closet from which I could listen. I heard the queen say that a doctor of theology named Olivé had predicted, in a book dedicated to Philip III, that the king would die in 1610. Furthermore, the king would die in a carriage—and the king knew of this prediction."

"Did you ever hear tell of a man named Lagarde?" asked the cardinal.

"Yes, Monseigneur," said Latil, "and that reminds me of a detail I'd forgotten, one that greatly disturbed Monsieur d'Épernon. This Lagarde, upon returning from the wars against the Turks, settled in Naples, where he lived with a man named Hébert, who'd been secretary to the conspirator Biron. As the latter had been executed only two years before, his accomplices were still in exile. One day Hébert invited Lagarde to dinner, and while they dined a big man dressed in purple entered the room and announced that all refugees would soon be able to return to France, because before the end of 1610, he would kill the king. Lagarde asked his name, was told he was called Ravaillac, and that he served Monsieur d'Épernon."

"Yes," the cardinal said, "I knew about that."

"Monseigneur would like me to be more succinct?"

"No, don't leave out a word. Too much is better than not enough."

"While Lagarde was in Naples, he was taken to visit a Jesuit named Père Alagon. This Jesuit was committed to the assassination of Henri IV. 'We'll choose a hunting day,' he said. 'Ravaillac will strike him on foot, and I from horseback.' On his way to France, he received a letter outlining the same plan. When he reached Paris, he took the letter to the king. Ravaillac and d'Épernon were both named."

"Did you hear whether the king took this letter seriously?"

"Oh, very seriously! Nobody in the Louvre knew why he was so melancholy. For a week, he kept the fatal secret to himself. Then he left the Court to spend some time alone in Ivry, at a small house of the captain of his guards. Finally, too worried to sleep, he came to the Arsenal and told everything to his minister Sully, begging him to lend him a place to stay, just three or four rooms, where he could rest and change his clothes."

"To this," murmured Richelieu, "to this he came, so good a king, the best France has had, obliged like the wretched Tiberius to sleep in a different room every night for fear of being murdered! And yet I complain of my problems!"

"Finally, as the king passed by the Cemetery of the Innocents one day, a sullen man wearing a green coat cried out, 'In the name of our Lord and the Blessed Virgin, Sire, I must speak. Is it true that you plan to make war on the pope?' The king wanted to stop and talk with this man, but we wouldn't let him.

"It was these things that made him as sad as a man marching to his death when, on that unfortunate Friday of May 14, I saw him come down the stairs of the Louvre and get into his carriage. It was then that Monsieur d'Épernon called me and told me to get on the running board."

"Do you recall," asked Richelieu, "how many people were in the carriage, and how they were sitting?"

"Three people, Monseigneur: the king, Monsieur de Montbazon, and Monsieur d'Épernon. Monsieur d'Épernon was on the left, and the king in the middle. I distinctly saw a man leaning against the wall of the Louvre, as if waiting for the king to come out. Seeing the open carriage, which enabled him to recognize the king, he left the wall and followed us."

"This was the assassin?"

"Yes, though I didn't know it at the time. The king was without guards. He was on his way to see Monsieur de Sully, who was ill, but on the Rue de l'Arbre-Sec he changed his mind and directed them to take him to visit Mademoiselle Paulet, saying he wanted to ask her to undertake the education of his son Vendôme, who was developing nasty Italian tastes."

"Continue, continue," the cardinal insisted. "Don't leave out a single detail."

"Oh, Monseigneur! It's as if I'm still there. It was a beautiful day, about four o'clock in the afternoon. Though everyone recognized Henri IV, no one shouted 'Vive le roi!' The people were surly and defiant."

"When you reached the Rue des Bourdonnais, didn't Monsieur d'Épernon bring something to the king's attention?"

"Ah, Monseigneur," Latil said, "it seems you know as much as I!"

"On the contrary, as I said, I know nothing. Continue."

"Yes, Monseigneur, the duke gave him a letter. The king began to read it, and paid no further attention to what was happening around him."

"That's it," murmured the cardinal.

"About a third of the way up the Rue de la Ferronnerie, a wine cart and a hay wagon had collided. There was quite a commotion. Our driver steered to the left, his wheels almost touching the wall of Saints-Innocents. I leaned against the door for fear of being crushed. The carriage slowed to a halt. Just then, a man stepped up on a borne, thrust me aside, pushed himself in front of Monsieur d'Épernon, who leaned back, and struck the first blow at the king. 'To me,' the king cried, 'I'm hurt!' And he raised the arm that held the letter. This gave the assassin the opening for a second blow. He struck. This time the king could utter nothing but a sigh—he was slain.

"'The king is only wounded!' Monsieur d'Épernon cried, and threw his cloak over him. Meanwhile I fought with the assassin and tried to hold him, as he carved my hands with his knife. My life was nothing. I finally let go when I saw they had him. 'Don't kill him,' cried Monsieur d'Épernon. 'Take him to the Louvre.'"

Richelieu placed his hand on that of the wounded man, as if to interrupt, and asked, "The duke said that?"

"Yes, Monseigneur, but only after the murderer was already taken and there was no danger they'd kill him. They took him to the Louvre. I followed. I thought of him as my captive. I waved my bloody hands and cried, 'That's him, he's the one who killed the king!' 'Who?' the people cried. 'Who?' 'Him, the one dressed in green!' They wept, they screamed, they threatened the assassin. At times, the king's carriage couldn't even move, so great was the press around it.

"Halfway back, I saw Concini, the Maréchal d'Ancre. Someone told him the fatal news, and he forced his way to the castle. He went straight to the queen's chambers, opened her door, and, without mentioning any names, as if she'd know who he meant, he cried in Italian, 'E amazzato.'"

"He is slain!" repeated Richelieu. "This matches the other reports perfectly. Now for the rest."

"They took the assassin to the Hotel de Retz, next to the Louvre. They put guards at the door but left it open, so anyone could come in. It seemed to me that this man was my captive, so I stationed myself at his door. Among his visitors was Father Coton, the king's confessor."

"Coton himself? Are you sure?"

"He came, yes, Monseigneur."

"Did he speak with Ravaillac?"

"He spoke with him."

"Did you hear what they said?"

"Yes, certainly, and I can repeat it word for word."

"Do so!"

"Coton said, with a paternal air, 'My friend . . .'"

"He called Ravaillac his friend!"

"Yes. He said, 'My friend, take care not to upset your betters.'"

"And how did the assassin take this?"

"Calmly, like a man who felt he was well protected."

"Did he stay in the Hotel de Retz?"

"No. Monsieur d'Épernon took him back to his own mansion, where he was kept from the 14th through the 17th. The duke had plenty of time to talk to him in private. It wasn't until the 17th that he was taken to the Conciergerie."

"At what time, exactly, was the king slain?"

"At twenty minutes past four."

"And by when was his death known throughout Paris?"

"Within nine hours. By half past six the queen had been proclaimed regent."

"Proclaimed regent, a foreigner who still spoke Italian," Richelieu said bitterly. "An Austrian, the grand-niece of Charles V, cousin of Philip II—in other words, the Catholic League incarnate. But let's deal with Ravaillac's end."

"No one can tell you better than I how it happened. I was there when he was on the wheel. I had privileges, they said; 'This is Monsieur d'Épernon's page, who arrested the murderer,' and the women kissed me, while the men shouted 'Long live the king,' though he was dead. The people, who at first had been stunned and oppressed by the news, had gone insane with fury. There were demonstrations outside the Conciergerie, where the people, unable to stone the culprit, stoned the walls in his place."

"Ravaillac never named any accomplices?"

"Not during the interrogations. To me it was evident that, until the very end, he expected some sort of last-minute reprieve. He did say he'd spoken to some priests at Angoulême, confessing that he hoped to kill a heretic king, and instead of dissuading him, they'd given him absolution and a small reliquary that they said contained a piece of the true cross. This reliquary, when opened before the court, was empty. Thank God that at least the priests hadn't dared to make the Lord Jesus an accomplice in such a crime."

"What did he say when he saw he'd been deceived?"

"He only said, 'The guilt of fraud is on the fraudulent.'"

"I've seen myself," the cardinal said, "only a summary of the 'process verbal,' which said, 'What happened when the prisoner was put to the question is the secret of the court.'"

"I wasn't there when the question was put," Latil said, "but I was next to the executioner at the wheel. The sentence was that the prisoner be tortured and quartered, but they didn't limit themselves to that. The king's attorney, Monsieur La Guesle, proposed adding molten lead, pitch, and boiling oil, accompanied by a mixture of wax and sulfur. His proposal was adopted with enthusiasm.

"If we'd let the people handle things, Ravaillac would have been torn to pieces in five minutes. When he came out of the prison and marched to the scaffold, there was such a storm of curses, threats, and cries of rage, that only then did he realize the magnitude of his crime. On the scaffold, he turned to the people and begged for mercy, asking, in a doleful voice, for the consolation of a Salve Regina."

"And was he granted this consolation?"

"Oh, yes! With one voice the entire crowd around the scaffold shouted, 'Damnation to Judas!'"

"Continue," Richelieu said. "You were on the scaffold, near the executioner, you say?"

"Yes, I was granted that favor," Latil said, "for having arrested, or at least helped to arrest, the murderer."

"Quite so," the cardinal said. "I've been told he was confessed on the scaffold?"

"Here's what happened, Monseigneur. Your Eminence understands that, when one has witnessed such a scene, days, months, and years may pass, but it will be remembered for a lifetime.

"After the first tugs of the horses, which failed to pull off any of his limbs, wounds were slashed into his arms, chest, and thighs with a razor, into which they poured, successively, molten lead, boiling oil, and sulfur. By then his body was one great wound, and he cried out to the executioner, 'Stop! Stop! I'll talk!' The executioner paused. The court clerk, who was at the foot of the scaffold, came up and, on a sheet separate from the official process verbal, took down what the prisoner said."

"Well," the cardinal asked eagerly, "in that final moment, what did he confess?"

"I wanted to get closer," Latil said, "but they stopped me. The only words I could clearly hear were the names of d'Épernon and of the queen."

"But the process verbal? And this separate sheet? Did you never hear of them while in the house of the duke?"

"In fact, Monseigneur, I heard them spoken of often."

"What was said?"

"It was said that the court reporter kept the process verbal hidden in a strongbox in the wall next to his bed. As for the single sheet, it was reputed to be in the possession of the family of Joly de Fleury, who denied having it. However, much to Monsieur d'Épernon's dismay, he was said to have shown it to some friends, who, due to the clerk's poor handwriting, had found it very difficult to make out the names of the duke and the queen."

"So, after this sheet was written?"

"When the dictation was complete, the execution resumed. The horses provided by the provost were bags of bones, too weak to pull the prisoner apart, so a gentleman offered to lend his own horse to the procedure, and at the first pull it tore off a thigh. As the prisoner was still alive, the executioner moved to finish him, but the lackeys of all the lords attending the execution jumped the fence, climbed the scaffold, and cut his body to pieces with their swords. Then the people rushed in and tore it into smaller pieces, and carried off bits of the regicide to burn at the crossroads. On returning to the Louvre, I saw the Swiss Guard roasting a leg right under the queen's windows. So there!"

"And that's all you know?"

"Yes, Monseigneur, except I've often heard tell how the treasury Sully had gone to such trouble to amass was divided up among the great nobles."

"Indeed. The Prince de Condé alone walked off with four million—but that's not what concerns me. Let's return to the business at hand. Tell me, amid all this, did you ever hear anything about a certain Marquise d'Escoman?"

"Yes, I believe I did!" Latil said. "A small woman, with a bent back, whose maiden name had been Jacqueline Le Voyer—and her name wasn't Escoman, it was Coëtman. She was the duke's mistress. And though she was called a marquise, she wasn't really, as her husband's name was just Isaac de Varenne, period. Ravaillac had spent six months at her house. She was accused of being his accomplice in the king's assassination. She told everyone who'd listen that she barely knew Ravaillac, and that it was the queen mother who was behind the plot."

"What happened to this woman?" the cardinal asked.

"She was arrested several days before the king's murder."

"Yes, and she remained in prison until 1619, when she was abducted and taken to some other prison, I don't know which. Do you know?"

"Monseigneur will recall that in 1613, Parliament called a halt to the investigation, due to the sensitivity of the case. They considered the accusations a threat to the realm. After Concini was killed and Luynes was in the ascendant, the case could have been reopened, but Luynes preferred reconciliation with the queen mother to risking an open break that would expose her to Louis XIII's wrath. Luynes, therefore, pushed Parliament into declaring that accusations against the queen were libelous. Marie de Médicis and d'Épernon were cleared, and Madame Coëtman was condemned in their place."

"Indeed, that's when she disappeared. But to what prison was she taken? That's what I asked, and I assume you know the answer, since you evaded the point."

"You're right, Monseigneur. I can tell you where she is—or at least where she was, for since it's been nine years, only God knows if she's alive or dead."

"God must grant that she lives!" the cardinal exclaimed, with a fervor that showed that his faith was driven by his need. He added, "I've observed that the more the body suffers, the more the soul takes command."

"Well, Monseigneur," said Latil, "she was confined in a place where the bones can't rest until the flesh is gone."

"And you know where this place is?" the cardinal asked eagerly.

"It was built on purpose to hold her, Monseigneur, in an angle of the courtyard in the Convent of Repentant Daughters. She was put in a mausoleum whose door was walled shut. She was given food and drink through a window with iron bars."

"You saw this yourself?" demanded the cardinal.

"I saw it myself, Monseigneur. When we left, children were throwing stones, as if at a wild beast, while she cried, 'They lie! I wasn't the assassin, it was the ones who put me here.'"

The cardinal rose. "There's not a moment to lose," he said. "This is the woman I need." Then, to Latil: "Heal and recover, my friend. And once recovered, have no fears for the future."

"*Peste*! With a promise like that, I certainly won't, Monseigneur. To be sure, it's time."

"Time for what?" Richelieu asked.

"Time we finished. I feel weak and . . . well . . . am I dying?" With a gasp, his head fell back on the pillow.

The cardinal looked around until he found a small bottle that seemed to contain a cordial. He poured a few drops of the liquor onto a teaspoon and made the man swallow it. Latil opened his eyes and gasped again, but in relief.

The cardinal then put his finger to his lips to enjoin the man to silence, pulled up the hood of his cloak, and went out.

XXII

The *In Pace*

It was about one-thirty in the morning or so, but the advanced hour was just one more reason for the cardinal to continue his investigations. If he presented himself at the door of the infamous convent in the daytime, wherein were collected the most immoral women from the worst places in Paris, he feared he might be recognized, and there might be speculation as to the reason for his visit. He knew the curtain that Concini, the queen mother, and d'Épernon had tried to draw across the terrible tragedy of the assassination of Henri IV. He knew, as we saw in the previous chapter, that all the written evidence had disappeared. He feared that the last living evidence might disappear as well. The attack on Latil demonstrated that he was following a thread that, at any moment, the hand of death could break. Here was this woman whose house, it was said, Ravaillac had shared for six months, and who, having learned a state secret, was now dead or dying in an *in pace*—for so they called those tombs devised by monks, those expert tormenters, to impose physical and mental suffering to the limit of what's possible for strength to endure.

The Rue des Postes, the site of the Convent of Repentant Daughters (later replaced by the Madelonettes), was far from the Rue de l'Homme-Armé—or rather the Rue du Plâtre, where the false friar's sedan chair awaited him. But the cardinal forestalled any objections from his porters by placing a silver crown in each one's hand. They took a moment to discuss which route would be shortest, then decided to take the Rue des Billettes to the Rue de la Coutellerie, cross the Pont Nôtre-Dame, and take Rue Saint-Jacques and the Rue de l'Estrapade to the Rue des Postes, where they'd find, on the corner of the Rue du Chevalier, the Convent of Repentant Daughters.

When the sedan chair stopped at the gate, two o'clock was sounding from the nearby Church of Saint-Jacques du Haut-Pas. The cardinal stuck his head out the door and ordered one of the porters to ring the gate bell loudly. The larger of the two obeyed.

After a few minutes, during which the cardinal, impatient, had had the bell rung twice more, a small barred window opened in the gate and the head of the sister on duty appeared to ask what they wanted. "Ask her to tell the mother superior it's a Capuchin monk sent by Father Joseph to speak to her about an important matter," the cardinal said to one of the porters. The man repeated the sentence word for word.

"Which Father Joseph?" the sister asked.

"It seems to me there's only one who matters," said a commanding voice from within the chair. "The one who's the cardinal's secretary."

This voice had such a tone of authority that the sister asked no further questions, just closed her window and disappeared.

The chair was set on the ground and the false monk climbed out. "Is the superior coming down?" he asked the sister when she reappeared at the window.

"This very instant. But if Your Reverence has just come to call on one of our prisoners, there was no need to wake the mother superior: I have the authority to let any worthy servant of God into one of our cells, whether that servant wears a frock or a robe."

The cardinal's eyes flashed like lightning. He knew she spoke the truth: the unlucky women who were locked in the convent in order to repent of their sins were often led, on the contrary, to commit new ones. His first indignant reaction was to refuse, but then it occurred to him that this might more easily get him to his goal. "Very well," he said. "Lead me to the cell of the Dame de Coëtman."

The sister stepped back. "*Jésus-Dieu!*" she said, crossing herself. "What name did Your Reverence say?"

"That is the name of one of your prisoners, I believe."

The sister said nothing.

"Is the prisoner I wish to see dead?" the cardinal asked anxiously, for he feared the answer might be yes.

The sister continued to remain silent.

"I am asking if she is alive or dead," the cardinal said, in a voice beginning to reveal his impatience.

"She is dead," said a voice from the darkness of the convent beyond the window.

The cardinal thrust his keen gaze into the darkness whence the voice came, and saw a human form he recognized as that of another sister. "Who are you," Richelieu demanded, "who respond so peremptorily to a question not addressed to you?"

"I am the proper person to answer questions of this nature, though I don't recognize you as one with the right to ask them."

"I have that right," the cardinal replied, "and you will answer my question, whether you like it or not." Then, turning to the first sister, he said, "Bring a light."

There was no mistaking the tone of the speaker: here was a man who had the right of command. The sister, without waiting for confirmation from her superior, went back inside and came out with a lighted candle.

"By Order of the Cardinal," said the false monk, drawing a letter from within his robe. He unfolded it to reveal, beneath a few lines of writing, a large red wax seal that gleamed in the light from the candle. He held up the letter to the superior where she could see it through the bars of the window. Meanwhile, the sister passed the candle through the grill, so the superior could read the following lines:

By order of the Cardinal Minister, all are directed, in the name of his spiritual and temporal power, on behalf of

the Church and the State, to answer any questions whatso-
ever, on any subject whatsoever, the bearer chooses to ask,
and to bring him to any and all prisoners he shall name.
December 13 in the Year of Our Lord Jesus Christ, 1628

—Armand, Cardinal de Richelieu

"Before commandments like these," said the superior, "I have no choice but to bow."

"Then please order the sister to return inside and lock up."

"You heard, Sister Perpetua?" the superior said. "Obey."

Sister Perpetua placed her candle on top of the stairs leading up to the gate, returned inside, and locked the door behind her.

The cardinal, meanwhile, ordered his porters to pick up the sedan chair, back away from the door, and await his signal.

The superior opened the gate, and the cardinal entered. "Why did you say, my sister," he asked in a stern voice, "that the Dame de Coëtman was dead when she is not?"

"Because," the superior replied, "I regard as dead anyone whom society has completely rejected."

"The only ones who are truly denied the company of their fellows are the dead and buried," said the cardinal.

"The stone of the tomb was closed over the one you named."

"That stone closed on a living person is not a tombstone, it's the stone of a prison—and any prison door can be reopened."

"Even," said the nun, looking the pretend monk in the face, "when a parliamentary decree has ordered that door shut for all time and eternity?"

"There is no judgment higher than justice—and I am the one the Lord has given the power to judge the judges."

"There's only one man in France who has that power."

"The king?" asked the monk.

"No: one who, though below him in rank, is above him in genius. Cardinal Richelieu. Are you the cardinal in person? If you are, I'll obey, but my orders are so precise that I must refuse anyone else."

"Take that light and lead me to the Dame de Coëtman's prison, which is in the left corner of the courtyard. I am the cardinal."

And he removed his hood and uncovered his head, with a result much like that of the revelation of Medusa of antiquity.

The superior remained motionless for a moment, paralyzed not by resistance but by surprise. Then, with that passive obedience that generally followed a command from Richelieu, she bowed, took the candle and his arm. Leading the way, she said, "Follow me, Monseigneur."

Richelieu followed. They crossed the forecourt. The night was calm, but cold and dark, the stars shining in a black sky, with the sharp glints that foretoken the arrival of the winter frost. The candle flame rose vertically into the air, bent by no breath of wind. It cast a circle of light around the monk and the nun who moved with them, lighting objects as they approached and leaving them in shadow when they passed.

Finally, they began to glimpse a small round building like an Arab hut. In the center of it, about the height of a man's chest, a small black square took shape. It was the window, and as they approached they could see that it was closed by a grid of iron bars, so tight one could barely pass a fist between them.

"She's here?" the cardinal asked.

"She's here," the superior replied.

As they got closer, it seemed to the cardinal that two pale hands grasping the bars suddenly let go, and a dim figure within disappeared back into the dark interior of the tomb.

The cardinal approached first and, despite the stench issuing from the tomb, put his face to the bars to try to see inside. But the night was so black, he could see nothing but two greenish lights shining in the darkness like the eyes of a wild beast.

He stepped back, took the candle from the superior, and passed it through the bars and into the mausoleum. But the air inside was so noxious, so thick, that inside the tomb the flame grew pale, dwindled, and almost went out.

The cardinal drew the candle back out, and the flame returned to life. Then, in order to clear the air and light up the interior, he took his signed order, which he no longer needed once it had been acknowledged, set it afire, and threw it into the tomb.

Despite the thickness of the atmosphere within, the letter gave off enough light for the cardinal to see, crouched against the wall opposite the window, a figure, elbows on knees, chin on fists, and naked but for a scrap of damp cloth that covered her from waist to knees.

This figure, pale, hideous, and shivering, watched the monk from hollow eyes with the night inside them, their gaze fixed, almost insane.

A groan came from her with every exhalation, painful as the breath of the dying. She had been in constant pain for so long that this groaning had become a part of her.

The cardinal, though not particularly sensitive to others' pain, or even his own, shivered from head to toe at this sight. He turned a menacing gaze on the superior, who said, "That was the order."

"Whose order?" demanded the cardinal.

"The order of judgment."

"And what did this order of judgment say?"

"That Jacqueline Le Voyer, called the Marquise de Coëtman, is to be enclosed in a structure of stone, sealed behind her so no one can enter, and she shall be fed only bread and water."

The cardinal passed his hand across his brow. Then, approaching the barred window, within which the night had returned, he said, "Is that you?" He turned his face toward where he'd seen the pale figure. "Are you Jacqueline Le Voyer, Dame de Coëtman?"

"Bread! Heat! Clothing!" gasped the prisoner.

"I asked you," repeated the cardinal, "if you are Jacqueline Le Voyer, Dame de Coëtman."

"I'm hungry! I'm cold!" replied the voice, ending in a sob.

"First answer my question," the cardinal insisted.

"If I say I'm the one you named, you'll just let me starve. For two days they've ignored me, despite my cries."

The cardinal glared again at the superior, who murmured, "The order! The order!"

"The order was she's to live on bread and water, not be starved."

"Why is she so stubborn as to go on living?" said the superior.

The cardinal very nearly said something close to blasphemy. Instead, he crossed himself, saying "If you tell me that this order gives you the right to let her die, I swear to God, you'll take her place in that tomb."

Then, turning back to the wretch who was the object of their discussion, the cardinal said, "If you admit you're really the Dame de Coëtman, and if you answer my questions honestly and faithfully, within an hour you'll have clothing, heat, and bread."

"Clothing! Heat! Bread!" cried the prisoner. "Do you swear it?"

"On the five wounds of Our Lord."

"Who are you?"

"I am a priest."

"In that case, I don't believe you. It's priests and nuns who've tortured me for nine years. Let me die. I won't talk."

"But I was a gentleman before taking orders," said the cardinal, "and I swear on my honor as a gentleman."

"And what do you think would happen to you if you betrayed these promises?" said the prisoner.

"Then I would be dishonored in this world and damned in the next."

"All right, then, yes!" she cried. "Yes! No matter what happens, I'll tell everything!"

"And if I'm pleased with what you tell me, then in addition to bread, clothing, and heat, you'll have freedom."

"Freedom!" the prisoner cried, rushing to the window and pressing her pale face against the bars. "Yes, I'm Jacqueline Le Voyer, Dame de Coëtman! Yes, I'll tell everything, everything, everything!"

Then, in a fit of crazy happiness, she yelled "Freedom!" Her laugh was mad, sinister, and she shook the bars with a strength that should have been impossible to a body so lean and feeble. "Freedom! Oh, you must be Our Lord Jesus Christ himself, if you can say to the dead 'Get up and walk from your graves!'"

"My sister," said the cardinal, turning toward the superior, "I will forget everything if, within five minutes, you have tools brought that will enable an opening to be made in this tomb large enough for this woman to get out."

"Follow me," the superior said.

The cardinal turned to follow. "Don't leave me! Don't leave me!" the prisoner said. "If she takes you with her, you'll never return, I'll never see you again. The heavenly light that came into my tomb will go out and I'll be buried once more."

The cardinal gave her his hand. "Rest easy, poor creature," he said. "With God's help, your martyrdom is almost over."

But, seizing his hand between two fleshless claws that gripped like a vise, she cried, "A hand! I hold a hand! The first human hand that's been extended to me for ten years! The others were nothing but tigers' paws. Be blessed, O be blessed, human hand!" And she covered his hand with kisses.

The cardinal didn't have the courage to remove it. He called out to his porters, saying, "Follow this woman," indicating the superior. "She'll give you the tools necessary to rip open this tomb. There are five *pistoles* in it for each of you."

The two men followed the superior who, light in her hand, led them to a sort of shed where they kept the garden tools. In much less than five minutes they reappeared, the larger of the two with a pickaxe on his shoulder, the other with a crowbar.

They sounded the wall with the tools, and where it seemed to be thinnest, they began to work.

"What should I do now, Monseigneur?" asked the superior.

"Go heat up your room," the cardinal ordered, "and prepare some food."

The superior withdrew.

The cardinal's eyes followed her, glinting from the candle she carried. He watched her enter the convent. Probably it never even occurred to her to resist what was happening. She knew too well what her situation was, and though the power of the cardinal was far from the height it would reach later, she knew she was at his mercy, as his ecclesiastical power at this time was even greater than his temporal power. He was within his rights, having temporal authority over a prison, and religious authority over a convent.

When the prisoner heard the pickaxe and the crowbar echoing from the stone, only then did she believe what the cardinal had promised. "So it's true! It's true!" she cried. "Oh, who are you, that I may bless you in this world and through all eternity?"

Then she heard the first stones crack and tumble into the interior, and her eyes, accustomed to darkness like those of night birds, saw light infiltrating her tomb from an opening other than her barred window, which for nine years had been her only source of light and air. She dropped the cardinal's hand, rushed to the opening, and despite the risk of being struck by the pickaxe, she grabbed the stones and tugged on them, doing whatever she could to hasten her deliverance.

Even before the hole was big enough for her to get out, she stuck her head through, then her shoulders, ignoring cuts and bruises, and saying through her tears, "Help me! Oh, help me! Pull me from my grave, blessed saviors, beloved brethren!" And since she was already halfway out, they took her under the arms, her body as cold as the stone from which she issued, and dragged her out.

Once she was out, the poor creature's first act was to fill her lungs with the clean air. She extended her arms to the stars with a painful cry of joy, and fell on her knees to thank God. Then, seeing her savior, she held out her arms and rushed toward him.

But he, either out of pity for this half-naked woman, or out of shame for her condition, had already taken off his monk's robe, which for convenience opened in front. He cast it over her shoulders, leaving him in the clothes he wore beneath, a cavalier's outfit in black velvet with purple ribbons.

"Cover yourself with this robe, my sister," he said, "until you receive the clothes you've been promised." Then, as she staggered from either emotion or lack of strength, he called, "Good men, come here." Giving them twice what he'd promised, he said, "Take this woman, who's too weak to walk, and carry her to the superior's room."

He went up to the room where, according to his orders, the superior had laid a fire in the hearth, while two candles burned on a table. "Now," the cardinal said, "bring paper, pen, ink, and leave us!"

The superior obeyed. Left alone, leaning on the table, the cardinal murmured, "This time, I think the spirit of the Lord is truly with me."

At that moment, the larger of the two porters came in, carrying the unconscious prisoner as if she were a child. He placed her where the cardinal indicated, still wrapped in the monk's robe, near but not too close to the fire. Then, bowing as if aware he was in the presence of great rank, he went out.

XXIII

Her Story

The cardinal remained alone with the poor creature, who lay so motionless that one might have thought her dead but for the nervous chills that occasionally agitated the coarse cloth of the robe that covered her. She was so shrouded that no part of her body was showing, and her shape, revealed in relief, seemed more like that of a corpse than a living person.

But, little by little, as the warmth of the fire penetrated the robe, the trembling beneath it became more frequent. Two hands, which might have been taken for a skeleton's if they hadn't had such long nails, emerged from the sleeves, stretching instinctively toward the fire, proving that the body they belonged to had not yet reached its limit of suffering. Then the pale face, eye sockets wide with pain, swarthy cheeks and lips drawn back from the teeth, appeared in its turn, like the head of a turtle protruding from its shell. Legs as well stretched toward the fire, revealing from under the hem of the robe two feet as cold and hard as marble. Then, stiffly, the figure sat up, and a voice came as if from the chest of a corpse: "The fire! Oh, how good is the fire!"

She crept closer to the flames, like an infant unaware of the danger, too chilled to really feel its heat.

"Take care, my sister," said the cardinal, "lest you burn."

The Dame de Coëtman shuddered and turned rigidly toward the voice. She hadn't noticed that anyone else was in the room, hadn't seen anything but the fire that to her was as compelling as the dizzying edge of an abyss.

She gazed for a moment at the cardinal, but didn't recognize him in his cavalier's outfit, having seen him only in a monk's robe. "Who are you?" she asked. "I know your voice, but not your look."

"I'm the one who has already given you clothing and heat, and next will give you bread—and freedom."

She made a mental effort to remember, then said, "Oh, yes!" She dragged herself toward him. "Yes, you promised."

But then she looked around and, lowering her voice, said, "But can you keep your promise? I have enemies, terrible and powerful enemies."

"Don't worry—you have a protector more terrible and powerful than they are."

"Who is that?"

"God!"

The Dame de Coëtman shook her head. "He's forgotten me for a very long time," she said.

"Yes, but once He remembers, He won't forget again."

"I'm very hungry," she said.

At that moment, as if at her order, the door opened and two nuns came in, bringing bread, wine, a cup of broth, and a plate of cold chicken.

At the sight of them, the Dame de Coëtman screamed with fright. "My tormentors!" she cried. "Protect me!" And she crouched behind the cardinal's chair, placing her unknown defender between her and the nuns.

"Is that enough, Monseigneur?" the superior asked from the doorway.

"Yes, but you see how the sisters are frightening the prisoner. Have them put what they've brought on the table and go."

The nuns placed the broth, chicken, bread, and wine on the table opposite the Dame de Coëtman, with a spoon in the broth, and a fork and knife with the chicken. "Go," said the superior. The nuns departed.

The superior turned to leave, but the cardinal raised a finger. The superior saw that the gesture was directed at her and stopped. "Keep in mind," he said, "that I will taste everything this woman will eat and drink."

"There's nothing to fear, Monseigneur," replied the superior. And, with a curtsy, she withdrew.

The prisoner waited until the door was closed before reaching a lean arm toward the table. But she stopped short. The cardinal picked up the cup of broth and took a sip from it, and then turned toward the starving woman, whose arms were stretched toward him. "You say you haven't eaten for two days?"

"Three, Monseigneur."

"Why do you call me Monseigneur?"

"I heard the superior call you that—and, indeed, you must be a great noble to dare to defend me like this."

"If you haven't eaten for three days, you must be cautious. Take this cup, but drink the soup one spoonful at a time."

"I'll do whatever you tell me, Monseigneur, in this and in everything." Eagerly, she took the cup from the cardinal's hand and brought the first spoonful to her mouth. But her throat was so tight, her stomach so shrunken, that the broth went down painfully and with difficulty.

Gradually, however, it eased, and by the fifth or sixth spoonful, she was able to drink right from the cup. But by the time she finished it, she was so weak that a cold sweat burst from her forehead, and she was ready to faint.

The cardinal tasted the glass of wine, and then passed it to her, telling her to take only a sip.

She drank several sips. Her cheeks flushed with sudden fever, and, placing a hand to her chest, she said, "Oh, I'm drinking fire!"

"And now," said the cardinal, "after a moment more, we will talk." And he helped her to get up and sit in a chair near the fireplace.

No one, seeing this man gently nursing this human debris, would recognize in him the terrible prelate, the terror of the French nobility, who had struck off heads that even royalty had been unable to bend.

You may say he was a cruel man, and this show of mercy was entirely in his own interest. But to this we answer that a policy of cruelty is only necessary where it serves justice.

"I'm still hungry," said the poor woman, looking avidly at the food on the table.

"You'll have plenty of time to eat," said the cardinal. "Meanwhile, I've kept my promise: you're warm, you're fed, you'll have clothes, and you'll be free."

"What do you want to know?"

"How did you know Ravaillac, and where did you first meet him?"

"In Paris, at my home. I was the confidante in all matters of the king's former mistress, Madame Henriette d'Entragues. Ravaillac had been living in Angoulême under the protection of the Duc d'Épernon. He'd been involved in two felonies: he'd spent a year in prison on a murder charge and racked up a number of debts. Though he'd been released, he was due to go back inside."

"Have you ever heard about his visions?"

"He told me of them himself. In the first and most important, he lit a fire and, bending over it, saw a vine grow out of it and change shape, becoming the sacred trumpet of the Archangel. It formed itself to his mouth and, without his blowing into it, sounded the fanfare of holy war, while out of it a torrent of the hosts burst right and left."

"Had he studied theology?" asked the cardinal.

"He'd confined his studies to a single question of law: when was it the duty of a Christian to kill an enemy of the pope? When he was released from prison, Monsieur d'Épernon, knowing he was a religious man who'd been visited by the spirit of the Lord—and knowing the solicitor in charge of his case—had him brought to Paris for the next phase of his trial. As he had to pass through Orléans, Monsieur d'Épernon arranged for Monsieur d'Entragues and his daughter, Henriette, to give him a letter of passage allowing him to travel to Paris and lodge in my home."

"What was the first impression he made upon you?" the cardinal asked.

"At first I was scared of him. He was a tall man, powerfully muscled, with brown skin and a dark visage. When I saw him, I thought I beheld Judas. But after I'd opened the letter from Henriette, read that he was very devout, and saw how mildly he behaved, I had no more fear."

"And from your home he went to Naples?"

"Yes, on behalf of the Duc d'Épernon. He lodged with a man named Hébert, the traitor Biron's secretary. It was there that he first announced that he planned to kill the king."

"Yes, a certain Latil told me the same thing. Do you know this Latil?"

"Oh, yes! At the time I was arrested, he was Monsieur d'Épernon's confidential page. He must know quite a lot."

"And what he knows, he's told me. Continue."

"I'm hungry," said the Dame de Coëtman. The cardinal poured her a glass of wine and allowed her to dip some bread in it. After eating the bread and drinking the wine, she felt more composed.

"He sought you out when he returned from Naples?" the cardinal asked.

"Who? Ravaillac? Yes, and twice, on Ascension Day and Corpus Christi, he told me he—that is to say, it had been decided—was to kill the king."

"And why do you think he took you into his confidence?"

"He said he was torn by doubts, but he was obliged to do it."

"By what?"

"By the debt he owed Monsieur d'Épernon, who wanted the king assassinated to get the queen mother out of danger."

"And what danger was the queen mother in?"

"The king wanted to put Concini on trial for extortion and condemn him for treason, and accuse the queen mother of adultery and send her back to Florence."

"And given his revelations, what did you decide to do about it?"

"Ravaillac didn't seem to realize that the queen mother was involved in the plot, so I thought about telling him all. Instead, I wrote to the king, requesting an audience, but received no response. And indeed, at that time he was completely preoccupied by his infatuation for the Princesse de Condé. So I wrote to the queen, saying that I had something important to tell her, and waited three days for an audience. But the three days passed without a response; and on the fourth, she left for Saint-Cloud."

"Who told you of this?"

"Vautier, who was the queen's apothecary at the time."

"And what conclusion did you draw?"

"That Ravaillac was wrong, and that the queen mother really was involved in the plot."

"So, then?"

"I resolved to talk to the king at any cost, so I went to the Jesuits of Rue Saint-Antoine and asked to speak to the king's confessor."

"And how were you received?"

"Poorly."

"But were you able to speak to Father Coton?"

"No, Father Coton was away. I was taken to the father examiner, who told me I was imagining things. 'What, disturb His Majesty's confessor?' he said. 'On what grounds?' 'Because they plan to kill the king!' I cried. 'Bah. Tend to your own affairs,' he said. 'Take care,' I said, 'if any harm comes to the king, I'll go straight to the judges and tell them you refused to listen.' 'Well, then, go tell

Father Coton yourself,' he said. 'Where is he?' 'At Fontainebleau. But there's no point in your going there, so I'll go myself.'

"However, I didn't trust the father examiner, so the next day I hired a carriage to take me to Fontainebleau. I was preparing to leave when I was arrested."

"What was the name of this Jesuit examiner?"

"Father Philippe. Then, from prison, I wrote two more letters to the king, and I'm sure one of them got through."

"And the other one?"

"The other letter I sent by way of Monsieur de Sully."

"Who carried it?"

"Mademoiselle de Gournay."

"I know her—an old lady who writes books?"

"Exactly. She took it to Monsieur de Sully at the Arsenal; but as the letter mentioned the names of d'Épernon and Concini and repeated the warning I gave about the queen, Monsieur de Sully didn't dare show it to the king. However, he said if there was a real threat, he could send to have me and Mademoiselle de Gournay brought to the Louvre. But as the king had received so many such warnings, he just shrugged and dismissed our letter as unreliable."

"What was the date of this letter?"

"That must have been May 10 or 11."

"Do you think Mademoiselle de Gournay might have kept it?"

"It's possible, but I wouldn't know. I was in prison. One night— it was October 28, 1619, as I know because that was when I could still keep track of time—I was taken from my first prison. A bailiff came into my cell, ordered me to stand, and read me a Parliamentary decree that condemned me to spend the rest of my life bricked up in a tomb, with only a barred window for light and air, and only bread and water for nourishment. I thought it was bad enough to have been imprisoned for trying to save the king, but this new sentence almost destroyed me. On hearing it read, I fell unconscious to the floor. I was only twenty-seven years old—how many more years would I have to endure such a sentence?

"While I was unconscious, they carried me out and put me in a carriage. The breeze blowing across my face from the window brought me around. I sat between two officers, each of whom held a chain gripping one of my wrists. I was dressed in a black frock, the remnants of which I still wear. I knew I was being taken to the Convent of Repentant Daughters, but I had no idea where that was located. The carriage went through a gate that opened before it, clattered through a passage into a courtyard, and stopped at the tomb you took me from.

"They forced me into it through a hole in the wall, and one of the officers came in behind me. I was half-dead, I made no resistance. I leaned against the window. One of my wrist-chains was tied around my neck, and the other was linked to it and passed through the window to the second officer. The first officer went out, and two other men I'd glimpsed in the darkness began to work. They were two masons, and they began walling up the opening.

"Only then did I really come to myself. I uttered a terrible cry and tried to rush toward them. I was stopped by the neck chain. For a moment I thought I'd strangle myself and pulled with all my strength. The links of the chain bit into my neck, but as the chain had no noose it didn't tighten and I just kept pulling forward. My breath gasped, my vision turned red. The officer yanked back on the chain. I fought toward the opening, but by the time I reached it the masons had already gotten it three-quarters closed. I thrust my hands through the gap, trying to pull down the stones while the mortar was still wet. One of the masons covered my hands with mortar and the other pinned them under a heavy rock. I was caught as if in a trap. I cried, I yelled. I foresaw what would happen: since no one would be able to enter my cell, if I was mortared into the wall away from the window, I'd die of hunger, hanging from my hands. I prayed for release.

"One of the masons, without saying a word, thrust a crowbar under the stone and lifted it. With a violent effort, I tore my half-crushed hands from the wall and collapsed back beneath the window, exhausted by the double effort to try to strangle myself and to stop the masons from walling me in.

"Meanwhile, they finished their dark and fatal labor. When I came to, I was entombed. The sentence of Parliament had been carried out.

"For eight days, I was raving mad. The first four, I rolled around the floor of my tomb, howling desperately, and for those four days I ate nothing—I wanted to starve, and thought I'd have the strength to do it.

"It was the thirst that broke me. On the fifth day, my throat was on fire. I drank a few drops of water, and that was my commitment to continuing to live.

"Then for a while I thought it was all some kind of error, a mistaken sentence that would soon be overturned. Such a thing had to be impossible in the reign of King Henri's son, under the regency of King Henri's wife. I'd just wanted to save Henri IV; it couldn't be that they'd want to punish me more than they'd punished his murderer, a man whose ordeal had lasted only an hour, while God knows how many hours, how many days, how many years my own ordeal would last.

"But eventually this hope, too, dwindled and died.

"Once I'd resolved to live, I asked for straw to make a bed, but the superior said I'd been sentenced to bread and water, and if Parliament had wanted me to have straw, they'd have put it in the sentence. So I was refused what we grant to our lowest animals: a mere bundle of straw.

"I'd hoped that when the harsh winter nights came, I'd die of cold. I'd heard that freezing to death was a gentle way to go. At times during that first winter, chilled to the bone by the freezing temperatures, I drifted into sleep, or rather unconsciousness. But, every time, I awoke—cold, stiff, almost paralyzed, but alive.

"I lived till the rebirth of spring. I saw the flowers reappear. I saw the trees grow green. Gentle breezes penetrated to me, and I felt my cheeks dampen with tears. I thought the winter had dried up my tears, but with spring, with life, they returned.

"It's impossible to describe with what sweet melancholy I watch-ed the first ray of spring sunshine slant through my window and into my tomb. I reached my arms into it. I tried to grab it and take it into my heart. Alas! It escaped me, as ephemeral as the hopes of which it seemed a symbol.

"For the first four years, and part of the fifth, I marked the passing days on the wall with a piece of stone the children had thrown at me during my madness. But when I saw winter return for a fifth time, the heart went out of me. What matter the count of days past? Better to think only of the days I had left.

"After a year of sleeping on bare stone and leaning against damp walls, my clothes began to wear thin. After two years, they tore like wet paper, and fell to pieces. I waited till my clothing was nearly gone before asking for more, but the superior said the sentence spoke of bread and water, and nothing else.

"Little by little, my clothes tore and fell apart. Winter came again. The terrible nights I'd previously endured wearing a warm woolen dress, I now suffered naked, or nearly so. I picked up the tattered rags that fell from me and tried to reattach them, but they fell like leaves in autumn, leaving me bare.

"Sometimes priests came to peer at me through my window. When I first saw them, those men of God, those angels of humanity, I begged for mercy. They laughed. More of them came after I was naked, but I gave up talking to them, and just tried to cover myself with my hands and my hair.

"I lived the simple, mechanical life of an animal. I drank; I ate; I barely even thought. I slept as much as I could for, while asleep, I couldn't feel the pain of life.

"Three days ago, they failed to bring me my food at the usual time. I thought it was just some kind of mistake. I waited. Evening came. I was hungry, I called out. There was no answer. That night, though already suffering, I was still able to sleep. The next morning at daybreak, I was waiting at the bars of my window for my food. It didn't come. Nuns passed by; I called to them, but they just told their rosaries and said nothing. Night came again, and I saw they planned to starve me. What a sad and weak nature is ours! Once I would have welcomed death, but now I was afraid.

"That second night I slept only an hour or two, and when I did I had terrible dreams. The pain in my stomach and belly was excruciating, and woke me whenever sleep closed my eyes. At daybreak I rose to see if they might bring food, though I knew they wouldn't. That day was one long agony. I cried out, not for bread, but because the pain made me scream.

"Needless to say, no one responded to my cries.

"I tried to pray, over and over, but it was useless. I couldn't find the name of God—that name that comes so easily to me now.

"Again the day grew dim, the shadows entered my tomb, darkness fell, and it was night. I was in such pain, I thought this night was my last. I could cry no more—I hadn't the strength. I surrendered.

"Wrapped in agony, I counted each hour of the night, unable to escape a single moment of my pain. Each tolling of the bell seemed to strike in my skull and explode into millions of sparks. Finally, midnight having struck, I heard the sound of the outer gate open and close. It was an unusual noise at that hour, so I dragged myself to my window and peered out, hanging on the bars with both hands and clinging to the sill with my teeth. I saw a light come in the gate, enter the parlor, then come down into the courtyard and approach. For a moment I dared to hope, but when I saw the man with the superior was a monk, it was all over. I let go of the bars, pried my teeth from the sill—they seemed stuck there, as if welded to the stone—and then fell back to where you saw me.

"It was high time. Twenty-four hours later, you would have found nothing but a corpse."

As if she'd been waiting for the Dame de Coëtman's story to end—and, indeed, perhaps she was—upon these last words, the superior appeared in the doorway. "Monseigneur's orders?" she asked.

"First, a question—and, as I've stated, you must reply truthfully."

"I hear you, Monseigneur," the superior replied with a bow.

"Who was it who came to you, astonished to find this poor creature still alive, though naked, fed on bread and water, and buried in a tomb?"

"Is it Monseigneur who orders me to talk?" said the superior.

"In my dual authority, both spiritual and temporal, I demand to know the name of this woman's executioner—you others being no more than her torturers."

"It was Messire Vautier, astrologer and doctor to the queen mother."

"He's the one I sent my letters to," said the Dame de Coëtman, "though at the time he was only her apothecary."

"Very well," the cardinal said. "The orders of those who've demanded this woman's execution shall be fulfilled." He waved a hand toward the Dame de Coëtman. "For everyone in the world but you and me, this woman has died. That's why you had her tomb opened tonight: to bring out her corpse. And in her grave you will bury a stone, or a log, or an actual corpse you get from a hospital—that's entirely up to you."

"As you command, Monseigneur."

"Three of your nuns are in on the secret: the one who opened the gate and the two sisters who brought the food. You will explain to them what happens to those who speak when they should remain silent. After all," and he pointed angrily at the Dame de Coëtman, "they've seen an example with their own eyes."

"And is that everything, Monseigneur?"

"Everything! When you go down, have the goodness to tell the taller of my porters that I need, within the quarter of an hour, another sedan chair like the first—only one that can be locked, and has curtains over the windows."

"I will relay Monseigneur's orders."

On the side of his face away from the superior, the cardinal showed the jovial smile we saw the night he gave Souscarrières and Madame Cavois the patent for sedan chairs. It's an expression we'll see again, and more than once, as our story unfolds.

"Now," the cardinal said to the Dame de Coëtman, "I think you're well enough to eat a chicken wing or two, and even drink half a glass of wine to the health of our good superior."

Three days later, the chronicler L'Estoile wrote the following in his journal, based on information received from the Convent of Repentant Daughters:

> *On the night of December 13 to 14, in the little stone cell built in the courtyard of the Convent of Repentant Daughters, where she'd been confined for nine years since Parliament sentenced her to bread and water, died the Demoiselle Jacqueline Le Voyer, known as the Dame de Coëtman, wife of Isaac de Varenne, suspected of complicity with Ravaillac in the assassination of good King Henri IV. She was buried that same night in the convent's cemetery.*

XXIV

Maximilien de Béthune,
Baron de Rosny, Duc de Sully

The entire time the Dame de Coëtman was telling her story, the cardinal had listened with the utmost attention to her long and sorrowful tale. But though every word the poor victim spoke was a moral proof of the complicity of Concini, d'Épernon, and the queen mother in the assassination of Henri IV, no physical evidence—nothing visible, tangible, and irrefutable—had come out of it.

But what was clear as day, more clear than crystal, was not only the innocence of the Dame de Coëtman, but her dedication to preventing the terrible regicide of May 14—a dedication that was paid for by nine years imprisoned in the Conciergerie and nine years in a tomb at the Repentant Daughters.

And since the process verbal from Ravaillac's trial was burned and lost, it remained essential for the cardinal to obtain, at all costs, that sheet of Ravaillac's final revelations written when he was on the wheel.

This, then, was the difficulty, one might even say the impossibility, that the cardinal faced; it seemed that after all his efforts, he was back where he'd started. But Richelieu had known from the first that the difficulties he faced were almost insurmountable.

We believe we've said this sheet had been in the hands of Parliament's court reporter, Messire Joly de Fleury. Unfortunately, Messire Joly de Fleury had died two years before, and it was only after his return from Chalais's trial in Nantes that the cardinal had thought to begin collecting evidence against the queen mother—for it wasn't until Chalais's trial that he'd fully appreciated the extent of Marie de Médicis's hatred for him.

Messire Joly de Fleury was survived by a son and a daughter. The cardinal had summoned both of them to his office at his house in the Place Royale to interrogate them about the fate of this sheet, so important to him, and, indeed, to history. But Joly de Fleury's children said the sheet was no longer in their hands.

The cardinal had been told that eleven years before, in March 1617, a young man of fifteen or sixteen, dressed all in black and with a large hat pulled down over his eyes, had called on Messire Joly de Fleury, accompanied by another man ten or twelve years his senior. The Reporter of Parliament had received them in his office, where he'd spoken to them for nearly an hour. He'd then conducted them, with every mark of respect, out to the street, where a carriage—a rarity at the time—awaited the pair.

At dinner that evening, the worthy solicitor had told his son and daughter, "My children, if anyone ever comes to you after my death to claim the sheet containing Ravaillac's last confession on the wheel, say that it's no longer in your possession—or, better yet, that it never existed."

So the cardinal had been told, five or six months before the start of our story, when he'd interviewed the son and daughter of Messire Joly de Fleury. They'd tried at first to deny even the existence of the sheet, but when pressed by the cardinal they'd consulted with each other for a moment, then decided to tell him everything.

However, they were entirely ignorant of the identity of the two mysterious visitors who, it appeared, had come to demand that important piece of evidence from their father.

It was only six months later that the seriousness of the threats against him had forced the cardinal to reopen his investigation.

More than ever, as we've seen, this piece of evidence was essential to completing the case he was building to defend himself against Marie de Médicis. But more than ever, he despaired of finding it.

However, as Father Joseph had said, Providence had already

carried the cardinal this far, and surely he could hope it wouldn't stop halfway to his goal.

Meanwhile, as supporting evidence, he would go after the letter Madame de Coëtman had written to the king, sending it to Sully by way of Mademoiselle de Gournay—a letter which Sully might have kept.

If so, it should be easy to obtain. The old minister, or rather the old friend of Henri IV, was still alive, dividing his time between his château in Villebon and his winter house on the Rue Saint-Antoine, between the Rue Royale and the Rue de l'Égout-Sainte-Catherine. It was said that, faithful to his lifelong habits, he was always in his office by five in the morning. The cardinal drew an exquisite watch from his pocket: it was four o'clock.

At half past five exactly—after stopping at his house in the Place Royale to get a hat, and to leave word for his crony, Père Mulot de Lafollone, that he'd see him for lunch, and to his jester, Bois-Robert, that he needed to speak to him before noon—the cardinal knocked on the door of the Hotel Sully, which was opened by a Swiss Guard dressed in the uniform worn during the reign of Henri IV, the monarch people were already beginning to call *le Grand Roi.*

Let's take advantage of Richelieu's visit to Sully, a minister too often lost in the shadow of the minister who followed him, to present to our readers one of the most interesting personalities of the late sixteenth and early seventeenth centuries, a man whose character is often misunderstood—especially by historians who have been content to judge him by the face he presented to the public, without bothering to walk around and observe his other sides.

Maximilien de Béthune, Duc de Sully, who was, at the time of our story, sixty-eight years old, had singular pretensions regarding his birth. Instead of simply accepting that his father and grandfather were descended from the Comtes de Béthune in Flanders, he had concocted a family tree showing that he was descended from a Scotsman named Bethun, which would make him a cousin of the Archbishop of Glasgow. He also tried to show he was related to the great House of Guise through the House of Coucy, which was connected to the Emperor of Austria and the King of Spain.

Sully, who was called Monsieur de Rosny because his birthplace was the village of Rosny, near Mantes, was only moderately wellborn, despite his purported connections with the Archbishop of Glasgow and the houses of Austria and Spain. When Gabrielle d'Estrées, the king's mistress, took offense at some rude remarks by Monsieur de Sancy, the Surintendant des Finances, she'd had Henri IV replace him with Sully, believing him her devoted servant. Henri IV was oblivious to pettiness and ingratitude in his mistresses—it was one of the great faults of this great king—and due to the selfish wheedling of Gabrielle, he'd forgotten that Monsieur de Sancy, in order to buy the loyalty of the Swiss, had personally pawned the great diamond that still bears his name and was part of the Crown Jewels. In carrying out these sacrifices for France, the poor Surintendant des Finances had so impoverished himself that, in order to provide funds for his successor, Henri IV was obliged to resort to an expedient called a stop-defense, which was basically a delaying tactic deployed against his creditors. In fact, when confronted by the king's creditors, the irreverent Sancy sometimes had himself arrested as a common debtor. When conveyed to the door of the prison, he would show the warders the order for his arrest, and then, bowing to the officers, release himself and go on his way.

Sully was his successor. But the first time the upright Sully was called upon to prove his loyalty to his patron, it was in a matter that would have required him to be disloyal to his religion. When Henri IV, hoping to convert his children to legitimate heirs, spoke seriously of marrying Gabrielle, he found in Sully one of the fiercest opponents to the union.

King Henri's idea of marrying Gabrielle was more than just a lover's fancy: he wanted to give France a French queen, something it had never had.

Henri IV, politically astute and aware of his own weaknesses, didn't pretend that the woman he married would have no influence on the destiny of the State. In the two hours per day that he devoted to the business of rule, he settled even the most difficult questions with the decisiveness of a military commander—but everyone knew that this forceful captain, who wanted to be regarded as an absolute ruler, had at home a wife or mistress who was also, in her bedroom, a ruler quite as absolute.

With a king like that, who he married mattered a great deal.

It wouldn't matter that the Spanish had been beaten at Arques and Ivry if a queen, Spanish by birth or temperament, ruled the king's bed, and from that bed stretched her hand over the realm.

When Henri IV decided to remarry, he was virtually the only sovereign in Europe who'd borne a sword in battle. He was a conqueror on horseback, wearing the white plume of Ivry, the only man of his kind on the continent. But that sword, that French sword, was no threat if it was stolen from his bedside by a queen with foreign loyalties.

This is what a great politician, a man of genius like Richelieu, would have understood—but which Sully did not.

Sully, whose cold blue eyes and ruddy complexion, even at age sixty, might justify his claim to be of Scottish descent, was more feared than loved, even by Henri IV. As Duplessis-Mornay's secretary Marbault testified, he brought fear with him wherever he went: fear of his deeds, fear of his decisions, fear even of his gaze.

He was a soldier first and foremost, having been at war his entire life; as a minister he was active, energetic, and, rarest of all, an able financier. He exercised general command over all matters military, financial, and nautical—and personal command over his first love, the artillery.

He'd come to command the artillery because Gabrielle, who'd wanted higher honors for her sadly mediocre father, had been foolish enough to allow Henri IV to offer the position of Grand-Master of the Artillery to Sully instead—and Sully was wise enough to seize that opportunity without feeling the least bit grateful to Gabrielle. The day Gabrielle decided to insult Sully by offering him his first important office as a throwaway was the day she ensured that she would never become Queen of France.

Henri IV had attempted to legitimize his two sons by Gabrielle, granting them the title of prince and having them baptized as such. Afterwards Fresnes, Henri's Secretary of State, had sent Sully the documents recording their baptism as official Children of France.

But Sully had said "There are no Children of France," and sent the documents back. And the king hadn't dared to insist otherwise.

It was Sully's way of testing his master. Perhaps, if Henri IV had insisted, Sully might have given way. But in the event, it was King Henri who backed down. Sully then realized that the king didn't love Gabrielle quite as much as he respected Sully.

Gabrielle was beginning to age—and to sour. So Sully brought in, to oppose her, a rival who was still young, still beautiful, still seductive—in short, the complete package.

Gabrielle, alas, was a package plundered, opened, and emptied.

The new package came straight from the Grand Duke of Tuscany. He'd sent the king a portrait of his niece, a charming miniature of Marie de Médicis in her girlhood, radiating youth and freshness, in which her incipient obesity could be regarded as evidence of health.

Gabrielle brushed it off. "It's not her portrait I fear," she said, "it's her coffers of cash."

Indeed, Henri IV was in a position where he had to make a choice between love and money. And he had to decide quickly, before his love's love of money poisoned his own love.

In Paris at that time there was a man of Moorish race, an ex-cobbler from Lucca named Zamet who'd made a fortune in France and was now master of over 1.7 million crowns. Zamet had first found success as shoemaker to Henri III, employing his mastery of the tongue (to use a term from the cobbler's trade) in making charming, feminine shoes for the royal foot. Henri III, flattered by this delightful footwear, had made Zamet Preceptor of the Inner Chambers and Director of the Royal Boys' Choir—for this great king was a lover of music.

That was the beginning of Zamet's fortune. During the insurgency of the Catholic League, when everyone needed money, Zamet lent money to everyone: the Leaguers, the Spaniards, even the King of Navarre, who hadn't even asked for it. Had Zamet foreseen the greatness of Henri of Navarre, as Croesus had of Caesar? It seems an apt comparison.

Ultimately, Zamet was a tool of Grand Duke Ferdinand of the Empire. But Sully and Zamet understood each other. Sully was just waiting for his opportunity; if it came, and he seized it with a steady hand, he'd win.

To Gabrielle, Sully was little more than a servant, as he himself said in his memoirs. One memorable day, Gabrielle had referred to Sully as a mere "valet"—and though Sully might actually be a servant, he certainly didn't want to be called one. He complained about this remark to Henri IV, and the king told Gabrielle, "Better a 'valet' like Sully than ten mistresses like you."

Sully's time had come. Duke Ferdinand was on the move and, though an ex-cardinal, had reached across the Alps to poison his brother Francis and his sister-in-law Bianca.

Gabrielle was at Fontainebleau with the king. Easter was nigh. Her confessor demanded that she celebrate Easter in Paris. She had the fatal idea of staying at the home of Zamet the Moor—which sealed her fate.

Sully, who had quarreled with her, nonetheless went to see her there. Why? Perhaps because he couldn't believe she'd be so imprudent.

The poor woman thought she was already the queen. She acted as if she was, and told Sully she would always be happy to receive the Duchesse de Sully at her *levers* and *couchers*, her morning and evening audiences.

The duchess was furious at this impertinence. To appease her, Sully said, "Things are not as she believes, and soon you'll see a game well played, so long as the ball keeps moving."

Obviously, he knew everything.

What, you say? Sully knew Gabrielle would be poisoned?

No doubt about it. Sully was a statesman, and was careful to leave Paris so the poisoners could operate freely, though he left word that he be kept informed.

We say "poisoners" because there were two: the second was named Lavarenne, who died of shock because gossip named him, not a man, but a fish: *poisson*.

Just as Zamet was an ex-cobbler, Lavarenne was an ex-cook. Ironically, Henri had recommended him to the kitchens of his sister Madame, where he'd earned a reputation as a judge of chickens. She encountered him one day, after he'd made his fortune, and said, "Well done, my dear Lavarenne: you've plucked more chickens than my brother has plucked chicks."

Droll; very droll indeed. But Madame's anecdote highlights the ambitious nature of the former chicken chef.

It was to Lavarenne that Sully had said, "Let me be the first to know if by some chance an accident should befall Gabrielle—that is, the Duchesse de Beaufort."

Lavarenne took the hint. Thus Sully was one of the first informed; Lavarenne wrote him that Gabrielle had suddenly fallen ill, with a strange malady that had so disfigured her features that he "feared that if King Henri IV came back to Paris, viewing her would repulse him, so he dared to beg him to stay in Fontainebleau, especially since she was dead."

And he added to Sully, "And here I am, holding this poor dead woman in my arms, hardly able to believe that she won't be alive in another hour or so."

Yes, the two were so certain of the quality of their poison that, while Gabrielle was still alive, one of them wrote to tell the other that she was dying and the king that she was dead. Very droll indeed.

But she didn't die as quickly as they thought she would. She lingered on, in agony, until Saturday morning. Lavarenne had sent his message to Sully on Friday evening, and it arrived before the night was over. Sully kissed his wife, who was in bed, and told her, "My dear, you will not have to attend the *levers* and *couchers* of the Duchesse de Beaufort after all. That cord has broken. Now that she's dead, God grant our king a good life and a long one!"

Sully himself spoke of the matter, in more or less these words, in his own memoirs.

With Gabrielle dead, Sully had little trouble persuading Henri to settle on Marie de Médicis. But before Sully could proceed with that marriage, he had one more cord to break: that of Henriette d'Entragues.

Of all our Kings of France, it was Henri IV who was most susceptible to *amours*. Gabrielle was barely dead before he fell hard for Henriette d'Entragues, the daughter of Marie Touchet. Before she would give up herself, she asked for a promise of marriage; before he would give up his daughter, her father demanded five hundred thousand francs.

The king sent a proposed marriage contract to Sully, and ordered him to pay five hundred thousand francs to the father.

Sully tore up the marriage contract, then had half a million silver francs poured into the antechamber outside Henri's bedroom.

Henri IV, on returning to his room, stepped knee-deep into a pile of coins and looked down into the faces of French kings. There were even some guilders, as some of the money had come from Tuscany.

"*Ouais!*" he said. "What's all this?"

"These are the five hundred thousand francs you intend to pay to Monsieur d'Entragues for the possibility his daughter will love you."

"*Ventre-saint-gris!* I'd never imagined five hundred thousand francs took up so much room," the king said. "See if you can arrange it for half this much, my good Sully."

Sully arranged the matter for three hundred thousand francs, and it goes without saying that Henri IV, ignoring the risks, had rewritten his promise of marriage. But as Sully had predicted, despite paying the price, Henriette d'Entragues didn't deliver much in the way of love.

Sully was hailed as the restorer of the state's fortunes, and, unlike Monsieur de Sancy, he didn't expend any of his own money in that restoration. We wouldn't call him a thief or embezzler, rather a canny businessman, who never let an opportunity go missed. Henri was aware of this and often joked about it. In crossing the court of the Louvre one day, while saluting the king, who was watching from a balcony, Sully missed his footing and stumbled. "I'm not surprised to see you stumble," called the king. "If my strongest Swiss Guard had as many drinks in his belly as you have payoffs in your pocket, he wouldn't stumble: he'd fall flat on his face."

Despite being Superintendent of Finance, Sully was as stingy on his own behalf as he was on the state's, and rather than buy a carriage, he always rode across Paris on horseback. And as he was a terrible rider, everyone laughed at him, even the children.

But there had never been a Superintendent so tightfisted as he. An Italian, returning to the Arsenal for the fifth or sixth time to try to get the money that was owed him, saw three criminals being hanged at the Place de Grève and cried out, "Look at those lucky devils! At least they don't have to deal with that scoundrel Sully."

However, Sully didn't treat everyone the way he had the worthy Italian who'd envied the hanged men. A certain Pradel, who'd been head butler to the old Maréchal de Biron, kept trying to collect his back wages. Sully didn't want to pay these back wages, and one day went so far as to have the man marched out of his chambers. As he was being escorted through Sully's dining room, Pradel took a knife from the table setting and turned back toward Sully, who slammed the door on his aggrieved petitioner. Pradel went directly to an audience with the king, knife in hand, and told him the king was welcome to hang him, so long as he was first allowed to leave the knife in Sully's belly.

Sully paid him.

The Duc de Sully was the first to plant the famous elms that line France's highways, but he was so hated by some that they would chop them down, saying, "This for Rosny, may he be beheaded like Biron."

Speaking of Biron, Sully said in his memoirs that the marshal, with the twelve leading gallants of the Court, once undertook to put on a ballet they couldn't afford to pay for. The king told them, "You can't get anywhere without a Rosny at your side," and funded the ballet himself.

It may be hard to believe it of the man who historians have portrayed as such a grim and austere figure, but Sully loved to dance. Every night until the death of Henri IV—and after his death, even more so—a royal valet named Laroche would play the lute for Sully, performing all the latest dance tunes. From the first note, Sully was up on his feet, dancing alone, waving the extraordinary cap he usually wore in his office. He had as spectators only his two closest cronies, and though the party might have been more complete with a few women in attendance, the duke didn't want to endanger his reputation—or so says Tallemant des Réaux, who is rather hard on Sully. We are entitled to be skeptical of this. The two spectators, who may or may not have contented themselves with merely watching, were his friends the Président de Chevry and the Seigneur de Chevigny.

Since he was unwilling to dance with loose women, one assumes he could have asked the Duchesse de Sully, but he doesn't seem to have been bothered by his lack of a female partner. When handing out his monthly paychecks, he used to say to his people, "Some for the market, some for your wife, and some for your lovers. Don't mix them."

One day, tired of meeting people on the stairs who were on their way to see his wife rather than him, he asked to have a separate staircase built that led to the chambers of the duchess. When it was completed, he said, "Madame, I have had a staircase made expressly for you. Please have your callers use these stairs, because if I meet one of them on my own, I'll hurl him down to the bottom."

The day he was appointed Grandmaster of the Artillery, he took as his seal an eagle holding a bolt of lightning, with the motto *Quo Jussa Jovis*—"I fly at Jupiter's orders."

The seal of Cardinal Richelieu, whom we left ascending Sully's staircase at half past five in the morning, was, we recall, an eagle in the clouds—*Aquila in Nubibus.*

"Whom shall I announce?" a servant inquired of the morning visitor.

"Announce?" he replied, smiling in advance at the effect the news would produce. "Announce Monsieur le Cardinal de Richelieu!"

XXV

The Two Eagles

In truth, Sully had never heard an announcement quite so unexpected. When it struck his ear, he turned to see who had come to disturb the beginning of his day.

He'd been occupied in writing those voluminous memoirs he left to us, but rose from his chair at the valet's announcement.

Sully was dressed in the fashion of 1610, eighteen or twenty years before, in black velvet with slashed breeches and a purple satin doublet below a starched neck ruff, short hair, and a long beard, curled up out of the way and held in place, in the manner of Coligny, with a long toothpick. On top he wore an old-fashioned house-robe, while around his neck hung the gold chains bearing the diamond-studded symbols of his orders and offices, as if he were about to attend the King's Council of Henri IV. Dressed this way, except for the house-robe, he would often step out of his mansion (if the weather was good) at around one o'clock in the afternoon. Followed by his four Swiss Guards, he would walk from his hotel to the Place Royale, where he would march slowly around the square under the arcades. Everyone stopped to watch as he walked by, slow and grave, like a ghost of the previous century.

The two ministers, who stood in each other's presence for the first time, resembled the eagle each had taken as his symbol: *Aquila in Nubibus,* the eagle in the clouds, who ruled all he surveyed while hidden in the heights, was an apt representation of the minister who was all things to Louis XIII, his king; while on the other side, *Quo Jussa Jovis,* the eagle casting lightning at the behest of Henri IV, described Sully as that king's strong but obedient right arm.

(Readers who already know these historical facts may complain that these are unnecessary details that just get in the way of the picturesque and the novel. Such readers are welcome to pass over these details, but we include them for those unfamiliar with history or for those who, attracted by the ambitious title of this historical romance, hope to learn something from it.)

Richelieu, who was relatively young compared to Sully—the cardinal was only forty-two, while Sully was sixty-eight—approached the old friend of Henri IV with the respect due to both age and reputation.

Sully gestured toward a chair, and Richelieu sat in it. The proud old man, familiar with the etiquette of courts, appreciated this.

"Monsieur le Duc," said the cardinal, smiling, "does my visit surprise you?"

"I admit," Sully replied, with his typical bluntness, "that it is unexpected."

"But why, Monsieur le Duc? All ministers who work or have worked for the benefit of posterity—and we are among them—are dedicated to the happiness, glory, and greatness of the kingdom of France which they serve. Why shouldn't I, who humbly serve the son, seek out the support, advice, and knowledge of one who so nobly served the father?"

"Who remembers the services of one who is no longer able to serve?" Sully asked bitterly. "The old, dead tree is no good even for firewood, not worth the trouble to put it out of its misery."

"Ah, but wood in decay can shine at night, Monsieur le Duc, when living wood is lost in darkness. But I accept the comparison, because you, thank God, are still an oak, and I hope the birds who sing in your branches are the birds of memory."

"Yes, they told me you wrote poetry, Monsieur le Cardinal," Sully said disdainfully.

"I do, Monsieur le Duc, in my spare time, but not for myself. I study poetry, not to be a poet, but so I can judge poems fairly and reward poets as they deserve."

"In my time," said Sully, "gentlemen did not bother with such things."

"Your time, sir," replied Richelieu, "was a glorious time, when they fought battles such as Coutras, Arques, Ivry, and Fontaine-Française. It was the time when the old policy of François I and Henri II, that is, opposition to the House of Austria, was taken up once more, a policy of which you were one of the leading supporters."

"Over which I quarreled with the queen mother."

"That policy established French influence in Italy," the cardinal continued without seeming to notice the interruption, though he took careful note of it. "It brought us Savoy, Bresse, Bugey, and Valromey. It supported the Dutch revolt against Spain and encouraged the Lutherans in Germany against the Catholics. You were the instigator of the latter effort, which aimed to create a sort of Christian Republic in which all disputes would be resolved in a congress, a body where all sects would meet on an equal footing, and the estates confiscated by Emperor Mathias might be restored to their rightful heirs."

"Yes, and it was amid these glorious efforts that the assassin struck down the king."

Richelieu noted this second interruption as he had the first, intending to return to both matters, but for now he continued: "In such glorious days one has little time for literature, for it wasn't under Caesar that Horace and Virgil were born, or rather it wasn't Julius who was their Caesar, but Augustus. I admire your generals and your ministers, Monsieur de Sully, but do not disdain my poets. The generals and ministers make empires great, but it's the poets who kindle a civilization's lights. The future and the past are both dark as night, and only the poets brighten them. Ask now who were Augustus's generals and ministers, and the only one anyone can name is Agrippa. Ask who were the protégés of Augustus's friend Maecenas, and we remember Virgil, Horace, Varius, Tibullus . . . even those exiled by Augustus included the immortal Ovid. I can't be an Agrippa, or even a Sully, so let me be Maecenas."

Sully looked with astonishment at this man who had twenty times the authority Sully had known, but had come to remind him of his days of power and glory while sitting at the feet of their former master. He drew his toothpick from his beard and slid it between his teeth, which were as sound as those of a much younger man, and said, "Very well, you may have your poets, though I'm not sure their works are quite the marvels you say."

"Monsieur de Sully," said Richelieu, "when was it you planted the elms that today shade our roads?"

"Monsieur le Cardinal," said Sully, "that would have been from 1598 through 1604, so twenty-four years ago."

"Are they as beautiful and strong today as the day you planted them?"

"They were well planted and well grown, my elms."

"I know there were people who mistook your intentions and chopped some down, blind to the provident hand of the great man who was sowing shade for the aid of weary travelers. But the ones that survived, they've grown tall, spread their branches, flourished their leaves?"

"In fact, they have," Sully said proudly; "and when I see them so strong, so healthy, so green, I'm almost consoled for the ones that were struck down."

"That's how it is, Monsieur de Sully, with me and my poets. The critics may tear one down but they exalt another, and those who remain grow ever stronger and more fruitful. Today I planted an elm named Rotrou; tomorrow I will likely plant an oak called Corneille. I water them and wait. I can't say which ones would have flourished under your reign: Desmarets, Bois-Robert, Mairet, Voiture, Chape-lain, Gombauld, Baro, Raissiguier, La Morelle, Grandchamp—I couldn't say. It's not my fault if some grow into briars rather than a forest."

"Yes, yes, yes," said Sully. "The greatest laborers—and they say you do know how to work, Monsieur le Cardinal—need such distractions in their spare time. It's no worse, I suppose, than gardening."

"May God bless my garden, Monsieur de Sully, and make it one for the ages."

"But I don't imagine," said Sully, "that you got up at five in the morning to come pay me compliments and tell me all about your poets."

"First of all, I didn't get up at five in the morning," said the cardinal, smiling, "as I haven't yet been to bed. Perhaps in your time you got to sleep late, Monsieur de Sully, although you did work late. In my time, we don't sleep at all. No, I didn't come to pay you compliments and tell you about my poets. But the opportunity arose, and I was careful not to let it escape. In fact, Monsieur, I came to speak with you about two things you first brought up yourself."

"I brought up two things myself?"

"Yes."

"But I haven't said anything!"

"Begging your pardon, but when I mentioned your efforts against Austria and Spain, you said, 'Over which I quarreled with the queen mother.'"

"That's true. For isn't she Austrian by her mother Jeanne, and Spanish by her uncle Charles V?"

"Exactly—but it was because of you, Monsieur de Sully, that she became Queen of France."

"And I was wrong to advise that course to my august master, King Henri IV. Since then, many times, I have repented it."

"Well, today I fight the same struggle you faced twenty years ago, one to which you succumbed. And I may yet succumb in my turn, for I have two queens opposing me, the young and the old."

"Fortunately," Sully said, grinning and chewing his toothpick, "this time it's not the younger who has the more influence. King Henri IV loved too well, but his son doesn't love much at all."

"Have you ever thought, Monsieur le Duc, about this difference between the father and the son?"

Sully looked quizzically at Richelieu, as if to say "Are you serious?" Then he said, with a strange accent, "The difference between father and son? Yes, I have thought about it, and often."

"You recall the father: all activity, riding twenty miles on horse-back by day and then playing tennis in the evening, consulting with ministers and receiving ambassadors as he walked, busy from morning till night, playing to win, cheating when he lost without the slightest remorse, then generously returning his ill-gotten gains. Hurt by slights but reacting with a smile, though his smile was never far from tears. Never doing anything with half a heart, even if his whims led him to mad caprices. Deceiving women, but honoring them. He was born with the heaven-sent gift of loving, that same gift that made Saint Thérése weep for Satan, who could only hate."

"Did you know King Henri IV?" Sully asked in surprise.

"I saw him once or twice in my youth," Richelieu said, "that's all. But I have made him my special study. In contrast to him, behold his son: slow as an old man, dour as the dying, standing rather than walking, gazing out a window, looking without seeing. He moves like an automaton, games without caring if he wins, though hating to lose. Sleeping long, crying little, loving nothing and, worst of all, no one."

"I understand," said Sully. "Over a man like that, you can have little influence."

"If I do, it's because, despite all this, he has two virtues: pride in the monarchy and a jealous sensitivity to the honor of France. These are the two spurs with which I drive him. And they would be enough if it were not for his mother, always defending Spain and promoting Austria, though I, pursuing the policy of the great King Henri and his minister Sully, want only to oppose these two eternal enemies of France. So I come to you, my master, whom I study and admire, especially in financial matters, to ask for your aid against that evil genius who was your enemy then and is mine today."

"And how can I help you," Sully asked, "you, who are more powerful than the king?"

"You said it was amid your glorious campaign that the assassin struck down the king."

"Did I say assassin or assassins?"

"You said assassin."

Sully paused.

"So," Richelieu continued, drawing his chair closer to Sully's, "recall if you can all your memories of that fateful May 14, and tell me what warnings you had in advance."

"We had many warnings, but unfortunately we paid little attention to them. When men trust in Providence, they let their wits sleep. However, as I see it King Henri committed two key indiscretions."

"What were those?"

"He promised Pope Paul V he would restore the Jesuits to favor, but when the Pope pressed him to comply, he refused, saying, 'If I had two lives, I would gladly give one to satisfy Your Holiness, but as I have only one, I must preserve it for your service and for the sake of my subjects.' The second mistake was to insult Concino Concini, the queen's favorite, in open Parliament. When her gallant cavalier, a man who set fashions, won tournaments, and eclipsed even the princes, was insulted before mere men of the robe, she took it as a personal affront and vowed revenge—an Italian vendetta, no less. After that, she closed her heart to the king."

"The warnings that were ignored," Richelieu asked: "were any of them delivered by a woman named the Dame de Coëtman?"

Sully started. "Yes, in fact," he said. "But they weren't the only ones. There was a man named Lagarde in the Hébert household in Naples who warned the king that d'Épernon plotted to assassinate him. There was a certain Labrosse, whom we never found, who warned Monsieur de Vendôme on that May morning that a transition from 13 to 14 would be fatal to the king. I don't know if you've considered the influence of the number 14 on the birth, life, and death of King Henri IV."

"No," replied Richelieu, loosing the reins to let Sully run to his goal.

"Then listen," said that supreme calculator, who had reduced everything to the science of numbers. "First: King Henri IV was born fourteen centuries, fourteen decades, and fourteen years after the nativity of Our Lord Jesus. Second: his first day was December 14 and his last May 14. Third: there were fourteen letters in his name, Henri de Navarre. Fourth: he lived four times fourteen years, four times fourteen days and fourteen weeks. Fifth: he was wounded by Jean Chatel in 1594, fourteen days after December 14, between which and the time of his death was fourteen years, fourteen months, and fourteen times five days. Sixth: he won the Battle of Ivry on March 14. Seventh: Monsieur le Dauphin, who is now the reigning king, was baptized on August 14. Eighth: the king was killed on May 14, fourteen centuries and fourteen lustrums since the incarnation. Ninth: Ravaillac was executed fourteen days after the king's death. Tenth and finally: one hundred fifteen times fourteen is 1610, the year in which he died."

"Yes," said Richelieu, "that is both curious and strange. But everyone has a magic number. This Dame de Coëtman," he continued, "did she not also address you directly, Monsieur le Duc?"

Sully looked down. "Even the best and most devoted have their blind spots. I did mention her to the king. But the king just shrugged and said, 'What would you have, Rosny'—he continued to use my birth name though he'd made me Duc de Sully—'What would you have, Rosny? It's all in God's hands.'"

"This warning came in the form of a letter, did it not, Monsieur le Duc?"

"Yes."

"To whom was this letter addressed?"

"To me, to be passed on to the king."

"Who did it come from?"

"From the Dame de Coëtman."

"Did another copy come from another woman?"

"From Mademoiselle de Gournay."

"Then I must ask you, Monsieur le Duc—and I do so in the name and the honor of France. . . ."

Sully nodded, indicating that he was ready to answer.

". . . This letter, why did you not pass it on to the king?"

"Because it openly accused Queen Marie de Médicis, Épernon, and Concini."

"This letter, Monsieur le Duc—did you keep it?"

"No, I gave it up."

"May I ask to whom?"

"To the one who brought it—to Mademoiselle de Gournay."

"Do you have any reluctance, Monsieur le Duc, to write me the following note: 'Mademoiselle de Gournay is authorized to deliver to Monsieur le Cardinal de Richelieu the letter sent on May 11, 1610, from the Dame de Coëtman to the Duc de Sully'?"

"No, if Mademoiselle de Gournay refuses you. But she won't, as she is poor and in need, so it's unlikely you'll need my authorization."

"But if I do?"

"Send me a messenger and he'll return with the note."

"Now, one final matter, Monsieur de Sully, and you will have earned my heartfelt gratitude."

Sully bowed.

"In the house of Joly de Fleury, at the corner of Rue Saint-Honoré and Rue des Bons-Enfants, behind a brick in the wall, was hidden the process verbal of Ravaillac to Parliament."

"No: that document had been kept in the Palais de Justice, where it was destroyed in a fire. What Joly de Fleury had was the statement Ravaillac dictated at the scaffold, in between the tongs and the molten lead."

"That statement is no longer in the Fleury family's hands."

"It was, in fact, given up by Monsieur de Fleury before he died."

"You know that for certain?" asked Richelieu.

"Yes."

"You know it!" he cried, unable to suppress a gesture of joy. "So, then, you can tell me where it is? This sheet, it would be my saving grace. It is nothing less than the glory, the grandeur, and the honor of France—it is everything! In the name of Heaven, tell me I may have it."

"Impossible."

"Impossible? Why?"

"I have sworn a vow."

The cardinal rose. "If the Duc de Sully has sworn a vow, then I must honor the oath of the Duc de Sully. But in truth," he said, "this may be fatal for France."

And, without attempting to appeal to Sully by so much as a single word, he bowed deeply, receiving from the old minister in return a polite but moderate salute, and withdrew, beginning to doubt in that Providence that Father Joseph had promised would help him.

XXVI

The Cardinal in His Dressing Gown

At about seven in the morning, the cardinal returned to his house in the Place Royale and discharged his chair porters, who found themselves well paid and were therefore satisfied with their night. He slept for two hours and then went down to his study, in his dressing gown and slippers, at about half past nine.

This office, where he worked twelve to fourteen hours a day, was the center of Richelieu's world. He broke for lunch with his confessor, along with his cronies, clowns, and hangers-on. Then back to his study, where he would nap on his couch, which was as large as a bed, when politics kept him too long at his desk. He usually had dinner with his niece.

No one was allowed in his study, which was full of state secrets, unless Richelieu was there, the exception being Charpentier, his secretary, whom he trusted as he did himself. Once inside, Charpentier would unlock all the connecting doors, except for the one which led to Marion Delorme's house, of which only Richelieu had the key.

Cavois had been indiscreet enough to say that sometimes, instead of going up to sleep in his bedchamber, the cardinal would rest in his clothes on the couch in his office. And once, during the night, Cavois had heard the cardinal conversing with someone else, a voice he'd recognized as a woman's.

Word quickly got around, and the gossips all said that the woman had to be Marion Delorme, who was barely eighteen and was then in the flower of her youthful beauty. She was said to pass through the wall like a fairy, or like a sylph through a keyhole, and to talk with the cardinal about matters that had nothing to do with politics.

But no one had ever actually seen her within the cardinal's house.

However, we who have entered the notorious office and know all its secrets are already aware that it had a private mailbox which the cardinal used to correspond with his beautiful neighbor. Marion Delorme had no need to come to the cardinal, nor the cardinal to go to Marion.

That day, he seems to have had something to tell her, for upon entering his study he wrote two lines on a piece of paper, opened the near side of the private mailbox, slipped the sheet within, rang the bell, and closed his door.

This sheet, as we can report to our readers, from whom we have nothing to hide, contained the following question: "How many times in the last week has the Comte de Moret visited Madame de la Montagne? Is he faithful or unfaithful? In short, what do we know about him?"

It was signed, as usual, "Armand." However, both handwriting and signature were disguised, and had nothing in common with the handwriting and signature of the great minister.

Then he called Charpentier and asked who was waiting in the antechamber. "The Reverend Father Mulot, Monsieur de Lafollone, and Monsieur de Bois-Robert," the secretary replied.

"Very well," said Richelieu, "have them come in."

We've said that the cardinal usually had lunch with his confessor, his cronies, clowns, and hangers-on, and perhaps our readers were surprised to find His Eminence's confessor in such company, but Father Mulot wasn't one of these stuffy clerics who burdened his penitents with litanies of *pater nosters* and *ave marias*.

No, Father Mulot was, above all else, the cardinal's friend. Eleven years earlier, after the assassination of the Maréchal d'Ancre, Concino Concini, when the queen mother was exiled to Blois and the young Richelieu, who was then Bishop of Luçon, to Avignon, Father Mulot had done something extraordinary. Either out of friendship for Richelieu or from confidence in his genius to come, Mulot had sold everything he owned, raising three or four thousand crowns, then brought all this money and placed it in the hands of the cardinal-to-be. Thereafter, he became one of Richelieu's closest and most outspoken advisers.

And he was a good courtier, though on the subject of bad wine he was quite insufferable. One day while dining at the house of Monsieur d'Alaincourt, the Governor of Lyon, he was outraged by the wine that was put before them. He called over the servant who'd brought it, grabbed him by the ear, and said, "My friend, only a scoundrel would serve such wine to his master. Maybe he doesn't know any better, but I do, so take away this swill and bring us some decent wine."

As an enthusiast of the vine, the worthy chaplain had earned a nose like that of Bardolph, the jolly companion of England's Henry V, so red it could almost serve as a lantern. One day, when he was still Bishop of Luçon, Richelieu was trying on some beaver hats, and asked Father Mulot what he thought. "Do you think this one suits me?" he asked.

"It would match your robes better, Your Grandeur," Bois-Robert had interrupted, "if it was the same color as your confessor's nose."

The stalwart Mulot had never forgiven Bois-Robert this little jest.

The second guest waiting on the cardinal was a gentleman of Touraine named Lafollone. He was a sort of watchdog the king had given the cardinal to make sure no one bothered him unnecessarily or disturbed him with trivial matters. This Lafollone was as great an eater as Mulot was a drinker, and to watch the one drink and the other eat was one of the cardinal's daily amusements. Indeed, Lafollone thought of nothing but the table. When others said it was a good day for a walk, a nice day for a hunt, or good weather for a swim, he always replied that it was a good day to eat. The cardinal had other guardians, but with Lafollone around he never needed a taster.

The third guest, or rather the third person waiting on the cardinal, was François Le Métel de Bois-Robert, one of his literary collaborators as well as his jester. Though no one could say why, Bois-Robert was always irritable. He had come from Rouen, where he'd been a lawyer, but had left that city after having been accused by a woman of fathering her two children. Upon arriving in Paris, he first attached himself to Cardinal du Perron, but then decided he'd rather enter the service of Cardinal Richelieu. But, as we said, he was an irritable man, whose tongue was sharp when he wasn't accorded the respect he thought he deserved. "Eh, Monsieur," he said one day to the cardinal, "you let dogs eat the crumbs from your table. Am I worse than a dog?"

This humility disarmed the cardinal, who took Bois-Robert into his friendship, and soon found he couldn't do without him. When the cardinal was in a good mood, he called him "Le Bois" for short, repeating a joke made by Monsieur de Châteauneuf about the wood that comes from Normandy.

Bois-Robert was the cardinal's morning paper: thanks to him, the cardinal knew everything that was happening in the republic of letters he was nurturing. Bois-Robert, who had a great heart beneath his prickly exterior, guided the cardinal's hand in his efforts as a patron of the arts, sometimes even forcing that hand to open when it was clenched due to hostility or jealousy. Bois-Robert, in his way, helped Richelieu rise above hostility, and convinced him that the powerful should put themselves beyond jealousy.

One understands how, given the eternal tension of politics, the continual threat of conspiracy, and his endless struggle against the enemies who surrounded him, the cardinal needed from time to time to escape into levity. It was almost, for him, a matter of mental health: for the bow that is strung too tight can break.

It was especially after nights like the one he'd just endured that the cardinal sought the company of these three, who afforded him a few moments of rest from his duties, his cares, and his labors. More-over, besides the tales he anticipated from the witty and energetic Bois-Robert, he hoped to be able to learn from him where he could find what remained of the former Demoiselle de Gournay.

As soon as his letter to Marion Delorme was deposited in their private mailbox, as we've said, he ordered Charpentier to admit his three guests.

Charpentier opened the door. Bois-Robert and Lafollone deferred to each other, each desiring the other to enter first, but Mulot, who seemed to be in a bad mood, pushed both aside and entered before them.

He had a letter in his hand. "Oh, ho!" said the cardinal. "What have you there, my dear abbot?"

"What have I here?" Mulot cried, stamping his foot. "What I have here makes me furious!"

"And why is that?"

"Those who wrote this will never write me another!"

"Who?"

"The ones who write to me on your behalf!"

"*Bon Dieu!* What have they put in this letter?"

"What's in the letter is not the problem. In fact, for a letter from some of your people, it's quite polite for a change."

"What's the problem, then?"

"The way it's addressed! You know perfectly well I'm your con-fessor, not your almoner, since if I ever consent to be someone's almoner, it'll be for someone more important than you. I am a Canon of Sainte-Chapelle!"

"So, how was this addressed?"

"They wrote: *To Monsieur Mulot, Almoner to His Eminence*— the dolts!"

"Well," said the cardinal, laughing, as he'd expected some such response, "what if it was me who addressed the letter?"

"If it was you, then I am astonished. Though it wouldn't be, God knows, the first nonsense you've ever perpetrated."

"It's good to know just what sort of thing irritates you."

"This doesn't irritate me; it infuriates me!"

"All the better!"

"Why all the better?"

"Because you're so amusing when you're angry. And since I love to see you angry, I will address you from now on as Monsieur Mulot, Almoner to His Eminence."

"Just try it, and you'll see."

"I'll see what?"

"You'll see me leave you to eat lunch by yourself."

"I'll just send Cavois to fetch you."

"I'll refuse to eat."

"He'll force you to eat."

"I won't drink, either."

"He'll shove bottles of Romanée, Clos-Vougeot, and Chambertin right up your nose."

"Quiet, you!" Mulot cried, overwhelmed with fury and advancing on the cardinal with clenched fists. "You, why, I'll tell the world you're a—a terrible man!"

"Mulot! Mulot!" The cardinal was overcome with laughter at Mulot, who was beside himself. "Take care, or you'll find yourself hanged!"

"Hanged? On what pretext?"

"On the pretext that you reveal the secrets of the confessional!"

The other guests burst out laughing as Mulot tore the letter in pieces and threw them into the fire.

During this incident, the servants had brought in a table already set. "Ah, let's find out what's for lunch," said Lafollone, "and see if there's anything that will tempt a gentleman who's already had an excellent breakfast." Raising the covers of the dishes one after another, he said, "Ah-ha! White capons *royale*, a sausage of plovers and larks, two roasted woodcocks, mushrooms stuffed with Provençale crayfish *à la Bordeaux*—one could have lunch with that, in a pinch."

"Eh, *pardieu!*" Mulot said. "As to food, there will always be plenty of that. Everyone knows the cardinal indulges in all the mortal sins, especially gluttony, but let's see what he has to offer us in the way of wine. H'mm, a Bouzy red, a Bordeaux *grand cru*—excellent for those who suffer from stomachache, like all the wines of Bordeaux. Long live the wines of Burgundy! A Pommard, a *moulin-à-vent* . . . could be better, I suppose, but it will do."

"So, abbot, for lunch we have champagne, Bordeaux, and burgundy, and that isn't enough for you?"

"I'm not saying it isn't enough," Mulot said in a conciliatory tone; "I'm just saying the choices could be better."

"Are you lunching with us, Le Bois?" asked the cardinal.

"Your Eminence will excuse me. You asked me to come by this morning but said nothing of lunch, so I've already eaten with Racan, whom I met sitting with his heels up on the corner of Rue Vieille-du-Temple and Rue Saint-Antoine."

"The devil you say! Come to the table, Mulot, take a seat, Lafollone, be quiet and listen, as Monsieur Le Bois is going to regale us with some pretty tale."

"The tale, the tale," Lafollone said. "I'm not the one to interrupt you."

"I raise this glass of Pommard to your tale, Master Le Bois," said Mulot, still a trifle cross. "I hope this one is better than usual."

"I'm not here to amuse you," said Bois-Robert. "I speak only the truth."

"The truth," said the cardinal, "is that it's just like you to be sitting with your heels up on a street corner at half past eight in the morning!"

"Monseigneur shall judge for himself. Your Eminence knows that

Malherbe lives not a hundred paces from here, in the Rue des Tournelles."

"I'm aware of that," said the cardinal, who ate very little because
of his bad stomach, and thus could talk while eating.

"Well! It seems that last night he was carousing with Ivrande and
Racan at his place, and all three ended up sleeping, dead drunk, in
Malherbe's bedchamber. Racan is the first to awaken—he had business at an early hour. He gets up and puts on Ivrande's trunk-hose for
trousers without noticing the mistake, puts on Ivrande's shoes into
the bargain, washes his face, and leaves. Five minutes later Ivrande
wakes up and can't find his shoes. '*Mordieu!*' he says to Malherbe.
'I'll bet that absent-minded Racan took them!' So Ivrande puts on
Malherbe's breeches, despite the poet's protests from his bed, and
races off after Racan, whom he can see going down the street in
clothes far too large for him.

"Ivrande catches up to Racan and demands the return of his
clothes. 'My faith, you're right!' Racan tells him. And without
further ado, as I've had the honor to tell Your Eminence, he sits
down on the corner of Rue Saint-Antoine and Rue Vieille-du-
Temple, in the view of all the passersby of Paris, takes off his pants
and shoes and trades them with Ivrande.

"I arrived right about then and offered to buy Racan some lunch.
At first he refused, saying he'd risen early because he had a matter
of utmost importance to attend to; but when he tried to remember
what it was, it slipped his mind entirely. It wasn't until we were
almost finished with lunch that he slapped his forehead and said,
'Oh, now I remember what I had to do.'"

"And what was that?" asked the cardinal, who, as usual, took the
greatest pleasure in Bois-Robert's stories.

"He'd planned to go inquire about the health of Madame la Marquise de Rambouillet, who, since the misfortune that occurred to the
Marquis de Pisany, had come down with a fever."

"Indeed," the cardinal said, "I heard from my niece that she was quite ill—as you probably already know, Le Bois. Please check on her if you pass by her house."

"No need, Monseigneur."

"No need? Why?"

"Because she has recovered."

"Recovered! Who treated her?"

"Voiture."

"Bah. Since when is he a doctor?"

"Never, Monseigneur, but Your Eminence knows that you don't need a doctor to cure a fever."

"How's that?"

"All you need are two bears."

"What? Two bears?"

"Quite so. Our friend Voiture heard that you could cure a person of fever by giving them a great surprise, so he went out into the streets looking for something Madame de Rambouillet would find surprising. That's where he encountered a traveling animal show. 'Pardieu!' he said. 'That's just the thing.' He hired this Savoyard and his animals and led them to the Hotel de Rambouillet. The marquise was within, sitting by the fire behind a folding screen. Voiture entered quietly, bringing the bears in behind the screen, and sat them up in two chairs behind the marquise. Madame de Rambouillet heard snuffling behind her, turned around, and saw two beastly snouts in her face. She nearly died of fright, but the fever was broken."

"A fine story!" said the cardinal. "What do you think, Mulot?"

"I think that in the eyes of God, all means are good," said the chaplain. Wine tended to bring out the religion in him, as it put him in a state of grace.

"God? You backwoods preacher! You'd put God into the low company of Voiture, a Savoyard, and two bears, all in Madame de Rambouillet's parlor?"

"God is everywhere," the chaplain said beatifically, raising his eyes, and his glass, to heaven. "But you, Monseigneur—you don't believe in God!"

"What?" the cardinal cried. "I, not believe in God?"

"Are you telling me now that you do believe?" the priest said, regarding the cardinal with a pair of small black eyes illuminated by his nose.

"Of course I believe!"

"Come now, in your last confession you admitted you didn't believe."

"Lafollone! Le Bois! Don't believe a word of what Mulot says. He's so drunk he confuses a confession with a test of conscience," the cardinal cried, laughing. "Are you nearly finished, Lafollone?"

"I am done, Monseigneur."

"Good. Once you're finished, say your goodbyes and leave us alone. I have to charge Le Bois with a secret commission."

"And I, Monseigneur," said Le Bois, "have a small petition to present to you."

"Yet another protégé?"

"Say, rather, a protégée, Monseigneur: a lady."

"Le Bois! You go too far, my friend."

"Oh, Monseigneur! She's seventy years old!"

"And what does this protégée do?"

"She writes verses, Monseigneur."

"Verses?"

"Yes, and they're quite beautiful! Would you like to hear them?"

"No, they would put Mulot to sleep and give Lafollone indigestion."

"Please? Just four?"

"Oh, well—four should be no problem."

"Here, Monseigneur," said Bois-Robert, and he presented the cardinal with an engraving of Joan of Arc.

"But this is an engraving," said the cardinal, "and you spoke of verses."

"Read what is below the engraving, Monseigneur."

"Ah! Very well." The cardinal read the following four lines:

> Can you grant me, Virgin adored,
> Both your sweet eyes and the shining sword?
> My sight is sweetest when I see my kingdom,
> And my sword in fury shall give her Freedom!

"Well, well," said the cardinal, and he read the lines again. "They're quite good, these lines. Proud and powerful. Who wrote them?"

"Read the author's name—it's written below, Monseigneur."

"Marie Le Jars, Demoiselle de Gournay. What!" the cardinal cried. "These lines are by Mademoiselle de Gournay?"

"By Mademoiselle de Gournay, yes, Monseigneur."

"The same Mademoiselle de Gournay who published a volume titled *The Shadow*?"

"Yes, the one who published *The Shadow*."

"But she's the exact person I planned to send you to, Le Bois."

"Really!"

"Take my carriage and bring her to me."

"More down-at-heels wretches!" said Mulot. "If you send him chasing after every luckless poet, it will kill Monseigneur's horses."

"Monsieur Abbot," said Bois-Robert, "God created monseigneur's horses to be used, just as he did almoners of Sainte-Chapelle."

"Ha! For once you have him, *compère*," Richelieu laughed, while Mulot sputtered, speechless.

But the chaplain pulled himself together. "I am not the cardinal's almoner!" he cried, exasperated.

"The Demoiselle de Gournay is already here," Bois-Robert said.

"What? The Demoiselle de Gournay is here?" asked the cardinal.

"Yes. I expected, this morning, to solicit a favor for her from Your Eminence. Knowing Monseigneur's generosity, I was sure you would grant it, so I asked her to come here between ten o'clock and ten-thirty. So she must be waiting."

"Le Bois, you're a gem of a man. Come, Father, one last glass. Lafollone, one more spoonful of the *confit* and then say grace. I must give an audience to Mademoiselle de Gournay, who is a noble lady and the adopted daughter of Montaigne."

Lafollone beatifically crossed his hands on his belly and raised his eyes devoutly to heaven. "Lord God," he said, "please grant us the grace to digest this good lunch upon which we have dined so well."

This was what the cardinal called Lafollone's grace. "And now, Messieurs," said the cardinal, "you may leave."

Lafollone and Mulot both rose at this dismissal, Lafollone beaming, Mulot still surly, and made for the door. Lafollone rolled out, saying, "Decidedly, His Eminence spreads an excellent lunch."

Mulot, staggering like Silenus, raised his hands to heaven and sputtered, "A cardinal who doesn't believe in God! It's an abomination!"

As for Bois-Robert, he had already left His Eminence's office, eager to announce his good news to his protégée.

For a moment, the cardinal was alone. But this was enough time for him to arrange his angular features, though his eyes remained thoughtful in his pale, severe face. "Ravaillac's statement still exists," he whispered. "Sully knows who has it. And, oh—I too shall know!"

And as Bois-Robert returned, leading the Demoiselle de Gournay by the hand, a smile, an unusual sight on his somber countenance, appeared momentarily on his lips.

XXVII

The Demoiselle de Gournay

As we have said, the Demoiselle de Gournay was a spinster, born in the mid-sixteenth century. She was of a good family from Picardy.

At the age of nineteen she had read, and been amazed by, Montaigne's *Essays*. She decided she had to meet the author.

At that very time, Montaigne came to Paris. She quickly found out his address and sent him a letter of greeting, in which she declared her high esteem for him and his book.

Montaigne came to see her the next day and was so taken with her youth and enthusiasm that he offered to regard her as a father does a daughter, an offer she gratefully accepted. From that day forward, she added to her signature, "Adopted Daughter of Montaigne."

She wrote fairly good verse, as we have seen. But she had fallen into a state of misery and starvation by the time Bois-Robert, who was known as the Angel of Afflicted Muses, learned of her distress and decided to present her to Cardinal Richelieu.

Bois-Robert had seen the power of the cardinal, and he'd told her "To be blessed in this world by Monseigneur le Cardinal is nearly as good as to be blessed in the next by Our Lord Jesus Christ."

Bois-Robert didn't hesitate to introduce his protégée to the Place Royale, and by a strange coincidence he'd brought her to the cardinal's waiting room on the very day His Eminence meant to send him to summon her.

The needy spinster was punctual, as if having been warned of the habits of the cardinal.

So it was, as we've said, that he received her with a smile and, knowing literary Paris as he did, added an *à propos* compliment about her book, *The Shadow.*

But the lady, unabashed, said, "You laugh at a poor old woman—but I suppose a genius must laugh, and who in all the world would begrudge you entertainment?"

The cardinal, astonished at such humility combined with presence of mind, was moved to apologize. Then, turning to Bois-Robert, he said, "Come, Le Bois, what would you ask of us for Mademoiselle de Gournay?"

"It is not for me to set bounds on Your Eminence's generosity," said Bois-Robert with a bow.

"Well, then," said the cardinal, "I shall grant her a pension of two hundred crowns."

That was a great deal at the time, especially for a poor spinster. Two hundred crowns in that period were twelve hundred *livres*, equal to four to five thousand francs in our time.

The Demoiselle de Gournay made a gesture of gratitude and began to utter her thanks, but Bois-Robert, who was not yet satisfied, interrupted her in mid-sentence. "Monseigneur said two hundred crowns?"

"Yes," said the cardinal.

"That's all very well for her, Monseigneur, and thank you. But Mademoiselle de Gournay has dependents."

"Ah, she has servants?" said the cardinal.

"Yes, a daughter of the nobility cannot serve herself. Monseigneur understands that."

"I do indeed. And how many domestics does Mademoiselle de Gournay have?" The cardinal was determined to meet if not exceed whatever Bois-Robert asked for.

"Well, she has Mademoiselle Jamyn," replied Bois-Robert.

"Oh! Monsieur Bois-Robert," murmured the spinster, "please don't take liberties with the cardinal's charity."

"Trust me, trust me," said Bois-Robert, "I know His Eminence."

"And who is this Mademoiselle Jamyn?" asked the cardinal.

"The illegitimate child of Amadis Jamyn, and Mademoiselle de Gournay thanks you on her behalf," said the persistent muse. "But there is also darling Piaillon."

"Darling Piaillon?" asked the cardinal, while poor Mademoiselle de Gournay desperately gestured at Bois-Robert to stop, signals which Bois-Robert ignored.

"Darling Piaillon. Your Eminence doesn't know darling Piaillon?"

"I must admit I do not, Le Bois."

"But that is Mademoiselle de Gournay's cat."

"Monseigneur!" cried the poor spinster. "I must apologize!"

The cardinal waved his hand reassuringly. "I grant darling Piaillon an annual pension of twenty pounds, on the condition she be served tripe often."

"Tripe it shall be, even *à la mode de Caen,* if Your Eminence demands it."

"Thank you on behalf of my darling Piaillon," said Mademoiselle de Gournay, "but . . ."

"What, Le Bois?" said the cardinal, who couldn't help laughing. "There is a 'but'?"

"There is, Monseigneur. For darling Piaillon has just had kittens."

"Oh!" said the Demoiselle de Gournay, chagrined and rubbing one hand over the other.

"How many kittens?" asked the cardinal.

"Five!" said Bois-Robert.

"My!" said the cardinal. "Darling Piaillon is fruitful. No matter, Le Bois, I add a *pistole* for each kitten."

"And now, Mademoiselle de Gournay," said Bois-Robert, delighted, "I permit you to thank His Eminence."

"Not yet, not yet," said the cardinal. "It's too soon for Mademoiselle de Gournay to thank me, as I hope to soon be thanking her."

"What?" said Bois-Robert.

"Leave us alone, Le Bois. I have a favor to ask of mademoiselle."

Bois-Robert gazed in surprise, first at the cardinal, then at Mademoiselle de Gournay.

"Oh, I see what's in your mind, Master Droll," said the cardinal. "But if I hear any remarks from you about Mademoiselle de Gournay's honor, you'll have me to deal with. Await mademoiselle in the antechamber."

Bois-Robert bowed and left. He had no idea what this was about.

The cardinal waited until the door was closed before approaching Mademoiselle de Gournay, who had no more idea than Bois-Robert what he had in mind. "Yes, Mademoiselle," he said, "I have a favor to ask of you."

"What is it, Monseigneur?" the poor spinster asked.

"I need you to recall some memories. I'm sure it will be easy, for you have a good memory, don't you?"

"Excellent, Monseigneur, so long as we don't go back too far."

"What I'd like to ask you about is something, or rather two things, that happened between May 9 and 11 in 1610."

Mademoiselle started at that date, and looked anxiously at the cardinal. "May 9 to 11," she repeated. "May 9 to 11, in 1610—that is to say, the year they assassinated our poor dear King Henri IV, the Beloved."

"Exactly, Mademoiselle. And the question I need to ask you relates to his death."

Mademoiselle de Gournay said nothing, but her anxiety increased.

"Don't be upset, Mademoiselle," said Richelieu. "My investigation doesn't concern you and yours, only your devotion to the truth. The awards that Bois-Robert has solicited for you are not in question, for what I've granted you is far below your merit."

"You must pardon me, Monseigneur," said the poor spinster, "for I don't understand."

"Two words will make you understand. You knew a woman named Jacqueline Le Voyer, Dame de Coëtman, did you not?"

Mademoiselle de Gournay started and turned pale. "Yes," she said. "She was from the same province as I. But thirty years my junior, if yet she lives."

"I believe it was on the 9th or 10th of May, I'm not sure which, that she sent a letter addressed to Monsieur de Sully, to be given to the king."

"Yes, it was on May 10, Monseigneur."

"You know what was in that letter?"

"It was a warning that the king would be assassinated."

"The letter named the conspirators?"

"Yes, Monseigneur," the Demoiselle de Gournay said, trembling.

"You remember whom the Dame de Coëtman denounced?"

"I remember."

"Would you tell me their names?"

"This is a very grave matter you ask me about, Monseigneur."

"Indeed it is. I will name them, and I will be satisfied if you answer, yes or no, by a nod." He paused. "Those named by the Dame de Coëtman were the queen mother, Concini the Maréchal d'Ancre, and the Duc d'Épernon."

The Demoiselle de Gournay, more dead than alive, nodded her head in the affirmative.

"That letter," continued the cardinal, "you gave to Monsieur de Sully, who to the fatal harm of the king did not show it to him—but you felt you had done all you could."

"That's it exactly, Monseigneur," said Mademoiselle de Gournay.

"This letter—you kept it?"

"Yes, Monseigneur, for only two people had the right to ask it of me: the Duc de Sully, to whom it was addressed, and the Dame de Coëtman, who had written it."

"You never heard a word about this from the Duc de Sully?"

"No, Monseigneur."

"Nor the Dame de Coëtman?"

"I heard she'd been arrested on the 13th. I haven't seen her since and have no idea if she's dead or alive."

"So you have this letter?"

"Yes, Monseigneur."

"Then I must ask, my dear Demoiselle, for you to give it up to me."

"Impossible, Monseigneur," said the Mademoiselle de Gournay, with a firmness that, a moment before, would have seemed inconceivable.

"Why is that?"

"Because, as I've had the honor to tell Your Eminence a moment ago, only two people have a right to ask it of me: the Dame de Coëtman, who has been accused of complicity in this dark and terrible affair, and for whom it may serve as an exoneration; and Monsieur le Duc de Sully."

"The Dame de Coëtman no longer needs exoneration, as she died last night between the hours of one and two in the morning, at the Convent of the Repentant Daughters."

"God rest her soul," said Mademoiselle de Gournay, crossing herself. "She was a martyr!"

"And as for the Duc de Sully," continued the cardinal, "since he hasn't cared about this letter for the last eighteen years, it's unlikely he cares about it today."

Mademoiselle de Gournay shook her head. "I can do nothing without the permission of Monsieur de Sully," she said, "especially since the Dame de Coëtman is no longer of this world."

"But suppose," said Richelieu, "I said that the pensions I've granted you are the price of this letter?"

Mademoiselle de Gournay rose with supreme dignity. "Monseigneur," she said, "I am a daughter of the nobility and therefore a gentlewoman, as you are a gentleman. I will starve to death if I must, but I will do nothing to betray my conscience."

"Daughter of the nobility, you shall not starve to death, nor need you do anything to betray your conscience," said the cardinal, visibly pleased to see such courage in a poor writer of books. "I guarantee that Monsieur de Sully will give you the permission you require. You may go yourself to the Hotel de Sully, with my Captain of the Guards as your escort, if you wish."

He called Cavois and Bois-Robert, who each entered through a different door. "Cavois," he said, "take my carriage and drive Mademoiselle de Gournay to the home of Monsieur le Duc de Sully. Announce that you've come in my name and you'll be admitted immediately. Then accompany her, again in the carriage, to her home, where she will give you a letter that you will bring directly to me."

Then, addressing Bois-Robert, he said, "Le Bois, I hereby double the pensions of Mademoiselle de Gournay, of the bastard of Amadis Jamyn, of darling Piaillon, and of her kittens. Is that correct? Did I forget anyone?"

"No, Monseigneur," said Bois-Robert, overcome with joy.

"Work it out with my treasurer so they will begin on January 1, 1628."

"Ah! Monseigneur!" cried Mademoiselle de Gournay, seizing Richelieu's hand and kissing it.

"It's I who should kiss your hand, Mademoiselle," said the cardinal.

"Monseigneur! Monseigneur!" said Mademoiselle de Gournay, clasping his hand in hers. "For an old woman of my age . . . !"

"A noble hand is ever youthful," said the cardinal. And he kissed her hand as earnestly as if she were a maid of twenty-five.

Then Mademoiselle de Gournay left with Cavois by one door, while Bois-Robert went out another.

XXVIII

Souscarrières's Report

Left alone, the cardinal called his secretary, Charpentier, and asked
him to bring in the day's correspondence. It contained three letters
of importance.

One was from Bautru, ambassador to Spain—or rather envoy, as
ambassador was never his official title. He was known most as a wit
about Court, and we could call him Court Comedian, but such a
title is incompatible with high diplomacy, so we'll just refer to him
as ambassador.

The second was from La Saludie, Envoy Extraordinary to Piedmont, Mantua, Venice, and Rome.

The third was from Charnassé, a confidential agent sent through
Germany on a secret mission to Gustavus Adolphus.

Bautru was one of Richelieu's favorites, possibly because he was
one of the greatest enemies of Monsieur d'Épernon. Having made
some jokes about the duke, the duke had sent his man Simon to
visit him with an "accident"—that Simon, we recall, whom Latil
described as the duke's thug-in-residence. Still struggling to recover
after his "accident," bruised, with sore kidneys, and leaning on a
cane, Bautru went to visit the queen mother.

"Do you have the gout, Monsieur de Bautru?" asked the queen
mother. "Is that why you resort to a cane?"

"Madame," interrupted the Prince de Guéménée, "Bautru doesn't
have gout. He bears a stick for the same reason Saint Lawrence bore
a grille, as a symbol of his means of martyrdom."

In Bautru's provincial domain, the judge of a nearby small town
came to pester him so often that he ordered his valet not to admit the

284

man. But despite his orders, the next time the judge came, the valet announced him.

"Didn't I order you, buffoon, to find some reason to turn him away?" Bautru cried.

"My faith, yes, that's what you told me. But I didn't know what to say!"

"*Pardieu*! Tell him I'm still in bed."

The valet left, then returned. "Monsieur, he says he'll wait till you get up."

"Tell him I'm sick, then."

The valet left, and came back again. "Monsieur, he says he'll teach you a sure cure."

"Tell him I'm dying."

The valet withdrew, then returned again. "Monsieur, he says he wants to make his final farewell to you."

"Tell him I'm dead."

The valet left, and returned yet again. "Monsieur, he says he wants to bless your body with holy water."

"All right, let him in," Bautru said with a sigh. "I never thought I'd meet a man more stubborn than I."

One of the things the cardinal valued most in him was his honesty. The cardinal said of him, "Bautru, whom everyone calls a fool, has more integrity than two Cardinal Bérulles." The cardinal also appreciated his utter contempt for Rome, which Bautru called the Apostolic Fool's Paradise. One day Richelieu told him about the promotion of ten new cardinals appointed by Pope Urban XII, the last of whom was named Farcetti.

"I count only nine," Bautru said.

"What about Farcetti?" said the cardinal.

"Your pardon, Monseigneur—I thought that was his title."

Bautru wrote in his letter that Spain did not seem to take his mission seriously. The Count-Duke of Olivares had taken him to the royal henhouse, which he said was appropriate because, once His Majesty Philip IV arrived, he would send him back to the cocks—that is, to *los gallos,* which in Spanish is a sorry pun for France. He added that Olivares's invitation to the cardinal to review Spain's many proposals was just a means of playing for time, as Madrid was bound by treaty to help Charles-Emmanuel take Montferrat and partition it with Savoy once it was taken. He particularly warned His Eminence not to trust Ambassador Fargis, who belonged body and soul—well, body at least; Bautru had doubts about his soul—to the queen mother. Fargis did nothing without instructions from his wife, which were just orders passed on from Marie de Médicis and Anne of Austria.

Richelieu, having read Bautru's dispatch, shrugged slightly and muttered, "I would prefer peace, but I'm prepared for war."

La Saludie's dispatch was even more explicit. In exchange for renouncing his claims on Montferrat and Mantua, Richelieu had offered Duke Charles-Emmanuel the city of Trino, with its annual income of twelve thousand crowns. The duke had refused, replying that he preferred Casale to Trino, and Casale would be his before King Louis's troops had gotten as far as Lyon.

Nevers, the new French duke in Mantua, was becoming desperate, though he'd taken heart a bit at the arrival of La Saludie. But the envoy feared they would have to give up their first plan to help him, which was to land the Duc de Guise in Genoa with seven thousand men, as the Spanish were guarding all routes from Genoa to Montferrat. The king would have to settle for forcing the Pass of Susa in the Alps, which was fortified but not impregnable.

Having seen both the Duke of Savoy and the Duke of Mantua, La Saludie announced that he was departing next for Venice.

Richelieu took up his notebook and wrote: *Write to Chevalier Marini, our Ambassador in Turin, and order him to declare to Charles-Emmanuel that the king regards him as an enemy.*

Charnassé, in whose intelligence the cardinal had great confidence, had been gone longer than the other two, having visited, before arriving in Sweden, both Constantinople and Russia. Baron de Charnassé, in the grip of sorrow for the loss of a woman he loved, had asked the cardinal for a long mission away from Paris. From Constantinople he had crossed Russia and had now reached King Gustavus.

The letter from the baron was full of acclaim for the King of Sweden, described to Richelieu as the only man capable of stopping the progress of the Imperial Army in Germany, if the Protestants were willing to ally with him.

Richelieu thought for a moment; then, as if breaking a final scruple, he said to himself, "Well, the Pope can say whatever he wants. I may be a cardinal; but though I risk losing that title, I must still place the glory and grandeur of France first."

And taking a sheet of paper, he wrote:

> *Urge King Gustavus, when he's finished with the Russians, to enter Germany to rescue his co-religionists, whom the Emperor Ferdinand plans to destroy.*
>
> *Promise King Gustavus that Richelieu will provide the funds to support this policy, and intimate that the King of France may at the same time attack Lorraine as a diversion.*

The cardinal, as we see, remembered the coded letter that Rossignol had deciphered the week before.

Finally, the cardinal added:

> *If the enterprise with the King of Sweden ends as well as it has begun, the King of France may cease to worry about the House of Austria.*

꧁

The letter to Chevalier Marini and the dispatch to Charnassé went out that same day.

The cardinal was still at his diplomatic work when Cavois returned bearing the letter from the Dame de Coëtman, for which Mademoiselle de Gournay had received permission from Monsieur de Sully.

It read as follows:

> *To King Henri IV, Beloved Majesty*
>
> *I pray that you will instantly, in the name of France and in defense of your life, have arrested a man named François Ravaillac, known everywhere as the king-killer. He has confessed to me his horrible scheme, and has been, I dare to say it, driven to regicide by Queen Marie, by the Maréchal d'Ancre, and by the Duc d'Épernon. I, a humble servant of Her Majesty, have written three letters to the queen, but as they remain unanswered I must address the king directly. I beg and implore Monsieur le Duc de Sully, whom I believe to be His Majesty's loyal friend, to place this letter before the king.*
>
> *I am your very humble subject and servant,*
>
> > *Jacqueline Le Voyer,*
> > *Dame de Coëtman*

Richelieu nodded in satisfaction, as the letter was all he'd hoped. He opened the secret drawer that contained the end of the wire that led to his niece's apartments, and then, after a moment's hesitation as to whether she should be summoned, closed it again.

Then he noticed that Cavois still stood before him and seemed to have something else to say. "Well, Cavois, what do you want now, you pest?" he said, in a tone his associates recognized as showing he was in a good mood.

"Eminence, it is Monsieur de Souscarrières, who wishes to deliver his first report."

"Ah, right! Go collect this first report of Monsieur de Souscarrières and bring it to me."

Cavois left.

As if Cavois's announcement had reminded him of something, the cardinal got up, went to the door of the private mailbox that communicated with Marion Delorme, opened it, and picked up a note lying within. It contained the following information:

He has visited Madame de la Montagne only once in the last week. He is believed to be in love with one of the queen's ladies, a young woman named Isabelle de Lautrec.

"Oh, ho," said the cardinal, "the daughter of Baron François de Lautrec, who is with the Duc de Rethel in Mantua."

And he wrote the following memo: *Instruct Baron de Lautrec to summon his daughter to him.*

Then, to himself: "I intend to send the Comte de Moret to war in Italy, and he will go all the more readily if it takes him closer to his beloved."

As he finished this memo, Cavois returned and handed him an envelope sporting the arms of the Duc de Bellegarde.

The cardinal tore open the envelope, removed a letter, and read:

Report of Sieur Michel, called Souscarrières
To His Eminence Monseigneur le Cardinal de Richelieu

Yesterday, December 13, first day of the service of Sieur Michel, called Souscarrières:

Monsieur Mirabel, the Spanish Ambassador, took a sedan chair in Rue Saint-Sulpice and was carried, at eleven o'clock in the morning, to the shop of the jeweler Lopez.

At the same time, Madame de Fargis hired a chair in the Rue des Poulies and was also taken to Lopez's shop.

One of the porters saw the Spanish Ambassador chat with the queen's lady and pass her a note.

At noon, Monsieur le Cardinal de Bérulle hired a chair at the Galleries of the Louvre and was taken first to the home of the Duc de Bellegarde, then the home of Maréchal de Bassompierre. Through my contacts in the household of Monsieur de Bellegarde, who continues to believe me his son, I learned they discussed a secret conclave to be held in the Tuileries regarding the war in Piedmont. At this conclave will be Messieurs de Bellegarde, Bassompierre, de Guise, and de Marillac. Monseigneur le Cardinal will be notified of the day.

"Ah!" said the cardinal. "I suspected this fellow Souscarrières would be useful."

Madame de Bellier, the queen's confidential maid, took a chair at about two o'clock to see Michel Dause, the queen's apothecary, who that evening hired a sedan chair on his own account to take him to the Louvre.

"Good!" whispered Richelieu. "So the reigning queen wants to have her own Vautier, like the queen mother? We will keep an eye on him." He wrote in his notebook: *Buy the loyalty of Madame de*

Bellier, the queen's confidential maid, and her lover Patrocle, the esquire in the royal stable.

Then he continued his reading.

> *Last night at about eight o'clock, Her Majesty the Queen Mother took a chair to the home of the President of Verdun, which connects to the house of a famous astrologer known as "The Forbidden." Their interview lasted an hour. The Forbidden came out afterward, and was seen by the light of the chair lantern to be wearing a beautiful diamond ring, a gift in all probability from Her Majesty the Queen Mother. The subject of their conversation is unknown.*
>
> *Last night, the Comte de Moret hired a chair in Rue Saint-Avoye and was taken to the Hotel de Longueville, where there was a large gathering that included Monsieur Gaston d'Orléans, the Duc de Montmorency, and Madame de Fargis, all of whom also arrived by chair.*
>
> *Upon leaving, Madame de Fargis exchanged a few words with the Comte de Moret in the vestibule. Whatever was said seemed to please them both, as Madame de Fargis went away laughing, while the Comte de Moret left singing to himself.*

"This is all excellent," murmured the cardinal, and continued.

> *Last night, between eleven o'clock and midnight, Cardinal Richelieu, disguised as a Capuchin . . .*

"What's this?" said the cardinal, then continued with mounting curiosity.

. . . as a Capuchin, took a chair in the Rue Royale and was carried to the Rue de l'Homme-Armé, to the Inn of the Painted Beard . . .

"H'mm," said the cardinal.

. . . to the Inn of the Painted Beard, where he visited the room of Étienne Latil. At half past one, His Eminence came down and ordered the porter to take him to the Convent of the Repentant Daughters in the Rue des Postes.

"The devil!" the cardinal muttered. Then, driven on by curiosity:

Upon arriving, he persuaded the sister at the door to summon the superior, who opened it. He was then taken to the cell of the Dame de Coëtman. After a quarter of an hour's conversation at the cell's barred window, he called in his two porters and ordered them to break a hole in the wall large enough to allow the Dame de Coëtman to get out. Half an hour after His Eminence's order, this was completed.

The cardinal stopped to think a moment, and then continued.

Upon her release from the cell, the Dame de Coëtman being unclothed, the cardinal wrapped her in his robe, and then, attired only in black, escorted her to the superior's room, where the lady was warmed by a large fire and regained her strength. At three o'clock Monseigneur sent for a second chair for the Dame de Coëtman. He accompanied her in his own chair to the hostel and beauty salon of Madame Nollet, opposite the Pont Nôtre-Dame. There he left her, with some instructions, and went on his way.

"Not bad, not bad," muttered the cardinal. "One must admit, at least, that he is amusing. Onward."

> *At a quarter past five, His Eminence returned home to the Place Royale. Five minutes later, dressed in his usual attire, he was taken to the Hotel de Sully, where he remained for about half an hour. Around a quarter past six, he returned to the Place Royale.*
>
> *Ten minutes after his return, Madame de Combalet left in another chair and was taken to the house of Madame Nollet. After remaining about an hour she brought back, at around eight in the morning, the Dame de Coëtman attired as a Carmelite nun.*
>
> *This is the report which Sieur Michel, called Souscarrières, has the honor to submit to His Eminence, with the assurance that the facts are exactly as stated.*
>
> *Signed,*
> *Michel, called Souscarrières*

"By God," said the cardinal, "he is a cunning rascal. Cavois! Cavois!"

His guard captain entered. "Monseigneur?"

"The man who brought this report, is he still here?"

"Monseigneur," Cavois replied, "unless I'm mistaken, it is Monsieur de Souscarrières himself."

"Bring him in, my dear Cavois, bring him in."

As if the Seigneur de Souscarrières had anticipated this very invitation, he appeared at the office door, wearing an outfit simple yet elegant, and bowed deeply to the cardinal.

"Come in, Monsieur Michel," said His Eminence.

"Here I am, Monseigneur," said Souscarrières.

"It was no mistake to place my trust in you. You're a clever man."

"If Monseigneur is pleased with me, I'm also a happy man."

"Quite pleased. But I don't like riddles, as I don't have time to solve them. How can you recount all my personal details so accurately?"

"Monseigneur," Souscarrières replied with a self-satisfied smile, "I had no doubt Your Eminence would personally avail himself of this new form of transport which you have authorized."

"So?"

"So I tarried in the Rue Royale until I saw His Eminence come out."

"And thereafter?"

"Thereafter, Monseigneur, the largest porter, who knocked on the convent door, who carried the Dame de Coëtman to the hearth, and so forth—that was me."

"My faith!" said the cardinal. "Is that so?"

XXIX

The King Goes Larding

And now, for the purposes of our story, our readers must allow us to better acquaint them with King Louis XIII, whom we've only glimpsed at night in the queen's bedchamber, where he was driven by Cardinal Richelieu's suspicions that she might be plotting against him. We recall him announcing that, by order of Doctor Bouvard, he would be purged the next day and bled the day after that.

He was purged, he was bled, and it made him neither happier nor healthier: on the contrary, his melancholy and his pallor had only increased.

No one knew the cause of this melancholy, though it had afflicted the king since he was fourteen or fifteen. The mood drove him to try, one after another, every form of diversion or amusement he'd never tried before. Worse, in the middle of his crowded court he was virtually alone and friendless, accompanied only by his fool l'Angely, who always dressed in black, which added to the general air of gloom.

Nothing could be sadder than his lonely suite of rooms, where no woman ever entered, with the exception of Queen Anne and the queen mother, who did so only to keep him from coming to their own apartments.

If you had an audience scheduled with him, upon arriving at the designated time, often you would be received first by Monsieur de Tréville, or Monsieur de Guitaut, or by Beringhen, who in his capacity as Premier Valet de Chambre was known as "Monsieur le Premier." One or another of these gentlemen would introduce you into a seemingly empty chamber where you might look about and wonder if the king was there at all. Then you would notice him, standing in an embrasure and staring out the window, possibly with one of his gentlemen, whom he has honored by saying, "Come, Monsieur So-and-So, let us be weary together." Anyone who heard the tone in which he said this knew he spoke with complete sincerity.

More than once, the queen, trying to gain some leverage over this dreary personality and none too sure of being able to do it herself, had, on the advice of the queen mother, brought in a young beauty of whose loyalty she was certain in hopes that the girl might catch his eye, then exert some influence, but always in vain.

This was the king whom Luynes, after four years of marriage, had been forced to carry into his wife's bedchamber. This was a king whose favorites were always men, never women. The Italians thought they understood his preferences and summed him up with a phrase, *La buggera ha passato i monti*—that is, "Sodomy has come over the mountains."

Even "La Irresistible," the stunning Madame de Chevreuse, had tried to catch his eye; but despite the triple allure of youth, beauty, and wit, she had failed.

"But Sire," she said to him one day, exasperated by his chilly indifference, "wouldn't you like to have a mistress?"

"Yes, Madame, I would," the king said.

"Ah! And how would you like to have her, then?"

"Only above the belt," replied the king.

"Well," said Madame de Chevreuse, "the next time I come to the Louvre I'll dress like the actor Gros-Guillaume, who's so fat he wears a belt above and a belt below: but I'll just wear the belt below, on my thigh."

It was in the hope of engaging the king that the chaste and beautiful damsel we have presented to our readers as Isabelle de Lautrec had been brought to Court. We have seen how devoted she was to the queen, though her father was a retainer of the Duc de Rethel.

And indeed, Isabelle was so lovely that even Louis XIII had noticed. He'd chatted with her and found her personality quite charming. She, for her part, quite ignorant that she was part of a scheme, had spoken to the king with modesty and respect. But that was all six months before the time of our story, and since then the king had acquired a new page as a personal servant, with whom he was so taken that he had little time for Isabelle, let alone the queen.

In fact, with this king, favorite succeeded favorite so rapidly that at any given moment it was hard for the courtiers to know who, as they say at the horse races, had the inside track.

First there had been Pierrot, the peasant farmer we mentioned.

Then had come Luynes, the chief of his Cabinet of Birds.

Then came d'Esplan, his Arbalest Bearer, whom he made Marquis de Grimaud.

Then Chalais, who wound up beheaded.

Then Baradas, the favorite of the moment.

And now, at last, came Saint-Simon, who, hoping to become a permanent favorite, was conspiring at the disgrace of Baradas—a disgrace that was all too predictable, given the fragile moods of King Louis XIII, a man who kept his favorites in that impossible place between friendship and love.

Next beyond his favorites was his loyal entourage. This included Monsieur de Tréville, his Captain of Musketeers, who may be familiar to the reader from some other books we won't bother to mention here; the Comte de Nogent-Bautru, brother of that Bautru the cardinal had sent to Spain, a man who, the first time he'd been presented at Court, had chanced to meet the king at a path in the Tuileries flooded with water, and had carried the king over it on his shoulders as St. Christopher had carried Jesus Christ, and who had the rare privilege, shared only with the fool l'Angely, of being allowed to say anything in the presence of the king, even attempt to jolly him out of his gloomy moods; Bassompierre, made a marshal in 1622, more for service in the bedchamber of Marie de Médicis than for his exploits in battle, a man, moreover, of wit, charm, and heart who kept an outstanding memoir of his time, from the end of the 16th century through the early part of the 17th; Sublet-Desnoyers, the king's secretary, or rather his valet; La Vieuville, Superintendent of Finances; Guitaut, his Captain of the Guards, a man entirely devoted to him and to Queen Anne of Austria, who replied to all offers to join the service of the cardinal with "Impossible, Your Eminence—I'm a man of the king, and the Gospel says no one can serve two masters"; and finally Maréchal de Marillac, brother of the Keeper of the Seals, whose execution was later to be a bloody stain on the reign of Louis XIII—or rather the ministry of Cardinal Richelieu.

It so happened that, the day after Souscarrières had delivered his uncannily accurate report to Richelieu about the events of the night before, the king, after lunching with Baradas, had formed an impromptu party with Nogent and called for two of his musicians, Molinier and Justin, to accompany them with lute and viola while he engaged in his latest diversion. He then turned to Bassompierre, Marillac, Desnoyers, and La Vieuville, who had just come in, and said, "Gentlemen, let's go to the kitchens and lard some meat."

"Yes, gentlemen, let's go larding!" said l'Angely in snotty hauteur. "How well they go together: royalty and larding."

And, with this rather mediocre joke, he popped his hat on his head and pulled Nogent's down over his ears. "What are you doing, buffoon?" Nogent said.

"Covering your head and mine," said l'Angely.

"In front of the king? What are you thinking?"

"Bah! Etiquette doesn't apply to buffoons like us."

"Sire, please silence this insolent clown!" Nogent cried, furious.

"What, Nogent?" said Louis XIII. "You think anyone could keep l'Angely quiet?"

"You pay me to speak my mind," l'Angely said. "If I shut up, I'd be as dull as Monsieur de La Vieuville, whom you made Superintendent of Finances even though he has no finances and has to pay himself from yours. At least I steal my money honestly."

"Didn't Your Majesty hear what he said?" Nogent persisted.

"I did, but I think you should mind how you speak yourself."

"How I speak . . . to you, Sire?"

"Indeed. When we were playing tennis and I just missed the ball, you said, 'See that? There's Louis the *Just Missed*.' You must be a buffoon just like l'Angely, Nogent, if I allow you to say such things to me. Now come, gentlemen, let's go larding."

These words, *let's go larding*, deserve an explanation, as we don't want to leave our readers in the dark. The explanation is as follows.

As we've already mentioned, to fight his melancholy the king engaged in all kinds of diversions, though he was rarely diverted by them. As a child he'd made squirt-guns out of leather scraps, as a young man he'd daubed colors on canvas that his courtiers were required to call "paintings," then played what they were obliged to call "music" (though he was quite a good drummer, according to Bassompierre). He had hammered together frames and cages with Monsieur Desnoyers; he had made preserves and jam, and excellent jam at that; he had taken up gardening, managing to grow green peas in February, which were sold at market, where Monsieur de Montausson had bought some; and finally, he had learned how to be a barber. One day, in his enthusiasm for this new hobby, he had summoned and shaved all his officers, leaving on each chin only that slim goatee that became known as the "royale."

A satire about this went briefly around the Louvre:

> Alas, my poor beard!
> Who trimmed you thusly?
> The great King Louis,

Thirteenth of the name,
Chief barber of his manse.

"Monsieur de La Force,
You should do it, too!"
"Alas, Sire, thank you,
I don't dare to try,
Your soldiers won't give me the chance."

Let's all wear the beard
Of Cousin Richelieu.
Yes, that will do.
For only a fool would dare
To out-barber the King of France!

However, King Louis had tired of shaving his men's beards, as he tired of everything. A few weeks before this, he had gone down to the kitchens to test a theory of more economical recipes, so General Coquet could afford his milk soup and Monsieur de La Vrillière could still have his biscuits in the morning. There he saw his chef and his cooks larding bacon and pork fat into cutlets of veal, loins of beef, and whole hares and pheasants, a process he found fascinating. As a result, for the last month His Majesty had been larding meat in his kitchens, and had insisted that his courtiers go larding with him.

I don't know if the art of cooking was improved by the involvement of the royal hands, but the king certainly improved its presentation. Loins of veal and beef fillets, which were large enough to be trimmed artistically, started coming up from the kitchens in novel shapes: trees, houses, dogs, wolves, deer, and *fleurs de lys* were seen. Nogent and some of the others went from cutting heraldic shapes to making rather lewd images, which earned them severe reprimands from the priggish Louis, who forbade such tasteless viands from being served on the royal tables.

And now our readers know enough that we can proceed with our story. When the king said "Gentlemen, let's go larding," his entourage hastened to follow him down the stairs.

Bassompierre took advantage of the time it took to get the chamber prepared for the king's latest pursuit, where there were five or six marble-topped tables, each with its loin of veal, its fillet of beef, its hare or its pheasant, and where the squire Georges waited with plates of precut bacon and larding needles, which he handed to those who wished to humor His Majesty by submitting to his latest whimsy—Bassompierre, we say, took advantage of this moment to place a hand on the shoulder of the Superintendent of Finance and say, in a low voice but loud enough to be heard by everyone, "Monsieur le Surintendant, if it's not being too curious, might I ask when you plan to pay me my quarterly stipend as Colonel-General of the Swiss Guard, an office for which I paid a hundred thousand crowns in cash?"

Instead of answering, Monsieur de La Vieuville, who, like Nogent, was sometimes given to playing the fool, began to spin his arms like the hands on a clock, saying, "I'm late, I'm late, I'm late . . . !"

"My faith," said Bassompierre, "in my life I've solved many a riddle, but I don't know the answer to this one."

"Monsieur le Maréchal," said La Vieuville, "when one is late, he is not current, no?"

". . . Yes."

"Well, I have no currency, so I'm late, I'm late, I'm late!"

Just then the party was joined by the Duc d'Angoulême, the bastard of King Charles IX and Marie Touchet, and the Duc de Guise, whom we last saw at the soirée for Princess Marie and whom the Duc d'Orléans had promised a corps in the army, assuming he would be lieutenant general to the king in the Italian offensive. Both waited to approach until they were recognized by the king.

Bassompierre, who was at a loss for a reply to La Vieuville, bravely went up to the Duc d'Angoulême—we say bravely, because as Angoulême turned to face him, he brought to bear one of the most formidable noses of the époque. "You're late, you're late, you're late—fine, so's your wife," said Bassompierre. "What's that to me? Ah, *pardieu,* if I could only counterfeit money like Monsieur d'Angoulême, here, I'd have no worries."

The Duc d'Angoulême, who had no ready response, turned his nose and looked away, pretending he hadn't heard—but King Louis XIII had heard, and maliciously interjected, "Cousin, did you hear what Monsieur de Bassompierre said?"

"No, Sire, I am deaf in my right ear," replied the duke.

"Like Caesar," said Bassompierre.

"He wonders if you make counterfeit money."

"Pardon, Sire," replied Bassompierre. "I do not wonder if Monsieur d'Angoulême makes counterfeit money, I assert it as a known fact."

The Duc d'Angoulême shrugged. "For twenty years I've been putting up with this nonsense."

"Is there some truth to it, Cousin? Tell us," said the king.

"Ah, *mon Dieu,* very well: here is the truth. In my Château de Grosbois I rented a room to an alchemist called Merlin who claimed the location was perfect for finding the Philosopher's Stone. He gave me four thousand crowns a year on condition I not inquire into what he was doing, and allow him to live in a house of a Son of France where the law couldn't reach him. You understand, Sire, that since I was being paid more for a single room than I could get for the whole mansion, I wasn't about to pry and risk losing such a good tenant."

"You see how you slander him, Bassompierre?" said the king. "What could be more honest than the entrepreneurship of our cousin?"

"Besides," said the Duc d'Angoulême, "what's a little counterfeit money to me, the son of King Charles IX of France, when your father, of glorious memory, son of Antoine de Bourbon and King of Navarre, was such a thief?"

"What—my father, a thief!" cried Louis XIII.

"Aha!" said Bassompierre. "Perhaps that's why he said to me one day, 'It's a good thing I'm the king, or else I'd be hanged!'"

"Sire, with all due respect owed to Your Majesty," continued the Duc d'Angoulême, "the king, your father, was a thief when gaming."

"And I," said Louis XIII, "I'll just point out to you that stealing in a game isn't stealing, it's just cheating. Besides, after the game, he returned the money."

"Not always," said Bassompierre.

"What do you mean, not always?" said the king.

"Upon my word, it's the truth, and your august mother will support me. One day, or rather one night, I had the honor of playing with the king. There were fifty *pistoles* in the pot, but we noticed some half-*pistoles* were mixed in. 'Sire,' I said to the king, 'is Your Majesty trying to pass off half-*pistoles* as full *pistoles*?' 'No, it's you,' replied the king. So I took all the half-*pistoles,* opened a window, threw them down to the servants waiting in the courtyard, and then returned to the game with all the full *pistoles*."

"You did that, Bassompierre?" said the king.

"Yes, Sire, and your august mother said, 'Today Bassompierre is the king, and the king is Bassompierre.'"

"Faith of a gentleman, that was well said," cried Louis XIII. "And what did my father say?"

"Sire, no doubt memories of his marital woes with Queen Marguerite led him to speak unfairly, for he said, 'Yes, you'd like it if he was the king, as you'd have a younger husband.'"

"So, who won the game?" asked Louis XIII.

"King Henri IV, Sire. He took the entire pot, and he must have been preoccupied by Her Majesty's remarks, as when he pocketed his winnings he also took some of my spare coins that were still on the table."

"Oh," said the Duc d'Angoulême, "I saw him steal much more than that. . . ."

"My father?" asked Louis XIII.

"I once saw him steal a cloak."

"A cloak . . . ?"

"Though it's true that, at the time, he was still just King of Navarre."

"Very well," said Louis XIII, "tell us about that, Cousin."

"King Henri III was dying in Saint-Cloud, assassinated in the same house where he and Monsieur de Gondy had plotted the Saint Bartholomew's Day massacre, though he was then still just Duc d'Anjou. Anyway, it was the anniversary of the day of the decision, and the King of Navarre was there; it was in his arms that Henri III died, bequeathing him the throne. Navarre's outfit of purple velvet wasn't appropriate for mourning, and he didn't have enough money to buy a black doublet and breeches, so he rolled up the dark mantle of death that covered the king, put it under his arm, and stole away, thinking no one would be paying attention to him. But His Majesty had an excuse—assuming kings need an excuse to steal—as, without that cloak, he wouldn't have been able to mourn properly!"

"And now you complain, Cousin, that you can't afford to pay your servants," said the king, "when you have a room you could rent for four thousand crowns a year to a counterfeiting alchemist."

"Your pardon, Sire," said the Duc d'Angoulême. "It's possible my servants complain that I can't pay them, but I've never complained about it. The last time they came to me to demand their wages, saying they didn't have so much as a silver piece between them, I simply replied, 'This is within your own power to solve, fools that you are. Four dark streets lead to the Hotel d'Angoulême, a perfect setup. Put yourselves to work there.' They took my advice. There have been some complaints lately about robberies in the Rue Pavée, the Rue des Francs-Bourgeois, the Rue Neuve-Sainte-Catherine, and the Rue de la Couture, but those clowns no longer bother me for their wages."

"Yes," said Louis XIII, "and one day I'll hang your clowns from the gate of your hotel."

"If you can get the cardinal's permission, Sire!" laughed the Duc d'Angoulême.

"Gentlemen, let's lard," said the king, furious. And he threw himself on a loin of veal and began to pierce it with no less fury than if his larding needle was a sword and the veal was the cardinal.

"My faith, Louis!" said l'Angely. "I think this time it's you who got larded!"

XXX

As the King Was Larding

It was remarks like these—from his own entourage, even, who spared him nothing—that put the king into a rage against his minister and made him take those sudden and unexpected resolutions that were the bane of the cardinal's policy and patience.

If the enemies of His Eminence took advantage of Louis XIII in one of those moments of fury, he could be persuaded to adopt the most desperate decisions, or make them the most wonderful promises, even if he couldn't keep them.

However, as the bile evoked by the Duc d'Angoulême's words rose in his throat, the king, still stabbing his loin of veal, looked around, seeking someone who would give him a plausible excuse to vent his anger. His eyes fell on his two musicians, who stood on a low dais, one scratching at his lute and the other scraping his viola, with the same ill-temper as the king stabbing his veal.

He noticed something he'd paid no attention to earlier: each was only half-dressed. Molinier wore a doublet but no hose, while Justin, clad in a jerkin and hose, had no doublet.

"Hey!" said Louis XIII. "What is this, a masquerade?"

"Hold on!" said l'Angely. "I've got the answer to that."

"Fool," said the king, "you'd better not disappoint me."

Louis XIII gave privileges to l'Angely granted to no one else. Unlike other kings, when he was alone with his fool, instead of being amused, Louis XIII usually talked with him of death. The king was fascinated by the most morbid and fantastic concepts. L'Angely often accompanied him on his thought-journeys beyond the grave. He was the Horatio to this other Prince of Denmark who was seeking—who can say?—perhaps, like the first, the murderers of his father. Their talks were like Hamlet's conversation with the gravedigger, but far more grave.

In verbal jousts with l'Angely, it was usually the king who eventually gave up and gave in to the jester. This occasion was no different.

"Come," said Louis XIII, "explain yourself, fool!"

"Louis, called Louis the Just because you were born under the sign of Libra, be worthy for once of that name, despite the way my colleague Nogent insulted you earlier. Yesterday, based on who knows what folly, you, King of France and Navarre, pleading poverty, cut the annual salary of these musical wretches in half. However, Sire, people who are paid only half their salaries can only halfway afford to dress. So you see, if you must quarrel with someone about their outfits, quarrel with me, as I was the one who advised them to dress this way."

"The advice of a fool!" said the king.

"Only if it fails them," replied l'Angely.

"Well, then," said the king, "I forgive them."

"Thank His Most Gracious Majesty Louis the Just," said l'Angely. The two musicians stood up and bowed.

"Fine, fine!" said the king. "Enough!"

Then he looked around to see who was properly imitating him in his diversion.

Desnoyers prodded a hare, La Vieuville a pheasant, Nogent a beef tenderloin, while Saint-Simon, who wasn't too proud for it, assailed the plate of bacon. Bassompierre was talking with the Duc de Guise, Baradas was playing with a cup-and-ball, while the Duc d'Angoulême lay back in a chair, sleeping or pretending to sleep.

"What are you saying to the Duc de Guise, Marshal?" asked the king. "It must be very interesting."

"It is to us, yes," replied Bassompierre. "The Duc de Guise is seeking to quarrel with me."

"About what?"

"It seems Monsieur de Vendôme is bored in his prison."

"Good!" said l'Angely. "Though he always seemed equally bored at the Louvre!"

"And so," continued Bassompierre, "he wrote to me."

"To you?"

"He probably thinks I'm in favor."

"And what does my brother of Vendôme want?"

"He wants you to send him one of your pretty pages," said l'Angely.

"Quiet, fool!" said the king.

"He wants to be released from Vincennes to join the Italian campaign."

"Right!" said l'Angely. "Let the Piedmontese watch out if they turn their backs on him."

"And you replied to him?" asked the king.

"Yes, saying it was a waste of time unless he wanted to try asking to join the staff of Monsieur de Guise."

"Why is that?"

"Because Madame de Conti, the duke's sister, is my mistress."

"And how did you respond to that, de Guise?"

"I told him that meant nothing, as all Vendôme's aunts have been my mistresses, and I didn't like him any the better for it."

The king turned. "And you, my cousin of Angoulême, what are you doing?"

"I dream, Sire."

"Of what?"

"Of the war in Piedmont."

"And what do you dream?"

"I dream, Sire, that Your Majesty leads his army on a march into Italy, and on one of the highest rocks in the Alps he finds his name inscribed beside that of Hannibal and Charlemagne. What do you think of my dream, Sire?"

"We approve of this dream," said l'Angely. "See to it that others dream the same way."

"And who commands the troops for me? My brother, or the cardinal?" asked the king.

"Pay attention," said l'Angely. "If it's your brother, he'll command as your subordinate, but if it's the cardinal, he'll be your superior."

"Where the king is," said the Duc de Guise, "no one else commands."

"Right!" said l'Angely. "That's exactly how it was with your father, General Scarface, in the time of King Henri III."

"Which didn't turn out very well for him," said Bassompierre.

"Gentlemen," said the king, "the war in Piedmont is no small affair, and despite the disagreement between me and my mother, it has been decided upon in the King's Council. My Cousin of Angoulême and Monsieur de Guise, I must warn you, the queen mother's party is very much in favor of Monsieur having the command."

"Sire," replied the Duc d'Angoulême, "I say openly and in advance, I believe it should be Monsieur le Cardinal. After his success at La Rochelle, I think it would be doing him a great disservice to deprive him of the command—subordinate to the king, of course."

"That's your opinion?" said the king.

"Yes, Sire."

"Do you know that two years ago, the cardinal wanted to put you in Vincennes, and I was the one who prevented it?"

"Your Majesty was in error."

"How so?"

"If His Eminence wanted to put me in Vincennes, I'm sure I deserved it."

"Profit from the example of your cousin of Angoulême," said l'Angely. "He is a man of experience."

"I presume, Cousin," said the king, "that if I offered you command of the army, your opinion would be different?"

"If my king, whom I respect and must obey, ordered me to take command of the army, I would do so. But if I could, I would take that command and offer it to His Eminence, saying, 'Just give me a subcommand equal to that of Messieurs de Bassompierre, de Belle-garde, de Guise, and de Créqui, and I will be happy.'"

"*Peste!*" said Bassompierre. "Monsieur d'Angoulême, I had no idea you were so modest."

"I am modest in my judgments, Marshal, but proud when I compare myself to others."

"And you, Louis, who would you choose?" asked l'Angely. "The cardinal, Monsieur, or yourself? As for me, as I've told you, I'd pick Monsieur."

"And why is that, fool?"

"Since he was 'ill' all through the Siege of La Rochelle, he should be well rested in time for Italy. Perhaps hot countries suit your brother better than cold countries."

"Not when they're too hot," said Baradas.

"Oh, so you decide to get a word in, then?" said the king.

"Yes, when I have something to say," Baradas replied. "Other-wise, I am silent."

"And why aren't you larding?"

"Because my hands are clean and I don't want to soil them, and because I'm in a good mood and don't want to be in a bad one."

"Well," said Louis XIII, drawing a flask from his pocket, "this will restore your scented hands."

"What's that?"

"Orange-water."

"You know I detest your orange-water."

The king stepped up to Baradas and splashed orange-water on his face. Scarcely had the drops touched the young man when he leaped up, snatched the bottle from the king's hands, and smashed it on the floor.

"See, gentlemen," said the king, turning pale. "What would you do to a page if he was as guilty of such an insult to you as this ruffian has been to me?"

Everyone was quiet. Only Bassompierre was unable to keep his tongue still. "Sire, I would thrash him."

"So, you would thrash me, Monsieur le Maréchal?" Baradas cried. And drawing his sword in the presence of the king, he charged the marshal. The Duc de Guise and the Duc d'Angoulême seized him.

"Monsieur Baradas," said Bassompierre, "as it is forbidden, under penalty of the loss of the offending hand, to draw a sword before the king, for the respect that I owe him I will stand in his place and give you the lesson you've earned. Georges, give me a larding needle."

Taking the small cooking implement from the squire, Bassompierre said, "Release Monsieur Baradas."

They let Baradas go, and, despite the king's cries, he made a furious attack upon the marshal. But the marshal was an old and experienced fencer who, if he'd rarely drawn sword against an enemy, had often sparred with his friends. With perfect form, and without taking so much as a step back, he parried the favorite's every blow, and at the first opportunity thrust the needle into his opponent's shoulder and left it there.

"Take that, little man," he said. "It's better than a thrashing, and you'll remember it longer."

Seeing the blood stain Baradas's sleeve, the king let out a cry. "Monsieur de Bassompierre," he said, "leave me, and never return!"

The marshal took up his hat. "Sire," he said, "will Your Majesty allow me to appeal this judgment?"

"To whom?" asked the king.

"To the king—once he awakes."

And while the king shouted, "Doctor Bouvard! Get Doctor Bouvard," Bassompierre shrugged and went out, waving adieu to the Duc d'Angoulême and the Duc de Guise, while muttering, "Him, the son of Henri IV? Never!"

XXXI

The Shop of Ildefonse Lopez

Our readers may recall from Souscarrières's report to the cardinal that Madame de Fargis and Monsieur de Mirabel, the Spanish Ambassador, had exchanged a letter in Lopez's jewelry store.

But what Souscarrières didn't know was that the jeweler Lopez belonged body and soul to the cardinal, which was very much in his interest, because in his dual capacity as a Muslim and a Jew—he could pass at will for either a Jew or a Mohammedan—he needed a patron who could defend him in the event of an accusation of heresy, despite the care he took to eat pork every day to prove he was a follower of neither Moses nor Mohammed.

And yet, one day, he almost fell afoul of the stupidity of a Master of Requests. He was accused of secretly paying agents on Spain's behalf, so the Master of Requests appeared one day, audited his books, and found the following entry incriminating: "Guadamassil for Señor de Bassompierre."

Lopez, warned that he could be accused of high treason on the basis of this "payment" to Marshal Bassompierre, hastened to consult Madame de Rambouillet who was, along with the lovely Julie, one of his best customers. He begged for her protection, protesting that his only crime was the entry in his ledger that read, "Guadamassil for Señor de Bassompierre."

Madame de Rambouillet called down her husband and told him about the case. He immediately went to the Master of Requests, who was his friend, and asserted Lopez's innocence.

"And yet, my dear Marquis, one thing is clear," said the Master of Requests. "Guadamassil!"

The marquis paused. "Do you speak Spanish?" he asked the court official.

"No."

"Do you know what 'Guadamassil' means?"

"No—but by the name alone, I deem it must be very significant!"

"Well, my dear sir, it means that Monsieur de Bassompierre ordered . . . a Guadamassil tapestry for his wall."

The Master of Requests refused to believe it. The marquis had to bring him a Spanish dictionary so the Master of Requests could see for himself what the word meant.

In fact, Lopez was of Moorish origin; but as the last Moors were expelled from Spain in 1610, Lopez had gone to France to plead for the interests of the fugitives. It was then that he'd become acquainted with the Marquis de Rambouillet, who spoke Spanish.

Lopez was sharp. He advised a Parisian merchants' guild on a fabric shipment to Constantinople, and the enterprise was successful. The merchants cut him in on the profits. With this he bought a diamond in the rough and had it cut, polished, and sold so profitably that soon everyone was sending him their raw diamonds. In no time he was the leading jeweler in Paris, and since he employed the most skilled gem-cutters, all the most beautiful jewels of the era passed through his hands. One of his men was so skilled that he was able to split a flawed diamond into two perfect halves with a single blow.

During the Siege of La Rochelle, the cardinal had sent Lopez to Holland to commission new ships and buy up everything available that could float. While he was there, he acquired a large collection of items from India and China and brought them back to France for sale, thus creating the French market for Oriental bric-a-brac.

By the time he'd finished his sojourn in Holland, he'd made his fortune as an importer, meanwhile covertly completing his mission for the cardinal.

Lopez had also taken note of the coincidence of the simultaneous visits to his shop of the Spanish Ambassador and Madame de Fargis, and his diamond cutter had spotted the exchange of the letter. Thus the cardinal had dual confirmation of this intelligence, which only gave him a greater regard for the efforts of Souscarrières.

The cardinal therefore knew that, when the queen, on the morning of the fourteenth, ordered sedan chairs for guests to be carried to Lopez's shop, it wasn't a sign of a woman who wanted to buy jewelry, but rather of one who wanted to sell a kingdom.

Thus on December 14, at around eleven in the morning, while Monsieur de Bassompierre was planting a larding needle in Baradas's shoulder, the queen was stepping out with Madame de Fargis, Isabelle de Lautrec, Madame de Chevreuse, and Patrocle, her first esquire.

Madame de Bellier, her premier lady-in-waiting, arrived with a covered parrot cage in one hand and a letter in the other.

"Oh, *mon Dieu*, what do you have there?" asked the queen.

"A gift for Your Royal Majesty from Her Highness the Infanta Claire-Eugénie."

"So this comes from Brussels?" the queen asked.

"Yes, Your Majesty—and here is a letter from the princess explaining the gift."

"Let's have a look," said the queen, overcome by feminine curiosity and reaching for the cage's cover.

"Not yet," said Madame de Bellier, drawing back the cage. "Your Majesty must read the letter first."

"And who brought this cage and its letter?"

"Michel Dause, Your Majesty's apothecary. Your Majesty knows that he is our correspondent in Belgium. Here is Her Highness's letter."

The queen took the letter, opened it, and read:

My Dear Niece,
I send you a wonderful parrot which, if you do not frighten

it, you will discover can compliment you in five different languages. It is a good little animal, very sweet and loyal. You will never, I am sure, have reason to complain of it.

Your Devoted Aunt,
Claire-Eugénie

"Ah!" said the queen, "it talks, it talks!"

Immediately, a small voice came from under the cloth that said, in French, "Queen Anne of Austria is the most beautiful princess in the world."

"Ah! How wonderful!" cried the queen. "Now I would like, my dear bird, to hear you speak Spanish."

"*Yo quiero Doña Ana hacer por usted todo para que sus deseos lleguen.*"

"Now in Italian," said the queen. "Do you have something to say to me in Italian?"

The bird didn't delay—immediately they heard the same voice say, in an Italian accent, "*Darei la mia vita per la carissima padrona mia.*"

The queen clapped her hands with joy. "And what are the other languages my parrot speaks?" she asked.

"English and Dutch, Your Majesty," replied Madame de Bellier.

"In English, in English!" said Anne of Austria.

And the parrot, without further ado, immediately said, "*Give me your hand and I shall give you my heart.*"

"Ah!" said the queen. "I didn't quite understand. Do you know English, my dear Isabelle?"

"Yes, Madame."

"What did it mean?"

"The parrot said, 'Give me your hand and I shall give you my heart.'"

"Oh! Bravo!" said the queen. "And now, what was that last language you said it speaks, Bellier?"

"Dutch, Madame."

"Oh, what bad luck!" cried the queen. "None of us here understands Dutch."

"Wait, Your Majesty," said Madame de Fargis. "Beringhen is from Friesland, he knows Dutch."

"Call Beringhen," said the queen. "He should be in the king's antechamber."

Madame de Fargis went and brought back Beringhen. He was a tall and handsome lad, with blond hair and a red beard, half Dutch and half German, though he'd been raised in France. The king was very fond of him, and he was devoted to the king in return. Madame de Fargis came in tugging him by the sleeve; he didn't know what he was wanted for and, faithful to his orders, it was only at the express command of the queen that he left his post in the royal antechamber.

But the parrot was so smart that the moment Beringhen entered, it knew he could speak Dutch, and without waiting for a request for the fifth compliment, it said, *"Och, myne welbeminde koningin, ik bemin u, maar ik u meer in hollandsch, myne liefste geboorte taal."*

"Oh!" Beringhen said, astonished. "This parrot speaks Dutch as if it was from Amsterdam."

"And what did it say to me, if you please, Monsieur de Beringhen?" the queen asked.

"It told Your Majesty, 'Oh, my beloved Queen, I love you, but I love you most of all in Dutch, my dear native language.'"

"Well done!" said the queen. "And now we shall see it! I have no doubt it's as beautiful as it is well-educated." And so saying, she drew back the cloth to reveal what she already suspected: in the cage, instead of a parrot, was a pretty little dwarf woman, barely two feet tall and wearing a Frisian outfit.

She made a nice bow to Her Majesty. She then stepped out of the cage through the door, which was tall enough for her to use without stooping, and made a second bow, even more graceful than the first.

The queen took the dwarf in her arms and kissed her just as she would a child, and in fact, though she was fifteen years old, she was no bigger than a girl of two.

At that moment, someone was heard calling from the corridors, "Monsieur le Premier! Monsieur le Premier!"

According to the custom of the Court, that was the title of the king's Premier Valet de Chambre. Beringhen, who had finished his service to the queen, stepped quickly to the door and met the Second Valet, who was looking for him. Through the open door, the queen could hear the following exchange:

"What is it?"

"The king is asking for Doctor Bouvard."

"*Mon Dieu*!" said the queen. "Has some misfortune happened to His Majesty?" She went to the door to inquire further, but all she saw was the backs of the two valets as they raced off, each in a different direction. "Oh!" she said. "How can I find out what's happened to the king?"

"Is Your Majesty going to see?" asked Mademoiselle de Lautrec.

"I dare not," said the queen. "The king hasn't called for me."

"It's a strange country," murmured Isabelle, "where a worried wife dare not ask about her husband."

"Do you think I should go take a look?" said Madame de Fargis.

"But what if the king is angry?"

"Well, he's not likely to eat me—not King Louis XIII!" Then, approaching the queen, she whispered, "I'll just take a couple of peeks and find out what's happening."

And just like that, she was gone.

Five minutes later, she returned, laughing all the way.

The queen breathed a sigh of relief. "So it was nothing serious, then?"

"Oh, quite serious: there was a duel."

"A duel?" said the queen.

"Yes, in the presence of the king himself."

"Who dared to do that?"

"Monsieur Baradas and Monsieur de Bassompierre. Monsieur Baradas was wounded."

"By a sword?"

"No, a larding needle." And Madame de Fargis, who had assumed a serious look, broke out again into one of those rippling laughs like a string of pearls, a hallmark of those of joyous nature.

"Well, ladies, now that we've been informed," said the queen, "I don't think we should let this accident interfere with our visit to Señor Lopez."

Baradas, handsome though he was, didn't inspire much sympathy in the queen or the ladies of her suite, so nobody had any objection to the queen's proposal.

She set the dwarf in Madame de Bellier's arms and, asking her name, was told it was Gretchen, which means both "Daisy" and "Pearl."

The sedan chairs were waiting at the foot of the Louvre's grand staircase. Each could carry two passengers. The queen went with Madame de Fargis and tiny Gretchen.

Ten minutes later, they were at Lopez's place, which was at the corner of Rue du Mouton and the Place de Grève. When the porters set the queen's chair down in front of Lopez's door, a young man who stood on the threshold, hat in hand, stepped forward to open the chair and offer his arm to the queen.

This young man was the Comte de Moret.

A note from "Cousin Marina" to "Cousin Jacquelino" had apprised him that the queen would be at Lopez's shop from eleven to noon, and he had hastened to be there.

Had he come to greet the queen and salute Madame de Fargis, or to exchange glances with Isabelle? We cannot say—but what we can say is that as soon as he had bowed to the queen and shaken hands with Madame de Fargis, he ran to the chair that followed and offered his arm to Mademoiselle de Lautrec with as much respect as he had paid to the queen.

"Pardon me, Mademoiselle," he said to Isabelle, "for not coming to you first, as my heart desired; but in the presence of the queen, respect must come before all, even love."

And bowing to the young woman, he conducted her to the entourage forming around the queen, and then took a step back before she could answer with anything but a blush.

The attentions of the Comte de Moret were so different from those of other gentlemen, and on the three occasions in which he'd been face-to-face with Isabelle, he had shown her so much love and respect that it was impossible that these meetings could have failed to leave an impression on the girl's heart. She spent the entire time in Lopez's shop standing in a corner, preoccupied, oblivious to the treasures displayed around her.

Once inside, the queen looked around until she spotted the Spanish Ambassador, who was chatting with the diamond cutter, apparently asking the value of some of the stones.

She, for her part, had brought Lopez a beautiful string of pearls, some of which were damaged and needed to be replaced. But the price of replacing the eight or ten damaged pearls was so high that she was reluctant to give Lopez permission to do it.

Madame de Fargis, conversing with the Comte de Moret, had been listening to him with one ear and to the queen with the other. She came over and asked, "Begging your pardon, Your Majesty, but how much are you short of what you need?"

"Look here, my dear," said the queen. "I desire this beautiful crucifix, but this Jew of a Lopez won't sell it to me for less than a thousand *pistoles*."

"Bah!" said Madame de Fargis. "It's quite unreasonable of you, Lopez, to sell this imitation cross for a thousand *pistoles* when your kind paid only thirty silver pieces for the original."

"First of all," said Lopez, "I am not a Jew, I'm a Muslim."

"Jew, Muslim, it's all one to me," said Madame de Fargis.

"And then," continued the queen, "I need a dozen pearls to repair my necklace, and he wants to charge me fifty *pistoles* apiece."

"Is that all you need?" asked Madame de Fargis. "I have seven hundred *pistoles* of yours right here."

"Where is it, my dear?" asked the queen.

"In the pockets of that big dark fellow there, standing by that tapestry from India."

"Ah! Isn't that Particelli?"

"No, Madame, that is Monsieur d'Émery."

"Particelli or d'Émery, does it matter?"

"Only to the king, Madame."

"I don't understand."

"You may not know that when the cardinal appointed Monsieur d'Émery to be the Keeper of the Cutlery, the king said, 'Good, let us have this Monsieur d'Émery in the position as soon as possible.' 'Why is that?' asked the cardinal, astonished. 'Because I'd heard that a rascal named Particelli wanted the post,' said the king. 'Particelli? He was hanged,' said the cardinal. 'I'm glad,' said the king, 'because it's said he was a terrible thief.'"

"Yes, well, so . . . ?" said the queen.

"So," said Madame de Fargis, "you have but to whisper in the ear of Monsieur d'Émery and he will give you your seven hundred *pistoles*."

"But how will I repay him?"

"Simply by not pointing out to the king that d'Émery and Particelli are one and the same."

Madame de Fargis then ran over to d'Émery, who had not noticed the queen, occupied as he was with inspecting some fabrics. But as soon as he saw her, and Madame de Fargis had whispered a few words in his ear, he came over as quickly as his short legs and big belly would allow.

"Now, Your Majesty," said Madame de Fargis, "you remember Monsieur Particelli!"

"D'Émery," said the bursar.

"*Mon Dieu,* of course," said the queen.

"As soon as Monsieur Particelli knew of your embarrassment . . ."

"D'Émery, d'Émery," repeated the bursar.

". . . He offered to open for Your Majesty a line of credit with Monsieur Lopez for twenty thousand *livres.*"

"Twenty thousand *livres!*" cried the little man. "The devil!"

"Do you feel that isn't enough for such a great queen, Monsieur Particelli? Do you think it should be more?"

"D'Émery, d'Émery, d'Émery," he repeated despairingly. "Only too happy to be of assistance to Her Majesty; but in the name of heaven, call me d'Émery."

"Oh, that's right," said Madame de Fargis. "Particelli was hanged, wasn't he?"

"Thank you, Monsieur d'Émery," said the queen. "In truth, you're doing me a genuine service."

"It is I who am obliged to Your Majesty—but I would be very grateful if you were to ask Madame de Fargis, who is quite mistaken, not to call me Particelli."

"Agreed, Monsieur d'Émery, agreed," said Madame de Fargis, "so long as you tell Monsieur Lopez that you're covering the queen for up to twenty thousand *livres.*"

"Yes, yes, but there will be no more talk of Monsieur Particelli, no?"

"No, Monsieur d'Émery! Of course not, Monsieur d'Émery!" said Madame de Fargis, steering him over to Lopez.

Meanwhile, the queen and the Spanish ambassador had exchanged a glance, then gradually moved toward each other. The Comte de Moret was leaning against a pillar and watching Isabelle de Lautrec, who was pretending to play with the dwarf and talk with Madame de Bellier, though she, feeling the burning gaze of Antoine de Bourbon upon her, was unable to play with the one nor converse with the other. Madame de Fargis was ensuring that Her Majesty would have twenty thousand *livres* credit, and d'Émery and Lopez were discussing the terms. Everyone was so busy with their own affairs that no one paid any attention to the ambassador and the queen, who drifted together until they were side by side.

There was a brief exchange of compliments before they passed on to more interesting matters. "Her Majesty has received a letter from Don Gonzalès?" the ambassador asked.

"Yes, by way of the Comte de Moret."

"And Her Majesty read not only the visible lines, written by the Governor of Milan . . ."

". . . But also the invisible lines written by my brother."

"And the queen has considered the advice she was given?"

The queen blushed and looked down.

"Madame," the ambassador said, "there are necessities of State before which even those of the highest rank must bow. If the king died . . ."

"God save us from that misfortune, Monsieur!"

"But—if the king did die . . . what would happen to you?"

"God would decide that."

"We need not leave the decision to God, Madame. Do you trust Gaston's word?"

"That wretch? No!"

"They would send you back to Spain, you know, or confine you in a French convent."

"I do not hide from myself that that would be my fate."

"Could you depend on support from your mother-in-law?"

"Oh, no. She pretends to love me, but I know that beneath it all she hates me."

"Indeed. But if Your Majesty were with child at the time of the king's death, you would be declared regent, and everyone would fall at your feet."

"I know that, Monsieur."

"Well?"

The queen sighed. "But . . . there's no one I love who . . ."

"What you mean is that you still love someone who, unfortunately, it's futile to love."

Anne of Austria wiped away a tear.

"Lopez is looking at us," said the ambassador. "I don't much trust this Lopez. We must part, but first promise me one thing."

"What's that, Monsieur?"

"I ask only this, but I ask it at the behest of your august brother, and on the behalf of both Spain and France."

"What do you want me to promise, Monsieur?"

"That, if the grave circumstances we've discussed come to pass, you will close your eyes and allow yourself to be led by Madame de Fargis."

"You have the queen's promise on that," said Madame de Fargis, appearing between the queen and the ambassador. "I promise it myself, in the name of Her Majesty."

Then she added in a whisper, "Lopez is looking at you—and the diamond cutter has been listening."

"Madame!" said the queen loudly. "It must be two o'clock in the afternoon. We must return to the Louvre for dinner, and to inquire after poor Monsieur Baradas!"

XXXII

Advice from a Jester

As we have seen, King Louis XIII was offended at first by the insolence of his favorite Baradas, when he tore the bottle of orangewater from the king's hands and threw it at his feet. But as soon as he saw the wound inflicted by Monsieur de Bassompierre, spilling the precious blood of his precious Baradas, his anger changed to agony. Throwing himself upon the wounded youth, he drew the larding needle from his shoulder and, against all advice, citing his knowledge of medicine, insisted on treating the wound himself.

But the gifts and privileges Louis XIII had showered on his favorite, reminiscent of the favors Henri III had granted his *mignons,* had turned him into a spoiled child. Baradas pushed the king away, pushed everyone away, vowing he would never forget this insult to himself and to the king. He shouted that justice demanded the Maréchal de Bassompierre must be sent to the Bastille, unless he agreed to a public duel to settle the matter, like the one under Henri II that had ended in the death of La Châtaigneraie.

The king tried to calm him, but Baradas, who might have forgiven a wound from a sword, even from the proud Marshal Bassompierre, couldn't forgive being wounded with a larding needle. He gave the king an ultimatum: nothing would do but either a legal duel in the presence of King and Court, or Bassompierre sent to the Bastille.

Baradas then stalked off to his room, like the majestic Achilles retiring to his tent after Agamemnon refused to give up the lovely Briséis.

This event threw all the larders into disarray, even those who weren't larding. The Duc de Guise and the Duc d'Angoulême, wanting no part of this domestic quarrel, put on their hats, walked to the door, and went out together.

Once the door had closed behind them, the Duc de Guise paused and asked the Duc d'Angoulême, "So, what do you think of that?"

Angoulême shrugged his shoulders. "I say that poor old King Henri III, much maligned though he is, was less dismayed by the deaths of his favorites Quélus, Schomberg, and Maugiron than our good King Louis XIII is by a scratch to Monsieur Baradas."

"Is it possible for a son to be so unlike his father?" said the Duc de Guise in a low voice, glancing around as if looking for an escape route. "My faith, I must admit I preferred King Henri IV, even if he was still a Huguenot at heart."

"You say that now that he's dead; but when he was alive, you detested him."

"He'd done so much damage to our noble house, it was impossible to be friends."

"I can accept that," said the Duc d'Angoulême, "but what I can't accept is this insisting on a similarity between a child and his father. Such a resemblance is not granted to every family. Let's take you, for example, my dear duke," said Angoulême, gently prodding de Guise's arm. "I, who have had the honor of knowing your mother's husband, and the pleasure of knowing you, I dare say, without the slightest malice intended, that there is no resemblance at all between you and him."

"My dear Duke!" said Monsieur de Guise, not quite sure whether Angoulême was mocking him.

"But no!" Angoulême insisted, with that air of bonhomie of which he was a master, so that no one could ever tell whether he was quite serious. "But no! It's obvious enough, *pardieu*. Your late father was large where you are small, had an aquiline nose where yours is snubbed, and had dark eyes where yours are gray."

"Next you'll say he had a scar on his cheek, where I do not!"

"Only because you've never gone to war as he did."

"What!" cried de Guise. "I, never gone to war? And what of La Rochelle, then?"

"That's right, I forgot. You have seen war—from the battlements."

"Duke," said Monsieur de Guise, detaching his arm from Angoulême's, "I think you're having a bad day, and it's time we parted."

"Me, having a bad day? Is that what you think? If I said anything disagreeable, that was certainly not my intention. If you don't look like your father, you must understand that that's just a matter of chance. For example, do I resemble my father, Charles IX, who had red hair and a ruddy complexion? Not a bit. There's no point in getting upset about it—everyone must look like someone. Our king, for example, looks a lot like Virginio Orsini, that cousin of the queen mother who came to France with her. You remember Orsini, don't you? While Monsieur, in turn, looks as much like Concino Concini as one drop of water does to another. You yourself can have no doubt whom you resemble."

"No, I've no idea, and I don't care to know."

"Quite so, you couldn't have known, since six months before your birth he was killed by your uncle Mayenne. Well, you resemble no one so much as the Comte de Saint-Mégrin. Or did you know that already?"

"I am sorry, my dear Duke, but I must warn you to stop there."

"I'm afraid that now you're the one speaking in anger and malice, not I. Did I lose my temper when Monsieur de Bassompierre said I was passing counterfeit money? I did not. I'm afraid it's you who've fallen into a bad mood, not me, and I who should take my leave."

"I believe you're right," said Monsieur de Guise, who strode off down the Rue de l'Arbre Sec, which led to the Rue Saint-Honoré. In fact, he left his caustic interlocutor so rapidly that Angoulême stood there for a moment wearing the astonished look of one surprised not to have gotten the last word. Eventually he walked on toward the Pont Neuf, hoping to find there another victim upon whom he could resume the petty torment he'd inflicted on the Duc de Guise.

Meanwhile, the other courtiers had left one by one, until the king found himself alone with l'Angely. The jester, pleased to find himself in sole possession, planted himself before the king, who was sitting with his head down, melancholy eyes fixed upon the ground.

"Hum!" l'Angely sighed heavily.

Louis raised his head. "Well?" he asked, in the tone of a suffering man who expects sympathy.

"Well!" l'Angely repeated in the same tone.

"What have you to say about Monsieur de Bassompierre?"

"I say," l'Angely replied, in a tone that betrayed a mocking admiration, "that anyone so adept with a larding needle must have been a cook in his youth."

A flash briefly lit the dull eyes of Louis XIII. "L'Angely," he said, "I forbid you to joke about Monsieur Baradas's accident."

L'Angely's face assumed an expression of deepest pain. "Because the Court cannot bear to lose him?"

"One more word, Fool," said the king, rising and stamping his foot, "and I'll thrash you till you bleed."

He began marching around the room in agitation. "I see," said l'Angely, hopping up onto the chair the king had just left. "First your pages misbehave, and who do you threaten to thrash? Me. And now here I am, threatened again. Ah! My colleague Nogent was right: they don't call you Louis the Just for nothing. Plague take it!"

"Oh!" cried Louis XIII, without bothering to reply to his fool's jests, not that he would have known what to say. "I shall have my revenge upon Monsieur de Bassompierre!"

"Did you ever hear the story about the snake who bit a steel saw, and found out he wasn't the only one who had teeth?"

"What do you mean? Are you making excuses for him?"

"I mean, my son, that king though you are, you can't afford to throw away your true friends in order to preserve your false ones. Consider our minister, Richelieu. Though you're the one who's called the Just during your lifetime, it may well be that he will be the one called the Just after his death."

"What?"

"You don't see it that way, Louis? I certainly do. Remember when the cardinal came and told you, 'Sire, while I've been laboring on your behalf and for the glory of France, your brother has been conspiring against me, which is to say against you. He came to my château of Fleury with his entourage in order to dine with me, during which Monsieur de Chalais was to pass his sword through my body. Here's the proof. Ask your brother about it.' So you interrogated your brother. He collapsed in terror, as always, fell at your feet, and confessed to everything. Ah! It was a crime of high treason, and he should have lost his head on the block.

"And now you will go tell Monsieur de Richelieu, 'I went larding, but Baradas wouldn't lard. I tried to make him, but he snatched my orange-water, without any respect for my majesty, and smashed the bottle on the floor. I asked what a page who so insulted his king deserved, and Marshal Bassompierre, a sensible man, replied, "The whip, Sire." Upon which Monsieur Baradas drew his sword and lunged at Monsieur de Bassompierre who, in deference to my majesty, declined to draw his own blade, merely taking a larding needle from the hands of Georges and planting it in Monsieur Baradas's shoulder. I demand, therefore, that Monsieur de Bassompierre be sent to the Bastille.'

"But your minister—whom I will support against everyone, even you—your minister, who is the personification of justice, will say, 'But it is Monsieur de Bassompierre who is in the right. Though I have sent other nobles and even princes to the Bastille, I will not send him. However, I will have your page beaten for having snatched your bottle from your hand, and put in the pillory for drawing his sword in your presence—this, I, your minister, the most important man in France after you—this I will do.' And how will you reply to him, your loyal minister?"

"All I can say is, I love Baradas and hate Monsieur de Richelieu."

"So you can't just be wrong, you have to be wrong twice over: you hate a great man who does everything he can to make you great as well, and you love a little lout who can't advise you as well as Luynes, or even betray you as well as Chalais."

"Didn't you hear his request for a trial by combat? There's a precedent for it, the duel of Jarnac and La Châtaigneraie, under Henri II."

"Sure. But you forget that that was seventy-five years ago, before the edicts against dueling, back when two chivalrous lords like Jarnac and La Châtaigneraie were entitled to draw swords against each other. But since then, by your decree, de Bouteville, a Montmorency no less, has paid with his head for dueling. Just go tell Monsieur de Richelieu that he should let Monsieur Baradas, a king's page, fight a duel against Monsieur de Bassompierre, a Marshal of France, and see where it gets you!"

"But I must allow my poor Baradas some satisfaction, or he'll do what he says he will."

"And what is that?"

"He'll stay in his rooms!"

"Oh, and will the Earth stop rotating because this Monsieur Galileo says it must? No, Sire. Monsieur Baradas is a selfish ingrate just like those before him, and in time he will disgust you as they have. As for me, my son, if I were in your place, I know what I'd do."

"Well, what would you do? Because I must admit, l'Angely, that sometimes you do give me good advice."

"You might even say I'm the only one who does."

"All but the cardinal—you were just talking about him."

"Oh, don't ask him. This isn't his affair."

"But see here, l'Angely—in my place, what *would* you do?"

"If having favorites doesn't make you happy, try having a lover instead."

Louis XIII recoiled, with an expression somewhere between prudishness and repugnance.

"I swear, my son, you don't know what you're missing," said the jester. "A woman is a fine thing, and not to be despised."

"Not the women in this Court!"

"What's wrong with the women of the Court?"

"They're so shameless, it disgusts me."

"Indeed, my son? I hope you're not referring to Madame de Chevreuse."

"Oh, yes! Let's hear you defend Madame de Chevreuse."

"Well," said l'Angely, with the most naïve air in the world, "I understand she is quite clever."

"Huh. Tell that to Milord Henry Rich, and to Châteauneuf. Tell that to the old Archbishop of Tours, Bertrand de Chaux, in whose papers they found a note signing over twenty-five thousand *livres* to Madame de Chevreuse."

"Yes, that's all true—I remember how the queen, who could deny her favorite nothing, asked you for a cardinal's hat for the worthy archbishop. But you refused, and the poor fellow was heard to say, 'If Madame were the king's favorite instead of the queen's, I'd be a cardinal today.' But three lovers, even if one is an archbishop, isn't too many for a woman of twenty-eight who's already had two husbands."

"Oh, that's hardly the complete list! Ask Marillac, ask her knight-gallant Crufft, ask . . ."

"No, that's quite enough," said l'Angely. "I'm far too lazy to speak to so many people. Let's move on. There's Madame de Fargis, though I will admit from the start that she is not exactly a vestal virgin."

"Now I know you're not serious, Fool. Have you seen her with Créqui? And Cramail? And the other Marillac, Keeper of the Seals? Haven't you heard the Latin lyric about her? *'Fargia di mihi sodes, quantas commiosti sordes, inter primas atque laudes, quando'* . . . I can't repeat the rest."

"No, I hadn't heard that!" said l'Angely. "Sing the rest of it, all the way to the ending. I find it enchanting."

"No, I can't," said Louis, blushing. "There are words no proper person can speak."

"Though I see you know it by heart, every syllable. Hypocrite! But let's move on. What do you think of the Princesse de Conti? She is rather mature, but that just means she has more experience."

"After what Bassompierre said, it would be crazy. And after what she's said herself, it would be stupid!"

"I heard what the marshal had to say, but I don't know what she said. Come, my son, give me the whole juicy anecdote—you tell them so well!"

"Well, she said to her brother, who was gambling but losing, 'Perhaps you've played enough, brother.' And he replied, 'I'll give up playing at cards when you give up playing at love.' And the wicked woman didn't even reproach him! . . . Anyway, my conscience wouldn't allow me to speak of love to a married woman."

"Is that why you don't speak of love to the queen? But very well, let's move on to the unmarried ladies. What do you think of the beautiful Isabelle de Lautrec? You can't accuse her of such follies." Louis blushed to the tips of his ears. "Ah-ha!" said l'Angely. "Have I hit the bull's-eye?"

"I have nothing to say against the virtue of Mademoiselle de Lautrec. On the contrary," said Louis XIII, in a voice in which one could discern a slight tremor.

"Against her beauty, then?"

"Even less so."

"Against her wits, perhaps?"

"No, she is quite charming, but . . ."

"But what?"

"I don't know if I should tell you this, l'Angely, but. . . ."

"Come on!"

"I don't think she really likes me very much."

"Well, my son, you have nothing to lose by trying, except some false modesty."

"And the queen—if I listen to your advice, what will she say?"

"If someone is going to hold Mademoiselle de Lautrec's hands, it might as well be you. Anything to get you out of the clutches of these villainous pages and squires."

"But Baradas. . . ."

"Baradas will be jealous as a tiger, and probably try to stab Mademoiselle de Lautrec. But I think he'll find he's only rousing a Joan of Arc. Come on, give it a try!"

"But I'm afraid that Baradas, instead of coming back to me, will just stay angry."

"Well, there's always Saint-Simon."

"Yes, he's a fine lad," said the king, "and when we go hunting, he's the only one who knows how to blow the horn properly."

"You see? There are always consolations."

"So what should I do, l'Angely?"

"You should follow my advice, and the advice of Monsieur de Richelieu. Why, with a minister like him, and a fool like me, within six months you'll be the leading monarch in Europe."

"All right," Louis said with a sigh. "I'll try it."

"Starting when?" asked l'Angely.

"Starting tonight."

"Good! Be a man tonight, and you'll be a king tomorrow."

XXXIII

The Confession

The day after King Louis XIII, on the advice of his fool l'Angely, had resolved to make Monsieur Baradas jealous, Cardinal Richelieu sent Cavois to the Hotel de Montmorency with a letter to the duke, which read as follows:

Monsieur le Duc,

Permit me to employ one of the privileges of my office as minister to express to you my great desire to see you for a serious talk with one of our most distinguished captains about our imminent campaign.

Permit me, in addition, to request that this interview take place in my house in the Place Royale, which is near your hotel, so you need not come far. I hope that our meeting will be to your satisfaction, and that you will keep it a secret between us. If nine o'clock in the morning is convenient for you, it is for me as well.

If you wish company, and it is not inconvenient, please bring your young friend the Comte de Moret, if he will do me the honor, as I have a task worthy of his name and his ancestry.

Believe me, Monsieur le Duc, I am your most sincere and devoted servant.

—Armand, Cardinal de Richelieu

A quarter of an hour after having been charged with delivery of this letter, Cavois returned with the duke's answer. Monsieur de Montmorency had been most receptive and wished to convey to the cardinal that he accepted the invitation and would be there on time, accompanied by the Comte de Moret.

The cardinal seemed quite satisfied with this response. He asked Cavois for news of his wife, and heard with great pleasure that, since during the last eight or ten nights Cavois had been required to work at the Place Royale only two, domestic tranquility reigned in his household. Richelieu then began his usual work.

That evening, the cardinal sent Father Joseph to find out how the wounded Latil was doing. He was healing, but was still unable to leave his room.

The next morning at dawn, the cardinal, as usual, came down to his study, but despite the early hour someone was already waiting for him. A veiled lady, who said she wished to remain incognito, had arrived about ten minutes earlier, and was waiting in the antechamber.

The cardinal employed so many different people as his agents that, rather than try to guess which one of them this might be, he just ordered his valet, Guillemot, to bring her in and make sure no one interrupted their talk. If he wanted anything, he would knock on the wall.

Glancing at the clock, he saw that he still had more than an hour before his appointment with Montmorency, and, thinking this would be plenty of time to deal with the veiled lady, gave no more instructions.

Shortly thereafter Guillemot entered, leading the person he'd mentioned.

She remained standing by the door. The cardinal gestured to Guillemot, who went out and left him alone with his visitor.

As his visitor came further into his study, the cardinal knew at a glance that she was young and of noble birth, despite the veil that covered her face—and also that she seemed intimidated. "Madame," he said, "you wanted an audience with me. Well, here I am—speak." As he said this, he beckoned to her to approach.

The veiled lady stepped forward but faltered a little, supporting herself with one hand on the back of a chair, while with the other she tried to calm the beating of her heart. Meanwhile her head tilted back slightly, as if she was experiencing a spasm of emotion or fear.

The cardinal was too sharp an observer to miss these signs. "From the terror I inspire in you, Madame," he said with a smile, "I am tempted to believe that you come to me from my enemies. Have no fear, of them or of me; for from the moment you enter my house, you are received as the dove was in the Ark."

"I may, in fact, come to you from the camp of your enemies; but if I do, I come as a fugitive. I ask your help as both priest and minister; as a priest I beg you to hear my confession, and as minister I plead for your protection." And the unknown clasped her hands as if in prayer.

"I may certainly hear your confession, even if you remain incognito, but it will be hard to protect you unless I know who you are."

"Since I have your promise to hear my confession, Monseigneur, I have no reason to remain incognito, since the confession puts your lips under sacred seal."

"So," said the cardinal, sitting, "come here, my daughter, and place your trust in me twice over, since you call on me as both priest and minister."

The woman approached the cardinal, knelt beside him, and lifted her veil.

The cardinal knew he wasn't dealing with an everyday penitent and watched her keenly; but when the veil was raised, he couldn't help uttering a low cry of surprise. "Isabelle de Lautrec," he murmured.

"Yes, Monseigneur. Dare I hope that the sight has not changed Your Eminence's good intentions?"

"Not at all, my child," said the cardinal, with a lively gesture. "You come from a family who are loyal servants of France, and are the daughter of a man I respect and admire. I admit that when you first came to the Court of France, I regarded you with some suspicion; but since you have been here, I have nothing but approval for your conduct."

"Thank you, Monseigneur—that restores my confidence. I am here to beg for your aid, for I find myself doubly in danger."

"If it is a prayer that you seek, my child, or advice I can offer you, arise from your knees and sit beside me."

"No, Monseigneur, please allow me to remain as I am. I want what I have to say to retain the character of a confession. Otherwise it may sound more like a denunciation, which is not what I desire."

"Speak, then, my daughter, and I will listen," said the cardinal. "God forbid that I should ignore such strong feelings, even if they should be exaggerated."

"When I was told to stay behind in France, while my father went to Italy with the Duc de Nevers, Monseigneur, he argued his case with two points: First, that the long journey would fatigue me, and only end at a city that might be besieged and sacked. Second, that he had found for me a place near Her Majesty, a position that ought to satisfy any young woman, even one more ambitious than I."

"Go ahead and tell me of the dangers you perceive in this new position of yours."

"Yes, Monseigneur. It seemed to me that there was some uncertainty about my youth and the sincerity of my devotion to my royal mistress. The king, either on his own account or pressed by others' advice, seemed to pay me more attention than I deserved. My respect for His Majesty blinded me at first to the meaning of these attentions, though his shyness always kept him within the bounds of gallant courtesy. However, one day I felt as if I needed to account to the queen for the kind of things the king was saying to me. But to my amazement, the queen just laughed and said, 'It would be quite marvelous, dear child, if the king were to fall in love with you.'

"I thought about her words all night long, and it seemed to me that in my sojourn at Court and my position near the queen, there was more than had appeared at first. The next day, the king redoubled his attentions. That week, he had visited the queen's inner circle three times, something that never happened. This time he approached me directly, and spoke to no one but me. But at the first word he said to me, I bowed and excused myself on the pretext of being indisposed, asking the queen for permission to withdraw.

"Queen Anne seemed to disapprove of my behavior. When I asked her why she was so cool to me, she replied, 'I have nothing against you; I only regret that you seem unable to do for us something that would be of genuine service.' The queen mother was even colder to me than the queen."

"And," asked the cardinal, "did you understand what kind of service the queen had hoped for?"

"I had a vague idea, Monseigneur, and at the realization I felt myself blush to my brows. However, as the queen continued to favor me, I set my qualms aside and have tried to serve her these past months as best I could. But yesterday, Monseigneur, to the amazement of myself and of the two queens, His Majesty, who for weeks had not come near the queen's circle of ladies, unexpectedly showed up, and for once he was smiling. He greeted his wife, kissed his mother's hand, and walked straight up to me. The queen has allowed me to sit in her presence, but at the sight of the king I stood up. But he made me sit down again and, while playing with Gretchen, the dwarf who'd been sent to the queen by her niece, the Infanta Claire-Eugénie, the king spoke to me. He inquired after my health, and told me that the next time he invited the queens to join him in a hunt, he would like me to accompany them.

"These attentions from the king to a woman were so extraordinary that I felt all eyes were upon me, and I blushed more fiercely than ever. I don't know what I said to His Majesty—or, rather, I didn't say anything, just stammered disconnected words. I tried to get up. The king held me by the hand. I felt paralyzed on my chair. To hide my embarrassment, I took little Gretchen in my arms. But to do that, I had to look up, and when he saw my face, he said, 'Why are you crying?' And I realized that tears were flowing silently from my eyes and rolling down my cheeks.

"I don't know what meaning the king gave to my tears, but he stroked my hand and gave a bonbon to the dwarf, who took it with a wicked laugh, and then she slid from my arms and went to whisper to the queen. I felt I had no one to turn to; I didn't dare to get up and I didn't dare to stay. It was unbearable—I felt the blood roaring in my ears, my temples throbbed, the furniture seemed to tremble and the walls to sway. My senses left me, and I fainted.

"When I came to myself, I was lying on my bed, with Madame de Fargis near at hand."

"Madame de Fargis," repeated the cardinal, with a smile.

"Yes, Monseigneur."

"Go on, my child."

"I ask nothing more. For what she told me was so astounding, her knowing congratulations were so humiliating, her suggestive advice so strange and unforeseen, that I hardly know how to describe them to Your Eminence."

"Yes," said the cardinal. "She told you the king was in love with you, did she not? She congratulated you for accomplishing a miracle that even the queen could not, and encouraged you to return His Majesty's love as best you could, so that once you were within his good graces you could replace his sulky favorites and apply your newfound influence to serve the political interests of my enemies."

"Your name was not mentioned, Monseigneur."

"No, it wouldn't be, not at first. But otherwise I guessed what she told you, did I not?"

"Almost word for word, Monseigneur!"

"And how did you reply?"

"I didn't. All the vague premonitions of evil I'd felt when the king was first paying me his attentions were coming true. They wanted to make a political tool out of me. I started to cry and couldn't stop. The queen came in and hugged and kissed me, but this embrace, instead of consoling me, froze me to the heart. It seemed to me that such a kiss must hide a secret poison, a kiss given from a queen to encourage a girl to love and desire her own husband!

"The queen took Madame de Fargis aside and exchanged a few quiet words with her, and then said, 'Good night, dear Isabelle. You can believe everything Fargis says, especially when she assures you of the appreciation we shall have for your devotion.' And she left the room.

"Madame de Fargis remained. She told me that I was free to do what I wanted—in other words, free to love the king. She spoke for a long time while I remained silent, trying to make me understand that it was a good thing to have won the king's love and would all be for the best. No doubt she thought she had me convinced, for finally she kissed me in her turn and left. But no sooner had she closed the door behind her than my mind was made up: I would come to you, Monseigneur, to throw myself at your feet and tell you everything."

"What you have told me, my child," said the cardinal, "is no more than the story of your fears. These fears are neither a sin nor a crime, but, on the contrary, proof of your innocence and your loyalty, so I don't see why you need to come to me on your knees and tell your story in the form of a confession."

"But I haven't told you everything, Monseigneur. This antipathy, or rather this fear the king inspires in me, is not something I feel toward all men. My only hesitation in coming to you, Your

Eminence, is not that I must tell you 'The king loves me,' but rather that I must say 'Monseigneur, I fear because I love another.'"

"And this other, is it a crime to love him?"

"No, Monseigneur—but it is . . . dangerous."

"Dangerous? Why? At your age, both society and nature agree that it's the purpose of a woman to love and to be loved."

"But not when she fears that her love is above her in rank and in birth."

"Your birth, my child, is quite good, and your family name, though it doesn't shine with the luster it did a hundred years ago, is still on par with the finest names in France."

"Monseigneur, Monseigneur, don't encourage me in a foolish and dangerous hope!"

"Do you fear the one you love does not love you?"

"On the contrary, Monseigneur, I believe he does love me . . . and that's what frightens me."

"You believe in this love?"

"I have confessed it to you."

"And now that your confession is made, you said you had a plea for me."

"A prayer, rather, Monseigneur: the king's love has put me in a position where, even if he doesn't pursue it, I will be pressured into returning it. And while I may manage to put them off for a while, at some point they'll see that I'm not going to do what they wish, and then . . . My prayer, Monseigneur, is that you will send me to join my father. However dangerous it is there, it is less dangerous for me than here."

"If I were dealing with a heart less pure and less noble than yours, I would join with those who aren't afraid to tarnish your purity and break your heart—I too would say, let this king, who has never loved anything in the world, fall in love with you, and maybe, in time, you will love him in return. I would say, pretend to be the tool of these women who conspire at the humiliation of France, while working for her greatness as my secret ally. But you are not made for such intrigues. If you want to leave France, you shall go. If you want to join your father, I will give you the means to do so."

"Oh! Thank you!" the girl cried, seizing the cardinal's hand and covering it with kisses before the cardinal could do anything to resist.

"The road you choose will not be without danger."

"For me, Monseigneur, the real dangers are at this Court, where I feel threatened by mysterious and unknown perils, where I feel as if the ground trembles beneath me as I walk, and where I fear I shall lose the innocence in my heart and the purity of my thoughts. Keep me from these queens who conspire, these princes who pretend love they do not feel, these scheming courtiers who advise women to do impossible things as if they were easy and natural, these regal voices that promise to reward shame with honor. Save me from all this, Monseigneur, so that I may keep what the Lord has given me honest and pure, and I will be forever grateful."

"I am unable to refuse one who makes me such a plea as that. Rise. Everything will be ready for you within the hour—at least, there will be nothing to prevent you from leaving."

"Am I absolved, Monseigneur?"

"One who is not at fault needs no absolution."

"Bless me, at least, and your blessing will ease my troubled heart."

"The hands I extend to you, my child, soiled as they are with politics and worldly concerns, are less pure than your heart, troubled though it is. It is up to God to bless you, not to me, and I pray that he will bless you with his supreme goodness rather than my poor reverence."

At this, the clock struck nine. Richelieu went to his desk, rang a bell, and Guillemot stepped in. "Have the people I was expecting arrived yet?" the cardinal asked.

"This very moment. The duke is in the portrait gallery."

"Alone or accompanied?"

"With a young man."

"Mademoiselle," said the cardinal, "before answering you fully, or at least in more detail, I need to speak with the two people who have just arrived. Guillemot, escort Mademoiselle de Lautrec to my niece's house, and return in half an hour to see if I'm free."

And, bowing respectfully to Mademoiselle de Lautrec, who followed his footman out, he opened the door to the portrait gallery where he'd kept waiting, albeit briefly, the Duc de Montmorency and the Comte de Moret.

XXXIV

In Which Cardinal Richelieu Writes a Comedy
Without the Help of His Collaborators

The two princes had been waiting only a moment, and as they were aware of the cardinal's many responsibilities and how much his time was in demand, they would have been willing to wait considerably longer before taking offense. Though he hadn't yet reached the heights of power he would command after the famous event that history would call the Day of Dupes, the cardinal was already regarded, in fact if not officially, as the prime minister. This was especially true in matters of peace and war, where his opinion and the weight of his genius were eternally opposed by the hatred of the two queens and their allies on the Council of State, who met at the queen mother's Luxembourg Palace under the leadership of Cardinal Bérulle. When the two sides could not agree, the king intervened, approving or disapproving. This approval sometimes favored Richelieu and sometimes the queen mother, depending on the mood of King Louis XIII.

The critical matter to be decided in the next two or three days was not whether to go to war in Italy—that had already been decided on—but who would command the army. It was this important issue as regarded the two princes that the cardinal had in mind when he had written to ask the Duc de Montmorency to visit him, along with the Comte de Moret; but his interview with Isabelle de Lautrec had caused him to alter his intentions for the count.

This was the first time Montmorency had come face to face with Richelieu since the execution of his cousin, the duelist Bouteville, but we have seen that the noble Governor of Languedoc had taken the first step toward a reconciliation at Princesse Marie de Gonzague's soirée, where he had approached Madame de Combalet, who hadn't failed to report such an honor to her uncle. The cardinal was too wise a politician not to recognize that this show of respect for the niece was a message to the uncle, and that the prince was making an overture of peace.

As for the Comte de Moret, that was something else. This young man, so forthright, so French in character though surrounded by Italians and Spaniards, only twenty-two yet already known for his courage, was someone the cardinal wanted to conciliate, protect, and encourage—especially since he was the only son of Henri IV who had never openly conspired against him. The Comte de Moret, away from court intrigues, honored with a command in the army, serving France and the policies of the Duc de Richelieu, would be a counterweight against his half-brothers the Vendômes, who were in prison for conspiring against the cardinal.

In the cardinal's opinion, it was high time the young prince was taken in hand. Embroiled in the intrigues of Queen Anne and the queen mother, or taken as a lover by Madame de Fargis or Madame de Chevreuse, he would soon be bound too tightly to escape, even if he wished to do so.

The cardinal offered his hand to Monsieur de Montmorency, who accepted it and shook it sincerely, but he did not allow himself such familiarity with the Comte de Moret, who was of royal blood, and bowed almost as if he was before Monsieur.

After the initial exchange of compliments, the cardinal said, "Duke, when it came to war at La Rochelle, I wanted sole command of the naval campaign, so I purchased the title of Admiral of France from you and paid the price you requested. Today, I'm not here to sell you something, but to give you better than I've taken."

"His Eminence believes," said the duke with his most gracious smile, "that when it comes to service and the good of the State, to ensure my dedication it would be best to start with a promise?"

"No, Monsieur le Duc, I know that no one is more generous than you with your energy and blood. And it is because I recognize your courage and loyalty that I speak to you so directly."

Montmorency bowed.

"When your father died, though you were heir to his fortune and his titles, there was one charge you could not inherit because of your extreme youth: that of Constable of France. The *fleur de lys* sword cannot be borne by a child. Moreover, there was a strong arm already available to take it and wield it faithfully, that of the Seigneur de Lesdiguières. He was appointed constable, and retired only when he reached the age of eighty-five. Since then his son, Marshal Créqui, has aspired to replace him. But the sword of the constable is no family heirloom. This year, Monsieur de Créqui had his chance at conquest when he was offered the command of the expedition formerly led by the Duc de Nevers, but instead he declared for the queen mother, against me and against France. While I live, he will never be constable!"

The Duc de Montmorency could not contain his gasp of pure joy, an evidence of his satisfaction that did not escape the cardinal's notice. Richelieu continued, "The dedication I failed to find in Marshal Créqui I expect to find in you, Prince. Your relationship with the queen mother must not influence your love for France, because, make no mistake about it, the result of this war in Italy is crucial to the power and standing of France."

The Comte de Moret appeared to be listening attentively, so the cardinal turned to him. "You do well to pay heed, my young prince, for no one should love our France more than you, that France for which your august father gave everything, even his life."

And then, as he could see that the Duc de Montmorency eagerly awaited the conclusion of his speech, he said, "To get to the point, with the same frankness and honesty I hope for in return, if I am granted responsibility for the conduct of this war, you, my dear Duke, will have the main command of the army. And if, when the siege of Casale is lifted, you are the first one through the gate, you will find behind that door the sword of the constable, which will thus be borne by your family for the third time. If you wish to pass that sword on to someone else, you may, but I want you to bear it, and I offer it freely. Reflect on that, Monsieur le Duc."

"Your hand, Monseigneur," said Montmorency. The cardinal held out his hand. "In the name of France, Monseigneur, be my liege and accept my service. I swear to obey Your Eminence in every respect, except where it would compromise the honor of my name."

"I am no prince to be a liege, Monsieur le Duc," said Richelieu with supreme dignity, "but I am a gentleman. Rest assured, I would never ask a Montmorency to do anything he would be ashamed of."

"When do we move, Monseigneur?"

"As soon as we can, Monsieur le Duc. Assuming the direction of the war is entrusted to me, I expect to take the field at the beginning of next month."

"Then there is no time to lose, Monseigneur. I shall depart for my province this evening, and on the tenth of January I will be in Lyon with a hundred gentlemen and five hundred cavalry."

"But shouldn't you consider that someone else might be put in charge of directing the war?" said the cardinal. "What would you do if that happened?"

"No one but Your Eminence deserves to lead this enterprise, and I will obey no one but you and His Majesty Louis XIII."

"Go, then, Prince. And know that I fully expect you to earn the constable's sword."

"Shall I take my young friend the Comte de Moret with me?"

"No, Monsieur le Duc. I have a particular mission in mind to offer Monsieur le Comte de Moret. If he turns me down, he will be free to join you. I intend to propose a mission to him that will require courage, a steady hand, and the dedication of those who accompany him."

The duke and the Comte de Moret exchanged a few words in voices too low for the cardinal to hear, and Moret said to the duke, "Lend me Galaor."

Then, with joy in his heart, the duke seized the cardinal's hand, gripped it gratefully, and rushed from the study.

Left alone with the Comte de Moret, the cardinal approached him and said, with respect and warmth, "Count, given my position and my age, which is twice yours, I hope you will pardon me when I say that of all King Henri's children, you are the only one who truly resembles him, and I hope to love the son as I loved the father."

The young prince was facing Richelieu for the first time, hearing for the first time that voice against which everyone had warned him, and he was astonished at how that stern face could brighten with warmth, and how that commanding voice could soften.

"Monseigneur," he replied, with a laugh edged with emotion, "Your Eminence is very good to concern himself with a young fool whose only thought is to amuse himself as best he can, and who, if asked how he might do better, wouldn't know what to say."

"A true son of Henri IV is good at everything, Monsieur," said the cardinal, "because with that blood comes courage and intelligence. And that is why I cannot stand idly by and watch you go wrong, falling prey to the dangers that surround you."

"Me, Monseigneur?" said the young man, surprised. "What are these dangers, and in what way might I go wrong?"

"Will you grant me a few minutes of your attention, Monsieur le Comte? And for those few minutes, will you listen to me seriously?"

"At my age and with my heritage, Monseigneur, that is my duty, even if you weren't a minister of state and a man of genius. So I will listen to you—perhaps not seriously, but definitely with respect."

"You arrived in Paris at the end of November—on the 28th, I believe."

"The 28th, yes, Monseigneur."

"You came bearing letters from Milan and Piedmont for Queen Marie de Médicis, for Queen Anne of Austria, and for Monsieur."

The count stared at the cardinal, astonished and uncertain how to answer. But finally, faced by the truth and the brilliant man who spoke it, he said, "Yes, Monseigneur."

"But as the two queens and Monsieur had gone to meet the king, you were obliged to wait in Paris for a week. Rather than remain idle, you wooed Madame de la Montagne, the sister of Marion Delorme. Young, handsome, wealthy, and the son of a king, you didn't have too long to wait; within two days you were her lover."

"So is that the wrong track you worry about, and the danger from which you'd protect me?" laughed the Comte de Moret, surprised that an important minister would concern himself with such trivia.

"No, Monsieur—we're getting to it. No, I would hardly call taking a courtesan's sister as a lover a dangerous diversion, though it was not entirely free of peril. That madman Pisany thought you were Madame de Maugiron's lover, and wanted to murder you out of jealousy. Fortunately, his chosen assassin turned out to be more honest than heinous and, faithful to the memory of the great king, refused to lay a hand on his son. In the end he was a victim of his honesty; you saw him yourself, lying on a table and making his dying confession to a Capuchin."

"Did I? And just exactly when was it," said the Comte de Moret, hoping to embarrass Richelieu, "that I witnessed this painful spectacle?"

"December 5, at about six in the evening, in the common room of the Inn of the Painted Beard. Disguised as a Basque gentleman, you had just left Madame de Fargis who, herself disguised as a Catalan, had instructed you to meet with Queen Anne of Austria, Queen Marie de Médicis, and Monsieur at the Louvre between eleven o'clock and midnight."

"My faith, Monseigneur! I have to admit the reputation of your police is entirely justified."

"You are kind, Count. Now, do you think I went to the trouble to gather such information because I was worried you might become a threat to me?"

"I don't know. It seems Your Eminence has taken a great deal of interest in me."

"A great deal, Count. I wanted to save the son of Henri IV from becoming a threat to himself."

"How so, Monseigneur?"

"The fact that Queen Marie de Médicis, who is Italian and Austrian, and Queen Anne, who is Austrian and Spanish, conspire against France is a crime—but family ties often outweigh even the duties of a crown. But to have the Comte de Moret, son of a Frenchwoman and of the most French king who ever lived, conspire with those two queens on the behalf of Spain and Austria, that I must prevent—by persuasion and prayer if possible, but by force if necessary."

"Who told you I was conspiring, Monseigneur?"

"So far you have not conspired, Count, possibly thanks to your inborn noble instincts. And what these instincts should be telling you is that, as the son of Henri IV, who dedicated his life to opposing domination of France by Spain and Austria, you should not be serving their cause at the expense of the interests of France. Son of Henri IV, your father was murdered by Austria and Spain—do not sink so low as to ally with his assassins!"

"But why does Your Eminence say this to me instead of to Monsieur?"

"Monsieur has nothing to do with it—he is the son of Concini, not of Henri IV."

"Monsieur le Cardinal, consider what you're saying!"

"Yes, I know I risk the wrath of the queen mother, the wrath of Monsieur, even the wrath of the king, if the Comte de Moret leaves here determined to do me ill. But I prefer to think the Comte de Moret will be grateful for my concern, which has no source other than the great love and admiration I had for the king his father. I think, rather, that the Comte de Moret will keep what I say to himself, for his sake and for the sake of France."

"Is Your Eminence asking me to give him my word?"

"We do not ask for such things from the son of Henri IV."

"But Your Eminence didn't invite me here just to give me advice. I believe I heard something about entrusting me with a mission."

"Yes, Count, a mission that will take you far away from the dangers I fear."

"So you wish me to put this danger behind me?"

Richelieu nodded.

"And therefore I am to leave Paris?"

"I would have you return to Italy."

"Hmph!" said the Comte de Moret.

"Is there some reason why you don't wish to return to Italy?"

"No, I would just rather stay in Paris."

"So you refuse, Monsieur le Comte?"

"No, not completely—not if the mission can be delayed."

"You must leave tonight; tomorrow, at the latest."

"Impossible, Monseigneur," said the Comte de Moret, shaking his head.

"What?" cried the cardinal. "France goes to war, and you decline to take part?"

"Not at all. But I intend not to leave Paris until the last possible moment."

"This is your firm resolve, Monsieur le Comte?"

"It is my firm resolve, Monseigneur."

"Your reluctance to leave is a sad blow to me. I was counting on your courage, your devotion, and your nobility in acting as escort for a young lady, the daughter of a man for whom I have the highest regard. I'm afraid I'll just have to look elsewhere for someone willing to safeguard the travels of Mademoiselle Isabelle de Lautrec."

"Isabelle de Lautrec!" cried the Comte de Moret. "It's Isabelle de Lautrec you wish escorted back to her father?"

"Her very self. Why? Does that name surprise you?"

"Oh, pardon, Monseigneur, pardon!"

"No, don't worry about it, Count. I'm sure I can find her another escort."

"No, no, Monseigneur, look no further—the escort, the protector, the defender to the death of Mademoiselle de Lautrec is here before you! It is me, Monseigneur! It is me."

"Oh?" said the cardinal. "So you'll do it, then? I have nothing to worry about?"

"Nothing, Monseigneur!"

"You accept this charge?"

"I accept!"

"Well. In that case, here are my instructions."

"I am listening."

"I place in your charge Mademoiselle de Lautrec who, during the course of this journey, you will hold as safe and sacred as if she were your sister. . . ."

"I swear it!"

". . . And conduct her to her father, who is in Mantua. Then you will return to join the army and take a command under the orders of Monsieur de Montmorency."

"Yes, Monseigneur."

"And if it should happen—for you understand, a man of foresight must take everything into account—if it should happen that you should fall in love . . ."

The Comte de Moret started.

"Just supposing, you understand, because such things have been known to happen. Well, if that occurs, understand there is nothing I can do for you, Monsieur, who are the son of a king—but there's a lot I can do for Mademoiselle de Lautrec and her father."

"You can make me the happiest of men, Monseigneur. For I already love Mademoiselle de Lautrec."

"Do you indeed? How are we to account for this? Is it, perhaps, that you came secretly to the Louvre one night, and were conducted up the back stair by Madame de Chevreuse disguised as a page, who admitted you to a dark corridor that led you to the queen's chambers, where you met a certain someone? Could that be it? Why, what a miraculous coincidence!"

"Monseigneur," said the Comte de Moret, regarding the cardinal with wonder, "my admiration for you almost matches my gratitude! But . . ." The count paused, worried.

"But what?" asked the cardinal.

"There's just one thing I'm anxious about."

"What's that?"

"I love Mademoiselle de Lautrec, but . . . I don't know if Mademoiselle de Lautrec loves me. I don't know if, despite my devotion, she'll accept me as her escort."

"Well, Monsieur le Comte, it seems to me that that part is up to you."

"But how? I don't see how I'll have a chance to make sure, if this departure, as Your Eminence says, must take place tonight, or tomorrow morning at the latest. How is this going to work out?"

"You're quite right, Monsieur le Comte, there must be an interview between the two of you as soon as possible. However, I have other things to attend to. Please wait here for a moment, as I must issue some instructions that cannot wait."

The Comte de Moret bowed, his eyes following this man in admiration mingled with astonishment, this man who manipulated all Europe from this study, and who, despite the threats that surrounded him, nonetheless found time to pay attention to the smallest of details.

The door closed behind the cardinal. The Comte de Moret remained behind, his eyes fixed on the portal until it opened again—and he saw in its frame not just the cardinal, but Mademoiselle de Lautrec herself.

The two lovers, simultaneously struck as if by an electric shock, gasped in astonishment. Then, with the rapidity of thought, the Comte de Moret darted to Isabelle, fell to his knees before her, seized her hand, and kissed it with such passion that the young woman knew she had found, not a dangerous heartbreaker, but an ardent admirer.

Meanwhile the cardinal, who had achieved his goal of prying the son of Henri IV away from the Court and making him an ally, celebrated the victorious conclusion to a heroic comedy written without the help of his usual collaborators, Messieurs Desmarests, Rotrou, L'Estoile, and Mairet.

(Corneille, it will be remembered, had not yet had the honor of being presented to the cardinal.)

XXXV

The King's Council

The next big event, anxiously awaited by all—especially Richelieu, who was as sure of the king as anyone could be of Louis XIII—was a meeting of the King's Council. This was to be held at the queen mother's Luxembourg Palace, which had been built during her regency on the model of the palaces of Florence, and which contained the gallery of paintings Rubens had done ten years before, those magnificent works depicting the most important events in the life of Marie de Médicis, and which are now among the principal ornaments of the gallery of the Louvre.

This event was to be held that evening.

The council was primarily composed of the creatures of Queen Marie de Médicis. It was chaired by Cardinal Bérulle but conducted by Vautier, and included Maréchal de Marillac, who had been made a marshal without ever having been in a battle, and who the cardinal, in his memoirs, always referred to as Marillac the Sword, since his duel at the tennis courts with one Caboche, whom he'd killed before he had a chance to defend himself. The other member of the council was the Sword's elder brother, Michel de Marillac, Minister of Justice and Keeper of the Seals, who was one of Madame de Fargis's lovers.

When meeting on important matters, the King's Council was augmented by some others our readers already know, namely the Duc d'Angoulême, the Duc de Guise, the Duc de Bellegarde, and Marshal Bassompierre.

Monsieur, also, had returned to the council, as it was now some time since his disgrace in the Chalais conspiracy. The king attended whenever there was a decision before the council important enough to require his presence. The council's decisions had to be ratified by the king, who could approve, disapprove, or even completely change whatever it resolved.

Cardinal Richelieu, who was prime minister in practice if not yet in name, and who was to gain absolute power in later years, was at this point just one more voice in the council, though he was usually able to persuade the king to adopt his position, supported by the Marillacs, the Duc de Guise, the Duc d'Angoulême, and sometimes Marshal Bassompierre. He was consistently opposed by the queen mother, Vautier, Cardinal Bérulle, and two or three others who took their cues from Marie de Médicis.

This evening, Monsieur, on the pretext of his pretended quarrel with the queen mother, had sent word that he would not attend the council, though he knew that despite his absence, his mother would look out for his interests.

The King's Council was scheduled to begin at eight o'clock. By a quarter past eight, everyone summoned was in attendance, standing behind their chairs and waiting for the queen mother to take her seat.

At half past eight, the king arrived. He saluted his mother, who rose to greet him, kissed her hand, and then sat beside her on a chair slightly higher than hers. Then he pronounced the traditional words, "You may take your seats, Messieurs."

The ministers and the honorary councilors all sat in the chairs provided for them around the table, one for each member.

The king slowly looked around at everyone present, then said, in the same flat and melancholy tone in which he said everything, "I do not see my brother Monsieur. Where is he?"

"He has disobeyed your orders, so doubtless he dares not appear before Your Majesty," said Vautier. "Is it your pleasure that we proceed without him?"

The king nodded. Then, addressing both the ministers and the honorary members, he said, "Messieurs, you all know why we are here today. We are considering whether we shall raise the siege of Casale and rescue Mantua in the name of the claims of the Duc de Nevers—claims we have affirmed and supported—and oppose the schemes of the Duke of Savoy in Montferrat. Although the right to declare war and peace is a royal right, we wish to hear your opinions in the hope they will cast some light on the matter before we make our decision, while reserving the right to make that decision regardless of your advice. I call upon our minister, Cardinal Richelieu, to summarize the state of affairs."

Richelieu rose, bowed to the king and the queen mother, and said, "I will keep this brief. In his dying statement, Vincent de Gonzague, the Duke of Mantua, bequeathed all his rights to the Duchy of Mantua to the Duc de Nevers, who was his closest relative since he had no male heir. The Duke of Savoy had hoped to marry his son to Gonzague's daughter, who as heiress to Mantua and Montferrat would thus augment his domain and make him a power in Italy. It is that ambition that has so often led him to betray his promises to France. This minister of His Majesty Louis XIII thinks it good policy to support Nevers, as placing a Frenchman on the thrones of Mantua and Montferrat will give us a position of strength in Lombardy. There, in between the Pope and the Venetians, we will be able to offset the power of Spain and Austria and neutralize their influence in northern Italy.

"The recent actions of this servant to His Majesty have been in service to this policy. It was to prepare the way for this Italian campaign that we sent a preliminary force south several months ago. That army, under the command of Marshal Créqui, was defeated, not by the Duke of Savoy, as the enemies of France have been quick to declare, but by incompetence almost amounting to treason, as our infantry and knights, unfed and unsupplied, deserted in the face of starvation.

"However, our policy is unchanged, and we have only been awaiting a favorable opportunity to continue the campaign. This minister of His Majesty believes that that time has come. With La Rochelle taken, our army and fleet are freed up for new commitments. The question before Your Majesty is, do we act now, or do we wait? This minister believes we should proceed with the war immediately, and I am ready to respond to any and all objections."

And then, bowing to the king and to Queen Marie, the cardinal resumed his seat, leaving the floor to his opponents—or rather his only opponent, Cardinal Bérulle.

The latter, in his turn, knowing that this was his cue to respond, glanced at the queen mother. She replied with a small gesture, at which he rose, bowed to Their Majesties, and said, "This project of pursuing a war in Italy, despite the apparent good reasons put forth by Cardinal Richelieu, seems upon closer inspection not only dangerous, but outright impossible. Germany is now nearly subdued, which provides the Emperor Ferdinand with far more armies than France can muster. Moreover His Majesty Philip IV, the august brother of the queen, has from the mines of the New World sufficient treasure to raise more armies than even the ancient kings of Persia.

"Instead of meddling in Italy, the Emperor is certain to devote his efforts to further suppression of the unruly Protestants, to recover the bishoprics, monasteries, and other Church property they have unjustly seized. Why should France, the eldest daughter of the Church, oppose such a noble and Christian pursuit? Wouldn't it be better for the king to emulate this policy and devote our efforts to eradicating heresy within our own borders, while the Emperor and the King of Spain do the same within the borders of Germany and the Netherlands? And yet, in direct opposition to such pious efforts, Monsieur de Richelieu proposes peace with England and an alliance with heretical powers, acts which can only tarnish His Majesty's glory. Instead of making peace with England, should we not, while we have the chance, continue our war against Charles I and stop his persecution of English Catholics? Must France forget how the ladies and servants of Queen Henriette were driven from her, in violation of a solemn treaty? Will not the Lord reward the restoration of the true religion in England, as well as the expungement of heresy in France, Germany, and the Netherlands? In the sincere belief that I speak in the interests of France and throne, I place my humble opinion at Their Majesties' feet."

And Cardinal Bérulle sat in his turn, after acknowledging the supporting nods of those in Queen Marie's faction, including that of Keeper of the Seals Marillac, brought into the fold thanks to Madame de Fargis.

The king then turned to Cardinal Richelieu. "You hear, Monsieur le Cardinal?" he asked. "If you have a response, respond."

Richelieu rose. "I think my honorable colleague, Monsieur le Cardinal de Bérulle," he said, "is misinformed about both the political situation in Germany and the financial condition of Spain. The armies of the Emperor Ferdinand, though formidable, are not yet in command of Germany. And this minister of His Majesty knows that some of these Imperial armies of which Cardinal Bérulle speaks really owe their allegiance to Maximilian, Duke of Bavaria and head of the Catholic League. Rather than siding with the emperor, we should press the lion of the north, the great Gustavus Adolphus, to move against him. A few hundred thousand *livres* in bright, shining gold are all it will take to persuade him. Between the Protestant forces of Gustavus Adolphus and the Catholic forces of Maximilian, Ferdinand's armies will have plenty to keep them occupied.

"As to the imaginary treasures of King Philip IV, allow this minister to clarify their true value. The King of Spain takes in just five hundred thousand crowns per year from the West Indies, and two months ago the Council of Madrid was quite dismayed to learn that

Admiral Hein of the Netherlands took and sank the Spanish treasure fleet from South America in the Gulf of Mexico, a loss of twelve million crowns. This was such a disaster that His Majesty the King of Spain found himself unable to send the Emperor Ferdinand the million in gold he had promised.

"Now, to address the second part of my colleague's discourse, this minister will humbly observe that His Majesty cannot submit with honor to the eviction of the rightful Duke of Mantua, whom we have not only recognized, but who was named heir thanks to the persuasive influence of our ambassador, Monsieur de Saint-Chamont, upon the late and former duke.

"His Majesty must not only come to the aid of his allies in Italy, but also protect that lovely European country from the schemes of Spain, who intends to subdue it forever, increasing its power where it is already too powerful. If we do not strongly support the Duke of Mantua, he will be unable to resist the power of Spain, and will be forced to become just one more tributary to the Court of Spain. Furthermore, don't forget that the late Duke Vincent was about to commit Montferrat to us as well, in order to spite Charles-Emmanuel and confound the plots of Savoy.

"Finally, it is the opinion of this minister of the crown that it is our duty to punish the temerity of the Duke of Savoy, who has opposed our interests for the past thirty years. If he is not called to account for his numberless intrigues against us, including his involvement in the conspiracies of Chalais and Biron, and his alliance with the English in their trespasses at the Island of Ré and at La Rochelle, it will be to France's eternal shame."

Then, turning to the king and addressing him directly, the cardinal said, "By taking the rebellious city of La Rochelle, Sire, you not only won glory, you put the State in a most advantageous position for Your Majesty's next move. Italy, oppressed for years by the troops of the King of Spain and the Duke of Savoy, cries out for the aid of your victorious arms. Will you refuse to take up the cause of your neighbors and allies, who are about to be unjustly stripped of their rightful heritage? As for me, Sire, I, your minister, dare promise you today that if you take up this noble resolution, your success will be no less than at the siege of La Rochelle. I am no prophet"—and Richelieu looked with a smile toward his colleague, Cardinal Bérulle—"nor the son of a prophet, but I can assure Your Majesty that, if we lose no time in carrying out this plan, you will deliver Casale and bring peace to northern Italy before the end of May. And then, returning with your army through Languedoc, you will finish by completely reducing the Huguenots in July. Then Your Majesty, victorious everywhere, can take his rest in Fontainebleau, or wherever he desires, during the beautiful days of autumn."

(Our readers may find this chapter a bit long and dry, but our respect for the facts of history leads us to reproduce every detail of this great meeting in the Luxembourg that decided on the war in Italy, including all the speeches of the two cardinals. Our claim is that a historical novel should entertain both those readers who know the history it's based upon, and those who are learning about it from what we write.)

At this, gestures of approval were seen among the auxiliary gentlemen invited to the meeting, especially from the Duc d'Angoulême and the Duc de Guise.

The king spoke. "His Eminence," he said, "when he speaks of himself and our policy, refers to himself as 'the minister of the king,' because that policy is based upon my direct orders. Indeed, we believe that this war in Italy is necessary, that we must support our allies, and that we must maintain our position by opposing both the power and the influence of Spain. Our honor is at stake."

Despite the respect owed to the king, the only applause to this came from the friends of the cardinal, while those of the queen mother's faction could barely restrain their mutterings of disapproval.

Marie de Médicis and Cardinal Bérulle exchanged a few words in a lively undertone.

The king's expression was stern. He cast a sidelong, almost threatening glance toward the mutterers, and continued: "The issue we must now deal with is not peace or war, as war has been decided upon, but rather when we shall take the field. Opinions will be solicited, on the understanding that we reserve the ultimate decision to ourselves. Please speak to this, Monsieur de Bérulle, recognizing the respect we have for your advice, even when we do not follow it."

Marie de Médicis made a nod of thanks toward Louis XIII, then said to Bérulle, "An invitation from the king is an order. Speak, Your Eminence."

Bérulle rose. "The minister of the king," he said, emphasizing the title, "proposes an immediate commencement to this war, but I am sorry to say that I am diametrically opposed to such haste. If I am not mistaken, His Majesty has expressed a desire to lead this war in person. However, there are at least two reasons to delay. The first is this: the king's army, fatigued from the long siege of La Rochelle, needs to recuperate in winter quarters. Marching the troops from the shores of the ocean to the foothills of the Alps, without giving them time to rest, risks seeing them desert in droves. It would be cruel to subject these good soldiers to the rigors of winter in the snow-covered mountains, even if led there by the king.

"Even if we had the necessary funds for this, which we do not, as shown by the fact that it's been barely a week since Your Majesty's august mother requested a hundred thousand *livres* and was told by his minister that she could have no more than fifty thousand—to summarize, even if we had the funds, all the mules in the kingdom would not suffice to carry the food the army would need. Not to mention the fact that it's impossible to move our artillery in the winter, especially along unknown routes our engineers have never studied. Wouldn't it be wiser to wait until the spring? In the meantime, we can make all the necessary preparations for moving our men and materiel by sea.

"The Venetians, who have a far greater stake in the affairs of Mantua than we do, have made no move to oppose the invasion of Montferrat by Charles-Emmanuel, and will do nothing to support this enterprise of the king. If the oppression of the Duke of Mantua is such an important issue, why does Venice, which is so much closer than France, do nothing?

"Finally, the matter that should concern His Majesty above all others should be to avoid an open break with that most powerful of all Catholic monarchs, the King of Spain. That would be a far greater injury to the State than the fall of Casale and Mantua. I have spoken!"

Cardinal Bérulle's speech made a definite impression upon the King's Council. Rather than opposing a war which the king supported, he had outlined the probable costs and liabilities of that war. The officers invited to the council—Bellegarde, the Duc d'Angoulême, the Duc de Guise, General Marillac—were no longer as young as they had been, and perhaps were less eager for the opportunities of war than to avoid its fatigues and dangers.

Cardinal Richelieu rose once more. "I will respond to all the points made by my honorable colleague," he said. "First, though I don't think His Majesty has made a final decision on the matter, I do believe he plans to conduct this war in person. His Majesty, in his wisdom, must make that decision, though I fear he may sacrifice his own interests to those of the State, as a king, in his duty, must do.

"As to the question of the army's fatigue, which Cardinal Bérulle is so anxious about, if the troops are transported by sea and landed at Marseilles, they will still have to march to our headquarters at Lyon. Better for them to march at a measured pace through France, well fed, well housed, and well paid. That addresses the issue of desertion. As to the difficulties of taking the army across the Alps, it is better to

he king his absence, had asked l'Angely to make his
inquir as why he'd called for his fool as soon as
return

t l'A ad no more luck than the others, had
ing to

fact, ss concerned about the absence of Made-
lle d was about that of Baradas, but he'd come
ieve nearly infallible, and was astounded by
ilure

he choly, bemoaning the way fate seemed
os when Beringhen gently scratched at
or g Beringhen's particular signal, and
nge devoted person to share his misery,
ou

ns. "What do you wish of me, Ber-
? you know that I hate to be dis-
nk in ennui?"

e," said l'Angely. "Welcome in,

bre, "I never permit myself to
you wish to be bored in peace,
heir Majesties Queen Marie de
"

eens, here?"

find some way to escape,
n came Marie de Médicis,

fight nature now than to fight through our enemies' defenses later, if
we give them time to fortify the route we must take.

"It's true that last week I had to grant the king's august mother
only fifty thousand *livres* when she asked for a hundred thousand,
but that reduction had been specifically approved by the king due
to the imminent expense of the coming war. The proposed campaign
is well within our means, especially since, by engaging my honor
and my property, I have managed to borrow six million crowns to
support it.

"As to the route we must take, it has in fact been surveyed and
mapped. His Majesty has long had this campaign under consideration, and ordered me to send people into Dauphiné, Savoy, and
Piedmont on reconnaissance. Monsieur de Pontis and Monsieur
d'Escures have already made detailed maps of the terrain.

"Thus all the preparations for war have been made: the money
for the campaign is in the coffers, the troops are ready, the maps
are made—and a foreign war, as His Majesty points out, adds much
more glory to the throne than a civil war such as that of La Rochelle.
Spain's efforts to occupy Italy are vulnerable if we act quickly, so I
implore His Majesty to undertake this campaign as soon as we can.
And so I, in my turn, have spoken."

The cardinal resumed his seat, while looking toward Louis XIII
with a gaze that seemed to plead with the king to support the proposal he had made.

The king seemed to pay no attention to the cardinal, raising his
hand as soon as the latter had finished speaking. "Messieurs," he
said, "it is my will that you pay heed to my minister, Cardinal Richelieu. We have decided upon war against the Duke of Savoy, and it is
our desire that we waste no time in taking the field. Those of you
who have requests for your preparations should make them to Monsieur le Cardinal. In good time, I will decide if I will lead this war
in person, and if so, who shall be my lieutenant general. Having so

decided, this council is at an end." The king rose. "Messieurs, I pray God shall keep you. Good night."

And with a bow to the queen mother, Louis XIII took his leave.

The cardinal had won both points he'd pressed: the war against the Duke of Savoy and the immediate commencement of the campaign. So he had no doubt that he would win the third—that is, he would be given charge of the war in Italy, as he had for the siege of La Rochelle.

Marie de Médicis marched out, gritting her teeth in anger, accompanied only by Bérulle and Vautier.

"I fear we must say," said Bérulle, "like François I after Pavia, 'All is lost save honor!'"

"Not so!" said Vautier. "All is not lost, as the king has not yet named Richelieu as his lieutenant general."

"Don't you see," said the queen mother, "that in the king's mind Richelieu's already been appointed to that post?"

"Maybe," said Vautier, "but it's not yet final."

"Do you see any way to prevent this appointment?"

"Perhaps," said Vautier, "but I need to speak to Monsieur, the Duc d'Orléans, right away."

"I'll get him," said Bérulle, "and bring him to you."

"Go," said the queen mother, "and don't waste a moment." Then, turning to Vautier, she said, "What do you have in mind?"

"When we are in a place where we can be sure of not being overheard, I'll tell Your Majesty."

"Come, then." The queen and her adviser hurried down a corridor leading to the private apartments of Marie de Médicis.

XXXVI

Vautier's Plan

Though he had rooms in the queen mother's Luxembourg Palace, the king returned to the Louvre to avoid what he felt were the inevitable objections that would come from the two queens.

And indeed, after Marie de Médicis returned to her chambers, where she heard and approved Vautier's latest plan, before resorting to it she decided to make one last attempt to change her son's mind.

As for Louis XIII, as soon as he returned home, he called for l'Angely. But only after he'd inquired if there had been any word from Baradas.

Baradas had said nothing, and sent no word.

It was the stubborn silence of his sulky page that had been the cause of his bad mood at the King's Council. Vautier had guessed that was the reason, and based his new plan upon it.

Indeed, Louis XIII, though he'd made a few advances toward Mademoiselle de Lautrec, following through on his promise to l'Angely, was still dreaming about Baradas. This was exactly what l'Angely feared, so when he was called, he made haste to come and throw himself at the king's feet.

For an unexpected obstacle had arisen in l'Angely's project, a mystery that no one had been able to explain, even to the king. The previous evening, though she was supposed to be attending the queen, Mademoiselle de Lautrec had been absent from her circle, and Louis XIII, asking about it, had gotten no answer from the queen's ladies beyond astonishment. Mademoiselle de Lautrec had not been seen at the Louvre all day. The queen had inquired at her rooms and around the palace, but no one had been able to give her any news.

The king, piqued by this absence, had asked l'Angely to make his own inquiries, and that was why he'd called for his fool as soon as he'd returned.

But l'Angely, who'd had no more luck than the others, had nothing to report.

In fact, Louis XIII was less concerned about the absence of Mademoiselle de Lautrec than he was about that of Baradas, but he'd come to believe that l'Angely was nearly infallible, and was astounded by his failure.

So he was sinking into melancholy, bemoaning the way fate seemed to oppose him at every turn, when Beringhen gently scratched at the door. The king, recognizing Beringhen's particular signal, and thinking that here was one more devoted person to share his misery, called out softly, "Enter."

Monsieur le Premier came in. "What do you wish of me, Beringhen?" the king asked. "Don't you know that I hate to be disturbed when l'Angely and I are sunk in ennui?"

"You didn't hear that from me," said l'Angely. "Welcome in, Monsieur Beringhen."

"Sire," said the Valet de Chambre, "I never permit myself to disturb Your Majesty when I know you wish to be bored in peace, but I couldn't disobey orders from Their Majesties Queen Marie de Médicis and Queen Anne of Austria."

"What!" cried Louis XIII. "The queens, here?"

"Yes, Sire."

"Both of them?"

"Yes, Sire."

"And they want to talk to me?"

"Yes, Sire. Together."

The king looked around, as if he might find some way to escape, but at his first move the door opened and in came Marie de Médicis, followed by Queen Anne of Austria.

The king turned pale and exhibited the slight tremor he suffered when agitated, but he drew himself together, resolving to be impervious to whatever plea was coming. He faced the danger like a sulky and stubborn bull lowering its horns.

He turned first toward his mother, his most dangerous antagonist. "Upon my honor as a gentleman, Madame," he said, "I thought that once the King's Council was over, I would be free from further persecutions. What do you want of me? Tell me quickly!"

"My son, I want nothing but you yourself," said Marie de Médicis, while Queen Anne, hands clasped, nodded in support and agreement. "Was it not enough that, weak and suffering though you are, that man forced you to endure six months in the swamps of Aunis? Now he wants to subject you to the cold and snow of the Alps in the dangerous depths of winter!"

"Bah, Madame," said the king. "When God spared me from the fevers of the swamp, was not the Cardinal taking the same risks? And now you say he will expose me and my household further. Well, I won't be braving the snow and ice of the Alps alone. I shall give the soldiers an example of courage and perseverance, and he will be there beside me."

"I don't doubt that, my son—the Cardinal himself made the same point. But how can you compare the importance of his life to that of risking yours? The monarchy can lose ten ministers like Monsieur le Cardinal without suffering, but you . . . ! At your least illness, France trembles with fear, and your mother and your wife pray to God to preserve you."

At this, Queen Anne fell to her knees. "Sire," she said, "we are on our knees not only before the Lord but before you, to beg you as we plead with God not to abandon us. Please consider that what Your Majesty may regard as your duty is to the rest of us a source of profound terror. If Your Majesty suffered a misfortune, what would happen to us, and to France?"

"The Lord God, if he permitted me to die, will have foreseen the consequences and will provide for them, Madame. It is impossible to change what has been resolved."

"Why is that?" asked Marie de Médicis. "If this unfortunate war is so necessary, despite your having decided on it against the advice of all your counselors—"

"You mean all *your* counselors, Madame," interrupted the king.

"If it is necessary," Marie de Médicis continued, ignoring the interruption, "why must you go in person? Can't your beloved minister—"

"You know, Madame," the king interrupted for a second time, "I don't particularly like Monsieur le Cardinal. But I respect him, I admire him, and after God, he is this realm's greatest defender."

"Well, Sire, Providence will watch over the realm, whether or not you are with the cardinal. Charge your minister with conduct of the war and stay safely near to us."

"Oh, yes, and open the way for insubordination among the generals! To enable your de Guise, your Bassompierre, and your Bellegarde to refuse to obey a priest and jeopardize the fortunes of France! No, Madame! To recognize the genius of Monsieur le Cardinal is not enough, I must support him as well. Ah, if only there was a prince of the house I could trust!"

"Don't you have a brother? Don't you have Monsieur?"

"*Umpf.* Permit me to tell you, Madame, you are too indulgent toward one who has been disobedient as a son and rebellious as a brother!"

"But that's just it, my son. To bring peace back to our family, we must embrace the exile, we must love even the son who, admittedly, deserves to be punished rather than rewarded. But it is at supreme moments like this when logic must cease to drive our policy, when to rule well means to love well. God himself shows us by example that sometimes we punish the good and reward the bad. Sire, charge your prime minister with the conduct of this war, and put Monsieur subordinate to him as lieutenant general. I'm certain that if you give your brother this responsibility, he will give up his insane pursuit of Princesse Marie de Gonzague."

"You forget, Madame," said Louis XIII, frowning, "that it is I who am king, and therefore the master—and if my brother wished to take part in this effort, he could long ago have done so, with my consent rather than at my orders. Defying my right to rule is not the way to earn the right to command. I am resolved, Madame. In the future, I will command, and he will obey. This has been my determination for the last two years—that is to say, since the incident in the garden at Amiens." He emphasized the last words, while looking meaningfully at Queen Anne of Austria. "And for the last two years, I have found this policy a good one."

Anne, who was still on her knees before the king, arose at these harsh words and raised her hands to her eyes, as if to hide her tears. The king made a motion toward her, but the move was barely visible and was immediately suppressed.

Nonetheless, his mother noticed it, and seized his hands. "Louis, my child," she said, "this is not a dispute, this is simply a plea. I'm not a queen speaking to a king, I'm merely a mother talking to her son. Louis, in the name of my love, which you sometimes slight though you always do it justice in the end, yield to our entreaties. You are the king—in other words, the source of all power and wisdom. Revoke your decision, as is your right, and believe me, not only your wife and your mother, but all of France will thank you."

"Very well, Madame," said the king, who just wanted this discussion to end. "I will sleep on it tonight, and reflect on what you've said." And to his mother and his wife he gave one of those curt gestures that kings use to indicate that an audience is finished.

The two queens withdrew, Anne of Austria taking the arm of the queen mother. But they'd gone no more than twenty paces down the corridor when a door opened, and around the jamb appeared the head of Monsieur, Gaston d'Orléans. "Well?" he asked.

"Well," said the queen mother, "we did what we could. It's up to you to do the rest."

"Do you know which room is Monsieur Baradas's?" asked the king's brother.

"I do. It's the fourth door on the left, almost directly across from the king's chamber."

"Good," said Gaston. "I'll get him to do what we want, even if I have to promise him my Duchy of Orléans—not that I'd give it to him."

The two queens and the young prince departed, the queens to return to their chambers, while His Royal Highness Monseigneur Gaston d'Orléans tiptoed in the opposite direction, to the apartment of Monsieur Baradas.

We don't know exactly what passed between Monsieur and the young page, whether Monsieur promised him the Duchy of Orléans, or one of his lesser duchies of Dombes or Montpensier; all we know is that half an hour after entering the tent of Achilles, the modern Ulysses made his way, still on tiptoe, to the chambers of the queens. Once there, he opened the door with a cheerful air and said, in a voice full of hope, "Victory! He's returned to the king."

And, indeed, at almost that very moment, surprising His Majesty when he least expected it, Monsieur Baradas, without bothering to scratch at the door as etiquette demanded, entered the chambers of King Louis XIII, who recognized his page with a cry of joy and welcomed him with open arms.

XXXVII

The Overlooked Wisp of Straw,
the Unnoticed Grain of Sand

While these low intrigues were plotted against him, the Cardinal was bent over and peering, by the light of a lamp, at a map of what were then called "the Marches of the Realm." This map showed, in great detail, the border between France and Savoy, as surveyed by the engineer-geographer Monsieur de Pontis. The Cardinal also had before him the route the army must follow, the towns and villages where it would stop, and the roads and paths by which the food necessary to feed thirty thousand men would get to them. This map, prepared by Monsieur d'Escures, accurately showed every valley, mountain, river, and even stream. The Cardinal was delighted: it was the most detailed map he'd ever seen.

Just as Bonaparte in March 1800, stretched out across the map of Italy, pointed at the plains of Marengo and said "This is where I will defeat Mélas," so Cardinal Richelieu, more a man of war than of the church, said "This is where I will defeat Charles-Emmanuel." Delighted, he turned to Monsieur de Pontis and said, "Monsieur le Vicomte, you are a loyal servant of the king—but more than that, you're clever, and if this war turns out as well as we hope, you are due for a reward. And as I have no doubt of the outcome, you may ask for your reward in advance."

Monsieur de Pontis bowed. "Monseigneur, every man has ambitions, in the head or in the heart. Mine is in my heart, and since Your Eminence asks, I will open my heart to you."

"Ah!" said the cardinal. "You are in love, Vicomte?"

"Yes, Monseigneur."

"And you love above your rank?"

"Not my rank, but perhaps my fortune."

"And how can I serve you in such a case?"

"The father of the woman I love is a faithful servant of Your Eminence, who will do nothing without your permission."

The cardinal thought for a moment, as if plumbing his memory. "Ah!" he said. "You've been close to the queen in the last year, haven't you—and so you've seen Mademoiselle Isabelle de Lautrec?"

"Yes, Monseigneur," said the Vicomte de Pontis, blushing.

"But I don't believe Mademoiselle de Lautrec has been presented to His Majesty as your fiancée, no?"

"No, Monseigneur—not as my fiancée. In fact, when I spoke to Monsieur de Lautrec of my love for her, at the first words he said, 'Isabelle is not yet sixteen. In a couple of years, after the affair in Italy is settled, we may discuss this again—and then, if you still love her, and you have the approval of the cardinal, I would be happy to call you my son.'"

"And Mademoiselle de Lautrec—what did she think of her father's promise?"

"When I told Mademoiselle de Lautrec of my love, and that her father permitted me to speak of it to her, she promised—or rather, I should say, admitted to me—that her heart was free, and she had too much respect for her father to disobey him."

"And when did she say that to you?"

"A year ago, Monseigneur."

"And have you discussed it with her since?"

"Not . . . frequently."

"When was the last time you spoke to her of your love?"

"Four days ago."

"How did she respond?"

"She blushed and stammered out a few words, which I put down to embarrassment."

The cardinal smiled and said to himself, "It seems to me she left something out of her confession."

The Vicomte de Pontis looked anxiously at the cardinal. "Does Your Eminence have an objection to my ambition?" he asked.

"Not at all, Vicomte, not at all. If you love Mademoiselle de Lautrec, there may be obstacles . . . but none of them will come from me."

The viscount appeared relieved. "Thank you, Monseigneur," he said, bowing.

At that moment, the clock struck two in the morning.

The cardinal dismissed the viscount with some sadness, for, based on Isabelle's confession, he knew it would be difficult, if not impossible, to grant this loyal servant the reward he desired.

He was preparing to retire to his chambers when the door to Madame de Combalet's chambers opened and she appeared on the threshold, a smile lighting up her face.

"My dear Marie," said the cardinal, "should you be disturbing yourself at this late hour, when you should be taking the opportunity to get some sleep?"

"My dear Uncle," said Madame de Combalet, "joy can displace sleep as much as sorrow. When you are sad, you let me share your sorrow. When you are victorious, shouldn't I share in your victory? And you won a victory today, did you not?"

"Yes, Marie—a genuine victory," he said, his heart swelling in his chest.

"Well," Madame de Combalet said, "when you are victorious, allow me to share your triumph."

"You have a right to share my joy, dear Marie, because you are entitled to it. You're part of my life, a part of everything that happens to me, happy or unhappy. However, for once I can breathe freely, for my victory comes untainted. This time I didn't have to climb by stepping on another, or by sending an enemy to the scaffold. The greatest victories, Marie, are achieved through peaceful means, and are due to persuasion alone. Those who are coerced by force become our enemies, but those who succumb to reason become our allies.

"If God guides me, my dear Marie, within six months there will be a new power in Europe, feared and respected by all other powers—and that power will be France. All I need is for Providence to protect me for six months more from those two treacherous women! In six months, the siege of Casale will be lifted, Mantua will be rescued, and the Protestants of Languedoc, seeing me return from Italy with a victorious army, will sue for peace without the need, I hope, of further warfare. And then the pope will cease to oppose me, the king will favor me as he does now, and I will be able to exercise both temporal and spiritual power in France. Unless His Majesty encounters on the road one of those overlooked wisps of straw or unnoticed grains of sand that can overthrow even the mightiest project, I will be master of France and Italy!

"So kiss me, Marie, and go sleep the sleep you deserve. As for me, I'm not sure I'll sleep, but at least I'll try."

"But tomorrow you'll be a wreck."

"No, in lieu of sleep, this joy will carry me through."

"May I be permitted, my dear Uncle, to check upon you when I awake tomorrow, to see how you passed the night?"

"Come in early to be my sunrise, or late to be my sunset—so long as I get to see your beautiful eyes, I know the day will be fine. May your night be fine as well."

And, kissing Madame de Combalet on the forehead, he led her to the door of his study and stood in the doorway, watching until she was lost in the darkness of the stairs. Only then did the cardinal close the door. He was about to go to his bedchamber, but as he was leaving he heard a small knock on the panel that led to Marion Delorme's house.

He thought he must have been mistaken, but, as he stopped and listened, the knock came again, louder and more urgent. He had not been mistaken: someone was at the door that communicated with the neighboring house.

Richelieu went to the main door to his office and turned the key in the lock, then approached the secret panel. "Who knocks?" he asked quietly.

"It's me," a woman's voice said. "Are you alone?"

"Yes."

"Then let me in. I have something to report that I think is more than a little important."

The cardinal looked around to make sure he was, in fact, alone, and then pushed a spring that opened the secret panel.

In the doorway waited a handsome young man, twirling a fake mustache. It was Marion Delorme.

"Ah! Here you are, the pretty page boy," Richelieu said smiling. "I confess that if I had been expecting someone at this hour, it wouldn't have been you."

"Didn't you say to me, 'Whatever the hour, if you have something important to tell me, ring the bell, and if that doesn't work, knock on the door'?"

"I said that, my dear Marion, and thank you for remembering it." And, taking a seat, the cardinal motioned to Marion to sit beside him.

"In this costume?" said Marion, laughing and pirouetting on tiptoe to show it off, displaying her natural elegance even in an outfit unsuited to her sex. "No, that would be disrespectful to Your Eminence. I will remain standing, if you please, Monseigneur, while I make my little report—unless you'd prefer I speak to you on one knee. But I suppose that would be too much like a confession, which would be taking things too far."

"Speak to me however you like, Marion," said the cardinal, concern lining his forehead, "and quickly, for if I'm not mistaken, you bring me bad news. And in order to react to it, one can never hear bad news too soon."

"I'm not sure whether the news is bad—though my feminine instincts tell me it isn't good. You understand."

"I'm listening."

"Your Eminence is aware that the king has quarreled with his favorite, Monsieur Baradas?"

"Say, rather, that Monsieur Baradas has quarreled with the king."

"That's so, since Monsieur Baradas has been the one who was sulking. Well, tonight, while the king was with his fool, l'Angely, the two queens went in and then, after half an hour, came out again. They seemed upset and paused for a moment to speak with Monsieur, the Duc d'Orléans, after which he went to speak with Monsieur Baradas. After talking in a window embrasure for nearly a quarter of an hour, the prince and the page reached an agreement, and came out into the hallway. Monsieur waited until he saw Baradas go into the king's suite, after which he went down the corridor leading to the chambers of the queens."

The cardinal brooded for some moments, and then said to Marion, without bothering to conceal his anxiety, "Your report is so detailed, I'm sure I have no need to ask if it is accurate."

"It is—and in any event, I have no reason to hide anything from Your Eminence."

"If it's not indiscreet to ask, my dear friend, I'd like very much to know how you learned this."

"It's not indiscreet at all, as I hope to be of service to both you and the friend who gave me this news."

"Who is this friend?"

"One who hopes to be a devoted servant to Your Eminence."

"His name?"

"Saint-Simon."

"The king's new page? The short one?"

"Exactly."

"Do you know him?"

"I know him, but not well. Tonight he came to my house."

"Before or after midnight?"

"I'll tell you what I'm able to say, Monseigneur, and you'll have to be satisfied with that. He came to my house tonight from the Louvre, all eager to tell me his story. On the way to visit his comrade Baradas, he saw the two queens come out of His Majesty's chambers. They were so agitated that they didn't notice him. He saw them stop in a doorway to speak with Monsieur, the Duc d'Orléans, but Saint-Simon continued on his way and went in to visit Baradas. The page was still sulking, and said that on the next day he planned to leave the Louvre. At that moment, Monsieur entered. He didn't see Saint-Simon, who is rather small. He stood there silently and, as I have said, watched his comrade talk with the prince in the recess of a window. Then both left, Baradas to go to the king, and Monsieur, in all probability, to run to the queens to report his success."

"And this rather small Saint-Simon came to tell you all this so you'd repeat it to me, you say?"

"My faith, I'll give it to you in his own words: 'My dear Marion, I think all these comings and goings portend a plot against Cardinal Richelieu. You are said to be one of his good friends—I don't ask whether this is true or not, but if it is, please tell him about it. And say that I am his humble servant.'"

"He's a clever lad. I won't overlook this service he's done me, and you can tell him I said so. As for you, my dear Marion, how may I prove my gratitude?"

"Oh, Monseigneur."

"I'll think about it, but in the meantime . . ." The cardinal drew from his finger a beautiful diamond ring. "Here," he said, "take this diamond as a remembrance of me."

But Marion, instead of offering her hand, put it behind her back. The cardinal reached around, took her hand, and put the ring on her finger himself. Then, kissing her hand, he said, "Marion, tell me you're still my good friend and always will be."

"Monseigneur," Marion said, "I am sometimes mistaken when it comes to lovers, but as to friends, never."

Then, hand on one hip and hat in the other, with the audacity of youth and beauty, she bowed like a real page, and with a wink and a smile returned home, admiring her diamond and singing one of Desportes's villanelles.

The cardinal was alone once more, and passed a hand over his darkened brow. "So this," he said, "is the overlooked wisp of straw, the unnoticed grain of sand. This," he said, with a contempt impossible to describe, "this . . . *Baradas.*"

XXXVIII

Richelieu's Resolution

The cardinal spent a very restless night. As the beautiful Marion had thought, based on her previous experience with him on momentous occasions, the news she brought was serious: the king had reconciled with his favorite through the intercession of Monsieur, the cardinal's bitter enemy. It opened the door to any number of disastrous possibilities, and the cardinal, restless, considered them all. By the next morning—not to say when he awoke, but rather by the time he got up—he had a contingency in mind for each of them.

Around nine o'clock in the morning, a messenger from the king was announced. The cardinal was already in his office, and the messenger was ushered in. With a deep bow, he handed His Eminence an envelope with a large red seal; without knowing what the letter contained, the cardinal gave him a purse of twenty *pistoles*, as he did whenever he received a letter from the king. The cardinal had purses prepared for these occasions in a nearby drawer.

A glance told him the letter came directly from the king, as the address was written in His Majesty's own hand. So he invited the messenger to wait in the office of his secretary, Charpentier, to carry back an immediate reply.

He paused for a moment; then, like an athlete preparing for a physical challenge by rubbing oil on his muscles, he passed his handkerchief over his high forehead, damp with sweat, and prepared to break the seal.

Meanwhile, without his noticing it, a door opened quietly, and the anxious face of Madame de Combalet appeared in the gap. She knew from Guillemot that her uncle had slept badly, and from

Charpentier that a message had arrived from the king. Thus she ventured to intrude into her uncle's office where, though uninvited, she felt sure of her welcome.

But, seeing her uncle seated and holding in his hand a letter he hesitated to open, her unease was redoubled. Though ignorant of Marion Delorme's visit, she nonetheless guessed that bad news had arrived since she'd last seen him.

Richelieu finally opened the letter. As he read, something like a shadow appeared on his brow and grew to darken his visage.

She slipped noiselessly into the room and along the wall, stopping a few feet from him and leaning on a chair. The cardinal started slightly, but as he remained silent, Madame de Combalet believed she hadn't been noticed.

The cardinal continued reading, wiping his brow every few seconds. He was obviously dismayed.

As Madame de Combalet approached, she could hear his ragged breathing. Then his hand seemed to lose the strength to hold it, and he dropped the letter on the desk.

His head turned slowly toward his niece, revealing his pale and feverish face, and he held out toward her a trembling hand. Madame de Combalet seized his hand and kissed it.

But the cardinal put his arm around her waist and drew her to him, pressing her hand against his heart, while with the other hand he offered her the letter. "Read it," he said, trying to smile.

Madame de Combalet read the letter to herself.

"Read it aloud," said the cardinal. "In order to face this, I need to hear it from another. And the sound of your voice will be reassuring."

Madame de Combalet read:

> *My good friend Monsieur le Cardinal,*
>   *After careful consideration of the issues, both foreign and domestic, both equally serious, I have concluded that*

of the two, the domestic question is the most important. Considering the troubles plaguing the heart of our realm at the hands of Monsieur de Rohan and his Huguenots, we have decided, having confidence in the political genius you have so often displayed, to leave you in Paris to conduct affairs of State in our absence. Meanwhile we shall march south, with our beloved brother Monsieur as lieutenant general, and Messieurs d'Angoulême, Bassompierre, Bellegarde, and de Guise as our captains, to raise the siege of Casale and thwart the ambitions of Monsieur the Duke of Savoy. We shall send daily couriers to you to maintain constant communication, and to ask for your advice should we find ourselves embarrassed by circumstance.

Please provide, at your earliest convenience, a report of the exact state of the troops composing our army, as well as the artillery available for the campaign and what funds are available for our disposition, while retaining those you feel necessary to administer your responsibilities.

I thought long and hard before making the decision of which I inform you, as I remembered the words of that great Italian poet, forced to stay in Florence due to the unrest in the city, yet wishing to go to Venice to complete an important negotiation: "If I stay, what will go on? If I go, what will stay behind me?" I am luckier than him, for I have you, my good friend Monsieur le Cardinal, another self whom I can leave in Paris, to do everything I would do if I stayed.

With that, my good friend Monsieur le Cardinal, as I have no further business with you, I pray the good Lord shall protect you and keep you.

Your affectionate,
Louis

As she read this, Madame de Combalet's voice gradually dwindled until, as she reached the last lines, she could barely be heard.

However, though the cardinal had read the letter only once, its contents were already indelibly engraved in his memory, and he had only asked Madame de Combalet to read it in her soft voice to calm his mind, which had an effect like that of the harp of David upon the tumult of Saul.

When she had finished, she pressed her cheek to the cardinal's brow. "Oh!" she said. "The scoundrels! They're out to drive you to your grave!"

"Well, then, Marie—what would you do in my place?"

"Are you seriously asking for my advice, Uncle?"

"Quite seriously."

"Well—if I were in your place . . . !" She hesitated.

"If you were in my place . . . what?"

"In your place, I'd abandon the whole lot of them to their fate. We'd soon see how they'd fare without you to manage things."

"That's your advice, Marie?"

She drew herself up and said, fiercely, "Yes, that's my advice! None of these people—kings, queens, princes—are worthy of the efforts you make for them."

"And what, then, will we do, if I take my leave of 'these people,' as you call them?"

"We'll go to one of your abbeys, whichever one is best, and live on our own. I will love you, and all we'll care about is nature and poetry, forgetting all about these worms."

"You are consolation personified, beloved Marie, and you've always been a good counselor to me. And this time, moreover, your advice and my will are aligned. Last night, after you left my office, I was informed, more or less, of the blow that was about to strike. So I had all night to prepare for it and make up my mind as to how to respond."

He reached out his hand, drew a sheet of paper to him, and wrote:

Sire,

I could not be more flattered by this new mark of esteem Your Majesty wishes to bestow, but unfortunately I cannot accept it. My health, always fragile, was taxed by the siege of La Rochelle, which by the grace of God we concluded with success. But the effort has exhausted me, and my doctor, my family, and my friends all plead with me to avail myself of the absolute rest I can find only in the solitude of the country. Thus I mean to set aside all business, Sire, and withdraw to the house in Chaillot that I purchased for my retirement. I beg you, Sire, to please accept my resignation, while continuing to believe me the most humble, and especially the most devoted, of all your subjects.

—Armand, Cardinal Richelieu

Madame de Combalet had discreetly withdrawn while he was writing. But having signed it, he handed her the letter. As she read it quietly, great tears rolled down her cheeks.

"You're crying!" the cardinal said.

"Yes," she said, "blessed tears!"

"Why do you call them blessed tears, Marie?"

"Because they spring from joy in my heart, despite the blindness of the king and the misery of his kingdom."

The cardinal looked up and placed his hand on his niece's arm. "You're right," he said, "but God, who may abandon a king, does not so easily abandon an entire kingdom. Our lives are short and ephemeral, but that of a realm lasts for centuries. Believe me, Marie, France has too great a role to play in Europe to think that the Lord would look away from her. What I have begun, another will finish, and one man more or less will not change her destiny."

"But is it fair," said Madame de Combalet, "that the man who prepared the path for his country's destiny should not be the one to accomplish it, that his should be the labor, while another reaps the glory?"

"Now there, Marie," said the cardinal, his brow clearing, "without intending to, you touch upon the great question men have asked the sphinx for three thousand years: why is it that those who create prosperity so often earn only misfortune? The sphinx in our hearts has another name: Doubt. Why should God, the supreme justice, allow such supreme injustice?"

"Dear Uncle, I have nothing to complain of God. I just want to understand."

"God has the right to be unjust, Marie, for he has all eternity in which to repair injustice. If we could understand His secrets, we would see that what seems unfair to us serves His purposes in the end. The tension between His Majesty and myself, whom God preserve, had to be settled, if not today, then another day. Will the king decide in favor of his family, or in favor of France? Well, I am for France. And God is with France. In the end, who can be against me if God is on my side?"

He rang a bell. At the second ring, his secretary, Charpentier, appeared.

"Charpentier," he said, "compile a list of the troops ready to march to the Italian campaign, with a list of available artillery. I need this within a quarter of an hour."

Charpentier bowed and left.

Then the cardinal returned to his desk, picked up his pen, and below the last line of his resignation, he wrote:

P.S.: Your Majesty will find enclosed a detailed list of the troops of the army, as well as their equipment. As for the funds, the remainder of the six million borrowed on my guarantee—the cardinal consulted a small notebook he always carried with him—3,882,000 livres, can be found in a strongbox, the key of which my secretary will have the honor to deliver directly to Your Majesty.

As there may be those in the Louvre who fear there are state documents entrusted to me that may go astray, I give not only my office, but my entire house to Your Majesty. As everything I have comes from you, all that I have is yours. My servants will continue their efforts on your behalf, and their daily reports will be sent to you.

As of two o'clock on today's date, Your Majesty may take full possession of my house.

I finish these lines as I finished those above, daring to name myself the most obedient, but also the most loyal, subject of Your Majesty.

—Armand, Cardinal Richelieu

As he wrote, the cardinal read what he was writing aloud, so his niece didn't need to read the postscript to know what it said.

Just then, Charpentier came in with his report: thirty-five thousand men were ready for the campaign, with seventy guns.

The cardinal sealed the letter, put it and the report in an envelope, recalled the courier, and gave it to him, saying, "To His Majesty, in person."

He gave him the usual purse, and added a second to the first.

His carriage, according to the cardinal's orders, was harnessed and ready. The cardinal went down to it, taking nothing from his house but the clothes he wore. He got into the carriage with Madame de Combalet and sent his single servant, Guillemot, up onto the box. He told the driver, "To Chaillot!"

Then, turning to his niece, he added, "If, within three days, the king himself has not come to Chaillot, we leave on the fourth for my bishopric of Luçon."

XXXIX

Birds of Prey

As we have just seen, the advice of the Duke of Savoy had resulted in complete success: "If an Italian campaign is decided upon despite your opposition, get Gaston command of the army as a pretext for separating him from La Gonzague. The cardinal-duke, whose sole ambition is to be the foremost general of our age, will resign in protest. The king will accept the inevitable!"

By ten in the morning, the royalty in the Louvre was awaiting the cardinal's decision, waiting impatiently but, strange to say, in perfect harmony. These royal personages were the king, the queen mother, Queen Anne, and Monsieur.

Monsieur pretended to find a reconciliation with the queen mother as insincere as their quarrel had been. However, no matter how he appeared to get along with others, well or ill, Monsieur despised everyone equally; his cowardly and treacherous heart knew that, despite others' smiles and praise, he was held in contempt, and he returned their contempt with hatred.

The four were gathered in Queen Anne's boudoir, wherein we last saw Madame de Fargis, with the casual depravity of her corrupt and lascivious nature, giving Her Majesty such good advice.

In the chambers of the king, of Marie de Médicis, and of Monsieur le Duc d'Orléans, their accomplices stood awaiting their orders: Vieuville, Nogent-Bautru, and Baradas, now ascended to the height of his power, in the king's suite; Cardinal Bérulle and Vautier in the queen mother's rooms; while in the Duc d'Orléans's suite waited Doctor Senelle, who had penned the letter in cipher wherein Monsieur was invited, in the event of disgrace at Court, to take refuge in Lorraine—Senelle, the man whose letter had been sold to Father Joseph, His Gray Eminence, by his valet who, having been well rewarded for his betrayal, stood ready to betray him again.

As for Queen Anne, she had her own confederates at hand: Madame de Chevreuse, Madame de Fargis, and the little dwarf Gretchen who, it will be remembered, had been a gift of the Infanta Claire-Eugénie, and who, thanks to her small stature, could be employed to go where those of ordinary size could not.

At around half past ten—the time, we recall, when the cardinal was expected—his messenger arrived. As the king ordered he be admitted to the queen's chambers, and as the cardinal had ordered him to deliver his letter directly to the king, he saw no reason to delay and immediately executed his mission.

Everyone stared anxiously at the envelope which contained the fate of all their ambitions and hatreds, while the king took the letter with visible emotion, saying to the messenger, "Did His Eminence charge you with anything to tell me in person?"

"Nothing, Sire, except to present his humble respects to Your Majesty, and to deliver this message to you personally."

"Very well," said the king. "Go!"

The messenger departed.

The king opened the letter and prepared to read it. "Aloud, Sire, aloud!" cried Queen Marie, in a voice strangely combining command and appeal.

The king appeared to consider whether reading it aloud was a good idea. "Sire," said Queen Anne, "do we not all share the same interests?"

A twitch of his brow seemed to indicate that the king did not entirely agree—but whether in deference to his mother, or for reasons of his own, he began to read the letter aloud. Our readers have already heard it, but the effect it produced on the listeners is worthy of attention.

"Sire . . ."

As he said this word, the room fell so silent that Louis looked up from his letter as if to make sure his listeners had not vanished like ghosts.

"We're listening, Sire," the queen mother said impatiently.

The king, the least impatient of the four, perhaps because only he bore the weight of the monarchy and understood the gravity of this event, resumed, slowly and with a slight tremor in his voice:

"I could not be more flattered by this new mark of esteem Your Majesty wishes to bestow. . . ."

"Oh!" cried Queen Marie de Médicis, unable to contain her impatience. "He accepts!"

"Listen, Madame," said the king. "There is a *but*."

"Then read on, Sire, read on."

"If you want me to read on, Madame, do not interrupt me." And he continued, with the grave lethargy he applied to everything:

". . . But unfortunately, I cannot accept it."

"He refuses!" cried Monsieur and the queen mother together, unable to contain themselves.

The king frowned irritably.

"Excuse us, Sire," said the queen mother, "and carry on, please!"

Anne of Austria, though as faithless as Marie de Médicis, but with more self-control, given what she had to hide, laid her white hand, trembling with emotion, on her mother-in-law's black satin skirts, enjoining caution and silence.

The king continued:

"My health, always fragile, was taxed by the siege of La Rochelle, which by the grace of God we concluded with success. But the effort has exhausted me, and my doctor, my family, and my friends all plead with me to avail myself of the absolute rest I can find only in the solitude of the country."

"Ah!" said Marie de Médicis, with a sigh from deep within her voluminous chest. "Such a rest will be for the good of the realm, and indeed, for all of Europe."

"Mother! Mother!" hissed the Duc d'Orléans, who saw the flash in the king's eyes.

Anne pressed down firmly on Marie's knee. But the latter, incapable of self-control, said, "Oh, my son! You have no idea how that man has affronted me."

"Not so, Madame," said Louis XIII, frowning. "I know." And he continued, somewhat peevishly:

"Thus I mean to set aside all business, Sire, and withdraw to the house in Chaillot that I purchased for my retirement. I beg you, Sire, to please accept my resignation, while continuing to believe me the most humble, and especially the most devoted, of all your subjects.

"Armand, Cardinal Richelieu"

The listeners all stood at once, believing the reading at an end. Both queens kissed the Duc d'Orléans and approached the king to kiss his hand.

But the king stopped them with a glance. "This isn't finished," he said. "There is a postscript."

Although Madame de Sévigné had not yet written her maxim that the most important part of a letter is always contained in the postscript, everyone froze at the phrase *There is a postscript.*

The queen mother could not help saying, "I hope, my son, that if the cardinal goes back on his word, you will stick to your own."

"I have promised, Madame," replied Louis XIII.

"Then let us hear the postscript," said Monsieur.

The king read:

"P.S.: Your Majesty will find enclosed a detailed list of the troops of the army, as well as their equipment. As for the funds, the remainder of the six million borrowed on my guarantee, 3,882,000 livres, can be found in a strongbox, the key of which my secretary will have the honor to deliver directly to Your Majesty."

"Almost four million!" exulted Queen Marie de Médicis, with an avarice she took no pains to conceal.

The king stamped his foot, and there was silence.

"As there may be those in the Louvre who fear there are state documents entrusted to me that may go astray, I give not only my office, but my entire house to Your Majesty. As everything I have comes from you, all that I have is yours. My servants will continue their efforts on your behalf, and their daily reports will be sent to you.

"As of two o'clock on today's date, Your Majesty may take full possession of my house.

"I finish these lines as I finished those above, daring to name myself the most obedient, but also the most loyal, subject of Your Majesty.

"Armand, Cardinal Richelieu"

⁕

"Well," said the king, with a dark look and a hoarse voice, "now you're all happy, and each of you is ready to believe that you're in charge."

Queen Marie, who considered herself the most important of the assembled royalty, was the first to reply. "You know better than anyone, Sire, that here you are the master, and I for one shall be the first to make an example of my obedience—but, upon the occasion of this historic retirement of Monsieur le Cardinal, allow me to give you some advice."

"And what is that, Madame?" asked the king. "Advice from you is always welcome."

"You should make haste to appoint a council who will manage the affairs of the realm in your absence."

"So now, when I march away to war with my brother, you no longer fear for my health and that of my realm, Madame, as when I planned to go with Monsieur le Cardinal?"

"My son, when you resisted my pleas and those of the queen, your wife, you seemed so resolved to go that I haven't dared to consider any alternative."

"And who, Madame, do you propose to include in this council?"

"Well," said the queen mother, "I certainly think Cardinal Bérulle can take the place of Monsieur de Richelieu."

"And who else?"

"You already have Monsieur de La Vieuville for finance and Monsieur de Marillac as Keeper of the Seals. They can stay."

The king nodded. "And the war?" he asked.

"For that you have Marshal Marillac, brother of the Keeper of the Seals. Such a council, consisting of dedicated men and chaired by you, my son, will provide for the safety of the state."

"Then for naval affairs," said Monsieur, "since Monsieur le Cardinal will probably resign his admiralties along with his ministry, you have Messieurs de Lorient and du Ponent."

"You forget, Monsieur, that he bought one admiralty from Monsieur de Guise and the other from Monsieur de Montmorency, paying them a million each."

"Then pay him back," said Monsieur.

"With his own money?" asked the king, who had enough of a feeling of justice to regard such an act as shameful, though he knew Monsieur was perfectly capable of it.

Monsieur felt the dig, and reared under the spur. "No, Sire," he sniffed. "With Your Majesty's permission, I will find the money for one, and I'm sure Monsieur de Condé will pay for the other. Unless the king would prefer that I purchased both. Brothers of the king are often great admirals of the realm."

"Very well," said the king, "we'll see."

"Only," said Marie de Médicis, "I must point out, my son, that before turning over all this wealth left by Cardinal Richelieu to Monsieur de La Vieuville in his capacity as Superintendent of Finance, the king could, on his own authority, make such gifts of largesse as seemed appropriate—with no one the wiser."

"Not for my brother, in any case—he is wealthier than we are, it seems! He just claimed he had two million on hand to buy admiralties for du Ponent and de Lorient!"

"I said I would find the money, Sire. If Monsieur de Richelieu was able to raise six million by pledging his word, I should certainly be able to raise two million by mortgaging my property."

"I, who have no property," said Marie de Médicis, "have great need of one hundred thousand *livres*, but Monsieur le Cardinal said he could spare only fifty. From the additional fifty thousand I intend to pay a deposit to my portrait painter, Monsieur Rubens, who has received only ten thousand *livres* for the twenty-two paintings he executed for the gallery in my Luxembourg Palace. These paintings are dedicated to the memory and greater glory of the late king, your father."

"And in the memory of the late king, my father, you will pay for them, Madame," Louis XIII said, in a tone that startled Marie de Médicis.

Then, turning to Anne of Austria, "And you, Madame?" he asked. "Do you have any claims to make?"

"You had allowed me, Sire," said Anne of Austria, lowering her eyes, "to take the string of pearls you gave me to the jeweler Lopez to inquire about replacing the missing ones. But these pearls are so rare and beautiful, that to replace them would cost more than twenty thousand *livres*."

"So your concern today, Madame, is to pay a jeweler ten times what he deserves, whereas yesterday it was a sincere interest in my health, which you begged me not to expose to the Alpine snow by going on campaign with Monsieur le Cardinal. Is this the only request you have to make of me?"

Anne was silent.

"I'm sure the queen, my daughter," said Marie de Médicis, speaking mostly to Anne of Austria, "would be delighted to reward the dedication of her maid of honor, Madame de Fargis, with a gift of ten thousand crowns, half of which she would send to her husband, our Ambassador to Madrid, who cannot worthily represent Your Majesty on his current low salary."

"Such a modest request," said the king, "I could scarcely refuse."

"As for me," said Monsieur, "given the high command Your Majesty awards me under his orders, I hope Your Majesty will be so generous as not to make me conduct the war at my own expense, and will help me commence the campaign with . . ." Monsieur hesitated to state a figure.

"How much?" asked the king.

"No more than one hundred fifty thousand *livres*." The king didn't grimace, so he added, "At a minimum!"

"I understand that, after spending two million for the admiralties," said the king with a touch of irony, "you might be a bit embarrassed for the price of the campaign—but I must observe that Monsieur le Cardinal, when he was my minister and had also spent two million to purchase these titles from Messieurs de Guise and de Montmorency, instead of asking for one hundred and fifty thousand *livres* to fund his campaign, instead lent six million to me and to France. But of course, he was not my brother and part of the family."

"But," said Marie de Médicis, "where should money go, but to your family?"

"Quite so, Madame," said Louis XIII. "Our emblem is the pelican, who, if she lacks food for her children, feeds them her own blood. It's true that she feeds it to her children, and I have no children of my own. But perhaps, if she had no children, she would feed her own blood to her family. Your son, Madame, will have the one hundred and fifty thousand *livres* to fund his campaign." Louis XIII emphasized the words *your son*, for everyone knew Gaston was Marie de Médicis's favorite.

"Anything else?" asked the king.

"Yes," said Marie. "I also have a faithful servant whom I would reward, though, dedicated as he is, he has always refused monetary rewards, despite his needs, which are dire. Today, Providence provides the money to meet these needs. . . ."

"Take care, Madame," said the king. "This money comes not from Providence, but from Monsieur le Cardinal. If you confuse one with the other, it would then be impious for us to reject the cardinal, for it would be rebelling against Providence."

"Nonetheless, my son, I must point out that in your distribution of largesse, Monsieur Vautier has received nothing."

"Then I award him the same amount I gave the queen's friend, Madame de Fargis—but wait a moment, Providence gave us only 3,882,000 *livres* . . . no, my mistake, after subtracting two hundred and forty thousand crowns, there is still enough to reward a faithful servant of my own. I speak of my fool l'Angely, who never asks me for anything."

"But, my son," said the queen mother, "he has the favor of your attention, which is worth much."

"A favor which no one else vies for, mother mine. But it is noon," said the king, drawing his watch from his pocket. "At two o'clock I must take possession of the cardinal's house and office. And here is Monsieur le Premier scratching at the door to tell me my dinner is served."

"*Bon appétit*, brother!" said Monsieur, who, seeing that he had acquired two admiralties, the office of Lieutenant General of the King's Armies, and one hundred and fifty thousand *livres*, was overjoyed.

"No need of that wish, Monsieur," said the king, "because in that respect, I'm sure to be gratified." And the king went out, surprised to find that his personal involvement in affairs of state had delayed his regular lunch service by ten minutes, from 12:00 to 12:10.

If the worthy Doctor Héroard had not died six months earlier, we would, no doubt, know to every spoonful of soup what His Majesty Louis XIII ate and drank at this meal which inaugurated the era of his true monarchy. But all that has come down to us is that he dined *tête-à-tête* with his favorite Baradas, and, after an hour and a half, got into his carriage and told his driver, "Place Royale, the house of Monsieur le Cardinal." At two o'clock, led by the secretary Charpentier, he entered the office of his disgraced minister and sat in his chair with a sigh of satisfaction. He then said, smiling and without understanding all it meant, "At last! Now I shall reign."

XL

The King Reigns

After the spending spree of the Regency, when all the funds of France were spent on fairs and festivals in honor of that handsome cavalier who'd gathered all power as queen's favorite; when France, impoverished by the pillaging of the treasury of Henri IV, which Sully had so painstakingly amassed, and then had to watch as the realm's gold passed into the hands of d'Épernon, of de Guise, de Condé, and the other great nobles; when whatever was necessary was spent to stave off the hatred of a populace that suspected the queen of murdering her king—after all that, Louis XIII had known nothing but poverty, until he appointed Richelieu as his minister. It was due to the cardinal's wise administration, learned from Monsieur de Sully but pursued with even greater integrity, that order had returned to the king's finances and he became familiar with a metal he'd previously believed belonged only to Spain: gold.

But what a price this iron minister exacted to reach that point! Nobility and clergy were exempt from taxes until 1795, after the general employee tax of 1789 had failed to stave off state bankruptcy. If the cardinal had proposed taxing the exempt classes, it would have been rejected out of hand. Driven by implacable necessity, he therefore turned to the very body of France: her people, the peasants and the poor.

The French people were surrounded by enemies—to the west, the English; to the north and east, the Austrians; to the south, the Spanish—and in order to save the people, the cardinal plundered them. In four years, he'd increased tax revenues by nineteen million, necessary to support the army and create a navy. He'd had to close his eyes to the people's misery, close his ears to the cries of the poor, ignoring their wretched figures and sullen gaze. He had to obtain the king's attention and favor; but without a magic potion or enchanted ring, he had to resort to money, so money Richelieu found—and Louis XIII, who'd never had any cash, suddenly found it in his hands.

This was the source of King Louis's admiration for his minister—and of his jealousy.

Who could fail to admire a man who could raise six million *livres* on his word alone, when the king, by word and even by signature, couldn't raise fifty thousand?

But the king had never quite been able to believe in the promised 3,882,000 *livres*—so the first thing he demanded from Charpentier was the key to this famous treasure.

Charpentier, without comment, begged the king to get up, and then pushed the desk aside. He lifted the carpet upon which yesterday the cardinal, and today the king, had rested his feet, revealing a trap door. He unlocked it with a key and pulled the door open, revealing a large iron chest.

This chest unlocked with a combination, which Charpentier shared with the king. It opened with the same ease as the door, and to the dazzled eyes of Louis XIII was revealed the sum he was so eager to see.

Then, presumably in response to orders he'd received, Charpentier bowed to the king, gave him the key, and withdrew, leaving the two majesties, monarchy and money, alone with each other.

In that era, when banking was in its infancy, before paper money backed by shareholders was widespread, cash money was rare in France. The cardinal's 3,882,000 *livres* was therefore in the form of about one million crowns bearing the images of Charles IX, Henri III, and Henri IV, plus almost a million Spanish doubloons and seven or eight hundred thousand *reales* in Mexican gold. The balance was contained in a small bag of diamonds, each twisted like a candy in a paper wrapper, wearing its value on a label.

Louis XIII, instead of feeling that joy which the sight of gold was supposed to evoke, was instead overcome with sadness; after seeing this wealth of coinage, recognizing the kings stamped upon their faces, plunging his hand into the coffer's depths to feel the weight of the bullion, and holding up the diamonds to view their clarity, he straightened and, standing, gazed down at those millions that had been garnered through such pain to the donors, and delivered by such devotion from their gatherer.

He thought how easily, from this sum, he had already promised nearly three hundred thousand crowns to reward the devotion of his enemies, who hated the man who'd raised those funds. He wondered, in spite of himself, if, in his hands, that money would be spent in a manner as beneficial to France as if he'd left it in the hands of his minister.

Then, without withdrawing a single coin, he knocked twice on the panel to summon Charpentier. He ordered the secretary to lock the chest and close the trap door, and then gave him the key. "You will disburse nothing from this chest," he said, "except on my written order."

Charpentier bowed.

"With whom will I work?" asked the king.

"Monseigneur the cardinal," replied the secretary, "always worked alone."

"Alone? And what was he working on, all alone?"

"All the affairs of the State, Sire."

"But no one could handle all the affairs of the State by himself!"

"He had agents who reported to him."

"Who were his chief agents?"

"Father Joseph, Lopez the Spaniard, Monsieur de Souscarrières, and others I shall have the honor of naming to Your Majesty as matters arise or they come to present their reports. All have been informed that they will now be dealing with Your Majesty."

"Very well."

"In addition, Sire," Charpentier continued, "there are the agents dispatched by the cardinal to the various powers of Europe: Monsieur de Bautru to Spain, Monsieur de La Saludie to Italy, and Monsieur de Charnassé to Germany. Letters have arrived announcing their return today, or tomorrow at the latest."

"Upon their return, after having given them the instructions from Monsieur le Cardinal, you will introduce them to me. Is there anyone currently waiting to report?"

"Monsieur Cavois, the Captain of the Cardinal's Guard, who wishes the honor of being received by Your Majesty."

"I have heard that Monsieur Cavois is an honest man and a courageous soldier. I shall be glad to receive him."

Charpentier stepped to the outer door. "Monsieur Cavois," he said. Cavois appeared.

"Come in, Monsieur Cavois, come in," said the king. "You wished to speak with me?"

"Yes, Sire. I have a favor to ask of Your Majesty."

"Say on. If it will help us to keep a good servant, we'll grant it with pleasure."

"Sire, I wish Your Majesty to accept my resignation."

"Your resignation! But why, Monsieur Cavois?"

"I belonged to Monsieur le Cardinal while he was a minister; but if he is no longer a minister, I belong to no one."

"I beg your pardon, Monsieur, but you belong to me."

"I know that if Your Majesty insists, I shall be forced to remain in his service, but I must warn him that I'll be a poor servant."

"And why would you be a poor servant in my service if you were not for Monsieur le Cardinal?"

"Because my heart was in my service to him, Sire."

"And it would not be with me?"

"For Your Majesty, Sire, I must confess I feel only duty."

"And how did you become so tied to Monsieur le Cardinal?"

"Well, it was because of his deeds."

"And what if I want to do good deeds, even more so than him?"

Cavois shook his head. "It wouldn't be the same."

"It wouldn't be the same?" repeated the king.

"I owe everything I have to Monsieur le Cardinal. He brought me into his household, provided for my children, and most recently endowed me, or rather my wife, with a privilege that will bring in twelve to fifteen thousand a year."

"What? Monsieur le Cardinal gave his servant's wives pensions from the State that pay twelve to fifteen thousand a year! That's good to know."

"I did not say a pension, Sire; I said a privilege."

"And what is this privilege that was granted to Madame Cavois?"

"The right, shared with Monsieur Michel, to the monopoly on all sedan chairs on the streets of Paris."

The king thought for a moment, his eyes cast down. Cavois stood, motionless, his hat held in his left hand, his right hand stiff at the seam of his breeches.

"And what if I offered you, Monsieur Cavois, the same high position in my guard that you have in the Cardinal's Guard?"

"You already have Monsieur de Jussac, Sire, an exemplary officer to whom I'm sure Your Majesty wishes no harm."

"I will promote Jussac to marshal."

"If Monsieur de Jussac, as I have no reason to doubt, loves Your Majesty as I do Monsieur le Cardinal, he will prefer to remain as a captain near to his king, rather than to become a marshal and leave him."

"But, if you leave our service, Monsieur . . ."

"Such is my request, Sire."

". . . Will you accept, as a reward for your time spent with His Eminence, a bonus of fifteen hundred or two thousand *pistoles*?"

"Sire," replied Cavois, bowing, "the time I spent with His Eminence has already been rewarded, for its merits and more. We're going to war, Sire, and war takes money—lots of money. Keep the rewards for those who will fight, not for those who, like me, having devoted their fortunes to a man, will fall with that man."

"Are all the servants of Monsieur le Cardinal like you, Monsieur Cavois?"

"I think so, Sire, though some are more worthy."

"So, you have no more ambitions or desires?"

"Nothing, Sire, other than the honor to follow Monsieur le Cardinal wherever he goes, and continue to be part of his household, no matter how humble."

"Very well, Monsieur Cavois," said the king, piqued at the stubbornness of a captain who refused everything. "You are free."

Cavois bowed and, backing out, ran into Charpentier as he came in.

"And you, Monsieur Charpentier," cried the king, "do you, like Monsieur Cavois, refuse to serve me?"

"No, Sire. I was ordered by Monsieur le Cardinal to stay with Your Majesty until another minister was installed in his place, or His Majesty had a firm grasp of the work involved with the affairs of state."

"And when I have a grasp of our affairs, or another minister is installed, what will you do then?"

"I will beg leave of Your Majesty to allow me to rejoin Monsieur le Cardinal, who is accustomed to my service."

"But what if I asked Monsieur le Cardinal to let you stay with me?" asked the king. "When I have a minister who, unlike Monsieur le Cardinal, doesn't do everything himself, I'll need an honest and intelligent man as aide, and I'm sure you qualify for the role."

"I have no doubt, Sire, that Monsieur le Cardinal would instantly grant the king's request, as I am not worth causing dissension between my master and the king. But then I would have to throw myself at Your Majesty's feet and say, 'I have a father of seventy years, and a mother of sixty. Monsieur le Cardinal has provided for them and rescued them from misery. Once I am no longer at the side of Monsieur le Cardinal, my place is with them. Sire, allow a son to tend to his parents, and close their eyes when the time comes.' And I'm sure Your Majesty would not only grant me my prayer, he would commend it."

"'To honor your mother and father, all their lives,'" said the king, piqued even further. "The day a new minister is installed in place of Monsieur le Cardinal, you will be free, Monsieur Charpentier."

"Shall I give Your Majesty the key he entrusted me with?"

"No, keep it. If Monsieur le Cardinal, who is so well served that the king must envy his servants, trusted you with it, I'm sure it couldn't be in more honest hands. Remember, do not dispense any funds except at my written order, in my own handwriting."

Charpentier bowed.

"Don't you have here," asked the king, "a certain Rossignol, who I'm told is clever at deciphering secret letters?"

"Yes, Sire."

"I want to see him."

"If you knock three times on the panel, you can summon him. Would His Majesty like to knock himself, or shall I do it?"

"Knock," said the king.

Charpentier knocked thrice on the panel and Rossignol came through the door. He had a paper in his hand.

"Shall I stay or go, Sire?" asked Charpentier.

"Leave us," said the king.

Charpentier left.

"You are called Rossignol?" asked the king.

"Yes, Sire," replied the small man, while continuing to scan the paper.

"They say you are clever at deciphering?"

"In that regard, Sire, I don't know anyone better."

"You can decode any code you are given?"

"There is only one that, till now, has resisted me, but with God's help, I hope to master it."

"What is the most recent letter you deciphered?"

"A letter from the Duc de Lorraine to Monsieur."

"To my brother?"

"Yes, Sire, to His Royal Highness."

"And what did the Duc de Lorraine have to say to my brother?"

"Your Majesty wants the full account?"

"Indeed!"

"I'll go get it." Rossignol turned to go, and then asked, "The original, or the translation?"

"Both, Monsieur."

Rossignol darted out with the speed of a ferret, albeit one with a furrowed brow, and returned almost immediately with two papers in one hand, while continuing to study the one in his other. "Here they are, Sire," he said, presenting the original from the Duc de Lorraine and its translation.

The king started with the original, and read, "'If Jupiter . . .'"

"*Monsieur*," said Rossignol, interrupting the king.

"'. . . Is exiled from Olympus . . .'" continued Louis XIII.

"The *Louvre*," said Rossignol.

"And why would Monsieur be exiled from the Court?" asked the king.

"Because he conspires," Rossignol said calmly.

"Monsieur conspires? Against whom?"

"Against Your Majesty and the State."

"Do you know what you are saying, Monsieur?"

"I am saying that Your Majesty should continue reading."

"'. . . He could,'" read Louis XIII, "'take refuge in Crete.'"

"In *Lorraine.*"

"'Minos . . .'"

"Duc Charles IV."

"'. . . Would take great pleasure in offering him hospitality. But the health of Cephalus . . .'"

"The health of Your Majesty."

"He calls me Cephalus?"

"Yes, Sire."

"I know who Minos was, but I've forgotten Cephalus. Who was Cephalus?"

"A Thessalian prince, Sire, husband of a beautiful Athenian princess, who drove her from him because she had been unfaithful, but with whom he was later reconciled."

Louis XIII frowned. "So," he said, "this Cephalus, husband of an unfaithful wife with whom he reconciles despite her infidelity—that's me?"

"Yes, Sire—that is you," Rossignol calmly replied.

"Are you sure?"

"*Pardieu,* yes! As Your Majesty will see."

"Where were we?"

"'If Monsieur is exiled from the Louvre, he can take refuge in Lorraine. Duc Charles IV would take great pleasure in offering him hospitality. But the health of Cephalus . . .'—that is to say, the king; that's where you were, Sire."

"'. . . Cannot last long.' What does that mean, *cannot last long*?"

"It means that Your Majesty is ill, very ill indeed—at least, such is the opinion of the Duc de Lorraine."

"Ah!" said the king, turning pale. "So I'm ill, very ill indeed!" He searched for and found a mirror, looked at himself, and then patted his pockets for medicinal salts. Finding none, he made an effort to pull himself together and, in an agitated voice, continued to read. "'Why, in the case of his death, should we not marry Procris . . .'—Procris?"

"That is, the queen," said Rossignol. "Procris was Cephalus's unfaithful wife."

"'. . . Why should we not marry Procris to Jupiter?' To *Monsieur?*" cried the king.

"Yes, Sire. To Monsieur."

"To Monsieur!" Sweat sprang from the king's forehead, and he wiped it with a handkerchief, then continued: "'The rumor at Court is that Oracle . . .'"

"His Eminence."

"'. . . Wants to replace Procris with a marriage to Venus . . .'"

The king looked at Rossignol, who continued, without replying to the king, to study the paper in his hand.

"*Venus?*" repeated the king, impatiently.

"Madame de Combalet, Madame de Combalet," Rossignol hastily replied.

"'. . . To Cephalus,'" continued the king. "Marry me to Madame de Combalet? Me? Where do they get these ideas? 'Meanwhile, Jupiter'—that is to say, Monsieur—'continues to court Hebe . . .'"

"Princesse Marie de Gonzague."

"'. . . Feigning passion, as well as a falling-out with Juno.'"

"The queen mother."

"'It is important that, to this end, Oracle'—that is, the cardinal—'must mistakenly believe that Jupiter loves Hebe. Signed, Minos.'"

"Charles IV."

"Ah!" murmured the king. "That explains his apparent reluctance to sacrifice his great love in order to become lieutenant general. So, my health cannot last, eh? And when I am dead, you will marry my brother to my widow! But, thanks be to God, though I may be ill, 'very ill indeed,' as they say, I'm not dead yet. So, my brother conspires, and if his conspiracy is discovered, he can escape to Lorraine and find refuge with the duke! Does he think France couldn't swallow a mouthful like Lorraine, duke and all? Isn't it enough that they gave us the Guises?"

Then, turning quickly to Rossignol, "And how," the king asked, "did this letter come into the hands of Monsieur le Cardinal?"

"He had it from Monsieur Senelle."

"One of my own doctors," said Louis XIII. "Truly, I am well served!"

"Foreseeing an intrigue between the Court of Lorraine and that of France, Monsieur Senelle's valet had been suborned in advance by Father Joseph."

"This Father Joseph seems to be a clever man," said the king.

Rossignol winked. "He's the shadow of His Eminence," he said.

"So Senelle's valet . . . ?"

"Stole the letter and sent it to us."

"Where was Senelle, then?"

"Not far from Nancy; the valet returned and said he'd inadvertently burned the letter with some other papers. The duke suspects nothing, and has sent a second letter to His Royal Highness Monsieur."

"And how has my brother *Jupiter* responded to the wise *Minos*?" asked the king, laughing nervously, mustache twitching as he awaited the reply.

"I don't yet know. This is his answer that I'm working on."

"What! You have his answer there?"

"Yes, Sire."

"Give it to me."

"Your Majesty won't understand it, given that I don't understand it yet myself."

"Why is that?"

"Because after they lost the first letter, fearing some accident, they invented a new code."

The king looked at the letter and read these completely unintelligible words: "'*Astra-so be-the-amb in joy as L.M.T. wants to be.*' When will you know what this means?"

"I'll have it by tomorrow, Sire."

"This is not my brother's handwriting."

"No, this time the valet didn't dare steal the letter, lest he be suspected, so he copied it."

"And when was this letter written?"

"Today at noon, Sire."

"And you already have a copy?"

"Father Joseph handed it to me at two o'clock."

The king remained thoughtful for a moment, then turned again to the little man, who had taken back the letter and was working to guess its meaning. "You'll stay on with me, won't you, Monsieur Rossignol?" he asked.

"Yes, Sire, until this letter is fully decrypted."

"What, only until this letter is decrypted? Are you planning to rejoin Monsieur le Cardinal?"

"Yes, in fact, but only if he is once more a minister. If he isn't a minister, he has no need for me."

"But I have a need for you!"

"Sire," said Rossignol, shaking his head so that his glasses nearly fell off, "I'm leaving France tomorrow."

"Why's that?"

"Because in serving Monsieur le Cardinal, and through him Your Majesty, in deciphering the codes invented for their intrigues, I've made terrible enemies of the Great Nobles, enemies against whom only the cardinal could protect me."

"But what if I protect you?"

"His Majesty may have the intention, but . . ."

"But?"

"But he does not have the power."

"What?" The king frowned.

"Moreover," continued Rossignol, "I owe everything to Monsieur le Cardinal. I was a poor boy in Alby when it chanced that the cardinal learned of my talent with ciphers. He took me on and gave me a position paying a thousand crowns, then two thousand, then added twenty *pistoles* for each letter I decoded. For six years I've deciphered one or two letters a week, so I have a tidy sum saved away."

"Where?"

"In England."

"So you'll probably go to England and enter the service of King Charles?"

"King Charles offered me two thousand *pistoles* a year and fifty *pistoles* per letter deciphered if I would leave the service of Monsieur le Cardinal. I refused."

"And if I offered you as much as King Charles has?"

"Sire, the most pressing need of a man on this earth is to stay above it. With Monsieur le Cardinal in disgrace, even with Your Majesty's royal protection—or perhaps because of it—I have less than a week to live. When he left this house, it took all of his authority to make me stay here as long as I have, but for Your Majesty, I am willing to risk my life . . . for another twenty-four hours."

"So you're not willing to risk your life for me beyond that?"

"We owe our devotion to our parents, and beyond that to a benefactor. Seek for devotion, Sire, from your parents, or from those for whom you have done good. I have no doubt Your Majesty will find it there."

"You have no doubt. Well, I have reason to doubt it!"

"Now that I have told His Majesty why I have stayed, that is, to perform a service—now that he knows the risks I run to remain in

France even this long, I beg His Majesty not to oppose my departure, for which everything is prepared."

"I will not oppose it, but on the express condition that you vow not to enter the service of any foreign prince who might use your talent against France."

"I give Your Majesty my word."

"Go. Monsieur le Cardinal is very lucky to have servants such as you and your colleagues." The king looked at his watch. "Four o'clock. I will be back here at ten in the morning; make sure the translation of the new letter is ready by then."

"It will be, Sire."

As the king was reaching for his hat, Rossignol asked, "Wouldn't His Majesty like to speak with Father Joseph?"

"Of course, of course," said the king, "and when he comes, ask Charpentier to send him in."

"He's right here, Sire."

"Then have him enter, and I'll speak to him at once."

"Here he is, Sire," said Rossignol, withdrawing to defer to His Gray Eminence.

The monk appeared, and stood humbly waiting on the threshold of the study. "Come, come, *mon Père*," said the king.

The monk approached with every appearance of humility, head down and hands crossed on his breast. "Here I am, Sire," said the Capuchin, stopping four paces from the king.

"You were waiting, Father," said the king, looking at the monk with curiosity, because for him a whole new world was opening before his eyes.

"Yes, Sire."

"How long?"

"For an hour or so."

"And you waited that long without anyone letting me know you were there?"

"A humble monk has nothing better to do, Sire, than to await orders from his king."

"I am told you are a man of great ability, *mon Père.*"

"My enemies may say that, Sire," replied the monk, eyes piously downcast.

"You helped the cardinal to bear the burden of his ministry?"

"As Simon of Cyrene helped Our Lord carry his cross."

"You are a great champion of Christianity, are you not, *mon Père*? If it was the eleventh century, you would, like Peter the Hermit, preach the crusade."

"I preach the crusade even in the seventeenth century, Sire, albeit without success."

"Indeed? How so?"

"I wrote an epic poem in Latin entitled the *Turciade* to inspire the Christian princes to take up arms against the Muslims. But much time has passed, and they show no signs of being inspired."

"You rendered great service to Monsieur le Cardinal?"

"His Eminence was blocked at every turn, but I helped as I could, according to my limited abilities."

"How much did His Eminence grant you per year?"

"Nothing, Sire. It is forbidden for our order to receive anything but alms. His Eminence paid only for my carriage."

"You have a carriage?"

"Yes, Sire, but not in gratification of pride. I formerly rode an ass."

"The humble mount of Our Lord," said the king.

"But Monseigneur found that I did not travel fast enough."

"And so he gave you a carriage?"

"At first, Sire, I refused the carriage out of humility, so he gave me a horse. Unfortunately, this horse was a mare, and one day my secretary, who was riding a stallion . . ."

"Yes, yes, I understand," said the king hastily. "And that's when you accepted the carriage offered by the cardinal?"

"Yes, Sire—I resigned myself to it. For I thought," said the monk, "it would be pleasing to God to see the humble glorified."

"Despite the cardinal's retirement, *mon Père,* I would like to keep you near me," said the king. "Tell me what you require."

"Nothing, Sire. For the sake of my salvation, I may already have been too forward in the acceptance of honors."

"Have you no desires I can satisfy?"

"Only to allow me to return to my monastery, which perhaps I never should have left."

"You are too useful in the affairs of state for me to allow that."

"I could see such things only through the eyes of His Eminence, Sire. With that illumination gone, I am blind."

"In every estate, *mon Père,* even the religious, it's possible to see ambition awarded according to its merits. God has not given you your talent in order for it to be wasted. Monsieur le Cardinal is an example of the heights one might achieve."

"And from which, therefore, one can fall."

"But no matter how far you fall, if you fall wearing a cardinal's red hat, the descent is bearable."

A flash of avarice glimmered beneath the Capuchin's lowered lashes.

This glimmer did not escape the king's notice. "Have you ever thought about a high-ranking post in the Church?" he asked.

"I might have had such thoughts, but only with Monsieur le Cardinal."

"Why only with Monsieur le Cardinal?"

"Because it would have taken all his influence with Rome to achieve such a goal."

"And you think my influence doesn't match his?"

"Your Majesty proposed to give the Archbishop of Tours a cardinal's hat, but he was an archbishop—not a poor Capuchin monk."

Louis XIII studied Father Joseph as closely as he could, but it was impossible to read anything in those downcast eyes or on those features of marble. Only the lips seemed alive.

"Furthermore," continued the monk, "there is the single grave fact that overshadows all others in accepting those tasks placed upon me by Monsieur le Cardinal and God; and that is the danger of committing sins that may jeopardize the salvation of one's soul. But with Monsieur le Cardinal, who wields the power of Rome for both penitence and remission, I need have no fear, for if I sin by day, I confess by night. Monsieur le Cardinal absolves me, and I sleep in tranquility. However, if I serve a secular master, even a king, well . . . a king cannot absolve me. I cannot sin for the state and retain a clear conscience."

The king continued to study the monk as he spoke, and the more he said, the more a certain repugnance grew on the king's face. "And when would you like to return to your monastery?" he asked, when Father Joseph had finished.

"As soon as I have Your Majesty's permission."

"You have it, *mon Père,*" the king snapped.

"Your Majesty overwhelms me," said the monk, crossing his hands on his breast and bowing to the ground. And, unlike how he'd entered, neither stiff nor humble, he strode out without even turning to say farewell from the doorway.

"Ambitious hypocrite! You, at least, I won't miss," murmured Louis XIII.

Then, after a moment surveying the shadows falling in the study, he said, "No matter. But one thing is certain: if I abdicated the throne tonight, as this morning the cardinal did this office, I wouldn't be able to find four men to follow me into exile and disgrace. Not three, not two, maybe not even one."

Then he said, "Well, maybe one—there's still my fool, l'Angely. Though of course, he's a fool!"

XLI

The Ambassadors

The next morning at ten o'clock, as he'd promised, the king was once again in the cardinal's office.

The lessons he was learning, while humiliating, were also fascinating.

On his return to the Louvre the day before, he had received no one, closeting himself with his page Baradas, whom he'd sent three thousand *pistoles* via Charpentier as a reward for his help in bringing down the cardinal. He thought it best to delay paying the others, so he'd given Baradas his reward first.

Before giving the queen her thirty thousand, the queen mother her sixty thousand, and Monsieur his one hundred fifty thousand *livres*, he wanted to read Monsieur's response to the Duc de Lorraine, which Rossignol had promised him by ten o'clock the next morning.

Thus, as we've said, at ten o'clock the king was once more in the cardinal's office, and even before he threw his cape over a chair and put his hat on the table, he knocked three times on the panel.

Rossignol appeared with his usual punctuality.

"Well?" the king asked eagerly.

"Well, Sire," Rossignol said, blinking behind his glasses, "we have cracked the code."

"Quick," said the king, "let's see it. The key first."

"Here it is, Sire." And he presented the key.

The king read:

❧

Je—	The King
Astre se—	The Queen
Be—	The Queen Mother
L'amb—	Monsieur
L.M.—	The Cardinal
T.—	Death
Pif-paf—	The War
Zane—	Duc de Lorraine
Gier—	Duchesse de Chevreuse
Oel—	Madame de Fargis
O—	Pregnant

"And now?" said the king.

"Apply the key, Sire."

"No," the king said, "you do it, you're used to it. My head would break at such a task."

Rossignol took the paper and read, "*The queen, the queen mother, and the Duc d'Orléans are in bliss. The cardinal is dead. The king wants to be king: he's decided on war against the Prince of Marmots, but with the Duc d'Orléans in charge. The Duc d'Orléans is in love with the Duc de Lorraine's daughter, but he'd rather marry the queen, even if she is seven years older than him. His only fear is that, following the advice of Madame de Fargis or the Duchesse de Chevreuse, she may be pregnant when the king dies. Signed, Gaston d'Orléans.*"

The king had listened without interrupting, though he had wiped his forehead several times and scored the floorboards with the wheel of his spur. "Pregnant," he murmured, "pregnant. If she becomes pregnant, it certainly won't be by me."

Then, turning to Rossignol: "Is this the first letter of this sort that you've decoded?"

"Oh, no, Sire! I've deciphered ten or twelve like this."

"What! And Monsieur le Cardinal never showed them to me?"

"Why torment Your Majesty with a misfortune that might never occur?"

"But when he was accused and harried by these people, why didn't he use these weapons against them?"

"He was afraid that would also make them enemies to the king."

The king took a few steps back and forth, from one end of the study to the other, his head low and his hat over his eyes.

Then, returning to Rossignol, he said, "Make me a copy of each letter, with its decoded version, and the key on top."

"Yes, Sire."

"Do you think there will be others like this?"

"Most certainly, Sire."

"Who are the people I'm to receive today?"

"That's not my concern, Sire. Ciphers are my only business. You should see Monsieur Charpentier."

Even before Rossignol was out the door, the king, with a feverish and trembling hand, struck two blows on the panel. These rapid, violent blows indicated his state of mind.

Charpentier appeared instantly, but stopped on the threshold.

The king's eyes were fixed on the floor, fist clenched on the cardinal's desk, while he muttered, "Pregnant . . . the queen pregnant . . . a foreign queen on the throne of France. By an Englishman, maybe!"

Then, in a lower voice, as if he was afraid himself to hear what he said: "Nothing is impossible. Not in this family, based on what has gone before."

Absorbed in his thoughts, the king hadn't noticed Charpentier. Thinking the secretary hadn't responded to his summons, he looked up impatiently and was about to knock a second time when, seeing the gesture and guessing the intention, Charpentier stepped forward and said, "Here I am, Sire."

"Good, good," the king said, trying to regain his composure. "What do we have before us today?"

"Sire, the Comte de Bautru has arrived from Spain, and the Comte de La Saludie from Venice."

"What were they doing in those places?"

"I don't know, Sire. Yesterday I had the honor to tell you that Monsieur le Cardinal had sent for them, as well as for Monsieur de Charnassé, who will be arriving from Sweden by tomorrow at the latest."

"You informed them that the cardinal was no longer a minister and that I would receive them in his place?"

"I sent them His Eminence's orders, which were to report on their missions to His Majesty as they would have done to himself."

"Who is coming first?"

"Monsieur de Bautru."

"As soon as he arrives, bring him in."

"He is here, Sire."

"Let him come, then."

Charpentier turned, spoke a few words in a low voice, and then stepped aside to let Bautru enter.

The ambassador was still in his traveling clothes, and apologized to appear so before the king, but it was thus that he had always met Cardinal Richelieu. Once he'd arrived in the antechamber, he hadn't wanted to keep His Majesty waiting.

"Monsieur de Bautru," the king said to him, "the cardinal spoke well of you, saying you were a trustworthy man, and that the honest opinion of a Bautru was worth two of Cardinal Bérulle's."

"Sire, I endeavored to be worthy of the confidence the cardinal placed in me."

"And you will prove worthy of mine as well, won't you, Monsieur, telling me everything you would have told him?"

"Everything, Sire?" Bautru asked, staring at the king.

"Everything. I'm looking for the truth and I want all of it."

"Well, Sire, you should start by recalling your Ambassador de

Fargis who, instead of following the instructions of the cardinal, to the benefit of Your Majesty's honor and glory, follows those of the queen mother, to the detriment of France."

"Others have already advised me of this. I will think about it. You've spoken with Count-Duke Olivares?"

"Yes, Sire."

"What were your orders regarding him?"

"To negotiate, if possible, a peaceful settlement on Mantua."

"And?"

"When I tried to talk business with him, he led me into the hen-house of His Majesty King Philip IV, which contains the most curious species in the world, and offered to give me samples to send to Your Majesty."

"So he was mocking you, then?"

"Both me, Sire, and he whom I represented."

"Monsieur!"

"You asked me for the truth, Sire. That's what I give you. Shall I lie? If the truth is unpleasant, I certainly have wit enough to replace it with pleasant lies."

"No, give me the truth, whatever it may be. What do people think of our planned Italian campaign?"

"People laugh, Sire."

"People laugh? Don't they know what we plan to do?"

"They do, Sire—but they say the queens will make you change your mind, and that Monsieur, placed in command, will obey the queens rather than you, so the expedition is bound to end up failing to support the Duc de Nevers."

"Ah! So they think in Madrid?"

"Yes, Sire, they think it and write it—as I know, since I suborned one of the Count-Duke's secretaries. Olivares wrote to Don Gonzalès de Cordova, 'If the king gives Monsieur control of the army, have no fear: that army will never cross the Pass of Susa. On the other hand, if the cardinal is in charge of the conduct of the war, with or without the king, the Duke of Savoy will need all the support you can send him.'"

"You're sure of this?"

"Quite sure, Sire."

The king resumed pacing back and forth, head down, hat pulled over his eyes, as was his habit when worried. Suddenly he stopped and, fixing Bautru with a penetrating look, asked, "And the queen—have you heard anything about her?"

"Only what's said at Court."

"And what do they say at Court?"

"Nothing I can repeat to Your Majesty."

"Never mind that. I want to know."

"Slander and calumny, Sire. Don't disturb yourself with such filth."

"I tell you, Monsieur," said Louis XIII, impatiently stamping his foot, "that slander or truth, I want to hear what is said of the queen!"

Bautru bowed. "Your Majesty orders, and a loyal subject must obey."

"Obey, then."

"It is said that Your Majesty's health is failing. . . ."

"My health is failing! So everyone seems to hope. It seems my death is their salvation. Go on."

"Since your health is failing, the queen will take steps to make sure . . ." Bautru hesitated.

"Make sure of what?" demanded the king. "Speak! Tell me!"

"To ensure the regency."

"But there's only a regency when there's an heir to the throne!"

". . . To ensure the regency," Bautru repeated.

The king stamped his foot. "So, the same rumor in Spain as in Lorraine—in Lorraine it's a fear, but in Spain, a hope. Indeed, if the queen becomes queen regent, then Paris will be Spanish. So that's what they're saying, Bautru?"

Bautru bowed to the king. "You ordered me to speak, Sire. I obeyed."

"You've done well. I told you I was looking for the truth, and you've put me on the trail—and now, thank God, I'm hunter enough to follow it to the end."

"Any further orders, Your Majesty?"

"Go and rest, Monsieur. You must be exhausted."

"Your Majesty hasn't told me whether I've had the good fortune to please him, or the misfortune to dissatisfy him."

"I can't say I enjoyed hearing what you had to tell me, Monsieur Bautru. But you've done your duty, which is better. The next time there is a vacancy among the Councilors of State, I think I may reward you with it." And Louis XIII, removing his glove, presented his hand for the Ambassador Extraordinaire to Philip IV to kiss.

Bautru, as etiquette required, backed out of the room so as not to turn his back on the king.

Left alone, the king murmured, "So—my death is others' hope; my honor is a joke; and the succession to the throne is a lottery. If my brother assumes the throne, he'll betray France and auction it to the highest bidder. And my mother, the widow of Henri IV, that great king who was killed because he planned to make France greater still—my mother will help him. Fortunately . . ." and the king gave a shrill laugh, ". . . when I die, the queen may be pregnant, which will upend everything. Oh, how happy I am in my marriage!"

Then his expression darkened even more, and his voice lowered. "Not so astonishing, then, that they all wanted me to get rid of the cardinal!"

He thought he heard a small sound from the door, and turned. The door opened. "Does Your Majesty wish to receive Monsieur de La Saludie?" Charpentier asked.

"I believe so," said the king. "Everything these gentlemen have to tell me is so very interesting." Then, with another shrill laugh: "They do say that a king never knows what's happening in his own castle! But though he may be the last to know, he can find out if he wants to." Then, as Monsieur de La Saludie appeared at the door, he said, "Come, come, Monsieur de La Saludie, I've been expecting you. You've been told, haven't you, to report to me in place of the cardinal? Speak, and keep no secrets from me that you would share with him."

"But, Sire," said La Saludie, "in the situation in which I find myself, I'm not sure if I should repeat . . ."

"Repeat what?"

"Words of praise from Italy for a man of whom it seems you had complaints."

"Ah! Do they praise the cardinal in Italy? And what do they say of the cardinal on the far side of the mountains?"

"Sire, they are unaware that the cardinal is no longer your minister, and they congratulate Your Majesty on being served by the leading political and military genius of our century. I was instructed by the cardinal to announce the fall of La Rochelle to the Duke of Mantua, to the Senate of Venice, and to His Holiness Urban VIII. The news was received with joy in Mantua, enthusiasm in Venice, and satisfaction in Rome. Your Majesty's planned expedition into Italy has terrified Charles-Emmanuel of Savoy, but reassured all the other princes. Here are letters from the Duke of Mantua, from the Venetian Senate, and from His Holiness, Sire, all of which express the utmost confidence in the plans of the cardinal. And each of these three powers, who wish to support this effort as much as they can, has instructed me to place drafts with their bankers for funds totaling one and a half million crowns."

"And these drafts are in whose name?"

"In the name of Monsieur le Cardinal, Sire. They are payable on demand—he has only to endorse them to collect the money."

The king took the drafts and turned away. "A million and a half," he said, "along with the six million he borrowed—it's with this that we're marching to war. And all the money raised by one man, as if that man was himself the grandeur and glory of France."

Then, at a sudden thought, Louis XIII stepped to the panel and knocked twice. Charpentier appeared. "Do you know," asked the king, "from whom the cardinal borrowed the six million with which he planned to finance the war?"

"Yes, Sire, from Monsieur de Bullion."

"Did it take much effort to persuade him to make the loan?"

"On the contrary, Sire, it was he who offered the money."

"How's that?"

"Monsieur le Cardinal complained that the army raised by the Marquis d'Uxelles had dispersed, due to their pay having been appropriated by the queen mother, and their food having not been delivered by Marshal Créqui. 'That army is lost,' said His Eminence. 'Well, then!' said Monsieur de Bullion, 'we must raise another, that's all.' 'And with what?' 'With what? I'll give you enough for an army of fifty thousand men, with a million in gold in reserve.' 'In that case, I'll need six million.' 'When?' 'As soon as possible.' 'Will tonight be too late?' Then the cardinal laughed. 'What, do you have that much in your pocket?' 'No, but there's that much in the Treasury. I'll give you a draft to present to Fieubet, the Exchequer.' 'And what guarantees do you require in return, Monsieur de Bullion?' He rose, bowed to His Eminence, and said, 'Merely your word, Monseigneur.' The cardinal embraced him. Monsieur de Bullion wrote a few lines on a piece of paper, the cardinal accepted it, and that was that."

"Very well! Do you know where I'd find Monsieur de Bullion?"

"At the Treasury, I suppose."

"Wait a moment." The king went to the cardinal's desk and wrote:

Monsieur de Bullion,
   I have a particular need for a sum of fifty thousand livres so I won't have to touch the money that you were kind

enough to lend to the cardinal. Please let me know if such
a loan would be possible; I give my word to repay it within
a month.

> *Your affectionate,*
> *Louis*

Then, turning to Charpentier, he asked, "Is Beringhen at hand?"

"Yes, Sire."

"Give him this note, and tell him to take a sedan chair to go see Monsieur de Bullion. He is to wait for a reply."

Charpentier took the note and left, but then returned almost immediately.

"Well?" said the king.

"Monsieur Beringhen is on his way, but I wanted to inform Your Majesty that Monsieur de Charnassé has arrived from West Prussia, with a letter for the cardinal from King Gustavus Adolphus."

Louis nodded. "Monsieur de La Saludie," he said, "do you have anything else to say?"

"Only, Sire, to assure you of my respect, and that I would like to add my voice to those who regret the departure of Monsieur de Richelieu; it is my duty as a faithful subject to tell Your Majesty that, as far as Italy is concerned, he was the man we needed. I would be happy if I could be allowed to send the cardinal my regards, even if he is in disgrace."

"I'll do better than that, Monsieur de La Saludie," said the king. "I'll give you the opportunity to see him personally."

La Saludie bowed.

"Here are the drafts from Mantua, Venice, and Rome. Go to Chaillot and present your regards to the cardinal, along with these notes. Ask him to endorse the drafts, then take them to Monsieur de Bullion and collect the money in the name of His Eminence. To speed you on your way, you may take my carriage, which is waiting at the door. The sooner you return, the better I'll recognize your zeal and devotion."

La Saludie bowed again and, without wasting another second on compliments and courtesies, left to execute the king's orders.

Charpentier was still at the door. "I will see Monsieur de Charnassé now," the king said.

Never had the king been obeyed at the Louvre as he was at the house of the cardinal; he had no sooner expressed his desire to see Monsieur de Charnassé than the man appeared before him.

"Well, Baron," said the king, "it seems you had a successful trip."

"Yes, Sire."

"Please make your report without losing a second. Only yesterday did I finally learn the value of time."

"Your Majesty is aware of why I was sent to Germany?"

"His Eminence, whom I trusted to act on his own initiative, thought it sufficient to announce your departure and notify me of your return. Otherwise, I know nothing."

"Would His Majesty like me to give him a detailed account of my instructions?"

"Speak."

"These were my orders, which I learned by heart in case the written instructions went astray: 'The frequent efforts of the House of Austria to undermine the allies of the king have forced him to take measures on their behalf; with the fall of La Rochelle, His Majesty has decided to muster his finest troops and personally lead them to the aid of his allies in Italy. Accordingly, the king has dispatched Monsieur de Charnassé to Germany to assure all his allies there of His Majesty's full support, if they will act in concert with the king in the interest of their mutual defense. The Baron de Charnassé is authorized to discuss the most suitable and appropriate means by which His Majesty might aid his allies.'"

"Those were your general instructions," said the king, "but no doubt you had others that were more specific?"

"Yes, Sire. For Duke Maximilian of Bavaria, whom His Eminence knew was very angry with the Emperor, I was to advise the creation of a Catholic League to oppose Ferdinand in both Germany and Italy, while Gustavus Adolphus was attacking the Emperor at the head of his Protestant troops."

"And what were your instructions regarding King Gustavus Adolphus?"

"I was instructed to promise King Gustave that if he would lead a Protestant League, as the Duke of Bavaria would with the Catholics, he would receive an annual subsidy of 500,000 *livres*, as well as the promise that Your Majesty would support him by attacking Lorraine, the neighboring province of Germany that has played host to so many conspiracies against France."

"Yes," the king said, smiling, "I see it: Crete and King Minos. But what would the cardinal, or rather I myself, gain by attacking Lorraine?"

"It would force the princes of the House of Austria to divert troops to the defense of Alsace, which would take their eyes off Italy and give France the freedom to finish her business in Mantua."

Louis took his forehead between his hands. The intricate plans of his minister staggered him with their size and complexity, until his brain seemed ready to burst.

"And," he said, after a moment, "did King Gustavus Adolphus accept?"

"Yes, Sire, but with certain conditions."

"What?"

"They are contained in this letter, Sire," said Charnassé, drawing from his pouch an envelope embossed with the arms of Sweden. "Would His Majesty prefer to read this letter himself, or shall I, as may be more appropriate, explain its meaning?"

"I want to read everything, Monsieur," said the king, taking the letter from his hands.

"Remember, Sire, that King Gustavus Adolphus is rather jolly and informal, indifferent to the forms of diplomacy, and speaks his mind as if from one soldier to another."

"If I'd forgotten that, I'll remember it, and if I'd never known it, I'll learn." And, unsealing the letter, he read it in a low voice:

[At Stuhm, after the final Swedish conquest of the forts of Livonia and Polish Prussia.]

The 19th of December, 1628

My dear Cardinal,

As you know, I'm a bit of a pagan, so don't be surprised by the informality with which I write to a Prince of the Church.

You are a great man—more than that, a man of genius— and more than that, an honest man, one with whom one can talk and do business. Let us talk, then, of the affairs of France and of Sweden, and of how they can march together. I am ready to negotiate, but only with you.

Are you sure of your king? Are you sure he won't turn, at the first cry, to his mother, his wife, his brother, his confessor, or his favorite—Luynes, is it, or Chalais? I can't keep them straight. Meanwhile you, who have more talent in your little finger than all these people, king, queens, princes, favorites, churchmen—don't you fear that someday you'll be brought down by some low intrigue hatched in the harem, as if you were no more than a pasha or vizier?

If you are sure of your position, do me the honor to say to me: Friend Gustave, I have at least three years more during which I can dominate these witless lords and ladies who give me so much work and yet make so much trouble. If you can give me your personal assurance that the king will support you, then I will begin my campaign without delay—but not if you tell me it's up to the king. On your word, I'll muster my army and mount my horse, and we will plunder Prague, burn Vienna, and sack Buda and Pest. But solely on the word of the King of France, I will not beat a single drum, load a single musket, or saddle a single horse.

If that's the way the wind blows, My Eminenceness, send your reply by way of Monsieur de Charnassé, and I will sheathe my sword, though it saddens me to do so. But if the Devil allows, we shall campaign together, and drink to each other in the spoils of Hungarian wine!

As a man of spirit, I commend you not to the mercy of God, but to the care of your own genius. I address you, with joy and pride, as,

> *Your affectionate,*
> *Gustavus Adolphus*

The king read this letter with increasing irritation, and when he was finished, he crumpled it in his hand. Then, turning to the Baron de Charnassé, he asked, "Are you aware of the contents of this letter?"

"I know the gist of it, Sire, but not the details."

"Barbarian! Uncouth northern bear!" the king whispered.

"Sire," Charnassé remarked, "this barbarian just defeated both the Russians and the Poles. He learned the arts of war from a Frenchman named La Gardie, but has exceeded him: he is the inventor of modern warfare and, in short, the only man who can thwart the ambition of Emperor Ferdinand and beat Tilly and Wallenstein."

"Yes, I know that's what they say," replied the king. "I know that in the opinion of the cardinal, the first man of war in Europe is King Gustavus Adolphus, but," he added with a laugh intended to be mocking but in the event only nervous, "I may not share that opinion."

"I sincerely regret that, Sire," said Charnassé, bowing.

"Ah!" said Louis XIII. "So, Baron, you wish to return to the King of Sweden on our behalf?"

"That would be a great honor for me and, I believe, of great benefit to France."

"Unfortunately, that is impossible," said Louis XIII, "as His Swedish Majesty wishes to deal only with Monsieur le Cardinal, and the cardinal is no longer involved in such affairs."

There was a scratching at the door. The king turned and said, "Well, what is it?" Then, recognizing the scratching as that of Monsieur le Premier, he said, "Is that you, Beringhen? Come in."

Beringhen entered. "Sire," he said, presenting a large letter with a broad seal, "Monsieur de Bullion's reply."

The king opened it and read:

> *Sire,*
>
> *I am in despair, but, in service to Monsieur de Richelieu, I have emptied my coffers down to the last crown, and though I wish to please His Majesty, I cannot say when I could give him the fifty thousand livres he asks for.*
>
> *It is with sincere regret and the most profound respect, Sire, that I have the honor to tell Your Majesty that I am his most humble, faithful, and obedient servant.*
>
> *—De Bullion*

Louis gnawed at his mustache. Gustave's letter told him how much political credit he had, and Bullion's told him how much financial credit.

At that moment, La Saludie returned, followed by four men, each bending under the weight of the bag he carried.

"What's this?" asked the king.

"Sire," said La Saludie, "it's the one-and-a-half million *livres* that Monsieur de Bullion sends to Monsieur le Cardinal."

"Monsieur de Bullion?" said the king. "He had this much money?"

"By our lady, Sire!" said La Saludie. "So it seems."

"And who did he send you to for the money this time? Fieubet?"

"No, Sire. He was going to at first, but then decided that for such a small amount it wasn't worth it, so he just wrote a note to his first clerk, Monsieur Lambert."

"Insolent dog!" murmured the king. "He has too little cash to give me fifty thousand *livres*, but he has a million and a half to pay Monsieur de Richelieu for the drafts from Mantua, Venice, and Rome."

He dropped onto a chair, crushed under the weight of the moral whiplash of the last two days. Beginning to glimpse the inevitable truth, he said to Charnassé and La Saludie, "Messieurs, my thanks. You are good and faithful servants. I'll call you within a few days to tell you my wishes." He gestured for them to withdraw; they bowed and went out.

The four porters had deposited their bags on the floor and were waiting. Louis stretched out his hand to the panel and knocked twice. Charpentier appeared. "Monsieur," said the king, "put away these one-and-a-half million *livres*—but first pay these men."

Charpentier gave each porter a silver crown, and they went out.

"Monsieur Charpentier," said the king, "I'm not sure if I will come tomorrow. I'm terribly tired."

"It would be unfortunate if Your Majesty couldn't come tomorrow," said Charpentier. "It is the day for reports."

"What reports?"

"Reports from the cardinal's chief agents."

"Who are these chief agents?"

"Father Joseph, though you have given him permission to return to his monastery, so of course he won't be reporting tomorrow; Monsieur Lopez the Spaniard; Monsieur de Souscarrières."

"Are these reports made in writing, or in person?"

"Since the cardinal's agents know that tomorrow they will be reporting to the king, it's likely they will report in person."

"I'll be here, then," said the king, rising with an effort.

"So if the agents come in person . . . ?"

"I'll receive them."

"I must warn Your Majesty about the nature of one of these agents, of whom I've not yet spoken."

"Is there a fourth agent, then?"

"An agent even more secret than the others."

"And who is this agent?"

"A woman, Sire."

"Madame de Combalet?"

"Your pardon, Sire, but Madame de Combalet is not an agent of the cardinal—she is his niece."

"Then who is this woman? Is she well known?"

"Yes, Sire."

"Her name?"

"Marion Delorme."

"His Eminence received that notorious courtesan?"

"She was one of his most effective agents. Indeed, it was through her that he was warned in advance that he was about to be disgraced."

"Through her?" said the king, astonished.

"When the cardinal wanted to learn secret news of Court intrigues, he turned to her. Perhaps knowing that Your Majesty is in this office in place of the cardinal, she will have something of particular importance to say to Your Majesty."

"I assume she doesn't come here publicly."

"No, Sire. Her house is adjacent to this one, and the cardinal had a door made in the adjoining wall so that one can pass between the houses."

"Are you sure, Monsieur Charpentier, that His Eminence wouldn't consider it a betrayal to reveal all these secrets to me?"

"On the contrary, I tell Your Majesty all this at his direct order."

"Where is this secret door?"

"Behind this panel, Sire. During work tomorrow, if the king is alone, hears a gentle knock at this panel, and wishes to honor Mademoiselle Delorme by receiving her, he can press this button and the door will open. If he does not wish to see her, he can respond with three equal taps on the button. Ten minutes later he will hear a bell, and between the doors he will find a written report."

Louis XIII thought for a moment. It was obvious that his curiosity was fighting a fierce battle with his repugnance for women—especially those in Marion Delorme's trade.

Finally his curiosity got the better of him. "If His Eminence, a holy Prince of the Church, was willing to receive Mademoiselle Delorme, it seems to me that I may receive her as well. And if that turns out to be a sin, I'll just confess it. Until tomorrow, Monsieur Charpentier."

And the king took his leave, even more pale, tired, and dazed than the day before, but with a better idea of how hard it is to be a great minister, and how easy to be a mediocre king.

XLII

A Royal Intermission

Anxiety permeated the Louvre: during the days the king went to the Place Royale, he didn't see any members of his family—not the queen mother, the queen, nor the Duc d'Orléans—and none of them had received the gifts he'd promised, which were to come from a treasure he alone could touch.

Furthermore, the new King's Council, reorganized with such enthusiasm by Bérulle and General Marillac after the cardinal's resignation, had received no orders to meet and, therefore, had not deliberated about anything.

Each day, according to the rumors spread by Beringhen, who dressed the king in the morning and undressed him at night, and saw him leave and return, His Majesty was sad each morning when he left, and even gloomier when he came back in the evening.

Only the king's fool, l'Angely, and his favorite, Baradas, had access to his inner chamber.

Of all the birds of prey extending their beaks and claws toward the cardinal's treasure, only Baradas had received his three thousand *pistoles* from Charpentier. It's true he had extended neither beak nor claw, the largesse having come without his asking for it. The page had his faults, but he also had the virtues of youth. He was prodigal when he had money, but unable to use his influence with the king to extend his extravagance. When money stopped flowing, he waited quietly—for he had fine clothes, beautiful hair, and a graceful form—and eventually the flow would resume, whereupon he would spend it as quickly as before.

During the king's absence, Baradas spent his time with his friend

Saint-Simon, awaiting the manna that would pour from heaven, and considering with his young comrade what he should do with it. The two youths—for they were barely men: Baradas, the elder, was scarcely twenty—discussed what might best be done with three thousand *pistoles*. They decided they would spend a whole month living like princes. Only one thing worried them: would the king actually pay up? Many a bill carrying the royal signature had been presented to the royal treasurer without being honored, and they feared that, despite the majesty of Louis's royal name, they might find themselves as disappointed as any minor merchant from the city.

Eventually Baradas had withdrawn to his room, taken up pen, paper, and ink, and undertaken the effort of writing a letter, a colossal undertaking for the average gentleman of his time. After much massaging of his brow and scratching of his head, he was finished; he put the letter in his pocket, waited bravely for the king to return, and then, even more bravely, had asked His Majesty when he might present himself to the treasurer to receive his promised sum of money.

The king said he could present himself whenever he liked, as the treasurer was his to command. Baradas had kissed the king's hand, then leaped down the stairs four at a time, jumped into one of the sedan chairs of the firm of "Michel and Cavois," and had himself taken immediately to the cardinal, or rather to the cardinal's former hotel.

There he found Secretary Charpentier, faithful to his duty, and duly presented himself. Charpentier received his note, read it, and recognizing the king's signature, bowed respectfully to Monsieur Baradas and asked him to wait for a moment. He left with the note and, five minutes later, came back with a bag of gold containing three thousand *pistoles*.

At the sight of this bag, Baradas, unable to believe it, felt his heart leap. Charpentier offered to count out the sum before his eyes, but

Baradas, who was eager to clutch the blessed bag to his chest, was willing to forego this. However, Charpentier insisted, and Baradas, who still felt weak after his wound, didn't feel that he could wrest the bag away from him. So he waited until Charpentier was done, and then lugged the bag down to his waiting sedan chair.

There, Baradas reached into the bag and drew out a handful of gold and silver crowns, which he offered to Charpentier. The secretary merely bowed and refused. Baradas was astonished at this, staring at Charpentier as he went back through the door of the hotel.

But bit by bit, Baradas got over his amazement. Once recovered, he ordered the chair porters to guard his bag, then went to the next house over, stepped up to the door, and knocked. He drew his laboriously written letter from his pocket and presented it to the elegantly dressed doorman who answered his knock, saying "For Mademoiselle Delorme."

He accompanied the letter with two crowns, which the doorman refused as scrupulously as Charpentier had. Then Baradas returned to his chair and, with that commanding voice that belongs only to those who have money in their pockets, called out to his porters, "To the Louvre!"

And the porters, who hadn't failed to note the weight and rotundity of Baradas's bag, departed at a rate that would do credit to modern marathon athletes.

After a quarter of an hour, Baradas, who had not for a moment stopped stroking the bag that was his traveling companion, was at the door of the Louvre. There he met Madame de Fargis, who was just descending from another sedan chair.

The two recognized each other, and a smile curved the sensual lips of the mischievous young woman, as she saw the effort Baradas was making with his injured arm to lift the heavy bag. She asked, with mocking courtesy, "Would you like me to assist you, Monsieur Baradas?"

"Thank you, Madame," replied the page. "If, on your way, you should happen to see my comrade Saint-Simon, and could ask him to come down here, that would be much appreciated."

"Of course," replied the young coquette. "My pleasure, Monsieur Baradas." And she ran nimbly up the stairs, lifting the hem of her dress to reveal the curve of her calf, giving just enough of a look to enable one to guess the shape of the rest.

Five minutes later, Saint-Simon came down. Baradas had generously paid off his porters, and now the two men, joining their efforts, managed to lift the heavy bag up the stairs, much as in that painting of Paul Véronese where we see two young men in party dress carrying a large amphora containing enough wine to make twenty men drunk.

Meanwhile, Louis XIII had extended his evening dinner for five hours, during which he'd conversed with his fool, who hadn't failed to notice His Majesty's increasing sadness.

Louis XIII was sitting on one corner of the broad hearth in his parlor, behind the table, while l'Angely, on the other side, crouched in a high chair like a parrot on its perch, resting his feet on the lowest rung to make a table of his knees, on which he rested his plate with an aplomb in accord with his careful sense of balance.

The king lacked an appetite and merely nibbled at a few dried cherries, wetting his lips from a glass that glittered with the gold and blue royal crest. He wore atop his head his black felt hat adorned with black plumes, the broad brim casting a shadow over his features that matched their expression.

L'Angely, on the contrary, was ravenous, and had made up for missing his usual second dinner at five or six o'clock by sliding toward himself all the food the king disdained, mainly a huge pheasant paté and a woodcock stuffed with figs. After offering them to the king, who declined, he cut fat slices of both paté and fowl and transferred them to his plate. After attacking first the paté, then the woodcock, and finally the figs, he poured himself a glass of the cardinal's wine, which was none other than what we now call Bordeaux. The king and the cardinal, who had the two worst stomachs in the kingdom, always drank this fine wine watered, but l'Angely, who could digest anything, drank it straight, enjoying its bouquet and smooth savor.

The first bottle of this wine had already been set empty on the hearth, and was soon to be joined by a second—which l'Angely, as a connoisseur, kept at an appropriate distance from the fire. Though it was still standing on the table, it was sufficiently empty to show that it wouldn't be there long, as l'Angely's deep respect for its qualities caused him to give it frequent caresses as he filled his glass. The fool, who like the Greek philosophers was an enemy to redundancy, was almost inclined to set his glass aside and, like a child drinking from a stream, pour the wine directly into his cupped hand.

As l'Angely tenderly caressed the bottle once again, he uttered a sigh of satisfaction, just as Louis let out a sigh of sadness. L'Angely paused, the bottle in one hand, a wishbone in the other. "It seems," he said, "that being a king is no fun, especially if *you* happen to be the king."

"Ah, my poor l'Angely," said the king, "I'm so very unhappy."

"Tell me all about it, my son. It will console you," said l'Angely, placing the now-empty bottle on the hearth and cutting himself a slice of pie.

"Everyone steals from me, everyone lies to me, everyone betrays me."

"True! Did you only just notice this?"

"No, I've just been confirming it."

"Come, come, my son, do not succumb to pessimism. I confess that, for my part, I'm inclined to think things are not so bad. I've dined well, this pie is good, the wine was excellent, the Earth rotates slowly enough that it does not throw me off, and I feel in my whole body a warmth of pleasant well-being that enables me to view life through a rosy glow."

"L'Angely!" Louis XIII said tartly. "No heresy, or I'll have you whipped."

"What?" replied l'Angely. "Is it heresy to view life through a rosy glow?"

"No, but it's heresy to say the Earth rotates."

"Well, *ma foi*, I'm not the first man to say it. I believe Messieurs Copernicus and Galileo were ahead of me."

"Perhaps, but the Bible says otherwise, and you can't pretend that Copernicus and Galileo were wiser than Moses!"

"H'mm," said l'Angely.

"See here," the king insisted, "if the Earth turned and the Sun were immobile, then how was Joshua able to stop the Sun for three days?"

"Are you quite sure that Joshua stopped the Sun for three days?"

"Not Joshua, but the Lord."

"And you think the Lord gave him this extra time because he needed it to chase five Canaanite kings into a cave so he could wall them up? By my faith, if I were the Lord, instead of stopping the Sun, I would have brought on the night, to give those poor devils a chance to escape."

"L'Angely, l'Angely," the king said sadly, "you're worse than a Huguenot."

"Careful, Louis—you're closer to a Huguenot than I am, assuming you're the actual son of your father."

"L'Angely!" snapped the king.

"You're right, Louis," said l'Angely, renewing his attack on the figs. "Let's not talk about theology. So you say, my son, that everyone betrays you?"

"Everyone, l'Angely!"

"Even your mother?"

"Especially my mother."

"Bah! What about your brother?"

"My brother, more than anyone!"

"At last. And here I thought *you* thought it was only the cardinal who was deceiving you."

"On the contrary, l'Angely, I believe Monsieur le Cardinal was the only one who *wasn't* deceiving me."

"What? Is the whole world turned upside down, then?"

Louis nodded his head sadly.

"And yet I hear that, in your joy to be rid of him, you've promised grand gifts to your whole family!"

"Alas!"

"I hear you gave sixty thousand *livres* to your mother, thirty thousand to the queen, and one hundred fifty thousand *livres* to Monsieur."

"Well, l'Angely, that's what I've promised them."

"So you haven't given it to them yet? Good!"

"L'Angely," said the king, "I've had a sudden inspiration."

"Not to burn me as a heretic or hang me as a thief, I hope!"

"No, not that. Since I have some money . . ."

"*You* have *money*?"

"Yes, my child."

"Word of honor?"

"Faith of a gentleman! And plenty of it."

"In that case, see here," said l'Angely, caressing the bottle once again, "use it to buy more of this wine, my son. Invest it in the 1629 vintage!"

"No, that's not what I'm inspired to do. Besides, you know I drink only water."

"*Parbleu!* And that's why you're so sad."

"No, it would just be crazy for me to be happy."

"Well, I'm crazy, but I'm not happy about it. Come, tell me your inspiration!"

"I have decided to make your fortune, l'Angely."

"My fortune? Me? What do I need with a fortune? I have food and shelter here at the Louvre. When I need money, I probe your pockets and take what I find. Not that I ever found much. But it's enough for me, and I have no complaints."

"I know you never complain, and this saddens me."

"Why must you always grieve? What an awful personality you have."

"You never complain—you, whom I give nothing—but they complain continually, though I give to them constantly."

"Let them complain, my son."

"But if I died, l'Angely . . ."

"Great, another cheerful thought. At least wait until after Carnaval."

". . . If I died, they'd drive you away without a *sou*."

"Well, then, I'd go."

"But what would become of you?"

"I'd become a Trappist monk! Why not? They have a monastery right near the Louvre."

"They all hope I'll die, you know. What do you say to that, l'Angely?"

"I say you should continue to live, just to infuriate them."

"But life is not much fun, l'Angely."

"Do you think it will be better once you're buried at Saint-Denis?"

"It's no fun anywhere, l'Angely," said the king, mournfully.

"Louis, I warn you, you'll be even more bored when you're dead. You're starting to make my bones rattle."

"So you don't want me to make you rich?"

"I want you to let me finish my wine and my paté!"

"I could give you three thousand *pistoles*, like I gave Baradas."

"You gave Baradas three thousand *pistoles*?"

"Yes."

"Well, you must be proud. There's money well spent."

"You think it's a waste of money?"

"On the contrary! He'll share it out with all the pretty boys and beautiful girls."

"You know, l'Angely, I don't think you believe in anything."

"Not even the virtue of Monsieur Baradas."

"Just speaking with you is a sin."

"Quite so, if speaking truth is a sin. Shall I give you some advice, my son?"

"What's that?"

"Go to the chapel, pray for my salvation, and leave me to eat my dessert in peace."

"Good advice can come even from the mad," said the king, rising. "I will go and pray." And the king went off to his chapel.

"So you will pray for me," said l'Angely, "and I will eat, drink, and sing for you, and we will see which is of most benefit."

And, indeed, as Louis XIII, sadder than ever, closeted himself in his chapel, l'Angely, who had finished the second bottle, opened the third and began a song:

> When I'm weary, I invite
> Bacchus in for the night
> Then happily I rest
> As if I'd gold in my chest
> More gold in my coffer
> Than Croesus could offer
>
> I couldn't ask for more
> Dance around the floor
> No laurels I need
> No honors, no greed
> Kings, queens, nobles, princes
> Can't better my prances

So pour me champagne
To distract my brain
Draw out my troubles
With a glass full of bubbles
Better drunk in my room
Than stone dead in a tomb!

XLIII

Et tu, Baradas?

When Louis came out of his chapel, he found l'Angely slumped over the table, head resting on his arms, asleep or pretending to sleep.

He looked on sadly for a moment, and then this weak and selfish half-man, who despite his terrible upbringing was occasionally illuminated by an instinctive flash of truth and decency, was seized by a great compassion for his companion in misery. L'Angely was so devoted—not to cheering him up, as other fools had done for their kings, but to simply walking with him down the dark corridors of the monotonous hell of depression. Louis remembered the offer he'd made the fool with his typical recklessness, which l'Angely had not refused so much as evaded. He remembered the good humor and patience with which l'Angely suffered his bouts of ill temper, his selfless devotion though surrounded by ambition and greed—and then, picking up pen, ink, and paper, he wrote a draft granting l'Angely the same amount he'd given to Baradas, and slipped it into his pocket quietly, so as not to wake him. Then he returned to his suite, where he listened for an hour as his minstrel played the lute. After that, he called Beringhen to help him into bed, then sent for Baradas to come talk with him.

Baradas arrived, still gleeful from having counted and recounted his three thousand *pistoles,* stacking and restacking them.

The king had him sit on the foot of the bed, and said with an air of reproach, "Why are you so cheerful?"

"I'm cheerful," Baradas replied, "because I have no reason not to be—in fact, quite the contrary!"

"Why is that?" asked Louis with a sigh.

"Has Your Majesty forgotten that he granted me three thousand *pistoles*?"

"No, indeed. I remember."

"Well, then: three thousand *pistoles*! I must admit to Your Majesty that I wasn't really expecting it."

"Why not?"

"Ah, man proposes, but God disposes!"

"But if the man is a king?"

"Nonetheless, God is still God!"

"And so?"

"So, Sire, it was paid, every coin, cash on the barrelhead! *Peste*! Monsieur Charpentier is in my opinion a much greater man than Monsieur de La Vieuville, who when I asked for money just waved his arms and whispered, 'I swim, I swim, I swim. . . .'"

"So you got your three thousand *pistoles*."

"Yes, Sire."

"And so you're rich?"

"Yes, ha ha!"

"What are you going to do now? Are you going to act the bad Christian and spend it all on gambling and women, like the prodigal son?"

"Oh, Sire!" Baradas said, pretending to be hurt. "Your Majesty knows I never gamble."

"So you say, at least."

"And as for women, I can't stand them."

"Is that really true, Baradas?"

"I am constantly quarreling with Saint-Simon about this very subject, holding up Your Majesty to him as an example."

"It's true, Baradas: women were created for the peril of our souls. It wasn't woman who was seduced by the serpent—she is the serpent itself!"

"It's just as you say, Sire! I'm going to commit that maxim to memory and write it down in my prayer book!"

"Speaking of prayer, I had my eyes on you during mass last Sunday, Baradas, and you seemed quite distracted."

"If so, it was only because my eyes turned the same way as Your Majesty's, toward Mademoiselle de Lautrec."

The king bit his mustache and changed the subject. "So, what *will* you do with your money?"

"If it was three or four times as much, I'd use it to fund pious works," said the page, "like dedicating the foundation of a convent or the erection of a chapel, but with such a limited amount . . ."

"You know I'm not rich, Baradas," said the king.

"Oh, I'm not complaining, Sire, quite the contrary. But with, as I said, such a limited amount, I'll first give half of it to my mother and my sisters."

Louis nodded.

"Then," Baradas continued, "I'll divide the remaining fifteen hundred *pistoles* into two shares. The first seven hundred fifty will go to buy me two good horses to take on Your Majesty's Italian campaign, along with weapons, and pay and clothing for a lackey."

The king nodded his approval. "And as for the remaining seven hundred fifty, what will you do with that?"

"I will keep it as a reserve, with a bit for pocket money. God bless you, Sire," Baradas continued, raising his eyes to heaven, "for such good deeds that enable others to rescue orphans and console widows."

"Embrace me, Baradas—embrace me!" cried the king, moved to tears. "Use the money as you say, my child, and I will make sure you never want for more."

"Sire," said Baradas, "you are magnificent, majestic, and wise as Solomon—plus you have the advantage over him in the eyes of the Lord in not having three hundred wives and eight hundred . . ."

"The Lord preserve me!" cried the king, terrified by the mere idea, and raising his own hands to heaven. "But this conversation is a sin, Baradas, for it smacks of ideas that contradict morality and religion."

"Your Majesty is right," said Baradas. "Shall I go and do some pious reading?" The page knew that was the quickest way to quell the king. He got up, pulled down Gerson's *Eternal Consolation* from a shelf, sat down near but not on the bed, and began to read from it in a voice full of unction.

By the third page, the king was asleep.

Baradas stood up on tiptoe, replaced the book on the shelf, went quietly to the door to let himself out, and then returned to the dice game with Saint-Simon that the king's summons had interrupted.

The next morning, at ten o'clock, the king went down from the Louvre to his carriage, and was borne to the office where, for the last two days, so many things he'd never suspected had appeared in their true guise.

He found Charpentier awaiting him. The king was pale, tired, and depressed. He asked if the daily reports had arrived yet.

Charpentier replied that as Father Joseph had retired to his monastery, there would be no report from him, only from Souscarrières and Lopez.

"And have these reports arrived?" asked the king.

"As I had the honor to tell His Majesty," said Charpentier, "knowing that today they would be dealing with His Majesty himself, both Messieurs Lopez and de Souscarrières said they would bring their reports personally. The king may simply read their reports himself, and call upon them for further clarification."

"Where are these reports?"

"Monsieur Lopez is here with his; but in order to leave enough time for His Majesty to speak with him and then open the correspondence of Monsieur le Cardinal, I have made the appointment with Monsieur de Souscarrières for noon."

"Ask Lopez to come in."

Charpentier went out and, a few seconds later, announced Don Ildefonse Lopez.

Lopez came in, hat in hand and bowing to the ground.

"Fine, Monsieur Lopez, fine," said the king. "I know you of old, as one who's cost me dear."

"How so, Sire?"

"Isn't it at your shop the queen buys her jewelry?"

"Yes, Sire."

"Well, the day before yesterday, the queen asked me for twenty thousand *livres* for a string of pearls, which she wanted to buy from you."

Lopez laughed and, in laughing, revealed a set of teeth that could have passed for pearls.

"What are you laughing at?" asked the king.

"Sire, shall I speak with you exactly as I spoke with Monsieur le Cardinal?"

"Exactly."

"Well, then, in today's report to His Eminence is a full paragraph on this string of pearls—or rather, its significance."

"Read me this paragraph."

"As the king commands, but Your Majesty will understand it better if I explain a few things first."

"Proceed."

"On December 22, Her Majesty the Queen appeared at my shop, under the pretext of buying a string of pearls."

"Under the pretext, you say?"

"Under the pretext, yes, Sire."

"What was her real purpose?"

"To meet with the Spanish Ambassador, the Marquis de Mirabel, who happened to be there."

"He 'happened' to be there?"

"Of course, Sire. It is always by happenstance that Her Majesty the Queen meets the Marquis de Mirabel, who can only present himself at the Louvre with advance notice on certain days."

"That was done by my order—upon the advice of the cardinal."

"Therefore Her Majesty the Queen, if she has something to convey to the ambassador or to her brother the King of Spain, must meet the ambassador somewhere by chance, since she can't see him otherwise."

"And this 'happenstance' occurred at your shop?"

"With the permission of Monsieur le Cardinal."

"So the queen met with the Spanish Ambassador?"

"Yes, Sire."

"Did they have a long conference?"

"They had time to exchange only a few words."

"We desire to know what those words were."

"I've already told Monsieur le Cardinal."

"But he didn't tell me. His Eminence was very discreet."

"Let me say in advance that I don't wish to distress Your Majesty."

"Just tell me what they said."

"What I shall repeat to Your Majesty was overheard by my diamond cutter."

"He understands Spanish?"

"He does, since Monsieur le Cardinal ordered that he should secretly learn it. But as nobody knows this, the speakers were unguarded. They said:

"The ambassador: 'Her Majesty has received by way of the Governor of Milan and the Comte de Moret, a letter from her illustrious brother?'

"The queen: 'Yes, Monsieur.'

"'Has Your Majesty thought about its contents?'

"'I've thought about them, but must think some more before I answer him.'

"'Answer how?'

"'By means of a box supposed to contain fabrics, but which will actually contain this little dwarf you see playing with Madame de Bellier and Mademoiselle de Lautrec.'

"'You think she can be trusted?'

"'She was a gift to me from my aunt Claire-Eugénie, Infanta of the Netherlands, and acts in the interest of Spain.'"

"In the interest of Spain . . ." repeated the king. "It seems everything around me is in the interest of Spain—of my enemies, in other words. And this little dwarf?"

"She was sent off yesterday in her box, but before that, she told Monsieur de Mirabel, in very good Spanish, 'Madame my mistress told me she has considered her brother's advice, and if the king's health continues to deteriorate, she will take measures not to be caught off guard.'"

"Not to be caught off guard," the king repeated.

"We do not understand what that means, Sire," Lopez said, lowering his head.

"But I understand," said the king, frowning, "and that's enough. Did the queen mention that she'd soon be able to pay for this necklace she's buying from you?"

"I've already been paid, Sire," said Lopez.

"What, you've been paid?"

"Yes, Sire."

"By whom?"

"By Monsieur Particelli."

"Particelli? The Italian banker?"

"Yes."

"But I was told he'd been hanged."

"Quite so, quite so," said Lopez, "but before he died, he sold his bank to Monsieur d'Émery, a good honest man."

"Everyone," murmured Louis XIII, "everyone robs me and deceives me! And the queen has not seen Monsieur de Mirabel since?"

"The reigning queen, no; the queen mother, yes."

"My mother? When was this?"

"Yesterday."

"To what end?"

"To announce that the Cardinal was overthrown, that Bérulle had replaced him, and that Monsieur had been appointed lieutenant general, so the ambassador could write to King Philip IV or the count-duke and tell them the Italian war is as good as off."

"What, the war in Italy is off?"

"Those were Her Majesty's very words."

"Oh, I see. I understand. They will treat this second army like the first, leaving it without pay, without food, without clothes. Oh, the wretches! The wretches!" cried the king, pressing his forehead into his hands. "Do you have anything else to tell me?"

"Some minor matters, Sire. Monsieur Baradas visited my shop this morning to buy some jewelry."

"What kind of jewelry?"

"A necklace, a bracelet, and some hairpins."

"For how much?"

"For three hundred *pistoles.*"

"Why would he want this necklace, bracelet, and hairpins?"

"Probably for some mistress, Sire."

"What?" said the king. "Last night he told me he hates all women. Anything else?"

"That's all, Sire."

"To summarize: Queen Anne and Monsieur de Mirabel agreed that, if my condition worsens, she will not be caught off guard. The queen mother told Monsieur de Mirabel that he can report to His Majesty Philip IV that Monsieur de Bérulle has replaced Monsieur de Richelieu and my brother is lieutenant general, so the Italian war is as good as off. Finally, Monsieur Baradas is using the money I gave him to buy necklaces, bracelets, and hairpins. Well done, Monsieur Lopez; you've told me what I needed to know. Continue to serve me well—or serve Monsieur le Cardinal, which is the same thing—and don't miss a word of what passes at your shop."

"I hope Your Majesty will not endanger my business."

"Come, come, Monsieur Lopez. I merely hope to have an end to all these treasons. Now, on your way out, if you see Monsieur de Souscarrières, send him in."

"I'm here, Sire," a voice said. Souscarrières appeared in the doorway, hat in hand, bent in an elaborate court bow.

"Ah! You were listening, Monsieur," said the king.

"Not at all, Sire! It's just that my zeal for serving Your Majesty is so great that I guessed Your Majesty wished to see me."

"Ah-ha! And do you have plenty of interesting things to tell me?"

"Two days' worth of reports, Sire."

"Then tell me what happened two days ago."

"The day before yesterday, Sire, Your Majesty's august brother hired a chair and was taken to meet the envoy of the Duc de Lorraine and the Spanish Ambassador."

"No surprise there. Continue."

"Yesterday, at about eleven o'clock, Her Majesty the queen mother hired a chair to carry her to Lopez's shop, as did the Ambassador of Spain."

"I know what they said to each other. Continue."

"Yesterday, Monsieur Baradas took a chair from the Louvre to the house of Monsieur le Cardinal in the Place Royale. He went in and, five minutes later, came out with a heavy sack of money."

"I'm aware of it."

"From the cardinal's door, he went to the door of his neighbor."

"Which neighbor?" the king asked, agitated.

"Mademoiselle Delorme."

"Mademoiselle Delorme! Did he visit Mademoiselle Delorme?"

"No, Sire, he just knocked on the door, and when a servant answered, he gave him a letter."

"A letter!"

"Yes, Sire. Then, the letter delivered, he got back in the chair and was returned to the Louvre. This morning, he went out again. . . ."

"Yes. He was taken to Monsieur Lopez's shop, where he bought some jewelry, and then . . . and then where did he go?"

"He returned to the Louvre, Sire, but reserved the use of a chair for the entire night."

"Do you have anything else to tell me?"

"About what, Sire?"

"About Monsieur Baradas!"

"No, Sire."

"Then you may go."

"But, Sire, I need to report about Madame de Fargis."

"Go."

"About Monsieur de Marillac."

"Go."

"About Monsieur your brother!"

"That's *enough* for today. Go!"

"But what about that wounded Étienne Latil, who was taken to see Monsieur le Cardinal at Chaillot?"

"I don't care. Go."

"In that case, Sire, I withdraw."

"Yes. Withdraw."

"Can I, in withdrawing, dare to hope that the king is pleased with me?"

"Only too pleased!"

Souscarrières bowed and backed out.

The king didn't even wait till he was gone before knocking on the panel.

Charpentier appeared.

"Monsieur Charpentier," the king said, "when the cardinal had business with Mademoiselle Delorme, how did he call her?"

"It's quite simple," Charpentier said. He pressed the spring, opened the secret portal, rang the bell between the two doors, and said to the king, "If Mademoiselle Delorme is at home, she will come at once. Does His Majesty wish to receive her alone, or does he wish me to stay?"

"Leave me alone."

Charpentier left. As for Louis XIII, he waited eagerly in front of the secret passage.

After a few seconds, his eager ears heard the sound of a light step. "Ah," he said, "finally I'll know the truth."

He'd hardly finished when the door opened and Marion, wearing a white satin dress with a simple string of pearls at her neck, a forest of dark curls falling on her round white shoulders, appeared in all her eighteen-year-old beauty.

Louis XIII, though rarely susceptible to the beauty of women, stepped back, amazed.

Marion entered, made an adorable little bow in which respect was cleverly mingled with coquetry, then cast down her eyes, modest as a milkmaid. "My king, to whom I have always hoped to have the honor to appear," she said, "has sent for me. On my knees I must hear his words; at his feet I must receive his orders."

The king stammered out a few incoherent words, which gave Marion a chance to enjoy the effect of her entrance. "Impossible," the king said, "impossible. Am I wrong, or are you not Mademoiselle Marie Delorme?"

"But no, Sire! For you, I am just Marion."

"So, if you are Marion . . ."

Marion bowed, eyes downcast in perfect humility.

". . . If you are Marion," continued the king, "you should have received a letter yesterday."

"I receive many every day," said the courtesan, laughing.

"A letter that arrived between five and six o'clock."

"Between five and six o'clock, Sire, I received fourteen letters."

"Did you keep them?"

"I burned twelve of them. The thirteenth I keep near my heart. Here is the fourteenth."

"This is his writing," the king cried. Hastily he took the letter from Marion's hands. He turned it over and over, and said, "It's still unopened."

"As it came from someone near to the king, and as I was aware that today I might have the supreme honor of meeting Your Majesty, I was careful to keep the letter exactly as I received it."

The king looked at Marion in amazement, then shook the letter angrily. "Bah!" he said. "I want to know what this letter says."

"There is a way, Sire, to open it without breaking the seal."

"If I were a police lieutenant, I might do that," said Louis XIII, "but I am a king."

Marion gently took the letter from his hands. "But as it is addressed to me, I may open it." And she unsealed the envelope and gave the letter to Louis XIII.

Louis XIII hesitated a moment, but all the dark feelings that advise a jealous heart made that moment a short one. He read it aloud in a low voice, his tone sinking ever lower as he read.

We must admit, the contents of the letter were not the sort to bring a cheerful expression to Louis's face—a place where, if such an expression ever appeared, it didn't last more than a few minutes.

Herewith, the contents of the letter:

Lovely Marion,

I am twenty years of age; some women have not only been good enough to tell me that I'm a pretty lad, they have gone on to do such things that left no doubt but that they believed it. Also, I'm the leading favorite of King Louis XIII, who, though stingy, was just somehow inspired to give me the gift of three thousand pistoles.

My friend, Saint-Simon, informs me that you are not only the best-looking girl in the world, but moreover the best in every other way as well. Well, I propose we join together to take a month and spend those three thousand pistoles that idiot king gave me. Say, a thousand pistoles on clothes and jewelry, another thousand on horses and carriages, and the last thousand on games and parties. Does this proposition suit you? If you say Yes, I can be there in no time with the money bag. If you say No, I'll tie the bag around my neck and throw myself in the river.

But you will say Yes, won't you? You wouldn't wish to be responsible for the death of a poor lad who has committed no crime other than to love you madly without ever having seen you.

Reply by tomorrow night, and my money bag and I will be at your feet.

Your devoted,
Baradas

Louis read these last lines in a voice so tremulous that it was nearly unintelligible, even if he'd been speaking loud enough to be heard.

The letter ended, his arms dropped, nerveless, the hand holding the letter resting on his knee.

His face as white as the paper, his eyes rose toward heaven in despair, and, like Caesar, who, barely seeming to feel the stabs of the other conspirators, cried out *"Et tu, Brutus!"* when struck by the only hand that was dear to him, Louis XIII exclaimed, in an agonized voice:

"Et tu, Baradas!"

And, without sparing another glance for Marion Delorme, without seeming to even notice she was there, the king threw his cloak over his shoulder, put his hat on his head, pulling it down over his eyes, ran down the stairs, out the door, and into his carriage. A servant closed the door behind him as he cried, "To Chaillot!"

As for Marion, after seeing the king make this curious exit, she ran to the window, drew aside the curtain, and saw him drive off in his carriage. Then, with that mischievous yet charming smile that belonged only to her, she said, "No doubt about it: I shall have to become a page."

XLIV

How Étienne Latil and the Marquis de Pisany, Each Making His First Outing, Happened to Encounter Each Other

We have reported how the cardinal had retired to his country estate at Chaillot and left his house in the Place Royale—in effect, his ministry—to Louis XIII.

The rumor of his disgrace spread rapidly through Paris, and at a rendezvous between Madame de Fargis and Marillac the Minister of Justice at the Inn of the Painted Beard, she gave him the great news.

This great news quickly spread from the chamber where it was reported to the ear of Madame Soleil, and from her to Master Soleil. Together they carried it to Étienne Latil, who had just left his bed three days before and was walking around his room, leaning on his sword.

Master Soleil had offered to lend him his own cane, a handsome one with an agate set in the handle, like that of Mudarra the Bastard in Lope de Vega's play. But Latil refused, deeming it unworthy for a man of the sword to rely on something other than his sword.

At the news of Richelieu's disgrace he stopped short, leaned with both hands on the hilt of his sword and, looking keenly at Master Soleil, asked, "Is what you say the truth?"

"True as the Gospel."

"And where did you get this news?"

"From a lady of the Court."

Étienne Latil knew all too well that the house wherein he'd suffered the injury that had forced him to take up residence also played host to masked and incognito visitors from all walks of society. He took two or three thoughtful steps and then turned again to Master

Soleil. "And now that he's a minister no more, what do you think of the personal safety of Monsieur le Cardinal?"

Master Soleil grimaced and shook his head. "I think that if he hasn't taken his guards with him, he'd better take to wearing that breastplate he wore over his robes at La Rochelle."

"Do you think that's the only risk he runs?" Latil asked.

"Well, there's his food," said Soleil. "I imagine his niece, Madame de Combalet, will take the precaution of finding a reliable taster for him." Then he added, with that broad smile that often brightened his face, "Now, where do you suppose she might find someone like that?"

"He is found, Master Soleil," Latil said. "Call me a sedan chair."

"What, right now?" Master Soleil cried. "You're not recovered! Are you really reckless enough to leave?"

"Yes, I am that reckless, my host. And since I admit I'm reckless, and that such recklessness may cost me my life, we should settle our little account so that, in the event of my death, you've lost nothing. Let's see: three weeks of recuperation; nine pitchers of tea; two mugs of wine; and the devoted care of Madame Soleil, which is beyond price—does that come to more than twenty *pistoles*?"

"Monsieur Latil, please note that I ask no remuneration! The honor that it's been to house you, to feed you . . ."

"Ha! Feed me! That was easy enough."

". . . And to care for you, is quite sufficient! But of course, if you really insist on giving me twenty *pistoles* to acknowledge your satisfaction . . ."

"You won't refuse it?"

"God prevent me from insulting you so!"

"Then call me a chair while I count out your twenty *pistoles.*"

Master Soleil bowed and retired. Upon returning he went straight to the table upon which the twenty *pistoles* were lined up, counted them at a glance with that knack shared by innkeepers and tax collectors, and said, "Your chair is at hand, Monsieur."

Latil sheathed his sword, gestured for Soleil to approach, and said, "Lend me your arm."

"I'll give you my arm to help you leave my house, my dear Monsieur Étienne, but it's with great regret that I'll see you go."

"Soleil, *mon ami,*" said Latil, "I hate to see the slightest cloud cross your resplendent face, so I promise you that when I return to Paris I will stop here first—especially if you still have some of this lovely Coulange wine. I just made its acquaintance two days ago, and I regret not getting to know it more intimately."

"I've laid in three hundred bottles, Monsieur Latil. I'll save it for you."

"At three bottles a day, that will last me three months. So I'll stay with you for three months, Master Soleil, unless I run out of credit."

"You will never run out of credit. A man who is friends with Monsieur de Moret, Monsieur de Montmorency, and Monsieur de Richelieu—a prince, a duke, and a cardinal . . ."

Latil shook his head. "An honest farmer might give you less honor, but he'd be a better risk, Master Soleil," he declared, as he stepped into his sedan chair.

"Where should I tell the porters to take you, Monsieur?" asked the innkeeper.

"First to the Hotel de Montmorency, where I have a duty to perform, and then to Chaillot."

"To the hotel of Monseigneur le Duc de Montmorency," Soleil cried, "by way of the Rue des Blancs-Manteaux and Rue Sainte-Croix-de-la-Bretonnerie!"

The porters didn't need to be told twice, and furthermore they adopted Master Soleil's additional advice to go easy on their client, as he was recovering from a long and painful illness.

They stopped at Montmorency's door. The Swiss doorman, in full regalia, baton in hand, stood on the threshold. Latil beckoned to him, and he approached. "My friend," Latil said, "here's half a *pistole*. Be so kind as to announce me."

The Swiss doffed his hat, and asked whom he should announce.

"The wounded gentleman whom the Comte de Moret had the honor to visit during his illness, who promised to visit him as soon as he could stand. I am out today for the first time and, as promised, here I am. Please inquire if I may have the honor to be received by Monsieur le Comte."

"Monsieur le Comte de Moret left the hotel five days ago," said the Swiss, "and no one knows where he went."

"Not even Monseigneur le Duc?"

"Monseigneur left the previous day for his governorship of Languedoc."

"The dice are against me, but at least I've kept my promise to Monsieur le Comte. That's all you can ask of a man of honor."

"However," said the Swiss, stepping away from the door, "before departing with the page Galaor, the Comte de Moret did have Galaor leave a message with all the doormen and guards, one that may concern Your Lordship."

"What message is that?"

"He left orders that if a certain Étienne Latil presented himself at the hotel, he was to be offered room and board, and be treated as a man of confidence attached to the count's personal house."

Latil tipped his hat to the absent prince, and said, "Monsieur le Comte de Moret conducts himself like the worthy son of Henri IV he is. I am indeed that gentleman, and will have the honor, upon his return, to give him my thanks and enter his service. Here, *mon ami*, is another half a *pistole* for the pleasure of hearing that the Comte de Moret thinks kindly of me. Porters, on to Chaillot—to the estate of Monsieur le Cardinal!"

The porters picked up their poles and resumed their march, taking the Rue Simon-le-Franc, the Rue Maubué, and the Rue Troussevache so that, by the Rue de la Ferronnerie, they finally gained the Rue Saint-Honoré.

But as luck would have it, at the very moment that, at the doors of the Hotel de Montmorency, Latil cried, "On to Chaillot!"—as luck would have it, we say, the Marquis de Pisany, whom we temporarily lost sight of given the important events we had to relate, was just then rising for the first time since receiving his near-fatal sword thrust from Souscarrières. Resolving that his first action once back on his feet should be to apologize to the Comte de Moret, he summoned a chair and, after cautioning the porters to tread easily as he was recovering from a wound, concluded by crying, "On to the Hotel de Montmorency!"

Leaving the Hotel de Rambouillet, the porters went down the Rue Saint-Thomas-du-Louvre to the Rue Saint-Honoré, then made their way toward the Rue de la Ferronnerie.

The result of these reciprocal maneuvers was that the two chairs met at the head of the Rue de l'Arbre-Sec. The Marquis de Pisany, preoccupied with how to approach the Comte de Moret, failed to recognize Étienne Latil—but Latil, whose mind was free of care, instantly recognized the Marquis de Pisany.

One can imagine the effect this apparition had upon the irascible swashbuckler. He uttered a cry that stopped his porters in their tracks and, thrusting his head out the window, shouted, "Hey! Monsieur Hunchback!"

It might have been wiser for the Marquis de Pisany to pretend the insult was addressed to someone else, but he was so sensitive about his hump that his first impulse was to stick his head out the door of his chair, in order to see who was addressing him by his deformity rather than his title.

"To what do I owe the pleasure?" asked the marquis, as his porters settled to a stop.

"It would be my pleasure if you'd stop a moment. I have a score to settle with you," said Latil. Then, to his porters: "Quick! Set my chair down so my door is lined up with his."

The porters picked up their poles and aligned Latil's sedan chair with Pisany's. "How's this, Monsieur?" they asked.

"Perfect!" Latil said. "Ahh!"

This sigh came from his satisfaction at finally confronting his nemesis, whose name was yet unknown but whose rank had been revealed by the ring he'd been shown.

For his part, Pisany had finally recognized Latil. "Onward!" he shouted to his porters. "I want nothing to do with this man."

"Perhaps, but unfortunately, this man has dealings with you, my darling. Don't move, any of you!" he shouted to the porters of the other chair. "Don't you dare budge, or *ventre-saint-gris,* as Henri IV used to say, I'll cut off your ears!"

The porters, who'd been raising Pisany's chair, set it back on the pavement. Meanwhile passersby, attracted by the fracas, began to gather around the two chairs.

"And I say," Pisany cried, "that if you don't carry me on, I'll send my men to beat you!"

The marquis's porters all shook their heads. "Better to be beaten," one said, "than to lose our ears."

"Send your men," said another. "We have sticks of our own."

"Bravo, my friends!" said Latil, who saw that luck was with him. "Here are four *pistoles* with which to drink my health! Now, I dare to give my name, which is Étienne Latil. Do you dare to give yours, Monsieur Hunchback?"

"You wretch!" cried Pisany. "Wasn't being impaled on two swords enough for you?"

"It was not only enough," replied Latil, "it was too much. But I'll settle for impaling you just once."

"Would you abuse a man who can't even stand on his own two legs?"

"Is that the situation?" asked Latil. "In that case, the playing field is even. We shall fight while seated. *En garde*, Marquis . . . Oh, dear! Without your three accomplices, who will stab me from behind?" Latil drew his sword and hovered the tip beneath his opponent's eye.

There was no way to decline. Witnesses surrounded the two chairs. Moreover, as we've said, the Marquis de Pisany was no coward. He drew his sword.

The fighters, whose only doors faced each other, were obscured to all other observers, who could only glimpse two blades flashing between the chairs. They passed, crossed, parried, feinted, thrust, and riposted, while cries of rage came first from one door, then from the other.

Finally, after a duel that lasted nearly five minutes, to the great entertainment of the audience, there was a cry—or rather, a blasphemy—from one of the two combatants. Latil had nailed his opponent's arm to the frame of his chair.

"There!" said Étienne Latil. "Take that, my good Marquis—and remember that every time we meet, you'll be served the same way."

The common people love a winner, especially when he's good-looking or generous. Latil was reasonably handsome, and what's more, he'd thrown the porters four *pistoles*.

The Marquis de Pisany, on the other hand, was ugly, defeated, and had kept his *pistoles* to himself. If he called upon the audience for aid and justice, he would certainly be mocked and denied. So he made up his mind: "To the Hotel de Rambouillet," he said.

"To Chaillot!" said Étienne Latil.

XLV

The Cardinal at Chaillot

Arriving at Chaillot, the cardinal found himself in much the same situation as Atlas when, after bearing the weight of the world, he was able to place it for a few moments on the shoulders of his friend Hercules. He felt at last he could take a breath. "Ah," he whispered, "I shall have the time to write poetry."

Indeed, Chaillot was the retreat the cardinal had bought as an escape from politics, where he could write, if not true poetry, at least a little verse.

An office on the ground floor that opened onto a beautiful garden, with an avenue of lime trees dark and cool even in summer, was the sanctuary where he'd taken refuge one or two days a month.

Now he'd returned to that repose and renewal. For how long? He couldn't tell.

His first idea, upon setting foot in this poetic oasis, was to call for his usual collaborators, those writers who, in his battles of the mind, were like the generals he sent to war in Spain and Italy. Against such as England's Shakespeare, with Rotrou and Corneille he marshaled his French forces of letters.

Then it occurred to him that, though master of his house at Chaillot, he was no longer the powerful minister distributing largesse. Here he was only a private citizen with whom, suddenly, it was dangerous to associate. He therefore resolved to wait and see which old friends would come to him without being summoned.

So he drew forth the outline of his new tragedy, *Mirame*, which was nothing less than a retaliation in words against the reigning queen, and reviewed the scenes he'd already begun.

Cardinal Richelieu, poor Catholic though he was, was even worse when it came to the Christian virtue of forgiving one's enemies. He'd been devastated by the pernicious plot that had toppled him from power, and blamed Queen Anne as one of its prime movers. So he consoled himself with the idea of taking what revenge he could.

We are sorry to have to reveal this petty weakness in such a great minister, but we are his historian, not his apologist.

The first show of sympathy for his plight came from an unexpected quarter. Guillemot, his valet, announced that a sedan chair had arrived bearing a man who seemed to be recovering from serious illness or injury. He had gotten as far as a bench in the entry hall where he had sunk down in exhaustion, saying "My place is here."

The porters, paid off, trotted away as quickly as they'd come.

This man, who wore a somewhat battered felt hat and a cloak the color of Spanish tobacco, was dressed in a manner more military than civilian, and bore a rapier like those we see in the sketches of Callot, in the style that was just beginning to become fashionable.

When asked what name should be announced to the cardinal, "I am nobody," he replied, "so announce no one."

Asked why he had come, he said simply, "His Eminence is short of guards. I'll help ensure his safety."

This seemed strange enough to Guillemot that he thought he'd better inform Madame de Combalet and Monsieur le Cardinal. The cardinal ordered this mysterious guardian brought before him.

Five minutes later, the door opened and Étienne Latil appeared in the doorway, pale and leaning on the jamb, his hat in his right hand, the left on the pommel of his sword.

With his knack for remembering faces, Richelieu recognized him at a glance. "Ah!" he said. "Is that you, my dear Latil?"

"In person, Your Eminence."

"Are you doing better?"

"Yes, Monseigneur, so since I'm recovered I've come to offer my services to Your Eminence."

"My thanks, Monsieur," the cardinal laughed, "but there's no one I need you to rid me of."

"That may be," said Latil, "but aren't there those who'd like to be rid of you?"

"Now that you mention it," said the cardinal, "that seems quite likely."

Just then Madame de Combalet entered through a side door, her worried gaze darting quickly from her uncle to the unknown adventurer.

"Come, Marie," said the cardinal, "and help me welcome this brave lad, the first who's come to help me in my day of adversity."

"Oh, I won't be the last," said Latil, "but I'm not sorry to be counted as the first."

"Uncle," said Madame de Combalet, after regarding Latil with the sympathetic eye of a woman, "monsieur is pale and stricken with weakness."

"Which speaks all the better for him. I know from my doctor, who's been looking in on him, that he only got up for the first time three days ago. This visit, so early, is entirely to his credit."

"Oh," said Madame de Combalet, "so this is the gentleman who was wounded in the brawl at the Inn of the Painted Beard?"

"You're right, fair lady, and my hat's off to you," said Latil. "They got me in an ambush, but I finally caught up with that cursed hunchback, and sent him home just now with a sword thrust through the arm."

"The Marquis de Pisany?" said Madame de Combalet. "That poor wretch has no luck. He'd just spent over a week recovering from a wound he'd received the same night you were nearly murdered."

"The Marquis de Pisany, eh?" Latil said. "It's good to finally know his name. That explains why, when I told my porters 'To Chaillot,' he said to his 'To the Hotel de Rambouillet'—an address I took care to remember."

"If you were both recovering from wounds, how did you manage to have a duel?" asked the cardinal.

"We fought from our sedan chairs, Monseigneur. It was most convenient, just the thing for wounded swordsmen."

"And you're telling me this, after my edicts outlawing duels!" said the cardinal. "Though it is a fact that I'm no longer a minister, so it's not my problem. In fact, given a year . . ." And the cardinal sighed, which proved he wasn't so removed from worldly things as he wanted to believe.

"But didn't you say, dear Uncle, that Monsieur Latil—that is your name, is it not?—had come to offer his services?" asked Madame de Combalet. "What services does he offer?"

Latil raised his sword. "Services both offensive and defensive," he said. "Monsieur le Cardinal lacks both a Captain of the Guards, and guards for him to captain. I will take their place."

"A new Captain of the Guards?" said a feminine voice from behind Latil. "I don't think so. Not so long as he still has his Cavois! . . . Who is, of course, also *my* Cavois."

"Ah!" said the cardinal. "There's a voice I know. Come in, dear Madame Cavois, come in."

A lithe and pretty woman, though starting, in her thirties, to be more plump than lithe, slipped into the room, brushed past Latil, and presented herself to the cardinal and Madame de Combalet.

"At last," she said, rubbing her hands, "you're free from that awful ministry and all the trouble it gave us!"

"Gave us, you say?" said the cardinal. "So my ministry gave you troubles as well, dear Madame?"

"I should say so! I couldn't sleep day or night, I was so afraid some catastrophe would strike Your Eminence, and take my poor Cavois as well. All day I worried, and jumped at the slightest sound. All night I dreamed, and woke up with a start. You have no idea how bad a woman's dreams can be when she sleeps alone."

"But what of Monsieur Cavois?" asked Madame de Combalet, laughing.

"When he did sleep with me, you mean? Oh, Cavois! At least we never lost the will for it, thank God. Ten children in nine years, which shows we couldn't get enough, but as time went on, I was more and more troubled. Then Monsieur le Cardinal took him to the Siege of La Rochelle, which lasted eight months! Fortunately I was already expecting when he left, so no time was lost. But this time, Madame, His Eminence was going to take him away to Italy. Can you believe it? And for God knows how long! But I prayed to God for a miracle, and thanks to my prayers Monsieur le Cardinal has lost his position."

"Why, thank you, Madame Cavois!" laughed the cardinal.

"Yes, thank you," said Madame de Combalet. "It was a big favor, indeed, that God has granted us. It gives you your husband and me my uncle."

"Fah!" said Madame Cavois. "A husband and an uncle are not the same thing at all."

"But, Madame," said the cardinal, "unless Cavois goes with me into disgrace, he must follow the king."

"To where?" asked Madame Cavois.

"To Italy!"

"Him, go to Italy? Certainly not, Monseigneur. Him, leave me? Leave his little woman? Never!"

"But didn't he leave you to go on campaign with me?"

"Oh, with you, yes. I think you bewitched him somehow. His wits aren't that quick, poor man, and if he hadn't had me to manage our home and raise our children, I don't know what he would have done. But leave me to go with someone other than you? Never! He's as likely to risk God's wrath by sleeping with another woman."

"But what of his duties?"

"What duties?"

"If he's no longer in my service, he must serve the king."

"If he's no longer in your service, Monseigneur, he must serve me! I imagine that by this time he's already presented his resignation to His Majesty."

"Did he tell you he was going to do that?" asked Madame de Combalet.

"Does he need to tell me everything he's going to do? Don't I always know what he does before he does it? Isn't he as transparent to me as crystal? When I tell you that by now he's probably done it, then he has!"

"But, my dear Madame Cavois," said the cardinal, "as captain of my guards he earned six thousand *livres* per year. As a private citizen, I can't pay a captain of the guards six thousand *livres*. That's a lot to lose from your household budget. Think of your eight children!"

"Yes, but haven't you already covered that? Half the sedan-chair monopoly is worth at least twelve thousand *livres* a year—and isn't that preferable to depending on a position with the king, from which he might be dismissed at the slightest whim? Our children, thanks be to God, are plump and stout, and you shall see they lack nothing. If you have healthy children, you have everything!"

"What, are your children here?"

"All but the one who was born during the Siege of La Rochelle, who is only five months old and still with the wet nurse. But he's as healthy as the rest."

"With a wet nurse? Then, are you expecting again, Madame Cavois?"

"By the grace of God! After all, my husband's been back for nearly a month. Come in! Come in, everyone! By the cardinal's permission!"

"Yes, I will permit it—but at the same time I must permit, or rather command, Latil to take a seat. Take a chair and sit down, Latil."

Latil didn't speak, but he quickly obeyed. Another minute on his feet and he would have fainted.

Meanwhile, all the Cavois children trooped into the room in order of age, the eldest first, a sweet boy of the age of nine, then a girl, then another boy, then another girl, all the way down to an infant of two years.

Arrayed in front of the cardinal, from tallest to shortest, they looked like a set of pan-pipes.

"Now, then," said Madame de Cavois, "here is the man to whom we owe everything—you, me, and Papa. Kneel before him and offer him your thanks."

"Madame Cavois! We do not kneel save before the Lord."

"And before those who represent him. Kneel, you puppies."

The children obeyed.

"Now, Armand," said Madame de Cavois to the eldest boy, "repeat to Monsieur le Cardinal the prayer I taught you to say every morning and night."

"Lord God," said the child, "grant health to my father, my mother, my brothers, and my sisters, and see to it that His Eminence the Cardinal, to whom we owe everything, shall lose his ministry so that Papa can spend his nights at home."

"Amen!" the children replied in unison.

"Well," said the cardinal, laughing, "it's no surprise to me that such a prayer, offered so earnestly by so many voices, was granted."

"*Là!*" said Madame Cavois. "And now that we've said everything to Monseigneur that we had to say, get up and go on out." The children rose and left the room in the same order they'd come in. "Good!" said Madame Cavois. "Very obedient."

"Madame Cavois," said the cardinal, "If I'm ever restored to my ministry, I shall appoint you as drill instructor to the King's Infantry."

"God forbid, Monseigneur!"

Madame de Combalet kissed the children and their mother, who loaded them into three waiting sedan chairs, before entering a fourth herself with the two-year-old. The cardinal watched them go with some emotion.

"Monseigneur," said Latil, straightening himself on his chair, "you won't need me as a man of the sword, since Monsieur Cavois also follows you in your fall from grace, but it's not really steel that you have to fear. For your true enemy goes by the name of Médicis."

"I am entirely of the same mind," said Madame de Combalet, coming back into the room. "And I fear the same thing: poison."

"You need someone devoted to you, Your Eminence, who will taste everything you drink and everything you eat before you do. I offer myself for this role."

"I'm so sorry, my dear Monsieur Latil," smiled Madame de Combalet, "but you're too late. Someone else has already offered to do that."

"And has been accepted?"

"I sincerely hope so," Madame said, gazing tenderly at her uncle.

"And who is that?" asked Latil.

"Me," said Madame de Combalet.

"In that case," said Latil, "there's no need for me here. Adieu, Monseigneur."

"What are you doing?" the cardinal said.

"I'm leaving. You have a guard captain, and you have a devoted taster, so in what way could I serve Your Eminence?"

"As a friend. Étienne Latil, a heart like yours is hard to find, and having found it, I intend to keep it." Then, turning to Madame de Combalet, he said, "My dear Marie, I entrust to you, body and soul, my friend Latil here. Though right now I can't find a position equal to his merits, the opportunity may yet present itself.

"Now, let's see if my literary friends are as loyal to me as my guard captain and my lieutenant. I need to know how tomorrow will be spent."

"Monsieur Jean Rotrou," announced the voice of Guillemot.

"There, you see?" the cardinal said to Latil and Madame de Combalet. "One arrives already, and not one I expected."

"The devil!" Latil said to himself. "Thank God my father never taught me to appreciate poetry."

XLVI

Mirame

Rotrou did not arrive alone. The cardinal gazed curiously at the unknown companion who followed him, hat in hand, his half-bow indicating admiration rather than servility.

"So it's you, Rotrou," said the cardinal, taking his hand. "I won't hide from you that I rely on the loyalty of my fellow poets above that of all others. I'm pleased to see that you're the most faithful of my followers."

"If I could have predicted that this would happen to you, Monseigneur, I'd have been here even sooner! What I can predict is that if your fall from power closes some doors, it will open others. Now," Rotrou said, rubbing his hands together, "let's write some poetry!"

"And is this young man of the same opinion?" Richelieu asked, looking at Rotrou's companion.

"So much so, Monseigneur, that when he came running to tell me the news he'd heard at Madame de Rambouillet's, that Your Eminence was no longer a minister, he begged me to introduce him to you immediately. He hopes that, now that affairs of state no longer occupy your time, you'll be able to go see his comedy when it plays at the Hotel de Bourgogne."

This proposal to a Prince of the Church, which might appear improper today, seemed not at all strange or scandalous to Richelieu. "And what is this piece you've presented to the comedians at the Bourgogne?" asked the cardinal.

The young man dressed in black shyly replied, "It's called *Mélite*, Monseigneur."

"Ah!" Richelieu said. "Then you must be that Monsieur Corneille whom your friend Rotrou says will shortly surpass us all, himself included."

"Friends can exaggerate, Monseigneur—and Rotrou is even more than a friend to me: he's a brother."

"The ancients tell us of such friendships between warriors, but never between poets," Richelieu said to them, then turned to Corneille. "Are you ambitious, young man?"

"I am, Monseigneur. And I have one ambition above all that, if realized, will fill me with joy."

"And that is?"

"Ask my friend Rotrou."

"So! Ambitious yet shy," said the cardinal.

"Better than shy, Monseigneur," said Rotrou. "Modest!"

"And this ambition of yours," asked the cardinal, "is it something that I can grant you?"

"In a word, Monseigneur—yes," said Corneille.

"Then speak of it. I've never been more willing to realize the ambitions of others than since my own have been thwarted."

Rotrou said, "Monseigneur, my friend Corneille longs for the honor of being one of your collaborators. If Your Eminence had continued as a minister, he'd hoped that the success of his comedy would enable him to be presented to you. However, now that you are merely a man of greatness, with time for great works ahead of you, he said to me, 'Jean, *mon ami*, now the cardinal will turn to his real work. Introduce me to him while there is still a place by his side.'"

"There is still a place, Monsieur Corneille," said the cardinal, "and you shall have it. Dine with me, Messieurs, and if our other companions happen to join us, I'll share with all of you my new drama, of which I've already outlined a few scenes."

The cardinal was not disappointed in his hopes, for by supper-time he'd gathered around his table his five collaborators: that is,

Bois-Robert, Colletet, L'Estoile, Rotrou, and Corneille. Richelieu received them with as much honor as if he was dining with his peers. After dinner, he led them into his study, where Richelieu, burning with impatience to share his new project with his colleagues, drew forth a folio upon which was written, in large letters:

MIRAME

"Messieurs," said the cardinal, "everything we have done so far is just the prologue to this work. The name 'Mirame' means nothing to you, of course, as the name, like the play, is a work of pure invention. But it is not given to man to create, only to replicate creation, to the degree that the poet has talent and imagination. So you will probably recognize the real people and places represented by the fictitious names herein. I hope that will inform your comments, which are entirely welcome."

His listeners bowed. Corneille glanced at Rotrou, as if to say, "I have no idea what this means, but I trust you'll explain it later." Rotrou reassured him with a gesture.

Richelieu waited for the young men to complete their pantomime, then continued: "Imagine a King of Bithynia—or wherever—who is rival to the King of Colchis. The King of Bithynia has a daughter named Mirame, who has a confidante named Almire and a servant named Alcine. For his part, the King of Colchis, who is at war with Bithynia, has a sly, seductive, and elegant favorite named Arimant. You might find someone like him in a country neighboring our own France."

"The Duke of Buckingham," said Bois-Robert.

"Quite so," said Richelieu.

Rotrou bumped his knee against that of Corneille, who was still struggling to follow, though the name of Buckingham clarified things a bit.

"Now Azamor, the King of Phrygia, and ally to the King of Bithynia, is not only in love with Mirame, he is her fiancé."

"But she, of course, is in love with Arimant," said Bois-Robert.

"You've got it, Le Bois," said Richelieu, laughing. "You see the situation, don't you, Messieurs?"

"It's simple," said Colletet. "Mirame loves her father's enemy, and so betrays her father to her lover."

Rotrou again knocked his knee against Corneille's, but Corneille was all at sea.

"That goes too far, Colletet," said the cardinal. "A wife may betray her husband, but for a daughter to betray her father, that goes too far. No, in the second act, she merely receives her lover in the palace gardens."

"As a certain Queen of France," said L'Estoile, "received Milord Buckingham . . ."

"Hush, Monsieur de L'Estoile! One would think such a rumor was historical fact. Anyway, at last the two sides come to blows. Arimant wins the first victory, but then, in one of those reverses so common in the annals of war, he's defeated by Azamor. Mirame learns that her lover's victory has turned to defeat, and is overcome with sorrow. Arimant cannot face his defeat, throws himself on his sword, and is believed dead. Mirame wants to follow him in death, and turns to her confidante, Madame de Chevreuse . . . no, my mistake! 'Madame de Chevreuse,' what was I thinking? Mirame speaks to her confidante, Almire, and asks her to take poison with her, an herb she brought from Colchis. They consume the poison and fall into a swoon.

"Meanwhile, Arimant has recovered from his wounds, which weren't fatal. But he is stricken with despair upon learning of the death of Mirame. Everyone is in anguish until Almire reveals that she gave the princess a sleeping draught rather than poison, much like that which Medea gave the serpent that guarded the Golden

Fleece. So Mirame isn't dead after all, the King of Colchis makes peace with Azamor, and Mirame is united with Arimant."

"Bravo!" Colletet, L'Estoile, and Bois-Robert cried as one.

"It's sublime!" added Bois-Robert, hoping to take the lead.

"Indeed, it's not bad at all," said Rotrou. "What do you think, Corneille?"

Corneille nodded tentatively.

"You don't exactly seem thrilled, Monsieur Corneille," said Richelieu, a little piqued by the lack of enthusiasm on the part of his youngest listener.

"Not at all, Monseigneur," said Corneille. "I was just thinking about the play's structure."

"It's perfect," said Richelieu. "The first act ends with the scene between Almire and Mirame where Mirame agrees to receive Arimant in the palace gardens. The second ends when, having received him, she recoils from his impudence and cries, 'What have I done? I'm no better than a criminal!' Her infidelity is exposed to all!"

"Bravo!" applauded Le Bois. "Thesis and antithesis! It's classical!"

"The third act," the cardinal continued, "ends in despair, as Azamor realizes that, despite his victory, Mirame prefers Arimant. The fourth act ends with the 'death' of Mirame, and the fifth, the King of Bithynia's consent to his daughter's marriage with Arimant."

"Exactly!" said L'Estoile. "The drama is complete, and couldn't be more perfect, Monseigneur!"

"Quite so," said Richelieu. "And I've already written a number of verses, which I'm quite fond of, that will put the story across."

"Will you share these verses with us, Monseigneur?" said Bois-Robert.

"Very well. Here's the first scene between the king and his confidant, Acaste, in which the king complains of his daughter's love for his enemy:"

⚜

THE KING: Arimant's plans will come to naught,
    His army's a figment that's never fought,
    Yet I fear no matter what I do,
    My daughter's love will blind her view.
    Indeed, it's due to my blood, I fear.

ACASTE: What, Sire, your blood?

THE KING: My blood. Now hear:
    Our royal blood is my enemy's aim
    It draws him on like a heavenly flame
    A flame that's fatal to all of my name
    To the State, and most of all, Mirame
    Whose heart is drawn by the ploys of this stranger
    Leading him on, increasing the danger
    Even when I gain the victory
    She gives it to him!

ACASTE: Lord! Can it be?

THE KING: Acaste, it's true. He works each day
    To subvert my state in every way
    To corrupt my folk, thwart my every effort
    Some plots we see, but others are covert!

To these verses, emphatically delivered, the applause of his listeners rang out.

At that time, dramatic verse was still far from the degree of perfection later reached by Corneille and Racine. The antithesis was the prevailing mode until the end of this period, when good poetry began to be preferred to pretty poetry, and verse that truly conveyed character and context came into its own.

Elated by the unanimous approval, Richelieu continued. "In the same act," he said, "I've sketched out a scene between Mirame and her father, a scene that I want you to keep, Messieurs, when I charge you with completion of the first act. This scene encapsulates my ideas, and must be retained as is."

"Read it to us, Monseigneur," cried L'Estoile, Colletet, and Bois-Robert.

"We are all ears, Monseigneur," said Rotrou.

"I forgot to mention that Mirame was originally engaged to the Prince of Colchis," said Richelieu, "but he has died, so she uses her loyalty to him as an excuse to stave off marrying Azamor and to flirt with Arimant. Now, here is the scene between her and her father. You may all read into it what allusions you like."

THE KING: Daughter, I am a soul all ambivalent
      Full of vain hope, vainglorious Arimant
      Comes to parlay with me, but hopes to see you
      What prospects for peace are really in view?

"In other words: Buckingham says he comes as ambassador to King Louis XIII, but actually to see Her Majesty," said Bois-Robert.

For the third time, Rotrou nudged Corneille's knee.

Richelieu said, "Mirame replies:"

      If he comes to make peace, then I rejoice
      Succeed, and to see him would be my choice
      But if he breaks with us, there's no reason why
      I'd receive this foreigner; I'd sooner die.

THE KING: What if it was he who was Colchis's king?

MIRAME: If he hates you, he earns my loathing

THE KING: Though born a subject, his aims are high

MIRAME: Against you, his plans will go awry

THE KING: He claims the favor of Venus and Mars

". . . I really want this to be kept as is," said Richelieu, interrupting himself.

"No one who understands its beauty would dare to touch it," said Bois-Robert. "Go on, go on!"

The cardinal, reassured, continued: He claims the favor of Venus and Mars

MIRAME: As do many who are varlets and beggars

"I beg you as well to make no changes," Colletet said. Richelieu continued:

THE KING: He boasts of having a secret bliss

MIRAME: No trustworthy lover would ever say this

"That was well put," murmured Corneille.

"Do you think so, young man?" Richelieu said complacently.

THE KING: He claims he holds the heart of a beautiful lady

MIRAME: It's not I; I'd never do something so shady

THE KING: Why do you blush if he's not your beau?

MIRAME: It's anger, it's fury that makes me blush so!

❧

Richelieu stopped. "That's as far as I got," he said. "In the second and third acts, I also roughed out some scenes that I'll share with those who will be finishing those acts."

"Who will complete the first act?" said Bois-Robert. "Who will dare to put his words next to yours, Monseigneur?"

"Ah, Messieurs!" Richelieu said, childishly happier about being praised by these poets than he'd ever been by political success. "If you find the first act too daunting, there are five of you, and five acts—you can draw lots!"

"Nothing is too daunting for youth," said Rotrou. "My friend Corneille and I will take the first two acts."

"You are bold!" Richelieu said, laughing.

"Not too bold, so long as Your Eminence will give us a detailed outline of the scenes, so we know how to conform to his intentions."

"Well, then," said Bois-Robert, "I'll take care of the third."

"I'll take the fourth," said L'Estoile.

"And me, the fifth," said Colletet.

"If you're taking the conclusion, Colletet," Richelieu said, "then I suggest . . ." And, placing his hand on Colletet's shoulder, he drew him into the embrasure of a window, where they spoke in low voices.

Meanwhile, Rotrou leaned over to Corneille and whispered, "Pierre, from here on, your fortune is in your own hands, and it's up to you not to let it escape."

"How do I do that?" Corneille asked innocently.

"Make sure you write no verse that is better than the cardinal's," said Rotrou.

XLVII

News from the Court

With the five acts of *Mirame* assigned, and suggestions on the fifth given to Colletet, the cardinal's collaborators took their leave, except for Corneille and Rotrou, whom he kept for part of the evening to explain his plans for the first two acts.

Corneille and Rotrou slept at Chaillot that night. Bois-Robert returned the next morning to receive instructions for himself and his two companions, as he was responsible for communication with them. All three had lunch with the cardinal, who gave them his final instructions. After lunch, Corneille and Rotrou took their leave, but Bois-Robert remained.

The cardinal had few secrets from Bois-Robert, and Bois-Robert had seen past the cardinal's pleasure in discussing his drama to the deep concern beyond.

Bois-Robert had talked with Charpentier and Rossignol, and knew all about the return reports of Bautru, La Saludie, and Charnassé. The day before, he had visited Father Joseph at his monastery, and could tell the cardinal the monk's thoughts about affairs. The news pleased Richelieu, who had full confidence in the monk's discretion and his lack of ambition—for though Joseph would eventually betray him, that time had not yet come. Finally, he'd brought the daily reports from Souscarrières and Lopez.

So all hope that the king might yet turn back to him was not lost, and though three days had passed, the cardinal wasn't ready to despair.

About two o'clock, they heard the gallop of an approaching horse, and the cardinal ran to the window, though of course such a rapid rider couldn't be the king.

The cardinal was so sure of himself that he couldn't contain a cry of joy, for he saw a young man wearing the livery of the king's pages jump lightly down from his horse and throw the reins to one of the cardinal's hostlers. Richelieu recognized the page as Saint-Simon, the friend of Baradas who'd carried an important note to Marion Delorme. "Bois-Robert," the cardinal said eagerly, "bring that young man to me, and make sure we are interrupted by no one."

Bois-Robert dashed down the stairs, and within moments the cardinal heard the footsteps of a young man climbing the stairs four at a time.

At the door of the cardinal's study, he received him face to face. The young man stopped short, snatched rather than doffed his hat from his head, and dropped to kneel before the cardinal. "What are you doing, Monsieur?" the cardinal asked, laughing. "I'm not the king!"

"Not any more, Monseigneur, it's true," said the young man, "but with God's help, you will be again."

A frisson of joy ran through the cardinal. "You've done me a service, Monsieur," he said, "and if I become a minister again, whether or not I deserve it, I'll try to forget my enemies—but I promise to remember my friends. So, do you have good news for me? But get up, I beg you."

"I come from a lady whom I don't dare to name before Monseigneur," Saint-Simon said, standing.

"Very well," said the cardinal. "I can guess."

"She asked me to tell Your Eminence that she spoke with the king for several hours, and would be very much surprised if, by half past three this afternoon, the king was not at Chaillot."

"This lady must not be a lady of the Court," Richelieu said, "as she ignores the rules of etiquette, which dictate that the king could not personally visit such a humble subject as I."

"She is not a lady of the Court, that's true," said Saint-Simon, "but many habitués of the Court honor her with their visits. So I think, if I might, that it's safe to place some credence in her predictions."

"Has she ever shared her opinions with you?"

"With me, Monseigneur?" Saint-Simon laughed heartily with the joy of youth, incidentally showing off a beautiful set of teeth.

"Did she ever tell you that, if Monsieur Baradas ever fell out of favor with the king, in all probability his successor would be Monsieur de Saint-Simon—especially if he was endorsed by a cardinal-minister recently restored to power?"

"She . . . may have mentioned something like that, Monseigneur, but it was nothing so strong as a prediction. It was more of a promise, and I trust less in the promise of a Marion Delorme . . . ah, *mon Dieu*, I've named her!"

"I am like Caesar," said Richelieu, "a little hard of hearing in the right ear. What was that?"

"Sorry, Monseigneur," said Saint-Simon, "but I thought Caesar was hard of hearing in the left ear."

"You may be right," said the cardinal. "In any case, I have the advantage over him, as I'm deaf in whichever ear I choose. But you come from the Court. What's the news? Of course, I'm only asking what everyone would know, since I'm way out here in provincial Chaillot."

"Here is the news, in a nutshell," said Saint-Simon. "Monsieur le Cardinal resigned, and for three days there was celebration at the Louvre."

"I've heard that."

"The king promised largesse to everyone: a hundred and fifty thousand *livres* to the Duc d'Orléans, sixty thousand to the queen mother, and thirty thousand to the queen."

"And has he given them the money?"

"Not yet. Those who received these promises were so incautious as to rely on the king's word, and didn't get him to sign vouchers to Charpentier on the spot. But . . ."

"But?"

"But the next day, after returning from the Place Royale, the king confined himself to his chambers, where he dined alone with l'Angely. There he offered thirty thousand *livres* to l'Angely, who refused it outright."

"Ah!"

"Is Your Eminence surprised?"

"Not at all."

"Then he received Baradas, to whom he'd promised thirty thousand *livres,* but he, less confident than Monsieur, the queen mother, or the queen, and who wasn't sure who had the key to the treasure, whether it was Marillac the Keeper of the Seals, his brother Marillac the general, La Vieuville, or even Monsieur de Bassompierre. . . ."

"It was the king! The king!"

"The king?" Saint-Simon repeated.

"Yes! Has His Majesty met with the Council?"

"No, Monseigneur, the king told them he was unwell."

"What did they want to discuss, do you know?"

"The war, probably."

"What makes you think that?"

"Monseigneur Gaston was furious because of something Monsieur de Bassompierre had said."

"What had he said?"

"Monseigneur Gaston, in his capacity as lieutenant general, was tracing out the army's route of march. At one point it involved crossing a river—the Durance, I think. 'Where shall we cross it?' Bassompierre asked. 'Here, Monsieur,' replied Monseigneur Gaston, placing his finger on the map. Bassompierre said, 'I beg you to observe, Monseigneur, that your finger is not a bridge.' Monseigneur Gaston stormed out of the council in a fury."

A wry smile lit up Richelieu's face. "Let them do as they please," he said. "They can cross the rivers wherever they want to, and I'll just laugh at their disasters from a safe distance."

"Please do not laugh, Monseigneur," said Saint-Simon, in an unexpectedly serious tone. Richelieu looked at him, surprised. "Their disasters," the young man continued, "would be France's disasters."

"Well said, Monsieur," the cardinal replied, "and I thank you. So you're saying the king hasn't seen anyone from his family since yesterday."

"No one, Monseigneur—I assure you."

"And only Monsieur Baradas has collected his thirty thousand *livres*."

"Of that I'm sure. He called me to the bottom of the stairs to help him carry up his new riches."

"And what will he do with his thirty thousand *livres*?"

"Nothing yet, Monseigneur. But in a letter, he offered to Marion Delorme—I mentioned her name once, so I may do so again, may I not?"

"You may. What did he offer to Marion Delorme?"

"To spend the money with her."

"And how did he make this offer? Verbally?"

"No. By letter, fortunately."

"And Marion kept this letter, I hope? She has the letter in her hands?"

Saint-Simon took out his watch. "Half past three," he said. "By this time, she must have given it up."

"To who?" the cardinal demanded.

"To who but the king, Monseigneur?"

"To the king!"

"That's what made her think the afternoon wouldn't pass without you receiving a visit from His Majesty."

"Ah! Now I understand."

Just then they heard the sound of a carriage arriving at speed.

The cardinal, suddenly pale, leaned on a chair.

Saint-Simon ran to the window. "The king!" he shouted.

A moment later, the door to the stairs opened and Bois-Robert rushed in, shouting, "The king!"

The door to Madame de Combalet's chambers opened and she whispered, in a voice trembling with emotion, "The king."

"Go, all of you," said the cardinal. "Leave me alone with His Majesty."

Each disappeared through a different door, while the cardinal mopped his brow.

Then steps were heard on the stairs, ascending, one at a time, in a measured meter.

Guillemot appeared at the door and announced, "The king."

"By my faith," the cardinal murmured, "in Marion Delorme, I have a great diplomat as a neighbor."

XLVIII

Why Louis XIII Always Dressed in Black

Guillemot disappeared. King Louis XIII came face to face with Cardinal Richelieu. "Sire," Richelieu said, bowing respectfully, "I was so surprised to hear that the king was at the door of my humble home that, instead of rushing downstairs as I should have, I stayed here, as if my feet were nailed to the floor, stunned and doubting that it could really be His Majesty himself who deigned to visit me."

The king looked around him. "We are alone, Monsieur le Cardinal?" he asked.

"Alone, Your Majesty."

"Are you sure?"

"Quite certain, Sire."

"So we can speak freely?"

"Entirely freely."

"Then close that door and listen to what I have to say."

The cardinal bowed and obeyed, shutting the door and indicating a chair to the king, who sat, or rather sank, into it. The cardinal stood by and waited.

The king slowly raised his eyes to the cardinal, regarding him for a moment, then said, "Monsieur le Cardinal, I was wrong."

"Wrong, Sire? In what?"

"To do what I did."

It was the cardinal's turn to stare at the king. "Sire," he finally said, "I believe a frank discussion, clear and precise, that leaves not a cloud, a doubt, or a shadow between us, has long been necessary. The words Your Majesty just said lead me to believe that the time for that discussion has come."

"Monsieur le Cardinal," said Louis XIII, drawing himself up, "I hope you will not go so far as to forget . . ."

". . . That you are King Louis XIII, and I am your humble servant Cardinal Richelieu? No, Sire, rest easy. However, given the deep respect I have for Your Majesty, I beg leave to tell him everything. If I have the misfortune to say something hurtful, I will retire to a place so remote, Your Majesty will never be troubled by me again, or even have the need to say my name. If, on the contrary, he recognizes that my reasons are good, my issues are real, he will only have to tell me in the same tone in which he just said 'I was wrong.' There's no need to say 'Cardinal, you were right.' We'll just consign what has passed to the oblivion of the past."

"Speak, Monsieur," said the king. "I'm listening."

"Sire, allow me to begin by saying that my honesty and integrity have always been beyond question."

"Have I ever attacked them?" asked the king.

"No, but Your Majesty has allowed them to be attacked, and it was a great wrong."

"Monsieur!" the king said.

"Sire, shall I speak, or shall I not? Does Your Majesty command me not to speak?"

"No, *ventre-saint-gris*, as my father used to say. On the contrary, I command you to talk—but please go easy on the reproaches."

"I am, however, obliged to treat Your Majesty as I think he merits."

The king stood, stamped his foot, marched to the window, from the window to the door, and from the door back to his chair, where he stared silently at Richelieu—and then finally sat down and said, "Speak. I sacrifice my pride on the royal crucifix. I will hear whatever you have to say."

"I said, Sire, that I would start with my honesty and integrity, so please consider the words that follow."

Louis XIII gave a formal nod.

"I have, from my estate," the cardinal continued, "some twenty-five thousand *livres* a year in rents. The king gave me six abbeys that generate another one hundred twenty-five thousand *livres*. So my annuities bring me one hundred and fifty thousand *livres.*"

"I know all that," said the king.

"Your Majesty no doubt also knows that, as your minister, I was surrounded by threats and plots, to the point where I had to have guards and a captain to defend myself."

"I know that as well."

"Then, Sire, I refused sixty thousand *livres* in pensions that you offered me after taking La Rochelle."

"I remember."

"I turned down the salary that came with the Admiralty, worth forty thousand *livres*. I refused the grant that came with the Admiralty, one hundred thousand *livres*—or rather, I donated it to the State. Finally, I refused a million that the bankers offered me to save them from being investigated. But they were investigated, and I forced them to disgorge ten million in fines into the king's coffers."

"No one could dispute any of this, Your Eminence," the king said, raising his hat. "You are the most honest man in my kingdom."

The cardinal bowed, and continued, "But that's not what is said by my enemies in Your Majesty's Court—even by those closest to Your Majesty. Who is it who libels me across France, and slanders me in the eyes of all Europe? Those who should be the first to honor me as you do, Sire: His Royal Highness Monseigneur Gaston, Her Majesty Queen Anne, and Her Majesty the Queen Mother."

The king sighed. The cardinal had touched the wound. Richelieu continued, "His Royal Highness Monsieur has always hated me. How have I responded to this hatred? The Chalais affair was nothing less than an attempt to murder me. Confessions from everyone involved, Monsieur included, made that clear. And what was my revenge? I made him marry Mademoiselle de Montpensier, the richest heiress in the kingdom, and persuaded Your Majesty to give him the honors and title of Duc d'Orléans. Monseigneur Gaston has, as a result, an annual income of a million and a half *livres.*"

"In other words, Monsieur, he's even richer than I am."

"The king doesn't need to be rich, he's the king; if he needs a million, he asks for a million, and it is found."

"That's true," said the king. "The day before yesterday, you gave me four million, followed by another half million yesterday."

"Must I remind Your Majesty also how much resentment Queen Anne of Austria holds against me? And what, in her eyes, is my crime? Respect must silence me on that score."

"No, speak, Monsieur le Cardinal. I shall, I must, I want to hear everything."

"Sire, the great misfortune of princes, and the calamity of states, is the marriage of a king with a foreign princess. Queens who come from Austria, from Italy, or from Spain, at some point become enemies of the State. How many queens, to the benefit of their father or brothers, have stolen the sword of France from under the king's pillow? And what happens then? Despite such treason, the real culprit goes unprosecuted, and it is always lower heads that fall. After conspiring with England, Queen Anne, who hates me because she sees me as the champion of France, now conspires with Spain and Austria."

"I know it—oh, I know it," said the king in a hushed voice. "But Queen Anne has no power over me."

"That's true. But what about Marie, the queen mother, Sire? Queen Marie, the cruelest of all my enemies, because it was to her I was most devoted—and so from her I've suffered the most."

"Forgive me, Monsieur le Cardinal."

"No, Sire, I cannot forgive you."

"Even if I beg?"

"Even if you command me. When you sought me out here, I told Your Majesty he shall have the entire truth."

The king sighed, and said, voice trembling, "Do you think I don't know the entire truth?"

"Not all of it. And this time, you shall hear it. Your mother, Sire, is the arch-nemesis of France. Your mother, Sire . . . it's terrible to say this to a son, but your mother . . ."

"What about my mother?" said the king, glaring at the cardinal.

This glare from the king, which would have silenced a man less determined than the cardinal, instead seemed to loosen his tongue. "Your mother, Sire," he said, "was unfaithful to her husband. Before her marriage, your mother, during her time in Marseilles . . ."

"Silence, Monsieur!" said the king. "The walls listen, they say, and sometimes they hear . . . what they should not hear. Nobody needs to know, beyond you and me, why I hesitate to give an heir to the crown, when everyone presses me on it, most of all you. And what I say is so true, Monsieur," the king said, rising and grasping the cardinal's hand, "that if I thought my brother the true son of King Henri IV, in other words, the only blood that has the right to rule France, then as God and you hear me, Monsieur, I already would have abdicated in his favor and retired to a monastery, to pray for my mother and for France. Now, do you have anything else to tell me? If so, after all that, then tell me now."

"Well, Sire, yes—I do have more to tell you," the cardinal said, surprised in spite of himself, "for I begin to understand that the instinctive respect I hold for Your Majesty has been justified, and my admiration is only deepened by this sharing of secrets. Oh, Sire! What worlds of sadness are revealed by your lifting of this veil! As God is my witness, if I didn't believe that the future of France depends on what else I need to tell you, I'd stop now and seal my lips forever. But, Sire . . . have you ever thought about the death of King Henri IV?"

"Alas! I think of it every day, Monsieur!"

"But, in thinking of his death, have you tried to unravel the terrible mystery of the Fourteenth of May?"

"Yes, and I have done so."

"So, you know who the real assassins are, Sire?"

"The assassination of Concini, le Maréchal d'Ancre, which I would approve again tomorrow if need be, proves that I know at least one of them—though I do not know the other."

"But I, Sire, I—who didn't have the same reasons as Your Majesty to look away—I've seen to the bottom of this mystery, and I can name *all* the assassins."

The king groaned.

"You remember, Sire, that there was a religious woman, a holy creature who, knowing that the crime was afoot, swore it would not be completed. Do you know the reward for her loyalty?"

"She was buried alive in a tomb at the Daughters of Repentance, the door walled up to keep her in, where she stayed for years on end, exposed to the scorching rays of the summer and the icy gales of the winter. Her name was Coëtman, and she died there ten or twelve days ago."

"And knowing this, Sire, Your Majesty still suffered such an injustice to occur?"

"The person of a king is sacred, Monsieur le Cardinal," replied Louis XIII, who believed in the cult of absolute monarchy—that terrible cult that, under Louis XIV, would become idolatry. "Woe to those who learn a king's secrets."

"Well, Sire, this is a secret known by someone other than you and me."

The king was suddenly alert, and fixed a clear eye on the cardinal. "You may have heard," Richelieu continued, "that on the scaffold, Ravaillac asked to be confessed."

"Yes," said Louis XIII, turning pale.

"You may even have heard that the clerk there listened while the condemned, already half dead, spoke the names of the culprits?"

"Yes," said Louis XIII, "which were written down on a sheet kept out of the record."

To the cardinal's eyes, he seemed even more pallid than before. "Then you may have heard that this sheet was kept and guarded very carefully by the clerk, Joly de Fleury?"

"I've heard all of this, Your Eminence. What else? What else?"

"Well, I tried to recover this sheet from the children of Monsieur Joly de Fleury."

"Why would you want to do that?"

"To give it to Your Majesty, in the event that you wanted it destroyed."

"Well?"

"Well, Sire, this sheet is no longer in the possession of Monsieur de Fleury's children. Two unidentified men, one a young man of sixteen, the other a man of twenty-six, came one day to try to persuade the clerk to give up the sheet. And they were successful."

"And Your Eminence, who knows everything, doesn't know the names of these two men?" the king asked.

"No, Sire," the cardinal replied.

"Then *I* will tell you!" the king said, grabbing the cardinal by the arm. "The elder of the two men was Monsieur de Luynes, and the younger—was me."

"*You*, Sire!" the cardinal cried, recoiling.

The king reached into his lapel and pulled out of an inside pocket a yellowed and crumpled paper, the process verbal Ravaillac had dictated on the scaffold, the sheet that named the culprits, and said, "Here it is."

"Oh, Sire! Sire!" Richelieu said, realizing what the pale king must have suffered during their talk. "Forgive me for what I've said to you. I truly thought you didn't know."

"Then how did you account for my sadness, my isolation, my grief? Is it usual for the Kings of France to dress as I do? Among other sovereigns, the death of a father, a mother, a brother, a sister, a parent, or another king, means wearing the purple. But for all men, whether kings or commoners, the death of happiness means wearing black."

"Sire," said the cardinal, "there's no need to keep this paper. Burn it."

"No, Monsieur. I may be weak, but fortunately I know myself. Despite everything, my mother is my mother, and sometimes she gets the better of me. But when I feel that her domination might push me to do something wrong, something unjust, I look at this paper, and it gives me strength. This paper, Monsieur le Cardinal," the king said in a voice gloomy but resolute, "I give to you to keep as a pact between us, for on the day I must finally break with my mother—exile her from Paris, hound her from France—I will do it with this paper in my hand. On that day I will ask you to return it, and you—you may ask me for whatever you want."

The cardinal hesitated. "Take it," said the king. "I want you to. Take it."

The cardinal bowed and took the sheet of yellowed paper. "As Your Majesty wishes," he said.

"And now, put me no more to the question, Your Eminence. I place France, and myself, in your hands."

The cardinal fell to his knees, took the king's hands, kissed them, and said, "Sire, in return for this moment, I hope Your Majesty will accept the entire efforts of the rest of my life."

"So I intend, Monsieur," said the king, with that supreme majesty he could sometimes assume. "And now, my dear Cardinal, let's forget all that has happened, set aside the wretched intrigues of my mother, my brother, and the queen, and occupy ourselves with the glory of our arms and the greatness of France!"

XLIX

In Which the Cardinal Audits
the King's Accounts

The next day, at two in the afternoon, King Louis XIII, sitting in a great chair, his cane between his legs, his black hat with its black plumes resting on his cane, his brows somewhat less furrowed, his face less pale than formerly, watched the cardinal as Richelieu worked at his desk.

Both were in the cardinal's office in the Place Royale, the same place we saw the king, during his three-day reign, pass such troubling hours.

The cardinal wrote, and the king waited. The cardinal looked up and said, "Sire, I've written to Spain, Mantua, Venice, and Rome, letters which Your Majesty has done me the honor to approve. Now I have just written, again at the approval of Your Majesty, to your cousin the King of Sweden. This response was more difficult than the others: His Majesty King Gustavus Adolphus isn't yet allied to us, and he is a suspicious man, who makes decisions based on actions rather than words, reserving judgment until he's had time to make up his mind."

"Read your letter to me, Monsieur le Cardinal," said Louis XIII. "I already know what was in the letter from my cousin Gustave."

The cardinal bowed and read:

> Sire,
>
> The familiarity with which Your Majesty deigns to write to me is a great honor, but assuming such familiarity in return would show a lack of respect, and be unbefitting of the humility appropriate to one in my position, even bearing the title Prince of the Church by which Your Majesty has been good enough to address me.

*Sire, I am not a great man! Sire, I am no genius! But I am,
as you were good enough to note, an honest man. And it is
this virtue that the king, my master, particularly appreciates, as
he need only resort to himself when greatness or genius is required. I will speak candidly to Your Majesty, as requested, but
as nothing more than a simple minister of the King of France.*

*Yes, Sire, I am sure of my king, more so than ever, as on
this day he has confirmed my power over the direct opposition of Marie de Médicis, his mother, against Queen Anne,
his wife, and against Monseigneur Gaston, his brother—he
has given me proof that if sometimes his heart yields to filial
piety, fraternal friendship, or conjugal affection, which are
the happiness and glory of common men and which God has
placed in every honest and well-born heart, reasons of state
outweigh those noble impulses. Kings must sometimes over-
ride their feelings when matters call for discipline and rigor
in the name of good government.*

*One of the great misfortunes of royalty, Sire, is that
God has placed his representatives here on Earth so high
that kings cannot really have friends, only favorites. But
far from being influenced by his favorites, on the contrary,
my master, who is called "the Just," is entirely capable of
bowing to the demands of criminal justice when a favorite
is accused of meddling with state business—as he proved
in the affair of Monsieur de Chalais. My master's eyes are
so vigilant, his grip so firm, that no matter how deep the
conspiracy, no matter how powerful the conspirators, they
cannot escape the justice of this king, whose heart and soul
are devoted to France. If, one day, I do fall from power, it
won't be because I was undermined from below.*

*So I say to you, Sire—as well as to my king, with whom
I had the honor to share your letter, and from whom I have*

no secrets—yes, I am quite sure. If God gives me permission to stay in this world for another three years, and if the king gives me permission to remain as minister—and, in fact, Louis XIII gave Richelieu a nod—I can assure you in the king's name and mine that we will be able to keep every one of our commitments to you, and I will deal with you as frankly as I do with my master.

As to calling Your Majesty "my friend Gustave," I know of only two men in antiquity—Alexander and Caesar—and three men of our modern monarchy—Charlemagne, Philippe-Auguste, and Henri IV—who would have had the stature for such flattering familiarity. I, who am so unworthy, can only call myself Your Majesty's most humble and obedient servant.

—Armand, Cardinal de Richelieu

P.S. If it please Your Majesty, my king has appointed the Baron de Charnassé to deliver this letter, and to be responsible for negotiating with Your Majesty the great matter of the foundation of the Protestant League. He does so with the full powers of the king and, if you absolutely insist, with mine as well.

While the cardinal was reading this long letter, which was in part an apology to the king for the way Gustavus Adolphus had rather freely shown his disregard for Louis XIII, the king, though occasionally gnawing at his mustache, nodded his general approval. But when the letter had been read, he stood for a moment in thought, and then asked the cardinal, "Your Eminence, in your capacity as a theologian, can you assure me that this alliance with a heretic does not imperil the salvation of my soul?"

"As I am the one who advised Your Majesty to do so," said the cardinal, "if there is any sin in it, I take it upon myself."

"That reassures me somewhat," said Louis XIII, "but having taken this path since you became my minister, and assuming I'll continue to follow your advice in the future, do you really think, my dear Cardinal, that one of us can be damned without the other?"

"The question is too difficult for me to answer. All I can say to Your Majesty is that I pray to God never to let me stray from Him, either in this world or the next."

"Ah!" said the king, breathing more easily. "Is our work done, my dear Cardinal?"

"Not quite, Sire," said Richelieu. "I must beg Your Majesty to grant me a few moments to make sure our commitments are maintained and our promises are kept."

"Are you talking about the sums requested by my brother, my mother, and my wife?"

"Yes, Sire."

"Traitors and disloyal deceivers! You, who preach about saving money, are you going to advise me to reward infidelity, lies, and betrayal?"

"No, Sire, but I will say to Your Majesty that a royal word is sacred, and once given, it must be upheld. Your Majesty promised one hundred and fifty thousand *livres* to his brother...."

"If he would be lieutenant general, but since then he's asked for more!"

"All the more reason to award him compensation."

"He's an impostor who pretended to fall in love with Princesse Marie de Gonzague just to cause trouble!"

"Trouble we are out of, I hope, since he himself says he's given up on that love."

"While demanding his price to renounce it."

"If he has his price, Sire, you have to pay the bill at the rate that was set."

"One hundred and fifty thousand *livres*?"

"It's expensive, I know, but a king must keep his word."

"In no time, he'll take that one hundred and fifty thousand to Crete and bank it with King Minos, as he calls the Duc de Lorraine."

"Then, Sire, that hundred and fifty thousand will have been well spent: for a hundred and fifty thousand *livres* will buy us the taking of Lorraine."

"Do you think the Emperor Ferdinand will let us get away with that?"

"Well, don't we have Gustavus Adolphus to oppose him?"

The king thought for a moment. "You are a canny chess player, Monsieur le Cardinal," he said. "My brother Monsieur shall have his hundred and fifty thousand. But as for my mother, she'll never see her sixty thousand *livres*."

"Sire, Her Majesty the Queen Mother has been in need of money for quite a while; she asked me for a hundred thousand *livres*, and at the time I was only able to give her fifty. But at that time we were strapped for cash, whereas now we are flush."

"Cardinal! Do you forget all you said to me yesterday about my mother?"

"But didn't I say she was still your mother, Sire?"

"Yes. Unfortunately for me, and for France, she is."

"Sire, you committed to give Her Majesty the Queen Mother sixty thousand *livres*."

"Maybe, but I didn't sign anything."

"A royal promise is far more sacred than a written contract, Sire."

"Then have it come from you instead of from me. Maybe then she'll give you some respect and leave the both of us alone."

"The queen mother will never leave us alone, Sire. She was born with the meddling spirit of the Médicis, and she'll spend the rest of her life pursuing the two things she cannot have: her vanished youth and her lost power."

"All right, I give in on the queen mother. But what about the queen, who wants me to pay Monsieur d'Émery for a string of pearls—just one example of her continual demands!"

"That proves to us, Sire, that the queen recognizes she has no power without the king. And since the king has the key to a box holding four million *livres,* we might as well remind her of it. So the queen owes someone twenty thousand? Then I'm sure Her Majesty will appreciate receiving fifty thousand! Send her fifty thousand as a sign of good faith, on condition that twenty thousand of it goes to Monsieur d'Émery. The Crown of France is pure gold, Sire, and must shine on both the king and the queen."

The king rose and held out his hand to the cardinal. "Monsieur le Cardinal, you are not only a great minister and a good counselor, you are a generous enemy. I authorize you, Your Eminence, to pay out the various sums we have discussed."

"It is the king who promised, and the king who will deliver. The king will sign vouchers to present to the treasury, where they'll be covered—but it seems to me His Majesty is forgetting another reward he promised."

"Which one?"

"I thought I heard that, in an hour of generosity, he'd promised his fool Monsieur l'Angely the same amount he'd given his favorite, Monsieur Baradas: thirty thousand *livres.*"

The king flushed. "L'Angely turned it down," he said.

"All the more reason, Sire, to show your generosity. Monsieur l'Angely turned it down because that was the crazy thing to do, and a fool has to act crazy to deserve a place with Your Majesty. But the king has two real friends he can depend on: his prime minister, and his fool. He shouldn't appear ungrateful to the one while rewarding the other."

"That's so. You're right, Your Eminence; the little clown has suffered so from my bad moods the last three months. . . ."

"Three months, Sire, that can be recompensed at a rate of ten thousand a month. Show him that the King of France remembers his friends, as well as his favorites."

"A favorite, who abandons me for Marion Delorme, a girl who is . . . who is . . ."

"Who is very useful, Sire, as she gave me the warning that I was about to be disgraced, and thus I was able to prepare a way to recoup my fortunes. Without her, Sire, I would have been caught unaware, and been unprepared to engage Your Majesty's wisdom while absent. Put Monsieur Baradas in command of a company of troops, Sire, and give him the opportunity to prove to Your Majesty that the student can give faithful service to his teacher."

The king thought for a moment. "Monsieur le Cardinal," he asked, "what do you think of this friend of his, Saint-Simon?"

"I think I should recommend him, Sire, as a person of goodwill and propriety who could fill the place left vacant by the ingratitude of Monsieur Baradas."

"And besides," the king added, "he really plays the horn quite beautifully. I'm glad you recommend him, Cardinal. I'll see what I can do for him. By the way, what shall we tell the King's Council?"

"Will Your Majesty be at the Louvre tomorrow at noon? By then, I'll be prepared to explain my plan of campaign, so we can propose something more practical than crossing rivers upon Monsieur's finger."

The king stared at the cardinal, astounded that he should be so well informed even when away from Court. "My dear Cardinal," he said with a laugh, "you must have actual demons in your service! Unless—as I've thought more than once—you're the Devil himself."

L

The Avalanche

Just as the King's Council, convened this time by Richelieu, came to order in Paris, at around eleven in the morning a small caravan, which had left the French town of Oulx at dawn, and then passed through Exilles, now approached the outlying houses of the small town of Chaumont, just short of the Piedmont border.

This caravan was composed of four people, two men and two women, mounted on mules. Both men wore Basque outfits, but rode with their faces uncovered, and it was easy to see that they were young, the eldest about twenty-three, the youngest only eighteen. As for the two women, determining their ages was harder, as over their dresses they wore capes with hoods that completely hid their faces, something that might just as easily be attributed to the cold as to a desire to go unrecognized.

Then as now, the Alps were crossed by magnificent roads from Simplon, from Mont-Cenis, and from Saint-Gothard, but one could also reach Italy by way of trails so narrow, it was sometimes necessary for travelers to march single-file, leading their mules. These animals were perfectly comfortable with the dramatic terrain, both well trained and amenable.

At the moment, the elder of the two cavaliers led the way on foot, holding the bridle of the mule ridden by the younger of the women. Seeing no one on the road but a kind of traveling merchant who preceded the caravan by five hundred paces, whipping along a little mule loaded with bales, she drew back her hood to reveal a head of soft blond hair and a face with a complexion so wonderfully fresh, it could belong to no one over the age of eighteen.

The other woman followed, her face completely covered by her hood. Head bowed, whether in thought or by fatigue, she seemed completely oblivious of the way her mount picked its way along the trail, the snow-covered mountain on one side, sheer cliff on the other. But the mule seemed to know its business, choosing its way carefully, occasionally turning its head and eyeing the abyss, as if it understood quite clearly the dangers of a misstep.

This danger was quite real; so, as a distraction, or to stave off the beckoning demon of vertigo, the fourth traveler, a young man with blond hair, a compact well-made figure, and the bright flashing eyes of youth, sat his mule side-saddle like a woman, his back to the abyss. A mandolin hung from his neck by a sky-blue ribbon, and as he rode he played it and sang, apparently to the fourth mule which, freed of its rider, followed contentedly along at the rear. And here is his song:

> Venus has a thousand names
> And a hundred thousand nicknames
> Poor outraged lovers cry
> These iron-heart ladies
> Are creatures of Hades
> Who make them want to die
>
> Love for one is worry and tears
> For another it's all pain and fears
> For a third it's agony and defeat
> But me, when I think of
> The woman that I love
> She's nothing to me but sweet!

As for the elder of the two young men, he neither played the viola nor sang—he was too busy for that. All his attention was concentrated on the young woman he was leading and the dangers that

threatened her and her mount on the narrow and winding path. All
the while, she gazed at him with that sweet and charming regard
with which a woman looks at a man who not only loves her, but
is devoted to her, body and soul—and for whom devotion to the
second outweighs even devotion to the first.

After a moment, at one of the kinks in the path, the small caravan
halted. There was a serious issue to be resolved. As we said, having
passed Exilles two hours earlier, they were approaching the town
of Chaumont, the last town in France, which meant they were only
half a league from the checkpoint that separated the French province
of Dauphiné from the Italian province of Piedmont.

Beyond that point, they would be in enemy territory, not only
because Charles-Emmanuel, the Duke of Savoy and Piedmont,
knew of the cardinal's preparations for war, but also because he'd
been officially notified by the French government that if he didn't
allow their troops to march through his domain to raise the siege of
Casale, it would be regarded as an act of war.

So the serious issue was this: should they try to ride openly
through Susa Pass, risking recognition and arrest by Charles-
Emmanuel, or should they find a guide who could take them, by
some other circuitous route that might avoid Susa and even Turin,
and get them across into Lombardy?

The young woman, with the charming confidence of a woman
who loves a man who loves her in return, abandoned all these concerns to her lover; she looked at him with her lovely dark eyes and
sweet smile and said, "You know better than I what to do—I leave
it in your hands."

The young man, anxious about the safety of the woman he loved,
turned to question the woman whose face was hidden by her hood.
"And you, Madame?" he asked. "What do you think?"

At these words the hood was raised, and one could see the face
of a woman of forty-five or fifty, aged, emaciated, and ravaged by

long suffering. The only part of her face that seemed alive was her eyes, which shone with a piercing force as if trying to see beyond the world and into the unknown. "What's that?" she asked. She hadn't been listening, and had only looked up because they'd stopped.

The young man raised his voice, for the noise of the cascading Doire tumbling through the canyon made normal speech impossible. He repeated his question.

"As long as you're asking," she said, "what I think is we should stop at the next town because, since it's on the border, we should be able to find out what you want to know. If there's a back way across the mountains, someone in the village will know about it, and if we're looking for a guide, that's where we'll find him. A few hours spent in discreet inquiry won't make any difference; what's important is that we, or rather you, aren't recognized."

"My dear Madame," the young man replied, "you are wisdom incarnate, and we shall do exactly as you say."

"So?" asked the young woman.

"So now we go on. But what are you looking at?"

"Something amazing on the mountain. That is amazing, isn't it?"

The young man looked to where she was pointing. "What is?" he asked.

"That there should be flowers blooming at this time of year!"

And indeed, just below the snow line, bright red flowers danced in the breeze.

"Up here, dear Isabelle, there are no seasons," the young man said. "It's always winter here, but life can't be quenched. Even in winter this flower grows in the snow, which is why we call it the Alpine Rose."

"It's beautiful," Isabelle said.

"Would you like one?" the young man said. And before the young woman could answer, he leaped up the slope, clambering over the rocks toward where the flowers grew.

"Count, Count!" cried the young woman. "In heaven's name! Don't be so foolish! I can't bear even to look!"

But he who was honored with the title of "count," and who we have no reason not to recognize as the Comte de Moret, had already reached the ledge, picked the flower, and like a true *montagnard* slid back down the slope—though he, a man who prepared for every contingency, had, like his companion, a rope coiled around his waist, in order to help with ascents and descents.

He presented the Alpine Rose to the girl who, blushing with pleasure, raised it to her lips, then slipped it inside her bodice.

At that moment, a sound like thunder rolled down from the peak of the mountain above. A cloud of snow billowed into the air, and a mass of white began racing like lightning down the slope, increasing in speed and force as it came.

"Look out! Avalanche!" cried the younger of the two cavaliers, leaping from his mule. His companion wrapped Isabelle in his arms and leaned back against the overhanging rock face. The pale older woman drew back her hood so she could see what was happening. And suddenly, she screamed.

The avalanche swept across the path about five hundred paces ahead of the small caravan, and though it was a minor one, the travelers felt the earth shake under their feet as the wind of death blew past. But the pale woman's scream hadn't been a cry of personal terror, as Galaor, the younger man, and the Comte de Moret, worried about Isabelle, had both thought; it was because she'd seen the devastating tempest sweep the merchant and mule ahead of them down into the abyss.

The Comte de Moret and Galaor thought they'd escaped all danger, and weren't sure why she'd screamed, so they turned to look. But they saw only the pale woman pointing and crying, over and over, "There! There! There!"

Then their eyes focused on the narrow path ahead. The peddler and his mule were gone, and the road was empty. Suddenly Moret understood everything. "Follow us slowly and carefully," he told Isabelle, "and you, my dear Madame de Coëtman, follow Isabelle. Galaor and I will run ahead—maybe there's something we can do to save the poor fellow."

And, leaping ahead with the agility of a mountain goat, the Comte de Moret, followed by Galaor, rushed to the place indicated by Madame de Coëtman—whom Cardinal Richelieu, confident though he was that Moret would respect Isabelle's chastity, had sent along as a chaperone as a concession to worldly propriety.

LI

Guillaume Coutet

Arriving at the spot indicated, the two young men gripped each other and peered down into the terrible abyss.

They saw nothing at first, for they were looking too far out. Then they heard, from directly below them, words spoken as clearly as possible, given the profound terror of he who was speaking. "If you are Christian men, for the love of God, save me!"

Turning their eyes toward the voice, they saw, ten feet below them, on a precipice over a drop of more than a thousand feet, a man hanging from a tree, half uprooted and bending under his weight. His feet rested on a shifting rock, but it was clear that it wouldn't support him once the tree came loose, which could happen at any moment.

The Comte de Moret grasped the situation at a glance. "Quick! Cut a staff eighteen inches long," he cried, "thick enough to support a man's weight." Galaor, a mountaineer like Moret, understood what the count wanted. He drew a broad poniard from his sleeve and attacked a broken oak, and in a few moments hacked off a limb that could serve as a rope-ladder rung. Meanwhile, the count had unwrapped the rope from around his waist, to a length twice that of the distance to the man they hoped to rescue, and attached the rung to the loose end. Looping the rope around a protruding rock, he immediately began to let himself down toward the man suspended between life and death, meanwhile calling out encouragement.

Moret passed the man the wooden rung on the other end of the rope, and he grasped it just as the tree's roots pulled from the earth and it tumbled into the abyss.

They weren't safe yet: the rock supporting them was sharp, and was fraying the rope as they climbed. Fortunately, the two women arrived, bringing the mules with them. One mule was willing to approach near enough to the edge that they were able to pass the rope over its saddle. While Isabelle prayed, Madame de Coëtman, with indomitable determination, hauled the mule by the bridle until, with its help, Moret made it back over the edge. Then, drawing the rope over the saddle like a pulley, after a few seconds appeared the pale face of the peddler who'd so miraculously escaped death.

A cry of joy greeted his appearance, to which Isabelle added, "Courage! Courage! You are saved!"

The man got to his feet, stumbled forward, dropped the rope, and draped his arms over the mule. The mule shied away, and the man, at the end of his strength, threw his arms up with a wordless cry and fainted into the arms of the Comte de Moret.

Moret opened a bottle of one of those invigorating liquors they distill in the Alps, held it to the man's lips, and made him drink a few drops. It was apparent that the strength that had sustained him while he was in danger had abandoned him once he'd realized he was saved.

The Comte de Moret set him down, leaning him against the rock, while Isabelle held a bottle of smelling salts under his nose. The count untied the rung from the rope and threw it away, with a man's disdain for something useful whose use was over, and re-coiled the rope around his waist. Galaor, for his part, slapped his poniard back into its sheath with the recklessness of youth.

In a few moments, after two or three convulsive twitches, the man opened his eyes. The expression on his face showed no recollection of what had happened to him, but gradually the memory returned. He realized he owed his life to those around him, and his first words were of thanksgiving and gratitude.

The Comte de Moret, whom the man took for a simple *montagnard,* asked him about himself. "My name is Guillaume Coutet," the man replied. "I have a wife who was almost a widow, and three children who were nearly orphaned. If there's anything I can do for you, by my life or my death, you have only to ask."

Then he got to his feet with the help of the count, and, subject to the retroactive terror that accompanies, or sometimes precedes, such an accident, he approached the precipice and gazed shuddering down at the broken tree roots below. Then he looked beyond at the shapeless chaos of snow, ice, boulders, and broken trees piled at the bottom of the valley, where the tumbling Doire backed up against this sudden unexpected obstacle to its course.

He sighed, thinking of the mule and its lost load, which was, in all probability, all the wealth he had. Then, recovering, he murmured, "Life is the greatest gift you give us, *mon Dieu.* I offer my thanks to you, and to those who helped me, for keeping me safe."

He turned back toward the path but, whether from shock or the concussion of the fall, he was too weak to take another step. "I've delayed you long enough," he said to the Comte de Moret and Isabelle. "Since I can't do anything for you in exchange for saving my life, I won't hold you up any longer. Only, please tell the innkeeper of the Golden Juniper of the accident that befell his cousin, Guillaume Coutet, who remains on the road and could use some help."

The Comte de Moret whispered a few words to Isabelle, who nodded her approval. Then, addressing the wounded man, "My dear friend," he said, "since God gave us the opportunity to save your life, we're not about to abandon you. We're no more than half an hour from the village; you can ride my mule, while I lead my lady by her bridle, as I was doing before the accident."

Guillaume Coutet started to protest, but Moret silenced him, saying, "I have need of you, my friend, and you may be able, within twenty-four hours, to repay the service I rendered you by doing me a greater one."

"Really?" asked Guillaume Coutet.

"Faith of a gentleman!" replied the count, forgetting that he was betraying his cover with those words.

"In that case," the peddler said, bowing, "I obey, as is my duty twice over; first, because you saved my life, and second, because you have the right by rank to command a poor farmer like me."

Then, with the help of the count and Galaor, Guillaume Coutet mounted the mule. The count resumed his place leading the mule that carried Isabelle, who was happy that the man she loved had had a chance to prove his skill, courage, and generosity.

After a quarter of an hour or so, the little caravan entered the village of Chaumont, and stopped at the door of the Golden Juniper.

At the first words Guillaume Coutet said to the host of the Golden Juniper, not about the rank of the man who'd saved his life, but rather the service he'd rendered him, Maître Germain put the inn entirely at the count's service. But the Comte de Moret didn't need the entire inn, just one large room with two beds for Isabelle and the Dame de Coëtman, and another room for him and Galaor. So he had the double satisfaction of getting what he wanted without disturbing anyone else.

As to Guillaume Coutet, he was put up in his cousin's own bedroom. A doctor was sent for, who examined him from head to toe, and declared that none of his two hundred and six bones were broken. He was told to bathe in water infused with aromatic herbs and a few handfuls of salt, and then rub his body with camphor. With this treatment, and a few glasses of mulled wine, the doctor was hopeful that within a day or two, the patient would be able to continue his journey.

The Comte de Moret, after taking care of the two lady travelers, made sure that the doctor's instructions were followed exactly. Once the patient felt a bit better, the count sat down at his bedside.

Guillaume Coutet repeated his protestations of gratitude and loyalty. Moret let him talk and, when he had finished, said, "It's God to whom you owe your thanks, my friend, for it was He who led me to your aid. However, perhaps God had a dual purpose: to save you, and to provide me with your help."

"If that were true," said the patient, "I would be the happiest man alive."

"I've been directed by Cardinal Richelieu—you see I'm keeping no secrets from you, and trust entirely in your discretion—I've been instructed by Cardinal Richelieu to escort to her father in Mantua the young lady you met, and to whom I am devoted."

"May God guide and watch over you on your journey."

"Amen—but we learned at Exilles that Susa Pass is blocked by barricades and heavily guarded fortifications. If we're recognized there, we'll be captured and held as hostages by the Duke of Savoy."

"Then you'd better avoid Susa Pass."

"Is there a way around?"

"Yes, if you trust me to lead you."

"Are you from this area?"

"I'm from Gravière."

"So you know the side roads?"

"In order to avoid the border tax, I've learned all the mountain paths."

"Will you act as our guide?"

"It's a rough road."

"We're not afraid of danger."

"All right, then, I'll do it."

The Comte de Moret nodded, indicating that the man's word was enough. "However," he said, "there's more."

"What else do you need?" asked Guillaume Coutet.

"I need information on the fortifications being built at Susa Pass."

"That's easy to get, since my brother is helping to build them."

"And where does your brother live?"

"In Gravière, like me."

"Can I seek out your brother, carrying a word from you?"

"Why not have him come here instead?"

"Could we do that?"

"It's easy. Gravière is only half an hour away; my cousin is going there on his horse, and can bring my brother back with him."

"How old is your brother?"

"Two or three years older than Your Excellency."

"And how big is he?"

"About the same size as Your Excellency."

"Are there a lot of people from Gravière working at Susa?"

"He's the only one."

"Do you think your brother might be willing to do me a favor?"

"Considering what you've done for me, he'd be willing to walk through fire for you."

"Well, then, send for him. Needless to say, he'll be well rewarded."

"No need for that; Your Excellency has already rewarded us both."

"Then I'll go speak to our host about bringing him."

"Please call him and let me speak to him alone, so he has no doubt but that I'm the one who's asking him."

"I'll send him in."

The Comte de Moret went out and, a quarter of an hour later, Maître Germain mounted his horse and took the road to Gravière.

One hour later, he returned to the Golden Juniper, bringing with him Guillaume's brother, Marie Coutet.

LII

Marie Coutet

Marie Coutet was a young man of twenty-six, which as his brother had said made him three or four years older than the Comte de Moret. He had the rugged good looks of the *montagnard:* his honest face indicated a warm heart, and he was compact but strong, with broad shoulders and sturdy limbs.

On the way back, he'd been brought up to date on the situation. He knew that his brother, swept away by an avalanche, had had the good fortune to catch hold of a tree, and had been rescued by a passing traveler. But why had his brother sent for him once he was out of danger? That's what he didn't understand. But he didn't hesitate for a moment, which showed how devoted he was to his brother.

As soon as he arrived, he went to the room where Guillaume Coutet was resting, and spent ten minutes with him, after which he asked Maître Germain if he could speak to the gentleman. The Comte de Moret was quick to respond to this invitation.

"Your Excellency," Guillaume said to him, "this is Marie, my brother. He knows I owe you my life, and, like me, he is at your disposal."

The Comte de Moret looked over the young mountaineer, and at first glance thought he saw in him both courage and honesty. "Your name," he said, "is French."

"Indeed, Your Excellency," Marie Coutet replied, "both my brother and I are French in origin. My father and mother were from Phénioux; they moved to Gravière, where both of us were born."

"So you still think of yourself as French?"

"In my heart as well as my name."

"But you're working on the fortifications at Susa."

"They pay me twelve *sous* a day to shovel dirt, so all day I shovel dirt, without worrying about why or whose dirt it is."

"But, then, aren't you working against your country?"

The young man shrugged. "Why doesn't my country pay me to serve it?" he said.

"If I ask you to give me the details of the work you're doing, will you share them with me?"

"Nobody asked me to keep it secret."

"Do you know anything about the language of fortifications?"

"I've heard the engineers talk about redoubts, demi-lunes, and counterscarps, but I have no idea what those words mean."

"Could you draw me a diagram of the fortifications of Susa Pass, particularly those defending the heights of Montabon and Montmoron?"

"I don't know how to read or write. I've never even held a pencil."

"Are foreigners able to approach the works?"

"No. There's a line of sentries a mile in front."

"Could I go with you as a new worker? I was told they were looking for more men."

"For how many days?"

"Just one."

"If you don't come back the next day, they'll be suspicious."

"What if you were sick for a day?"

"That might work."

"Could I fill in for you?"

"I think so. My brother could write a note for the overseer, Jean Miroux. The next day, I'll recover and return to work with no one the wiser."

"Could you do that, Guillaume?"

"Yes, Your Excellency."

"When do you start work?"

"Seven in the morning."

"So there's no time to lose. Get the note from your brother, return to Gravière, and at seven in the morning I'll be there in your place."

"What about work clothes?"

"Can you lend me some?"

"My wardrobe is rather empty."

"Can I get something tailor-made?"

"It will look too new."

"What if I have it stained?"

"If someone sees Your Excellency buying these things, they'll be suspicious. The Duke of Savoy has spies everywhere."

"Well, you're about my size—your clothes will do. Here, this ought to cover it." The count handed Marie Coutet a purse.

"But . . . but this is far too much!"

"Well, after you've bought yourself some new clothes, you can return whatever's left."

With matters thus arranged, Marie Coutet went out to go shopping, while Guillaume sent for a pen and ink to write the note. The Comte de Moret went to tell Isabelle why he needed to spend a day on reconnaissance, after which they would know which path to take.

The proximity forced by their travels, the necessities of their situation, and their mutual confession of love had put the two young people in a delicate position. The count's official mission as escort of his lady-love was sweet yet circumscribed. But the hours shared in intimate speech, head to head, were infinitely precious; they felt they looked into each other's hearts and saw in them deep lakes of love, the surface of which reflected a heaven that said "I love you."

Isabelle, accompanied by the Dame de Coëtman and Galaor, could cross the French border with nothing to fear, but not so the Comte de Moret, for whom passing into a foreign country was dangerous. This made the time he spent with his fiancée all the more precious, for any separation, however short, might be permanent. So the young man treasured the hours he spent with Isabelle until Germain came in to report that Marie Coutet had bought his clothes and was waiting below.

Though it mattered only to them, Isabelle made Moret promise that he wouldn't leave without saying goodbye. So, a quarter of an hour later, he presented himself before her dressed as a Piedmontese peasant.

Precious minutes were spent by the girl as she critiqued the count's outfit, in the end finding it perfect. In the glow of love, even a homespun coat beautifies the object of affection.

The hour of ten was striking in Chaumont, and he had to go. It would be eleven by the time he got to Gravière, and at seven in the morning the count was due to be at work.

Before leaving, he armed himself with the letter written by Guillaume Coutet, which read as follows:

My dear Jean Miroux,

The one who bears this letter will inform you that I've returned from Lyon, where I went to buy goods, and of my condition due to the accident that occurred between Saint-Laurent and Chaumont. I was hurled by an avalanche into an abyss, at the edge of which, by the grace of God, I clung to by a tree, but I was saved by passing travelers, good Christian souls whom I pray God will welcome into his paradise. As I'm injured from the fall, my brother Marie has to stay nearby to massage and tend to me. However, he doesn't want the work to suffer from his absence, so he's sending his friend Jacquelino to take his place. He hopes to return to work tomorrow. Alas for my poor mule, Hard-to-Trot—you remember, you gave him that name yourself—who plummeted to the bottom, lost with all my

goods under fifty feet of snow. But thank God I lost only
a mule and a few bales of cotton rather than my life. I can
rebuild my business.

> *Your cousin-german,*
> *Guillaume Coutet*

The Comte de Moret smiled more than once while reading this letter. It was just what he needed; though he admitted to himself that it wouldn't have sounded as natural if he'd dictated it.

Since this letter was the final thing he needed, and Maître Germain's horse was saddled and waiting at the door, at the end of the hall he kissed Isabelle's hand one last time, and then jumped into the saddle. He invited Marie Coutet to ride pillion behind him, and as a soft voice whispered "*Bon voyage,*" he rode off on the horse— which, by its looks, seemed likely to be the father of that poor mule which Jean Miroux, doubtless from experience, had named Hard-to-Trot.

One hour later, the two young men were in the village of Gravière, and the next morning, at seven o'clock, the Comte de Moret presented Guillaume Coutet's letter to Jean Miroux, and was admitted without question to the company of laborers as Marie Coutet's replacement. As Guillaume had predicted, Jean Miroux asked for details about his cousin's accident, which Jacquelino was happy to provide him.

LIII

Why the Comte de Moret Went to Work on the Fortifications of Susa Pass

As we might guess, it wasn't for the pleasure of the labor that the Comte de Moret took on the guise of a Piedmontese and went to work for a long day on the Susa Pass fortifications.

In the conversation Cardinal Richelieu had had with the Comte de Moret, the cardinal had deemed Moret's political instincts and aspirations worthy of the son of Henri IV; and the son of Henri IV, warmed by the great minister's admiration, had made up his mind to try to deserve it—and not just for his potential deeds, but for his actual ones.

Consequently, when he saw an opportunity to do a great service for the cardinal and for his brother the king, though it meant the risk of being captured as a spy, he resolved to see for himself the fortifications being built by the Duke of Savoy, and to send a detailed report to the cardinal.

Upon his return that evening, after saying goodnight to Isabelle like Romeo to Juliet, "Wishing sleep to dwell upon her eyes, and peace in her breast," he retired to his room, where he had earlier set out paper, ink, and pen, and wrote the following letter to the cardinal:

> To His Eminence, Cardinal Richelieu,
> Monseigneur,
> I take a moment before crossing the French frontier to address a letter to Your Eminence, to say that so far our journey has been without any trouble worth reporting.
> However, as we approached the border, I heard news

that I thought might be significant to Your Eminence, as you prepare to march across Piedmont.

The Duke of Savoy, who was just buying time when he promised to allow the passage of French troops across his states, is fortifying Susa Pass. I decided to see with my own eyes what he's building there.

Providence granted me the chance to save the life of a peasant of Gravière whose brother works on the fortifications. I took this brother's place and spent a day on the job among the other workers. But before I describe to Your Eminence what I saw today, I must first give him an account of the natural obstacles he will find in his path.

Chaumont, from which I have the honor to write to Your Eminence, is the last French town before the border. Just a mile beyond is the marker that divides Dauphiné from Piedmont. A bit further into the province ruled by the Duke of Savoy, in a canyon between two tall cliffs, one encounters a huge boulder, sheer on every side, its top reached only by a narrow stair. Charles-Emmanuel regards this great rock as a natural fortification against the French, and has placed a garrison atop it. This fortified rock is called Gélasse, and it guards the approaches to the mountains on its flanks, which are called Montabon Peak and Montmoron Peak.

The path between these two mountains is Susa Pass, the gateway to Italy—and that is where I helped work on the new fortifications.

The Duke of Savoy has blocked this pass with a demilune, a curved earthwork solidly entrenched, with a barricade on either end, overlooking a field about two hundred yards wide that would be subject to crossfire.

Montabon Peak is topped by a stone keep with a garrison of one hundred, and His Highness the Duke has built a series of additional redoubts on the slopes of both mountains manned by twenty to twenty-five troops each. The cannons of Susa sweep the entire valley, and we won't be able to deploy a single piece of our own without coming under fire. The valley before the pass is about a mile in length, and varies in width from twenty yards to as little as ten. The valley floor is covered in loose rocks and gravel that couldn't possibly be cleared away.

Upon arrival at the job this morning, I learned that the Duke of Savoy and his son would be visiting later, coming up from Turin to Susa to inspect our labors. And indeed, at about one o'clock they appeared, and immediately came into the works. They brought three thousand new troops to Susa, and announced that another five thousand would be arriving the next day.

I was sent up Montmoron Peak to announce the arrival of the duke, and there I saw they're building a new fort to match the one across on Montabon. This confirmed my opinion that Susa Pass cannot be forced directly, only turned by a flanking maneuver.

Tonight, at about three in the morning, taking advantage of a bright moon, we intend to leave Chaumont, led by the man whose life we saved, and who will conduct us by little-known paths around the Duke of Savoy's fortifications.

As soon as Mademoiselle de Lautrec is safe with her parents, I will leave Mantua and travel by the shortest path to join you, Monsieur le Cardinal, to take my place in the ranks of the army, and ensure Your Eminence of my deepest respect and admiration.

—Antoine de Bourbon, Comte de Moret

And in fact, by three in the morning the little caravan was leaving Chaumont in the same order it had entered it, but for the addition of Guillaume Coutet as a guide. All five were riding mules, though Coutet had warned them that in certain spots they would have to dismount.

The travelers went straight toward Gélasse, which loomed in the darkness like the giant Adamastor—but, five hundred yards ahead of the great rock, Guillaume Coutet led them onto a narrow path that branched off to the left. After a quarter of an hour, they heard the sound of rushing water ahead. A torrent ran across their path, one of the thousand tributaries of the Po; it was swollen by the rains and presented an unexpected obstacle.

Guillaume paused on the bank, looking upstream and down for an easier crossing—however, before he even had time to think, the Comte de Moret, burning with the knowledge that two loving eyes were upon him, goaded his mule into the stream. But in less time than it takes to tell it, Guillaume Coutet caught hold of his mule and halted it, and then said, in that tone that guides take in the presence of real danger, "This is my business, not yours. Wait here!"

The count obeyed. Isabelle dismounted and came down the embankment to stand by her young man. Galaor and the Dame de Coëtman stayed on the path. Madame Coëtman, even paler in the moonlight than she was by light of day, regarded the torrent the same way she'd peered into the abyss: with the impassivity of a woman who had lived for ten years with death at her side.

Guillaume, on his mule, began to pick his way through the stream, but about a third of the way across, the current began to take the animal. For a moment, the mule was swimming wildly, out of its master's control, but the smuggler was not new to this sort of emergency and kept his cool. He managed to keep the mule's head up and out of the water, and after being carried downstream twenty-five or thirty yards, it reached the other bank, dripping and panting, and carried its rider ashore.

Isabelle, seeing this, seized Moret's hand and gripped it with a force that showed, not her fear for the guide, or what danger she might experience herself, but fear for what her lover would have risked if he'd followed his first intentions.

Having arrived on the far bank, Guillaume came back to a point opposite the rest of the party. He motioned for them to wait, and then went upstream another fifty paces. Then he went back into the water, probing for a better place to ford, with happier results this time, as the mule didn't lose its footing, though it was in water up to its belly.

Reaching the shallows on the party's side, Guillaume gestured to them to come, and they hastened to join him; meanwhile he turned around and took careful note of his position, not wanting to lose sight of the route, lest one of his followers slip into a deep spot and be swept away.

The provisions were carried across the torrent, and then the two women. First, Isabelle, mounted on her mule, was placed between Guillaume and the Comte de Moret, so she had someone to lend a hand on either side of her. Then Guillaume crossed the torrent for the fourth time, and came back with the Dame de Coëtman on one side and Galaor on the other. The lady agreed to this arrangement with her usual disinterested nod of the head. Thus everyone reached the further side without mishap.

The Comte de Moret, despite his long boots, was drenched up to his knees and had no doubt that Isabelle was in the same condition. Worried she would take injury from the icy water, he asked Guillaume where they could stop and build a fire. Guillaume said that about an hour ahead there was a mountain lodge where smugglers often stopped; there they would find a hearth and everything else they might need.

The terrain was easy for a mile or two, so they put the mules into a trot until they arrived at the first slopes of the ridge. There they were forced to dismount and lead the mules up the path in single file. Guillaume, as usual, took the lead, followed by Isabelle, the Comte de Moret, Madame Coëtman, and Galaor. The rain had tamped down the snow, so they were able to walk without slipping, and at the end of an hour, as Guillaume had promised, they were at the door of a broad lodge.

The door was open, and within they could see a mixed company of rough-looking men. Isabelle hesitated, and asked if they could keep going, but Guillaume assured her there was enough space within that she wouldn't have to come in contact with anyone whose looks troubled her.

Besides, their party was well armed: they had hunting knives—like we saw Galaor wield when cutting an oak limb into a ladder rung—and in addition each of the cavaliers had a pair of wheel-lock pistols. Guillaume, for his part, had a pistol in his belt in between a hunting knife and a dagger, and a carbine slung over his back, of the type used in the Tyrol for hunting chamois.

They stopped at the door, where Guillaume dismounted and went in.

LIV

An Episode in the Mountains

After a moment, Guillaume came back out, put his finger to his lips, took his mule by the bridle, and beckoned to the travelers to follow him. They went around the lodge into a sort of stable-yard, where they put the mules into a shed that already housed a dozen more of the animals.

Guillaume helped the two women dismount, and then invited them to follow him. Isabelle turned to the count. A woman's loving heart takes some of the trust once placed in God and transfers it to the one she loves. "I'm afraid," she said.

"Don't be," said the count. "I'll watch out for you."

"Anyway," said Guillaume, who'd overheard, "if we had something to fear, it wouldn't be in this place; I have too many friends here."

"What about Galaor and me?" asked the count.

"Leave your pistols in your belts—you won't need them inside, though you might while we're traveling. Wait here." He untied the women's baggage from the mules and, followed by the ladies, approached the lodge.

A woman who was waiting by the back door led the way into a kitchen area, where a great fire crackled in a hearth. "Abide here, Madame," Guillaume said to Isabelle. "You're as safe as in the Golden Juniper Inn. I'll go take care of the gentlemen."

The Comte de Moret and Galaor had followed Guillaume's directions and had dismounted, shoved their pistols into their belts, and unstrapped their baggage. Guillaume's guarantee of safety covered the travelers, but didn't extend to their saddlebags.

The three walked around to the entrance to the lodge, but paused for a moment at the threshold: there was a reason why Isabelle had taken fright at the sight of the company within. But the two young cavaliers were less timid; they shared a look and a nod, smiled, touched their pistol grips, and fearlessly followed Guillaume inside.

As for him, a lifelong smuggler and poacher, he appeared to be in his element. With his elbows and shoulders he opened a path to the huge fireplace around which, smoking and drinking, a dozen men were gathered. Their mismatched outfits didn't seem to indicate any particular occupation, but rather all occupations at once.

Guillaume went up to the fireplace and spoke a few words into the ears of two men who were sitting there. They got up at once, without seeming bothered about it, and gave up their seats on a pair of hay bales. The Comte de Moret and Galaor set their luggage on the bales, and set themselves on their luggage. Then they finally had a chance to take a good look at the company that surrounded them—a look that fully justified Mademoiselle de Lautrec's fears.

Most of the men, like Guillaume, were apparently members of the honorable fraternity of smugglers, but the others were a mixed lot: poachers on the lookout for any kind of game, highwaymen, condottieri, mercenaries from all over—Spaniards, Italians, Germans— it was a strange mixture. They spoke loudly in every language at once, and in terms so outlandish and lurid, even a skilled linguist would have had trouble sorting it out. These rougher types, instead of joining comfortably with the pack, seemed determined to keep their status as lone wolves, each trying to look more dangerous than the next. Only those few who were related to each other hung together.

Spaniards predominated. Most had come from the siege of Casale, where the besieged were dying of starvation; they were deserters fleeing Italy in the guise of irregular soldiers who, once they reached the mountains, turned to one of those nocturnal pursuits for which, in every country, the mountains are the theater. There these men flowed together, mingling to form a river that ran toward the edge of the abyss. Around their heads swirled the vapors of tobacco, mulled drinks, and alcoholic breath. A few smoking candles on the walls or tables added their fetid fumes to the atmosphere, which they lit no better than the moon in a stormy sky.

From time to time, voices rose in shrill disagreement, as shadowy figures raised menacing arms in the gloom; if the argument turned into a fight between, say, a Spaniard and a German, all those who spoke Spanish or German rallied to the one who spoke their language. If both parties were of equal strength, the mêlée became general, but if one side was weaker than the other, the original opponents were left to settle the quarrel on their own, with either a handshake or a knife.

The two young cavaliers had just sat down and started to warm their hands when one of these quarrels, which were always ready to break out anew, flared up in a corner of the room. German and Spanish insults were exchanged, denoting the nationalities of the opponents. Immediately, a dozen men charged through the smoke toward the conflict, but as nine were Spaniards and only three Germans, the Germans quickly retreated to their benches, saying "It's nothing"— at which the Spaniards stood down, saying "Let them be."

Left on their own, the two disputants soon became combatants. Violent words turned to violent actions, and knife blades flashed in the candle light; curses bespoke wounds, their level of obscenity indicating the seriousness of the injuries. Finally a cry of pain rang out, stools and chairs were overturned as someone ran for the door, and a death rattle came from under the corner table.

As soon as he saw the knives flashing, the Comte de Moret had moved as if to intervene, but an iron hand gripped his arm and held him down on his luggage. It was Guillaume who was doing him this favor. "By Christ," he said, "sit still!"

"But . . . it's murder!" said the count.

"What business is that of yours?" Guillaume said quietly. "Let them be."

And, as we've seen, he did let them be. As the one who'd dealt the death wound escaped out the door, the one who'd received it slid down the wall until he fell beneath a table, where he gasped out his life.

Once the fight was over and the killer gone, there was no objection to providing some relief to a dying man. As it was the German who was dying, two or three of his compatriots lifted him up from under the table and laid him on the top.

The fatal wound was an upward stab, inflicted by one of those Catalan blades with a needle point that widens toward the hilt. It had gone in between the seventh and eighth ribs, right into the heart, and after the wounded man was set on the table, he gave a final spasm and quickly expired.

In the absence of friends and relatives, his compatriots acted as his heirs and, nobody objecting, his effects were claimed by his three fellow Germans. After searching the body, they divided his money, his arms, and his clothes, as if this were the most routine matter in the world. That accomplished, the three Germans dragged the corpse outside, in its shirt and breeches, to a place where the road overlooked a thousand-foot cliff. There the body was slid over the edge, just like the body of a dead sailor cast overboard from a ship sailing the high seas. Except that in this case, a few seconds later they heard the thud of the body striking the rocks below.

The dead man's father, mother, family, and friends were all unknown, and no one gave them a single thought. What was his name? Where was he from? Who was he, really? It no longer mattered. He was one less atom in the infinite, and only the eye of God counted him among the countless atoms of humanity. His death left no more mark on Creation than the swallow who, at the approach of winter, departs for the south, leaving only a whisper in the air, or the ant that a passing traveler unknowingly crushes beneath his tread.

However, the Comte de Moret was appalled by the thought that Isabelle was separated from this terrible event by nothing more than a thin wall. He rose stiffly and made his way to the door of the kitchen where she was hiding, and found the hostess sitting on the threshold. "Never fear, my handsome young man," she said. "I'm on watch."

At that moment, as if Isabelle had sensed right through the wall that her lover had come looking for her, the door opened, and she graced him with that sweet, angelic smile that brought Paradise to wherever it shone. "Welcome, my dear," she said. "We're ready, and waiting on your signal."

"Then close the door, dear Isabelle. Don't open it except to my voice. I'll tell Guillaume and Galaor."

The door was closed. Turning around, the count found himself face to face with Guillaume. "The ladies are ready to go," he said. "We should leave as soon as we can—this place makes my blood run cold."

"Good. But we'll make a gradual exit, and not go off all at once. You and the lad go first; in a couple of minutes, I'll follow with the luggage."

"Do you think there might be trouble?"

"There are all sorts here tonight—and you've seen the low value they place on a man's life."

"Why did you bring us in here, if you knew we'd find bandits like this?"

"I haven't passed this way for two months. Two months ago they weren't fighting in Italy yet. Where there's war, there are deserters, and deserters become dangerous bandits. If I'd known what awaited us, we would have kept going."

"All right. Send me Galaor. We'll prepare the mules and get ready to put this place behind us."

"I'm on my way."

Five minutes later, the four travelers and their guide left the smugglers' lodge as covertly, and most of all as quietly, as they could, and resumed their interrupted journey.

LV

Souls and Stars

Upon leaving the stable yard, Guillaume showed the count the long trail of blood that reddened the snow up to the edge of the precipice where the body had been thrown over. No words were necessary; the count looked around warily and instinctively placed his hand on his pistol.

Isabelle, who had heard nothing inside, saw nothing outside. The count had asked her to stay quiet, and so she was.

The moon cast its cold light on the snow-covered terrain and disappeared, from time to time, behind dark clouds that rolled across the sky like great waves.

The road was smooth enough that Isabelle was able to leave the mule in charge of following the path, and turn her eyes up to the celestial infinity. In winter in the mountains, when the air is crisp and cold, and the viewer is above the mists of the lowlands, the stars shine down with a pure and sparkling light. In a dreamy and melancholic mood, Isabelle was soon lost in contemplation.

Worried about her silence—because lovers worry about everything—the Comte de Moret hopped down from his mule. He took her mule by the bridle with one hand, while offering her the other. "What are you thinking about, beloved?" he asked her.

"What should I think about, my dear, when I gaze into the starry firmament, but the infinite power of God, and the tiny place we occupy in this universe that our pride leads us to believe was made just for us."

"What would you think, my dear dreamer, if you knew the actual size of those worlds rolling through the heavens, compared to the reality of our own globe?"

"You think you know, do you?"

The count smiled. "At Padua," he said, "I studied astronomy under a great Italian master, a professor who took me into his confidence. He told me a secret he hasn't yet dared to reveal, fearing it would be dangerous for him to do so."

"Can a scientific secret be dangerous?"

"It can be, if it contradicts the holy books!"

"One must have faith first and foremost! In the heart of the religious, faith takes precedence over science."

"But remember, dear Isabelle, you're talking to a son of Henri IV, whose father converted to the church under the duress of politics. His last words about me before he died—alas, he died so quickly he couldn't spare me any more thought than this—his final words were 'Let him study, let him learn, and let him make up his own mind.'"

"You mean you're not a Catholic?" Isabelle asked with some anxiety.

"No, I am—don't worry about that," said the count. "But my tutor, who was an old Calvinist, taught me to consider every belief in the light of reason, and to reject religious dogma if it required suppressing the mind in favor of faith. So I study, and learn, and am reluctant to accept any teaching that requires blind belief. But that doesn't stop me from glorying in the greatness of God, in whose mercy I would seek shelter if disaster ever struck me."

"That's a relief," Isabelle said, smiling. "I was afraid I'd fallen for a pagan."

"You may have fallen for worse than that, Isabelle. A pagan might agree to be converted, but a thinker seeks enlightenment. And enlightenment, as it approaches universal truth, moves farther from dogma. Had I lived in Spain in the time of Philip II, dear Isabelle, I'd probably have been burned as a heretic."

"*Mon Dieu*! But what about the stars I was gazing at, and what the Italian sage told you?"

"He told me something you're going to deny, though I think it's the absolute truth."

"I would never deny anything you tell me, my love."

"Have you ever lived by the side of the sea?"

"I've been to Marseilles twice."

"And what did you think was the most beautiful time of day?"

"Sunset."

"Wouldn't you have sworn that it was the Sun who moved across the sky, and then rushed down beyond the edge of the sea?"

"I would, and I still swear it."

"I'm afraid you're wrong, Isabelle: it's not the Sun that moves, it's the Earth."

"Impossible!"

"I told you you'd deny it."

"But if the Earth was moving, I'd feel it."

"No, for everything moves with it, including the atmosphere around us."

"But even if we're the world that's moving, we would still see the Sun."

"You're right, Isabelle, and your quick wit is almost the equal of science. But the Earth not only moves, it rotates; at this moment, for example, the Sun illuminates the Earth on the side away from us."

"If that's the case, why aren't we upside-down with our feet in the air?"

"In a relative sense, we are! But the atmosphere I mentioned surrounds us and sustains us."

"I don't understand a word of this, Antoine, and would prefer to talk about something else."

"What shall we talk about?"

"The thing I was thinking about when you asked me what I was thinking about."

"And what was that?"

"I was wondering if all these worlds scattered across the sky had been created as homes for our souls after death."

"Dear Isabelle, I never would have believed you were so ambitious."

"Ambitious? Why?"

"Only two or three of those worlds are smaller than ours: Venus, Mercury, the Moon—three in all. Others are eighty times, seven hundred times, even fourteen hundred times bigger than the Earth."

"If you mean the Sun, then certainly—it's the principal star of all the stars. From it we have everything that gives us existence: warmth, power, and the glory of the world around us. The Sun is not just in the beat of our hearts, it's the heartbeat of the Earth."

"Dear Isabelle, you just said more with your imagination and poetry than my Italian sage with all his knowledge."

"But," Isabelle demanded, "how can these points of light in the sky be bigger than the Earth?"

"Leaving out those we can barely see because they're so far from us, like Uranus and Saturn—do you see that golden star, there?"

"I see it."

"That's Jupiter; it is four hundred and fourteen thousand times larger than the Earth, and it has four moons that bathe it in eternal light."

"But how does it seem so small when the Sun seems so big?"

"Partly because the Sun is five times the size of Jupiter, and partly because we are only thirty-eight million leagues from the Sun, but we are one hundred and seventy million leagues from Jupiter."

"But who told you all this, Antoine?"

"My Italian sage."

"What's his name?"

"Galileo."

"And you believe what he told you?"

"Firmly."

"Well, my dear Count, you frighten me with your vast distances. I don't think my soul could ever make such a journey!"

"Assuming we have souls, Isabelle."

"Can you doubt it?"

"I've not seen it demonstrated."

"We'll not talk about that; Italian sage or no, I much prefer to believe I have a soul!"

"If you believe in your soul, I'll try to believe in mine."

"Well, suppose you have one, and after death you were free to choose between a temporary stay here, or eternity on another world. Which would you choose?"

"But you, my dear Isabelle: where would you go?"

"I admit that I lean toward the Moon, for it's the star of unhappy lovers."

"That would be a good choice insofar as it's the closest, Isabelle, being a mere ninety-six thousand leagues away, but it's the planet where your soul would fare the worst."

"Why?"

"Because it's uninhabitable, even for a soul!"

"Oh, how unlucky! Are you sure?"

"Judge for yourself. Currently, the best telescopes in the world are in Padua. When trained on your favorite planet, they see nothing but absolute sterility and solitude, at least on its visible hemisphere; no atmosphere, and thus no river, lake, or ocean; no vegetation; no life. It's true that the side we can't see may have everything that the near side lacks. But I doubt it, so I advise you not to send your soul there, because mine has to follow wherever yours goes."

"You seem to know all these worlds as if you'd lived there, my dear Count! In all these stars and constellations, these planets and these moons, where should I go, if your soul is determined to follow mine?"

"As to that," said the count, "I wouldn't hesitate for a moment: to Venus!"

"From a man who claims not to be a pagan, that's a bit compromising. So why is Venus the planet of your choice?"

"See there, dear Isabelle? That blue flame in the sky is Venus; it's the forerunner of the night, and the harbinger of the dawn, the most radiant planet in our system. It's only twenty-eight million leagues or so from the Sun, and receives twice as much heat and light as the Earth; it has an atmosphere much like ours, and though barely half the size of our planet, it has mountains reaching an altitude of a hundred and twenty thousand feet. Now Venus, unlike Mercury, is almost entirely enveloped in clouds, so it must be home to the streams and rivers that are missing from the Moon. Souls that walk along those banks would hear the water murmur with a lovely freshness."

"Very well: we go to Venus," said Isabelle.

This pact had just been concluded when they heard a sound rapidly approaching. The travelers instinctively stopped and turned to see where the sound came from. A man was running toward them at full speed, but he didn't cry out, just waved his hat wildly. They could see him clearly, as the Moon was sailing through a gap in the clouds, like a boat on a deep blue sea.

It was apparent that this man had something important to convey to the travelers. When he got close enough, he gasped out Guillaume's name. Guillaume got down from his mule and ran to meet the man, who was one of the two smugglers who had given up his place by the fire to the Comte de Moret and Galaor.

The two men met at about fifty paces away, exchanged a few words in an undertone, and then came toward the caravan. "Bad news, friend Jacquelino," said Guillaume, affecting an air of familiarity with the count that was meant to deceive his smuggler friend as to Moret's rank, a rank which the man seemed to guess nonetheless. "They're coming after us. We need to find a place to hide so we can let them go past."

LVI

The Giacon Bridge

Here, in fact, is what happened in the smugglers' lodge after the Comte de Moret, Galaor, and Guillaume Coutet left the common room. The front door reopened, and the face of the Spaniard who had fled after slaying the German reappeared there. The room was so quiet, it was as if nothing unusual had happened. "Hey!" he called. "You Spaniards!"

All the Spaniards got up at the summons of their compatriot and went toward him. A local smuggler, the friend of Guillaume Coutet, suspecting the Spaniards were up to no good, went out the back door and circled around the lodge until he could get close to the conspirators. He heard the murderer tell his compatriots that, through the window of the kitchen, he'd seen two women, one of whom looked like an aristocrat. These ladies, he said, seemed to be part of Guillaume's caravan. And that was an opportunity too good to pass up.

The murderer had little difficulty in persuading his comrades to seize the chance. There were ten Spaniards; they ought to be able to overwhelm three men without too much trouble, especially since one was a guide who probably wouldn't stick his neck out for people he didn't know. The gang went to gather their weapons.

The smuggler, meanwhile, took to his heels and raced up the road, hoping to reach the caravan before the Spaniards could come upon them. And indeed, he arrived ahead of them, but not by much.

Guillaume and the smuggler talked it over quickly. They were both intimately familiar with the local terrain; but where there's no foliage, it's not easy to hide five travelers and their mules. The two smugglers grimaced, and then both said "The Giacon Bridge."

The Giacon Bridge was a high stone arch across a mountain canyon that carried the road over a tumbling tributary of the Po. Beyond, the road forked, one path climbing toward Venaux, the other bending back toward Susa, approaching it from behind. When they arrived at that point, the Spaniards would just have to guess which way their prey had gone, and if they picked the wrong direction, the travelers might escape—especially since the Spaniards had no idea the little caravan had been warned of the pursuit. They would probably just pick one fork or the other and continue on.

Ten minutes' ride brought them to the Giacon Bridge. Guillaume took Isabelle's mule by its bridle, his comrade led the mule of Madame de Coëtman, and so they crossed the narrow span. Providence was on their side, for a sea of dark clouds, which eclipsed the constellations which the count and Isabelle had admired, were also about to swallow the Moon and its light. In five more minutes, it would be dark as pitch.

The smuggler let go of the bridle of the Lady Coëtman's mule, walked fifty paces away, dropped, and pressed his ear against the ground. The little caravan held still. After listening for a few seconds, the smuggler jumped up and ran back. "I heard them," he said, "but they're still six hundred yards behind us. In a minute, the Moon will disappear behind the clouds. There's not a moment to lose."

They resumed their ride. The clouds swept across the sky and the Moon disappeared; looking back, the travelers saw their pursuers arrive at the bridge just as darkness fell. Guillaume, who led the first mule, turned abruptly to the left, leading them onto a path cut into the rock that led down toward the tumbling torrent below.

This path, such as it was, must have been cut so that, in the heat of summer, mules could be led down to cool water. It was a steep descent, but they managed it without accident. At the bottom, the smuggler again pressed his ear against the stone. "They're coming," he said. "If one of our mules neighs and they spot us, leave it to me—I'll take that mule and lead them away."

Guillaume led the travelers under the arch of the stone bridge, where they bound kerchiefs around the mouths of the mules. Meanwhile his comrade went ahead to scout along the road to Venaux. Soon all the travelers could hear the Spanish bandits as they crossed the bridge. But as the travelers were doubly concealed by the darkness and the bridge, they were completely invisible, unless some unforeseen accident revealed their hiding place.

After crossing the bridge, the Spaniards fell to arguing about whether they should take the fork that went on toward Venaux, or back toward Susa. The discussion became heated, and those among the fugitives who understood Spanish could clearly hear the whole debate.

Suddenly, they heard a male voice rise in song from beyond the bridge. Guillaume placed a finger against the Comte de Moret's lips—he had recognized the voice of his comrade.

The song interrupted the debate at the fork in the road. Four of the Spaniards stepped forward to meet the singer. "Hey, you!" they called out in broken Italian. "Did you see any mounted travelers go by?"

"I saw two men and two women led by Guillaume Coutet, a merchant from Gravière," he said. "Is that who you mean?"

"Exactly!"

"Well, they're only about five hundred yards ahead along the road to Venaux," the smuggler said. This settled the argument, and the bandits rushed off down the road to Venaux.

The travelers peered warily out from the shadows beneath the bridge. As for the smuggler, he took the road toward Susa, gesturing to the travelers to follow him. The sound of the bandits receded into the distance, and after five minutes' wait, the caravan, led by Guillaume, went back up the steep path to the bridge. Five hundred yards down the Susa road, they caught up with the smuggler, who, unwilling to return to the lodge after misleading the bandits, asked if he could join the travelers' party. Permission was instantly granted, and the Comte de Moret promised him that, once they were over the border and into Piedmont, he would be well rewarded.

They continued on their way, pressing the mules for speed, which was easier as they approached Susa, where the road was better. As they got closer, the two guides advised caution, but the path they were following was so little known and even less frequented that the Savoyards had set no sentries on it, though it approached the northern ramparts.

The ramparts, when they reached them, were deserted, as the entire defense of the town of Susa was concentrated in the pass, a mile further ahead. Eventually, by following the rampart around to the east, they came down off the mountain and onto the road to the town of Malavet, where they spent the night.

The next morning, they took counsel. They could descend into the plain and go down to Lake Maggiore by way of Rivarolo and Joui, but that would be risking a danger of capture even worse than falling into the hands of Spanish bandits. It was true that the Comte de Moret had been charged upon his departure from France to carry a letter from Queen Anne to Don Gonzalès de Cordova, the Governor of Milan, and thus could pretend to be on a mission for the two queens to Rome or Venice. But that ruse would have galled him, as he was a true son of Henri IV and hated to lie.

Besides, that would have shortened the journey, which Antoine de Bourbon wished to prolong as much as possible. And since his advice carried the most weight, his will prevailed.

So they decided to go the long way around, through Aosta, Domodossola, and Sonovre, and by bypassing the Lombard basin make their way to Verona, where they'd be safe. After a couple of days of rest in Verona, the party would separate, the women continuing on horseback to their destination, Mantua.

At Ivrea, the smuggler who had joined their caravan went on his way, after being rewarded for his devotion with a money pouch that persuaded Guillaume Coutet all the more that he was guiding a nobleman who was traveling incognito. And to be fair we must say that it was to confirm this suspicion that he was determined to accompany the travelers to the end of their journey. As it happened, that confirmation wasn't hard to come by: if Guillaume Coutet had sworn to serve the count because the latter had saved Coutet's life, Antoine de Bourbon felt the strong sympathy and connection of the savior for the saved.

After twenty-seven days of travel, and a series of unimportant incidents we will spare the reader by omitting, as they lacked the drama of previous events, the party arrived in Mantua by way of Tordi, Nogaro, and Castellarez.

LVII

The Oath

No letter, word, or message had forewarned the Baron de Lautrec of the arrival of his daughter. As a result, though he wasn't always the most attentive of fathers, the first moments of their reunion were an outpouring of paternal and filial love.

It was several moments before the baron could acknowledge his daughter's traveling companions, and read the letter sent to him by Cardinal Richelieu. From this letter, he learned the name of the young man charged with the care of his daughter, and from that just how much the cardinal cared for his Isabelle.

Altogether he had more than enough reason to immediately notify Charles de Gonzague, the new Duke of Mantua, of the arrival of his daughter, and of the illustrious escort who'd brought her to his door. So he sent a servant to the Château de Té to tell the duke the news, which was bound to pique his interest, since the Comte de Moret, as the natural brother of Louis XIII, must be privy to the intentions of the cardinal and the king.

When he heard that the count requested an audience, the Duke of Mantua responded by mounting a horse and coming himself, accompanied only by one of his most faithful servants. He found that the Comte de Moret, despite being the son of Henri IV, refused to cover his head and take a seat before the duke did.

As it happened, the duke already knew, from an envoy, the news from Paris as of January 4, 1629—that is to say, several days after the departure of the Comte de Moret and Isabelle. The cardinal, on the strength of the king's promise to him, had conveyed France's full support to the Duke of Mantua, which had gone a long way to relieve him of his fears. And now here came not a mere courier, but an emissary from Richelieu himself, to assure him that the cardinal—and the king—were on their way.

History tells us that on Thursday, January 15, the king dined at Moulins and spent the night at Varenne. We don't know his exact whereabouts between January 15 and February 5—but we do know that in that time the plague, which had broken out in Italy, had crossed the Alps and reached Lyon. Would the king have enough courage, in the face of bitter cold and this deadly scourge, to carry him through Lyon and up into the frigid mountains?

For anyone who knew how changeable the king was, this was a real concern. But for those who knew the steadfast character of the cardinal, there was hope. The Comte de Moret could only repeat to the Duke of Mantua what he'd been told by the cardinal: that the French intended to raise the siege of Casale and bring immediate relief to Mantua.

There was no time to lose. Charles, the Duc de Nevers, knew from a reliable source that Prince Gaston, in a moment of anger, had sent a message reaching out to Wallenstein in Germany. Thus Monsieur unwittingly drew toward France those new Huns under their new Attila. For the last three months, two generals of these barbarians, Aldringen and Gallas, past masters of destruction and pillage, had been sacking their way through Worms, Frankfurt, and Swabia. To the poor Duke of Mantua, it was as if they were already looming across the Alps, more terrible than the savage tribes of the Cimbri and Teutons, who had sledded down mountains and across frozen rivers on their shields.

The Comte de Moret knew he shouldn't stay long in Mantua. He had promised the cardinal he would return to take part in the campaign—but against this, the duke urged him to lend his name to the defense of Mantua until it could be relieved by the king's forces. The situation in Mantua was so grave, the Baron de Lautrec almost regretted that he'd summoned his daughter into it.

The day after their arrival, her father summoned Isabelle for a private talk. He told Isabelle the commitments he'd made regarding her to the Vicomte de Pontis—and in return, Isabelle told him quite openly of the vow made to her by the Comte de Moret. Despite the excellence of the Monsieur de Pontis's birth and family, they were no match for that of Antoine de Bourbon, who outranked anyone of less than royal birth. The baron contented himself with bringing the Comte de Moret into his office to ask him about his intentions. Moret replied with his usual frankness, confessing that the cardinal had already forced his hand, and endorsed his commitment—so long as first he discharged his duty to the cardinal.

The Baron de Lautrec accepted this commitment, with the proviso that if the count was killed, or contracted to another, he would resume his authority to bestow his daughter's hand where he would. Barring that, he had no reason to resist the young count's suit for Isabelle.

The evening after this double discussion, the young couple, walking along the banks of the river Virgil, related to each other the talks they'd had with the baron. Isabelle made her lover promise not to get killed, he promised never to take another for his wife, and both were satisfied.

We must emphasize this promise "never to take another for his wife," because with every son of Henri IV other than Antoine de Bourbon, this would certainly have been a Jesuitical promise, adhered to in fact but not in spirit. There was certainly no ulterior motive in the promise not to get killed, but this promise to take no other wife but Isabelle de Lautrec—did it extend to mistresses, or those moments when the Devil might otherwise tempt him? The most faithful of lovers have such moments, even those who aren't sons of a freethinker like Henri IV. Could the young Basque Jacquelino resist the sultry attractions of his beautiful cousin Marina, whose hot eyes shot him flaming glances that set his heart afire?

What if another evening came like that after Marie de Gonzague's soirée, when La Fargis, her kiss still burning on his lips, was stepping into her chair—what if Satan tapped him on the shoulder and urged him to join her? Was he strong enough to send Satan back to Hell?

We can't say that, for Antoine de Bourbon, the words he'd spoken to Isabelle de Lautrec outweighed the attractions of Madame de Fargis, that Venus Astarte who whispered burning words of forbidden love into the ears of her lovers. What we can say is that the Comte de Moret felt the need of a witness other than the river the pagans called the Mincio, and other lights than those of Venus, Jupiter, Saturn, and Cassiopeia. And so he asked Isabelle to join him in a Christian church and, in the presence of God, reaffirm the solemnity of his oath.

Isabelle, like her compatriot Juliet, promised everything her lover asked, repeating to him the words of the English poet: "My bounty is as boundless as the sea, my love as deep; the more I give to thee, the more I have, for both are infinite."

The next day at the same hour, that is to say, about nine in the evening, two shadows, one walking a few steps behind the other, slipped into St. Andrew's Church through a side door. By the light of the ever-burning lamps and votive candles offered in memory of the many miracles commemorated there, they made their way toward the altar of Our Lady of the Angels, which was also known by the even more charming name of Our Lady of Love, since its first dedication in that name a half-century before had exposed the amorous susceptibility of a bishop.

First came a young woman, who knelt before it. The young man who followed knelt beside her, on her right. Both, radiant with youth and beauty, were bathed in the flickering light of the lamp, she with her head down, eyes moist with tears of joy, he with his face raised, his eyes sparkling with happiness.

Each said a silent prayer—though by "each," we really mean "Isabelle de Lautrec." For the words that overflowed her heart formed a prayer on her lips to the dear Mother of God. But men only know how to pray in misfortune; in happiness, their words are but a babble of desire amid sighs of passion.

Then, their first surge of love expressed, their trembling hands sought each other's grasp. Isabelle gasped with a joy that was almost pain, and then, with no thought of where she was, cried, "Oh, my love—how much I do love you!"

The count looked up at the Madonna. "See!" he cried. "The Madonna smiles! And so do I, for how much do I love you, my dearest Isabelle."

And their heads dropped to their chests, crushed beneath the weight of their happiness.

The count pressed Isabelle's hand against his breast, then gently pulled his hand from hers and pressed her fingers against his lips. And then, pulling the ring from the smallest of his fingers, he placed it on the second finger of her hand, saying "Holy Mother of God, patron saint of love both human and heavenly, you whose celestial smile echoes our own, be witness that I hereby pledge to have no wife but Isabelle de Lautrec. If I break that oath, may you punish me as I deserve."

"Oh, no, Virgin Mother," Isabelle cried, "never punish him!"

"Isabelle!" said the count, taking her fiercely in his arms, then gently releasing her before the holiness of the place.

"Madonna, holy and all-powerful," she said, "be witness in my turn to my oath. I swear here at your altar, before whose divine feet I kiss, that from today I belong body and soul to the one who just placed this ring on my finger, and that, even were he to die, or, worse, betray his oath, I will be no one else's wife, unless it be that of your divine son."

With this final word, Isabelle's lips were closed by a kiss. The sainted Madonna smiled down at the count's kiss and at Isabelle's gasp, as she remembered that she'd been called Our Lady of Love before she was called Our Lady of the Angels.

LVIII

The Journal of Monsieur de Bassompierre

As the Duke of Mantua learned from the envoy, the cardinal and the king had left Paris on the fourth of January and, on the fifteenth, they dined at Moulins and supped at Varenne, which is not to be confused with that Varennes in the Meuse later made famous by the arrest of a king.

For this commencement of the campaign, we have a reliable guide in the journal of Monsieur de Bassompierre. It is to him we turn for the historical part of our story.

The king, after making his fateful pact with Richelieu, left His Eminence's office, and outside encountered Monsieur de Bassompierre, who had come to pay his respects to the cardinal. Seeing him, the king paused and turned to Richelieu, who was escorting him to the door of the street. "Look, Monsieur le Cardinal—here's someone we can trust to go with us, and who will serve me well."

The cardinal smiled and nodded. "That is the marshal's way."

"Your Majesty will pardon me for asking, but where are we going?"

"To Italy," said the king. "I go in person to raise the siege of Casale. So prepare to depart, Monsieur le Maréchal. We'll take Créqui as well—he knows that country, and hopefully will tell us all about it."

"Your servant, Sire," Bassompierre replied with a bow. "I'll follow you to the end of the world, and even to the Moon, should you choose to mount so high."

"We go neither so far nor so high, Marshal. We rendezvous in Grenoble. If anything delays you from joining us there, please inform the cardinal."

"Sire," said Bassompierre, "with God's help, nothing will go amiss—especially if Your Majesty will order that old scoundrel La Vieuville to pay me what I'm owed as Colonel-General of the Swiss Guard."

The king laughed. "If La Vieuville won't pay you," he said, "the cardinal will."

"Is that so?" Bassompierre seemed skeptical.

"Quite so, Marshal. In fact, if you'll give me your bill now, you can leave here with the money. We depart in three or four days and have no time to lose."

"Monsieur le Cardinal," said Bassompierre, with that air of grand nobility unique to him, "I never carry cash with me when I go to play cards with the king. I'll leave the bill with you, if I may, and send a lackey around later to pick up the money."

The king departed. Bassompierre wrote out his bill for the cardinal, and sent for the money the next day.

The same evening that the cardinal had told Louis XIII that a king must always be true to his word, he sent one hundred fifty thousand *livres* to the Duc d'Orléans, sixty thousand to the queen mother, and fifty thousand to Queen Anne. Also, l'Angely received the thirty thousand *livres* the king had offered him, and Saint-Simon the appointment of King's Squire, with its fifteen thousand *livres* per year. As for Baradas, we know that he had been surprised to receive a bearer bond from the king for thirty thousand *livres,* and had collected it the same day.

The cardinal had also settled his accounts. Charpentier, Rossignol, and Cavois all shared in his success—but the payment to Cavois, generous though it was, was small consolation to his wife. For her, the cardinal's resignation had brought about a welcome return to quiet nights without disturbance, which was all she'd been praying for—with, as we've seen, the aid of the children. Unfortunately, Man, in creating a personal God who could respond to every person, had so overwhelmed the Deity with entreaties that sometimes even the holiest and most reasonable requests were overlooked. Poor Madame Cavois fell into this category, and, following His Eminence, Cavois once again left her a widow. Fortunately, he left her once again pregnant.

The king had previously bestowed on Monsieur the title of lieutenant general; but from the moment the cardinal rejoined the king, it was apparent that it would be Richelieu who would manage the conduct of the war, and that the office of lieutenant general would be an empty formality. So, though Monsieur sent his train by way of Montargis and then followed it beyond Moulins, upon arrival at Chavagnes he changed his mind and announced to Bassompierre that, considering the insult he had been offered, he was withdrawing to his principality of Dombes where he would await the orders of the king. Bassompierre implored him to reconsider, but to no end.

No one was surprised by Monsieur's decision, most seeing in it cowardice rather than wounded pride.

The king marched quickly to Lyon, where he found the plague was raging, and went on to stop in Grenoble. On Monday, February 19, he sent to the Marquis de Thoiras in Vienna to come join the army and oversee the passage of the artillery over the mountains.

The Duc de Montmorency had, on his part, informed the king that he would come by Nîmes, Sisteron, and Gap, joining the king at Briançon.

It was there that the real troubles began. The two queens, on the pretext that they feared for the health of the king, but actually to subvert the influence of the cardinal, had left Paris with the aim of joining the king in Grenoble. But he had ordered them to stop in Lyon, and they dared not disobey. However, in Lyon they made all the trouble they could, diverting Créqui's attention from preparing for the passage of the mountains, and delaying Guise from joining the fleet. However, nothing discouraged the cardinal: so long as the king was his ally, the king was his strength. He hoped that the king, by taking the personal risk of crossing the Alpine passes in winter, would attract from the neighboring provinces the help they needed—and it had been working before the two queens began to interfere.

When they got to Briançon, it was clear that the two queens' meddling had been so successful that nothing that was supposed to be there had arrived: no food, no mules, almost no ammunition, and no more than a dozen cannon.

Worse, there were only two million *livres* left of all the millions the cardinal had borrowed.

All this while, opposing the king was the Duke of Savoy, the most wily and deceitful prince of his time. He held Susa Pass, the way across the Alps to Casale and Mantua.

None of these obstacles stopped the cardinal for a moment. He convened their most skillful engineers and sought with them the means of doing everything men's effort could do. Charles VIII had been the first to carry cannon across the Alps, but that had been in good weather; it was hard enough to cross these almost inaccessible mountains in the summer, let alone in the winter. They affixed cables to the artillery and attached them to pulleys and winches; some men cranked winches, others hauled cables by hand. The cannon balls were hoisted up in baskets; barrels containing ammunition, powder, and more balls were loaded onto mules, bought at a ruinous price.

In six days, all this equipment was brought over Mont Genèvre and down to Oulx. The cardinal pushed on to Chaumont, where he hastily gathered what information he could and checked it against the intelligence sent on by the Comte de Moret.

It was there that, upon reckoning all the ammunition, he was told that there were only seven cartridges per man. "What of that," Richelieu replied, "so long as Susa is taken with the fifth?"

Meanwhile rumors of these preparations reached the ears of

Charles-Emmanuel, the Duke of Savoy; but the king and the cardinal were already in Briançon when Savoy thought them still in Lyon. Consequently he sent his son, Victor-Amadeus, to call on King Louis XIII in Grenoble; but once in Grenoble, he learned that King Louis had already left and was at that hour crossing the mountains.

Victor-Amadeus set out at once in pursuit of the king and the cardinal. He caught up with Louis XIII at Oulx and asked for an audience, just as the last pieces of artillery were descending from the pass.

The king received him, but refused to listen to him and sent him on to the cardinal. Victor-Amadeus left immediately for Chaumont. There the Prince of Savoy, raised by a master of the ruse, hoped to use on the cardinal the methods familiar to himself and his father—but this time he was outfaced, a serpent against a lion.

The cardinal understood from the prince's first words that the Duke of Savoy had but one reason for sending his son, and that was to gain time. But where the king might have been taken in, the cardinal saw clearly the negotiator's intentions.

Victor-Amadeus had come to ask for time so his father could find a way out of the promise he'd made to the Governor of Milan not to allow French troops to cross his domain. But even as he began to articulate his request, the cardinal brought him up short. "Your pardon, My Prince," he said, "but His Highness the Duke of Savoy asks for time to repudiate a promise he was in no position to give."

"How is that?" asked the prince.

"Because, in his recent negotiations with France, he agreed to allow my master the king passage through his domain, if needed to support his allies."

Victor-Amadeus was taken aback. "I must beg pardon of Your Eminence, but I've seen this clause nowhere in the treaties between France and Savoy."

"And you're well aware why you haven't seen it, Prince. It was a verbal agreement, and out of respect for the duke, your father, we were satisfied with his word of honor and didn't require that clause in writing. According to him, the King of Spain would take offense if he granted such a privilege to France and wouldn't give him a moment's rest until he'd obtained a similar right."

"But," ventured Victor-Amadeus, "the duke my father does not refuse passage to the king your master."

"Then," said the Cardinal, smiling as he recalled the details of the letter received from the Comte de Moret, "is it to honor the King of France that His Highness the Duke of Savoy has closed the pass of Susa with a demi-lune bastion large enough for three hundred troops, backed up by barricades with room for three hundred more, and on top of this the Fort of Montabon, built between two redoubts with outworks placed to create a crossfire? Is it to facilitate the passage of the king and the army of France that, in addition to blocking the valley, boulders so large that no engine could move them have been rolled down into the road? Is it to plant trees and flowers along our path that for the last six weeks, three hundred workers have plied pickaxe and spade at work that has attracted visits from both you and your august father?

"No, Prince, let us not mince words: speak frankly, as rulers should. You delay in order to give the Spanish enough time to take Casale, whose garrison is heroically dying of hunger. *Eh bien!* As it is in our interest, and is our duty, to rescue this garrison, we say to you that your father, His Highness the Duke, owes us this passage, and your father the duke will give it to us.

"We need two days for the rest of our materiel to arrive." The cardinal drew his watch. "It is now eleven in the morning. Eleven in the morning, the day after tomorrow, will be on Tuesday; at dawn on Wednesday, we attack. You may take it as written. Now, whether you go to open the pass, or to prepare to defend it, you have no time to spare for reflection, so I won't keep you. A frank and open peace, Monseigneur—or a good war."

"I fear it will be the good war, Monsieur le Cardinal," said Victor-Amadeus, rising.

"From the Christian point of view, and as a minister of the Lord, I hate war; but from the political point of view and as a minister of France, I think that war, though never a good thing, is sometimes a necessary thing.

"France is within its rights and will have them respected. When two states come to blows, bad luck comes to he who champions deceit and perfidy. God sees us; God will judge."

The cardinal saluted the prince, making it clear that further talk was futile. France would march on Casale, and no matter the obstacles, that was the path they'd chosen.

Callot

LIX

In Which the Reader Meets an Old Friend

Victor-Amadeus had scarcely left when the cardinal approached a table and wrote the following letter:

Sire,

If Your Majesty, as God gives me to hope, has fortunately completed transport of our materiel over the mountains, I humbly beg you will order the artillery, caissons, and all machines of war brought immediately to Chaumont. We pray the king will have the kindness to proceed here without delay, as the day of hostilities is to be Wednesday—subject to the will of Your Majesty, though it were best not changed without good reason.

I eagerly await Your Majesty's response—or, better still, Your Majesty himself.

I send a reliable man upon whom His Majesty can depend for anything, even as an escort should His Majesty choose to travel incognito by night.

I have the honor to be,
For Your Majesty,
Your most humble subject and most devoted servant,

—Armand, Cardinal de Richelieu

Once the letter was written and folded, the cardinal called, "Étienne!"

At once the door of the room opened, and on the threshold appeared our old acquaintance Étienne Latil, last seen entering the cardinal's study in Chaillot, pale, knees trembling, supporting himself against the wall, and feebly offering his devotion. But now with head high, mustache bristling, a spring in his step, hat in his right hand and the left on the pommel of his sword, he was once again that captain who might have stepped out of a sketch by Callot.

It had been fully four months since, struck at the same time by the Marquis de Pisany and by Souscarrières, he had fallen unconscious to the floor of Maître Soleil's inn. However, if a wound isn't fatal, it's not long before a man put together like Étienne Latil is back on his feet, more hale and hearty than ever.

The imminent hostilities lent a gaiety to his face that did not escape the cardinal. "Étienne," he said to him, "mount your horse this instant—unless you'd prefer, for your own reasons, to travel by foot—but however you wish, this letter, which is of the highest importance, must reach the king before ten this evening."

"Would Your Eminence tell me what time it is?"

The cardinal drew his watch. "It is nearly noon."

"And the king is in Oulx?"

"Yes."

"Unless I plunge down the Doire, the king will have his letter by eight."

"Try not to plunge down the Doire, as that would cause me grief; whereas if the king receives his letter, I'll be pleased."

"I shall hope to satisfy Your Eminence on both points."

The cardinal knew Latil for a man of his word, so judging that it was pointless to insist, he merely made a gesture of dismissal.

Latil ran to the stable to choose a good horse, stopping at the smithy only long enough to have it shod with crampons; that business finished, he sprang on its back and launched himself down the road to Oulx.

He found the track in better condition than he'd expected. With the aim of making it passable for the cannons and other equipment, the engineers had done everything feasible to improve it.

By four o'clock Étienne was at Saint-Laurent, and by half past seven he was at Oulx.

The king was at supper, served by Saint-Simon, who had succeeded Baradas in his favor. At the foot of the table was his fool and confidant, l'Angely. A message from the cardinal was announced, and immediately the king ordered that the messenger be brought before him.

Latil was fully conversant with all forms of etiquette, having spent his time as a page of the Duc d'Épernon, and thus was no man to let himself be intimidated by royal majesty. He entered boldly into the room, advanced toward the king, placed one knee on the ground, and presented him his hat with the cardinal's letter balanced atop it.

Louis XIII watched this with a certain astonishment: Latil had followed the rules of etiquette of the old-time court. "*Ouais!*" he said, taking the note. "Where do you come by these fine manners, my master?"

"Is not this the fashion, Sire, in which one presented letters to your illustrious father, of glorious memory?"

"Indeed! But the mode is a trifle passé."

"The respect is the same, Sire, so it seemed to me the etiquette should be the same."

"You seem well versed in etiquette for a soldier."

"I started out as page to Monsieur le Duc d'Épernon, and in that time I more than once had the honor to present a letter to Henri IV in the manner I have now had the honor to repeat to his son."

"Page to the Duc d'Épernon," repeated the king.

"And like him, Sire, I was on the running board of the carriage on May 14, 1610, in the Rue de la Ferronnerie, when Henri IV was slain; Your Majesty may have heard that it was a page who stopped the assassin by holding on to his cloak despite the knife-blows that slashed his hands."

"Yes. . . . This page, would he be you, by any chance?"

Latil, still on one knee before the king, drew off his deerskin gloves, revealing hands furrowed by scars. "Sire, see my hands," he said.

The king looked at the man with visible emotion, and said, "These hands are the hands of loyalty. Give me your hands, *mon brave.*" And taking Latil's hands in his own, he gripped them. "Now, rise," he said.

Latil rose. "A great king, Sire, was King Henri IV," he said.

"Yes, and God give me the grace to resemble him."

"The opportunity is here, Sire," replied Latil, indicating the note he had brought.

"Let us see," said the king, opening the letter.

"Ah!" he said, after reading it. "Monsieur le Cardinal says that he has engaged our honor, and that whether we disengage it or not, the matter will not wait. . . . Saint-Simon, inform Messieurs Créqui and Bassompierre that I must speak with them this very moment."

The two marshals were lodged in a house adjacent to that of the king, and were alerted within minutes; of the two other commanders, Monsieur de Schomberg was at Exilles, Monsieur de Montmorency at Saint-Laurent.

The king conveyed the contents of Richelieu's letter to the two marshals, and ordered them to get the artillery and munitions to Chaumont as quickly as possible, declaring that everything must be at Chaumont by the end of the next day.

As for the marshals, he expected them by Tuesday evening so they could take part in a council of war, in which they would decide the mode of attack for the following day.

At ten o'clock that evening, in a murky night swirling with snow, without moon or stars, the king departed on horseback for Chaumont accompanied only by Latil, Saint-Simon, and l'Angely. Having prepared his own horse for ice, Latil now took the same precautions with the king's horse. Then he set out on that route for the third time, leading on foot and probing the road.

Never had the king displayed such a bold demeanor, nor been so satisfied with himself. If he didn't have the strength of character for actual grandeur, he at least had a sense of it. He wore his hat with the black plumes, and thought of the white plumes his father Henri IV had worn during his great victory at Ivry. If his son could change his black plume for a white plume, why couldn't Susa be his Ivry?

Latil marched before the king's horse, sounding the road with an iron-shod staff, stopping from time to time to find better footing, taking the horse by the bridle and leading him over bad spots. At each guard post the king was recognized, and he gave the order to prepare the troops to march on Chaumont, enjoying in their obedience one of the sweetest prerogatives of power.

Just short of Saint-Laurent, Latil had an intimation, from the sharpness of the north wind, of the approach of one of those sudden whirlwinds that are dubbed in the mountains a "snowplow." He invited the king to dismount and take shelter between Saint-Simon, l'Angely, and himself, but the king wanted to stay on his horse, saying that if events called for him to be a soldier, he would act like a soldier. He wrapped himself in his cloak and waited.

The whirlwind didn't keep them waiting long; it came on with a whine.

L'Angely and Saint-Simon pressed themselves in on either side of the king, who was wrapped in his cloak. Latil seized the horse's bit with both hands and turned his back to the hurricane.

It arrived, terrible and howling.

In an instant, the road was covered with snow two feet deep. The riders felt their horses tremble between their legs: in such cataclysms of nature, the animals share the fright of man. The silk ribbon which held on the king's hat parted, and the black felt with its black plumes disappeared into the darkness like a night-bird.

Upon arrival at Saint-Laurent, the king asked to be led to Monsieur de Montmorency's quarters. It was one o'clock in the morning; Montmorency had thrown himself fully clothed onto his bed. At the first word of the king's presence, the duke sprang back up and stood in his doorway, awaiting the king's orders.

Such promptness pleased Louis XIII, and though not overly fond of Monsieur de Montmorency, who had at one time been enamored of the queen, he saluted him.

The duke offered to accompany the king and provide him with an escort. But Louis XIII replied that he was on the ground of France; and so long as he was on the ground of France, he felt safe; the escort he had seemed sufficient, being entirely devoted. He merely asked Montmorency to make his way to Chaumont in time for the council of war to be held at nine o'clock the following evening.

The only thing he agreed to accept was another hat. When placing it on his head, he realized that it had three white plumes, and once again he recalled Ivry. "It's a good omen," he said.

Upon leaving Saint-Laurent, the snow was so deep that Latil invited the king to come down from his horse. The king dismounted. Latil led, taking the king's horse by the bridle; l'Angely came after, then Saint-Simon. Louis XIII thus had a path to follow leveled for him by three men and three horses.

Saint-Simon, who was grateful to the cardinal for the favors he'd done him, praised to the king all the precautions Richelieu had taken and all the foresight he had shown. "Yes, yes," answered Louis XIII, "Monsieur le Cardinal is a good servant; I doubt that my brother, in his place, would have taken so many pains for me."

Two hours later, the king arrived without incident at the door of the Golden Juniper in Chaumont, as proud of his lost hat as of a wound, as proud of his night march as of a victory. He remarked that no one need awaken the cardinal.

"His Eminence is not asleep," replied Maître Germain.

"And what is he doing at this hour?" asked the king.

"I work for the glory of Your Majesty," said the cardinal as he appeared, "and Monsieur de Pontis aids me with all his power in this glorious task."

And the cardinal invited the king into his room, where he found a large fire to warm it, and an immense map of the country, drawn up by Monsieur de Pontis, unrolled on a table.

LX

In Which the Cardinal Finds the Guide He Needs

One of the great strengths of the cardinal was not to believe King Louis XIII had virtues that he lacked, but to make the king think he had them regardless.

Lazy and languid, he made the king believe he was active; timid and distrustful, he made the king believe he was brave; cruel and bloodthirsty, he made him believe he was just.

Richelieu said that, though the king's presence wasn't urgently required in Chaumont at that hour of the night, still he had exalted his glory and that of France by having made the trek, in such peril, on such roads and in the middle of such deep darkness, to answer the call of the nation. However, now the king must take to bed on the instant, as the day just beginning and the one to follow remained ahead of him.

By daybreak, the orders had been given all along the route, so that the troops bivouacked in Saint-Laurent, in Exilles, and in Séhault were all under way toward Chaumont.

These troops were under the command of the Comte de Soissons, the Ducs de Longueville, de la Trémouille, d'Halliun, and de La Valette, the Comtes d'Harcourt and de Sault, and the Marquises de Canaples, de Mortemar, de Tavaune, de Valence, and de Thoiras.

The four top commanders were the Duc de Montmorency and the three Marshals: Créqui, Bassompierre, and Schomberg.

The genius of the cardinal had planned it all; he conceived, the king commanded.

Since we've already told the story of the siege of La Rochelle, that glorious climax of the reign of Louis XIII, in our book *The Three*

Musketeers, we are permitted to dwell here at some length on the famous forcing of the Pass of Susa, about which the official historians have made much ado.

Upon leaving Richelieu, Victor-Amadeus, to cover his exit, as they say in the theater, had announced he was heading to Rivoli where the duke, his father, awaited him, and that in twenty-four hours he would announce Charles-Emmanuel's decision; but when he arrived in Rivoli, the Duke of Savoy, whose only goal was to draw things out, had already departed for Turin.

Thus around five in the evening, instead of Victor-Amadeus it was Savoy's prime minister, the Count of Verrue, who was announced at the cardinal's door. At this, the cardinal turned to the king. "Would Your Majesty," he asked, "prefer the honor of receiving him, or will you leave this burden to me?"

"If it was Prince Victor-Amadeus, I'd receive him; but since the Duke of Savoy sees fit to send me his prime minister, it's only right that my prime minister should answer him."

"Then does the king give me *carte blanche?*" asked the cardinal.

"Entirely."

"I'll leave the door open," continued Richelieu, "so Your Majesty will hear the entire exchange, and if anything I say displeases him, he'll be able to enter and contradict me."

Louis XIII gave a nod of assent. Richelieu, leaving the door ajar, went into the chamber where the Count of Verrue awaited.

This Count of Verrue should not be confused with his famous grandson, husband of the celebrated Jeanne d'Albert de Luynes, mistress of Victor-Amadeus II and known as the "Lady of Pleasure"— this Count of Verrue, whom history barely mentions, was a man of forty years, acute, discerning, and of proven courage. Charged with a difficult mission, he brought an essential candor to the tortuous negotiations required of an emissary of Charles-Emmanuel.

Seeing the grave figure of the cardinal, with that eye that saw to the bottom of hearts, faced with this genius who alone held in check the other sovereigns of Europe, he bowed deeply and respectfully. "Monseigneur," he said, "I come in place of Prince Victor-Amadeus, who is needed at the side of the duke, his father, who has fallen seriously ill. When his son, after having left Your Eminence, arrived last night at Rivoli, he found that his father had been taken to Turin."

"Then, Monsieur le Comte," said Richelieu, "you come charged with the full powers of the Duke of Savoy?"

"I come to announce that I precede his arrival, Monseigneur; ill as he is, the Duke of Savoy wants to plead his case to His Majesty in person. He is being carried here in a sedan chair."

"And when do you think he will arrive, Count?"

"His Highness's state of weakness, and the slowness of his means of transport, means that, in my opinion, he can be here no sooner than the day after tomorrow."

"At about what hour?"

"I wouldn't dare to promise before noon."

"I am in despair, Monsieur le Comte: I told Prince Victor-Amadeus that on that day at daybreak we would attack the entrenchments of Susa—and at daybreak we *will* attack."

"I hope Your Eminence will not be so inflexible," said the Count of Verrue, "since you know that the Duke of Savoy does not intend to deny passage."

"Ah, well, then," said Richelieu, "if we're in agreement, there's no need for further talk."

"It is true," said Verrue with some embarrassment, "that His Highness has one condition . . . or rather, one hope," added the count.

"Ah-ha!" said the cardinal, smiling. "And that is?"

"His Highness the Duke hopes that, due to the great sacrifice he is making, His Most Christian Majesty will cede from the Duchy of Mantua the same part of Montferrat that the King of Spain was allotting to Savoy if he prevailed—or if he does not want to grant it to the duke, that he will make a gift of it to Madame, your king's sister and our prince's wife. On this condition, the pass will be open tomorrow."

The cardinal looked for a moment at the count, who could not sustain his regard and lowered his eyes. Then, as if that was what he awaited, Richelieu said, "Monsieur le Comte, all Europe has such a high opinion of my master the king's regard for justice, that I don't know how His Highness the Duke of Savoy could imagine that His Majesty would consent to such a proposition. Personally, I'm certain that he would never accept it. The King of Spain may well grant part of what does not belong to him in order to engage Savoy to support an unjust usurpation; but God prevent that the king my master, who crosses the mountains to come to the aid of the oppressed Duke of Mantua, would treat his ally so. If the Duke of Savoy forgets what a King of France is capable of, the day after tomorrow he will be reminded."

"But may I hope at least that these final proposals will be presented by Your Eminence to His Majesty?"

"Useless, Monsieur le Comte," said a voice from behind the cardinal. "The king has heard, and is quite astonished that a man who must know better should make a proposal that would compromise France and stain its honor. If tomorrow the pass is not opened without condition, the next day, at daybreak, it will be attacked."

Then, drawing himself up and placing a foot before him with that majesty which he could sometimes assume, King Louis XIII added, "I will be there in person, and you'll be able to recognize me by these white plumes, as my august father was recognized at Ivry. I hope that His Highness the Duke will adopt a similar sign to identify him in the heat of battle. Take him my words, Monsieur: they are the only response I can and must make."

And he dismissed the count with a gesture, who responded with a deep bow and withdrew.

All that day and all that night, the army continued to assemble around Chaumont. By the following evening, the king commanded twenty-three thousand foot and four thousand horse.

Around ten at night, the artillery and all its materiel were lined up beyond Chaumont, the mouths of the guns turned toward the enemy. The king ordered a check of the caissons and crates for a report on how much ammunition was available. At this time the bayonet had not yet been invented, so the cannon and the musket decided everything. Today, the rifle has come forward as the weapon of choice for the modern warrior, becoming, as predicted by the Maréchal de Saxe, the handle of the bayonet.

At midnight, the council was convened. It was composed of the king, the cardinal, the Duc de Montmorency, and the three marshals: Bassompierre, Schomberg, and Créqui. Bassompierre, who was senior, took the floor. He cast his eyes over the map and studied the positions of the enemy—which they knew perfectly, thanks to the information sent by the Comte de Moret.

"Unless someone has a better idea," he said, "here is my proposal, Sire." And, saluting the king and cardinal to show that he was addressing them, he said, "I propose that the regiments of the French and Swiss Guards take the lead; the Regiment of Navarre and the Regiment d'Estissac, the left and right. The two wings will each be led by two hundred musketeers who will gain the summit of the two peaks of Montmoron and Montabon. Once at the top of the two mountains, nothing will be easier than for them to get the drop on the guards at the barricades. At the first shot heard from the heights, we move; while the musketeers fire on the barricades from behind, we will make a frontal assault with the two Guard regiments. Approach the map, Messieurs, look at the position of the enemy, and if you have a better plan than mine, speak up."

Maréchal de Créqui and Maréchal de Schomberg studied the map and supported Bassompierre's proposal.

That left the Duc de Montmorency.

Montmorency was better known for his dauntless courage and audacity on the field of battle than as a strategist and man of foresight; moreover, he spoke with a certain difficulty at first, with a stammer that he gradually lost as he went on. However, this time he found the courage to speak before the king.

"Sire," he said, "I respect the opinion of Monsieur de Bassompierre, and of Messieurs de Créqui and de Schomberg, and am well aware of their courage and experience; but while I don't doubt we can carry them, taking those barricades and the redoubts, especially the demi-lune that completely blocks the road, will be a difficult task indeed. Monsieur de Bassompierre has rightly said that we must take them; but is there no way to cut off these entrenchments? Can't we find, perhaps by a difficult mountain path, a way to turn the flank, to come down between the demi-lune and Susa and attack this position from behind? It would only be a question of finding a loyal guide and an intrepid officer, two things that don't seem impossible to me."

"You hear the proposal of Monsieur de Montmorency," said the king. "Do you agree?"

"Excellent!" replied the marshals. "But there's no time to lose in finding this guide and this officer."

At that moment Étienne Latil spoke a few quiet words in the cardinal's ear, and Richelieu's face brightened. "Messieurs," he said, "I believe Providence sends us our loyal guide and intrepid officer in one and the same person."

And turning toward Latil, who awaited his orders: "Captain Latil," he said, "bring in Monsieur le Comte de Moret."

Latil bowed.

Five minutes later, the Comte de Moret entered, and despite his disguise as a humble mountaineer, everyone could see the resemblance to his august father—a resemblance that was the envy of King Louis XIII, illustrious son of Henri IV. He had just arrived from Mantua, sent by Providence, as the Duc de Richelieu had said.

LXI

Susa Pass

The Comte de Moret, thanks to the route he'd taken to cross safely into Savoy, could be at once the loyal guide and the intrepid officer.

Indeed, the question had scarcely been stated before, taking a pencil, he traced on Monsieur de Pontis's map the path that led from Chaumont to the smugglers' inn. He paused to recount how he'd been forced to change his route to escape the Spanish bandits, and how this change of route had brought him to the path whereby one could slip past the ramparts that girdled the mountains above Susa.

He was authorized to take five hundred men with him, a larger troop being too awkward to maneuver on such a route.

The cardinal wanted the young prince to take a few hours of rest, but he refused, saying that if he was to arrive in time to create a diversion at the moment of the attack, he didn't have a minute to lose.

He requested the cardinal to give him, as second in command, Étienne Latil, whose devotion and courage were beyond question.

They agreed to all his desires.

At three in the morning, Moret's troop quietly departed; each man carried with him one day's rations.

Of the five hundred men who were to march under his orders, the Comte de Moret knew only the young captain; but once they were told they were to have the son of Henri IV as their leader, the soldiers crowded around him with cries of joy. They brought up torches so they could see his face, whose resemblance to that of the *Béarnais* redoubled their enthusiasm.

Immediately after the Comte de Moret's five hundred men marched out, under cover of a night so dark it was impossible to see ten paces before oneself, the remainder of the army was put in motion. The weather was terrible, and the ground was covered with two feet of snow.

Fifty men remained behind to guard the artillery park. The rest of the troops marched to within five hundred paces of the Rock of Gélasse, just short of Susa Pass. Six pieces of cannon and six pallets of balls were brought up to force the barricade.

The troops chosen to attack were seven companies of Guards, six of Swiss, nineteen of Navarre, fourteen of Estissac, and fifteen of Sault, plus the king's mounted musketeers.

Each unit was to throw out in front fifty storm troopers known as *"enfants perdus,"* supported by one hundred men, with those supported by five hundred more.

Around six in the morning, the troops were marshaled into order. The king presided over these preparations, detailing some of his musketeers to join the *enfants perdus.* Then he ordered the Sieur de Comminges, preceded by a trumpeter, to approach the border and ask the Duke of Savoy for passage for the army and the person of the king.

Monsieur de Comminges advanced, but a hundred paces from the barricade he was stopped by a challenge. The Count of Verrue appeared and called out, "What do you want, Monsieur?"

The herald responded, "We wish to pass, Monsieur."

"But," Verrue replied, "how do you wish to pass? As friends or as enemies?"

"As friends, if you open the pass to us; as enemies, if you close it. I am charged by the king my master to go to Susa and prepare lodgings for him, as he plans to sleep there tomorrow."

"Monsieur," answered the Count of Verrue, "the duke my master would hold it a great honor to host His Majesty, but he comes with so many followers that before I can respond, I must ask His Highness for orders."

"Well," said Comminges, "do you intend, by any chance, to dispute our passage?"

The Count of Verrue came forth and stood before him. "What would you have, Monsieur?" the herald asked the count.

"I have the honor to say to you, Monsieur," replied Verrue coldly, "that on this subject I must first know the intentions of His Highness, my master."

"Monsieur, I warn you," said Comminges, "that I must report your reply to the king."

"You may do as you please, Monsieur," responded Verrue. "You are master of yourself."

And with this, each saluted the other. Verrue returned to his side of the barricades, and Comminges returned to the king.

"*Eh bien,* Monsieur?" Louis XIII asked Comminges.

The herald related his discussion with the Count of Verrue: Louis XIII listened without missing a word, and when Comminges had finished, the king said, "The Count of Verrue answered not only as a worthy servant, but as a man of spirit who knows his duty."

At that moment the king was on the farthest frontier of France, between the *enfants perdus* ready to charge, and the five hundred men who were to support them.

Bassompierre approached, smiling and with hat in hand. "Sire," he said, "the dancers are ready, the violins are in tune, and the masks are at hand; when it pleases Your Majesty, we may commence the ballet."

The king looked at him, brow furrowed. "Monsieur le Maréchal, did you know I just received a report that we have only five hundred rounds in the artillery park?"

"Well, Sire," answered Bassompierre, "this is certainly the right time to consider that; if the masque isn't ready, the ballet shouldn't be danced. But let's do it. All will be well."

"Is that your answer to me?" said the king, fixing the marshal with a look.

"Sire, it would be beyond bold to guarantee something as doubtful as a victory; but my answer to you is that we will return with our honor, or I will fall or be taken."

"Make sure that if we are beaten, Monsieur de Bassompierre, that I am taken with you."

"Bah, what can happen to me worse than to be called a coward, as Your Majesty did the Marquis d'Uxelles? But don't worry, Sire, I'll try not to deserve such an insult. Let's just do it."

"Sire," said the cardinal, who held his horse close to the king's, "with an attitude like the marshal's, my hopes are high." Then, addressing Bassompierre: "Go, Monsieur le Maréchal, go—and do your utmost."

Bassompierre rode to where the other commanders awaited, and dismounted with Messieurs de Créqui and de Montmorency for the frontal assault on the trenches. Only Monsieur de Schomberg remained mounted, due to the gout in his knee.

They marched past the base of the Rock of Gélasse; for some reason the enemy had abandoned that position, strong though it was, perhaps afraid that those who defended it would be cut off and forced to surrender.

But as soon as the troops passed the rock, they were exposed, and fire commenced from the mountain and the broad barricade. And at the first volley, Monsieur de Schomberg was hit in the lower back.

Bassompierre followed the valley floor and approached the demilune that blocked Susa Pass from the front, Monsieur de Créqui close beside him.

Monsieur de Montmorency, as if he were a common soldier, sprang up the mountain on the left toward the peak of Montmoron.

Monsieur de Schomberg was tied to his horse, which was led forward by its bridle due to the difficulty of the terrain; he made his way up the right-hand slope in the midst of the *enfants perdus*.

Following Bassompierre's plan, these units were to flank the barricades, shooting the defenders from above while the others attacked the front.

The Valaisans and Piedmontese defended valiantly; Victor-Amadeus and his father commanded from the redoubt on the peak of Montabon.

Montmorency, reckless as always, quickly attacked and carried the first outwork on the left. As his armor had encumbered him while afoot, along the way he had dropped its pieces one by one, attacking the rampart in his simple buff jerkin and velvet trunk-hose.

Bassompierre, for his part, remained on the valley floor, weathering the fire from the demi-lune.

Behind came the king, with his white plumes, and Monsieur le Cardinal in a gold-embroidered robe of russet velvet.

Three times the center charged the demi-lune, and three times they were repulsed from that curved barricade. Musket balls leaped and ricocheted down the valley from rock to rock, killing one of Monsieur de Créqui's esquires within a few feet of the king's horse.

Bassompierre and Créqui then resolved to scale the slopes, each with five hundred men: Bassompierre the mountain on the left, to reinforce Monsieur de Montmorency, and Créqui the mountain on the right, to support Monsieur de Schomberg.

Two thousand five hundred men remained on the valley floor to maintain pressure on the demi-lune.

Bassompierre, overweight, fifty years old, and on the steepest slope, was climbing while leaning on his aide, when suddenly he lost his support: the aide beside him had taken a ball in the chest. He made it to the summit just as Monsieur de Montmorency was falling back from his third assault on the redoubt. They combined forces for a fourth.

Montmorency was lightly wounded in the arm, while Bassompierre's clothes were riddled with bullet-holes. But the redoubt on the left was carried, and the Savoyard defenders took refuge behind the demi-lune.

The two commanders looked across toward the mountain redoubt on the right. The battle there was hotly contested. Presently they saw two riders leave at a full gallop, making for a path that had apparently been prepared for their retreat down to the demi-lune. It was the Duke of Savoy, Charles-Emmanuel, and his son, Victor-Amadeus. A flood of fugitives followed them.

The redoubt on the right was taken. Only the demi-lune remained: the hardest nut to crack.

Louis XIII sent couriers to congratulate the marshals and Montmorency on their success, but telling them to retire and recover. Bassompierre replied on behalf of himself and Messieurs de Schomberg, de Créqui, and de Montmorency:

> *Sire, we are grateful for your concern, but at times like these the blood of a prince or a marshal of France is not worth more than that of the simplest soldier.*
>
> *We ask for ten minutes of rest for the men, after which the ball will start anew.*

And, indeed, after ten minutes of rest the trumpets sounded, the drums beat again, and the two wings, in two tight columns, closed on the now-reinforced demi-lune.

LXII

In Which It Is Shown That a Man is Never Hanged Until the Noose is Tightened

The approaches had fallen to the French—but the last entrenchment remained, teeming with soldiers, bristling with cannons, and anchored by the fort of Montabon, built atop an inaccessible rock; the fort had but one approach, a staircase that could be climbed only in single file.

Left far behind were any guns that might bear on either the valley floor or the mountain summits. The soldiers had to assault the demilune supported by nothing but what the Italians of the time called their *furia francese.*

From a low rise within range of the enemy's guns, king and cardinal watched the troops marching forward behind the flower of the nobility, the leaders' hats held high on the ends of their swords. The soldiers advanced head down, not asking if they were being led to butchery; their commanders led from the front, and that was all they needed to know.

His Eminence was with the king on his horse, and the cardinal saw the sudden gaps the cannon plowed through the ranks; the king clapped his hands, applauding the soldiers' courage while at the same time his innate cruelty awoke like a tiger scenting blood. When he'd had the Maréchal d'Ancre killed, though he was still too small to look out the window, he'd had some of his men lift him up so he could watch the bloody body carried past.

The troops reached the barricade; some carried ladders, and the escalade began.

Montmorency took a flag and was first upon the wall; Bassompierre, too old to follow, took a position halfway up the ramparts and exhorted the soldiers to do their utmost.

Some ladders broke beneath the weight of so many attackers, so keen were they to be the first to set foot on the rampart; others held back to allow time for their companions to go over, drawing up other ladders to mount the assault.

The besieged used whatever weapons they could. Some fired at the attackers at close range; others swung spades and picks, saw blood spout from their blows, and sometimes a man would throw his arms wide and fall backwards. Others hurled stones, or swung heavy poles that cleared two or three ladders at a time.

Suddenly the French could see disarray among the defenders, while from beyond them came shouting and a fusillade.

"Courage, *amis*," cried Montmorency, mounting another assault, "it's the Comte de Moret to our rescue!" And he sprang forward anew, ragged and bloody though he was, carrying along with him, by this supreme effort, all who could see and hear him.

The duke was not mistaken: it was Moret who had created the diversion.

The count had left at three in the morning, as we have seen, with Latil for captain and Galaor for aide-de-camp. They arrived at the bank of the torrent that had almost drowned Guillaume Coutet; but when the freeze had come, the water had dropped, and now one could cross by leaping from rock to rock.

Arriving on the other side of the torrent, the Comte de Moret and his men quickly crossed the field that separated them from the mountain. He found the rising path, and his men followed.

The night was dark, but the glimmer from the new-fallen snow lit the way.

The count, familiar with the difficult terrain, had provided his troops with long ropes, one for each twenty-four men. As each twenty-four-man unit marched along the brink, if one man slipped he was supported by the other twenty-three. Twenty-four others marched behind them, acting as another stay or support.

As they approached the smugglers' inn, he ordered the troops to be silent. Though they didn't know the reason, all remained quiet.

The count gathered a dozen men about him, explained to them that the inn before them was their objective, and ordered them to instruct their comrades to quietly surround it. If but one man escaped this nest of villains and gave the alarm, their mission could be compromised.

Galaor, who knew the place, took a score of men to surround the inn-yard; with twenty more Latil guarded the gate, while the Comte de Moret led a similar number to the only window that let daylight into the house, and by which those inside might escape. The window glowed brightly, indicating that the hosts were in residence.

The rest of the troop spread out along the road, in order to leave the bandits no route of escape.

The gate of the yard was closed; Galaor, with the lithe agility of a monkey, vaulted over, dropped into the yard, and opened it.

In a moment, the yard was full of soldiers, standing with muskets at the ready.

Latil arranged his men in two rows opposite the door, ordering them to fire on anyone who attempted to flee.

The count had slowly and quietly approached the window in order to see what was going on inside; but the heat of the room had fogged the glass, preventing a view of the interior.

One of the window's four panes had been broken in some brawl and replaced by a sheet of paper affixed to the frame. The Comte de Moret got up on the windowsill, cut a slit in the paper with the point of his dagger, and could finally glimpse the strange scene passing within.

The smuggler who had warned Guillaume Coutet when they'd passed through before that Spanish bandits were after them was bound and gagged on a table; the bandits whom he had betrayed, gathered *en tribunal,* had just pronounced judgment. As that judgment could not be appealed, the only question was whether he should be hanged or shot.

Opinion was almost evenly divided. However, as is well known, the Spaniards are a thrifty people. One made the point that you couldn't execute a man with fewer than eight or ten musket shots, which would cost them eight or ten charges of lead and powder—while to hang a man, not only did you need only one rope, but afterwards that rope, having been used in a hanging, multiplied its value by two, four, even ten times!

This sage advice, so economical, carried the day. The bandits chose the rope by acclamation, and the poor devil of a smuggler realized that his fate was sealed. His only recourse was the prayer of the dying: *My God, I place my soul within your hands!*

Then, amid the solemn silence that always precedes the terrible act of violent separation of body and soul, came the order: "Pull!"

But scarcely was this word pronounced when there came from the window the sound of tearing paper, and into the room stretched an arm pointing a pistol. The pistol fired, and the man holding the noose around the neck of the condemned man fell down dead.

At the same moment, a vigorous kick broke the window latches, and in two more blows it was open, letting in the Comte de Moret, who leaped into the room followed by his men. At the gunshot, like a signal, the front door and the yard door also burst open, so all exits were visibly barred by armed soldiers.

Within moments, the condemned was untied, and he passed from anguish to the giddy joy of the man who had made the march to the tomb, but leaps from the grave before the earth can cover him.

"Let no one try to escape," said the Comte de Moret, with a gesture of supreme authority that was his royal heritage. "Anyone who tries to flee will be killed."

Nobody moved.

"Now," he said, addressing the smuggler whose life he'd saved,

"I'm the traveler you so generously warned, two months ago, of the danger I was in, a warning for which you were just now about to die. It's only right that the roles be reversed, and this tragedy played out to its end. Point out to me the wretches who pursued us; their trial will be short."

The smuggler didn't wait to be asked twice; he indicated eight Spaniards—the ninth was dead.

These eight bandits, seeing themselves condemned, and understanding there would be no mercy, exchanged glances—and then with the energy of despair, drew their daggers and fell on the soldiers who guarded the door to the road.

But they had bitten off too much. As you may recall, Latil was in charge of guarding that door, and stood on the threshold with a gun in each hand. With two shots he killed two men.

The other six fought briefly with the men of the Comte de Moret and of Latil. For a few seconds there was the clash of steel, cries, oaths, two more gunshots, the thump of two bodies on the floor . . . and it was over.

Six were dead in their gore, and three others, still alive, were tied hand and foot and in the hands of the soldiers.

"Someone get that rope that was to be used to hang this honest man," said the Comte de Moret, "then find two more to hang these villains."

The muleteers, who were beginning to understand that they were not under suspicion, and that instead of seeing one man hang they were about to see three, a spectacle three times as entertaining, offered up the ropes on the instant.

"Latil," said the Comte de Moret, "I charge you with hanging these three gentlemen. I know you're efficient—don't let them linger. As for the rest of this honorable company, leave ten soldiers to keep them under guard. Tomorrow, no sooner than midday, if the prisoners have caused no trouble, they may be set free."

"And where will I rejoin you?" asked Latil.

"This brave man," answered the Comte de Moret, indicating the smuggler miraculously saved from the noose, "this brave man will lead you; but march double-time to catch up to us."

Then, to the smuggler, "Guide him along the same road you recall from before, my good man; later, at Susa, there will be twenty *pistoles* for you.

"Latil, you have ten minutes."

Latil bowed.

"Let's be on our way, Messieurs," said the Comte de Moret. "We lost half an hour here, though in a good cause."

Ten minutes later, Latil, guided by the smuggler, rejoined them; the task the count had left three quarters done was complete.

Latil and his guide caught up to Moret at the Giacon Bridge. The smuggler, who hadn't had time to thank him, threw himself at Moret's feet and kissed his hands.

"*C'est bien, mon ami,*" said the Comte de Moret. "Now, we must be at Susa within the hour."

And the troops resumed their march.

LXIII

The White Plume

We know the path the Comte de Moret had to follow: it was the same route he'd taken with Isabelle de Lautrec and the Dame de Coëtman. Strict silence was decreed, and no noise was heard but the sound of snow crunching under the soldiers' feet.

As they turned the shoulder of the mountain, the town of Susa came into view, limned by the first light of morning.

The ramparts, this far up the mountain, were deserted. The road, if the narrow furrow they followed no more than two abreast could be called a road, passed about ten feet above the parapet. From there, one could slip down to the ramparts.

The demi-lune, which, after the flanks were carried and the redoubts had been taken, still held off the French army, was nearly three miles from the town of Susa; and as no one could imagine an attack from the mountainside, no one was on guard there. However, by the light of dawn the sentinels in the town saw the small troop filing down the side of the mountain and raised the alarm.

The Comte de Moret heard their cries, saw their reaction, and knew there was no time to lose. Like a true mountaineer, he leaped from rock to rock and was the first to drop onto the ramparts.

Latil was right by his side.

At the cries of the sentinels, Piedmontese and Valaisans tumbled out of a guardhouse at the gate and formed into a troop of a hundred men, preparing to buy time for further reinforcements. The Comte de Moret gathered the first twenty men onto the rampart, and with this twenty he rushed the town gate.

In the gray dawn, the soldiers of Charles-Emmanuel saw a long dark file of men circling down the mountain, enemies who seemed to fall from the sky in numbers they couldn't tell, so they didn't put up much of a fight; however, thinking it was critical that the duke and his son be informed, they dispatched a rider to Susa Pass to warn them of what was happening.

The Comte de Moret saw this man being detached and tried to go after him, cutting his way through the mêlée; the courier was in full gallop, and the count suspected where he was going, but had no way to stop him.

It was just one more reason to secure the Susa town gate, below the pass into which Louis XIII, after flanking the barricades, had made a partial entry.

So he rushed the gate with what few men he had, and swarmed over the defenders. The fight was brief; surprised from the direction they least expected it, by a force of unknown size, and believing themselves betrayed, the Piedmontese and Valaisans, good soldiers though they were, cried "Alarm!" and ran for it, some through the town and others down the valley.

The Comte de Moret seized the gate, rallied his troops, and turned four guns to bear on the town. Then, leaving a hundred men to hold the gate and serve the guns, with the four hundred remaining he advanced to attack the fortifications at the pass from behind.

Cannon thundered from above, smoke wreathing Montabon peak. The two armies were in a death grip.

Moret doubled his men's pace; however, while still a mile from the entrenchments, he saw a corps of troops being detached from the Savoyard army and sent toward him. The unit was about equal in number to that of the Comte de Moret; at its head, mounted, was its commanding colonel.

Latil approached the count. "I recognize the officer leading that troop," he said. "He's a gallant soldier named Colonel Belon."

"And so?" said the count.

"I'd like Monseigneur's permission to take him prisoner."

"I'll allow you to do that—*ventre-saint-gris,* I could hardly ask for more! But how will you take him?"

"Nothing could be easier, Monseigneur; when you see the colonel fall beneath his horse, charge his men furiously; they'll think he's dead and will scatter. Swoop in and take the flag, while I take the colonel; though you might rather have the colonel and I the flag. The colonel will pay a fine ransom of three or four hundred *pistoles*— while the flag, for all its glory, is nothing but a flag."

"To me the flag, then," said the Comte de Moret, "and to you the colonel."

"Then let's beat the drums and sound the trumpets!"

Moret raised his sword, the drums beat, and the trumpets sounded the charge.

Latil took four men with him, each holding a musket, ready to pass a new weapon to him once he'd fired the first, the second, and even the third.

As for the enemy, at the sound of the French drums and bugles, the Savoyard troop seemed to quicken its step. Colonel Belon said a few words, the troops replied with "Long live Charles-Emmanuel!", and they came on at speed.

Soon the two troops were no more than fifty paces from each other. The Savoyard unit stopped to fire a volley. "This is the moment," said Latil. "Look out, Monseigneur! Take their fire, shoot back, and then charge the flag."

Latil had hardly finished when a hailstorm of balls passed like a hurricane—but mainly above the heads of the French soldiers, who held their ground.

"Aim low!" cried Latil. And as an example, aiming at the colonel's horse, he fired just as the officer shook the reins to charge.

The horse took the ball just below the shoulder; carried forward by its charge, it fell and rolled to within twenty paces of the French ranks.

"To me the colonel, to you the flag, Monseigneur," cried Latil, and he leaped, sword held high, upon the colonel.

The French soldiers had fired and, following Latil's advice, aimed low, so that nearly all their shots struck home.

The count took advantage of the chaos to hurl himself into the midst of the Piedmontese.

In a few bounds, Latil closed with Colonel Belon, who was pinned under his horse and stunned from his fall. Latil put his sword to his throat and said to him, "My prisoner, rescued or not?"

The colonel slid a hand toward his holster.

"One move, Colonel Belon," said Latil, "and you're dead."

"I surrender," said the colonel, handing his sword to Latil.

"My prisoner, rescued or not?"

"Rescued or not."

"Then, Colonel, keep your sword—one does not disarm a brave officer like you. We'll come to terms after the battle; if I'm killed, you are free."

With these words he helped the colonel out from under his horse, and having set him on his feet, he sprang into the midst of the Piedmontese ranks.

It played out the way Latil had predicted. The soldiers of Charles-Emmanuel, seeing the fall of the colonel, and unsure whether he was dead or alive, had lost their nerve. The count had attacked so furiously that the ranks had opened before him, and he'd reached the flag, around which a knot of Savoyards, Valaisans, and Piedmontese put up a brave defense. Latil threw himself into the thickest part of the mêlée, shouting in a voice like thunder, "Moret! Moret to the rescue! Strike for the son of Henri IV!"

This final onslaught broke the enemy troop. Cutting down the man who carried it, the Comte de Moret seized the Savoyard flag in his left hand. He raised it high and shouted, "Victory for France! Long live King Louis XIII!"

This cry was repeated by every Frenchman still upright. What followed was a rout: the troops who had been sent to oppose the Comte de Moret, diminished by a third, took to their heels.

"We mustn't lose a minute, Monseigneur," said Latil to the count. "After them, shooting as we go; we don't have to kill them, but it's important that our fire be heard in the entrenchments."

And indeed, their fire, heard in the demi-lune, spread chaos among the defenders.

Attacked from the front by Montmorency, Bassompierre, and Créqui, and from behind by the Comte de Moret and Latil, the Duke of Savoy and his son were afraid they'd be surrounded and captured; leaving the Count of Verrue to conduct a desperate defense, they went down to the stables, jumped into the saddle, and flew from the entrenchments.

They found themselves in the middle of Colonel Belon's soldiers, who were fleeing pell-mell with the French in pursuit, firing at will.

These two riders trying to reach the mountainside attracted the attention of Latil, who, thinking they looked important, sprang forward to cut them off; but just as he was about to grab the duke's horse by the bridle, he was dazed by a flash of light and a sharp pain in his left shoulder.

A Spanish officer in the service of the Duke of Savoy, seeing his master about to be taken, had jumped in and, swinging his long sword, gashed the shoulder of our swashbuckler.

Latil let out a cry, less of pain than of anger at seeing his prey escape. Sword in hand, he threw himself on the Spaniard.

Though Latil's sword was six inches shorter than that of his adversary, they'd barely met before Latil, a master of arms, knew himself master of his enemy. Twice wounded, the Spaniard fell within ten seconds, shouting "Save the duke!"

At these words, Latil leaped over the wounded man and resumed his pursuit of the two riders, but thanks to their hardy mountain horses they were already far enough down the road to be out of range.

Latil returned, furious at having missed such glorious prey; but at least he still had the Spanish officer who, unable to defend himself, surrendered "rescued or not."

Meanwhile, the demi-lune was in turmoil. The Duc de Montmorency, first onto the ramparts, held his position, dispatching with blows of an ax all who tried to approach him, and opening a space for those who followed him. Piedmontese, Valaisans, and Savoyards fled like a torrent out the postern gates toward the road down to Susa. But there they ran into the Comte de Moret, amid gunfire and cries of "Long live King Louis XIII!" Unaware of his true strength, they didn't even try to fight, they just ran, flowing around each group of French like water around rocks.

The Comte de Moret entered the demi-lune on the opposite side from Montmorency. They met in the middle, recognized each other, and embraced. Then, arm in arm, they marched victorious to the breach, one waving the French flag he'd first placed on the demi-lune's ramparts, the other the Savoyard flag he'd won. Saluting Louis XIII and lowering the two standards before him, together they cried "*Vive le Roi!*"

It was the same cry before which, three years later, both of them would fall.

The cardinal called out, "No one is to enter the redoubt before the king."

Just as these words were uttered, Latil slipped in through a postern.

Sentinels were placed at all entrances, and Montmorency and Moret went themselves to open the Gélasse gate for the king and the cardinal.

The two rode in, musketoon at the knee to signify that they entered as conquerors—and that the conquered, taken by storm, could expect only what was granted at the victors' good pleasure.

The king addressed the Duc de Montmorency first. "I know, Monsieur le Duc," he said, "that which is the object of your ambition. When the campaign ends, you shall be entitled to exchange your sword for one chased with golden *fleur de lys,* which will elevate you above all the Marshals of France."

Montmorency bowed. The Sword of the Constable was his sole ambition in the world, and this was the king's formal promise that he would have it.

"Sire," said the Comte de Moret, presenting the king with the flag won from Colonel Belon's regiment, "allow me the honor of placing at Your Majesty's feet this standard I have taken."

"I accept it," said Louis XIII; "and, in exchange, I hope you will be pleased to wear this white plume in your hat, in memory of the brother who gave it to you, and of our father who bore three of them at Ivry."

The Comte de Moret wanted to kiss the king's hand, but Louis XIII took him in his arms and embraced him warmly.

Then the king removed from his hat, the same one he'd received from the Duc de Montmorency, one of its three white plumes. He presented it, along with the diamond clip that held it on, to the Comte de Moret.

And that same day, around five in the evening, King Louis XIII made his entry into Susa, after having received from its authorities, on a silver platter, the keys to the town.

LXIV

What l'Angely Thought of the Compliments of the Duke of Savoy

King Louis XIII was delirious with joy. It was the second time in less than a year that he'd made a triumphal entrance into a town conquered by force of arms, thereby deserving the title of "the Victorious."

All that the cardinal had promised had been achieved, from first to last, the last promise being that on March seventh the king would sleep in Susa—and there he slept. But the cardinal, who knew secrets hidden to others, and who saw further than the king, was less at ease than this master. He knew—as did Louis XIII, though the triumph of the day had made him forget—that the fighting had nearly exhausted the army's ammunition.

He knew something else, which the king did not know: that the troops were short on food, and the bad weather and condition of the roads prevented the commissaries from bringing more.

He knew, moreover, that Casale was hard pressed by the Spanish. If the Duke of Savoy continued to resist them for another week or so, which wouldn't be hard, considering their lack of munitions, then Casale—reduced to the last extremity despite the heroism of its commander, Gurron, and despite the devotion of its people, who had joined the garrison in defending the city—might be forced to open its gates to the Spaniards. The latest intelligence from Casale reported that they'd eaten their horses and were down to the dogs and cats, the last resort of famine.

Thus, that evening, while Louis XIII was celebrating with his marshals, generals, and senior officers, Richelieu approached the king and asked if afterward, unless fatigue prevented it, His Majesty might spare a few moments.

The king, who seemed nearly as jubilant as the day he'd had the Maréchal d'Ancre killed, replied, "Since every time Your Eminence desires to speak with me, it's for the good of the state and the glory of the crown, I am and will always be willing to listen to you."

And indeed, when the soirée was over, the king, still glowing with praise, came to the cardinal. "And now, Your Eminence, it's just us," he said, sitting down and offering a chair to the cardinal.

Once the king was seated, the cardinal obeyed and took a seat as well. "Speak. I'm listening," said Louis XIII.

"Sire," said the cardinal, "I believe Your Majesty has now had satisfaction for the insult he suffered, and his desire for glory need not push him to continue a war that could immediately end in a glorious peace."

"My dear Cardinal," said the king, "I hardly recognize you: you call for war, despite all opposition; and now that the campaign's barely begun, you propose peace."

"Does it matter, Sire, whether peace comes sooner or later, so long as it brings us what we'd hoped?"

"But what will Europe say of us? To make such threats and demands and then give up after just one fight. . . ."

"Europe will say, Sire, and it will be the truth, that this one victory was so glorious and absolute that it decided the entire campaign."

"But still, to conclude the peace, we would have to present our demands."

"That is the grand prerogative of the victor."

"Do you think, Your Eminence, that we're in position to make such demands?"

"We're certainly in a position to open the negotiations, Sire."

"How so?"

"We can say it's in consideration of the best interests of your sister, Princess Christine."

"True enough," said the king, "she's married to Victor-Amadeus.

I always forget I have a family. It's also true," he added bitterly, "that it's a family I prefer to forget. So you think . . ?"

"I think, Sire, that though war is at times a cruel necessity, we belong to a church that abhors bloodshed, and it's our duty to curtail it when we can. That's within your power, Sire, after such a glorious day, for the God of Hosts is also the God of Mercy."

"How would you present this matter to the King of Marmots?" said the king, using the nickname concocted by Henri IV after his conquest of Bresse, Bugey, Valromey, and Gex.

"That's easily done, Sire. I'll write in the name of Your Majesty to the Duke of Savoy that he can choose between peace or war: if he prefers war, we will continue to fight as we did today and as your august father did in the past; but if, instead, he chooses peace, we will negotiate with him on the same basis as before our victory. To be specific, he is to allow the passage of French troops, and to assist with the relief of Casale, providing us food and ammunition at a fair market price; and furthermore Savoy will allow us, in the future, passage for whatever troops and materiel might be necessary for the defense of Montferrat, in the event that Montferrat were attacked or we thought such an attack likely; and that to ensure these two contingencies, Sire, the Duke of Savoy cedes to us Fort Gélasse and the Pass of Susa, to be occupied by a Swiss garrison commanded by an officer of your appointment."

"But the Savoyard is going to want something in return for all that."

"If you wish, Sire, we can meet one of his demands. We can offer, on behalf of the Duke of Mantua, in compensation for the House of Savoy's rights to Montferrat, to cede him the city of Trino, with its annual revenue of fifteen thousand crowns."

"We'd already offered him that, and he refused it."

"Sire, we were not then in possession of Susa."

"All thanks to you, and I'll never forget it."

"What must not be forgotten, Sire, is the risks Your Majesty faced, the courage of your troops, and the virtues of their commanders."

"If I ever had the misfortune to forget it, Your Eminence would remind me."

"So my proposal is acceptable?"

"Whom shall we send with it?"

"Doesn't it seem to Your Majesty that Marshal Bassompierre would be the best ambassador we could choose for this?"

"Perfect."

"Then, Sire, he will leave tomorrow morning to present our treaty to the duke. As for the secret articles . . ."

"There will be secret articles?"

"Every treaty has secret articles. Those will be negotiated personally between me and the duke or his son."

"Then everything is on hold!"

"Just for three days, Sire, until we arrange to receive a visit from the prince your brother, or your uncle the duke."

"That's right," said the king, "they are my family. But with one great virtue: they're family I can publicly make war against. And now, good evening, Monsieur le Cardinal. You must be tired and in need of a good night's sleep."

Three days later, in fact, as predicted by the cardinal, Victor-Amadeus came to Susa to negotiate with Richelieu, who obtained from him all the conditions he'd proposed to the king. As for the secret articles, they were granted as well, along with the public terms:

> *The Duke of Savoy engages to provide Casale with four thousand bushels of corn and wheat and five hundred casks of wine. In return, once this obligation is met, it is agreed that the troops of France shall not advance beyond Buno-*

longa, the village between Susa and Turin, and His Majes-
ty will allow the Prince of Piedmont time to persuade the
Spanish to lift the siege of Casale.

In addition, Charles-Emmanuel will be ceded the town
of Trino by the Duke of Mantua, Alba, and Montcalvo.

Eight days after this treaty was concluded, Don Gonzalès da Cordova personally raised the siege of Casale, thus preserving the honor of Spain.

On March 31 and April 1, respectively, the treaty was ratified by the Duke of Savoy and King Louis XIII.

However, the truth is that this treaty was regarded as no more binding than those made with the Duke of Lorraine. One day, when William III was telling Charles IV, Duc de Lorraine, that he'd signed a treaty in good faith, the duke said with a laugh, "So you'd rely on a treaty, then?"

"But of course," His Majesty naïvely replied.

"Well," replied Duke Charles, "whenever you like, I can show you a whole chest full of treaties that I've signed, none of which have been honored!"

And though Charles-Emmanuel had nearly as many treaties in his chest, he was happy to add one more, though he had no more intention of honoring it than any of the others. Nonetheless, he expressed the desire to embrace his nephew Louis XIII, so a meeting was arranged.

First came the Prince of Piedmont and the Cardinal of Savoy, who greeted the king when the treaty was signed; Victor-Amadeus brought his wife, Princess Christine, the king's sister. Louis accorded his sister all proper honors and every sign of friendship, delighted to show that he loved best this sister who'd made open war upon him, unlike the Queen of England and the Queen of Spain, who were content to conspire against him secretly.

Finally came the Duke of Savoy, who was received with open arms by his nephew Louis XIII, who had resolved to steal a march on him and surprise him before he was ready; but Charles-Emmanuel was warned in time and rushed down the stairs in a hurry, to meet the king on his doorstep.

"My dear Uncle," said Louis XIII, embracing him, "I'd intended to surprise you in your chamber!"

"You forgot, my dear Nephew," said the duke, "that it's not easy to move secretly when one is King of France."

The king climbed the stairs alongside the duke. But to reach the duke's chambers, he had to pass a row of courtiers and senior officers standing on a trembling balcony that barely supported them.

"Make haste, Uncle," the king said. "I'm not sure how long this will hold us up."

"Alas, Sire!" the duke replied. "See how all the world trembles before the might of Your Majesty."

The king, radiant with this praise, turned to l'Angely. "Hey, fool: what do you think of my uncle's compliments?"

"Oh, I'm not the fool you should ask," said l'Angely.

"Who, then?"

"Ask the two or three thousand fools who got killed to earn them!"

LXV

A Chapter of History

L'Angely, in his response to the king, had summed up the situation admirably.

After every war, no matter how long, even the Thirty Years War, a peace is signed, and, once signed, the kings who had made the war embrace each other, without a thought for the thousands of men sacrificed to the conflict, rotting on the battlefields, or the thousands of weeping widows, the thousands of mothers wringing their hands, or the thousands of children dressed in mourning.

And given the past history of the "good faith" of Charles-Emmanuel, one could be sure that this new peace would be broken the first time the Duke of Savoy found it advantageous.

A month or two passed in celebrations, during which the Duke of Savoy sent his emissaries to Vienna and Madrid.

In Vienna, his envoy delivered the message that King Louis's victory at Susa was not so much a humiliation of Savoy as it was of Emperor Ferdinand, as the Duke of Savoy had disputed the King of France's passage in order to sustain the Empire's rights in Italy. The aid France sent to the people of Casale was a clear attack on the emperor's authority, insofar as the place had been besieged by the Spanish in order to compel the Duc de Nevers, a Frenchman who'd claimed an Imperial fief, to bend the knee to His Imperial Majesty.

In Madrid, Savoy's envoy was charged to convey to King Philip IV and the count-duke, his prime minister, that the affront to Spanish arms at Casale was intended to weaken His Catholic Majesty's authority in Italy, an insult as yet unpunished. The King of France, goaded by Richelieu, planned to drive the Spaniards from

Milan, and the Court of Madrid should expect that once they were forced from Milan, then Naples would soon follow.

Philip IV and Ferdinand also exchanged emissaries.

Here's what they decided:

The Holy Roman Emperor would ask the Swiss Cantons to allow his troops free passage. If the Grisons refused, Imperial troops would attack by surprise, cross the Alps, and march immediately on Mantua.

The King of Spain recalled Don Gonzalès de Cordova and replaced him with the overall commander of the Spanish troops in Italy, the famous Ambrose Spinola, who was given orders to besiege and take Casale, while the Imperial troops besieged and took Mantua.

The French campaign, successfully completed in a matter of days, had caused quite a stir: the affair redounded to King Louis's credit across Europe, and he was acclaimed as the only sovereign, besides Gustavus Adolphus, willing to leave his palace to defend his realm, sword in hand.

Ferdinand II and Philip IV, in contrast, waged their cruel wars from a distance, kneeling safely at their altars.

If the king and his army had been able to stay in Piedmont, all their gains would have been preserved—but the cardinal was committed to suppressing the Protestants before summer. The Protestants had taken advantage of the absence of the king and cardinal to rally their forces, and fifteen thousand had gathered in Languedoc under the command of the Duc de Rohan.

The king bade adieu to "his good uncle" the Duke of Savoy, disregarding the intrigues the duke was brewing under his very nose in Piedmont. On April 22, he returned to France by way of Briançon, Gap, and Chatillon, and marched on Privas.

He avoided Lyon, from which the two queens had fled to escape the plague. As for Monsieur, still wallowing in his grievances, he'd left not only Paris, but France itself, accepting the hospitality of Duc

Charles IV of Lorraine in his city of Nancy. By leaving France, he'd abandoned his claim to Princesse Marie de Gonzague, transferring his attentions to Princess Marguerite of Lorraine, the duke's sister.

Pursued by forty thousand troops led by three Marshals of France and by Montmorency, to whom Richelieu had promised to present the Sword of the Constable, Rohan, the leader of the Protestants, fell into the same mistake made in the previous century by the leaders of the rebellious Catholic League: in return for funds that were never paid, he signed a treaty with Spain, mortal enemy of both France and her Protestants.

In the end, Privas, their greatest fortress, was taken. A third of its people were hanged, and the rest were stripped of all their property. On June 24, 1629, with a new Italian campaign pending, as the pot there was starting to boil, a final truce was signed, a peace whose primary condition was the demolition of the fortifications of every Protestant city.

Even before Privas, it was known that Emperor Ferdinand intended to send troops into Italy; it was said Wallenstein himself would lead fifty thousand men over the Alps of the Grisons. On June 5, Ferdinand published a decree stating that his troops marched into Italy not to make war, but to preserve the peace, sustaining the legitimate authority of the emperor and defending the empire's foreign fiefs from claims that infringed on his rights.

In the same statement, the emperor requested His Serenity the King of Spain, who possessed the chief stronghold of the Empire in Italy, to provide the Imperial troops with whatever food and ammunition they needed.

Everything France had done in Italy had to be done over again. Louis was willing, but couldn't be ready to undertake another foreign war in less than five or six months. Lacking money after Privas, Richelieu had been forced to discharge thirty regiments.

The envoy Monsieur de Sabran was sent to the Court of Vienna to discuss the emperor's ultimatum. Meanwhile, Monsieur de Créqui was dispatched to Turin to ask the Duke of Savoy to explain, frankly, which side he was on in the event of war.

The emperor replied:

> *The King of France entered Italy with a powerful army, without any declaration of war on Spain or the Empire, and overcame, by arms or agreement, several localities under the jurisdiction of the Emperor. If the King of France will withdraw his troops from Italy, the Emperor will be satisfied to allow all issues to be settled by a court of law.*

The Duke of Savoy replied:

> *The Imperial movement into the realm of the Grisons has nothing to do with the Treaty of Susa. But the King of Spain would like the French to leave Italy and give Susa back. If King Louis satisfies his brother-in-law Philip IV, the Duke of Savoy will persuade Emperor Ferdinand to withdraw his troops from the territory of the Grisons.*

Monsieur de Créqui sent this response to the king, who gave it to the cardinal and charged him with answering it. The cardinal replied:

> *Tell the Duke of Savoy this isn't a matter of what the King of Spain or the Emperor wants, it's about whether His Highness intends to keep his word by joining his troops with those of France to maintain the Treaty of Susa.*

The king returned to Paris, so angry with his brother Monsieur that he was ready to confiscate all his domains. But the queen mother went to work and mended the division between the brothers: Monsieur, as usual, humbly begged the king's pardon, presenting his conditions for returning, and instead of losing domains due to his escapade was instead granted a new fief in the Duchy of Valois, increasing his income by a hundred thousand *livres* a year, as well as the governorships of Orléans, Blois, Vendôme, Chartres, and the Château d'Amboise, the command of the Army of Champagne, and, in the absence of the king, the office of lieutenant general in charge of Paris and the surrounding region.

In addition, the accord included this curious clause: *Though reconciling with the king, Monsieur does not agree to overlook Cardinal Richelieu's many insults, affronts for which he will sooner or later be punished.*

The cardinal learned of this accord after it was too late to prevent it. He went to the king to see this agreement with his own eyes. Facing him, Louis bowed his head, aware of the weakness and deep ingratitude he'd shown in giving in to his brother's demands. "If this is what Your Majesty grants to his enemies," said the cardinal, "what is he willing to do for the man who has proven himself his best friend?"

"Anything such a man asks, if that man is you."

And indeed, the king awarded Richelieu the title of Vicar General in Italy and made him generalissimo of all his armies.

Upon learning of these concessions to her foe, Marie de Médicis accosted her son and, referring to the cardinal's new commissions, demanded haughtily, "What about us, Sire? In light of this, what rights do you grant to us?"

"The right of monarchs to cure scrofula," said l'Angely, who was present at the dispute.

By dint of incredible effort and by leveraging his new prestige, the cardinal found the wherewithal to mount another campaign. But a new enemy barred the path to Piedmont, an abyss that could swallow half an army. This enemy was the plague—that same plague which had forced the two queens to return to Paris and the king to withdraw through Briançon.

This plague arose in Milan—as depicted in Manzoni's novel *The Betrothed*—and passed from Milan to Lyon, where it wrought terrible havoc. It was said some soldiers had brought it over the Alps, where it broke out just outside Lyon in the village of Vaux. A *cordon sanitaire* was placed around the village, but this plague, like all plagues, had human vice as its ally. The plague found an accomplice in greed: some of the infected paid to be smuggled out of Vaux and into the Church of Saint-Nizier, which brought the contagion into the heart of Lyon.

It was the end of September. One would have said, watching workers fall as if struck by lightning all across the populous quarters of Saint-Nizier, Saint-Jean, and Saint-Georges, that nature was mocking humanity. For the weather was magnificent: never had a more beautiful sun lit so clear a sky; never had the air seemed so sweet and pure; never had the Lyonnais seen such lush vegetation. There were no sudden changes of temperature, no extreme heat or thunderstorms, none of those atmospheric disruptions so often associated with outbreaks of communicable disease. Radiant and smiling, nature watched as corruption and death came knocking at the doors of house after house.

Moreover, the spread of the scourge was inexplicable and oddly capricious. It spared one side of a street and ravaged the other. An island of homes would remain intact, while every house in the surrounding quarter was visited by the sinister guest. The plague passed over some of the most filthy and congested parts of the old city, only to break out in places like Bellecour and Terreaux, among the nicest, airiest, and most open neighborhoods.

Along the river quays, the entire lower part of the great city was devastated. No one knows why, but for some reason, the plague stopped dead at Rue Neyret. There, outside a small old house, is a statue bearing the Latin inscription: *Ejus præsidio non ultra pestis 1628.* Beyond, in Croix-Rousse, there wasn't a single case of plague.

Then, as if the plague hadn't done enough damage in its march, infection was followed by murder. As in Marseilles in 1720, as in Paris in 1832, the populace, ever suspicious and credulous, cried out that they'd been deliberately poisoned. But unlike in Paris, where it was said criminals had poisoned the fountains, or in Marseilles, where convicts were blamed for corrupting the harbor water, in Lyon it was meat vendors who were accused of spreading the plague. These street sellers were said to be the ones who'd passed the pestilence from house to house.

A Jesuit, Père Grillot, claimed the meat vendors were selling tainted lard and tallow. "It was in mid-September," he said, "that we began to notice the spoiled meat. The sacristan in the Jesuit church found a sack of greasy meat behind a bench, and when he burned it, the smoke was so foul that he had to bury what wouldn't burn."

Monsieur de Montfalcon's lovely history book provides us these details, but unfortunately doesn't tell us if Père Grillot was able to give absolution to those his claims assassinated. The very next day, an unlucky man who'd gotten tallow on his clothes from a lit candle was stoned by a mob. Then, in Guillotière, a doctor who'd concocted a potion for one of his patients was accused of poisoning him, and had to drink his own medicine to escape being killed. Any passing stranger might be accosted, pursued with the cry "Throw that poisoner into the Rhône!"

When the plague broke out in Marseilles, the city aldermen went to consult with Chirac, the municipal physician, who told them, "There's nothing to do but try to keep up your spirits." However, as they found in Lyon, staying cheerful wasn't so easy when the priests and monks advised giving up all hope, as the scourge was surely the instrument of God's wrath. So advised, the simple folk regarded the plague not as an epidemic that could be staved off, but as a destroying angel with a flaming sword that no one could escape.

The doctors who went on our expedition to Egypt learned a few facts about such plagues: they attack the weak, the feeble, and the afraid. Fear the plague, and you're as good as infected. And who wouldn't be afraid if they saw two Brothers of the Minimes chanting the General Atonement as they carried to Notre-Dame-de-Lorette a silver death lamp, on which were engraved the names of the city aldermen? Who wouldn't be afraid when monks on soapboxes in the squares and on street corners loudly preached the end of the world, while their priests granted final blessings to the dying city? When a monk or priest passed in the street, some knelt in their paths to ask absolution—but many fell before they could receive it. Penitents roamed the city in sackcloth and ashes, ropes around their waists and torches in their hands, and sick citizens, leaning against walls or lying in the street, without knowing whether these penitents were consecrated and had the right to absolve the dying, shouted their confessions to them, hoping to save their souls at the price of their dignity.

In such times we see how the grip of terror can sunder the bonds of nature, of friendship, and of love. Kin flees from kin, the wife abandons her husband, parents leave their children, the chaste surrender their modesty to any who will carry them away. One woman, laughing hysterically, told how she'd sewn into their funeral shrouds her four children, her father, her mother, and her husband. Another woman was widowed six times in six months, burying six husbands. Most citizens locked themselves in their houses or shuttered shops, jumping at every noise, eying passersby and gazing, haggard, from their windows, behind which they appeared as pale as ghosts. Few people were in the streets; those who had to go someplace did so at a run, with hardly a word for anyone they met. Anyone from outside Lyon who had to come into the city did so on a horse at the gallop, wrapped up to the eyes in a cloak. Gloomiest and most frightening of all were the physicians who made their rounds wearing a strange costume they'd invented, a beak wrapped in oilcloth that covered the mouth and nose, containing a handkerchief soaked in vinegar. Such a getup would have been laughable in ordinary times; but in this lethal atmosphere, it was terrifying.

After eight days, the city was almost depopulated, though more by flight than by death. All those who could afford to leave had left; even the judges had vacated, and the courts were quite empty. Women gave birth by themselves, for the midwives had all fled, and the physicians were busy with the plague. The workshops were silent: no laborers sang their work songs, no vendors cried their wares in the streets. Everything was still, everywhere was the silence of death, broken only by the dismal sound of the bell of the dead-cart as it collected the corpses, and by the tolling of the great bell of Saint-Jean, which rang every day at noon. These funereal sounds had a woeful effect on the nerves, especially those of women, who would sit gloomily counting their rosaries while uttering only an occasional moan. Some, when they heard the bell of the corpse-cart approaching, fell dead as if stricken by lightning. Others, leaving a church where the death bell tolled, fell ill on the way home and died soon thereafter. One frantic woman threw herself down a well; another young lady ran out of her house in a frenzy and hurled herself into the Rhône.

There were three main measures the citizens could take, and they took them: sequester the wealthy sick in their homes; lock up the sick poor in hospitals; and collect the bodies of those who had died. Some adopted a fourth course, skipping the first three, intruding into houses on the pretext of treating the sick or carrying out the dead, and instead carrying out anything of value they could find, breaking open desks, cracking safes, and relieving the dying of their rings and jewelry.

To sequester the sick, doors were walled up and food and medicines were passed in through the windows. New gallows were put up in every quarter, and looters caught in the act were taken to them and hanged without delay.

The hospitals were overwhelmed, so the city established a quarantine house on the right bank of the Saône. It had room for only two hundred beds, but had to accommodate four thousand patients: there were plague victims everywhere, in the rooms, in the corridors, in the cellars and the attics. Every victim who died and freed up a bed was replaced by two more. Doctors and nurses making their rounds could barely pick their way through the press. In between the stiffening corpses, which almost immediately began to rot, the dying trembled and shook, throats burning, crying out for water. Here and there a body would rise in a spasm from its mattress or pile of straw and, sunken-faced and wild-eyed, paw at the air with its hands, then utter a deep groan and fall back, dead. Other victims, if they had the energy, recoiled from these visions, tripping over their neighbors and dragging off those sheets that would soon serve as their shrouds.

And yet, the patients in the dreadful quarantine house were envied by those poor who were dying alone on street corners and in ditches.

Most wretched of all were the beggars and vagrants who were pressed into service as corpse collectors. They were paid three *livres* a day, plus whatever they found in the pockets of the dead. They had iron rakes and pitchforks that they used to drag out the bodies and pile them onto carts. Any bodies found above the ground floor were thrown out through the windows. The corpses were buried to overflowing in mass graves, which fermented and burst open, spewing out rotting human remains.

One old man by the name of Raynard had watched his entire family die, leaving him on his own. When at last he felt himself succumbing to the sickness, he was terrified of dying alone, being thrown into a mass grave, and denied a proper Christian burial. So he took a spade and a pick and used the last of his strength to dig his own grave. When the work was complete, he made a cross of his spade and pick and placed it at the head of his grave. Then he lay down on the edge of the pit, counting on his last convulsion to roll him in, in hopes that some passing Samaritan might see his body there and cover it with earth.

Most terrible of all, amid the agony of a dying people was the laughter and cheer of some of the corpse collectors, awful men who came to be known as "the crows." It was as if the dead were their friends, and the plague was their kin. They welcomed the coming of the plague to their city, and their admission into homes from which all their lives they'd been spurned. Like the Marquis de Sade, like the executioner of Mary Stuart, they wallowed in forbidden pleasures— and when a dead woman was pretty, when a corpse was beautiful, they celebrated a monstrous marriage of life with death.

Appearing in Lyon, as we said, in September, the plague peaked after about thirty days, but continued to rage for another month. Toward the end of December, when bitter cold came south, it tapered off. The citizens celebrated its departure with dances and bonfires, but then the warm weather came back, a heavy rain put out the fires, and the plague returned for another bout.

The epidemic revived to full force in January and February, then declined in the spring, only to reappear in August before finally disappearing in December. In just over a year, the plague in Lyon killed six thousand people.

Archbishop Charles Miron had been the first to die, on August 6, 1628, and was succeeded by the Archbishop of Aix, Alphonse de Richelieu, brother to the cardinal. It was to this brother that the cardinal naturally addressed himself to ask if it would be possible to attempt another campaign against Piedmont, marching thirty thousand men through Lyon and the Lyonnais. The archbishop replied that the threat of disease had passed, and there would be plenty of empty homes to house the troops—and even the Court, should the Court choose to follow the army.

When he received this response, the cardinal dispatched Monsieur de Pontis to Mantua that same day, to assure the duke that help was on its way. De Pontis was also ordered to place himself at the disposal of Duc Charles de Nevers to help plan the city's defenses.

M. ainé fc.   Cl. excu.

HENRY DVC DE MONTMORENÇY ET D'AM-
VILLE PAIR, ET MARESCHAL DE FRANCE.
Et Lieutenant gñal pour le ROY en Languedoc.

LXVI

One Year Later

A year had passed since Richelieu, satisfied with the Treaty of Susa, or at least pretending to trust in it, had been forced to leave Piedmont to go fight the Huguenots in Languedoc. During that year, as he'd promised King Louis XIII, the cardinal had crushed the hopes of the Protestants, already badly battered by the fall of La Rochelle. He had reorganized the army, refilled the coffers of the State with new money, and signed his famous treaty with Gustavus Adolphus, which supported the Catholics of France against the Protestants, and the Protestants of Germany against the Catholics. He had sent Marshal Bassompierre to the Swiss Council in Solothurn to complain about the passage of the Imperial Germans across the lands of the Grisons, and to see if he could bring back another five or six thousand Swiss mercenaries.

Finally, since he couldn't yet get to Mantua personally, the cardinal had sent the best help he could in the form of his finest engineer, Monsieur de Pontis, with military advice from Maréchal d'Estrées, sent from Venice. With the plague in Lyon exhausted, the French army was put back on the march, though, as mentioned, a year after forcing Susa Pass and imposing terms on Charles-Emmanuel, the cardinal found himself back where he'd started: except that with Susa Pass cleared, and Fort Gélasse in French hands, Piedmont was open to him—he should be able to get to Casale to rescue the Marquis de Thoiras, under siege by Spinola, who'd succeeded Gonzalès de Cordova as commander of the Spanish troops.

This time, the cardinal felt sure enough of the king that he could afford to leave him behind, having taken pains to reveal to him the treachery of Monsieur, Marie de Médicis, and Anne of Austria. And the cardinal's vanity played its part as well: newly empowered, he was able now to undertake a campaign on his word alone, and in the king's absence to reap its glory for himself. Every man of genius has a weakness, and Richelieu was so great that he had three: he wanted to be recognized not just as a great politician—which no one disputed—but also as a great general—making him a rival to his own commanders, Créqui, Bassompierre, Montmorency, Schomberg, and the Duc de Guise—and as a great poet, a title only posterity could award.

At the beginning of March 1630, the cardinal was back at Susa, exchanging ambassadors and envoys extraordinaire with that elusive chameleon called Charles-Emmanuel, that crowned snake who, for fifty years, had been slipping from the grasp of the Kings of France and Spain.

The cardinal had already spent a month in negotiations that had led nowhere. But he was compelled to be patient for fear the Duke of Savoy might prevent him from resupplying Casale with food and ammunition, where they were running out. The Duke of Savoy wasn't strong enough to resist the force of France without the support of Spain or Austria—but he had the support of Spain from Milan, and of Austria from Wallenstein's troops that had passed the Grisons. In fact, he might be better able to dispute the passage of Montferrat than he'd been to defend the Pass of Susa.

As the delays wore at his patience, the cardinal wrote to the Duc de Montmorency, in a tone more friendly than formal:

> *Monsieur le Duc, you know what we'd agreed between us: when the Italian campaign was over, you would be awarded the Sword of the Constable. But the Italian campaign, as you can see for yourself, won't be concluded until the Duc de Nevers is confirmed as the ruler of Mantua. Last year's*

campaign will be only a skirmish compared to this year's war, which must support Duc Charles in his claims. It's time we quit dealing with intermediaries and envoys while there's still a chance of success. Go to Turin under the guise of a pleasure trip and meet secretly with the Duke of Savoy. You are gallant, Monsieur, and the ladies of the Court of Savoy are beautiful, so I don't think you can complain too much of this task.

But let me speak frankly of the real mission, which is delicate. You are related, through your wife, to Queen Marie de Médicis, and are known to be a member of Queen Anne's circle—which will be a recommendation to the enemies of the king, though you are his friend as well. Try to arrange a direct meeting with the Duke of Savoy, or at least between his son and me, to find out his real position. Meanwhile, I, undistracted by beautiful ladies or lively music, will be sending scouts out in every direction. When you return, Duke, depending on what you find out, we'll know in which direction to march. Just try to keep the truth of your mission under your hat.

It was the kind of mission perfectly suited to the charming, elegant, and handsome Duc de Montmorency. He had, in fact, married the daughter of the Duke of Braciano, that same Vittorio Orsini who had been one of Marie de Médicis's lovers before her marriage, and perhaps even after—if the rumors about Louis's parentage were true, that made Montmorency the king's brother-in-law. He was, indeed, devoted to Queen Anne, though it was Buckingham who had stolen her heart when he had come to Court as ambassador of Charles I. Buckingham had scattered the pearls from his doublet across the Court of the Louvre, but had won a gem far more precious in the gardens at Amiens: a lady's love.

Yes, a man like the Duc de Montmorency would be welcomed at the Court of Savoy by all but the husbands of the beautiful Savoyard ladies. The duke therefore accepted this mission, half diplomacy and half gallantry, and departed for Turin, leaving the cardinal, as he'd said, to study the horizons to see which would be darkened by the oncoming storm.

On the northern horizon, in Germany, Wallenstein daily grew more powerful, becoming almost unstoppable. The Emperor had made him the Duke of Friedland, ruling the vast, rich regions he'd conquered for Ferdinand in Bohemia, domains confiscated from so-called rebels. At Wallenstein's own expense he'd raised an army of fifty thousand troops, repelled the Danes, beaten Mansfeld and his allies at the bridge of Dessau, defeated Bethlen Gabor, reoccupied Brandenburg, and conquered Holstein, Schleswig, Pomerania, and Mecklenburg—in token of which the Emperor named Wallenstein the Duke of Mecklenburg as well as of Friedland.

But there his series of conquests came to a halt, at least temporarily. Ferdinand was assailed with complaints against his bandit general from all sides; seeking a way to remove him from Austria, Denmark, Hungary, and Germany, he sent him east and south. Recruits flocked to Wallenstein: he sent a force of them to Italy, and another to Poland, where a huge garrison of forty thousand men camped on the Baltic, devouring a country already exhausted. To feed his troops he had to conquer or perish, so he went back to war, marching on the rich Imperial cities of Worms, Frankfurt, Schwaben, and Strasbourg. His western vanguard occupied a fort in the Diocese of Metz, and Richelieu learned that their Monsieur, when he was in Lorraine, had made contact with Wallenstein to invite his barbarians into France—ostensibly to overthrow Richelieu, though the real target was Louis XIII.

Wallenstein put two of his corps, those led by Gallas and Aldringen, under the command of Collalto, an Italian general, and dispatched them to Italy to besiege Mantua and support Charles-Emmanuel.

On the eastern horizon, Richelieu looked toward Venice and Rome. Venice had promised to create a diversion by attacking Milan, but Venice was no longer the power that once had made daring raids on Constantinople, Cyprus, and the Morea. But the Venetians fulfilled the rest of their promises, sending wheat, ammunition, reinforcements, and funds to Mantua, as well as cutting off food supplies to the besiegers.

Deprived of food, drink, and fodder, unable to breach Mantua's walls due to a lack of artillery, the Imperials were about to lift the siege when aid came from an unexpected quarter. The pope allowed them to resupply from the Papal States, provided they did so by buying bread, wine, and hay from one of his nephews (one of the few who hadn't been granted an ecclesiastical office). So as always, it was the pope, and an Italian pope at that, who betrayed Italy. He was a Barberini, naturally, of the same family that had stripped and sold the bronze plaques from the Pantheon of Agrippa.

Nearer to the cardinal, south of Savoy, was Spinola, the Genoese condottiere in the service of Spain. He'd marched into Montferrat when the Imperials had entered the Duchy of Mantua, more to block the relief of the city than to resume the siege of Casale. He had six thousand foot and three thousand horse, nine thousand troops with which to oppose the French if they tried to rescue Mantua. If Mantua fell, the twenty-five or thirty thousand Imperials who'd besieged it would be freed up to join Spinola in taking Casale and then driving the French from Italy.

To the west, Richelieu's horizons were darker still. At least Collalto and Spinola were visible enemies, openly opposed to him. That wasn't the case in France: there, the cardinal's enemies were like miners, digging underground in the dark to attack from hiding, while wearing a mask of friendship in the light. Louis, though aware that his life and reputation were linked to those of his minister, was worn out by these endless conspiracies—disgusted with everything, more melancholy than ever, he was prey to constant anxiety. His closest kin—mother, wife, and brother—all lived for a single hope: the fall of the cardinal. With every word and act devoted to that end, they made Louis's court a sour and bitter place, even while their efforts reinforced the king's conviction that he had no influence, no grandeur, and no royalty without the cardinal.

The king began to comprehend that these attacks on the cardinal were really just a prelude to their real aim, which was his own fall, by guile or by open attack. So Louis redoubled his defense of the cardinal, persuaded that to do so was to defend himself.

The flight of the Duc d'Orléans to Nancy, the secret letter decoded by Rossignol, and especially the treacherous negotiations between the Prince and Wallenstein, all convinced the king that a time was coming when Gaston, supported from outside by Austria, Spain, and Savoy, and from within by Queen Marie, Queen Anne, and malcontents of every stripe, would raise the banner of revolt.

And, indeed, there was no shortage of malcontents. The Duc de Guise was angry that he hadn't been given command of the army, and conspired with Madame de Conti and the Duchesse d'Elbeuf to plot against Richelieu. The judges at the Châtelet in Paris, incensed by new fees imposed on officers of the judiciary, refused to render justice. The lawmakers of Parliament were so upset by an increase in their taxes that they secretly offered to support the Duc d'Orléans if he promised to abolish the fees when he came to power.

We've gone into enough detail about the cardinal's police to make it clear that he was aware of all these malcontents, and had his eye on their intrigues. But despite these threats, he was convinced the king would nonetheless come to rejoin him, for two reasons: first, he knew the king's incurable melancholy and ennui would send him back to the army, if only to once again hear the glorious sound of victory, and the praise that goes with it; and second, since the king had named Gaston both Lieutenant General of Paris and Commander of the Army of Champagne, Gaston potentially had enough power, with the support of his mother and the queen, to drive the king from Paris, and maybe even from France. Gaston might take advantage of the king's absence to conspire against the cardinal and maybe even the king, but once Louis XIII had joined him, Richelieu feared nothing. He knew Gaston well enough to know that, if faced by an army commanded by the cardinal and the king himself, Monsieur would abandon his allies and accomplices and beg forgiveness, as he'd done before.

His review of the horizons of Europe complete, the cardinal turned from the dangers in the distance toward nearby Turin, to see how well Montmorency was following his instructions. Let's go and see for ourselves.

LXVII

Old Lovers Reunited

The Duc de Montmorency, without revealing the true nature of his trip, had invited his friend the Comte de Moret to accompany him to Turin, and Moret had accepted eagerly.

The gravity of the historical events we recount sometimes distracts us from the joys or sorrows they bring to the hearts of our characters. We mentioned the besieging of Mantua without relating how this siege dismayed the heart of the son of Henri IV.

Indeed, Isabelle, trapped in that city with her father, might suffer misery, famine, even death—all the risks associated with a siege by barbarians such as those who made up the Imperial hordes. So the Comte de Moret had volunteered to go and help defend Mantua—especially once he'd heard that Richelieu had sent his rival, Monsieur de Pontis, to that city as an engineer. Moret was eager not just to defend Isabelle against the besiegers, but also to oppose whatever influence de Pontis might gain with Monsieur de Lautrec.

But Richelieu didn't have so many loyal hearts and minds around him that he was willing to deprive himself of a man who, by rank alone, should stand near the king and cardinal—and who, by his courage and quick thinking, had already done great things, and might be called upon to do more. However, to reassure his young protégé, the cardinal informed him that he'd written to Monsieur de Lautrec, advising him to remember the promise the cardinal had made to the two young people, and to respect his daughter's commitment to the count.

Not that we wish to portray our hero as any better than he was: the blood of Henri IV flowed in his veins, and that made him, if not unfaithful, at least a little inconstant. Though he stuck to his oath to Isabelle never to have any wife but her, it would be untrue to say that, after the last campaign, thoughts of another hadn't entered his head while approaching Paris with his brother and the cardinal. Thoughts of a dark-haired woman, wearing a red Basque cap, whose red mouth had given him kisses at the Inn of the Painted Beard so bold that his lips burned again at the thought of them.

And more: he remembered the night when, leaving Princesse Marie de Gonzague's soirée, he and that enticing woman who'd played the role of his cousin had exchanged promises to meet again—promises that circumstances had forestalled, but which he intended to make good. But chance interfered once again: by the time the Comte de Moret had arrived in Paris, Madame de Fargis— we assume our readers had guessed it was her—had already left the capital, doubtless in the service of one of even higher rank. So Jacquelino, to his great regret, was unable to renew his acquaintance with his beautiful cousin Marina.

But the elegant court of the Duke of Savoy was a place he remembered fondly: he'd spent a month there two years before when on his way back from Italy, when he'd been given messages for Monsieur and the two queens. It was a court where opportunities for romance were not hard to find.

And, indeed, there were few courts as addicted to gallantry and romance as that of the Duke of Savoy. Dissolute himself, Charles-Emmanuel possessed that charm and urbanity that gave others the permission to indulge themselves. If, after all we've said about him, we wanted to further round out his personality, we would add that he was stubborn, ambitious, and wasteful. But he hid his hypocrisy under such an accomplished air of grandeur that his overspending passed for generosity, his ambition as a desire for glory, and his stubbornness as firmness and consistency. Unfaithful in his alliances, greedy for others' wealth, wasteful of his own, ever poor but lacking in nothing, he continually outfoxed Austria, Spain, and France, taking from whoever offered the most, and giving in return the least he could get away with, particularly in matters of war.

And he made war on his neighbors whenever it seemed to his advantage, because he was tormented by the need to increase his domains. Though forced eventually to sue for peace, in the subsequent treaty he always managed to insert a few ambiguous clauses that enabled him to violate it later. A master of delaying tactics, he was a modern Fabius of diplomacy. He had managed to marry himself to King Philip's daughter Catherine, and his son to King Henri IV's daughter Christine—though these two alliances provided only partial protection against the consequences of his habitual treachery. This time, at last, he faced his most formidable opponent, Cardinal Richelieu—and it would break him.

The Duke of Savoy gave a warm welcome to his two visitors: Montmorency, preceded by his reputation for courage, charm, and generosity; and Moret, who was remembered for his gallantry on his last visit. Madame Christine was particularly gracious to the young prince who so resembled Henri IV, and treated him like a brother.

Knowing Montmorency's romantic tendencies, Charles-Emmanuel had summoned to court all the most beautiful women of Turin and the surrounding area, in hopes of enticing the duke's interest from France to Savoy. But among all those beautiful faces, Antoine de Bourbon looked in vain for the one he'd hoped to see, that of the Countess Matilda of Espalomba.

There's a story about this lovely countess which, as it occurred before the opening chapter of this book, and didn't bear on the subsequent story of our prince, we haven't shared with our readers. One day, Charles-Emmanuel had seen a new star appear at his court, an unknown moon, pale and shining, in orbit around a planet that shed no light of its own. Though he came from one of the leading families of the realm, Count Urbain of Espalomba had married a commoner—Matilda of Cisterna, the loveliest flower of the Aosta Valley, to paraphrase Shakespeare—and brought his bride to Court.

Charles-Emmanuel, though sixty-seven, had preserved during his long reign those habits of gallantry that led him to treat his court like a private harem, where he had but to toss his ducal handkerchief to make his choice. Dazzled by the beauty of the Countess of Espalomba, he'd let her know that she had only to say the word to be the next Duchess of Savoy; but that word the lovely countess never said.

For once, the duke's heart was ignited, not by vulgar ambition, but by the burning flame of love. But the countess, just eighteen years old, had already set eyes on the Comte de Moret, a young prince of twenty-two: April and May came together, and spring was declared with a kiss.

The Count of Espalomba had his suspicions, but only about the Duke of Savoy. With his eye fixed on Charles-Emmanuel, he could see nothing else, and so it was that in the shadow of the old husband's jealousy, the two young lovers found happiness.

But the sovereign's eye was sharper than that of the husband—the duke suspected something, though he wasn't sure what. He mulled it over: Count Urbain was poor and avaricious, and had come to court seeking the duke's favor, so Savoy named the count Governor of Fort Pinerolo, with orders to take immediate command.

There the countess was sent as well to be locked away in a safe place, like a rich gem in a coffer to which only the duke held the key. Forced to separate, the young lovers had wept and promised each other eternal fidelity; we've seen how well the Comte de Moret kept his part of that oath.

Meanwhile, Matilda had no choice but to while away the time on her own; the chances for romance in Pinerolo were few and unappealing, especially after one had loved a young and handsome king's son. Matilda had learned that the count had left Savoy right after her departure, and she was grateful that her lover hadn't wanted to stay in a court that lacked her presence. For the past eighteen months, she'd dreamed of their reunion. So she was overjoyed when she learned her husband had been asked to leave Pinerolo and spend a few days in the capital during the fêtes planned to welcome the two princes to the Court of Turin.

At last the two lovers were reunited! Did each bring to this meeting an equal share of love? We dare not say—but each brought an equal share of youth, the thing that love resembles most.

However, once again their bliss was to be short-lived. The princes had only a few days to spend in Turin—but the Italian campaign could last for months, even years, so there might yet be opportunities for further reunions. They were careful to meet in secret, after which, thanks to information from his beautiful lover, the Comte de Moret was able to draw a detailed plan of Fort Pinerolo. Upon studying it, he was delighted to see that the bedchambers of the count and countess were at opposite ends of the château.

So the lovers set up a method of secret communication. When the young bride had left the lovely Aosta Valley, she'd brought along her slightly older foster sister, Jacintha—a standard precaution when a young woman married an older husband, as sisters made natural allies in marriages of convenience. Jacintha had a brother named Selimo who was two or three years older, so they arranged that he would bring the count, under the assumed name of Gaetano, to meet her at Pinerolo. What could be more natural than that a brother should come with his friend to visit his sister, especially when that sister lived with ten or twelve people in a grand abode that could easily house fifty? Once under the same roof, the youths would be poor lovers indeed if they couldn't manage to see each other three or four times a day, and at least once every night.

They worked all this out within the first day of seeing each other again. The young are said to be heedless of the future, but this pair of lovers, on the contrary, took the future quite seriously.

These arrangements were made right under Count Urbain's nose, whose suspicions were once again all directed at the Duke of Savoy. But the duke had either given up hope of winning the lady's love or, fickle as always, had decided that he preferred to torment Urbain by denying him his salary, on the pretext that money was so tight, he was going to have to beg his own subjects for contributions!

For his part, the Duc de Montmorency was the happiest man on earth. Young, handsome, wealthy, and wearing, after the royal houses, the greatest name in France, the ladies simply flocked to him. Flattered by the master of one of the most sophisticated courts in Europe, his vanity was stroked at every turn. For example, once, when leading the court from the table to the ballroom, the Duke of Savoy had called out, "Since you arrived, Duke, our ladies speak of nothing but how handsome you are, abandoning their husbands to worry and sorrow."

The eight days the two ambassadors spent at Turin or in Rivoli Castle passed in dinners, balls, cavalcades, and fêtes of every sort—and meanwhile the cardinal met with Victor-Amadeus in the castle or, as the cardinal preferred, in the village of Bunolonga. The cardinal liked Bunolonga better since it was only an hour's ride from Susa, and there the Prince of Piedmont came to him, rather than he to the Prince of Piedmont.

LXVIII

The Cardinal Takes the Field

The negotiations were intense. Each party had to deal with a formidable opponent. Charles-Emmanuel wanted peace for himself, but all-out war between France and the House of Austria, in hopes he could remain neutral until the opportunity came to reap the greatest reward by throwing his support behind one crown or the other. But the cardinal had already chosen the day he would go to war with Austria—the day that Gustavus Adolphus marched into Germany.

The cardinal turned the question from peace to war, asking Victor-Amadeus, "What price would the Duke of Savoy ask to declare for France, open his borders, and add ten thousand men to the army of the king?"

Since all possibilities, and this one in particular, had been foreseen by Charles-Emmanuel, Victor-Amadeus was ready with his answer: "It would take the King of France to attack Milan and the Republic of Genoa, with which Charles-Emmanuel is at odds, and to refuse all proposals of peace from the House of Austria until Milan is conquered and Genoa destroyed."

Here was a new proposal indeed, one that showed how the situation had evolved since the Treaty of Susa. The cardinal appeared surprised by this proposal, but quickly replied, in terms preserved for us by historians of the time: "What's this, Prince? My king sends his army to ensure the freedom of Italy, but the Duke of Savoy wants him to use it to destroy the Republic of Genoa, with whom His Majesty has no quarrel? France will willingly use its good offices and authority to negotiate with the Genoese to give satisfaction to the Duke of Savoy, but declaring war on them is out of the question.

Now, if the Spaniards put the king into the position of having to attack Milan, he'll probably do it, and pursue it with all rigor—and the Duke of Savoy can rest assured that once he prevailed, the king wouldn't keep any domains that didn't belong to him. The king, in the person of his minister, gives his word as to that."

The proposal had been quite specific, and so was the reply. Victor-Amadeus, backed into a corner, asked for a few days to consult with his father. Three days later, in fact, he was back in Buno-longa. "My father," he said, "fears that my brother-in-law Louis will come to terms with the King of Spain before the aims of the war are achieved. Prudence prevents him from declaring for France unless the king commits not to lay down arms until Milan has fallen."

Richelieu simply referred him back to the terms of the Treaty of Susa. Victor-Amadeus asked for more time to confer with his father, and returned again, saying "The Duke of Savoy is prepared to adhere to the terms of the treaty, provided the ten thousand infantry and one thousand horse he provides are used to help reduce the Republic of Genoa, that matter to be concluded before embarking on another."

"And this is your final word?" asked the cardinal.

"Yes, Monseigneur," replied Victor-Amadeus, rising from his seat.

Richelieu rapped twice on a panel behind him, and Latil appeared. The cardinal called him over and whispered, "The prince is leaving. Go ahead and make sure he receives no royal honors in passing."

Latil bowed and hurried out. The cardinal was satisfied: he knew an order given to Latil was as good as done. "Prince," the cardinal said to Victor-Amadeus, "I had for the Duke of Savoy, on the behalf of my master the king, all the regard a King of France can have for one who is not only a fellow sovereign, but an uncle. Add to this all the esteem the king has for Your Highness, who as the husband of his sister is no less than a brother. But in my double role as His Majesty's minister and generalissimo, I would fail in my duty if I didn't see Savoy severely punished for refusing to live up to its word. It's an insult to the king, and the Army of France won't stand for it. It's March 17." He drew out his watch. "Today, on March 17, as of six-forty-five in the afternoon, France and Savoy are at war. Take care! Because we mean business." And he bowed to the prince, who then left him.

Two sentries stood watch outside Cardinal Richelieu's door, halberds on their shoulders. Victor-Amadeus passed between them without either appearing to notice him or pay him the least regard. Other soldiers, who were playing dice on the stairs, didn't even pause their game to get out of his way. "Ah," murmured Victor-Amadeus. "So they've been ordered to insult me!" If he had any doubts that such was the case, they were settled at the gate, where the guards completely ignored him.

Prince Victor-Amadeus had scarcely left before the cardinal had summoned the Comte de Moret, the Duc de Montmorency, and the Marshals Créqui, la Force, and Schomberg. He explained the situation to them and asked for their advice. All were of the opinion that since the cardinal had committed them to war, they must go to war.

Ordering them to prepare to mobilize the following day, the cardinal dismissed them, keeping only Montmorency behind. Once they were alone, he asked, "Prince, would you like to be constable tomorrow?"

Montmorency's eyes flashed. "Monseigneur," he said, "the way Your Eminence phrases the question makes me wonder how that might be possible."

"It's not only possible, it's easy. We've declared war on the Duke of Savoy, as he'll learn at Rivoli Castle within two hours. Take fifty well-mounted cavaliers, gain entrée to the castle, seize the duke and his son, and bring them here. Once we have them, we can do as we like with them. They'll soon see reason."

"Monseigneur," said Montmorency, bowing, "just last week, in that same castle, I was the guest of the duke as your ambassador. It would be dishonorable to return there today as an enemy."

The cardinal shrugged. "You're right," he said. "One doesn't propose such things to a Montmorency. This is a mission for a swashbuckler—and I have one at hand. But I'll remember your refusal, my dear Duke. The next time you wish a favor, remember that I'd asked one of you."

Montmorency bowed and departed. "That was a mistake," the cardinal murmured thoughtfully as the door closed behind the prince. "Here is the price of relying so much on men of lower rank. Anyone else would have accepted the task, but men of high blood are too haughty. But he has an honorable heart, and though he doesn't like me, I'd trust him and his honest dislike before others who boast of devotion."

Then, knocking twice on the panel, "Étienne!" he called. "Étienne!"

Latil appeared.

"Do you know Rivoli Castle?" the cardinal asked.

"The château a league outside Turin?"

"Yes. Right now it houses the Duke of Savoy and his son."

Latil smiled. "So it's time to strike," he said.

"Meaning?"

"To take the two of them."

"You'd do that?"

"*Parbleu!* Would I?"

"How many men would you need?"

"Fifty, well-armed and well-mounted."

"Pick your men and your horses. If you succeed, there's fifty thousand *livres* in it for the men, and twenty-five thousand for you."

"The honor of the deed would be quite enough, but if Monseigneur insists on adding to that, I won't argue."

"Do you have anything else to say?"

"Just one thing, Monseigneur."

"What's that?"

"When undertaking a task like this one, one always hears 'If you succeed,' never 'If you don't succeed.' But no matter how well such a mission is performed, how skillfully managed, one of those unexpected events could occur that thwart even the greatest of captains. Then the men, through no fault of their own, get nothing, and that's discouraging. Promise us something even if we don't succeed, no matter how little."

"You're right, Étienne," said the cardinal, "and that's good advice. A thousand *livres* per man and twenty-five thousand for you if you succeed—and if you don't, two crowns per man, and twenty-five for you."

"Then here's how I see it, Monseigneur: it's seven o'clock now, and it'll take three hours to get to Rivoli, so we assail the castle at ten. The rest is up to luck, good or bad."

"Go, my dear Latil, and rest assured I believe that if you don't succeed, it won't be your fault."

"It's in God's hands, Monseigneur!"

Latil took three strides toward the door, then turned around. "Has Monseigneur mentioned this mission to anyone else?"

"Only one person."

"*Ventre-saint-gris,* as King Henri IV used to say. That cuts our chances by fifty percent!"

Richelieu frowned and said to himself, "If he turns this down, I must warn him that I'll take it hard." Then, to Latil: "Well, go anyway—and if you fail, I'll know that I'm the one to blame."

Ten minutes later, a troop of fifty cavalry led by Étienne Latil rode past the window of the cardinal, who watched them go from behind the blinds.

LXIX

The Empty Lair

Though in the shadow of a powerful and determined enemy who might declare war on him at any moment, it wasn't the Duke of Savoy's style to show fear; so while his son Victor-Amadeus was at Bunolonga negotiating with Richelieu, at Rivoli Castle the duke was throwing a grand party. On the evening of March 15, the prettiest women in Turin and the most elegant gentlemen of Savoy and Piedmont were all gathered at Rivoli, which was brilliantly lit, streams of light shining from the windows in all four directions.

The Duke of Savoy, charming, witty, and spry, despite his sixty-seven years, laughed and reveled with the vigor of a young man, and was the first to flatter his daughter-in-law, in whose honor the party was given. But occasionally, an almost imperceptible frown briefly darkened his face. He was thinking the French were only eight or ten leagues away—the French, who had forced the impregnable Pass of Susa within a matter of hours. Even now his fate hung in the balance in the secret struggle between Cardinal Richelieu and Victor-Amadeus, his son. Charles-Emmanuel had made excuses for his son's absence, saying he was expected back that evening—and meanwhile, he counted every passing moment.

Indeed, at about nine o'clock, the prince appeared in splendid attire. A smile on his lips, he greeted Princess Christine first, then the ladies, then those Savoyard and Piedmontese great nobles whom he honored with his friendship. Finally he approached Duke Charles-Emmanuel and, kissing his hand, spoke to him in a low voice as if inquiring about his health. His face was calm, but what he said was "France has declared war on us; hostilities begin tomorrow. We must take care."

The duke replied in the same tone, "Leave after the quadrille and give orders to concentrate the troops at Turin. As for me, I'll dispatch the governors of Forts Viellane, Fenestrelle, and Pinerolo to their posts."

Then he waved his hand to the musicians, who had paused when the prince had entered, and gave the signal to resume the dance.

Victor-Amadeus took the hand of his wife, Princess Christine, and without saying a word about the rupture between Savoy and France, led off the royal quadrille. Meanwhile, Charles-Emmanuel approached the governors of Piedmont's three main forts and ordered them to leave at once for their citadels.

The governors of Viellane and Fenestrelle had come without their wives, so they had but to saddle their horses and don their cloaks to follow the duke's command. This wasn't the case with Count Urbain of Espalomba; not only had he brought his wife, but she was dancing the quadrille with Prince Victor-Amadeus. "Monseigneur," he said, "your order won't be easy to follow."

"And why is that, Monsieur?"

"Because the countess and I came here from Turin dressed for the ball, in a hired carriage that doesn't come from Pinerolo."

"The wardrobe of my son and daughter-in-law will provide you with everything you need, and you can take a coach from my stables."

"I'm not sure the countess could undertake such a journey without risk to her health."

"In that case, leave her here and go alone."

The count gave Charles-Emmanuel a strange look. "Yes," he said, "I see how such an arrangement would be convenient for Your Highness."

"Any arrangement is convenient for me, Count, so long as you depart without wasting a minute."

"And the dishonor, Monseigneur?" the count demanded.

"Where is the dishonor, my dear Count, in ordering a commander to his post?" replied the duke. "On the contrary, it's a proof of confidence."

"That's no explanation for this sudden departure."

"A sovereign doesn't have to answer to his subjects," Charles-Emmanuel said, "especially when these subjects are in his service and he has orders for them. Now I order you to go at once to Pinerolo, and if the town and citadel are attacked you are to defend it until no stone is left standing upon another. You and Madame may ask for whatever you need, and it will be provided for you at once."

"Should I take the countess out of the quadrille, or wait until it's finished?"

"You can wait until it's finished."

"Very well, Monseigneur. When the quadrille is over, we'll depart."

"Go quickly, Count, and put up a strong defense." And the Duke of Savoy walked away, ignoring the oaths Count Urbain swore under his breath.

When the quadrille was finished, the count related the order he'd been given to his astonished countess. They left the hall by one door, while Victor-Amadeus went out the other.

The governors of Viellane and Fenestrelle, who'd had no part in the quadrille, were already gone.

The duke whispered a few words to his daughter-in-law, who followed the count and countess. Outside the hall, she assigned one of her maids to assist the countess, then returned to the fête to organize the next quadrille in place of Prince Victor-Amadeus.

Ten minutes later the prince was back in the ballroom, visibly paler than when he'd left. He went up to Duke Charles-Emmanuel, linked arms with him, and walked him to a window embrasure. There he gave the duke a note. "Read this, Father," he said.

"What is it?" asked the duke.

"A note that was just handed to me by a dust-covered courier who arrived on a horse coated with sweat. I tried to give him a purse full of gold for his effort, but he refused it, saying 'I serve a master who doesn't allow others to pay his servants.' And with that, having given his horse no more time to catch his breath than it took to say those words, he galloped off."

As he said this, Duke Charles-Emmanuel was reading the note. It was short:

A guest who was hospitably received by His Highness the Duke of Savoy takes this opportunity to pay for such hospitality by warning him that he and Prince Victor-Amadeus must depart Castle Rivoli this very night. There's not a moment to lose. To horse, and ride for Turin!

"No signature?" asked the duke.

"None. But it's obviously from the Duc de Montmorency or the Comte de Moret."

"What livery was the courier wearing?"

"No livery—but I thought I recognized him as one named Galaor who accompanied the duke."

"That must be it. Well?"

"Your opinion, Monseigneur?"

"My opinion, my dear Victor, is that we should follow this advice. Nothing bad will happen if we do, but we might suffer a terrible turn if we don't."

"Then let's be on our way."

The duke strode to the center of the ballroom, still smiling. "Ladies and gentlemen," he said, "I've just received information that I must respond to immediately, with the aid of my son. But don't concern yourselves—dance on, have fun, my palace is yours. Princess Christine, will you do the honors?"

Though couched as an invitation, it was a command. The ladies and gentlemen parted into two lines and bowed as the two princes passed, smiling and waving.

Once out of the ballroom, all pretense was abandoned. Father and son summoned their valets, who threw cloaks over their shoulders as they hurried down the stairs. They crossed the courtyard and went straight to the stables, saddled the two fastest coursers, slipped pistols into their holsters, mounted, and rode. They launched themselves at a gallop down the road to Turin, only a league away.

Meanwhile, Latil and his fifty men were also at the gallop along the road from Susa to Turin. Where the road forks, and one branch, lined with poplars, heads toward Rivoli Castle, Latil, who rode in the lead, thought he saw a shadow approaching.

On his side, the rider—for the shadow was that of a mounted cavalier—came to a halt, examining the band of riders with the same curiosity the riders were examining him.

Latil was about to cry "Who goes there?" when he stopped himself, for fear that his French-accented Italian would betray him. He decided to ride forward alone, and urged his horse toward the rider who stood in the road like an equestrian statue.

But as soon as the shadowy rider saw him coming, he drove in his spurs and left the Rivoli road, galloping cross-country toward the road to Susa.

Latil rode to cut him off, shouting "Halt!" But the shadow just rode all the faster. As they converged, Latil considered that the rider was now within pistol range, but two ideas gave him pause: first, the rider might not be an enemy; and second, a pistol shot this close to Rivoli might raise the alarm.

They reached the road, but the unknown rider was three lengths ahead of Latil, and he was better mounted; Latil pursued, but the rider not only maintained his lead, he increased it. After five minutes,

Latil gave up the pursuit and returned to his detachment. The darkness of night swallowed the rider and even the sound of his horse, leaving nothing behind.

Latil, shaking his head, resumed his position at the head of the troop. The event might mean nothing, but to Latil it was deathly important. He said to himself, "I'd wager anything the duke's been forewarned. Why would a cavalier riding from Rivoli be so desperate to hide his identity? Why would he ride to Susa, unless he'd come from Susa in the first place? By the sound of its breathing, his horse had clearly ridden a long way already."

His suspicions were further confirmed when, as they approached Rivoli, Latil saw not one, but two shadowy riders on the road ahead, who like the first stopped when they saw the approaching troop. But the pause was only momentary before they launched themselves in the opposite direction from the first rider, that is, toward Turin.

Latil didn't even consider pursuing them, as they rode fresh, first-rate horses whose hooves barely seemed to touch the ground. There was nothing to do but continue on to the château, whose windows glowed on the near horizon. But Latil was convinced that he knew the explanation for his encounters with these riders.

In ten minutes they were at the château gates. There was no sign of warning or alert. Latil rode around the compound, assigning six troopers to each door, and then, at the head of the final half-dozen, he rushed, sword in hand, up the stairs to the main doorway.

At the sight of armed men in French uniforms rushing into the ballroom, the astonished musicians abruptly stopped. The dancers, frightened, turned this way and that, but soldiers were coming in through every door.

Latil, having ordered his men to hold the doors, advanced, hat in one hand and sword in the other, toward the center of the room. But Princess Christine met him halfway. "Monsieur," she said to him, "I presume you come to call upon my father-in-law, the Duke of Savoy, and my husband, the Prince of Piedmont. I regret to say they're not here, having left for Turin no more than fifteen minutes ago, where I anticipate by now they've safely arrived. If you or your men are in need of refreshments, well, Rivoli Castle is famous for its hospitality, and I'd be happy to do the honors for an officer and soldiers of my brother Louis XIII."

"Madame," Latil replied, summoning all his memories of the old royal court so as to reply properly to the wife of the Prince of Piedmont, daughter-in-law of the Duke of Savoy and sister of his king, "we visit solely to bring news of Their Highnesses. We met them no more than ten minutes ago, on their way, as you did the honor to inform me, to Turin—and the way they spurred their horses, they were eager to get there. As for the hospitality you do us the honor to offer us, we must decline, as we are obliged to report our news to the cardinal."

And then, bowing to Princess Christine with an elegance one might find surprising in a mercenary captain, he withdrew. "Come on," he said, rejoining his men. "As I suspected, they were forewarned, and the lair is empty!"

LXX

In Which the Comte de Moret Offers to Take a Mule and a Million to Fort Pinerolo

When he heard the results of Latil's expedition, Richelieu was furious. Like Latil, he had no doubt but that the Duke of Savoy had been forewarned. But who could have alerted him? The cardinal had shared his plan with only one person, the Duc de Montmorency. Was he the one who'd warned Charles-Emmanuel? That seemed consistent with his exaggerated devotion to chivalry. But such chivalry on behalf of an enemy verged on treason to the crown.

Richelieu didn't reveal his suspicions about Montmorency, for he knew Latil was attached to the duke and to the Comte de Moret, but he asked a number of probing questions about this shadowy cavalier glimpsed in the dark.

Latil described what he'd seen: a young man aged seventeen or eighteen, wearing a large plumed hat and wrapped in a dark blue or black cloak, whose horse was as black as the night with which it had merged.

After Latil left, the cardinal sent to ask what orders the sentries had followed between eight and ten that night, and was told that no one could enter or leave the Susa garrison without the password, which that evening was "Susa and Savoy." Of course, the password was known to all the high officers: Marshals Schomberg, Créqui, and La Force, the Comte de Moret, the Duc de Montmorency, and so forth.

The cardinal called the sentries in and questioned them. From Latil's description, one of them recognized a youth who had gone out, giving the correct password. He'd left by the gate toward France rather than the gate to Italy, but that didn't mean anything: once outside the gate and into the town, he could easily have changed direction.

So they discovered at daybreak, when they found the tracks of a horse. The trail went out the France gate, around the town of Susa, and joined the road to Italy a mile beyond.

The cardinal lost no time in delays. The day before, he'd declared war to Victor-Amadeus; so by ten o'clock, his investigations having been concluded, he gave the order to march, and the drums and trumpets sounded.

The cardinal watched as the army passed, four corps commanded by Schomberg, La Force, Créqui, and the Duc de Montmorency. Among the officers standing near him was Latil. Montmorency was accompanied, as always, by a large entourage of gentlemen and pages. Among these pages was Galaor, wearing a wide plumed hat and mounted on a black horse. As the young man passed, Richelieu touched Latil on the shoulder. "Maybe," said the latter, "but I couldn't swear to it."

Richelieu frowned, and his eyes flashed in the direction of the duke. Putting his horse into a gallop, he rode to the head of the column, preceded only by the vanguard known as the *enfants perdus.* He was dressed in his usual wartime attire, a steel breastplate over a richly embroidered golden doublet. A feather floated from his broad felt hat. As they might meet the enemy at any moment, two pages went before him, one carrying his gauntlets and the other his helmet. At his side, two other pages led a rare and powerful war-horse. Cavois and Latil, the captain and lieutenant of his guards, followed close behind.

After an hour's ride, they reached a small river which the cardinal had had scouted out the previous day. Confident of his information, he was the first to ride into the water, and arrived without accident on the other side.

A heavy rain began to fall as the army crossed the river, but the cardinal, nothing daunted, continued his march. It would have been impossible to shelter an army in the few isolated houses that lined the road, but the soldiers, disregarding the possible, began to complain and wish the cardinal to the Devil. These complaints were loud enough that the cardinal could scarcely miss them.

"Well!" said the cardinal, turning to Latil. "Do you hear that, Étienne?"

"What, Monseigneur?"

"What those clowns are saying about me."

"Well, Monseigneur," said Latil, laughing, "it's the custom of suffering soldiers to wish their commanders to the Devil—but the Devil has no hold on a Prince of the Church."

"Perhaps, when I'm wearing my red robes—but not when I wear the uniform of His Majesty. Ride down the ranks, Latil, and advise them to be more patient."

Latil passed down the ranks, and then returned to his place by the cardinal. "Well?" asked the cardinal.

"Well, Monseigneur, they've decided on patience."

"Because you told them I was unhappy with them?"

"Not exactly, Monseigneur."

"What did you tell them, then?"

"That Your Eminence was grateful for how they endured the hardships of the road, so much so that when they arrive at Rivoli, they'll be issued a double ration of wine."

The cardinal gnawed at his mustache for a moment. "You may have hit on the answer," he said.

And indeed, the murmurs had subsided. Besides, the weather was clearing, and under a sunbeam in the distance, they could see the shining roofs of Rivoli Castle and the village that clustered around it.

Marching without pause, they arrived at Rivoli in just three hours. "Would Your Eminence like me to direct the distribution of wine?" Latil asked.

"Since you promised these buffoons a double ration, we must give it to them—but it must be paid for in cash."

"Indeed, they must have it, Monseigneur, but . . . cash?"

"Why, yes. Everything costs money."

The cardinal stopped, drew a tablet from his saddle, and wrote on the top sheet: *The Treasurer will pay Monsieur Latil the sum of one thousand* livres, *charged to my account.* Then he signed it.

Latil took the note and went on ahead.

When the army entered Rivoli three quarters of an hour later, the soldiers were struck dumb to see, in every tenth doorway, an open wine barrel surrounded by glasses. Their mute astonishment changed to loud satisfaction, the complaints about water were converted to cheers for the wine, and cries of *"Vive le cardinal!"* rang down the ranks.

Amid this ovation, Latil rejoined the cardinal. "Well, Monseigneur?" he said.

"Well, Latil, I think you understand soldiers better than I do."

"Pardieu! Each to his own! I know soldiers because I've lived among soldiers. Your Eminence understands churchmen, having lived among men of the Church."

"Latil," said the cardinal, placing his hand on the swashbuckler's shoulder, "if there's one thing I'm learning by living among soldiers, it's that the more one lives among churchmen, the less one knows about anything."

Having arrived at Rivoli Castle, the cardinal summoned his principal commanders. "Gentlemen," he said, "I think this castle is large enough to provide quarters for all of you. Messieurs Montmorency and Moret were guests here of the Duke of Savoy, and can show you around. In one hour, we'll convene for a war council. Be prompt; we have important matters to discuss."

The marshals and high officers, soaked to the bone and as eager to warm up as the soldiers, promised to be punctual and hurried away.

One hour later, the seven high commanders were gathered before Cardinal Richelieu in the audience chamber that just the day before had belonged to the Duke of Savoy. These seven were the Duc de Montmorency, the Marshals Schomberg, Créqui, La Force, and Thoiras, Monsieur d'Auriac, and the Comte de Moret.

The cardinal stood, gestured for silence, rested both hands on the table, and said, "Gentlemen, we have an open gate into Piedmont. This gate, Susa Pass, was unlocked with the price of our blood. However, when dealing with a man as devious as Charles-Emmanuel, one gate isn't enough—we need two. Here is my plan of campaign: before pushing further into Italy, I want to open another gate between Piedmont and Dauphiné so we can bring in further reinforcements, and in case we need a route for a withdrawal. For this purpose, I propose to seize Fort Pinerolo.

"You know, gentlemen, how the feeble Henri III ran afoul of the Duke of Savoy in his youth. Charles, the Duke of Mantua, whose claim we cross the Alps to support—his father, the old Duc de Nevers, Governor of Pinerolo and general of the armies of France in Italy, used his powers of eloquence to persuade Henri III to agree to a terrible mistake. Nevers foresaw the day that his son might lay claim to the Duchy of Mantua, and would want to control the passes to France. So he persuaded Henri III to trade away the governorship of Pinerolo in hopes it would fall to Mantua—despite the fact that this was not in France's best interest.

"So, Messieurs, it falls to us to return Fort Pinerolo to the crown of France. Should we attempt this by force, or by deception? If we choose force, it will cost us both time and troops. So I prefer deception.

"Philip of Macedon said there's no fort so impregnable it won't open its gates to a mule loaded with gold. I have the mule, and I have the gold, but I lack the man or the means to get it inside. Help me out: we need a way to turn a million in gold into the keys to this fortress."

As usual, the question was opened up to the floor, everyone having the opportunity to answer in order of seniority. Each commander asked for twenty-four hours to think about it, until they reached the Comte de Moret, who was youngest and therefore the last to speak. No one expected him to say anything, so he surprised everyone when he stood up, bowed to the cardinal, and said, "If Your Eminence will prepare the mule and million, I'll undertake to get those keys. All I'll need are three days."

LXXI

The Foster-Brother

The day after the council at Rivoli Castle, a young peasant named Gaetano, aged about twenty-four, dressed like a mountaineer from Aosta Valley and speaking with a Piedmontese accent, appeared at the gates of Fort Pinerolo at about eight in the evening. He said he was the brother of the Countess of Espalomba's chambermaid, Signora Jacintha, and asked to see her.

When informed of this by a soldier of the garrison, Signora Jacintha gave a little squeal of surprise that could easily have been mistaken for a cry of joy. Then, as if she had first to get her mistress's permission in order to respond to a summons of family at the fortress gate, she ran into the countess's bedroom. Five minutes later, she left by the door she'd gone in, while the countess darted out the opposite door and down the stairs to a charming little private garden, which happened to be overlooked by the windows of Jacintha's room.

Once in the garden, the countess made her way to its most secluded corner, a bower shaded by lemon, orange, and pomegranate trees.

Meanwhile, Jacintha ran down to the courtyard like a sister in a hurry to see her beloved brother, tenderly crying out "Gaetano! Dear Gaetano!"

The young man threw herself into her arms, just as Count Urbain of Espalomba returned from reviewing his sentries. He was in time to see the happy embrace of the young people, as they exclaimed that they hadn't seen each other for nearly two years, ever since Jacintha had left her mother's house to follow her mistress.

Jacintha approached the count with a pretty curtsy and asked permission to host her brother. He had, it seemed, some urgent business in the area, though he hadn't yet had time to explain it.

The count asked to speak with Gaetano and, after a few words, satisfied with the lad's demeanor, gave permission for him to stay in the fortress. Gaetano assured him that he wouldn't be there long, forty-eight hours at the most. Then the count, deciding he'd spent enough time with these commoners, dismissed them and went inside to his chambers.

Gaetano remarked that the count appeared to be in a sour mood, a fact that seemed to interest him more than one might expect from a farmer who had little to do with the affairs of the great nobles. Jacintha told him Urbain was angry with his sovereign, on two counts. First, for the arrogant way the Duke of Savoy had courted his wife in the very presence of her husband; and second, for the abrupt order to shut himself up in this citadel and defend it to the death against all comers. Count Urbain had said to his wife, in Jacintha's presence, that no noble of Spain, Austria, or France would stand for what he had to suffer in Piedmont—and neither should he.

Gaetano seemed so pleased with this news that, when they turned a dark corner of the corridor, as if in a surge of affection for his sister, he took Jacintha in his arms and gave her a big kiss on each cheek.

Jacintha's chamber was off that very corridor; she opened her door, ushered her "brother" inside, and shut it behind him. Gaetano said happily, "Here I am at last! And now, dear Jacintha, where is your mistress?"

"What? I thought you'd come to see me!" the young woman laughed.

"For you . . . and for her," said the Comte de Moret, for it was indeed him. "But mostly for her. I have political matters to arrange with your mistress, and, as you're the maid of a woman of affairs, you know business comes first."

"And where would you like to arrange these important matters?"

"Here in your room, if it's all right with you."

"What! In front of me?"

"Well, no. We have full confidence in you, my dear Jacintha, but some matters are too dangerous to share."

"Then what am I to do?"

"You, Jacintha, will sit outside your mistress's bed, where the curtains are drawn due to her sudden indisposition, keeping watch to make sure her husband doesn't intrude and wake her."

"Ah, Monsieur le Comte," Jacintha said with a sigh, "I had no idea you were such a clever diplomat."

"But I am, as you see. And for a diplomat, nothing is more precious than time, so tell me quickly—where is your mistress?"

Jacintha sighed even more deeply, opened the window, and said, "See for yourself."

The count then remembered the private garden Matilda had told him about, where she so often dreamed of him. She had spoken of a bower of pomegranate, orange, and lemon trees, where it was shady even in daytime, and more so at night. Jacintha had scarcely opened the window before he'd leaped to the ledge and down into the garden. Then, as Jacintha wiped away a tear she'd been unable to keep back, she watched him disappear into the little wood whispering, loudly, "Matilda! Matilda!"

At the sound of her name, Matilda instantly recognized the voice that spoke it and darted toward it, crying "Antoine!"

As the lovers met, they threw themselves into each other's arms, embracing against an orange tree, which rained a flurry of blossoms on their heads. There they remained for a time, if not silent, at least not quite talking, just uttering the vague murmurs that, on the lips of lovers, say so much without saying a word.

Finally both, as if awaking from a lovely land of dreams, said at the same time: "It's you!" And in a single kiss, both answered, "Yes!"

Then, as reality returned, the countess cried, "My husband?"

"All taken care of as planned—he took me for Jacintha's brother and has admitted me into the fortress."

Then they sat down side by side and hand in hand. The time had come for explanations.

Between lovers, explanations can take a long time. They started them in the garden but then took them into Jacintha's room, while Jacintha, as arranged, spent the night in her mistress's bedroom.

Around eight the next morning, a gentle knock sounded on the door of Count Urbain's bedchamber. He was already up and dressed, having been awakened at six o'clock by a message from Turin announcing that the French were at Rivoli and appeared to be in preparations to besiege Pinerolo.

The count was anxious, and showed it in the abrupt way he barked "Enter!"

The door opened, and to his amazement it was the countess. "It's you, Matilda!" he said, rising. "Have you heard the news? Is it to that that I owe the pleasure of this unexpected early visit?"

"What news, Monsieur?"

"Only that we're probably about to be besieged!"

"Yes, that's what I wanted to talk to you about."

"How and when did you learn this news?"

"Just last night, as I'll explain. It kept me awake all night long."

"As I can tell from your complexion, Madame—you look tired and pale."

"I was waiting impatiently for morning so I could speak to you."

"Couldn't you have awakened me, Madame? The news was important enough."

"But it stirred up such a tumult of doubts and worries, Monsieur, that I wanted to talk with you about the situation before sharing what I'd heard."

"I don't understand, Madame, and I confess that I can't think how a woman heard secret news about a matter of politics and war. . . ."

"Oh, I know you think we're not clever enough to think about such things."

"And you think that's wrong," said the count, smiling.

"I do, because women are capable of good advice."

"So, if I asked for your opinion on our situation, what advice would you give me?"

"First of all," the countess said, "I'd remind you of how shabbily the Duke of Savoy has treated us."

"No need of that, Madame—his disrespect was plain and clear, and I'll never forget it."

"I'd remind you of the festivities for the ambassadors at Turin, during which our sovereign made proposals to me that were an insult to both of us."

"I remember them, Madame."

"I would remind you of the brusque and uncivil way in which he ordered you to leave Rivoli and go to Pinerolo to be butchered by the French!"

"I haven't forgotten it, and I'm waiting for the chance to prove it to him."

"Well, that chance has come. You, Monsieur, are in one of those situations where a decisive man can be the arbiter of his own destiny and choose between two futures: servitude under a harsh and arrogant master, or freedom with dignity and an ample fortune."

The count looked at his wife in astonishment. "I confess, Madame, I have no idea where you're going with this."

"I will speak clearly about the matter. Jacintha's brother is in the service of the Comte de Moret."

Now the count was doubly astonished. "The natural son of King Henri IV?"

"Yes, Monsieur."

"And so, Madame?"

"So, the day before yesterday, Cardinal Richelieu declared before the Comte de Moret that he'd give a million in gold to anyone who would bring him the keys to Pinerolo!"

The count's eyes narrowed with greed. "A million," he said. "I'd like to see that."

"You can see it whenever you like, Monsieur!"

The count rubbed his hands together. "A million," he whispered. "You're right, Madame, this is a matter worthy of discussion! But how do you know this money is really . . . available?"

"That's easily explained. The Comte de Moret took charge of the affair and sent Gaetano ahead with orders to test the waters."

"And that's why Gaetano arrived to see his sister last night?"

"Exactly. His sister brought the proposal to me, so if it miscarried I'd be the only one who was compromised."

"How could it miscarry?" the count asked.

"It seemed possible . . . you might refuse it."

The count was thoughtful for a moment. "What guarantees am I offered?"

"Cash."

"But, then, what guarantees would they ask of me?"

"A hostage."

"A hostage? Who?"

"Me. It makes sense that you'd send your wife away from a fortress on the verge of a siege where you're planning to defend to the death. You can say you're sending me to my mother at Selimo, but actually let me know where to meet you later in France—since I assume you'll negotiate for a safe haven there."

"And how will the million be paid?"

"In gold."

"When?"

"As soon as, in exchange for the money Gaetano brings you, you sign an order of capitulation and hand me over as the hostage."

"Send him. When Gaetano returns tonight with the gold, be ready to go with him."

That night at eight o'clock, the Comte de Moret, still under the name of Gaetano, entered the gates of Fort Pinerolo with a mule loaded with gold, as he'd promised Cardinal Richelieu. And he left, as he'd promised himself, with the countess.

The capitulation came two days later, after the cardinal had placed the fortress under siege. The garrison was allowed to leave with their lives and all their baggage.

LXXII

The Eagle and the Fox

Two days later, Cardinal Richelieu occupied Fort Pinerolo just as Charles-Emmanuel was leading troops from Turin to lift the siege. When the latter was only three leagues from Turin, his scouts informed him that a body of eight hundred men under the Savoy banner was coming to meet him. He sent one of his officers forward on reconnaissance, and he reported back that, to his astonishment, the troops were the garrison of Pinerolo returning to Turin.

The fortress had surrendered.

This news was a terrible blow to Charles-Emmanuel. He paused, turned pale, put a hand to his forehead, and then called the commander of his cavalry. "Charge that rabble," he said, pointing to the poor devils who'd had no choice but to leave their garrison, since the governor had surrendered it. "And if possible, leave no one standing."

The order was executed to the letter: three-quarters of the wretches were put to the sword.

The fall of Pinerolo, the cause of which was still unknown to the Duke of Savoy, forced him to reconsider his position. It was disastrous. All the tricks and intrigue of a reign of nearly forty-five years—a reign composed entirely of tricks and intrigue—had come to this: the army of a terrible enemy was in the heart of his domain. His only recourse now was to throw himself into the arms of the Spaniards and Austrians, begging for aid from Spinola—a Genoese, and thus an enemy—or Wallenstein—a Bohemian, and thus a barbarian.

One must bend before the iron hand of necessity. The duke sent to Spinola, the Spanish commander-in-chief, and to Collalto, the German commander in Italy, asking them for aid against the French.

But Spinola, that canny warrior, was camped in Milan, from which he'd been keeping an eye on Charles-Emmanuel; he hadn't the least bit of sympathy for that intriguing and ambitious princeling, who had so many times, through his deceptions and reversals, caused Spinola to draw his sword and then put it back in its sheath. As for Collalto, he had but a single goal in Italy: equip and enrich his army and himself, and as a climax to the campaign, like a true condottiere, to take and pillage Mantua. Men of this stamp were understandably little moved by the pleas of the Duke of Savoy.

Spinola declared that he couldn't divide his army, as he needed all his troops for his operations in Montferrat.

Collalto was another matter. As we said, he could call on as many men as he needed from Germany. Wallenstein, at the head of the horde, led over a hundred thousand men—or rather was led by them— frightening Ferdinand with their power, sometimes even frightening himself, so he was willing to hire them out to whoever could afford them. So the negotiations between Collalto and Charles-Emmanuel were simply a matter of money; a few words and a large coffer of cash yielded the Duke of Savoy ten thousand men.

It was only Charles-Emmanuel's fervent hatred of France that allowed him to strike this terrible bargain, for he was bringing into Piedmont an enemy more terrible than the one he wanted to drive out. The French soldiers marched under rigorous discipline, plundering nothing but money; the Germans, on the contrary, stole everything they could carry.

The Duke of Savoy soon realized that his best chance was to make one last attempt to come to terms with Richelieu. Thus, two days after taking Pinerolo, as the cardinal worked in the same chambers where Count Urbain had received his countess on the morning after Gaetano's arrival, he was informed of the visit of a young officer in the service of Cardinal Antonio Barberini, the pope's nephew and his envoy to Charles-Emmanuel.

The cardinal immediately guessed what this was about. Latil had announced the officer, and as the cardinal had great confidence in both the courage and the insight of his lieutenant of the guards, he said "Come here."

"At your command, Your Eminence," Latil replied, touching his hat.

"Do you know this envoy from Monseigneur Barberini?"

"He's new to me, Your Eminence."

"And his name?"

"Also unknown to me."

"To you, but maybe not to me."

Latil shook his head. "There aren't many names I don't recognize."

"What's he called?"

"Mazarino Mazarini, Monseigneur."

"Mazarini! You're right, I don't recognize that name, Étienne. I don't like to play if I can't see my neighbor's cards. Is he young?"

"Twenty-six; twenty-eight at the most."

"Handsome or ugly?"

"Good-looking."

"Useful to both a woman and a prelate! What part of Italy is he from?"

"By his accent, I'd say the nobility of Naples."

"Sophisticated and subtle, then. Is he well groomed?"

"Like a coquette."

"So, to summarize: twenty-eight years old, handsome, well turned out, sent by Cardinal Barberini, the nephew of Urban VIII—he's either a useful idiot, or a capable agent, and we'll soon know which. In either event, thanks to you, he won't surprise me. Have him enter."

Five minutes later, the door opened again and Latil announced, "Captain Mazarino Mazarini!"

The cardinal glanced at the young officer. He was just as Latil had described him.

For his part, as he bowed respectfully to the cardinal, the young officer, whom we'll call Mazarin—for that was his name after he became a French citizen in 1639, and thus he is known to the history of the realm—made as complete a survey of His Eminence as a man with a quick and incisive mind can do at a glance.

We have once already, depicting Sully and Richelieu, showed the past meeting the present. Depicting Richelieu and Mazarin, we show the present meeting the future. But this time, instead of titling our chapter "The Two Eagles," we must call it "The Eagle and the Fox."

The fox came in with his astute and sidelong glance.

The eagle fixed him with his sharp and penetrating gaze.

"Monseigneur," said Mazarin, pretending to be flustered, "forgive my emotion in finding myself before the leading political genius of the century—I, a mere captain of the papal forces, and so young."

"Indeed, Monsieur," said the cardinal, "you're only twenty-six?"

"Thirty, Monseigneur."

The cardinal laughed. "Monsieur," he said, "when I went to Rome to be consecrated as a bishop, Pope Paul V asked me my age, and like you, I exaggerated—I said I was twenty-five though I was only twenty-three. He made me a bishop, and after the ceremony I threw myself at his feet and asked for absolution. I confessed that I'd lied and added two years to my age, and he gave it to me. Would you like absolution?"

"I will ask for that, Monseigneur," replied Mazarin with a smile, "on the day I'm made a bishop."

"Is that your ambition?"

"I hope, Your Eminence, to someday be a cardinal."

"That won't be hard, with the resources you have."

"And what would Monseigneur say these resources are?"

"First, the mission you've been given, which I'm told is on behalf of Cardinal Antonio Barberini."

"That rope is a thin one, since I'm merely a protégé of a nephew of His Holiness, and not of His Holiness himself."

"When I see a protégé of any of the nephews of His Holiness, I see the influence of His Holiness."

"However, you know what His Holiness thinks of his nephews."

"I recall that, in a moment of candor, he said that his first nephew, Francesco Barberini, when he left the Collegio Romano, was good only for saying paternosters; his brother Antonio, who sent you to me, was strong only in the stench of his trousers, which is why he'd given him a cardinal's robe; that Cardinal Antonio, when young, was nicknamed Demosthenes because he stammered and got drunk three times a day; and last of all Taddeo, who was named Generalissimo of the Holy See, was better with a knitting needle than a sword."

"Ah, Monseigneur! I'll press that question no further. But having said what the uncle thinks of his nephews, I imagine you can tell me what the nephews think of their uncle."

"That the favors they receive from Urban VIII are legitimate rewards for the pains they took to get him elected. On the first round of voting, the future pontiff had no supporters. But the nephews bought off the Roman populace, paying them to shout beneath the windows of Castel Sant'Angelo, "Barberini as pope, or death and fire!" At the next round, he got five votes, which was significant: only thirteen were needed. Two cardinals led the faction that was opposed to Barberini at all costs. Within three days, both cardinals passed away, one struck, they say, by apoplexy, while the other succumbed to an aneurysm. They were replaced by two Barberini supporters, which gave him seven votes. Two other opposing cardinals died soon thereafter. Then came word of an outbreak of plague; everyone was eager to get out, so the conclave was rushed to its conclusion. In the end, Barberini had fifteen votes, two more than the thirteen he needed."

"That wasn't too high a price, considering the great reforms proclaimed as soon as His Holiness Urban VIII assumed the papal throne."

"Yes, indeed," said Richelieu. "He forbade the Recollects to wear sandals and pointed hoods in the manner of the Capuchin Order; he defended the renaming of the Carmelites as the Reformed Carmelites; he demanded that the Spanish Premonstratensians revert to their old, somber habits and give up their proud new ones. He beatified two Theatine fanatics, André Avelino and Gaetano Tiane; a Barefoot Carmelite, Felix Cantalice; an Illuminatus, the Florentine Carmelite Corsini; two female ecstatics, Magdalena de Pazzi and Elizabeth, Queen of Portugal; and finally the blessed Saint Roch and his dog."

"Ah, well," said Mazarin. "It's clear Your Eminence is up to date on His Holiness, his nephews, and the Court of Rome."

"But you, who seem like a sensible man," said Richelieu, "why are you in the pay of such nonentities?"

"We start where we can with what we have, Monseigneur," said Mazarin with a sly smile.

"That's so," said Richelieu. "And now we've talked enough about them; what about us? What do you hope to get from me?"

"Something you'll never agree to."

"Why?"

"Because it's absurd."

"Why undertake such a mission?"

"Because it brings me before the man I admire most in the world."

"What is it, then?"

Mazarin shrugged. "I am to inform Your Eminence that due to the capture of Fort Pinerolo, the Duke of Savoy has become gentle as a lamb and supple as a serpent. Through this envoy, he begs Your

Eminence, who is known for his generosity, if, for the sake of the king's sister the Princess of Piedmont, you would return Fort Pinerolo, as this would greatly advance the cause of peace."

"My dear Captain," replied Richelieu, "it's as well that you started out as you did, or I'd have wondered why you were fool enough to take such a mission, or if you simply thought that I was a fool. In any case: no! Giving up Fort Pinerolo was one of Henri III's greatest shames, and regaining it will be one of the glories of the reign of Louis XIII."

"Are those the terms in which you would have me state your reply?"

"No, not exactly."

"Then how, Monseigneur?"

"Like this: His Majesty has not yet learned of our conquest of Pinerolo; I can do nothing until he informs me whether he wishes to keep it, or prefers to give it up as a courtesy to his sister. I'm told the king has left Paris bound for Italy, so we must wait until he arrives in Lyon or Grenoble. At that time, we can enter into serious negotiations and perhaps render a more positive response."

"Rest assured, Monseigneur, I shall deliver your response verbatim. Just allow me, if you please, to give them some hope."

"What will they do with that?"

"Nothing—but it may be useful to me."

"Do you plan to stay in Italy?"

"No, but I want to accomplish as much as I can before I leave."

"You don't think Italy has sufficient scope for your ambitions?"

"Italy is a shambles, and has been for centuries, Monseigneur. The last hundred years, as you know better than I, have been a disaster, the final collapse of all that remained from the feudal era. The two pillars of the Middle Ages, the Church and the Empire, are in disarray; once the pope and the emperor were the twin hands of God, but since Rudolph of Hapsburg, the emperors have been a series of despots, and since the rise of Luther, the pope is no more than the leader of a sect."

Mazarin appeared hesitant to continue. "Go on," said Richelieu. "I'm listening."

"You, listening to me, Monseigneur! Until today I doubted myself, but if *you* listen to me, I'll doubt myself no more.

"There are still Italians, but Italy is no more. Spain holds four of its capitals, Naples, Milan, Florence, and Palermo. France wants Savoy and Mantua. Venice is in decline, and Genoa gets by from day to day. A frown from Philip IV or Ferdinand II can shake even the pope, successor though he is to Gregory VII. Every man of leadership calls for freedom, but their voices lack strength; the nobles have crushed the people, and have themselves been reduced to mere courtiers. The nobility is powerless, seeing plots and invisible enemies on all sides, so they surround themselves with standing armies, with mercenaries and thugs, terrified of poison, cowering inside chain mail. Worse, they've handed over the Council of Trent to the Inquisition. The courage to fight in the open, to take the war to the battlefield, is gone, and with it the heart of the people. Maintaining order is everything, and order is the death of life."

"If you leave Italy, where will you go?"

"Wherever there are revolutions, Monseigneur: maybe England, but probably France."

"If you come to France, will you seek me out?"

"I would be happy and proud to do that, Monseigneur."

"Monsieur Mazarini, I hope we shall meet again."

"That is my one desire, Monseigneur."

And the artful Neapolitan bowed to the ground and backed out of the chamber.

"I had heard," the cardinal murmured, "that the rats were leaving the sinking ship; I didn't expect to meet one who might weather the storm." And he added softly: "This young captain will go a long way, especially if he trades his uniform for a cassock."

Then, rising, the cardinal stepped out into the antechamber, where he paced back and forth so thoughtfully that he almost overlooked the arrival of a courier, who gave him a letter from France. "Ah!" said the cardinal, seeing that the courier was covered in dust. "This letter must be urgent."

"Quite urgent, Monseigneur."

Richelieu took the letter and opened it; the letter was brief, but, as we shall see, was of some importance:

> *Fontainebleau, March 17, 1630*
> *The king has left for Lyon, but got no farther than Troyes before he returned to Fontainebleau. Beware: he's in love!*
> *P.S.: If the courier has arrived before the 25th, give him fifty pistoles!*

The cardinal read the letter over several times. He recognized the handwriting as that of Saint-Simon, who wasn't in the habit of conveying false information. But this news seemed so unlikely, he was doubtful.

"No matter," he said to Latil. "Get me the Comte de Moret; this is rather in his line."

"Has Monseigneur forgotten," Latil laughed, "that the Monsieur de Moret is escorting his beautiful hostage to Briançon?"

"Seek him out wherever he is and tell him to come without delay. I'm sending him to Fontainebleau with the news that we've taken Pinerolo!"

Latil bowed and went out.

LXXIII

"Aurora"

As we said in our previous chapters, King Louis XIII, harassed by his mother; fearful of his brother after granting him too much power; aware that Queen Anne, despite her disavowals, continued to meet and conspire with the Spanish ambassador—the king, separated from the cardinal, his political touchstone, had fallen into a melancholy that nothing could allay. What was especially irksome was the understanding, affirmed by the moral sense God gave him, that Richelieu was more essential to the survival of the State than he himself was. And yet everyone around him, with the exception of l'Angely, his fool, and Saint-Simon, whom he'd made grand equerry, either openly opposed this essential man, or conspired secretly against him.

In every society throughout history, there has always been a conservative or conventional party that opposes all new ideas as violations of tradition. This party prefers the known routine to an unknown future: that is to say, progress. The adherents of the status quo, favoring stagnation over movement, death versus life, saw in Richelieu a revolutionary whose efforts to reform society would just cause unrest. And Richelieu was not just the enemy of the conservatives, but of the entire Catholic world. Without him, Europe would have been at peace: Savoy, Spain, Austria, and Rome, all seated at the same table, would take turns plucking the leaves of the artichoke of Italy. Austria would have Mantua and Venice, Savoy would get Montferrat and Genoa, Spain would have Milan, Naples, and Sicily, and Rome would rule Tuscany and the minor duchies—while France, uninvited to the feast, could keep to herself on the other side of the Alps. Who opposed this peace? Richelieu, Richelieu alone. That's what the pope implied; that's what Philip IV and the Emperor proclaimed; that's what the choir of Queens Marie de Médicis, Anne of Austria, and Henriette of England all sang.

Beside these great voices who cried "Anathema!" against the minister were ranged lesser voices, such as that of the Duc de Guise, who'd hoped to lead the armies and had withdrawn, disgruntled, to his governance of Provence; that of Créqui, the Governor of Dauphiné, who thought he had the right to inherit the Sword of the Constable from his stepfather; of Lesdiguières and Montmorency, who at different times had been promised that sword, the latter now afraid it had slipped from his hands since he'd refused to abduct the Duke of Savoy for the cardinal; and all the Great Nobles, such as Soissons, Condé, Conti, and Elbeuf, who hated the cardinal's systematic dismantling of the rights and privileges of the dukes and princes.

Despite all these voices, or rather because of them, Louis was determined to leave Paris and keep the promise he'd made to his minister to join him in Italy. It goes without saying that this resolution, which would place the king under the influence of the cardinal, had been opposed with great outcry by the two queens, who declared that if the king went to Italy, they had no choice but to follow. For this they had the usual excuse, their fear for the king's health.

Despite these objections, the king had sent the cardinal notice of his intent to depart, and in fact had left for Lyon on February 21. His route would take him through Champagne and Burgundy; the two queens and the King's Council were to join him in Lyon.

But events didn't unfold quite so smoothly. The day after the king had left Paris, his brother Gaston, who until then hadn't dared to stray from his city of Orléans, left his post and marched with a great to-do to the capital, entering the city at about nine in the evening.

He went straight to the palace of the queen mother, where she was holding court.

Marie de Médicis rose, astonished, and, feigning anger, dismissed her ladies and shut herself up in her study with Gaston. Queen Anne joined them a few moments later, entering by a secret door.

There they renewed the pact, continually proposed by Queen Marie, that Monsieur would marry Queen Anne in the event of the king's death. This marriage would have been for Marie de Médicis a sort of prolonged regency, and she would gladly forgive God for carrying off her eldest son if that was her compensation. Blinded by her interests, Queen Marie was the only one who'd entered the pact honestly, as she couldn't see beyond her immediate desires.

The Duc d'Orléans had conflicting commitments to the Duc de Lorraine, whose sister he was in love with. He was in no hurry to marry his brother's widow, who was seven years his senior and who'd had, moreover, that deplorable affair with Buckingham. Queen Anne, for her part, hated Monsieur, despised him even more than she hated him, and didn't trust a word he said. Nevertheless, everyone repeated their promises.

No one outside really knew what happened in that chamber, and gossips, unaware of the presence of Queen Anne, spread the rumor the next day that the Duc d'Orléans had come to Paris to tell his mother of his undying love for Princesse Marie de Gonzague, and to take advantage of his brother's absence to marry her. This report seemed confirmed when, immediately after the duke's arrival, Marie de Médicis sent for the young princess and had her detained at the Louvre, where she was kept, to all intents, a prisoner.

For his part, Gaston loudly declared that such was his dearest desire. All the malcontents began to gather around him, insinuating that if, in the king's absence, he would openly declare against Richelieu, he would find himself at the head of a large and powerful party, one that would support him not only against the cardinal, but against

Louis XIII, whose fall might well follow that of his minister. Many chose to believe that Gaston had accepted these proposals. The Cardinal de La Valette, son of the Duc d'Épernon, and the Cardinal of Lyon, that brother of the Duc de Richelieu who led so bravely during the plague, arrived together to call upon the Duc d'Orléans; the latter paid a thousand compliments to Cardinal de La Valette, but the Cardinal of Lyon was left waiting in the hall without a word.

The day after Gaston's arrival in Paris, the queen mother wrote to Louis XIII to inform him of his brother's unexpected return— though it had probably been expected by her. Of course, nothing was said of the meeting and pact between her son and her stepdaughter, but she went on at length about Gaston's love for Marie de Gonzague.

Louis, who was already in Troyes when he received the letter from Marie de Médicis, announced that he would return to Paris; but at Fontainebleau he was met by a letter informing him that Gaston, hearing news of his return, had withdrawn to his estate at Limours.

Three days later came the news that the king, instead of continuing his journey south, would spend Easter at Fontainebleau.

What was behind the king's latest decision? We shall tell you.

The night of the meeting in Luxembourg Palace between the queen mother, Gaston d'Orléans, and Queen Anne, Madame de Fargis returned home from Spain, where she'd gone to support her husband's political efforts, which had appeared shaky. With the war between France and Piedmont seemingly over, her support was no longer needed in Madrid, and Madame de Fargis, to the great satisfaction of Anne of Austria, had been recalled to Paris.

When the queen saw her, she uttered a cry of joy, and as the lady ambassador knelt to kiss her hand, Anne lifted her up and embraced her.

"I see," Madame de Fargis said with a smile, "that my long absence hasn't cost me Your Majesty's good graces."

"On the contrary, dear heart," said the queen, "your absence just made me appreciate your loyalty all the more—and I've never had as much need for it as tonight."

"My arrival is timely, then, and I hope to prove to my sovereign that, far or near, I'll take care of her. But what's happened to make the presence of your humble servant so necessary?"

The queen told her of the king's departure, of Gaston's arrival, and of the pact they'd just renewed.

"So Your Majesty trusts her brother-in-law?" asked Madame de Fargis.

"Not for an instant; this pact is meant to quell my suspicions and keep me waiting off to the side."

"Has the king grown worse?"

"Morally, yes—but physically, no!"

"To the king, morality is all, as you know, Madame."

"What shall I do?" asked the queen. Then, in a lower voice: "You know, my dear, the astrologers claim that the king can't last beyond the next rise of Cancer."

"My lady," said Madame de Fargis, "you recall that I proposed a certain plan to Your Majesty."

The queen blushed. "But you know I could never go through with it," she said.

"That's a shame, because it's the surest method, and I even got the approval of the King of Spain, Philip IV."

"Dear God!"

"Or would you rather trust the word of a man who has never once kept his word?"

The queen was silent for a moment. "But, my dear Fargis," she said, resting her head on her confidante's chest, "even supposing I had the permission of my confessor—oh, just thinking about it makes me ashamed!—surely the plan you proposed should be the last resort, after we've tried everything else?"

"Will you allow me, dear mistress," said Madame de Fargis, taking advantage of the queen's position to drape an arm around her neck and gaze into her face, her eyes sparkling like diamonds, "to relate to you a story of the court of King Henri II, which says something about Queen Catherine de Médicis?"

"Speak, dear heart," said the queen, relaxing with a sigh upon the siren to whose voice she so unwisely listened.

"*Eh bien!* Now, the story goes that Queen Catherine de Médicis arrived in France at the age of fourteen, where she was married to the young King Henri II, and went, like Your Majesty, eleven years without children."

"I've been married for fourteen years!" said the queen.

"Well," Madame de Fargis smiled, "Your Majesty's marriage may have taken place in 1616, but it wasn't consummated until 1619."

"That's so," said the queen. "But what explains Queen Catherine's sterility? King Henri II didn't have the same . . . aversions as King Louis XIII, as proven by his mistress, Diane de Poitiers."

"He had no aversion to women, true—only to his wife."

"Do you think, Fargis, that the king's aversion to me is . . . personal?" the queen gasped.

"What, for Your Majesty? *Ventre-saint-gris*, as the king his father used to say! And as the sweet Comte de Moret still does, to whom Your Majesty should pay more attention. Anyway, don't even think it!"

Then, casting an eye like Sappho on her queen, anxious and piqued by doubt, she said, "And where would he find such eyes as yours, such a mouth, such lovely hair?" She ran her hand along the queen's arched neck. "Where would he find . . . such skin? No, Madame— no, my Queen, you are the loveliest of all, the beauty of beauties. But unfortunately for Queen Catherine, she had none of this. On the contrary, born of a diseased father and mother, she had the cold, slimy skin of a snake."

"Is this true, dear heart?"

"It's true. So when the young king, used to the pale and silky skin of Madame de Brézé, felt at his side a living corpse, he cried that he hadn't been sent a flower from the Pitti Gardens, but a worm from the Médicis tombs."

"Hush, Fargis! You give me a chill."

"So, my beautiful Queen, this revulsion King Henri II had for his wife, who was it helped him to overcome it? One who always had his interest at heart: that same Diane de Poitiers, she who, if the king died childless, would have fallen under the power of another Duc d'Orléans, one not much better than yours."

"Where are you taking this?"

"To here: if the king fell in love with a woman who he knew was devoted to you, a woman with the same religious convictions as the king, why, he would return from seeing her to Your Majesty, and then . . ."

"Well?"

"Well, a child would make the Duc d'Orléans beholden to us, rather than us to him."

"Ah, but my dear Fargis," said the queen, shaking her head, "King Henri II was a *man*."

"As King Louis XIII may yet be. . . ."

The queen replied with a sigh, "But where would you find a woman both pure and devoted?"

"I already have," Fargis said.

"One more beautiful than . . . ?" The queen stopped, biting her lip. She'd almost said, "One more beautiful than me?"

Fargis understood. "More beautiful than you, my Queen? Impossible! But one with beauty of another kind. You are the rose at the peak of its bloom, Madame; she, she is a bud, but with such a glow that her family and friends all call her the Aurora."

"And this marvel," said the queen, "is she at least of noble blood?"

"Of the highest class, Madame: she's the granddaughter of Madame de la Flotte, the queen mother's chief maid of honor, and the daughter of Monsieur de Hautefort."

"And you say this young lady is devoted to me?"

"She would give her life for Your Majesty," and she added, smiling, "maybe more."

"Is she aware of the role we want her to play?"

"Yes."

"And she accepts with resignation?"

"With enthusiasm, Madame—in the interest of the Church! We have her confessor on our side, who compares her to Judith of Bethulia, and the king's doctor. . . ."

"What does Bouvard have to do with it?"

"He will persuade the king your husband that he's sick due to chastity!"

"For a man who purges and bleeds him two hundred times a year, that will be difficult!"

"He'll manage it."

"So it's all arranged?"

"It lacks nothing but your consent."

"But I'd at least like to see and speak to this amazing Aurora!"

"Nothing simpler, Madame—she's here!"

"And she—she'll do it?"

"Yes, Madame."

The queen gave Fargis a look with just a touch of suspicion. "You arranged all this since your arrival tonight?" she said. "Truly, you don't waste any time, dear heart."

"I arrived three days ago, Madame, but I waited to see Your Majesty until everything was ready."

"And now everything is prepared?"

"Yes, Madame. But if Your Majesty prefers to adopt the first means I proposed, we can abandon this one."

"Not at all, not at all," the queen quickly said. "Perhaps you should bring in your young friend."

"Command your faithful servant, Madame."

"Bring her in!"

Madame de Fargis went to a side door and opened it. "Come in, Marie de Hautefort," she said. "Our beloved queen consents to receive your homage."

The young woman gave a cry of joy and rushed into the room.

The queen, seeing her, gasped in admiration and astonishment.

"Do you think her beautiful enough, Madame?" asked Lady Fargis.

"Maybe too beautiful," replied the queen.

LXXIV

The Letter and the Lure

And indeed, Mademoiselle Marie de Hautefort was wonderfully beautiful. She was a blonde of the South, with rose-petal skin and shining hair, and, as Madame de Fargis had said, she was called "Aurora."

It was Vautier who had discovered her on a trip to Périgord, and then come up with the scheme, remembering a look he'd seen the king give Mademoiselle de Lautrec one day. He had the idea that this invalid king, bled white as a ghost, might be susceptible to the infection of love. He'd arranged everything in advance, making sure no parent, lover, or friend would object to the young woman's commitment to the cause, but delayed, on the advice of Queen Marie, until the return of Madame de Fargis, who would coat the rim of the glass with honey before presenting the absinthe to the queen.

We've already seen how eager the queen was to swallow it.

But when she saw the beautiful girl at her feet, arms outstretched and crying "I would give my all, my everything for you, my Queen!"— she saw this delicate bud, heard that sweet voice that couldn't lie, and gently raised her up. That very evening, all was decided. Mademoiselle de Hautefort would do everything she could to make the king love her, and, once she was loved, use all her influence to urge him to reconcile with the queen and to dismiss Cardinal Richelieu.

They just had to set the stage for the enchanting scene that would captivate Louis XIII.

The queens announced that, as the king was at Fontainebleau, they would join him there for Easter. And in fact, they arrived on the eve of Palm Sunday.

The next day, the king attended services in the château chapel, and everyone was summoned to hear mass with His Majesty.

Just a few paces from the king, lit by a ray of sunlight through a stained-glass window that bathed her in a halo of gold and purple, was a young woman kneeling on the bare floor. He, the king, had his knees softly cradled on a gold-tasseled cushion. His chivalric instincts were awakened; he was ashamed to have a cushion under his knees when this beautiful girl had none. He had a page take it to her.

Mademoiselle de Hautefort blushed, considering herself unworthy to place her knees on a cushion where the king had knelt. She stood up, bowed to His Majesty, and respectfully placed the cushion on a chair, all with the innocent and virginal air of one of the noblest daughters of the South.

The king was moved by her grace. He'd been moved thus once before in his life, taken by surprise even more suddenly, which helps to explain the impression Mademoiselle de Hautefort made on this enigmatic man. On a journey to the provinces, he had, in a small town, attended a ball. Toward the end of the performance, one of the dancers, a certain Gau the Courtesan, had stepped gracefully onto a chair and raised a wooden candlestick holding a simple tallow candle. The king, when chaffed about his distaste for women, always recounted this story, saying this young woman had performed this act with such delicacy that he fell in love with her on the spot and, upon leaving the city, had sent her thirty thousand *livres* for her virtue.

Only he didn't say whether he sent her the thirty thousand *livres* because he wanted to defend her virtue, or possess it for himself.

The king was taken no less suddenly by the lovely Marie de Hautefort than he'd been by the virtuous Gau the Courtesan.

Upon returning to the château, he inquired as to who was the ravishing person he'd seen in the chapel, and learned she was the granddaughter of Madame de la Flotte, arrived that day in the household of Queen Marie de Médicis to be one of her maidens.

And that very day, to the astonishment of everyone, and to the great satisfaction of those involved in the matter, he made a complete change in the royal routine. Instead of staying locked in his darkest room, as he'd done for a month in the Louvre, and for the last week at Fontainebleau, he went out and about, in his carriage or walking in the park, as if seeking someone. And in the evening he came to visit the queens—as he hadn't done since the departure of Mademoiselle de Lautrec—to spend the evening chatting with the lovely Marie, and to inquire where she'd be the following day.

The next morning, he sent a letter by courier to Bois-Robert, summoning him to Fontainebleau with all haste.

Bois-Robert was amazed by this mark of favor, which was the sort of thing he expected from Richelieu, but not from the king. His surprise was even greater when Louis led him to a window embrasure, pointed out Mademoiselle de Hautefort, who was walking on the terrace, and told him he wanted a verse written about that particular lovely lady.

Astonished though he was, Bois-Robert didn't have to be asked twice. He praised Mademoiselle de Hautefort's beauty and, learning that she was called Aurora, said he could have sought high and low and found no better name for her dawn-like loveliness. It gave him, moreover, a subject for his verse.

In his poem, Louis XIII, under his sometime title of Apollo—Apollo was the god of the lyre, and Louis XIII, as we know, liked to compose music—begged Dawn not to rise so early and vanish so quickly. Desiring her since the beginning of the world, he pursued her daily in his horse-drawn celestial chariot without ever quite reaching her, always seeing her disappear just as he reached out his hand to touch her.

The king read this verse and approved it, except for one point. "This is fine, Le Bois," he said, "but remove the word 'desiring'."

"Why is that, Majesty?" asked Bois-Robert.

"Because I don't . . . desire."

There was no answer to that. "Desiring" was edited out.

As for the king, he set music to Bois-Robert's words, and words and music were sung by his official musicians, Molinier and Justin, who, given the importance of the matter, wore their most splendid attire.

The two queens, and especially Anne of Austria, applauded the poetry of Bois-Robert and the melody of the king.

Louis XIII performed his Easter rites. His confessor Suffren, who was in on the scheme, soothed His Majesty's conscience, citing the example of the Patriarchs, who were unfaithful to their wives without inviting the wrath of the Lord—but the king assured him that there was no such danger, as his love for Mademoiselle de Hautefort was pure and without sin.

Not so Madame de Fargis and company, who definitely had sin in mind. For a mind like La Fargis's, sin was always the object.

Once Easter was past, the cabal watched Louis XIII with some anxiety, but he made no move to continue his journey south; instead, he ordered hunts and banquets—but at both banquets and hunts, though he devoted himself exclusively to Mademoiselle de Hautefort, his conduct toward her was still perfectly respectful.

There was one gambit yet to try: to make the king jealous.

There existed a certain Monsieur d'Ecquevilly Vassé, of the family of Président Hennequin. Though never finalized, there had been some talk of marriage between him and Mademoiselle de Hautefort. He arrived at Fontainebleau, having been invited by Madame de Fargis with an eye toward making him an object of jealousy. And indeed, Monsieur d'Ecquevilly seemed inclined to revive his old courtship, despite the unusual attentions the king was paying his intended.

Louis XIII took pause and asked Mademoiselle de Hautefort about the matter, who confirmed that the families had discussed a marriage.

And so finally Louis XIII became jealous—and jealous of a woman!

The two queens met with Madame de Fargis to figure out how to exploit this jealousy. And Madame de Fargis came up with a scheme. That evening, Gretchen the dwarf, who could approach without question, would speak to Mademoiselle de Hautefort and awkwardly slip her a perfumed letter, in such a way that the king couldn't help but notice. The king would want to know who'd sent such a letter. The rest was up to the queen and Mademoiselle de Hautefort.

That evening, the usual circle gathered around Her Majesty Queen Anne. The king was sitting near Mademoiselle de Hautefort, cutting out paper dolls. Mademoiselle de Hautefort was carefully dressed, at the personal instruction of the queen. She wore a low-cut dress of white satin, and her dazzling arms and shoulders, whiter even than her dress, drew the lips like a magnet draws iron.

The king, from time to time, passed his eyes over these arms and shoulders, but no more than that.

Fargis stared openly. "Ah, Sire," she whispered to the king, "if I were a man . . ."

Louis XIII frowned.

Anne of Austria, adjusting the hem of her dress, also seemed to be looking at this beautiful image in rose-colored marble.

At that moment, little Gretchen crawled out on all fours from between the king's legs. The king thought it was Grisette, his favorite dog, and moved his feet to let her through. The dwarf shrieked as though the king had stepped on her hand.

His Majesty stood. Gretchen took advantage of the movement to slip the letter, as clumsily as instructed, into Mademoiselle de Hautefort's hand. The king couldn't fail to see it.

Taking part in this farce made the young woman blush, which served the conspirators' purposes perfectly. The king saw the letter pass from the dwarf's hand to Marie's, and from Marie's hand into a pocket.

"The dwarf gave you a letter?" he asked.

"Do you think so, Sire?"

"I know so."

There was a brief silence.

"Who is it from?" asked the king.

"I don't know," said Mademoiselle de Hautefort.

"Then read it, and you'll know."

"Later, Sire!"

"Why later?"

"There's no hurry."

"With me, there is."

"But it seems to me, Sire," said Mademoiselle de Hautefort, "I'm free to receive letters from whomever I like."

"Not so!"

"Why not?"

"Not when . . ."

"Not what?"

"Not when . . . not when . . . I love you!"

"What, you, love me?" said Mademoiselle de Hautefort, laughing.

"Yes!"

"But what will Her Majesty the queen say?"

"Her Majesty the queen says I can't love anyone; this will prove I can."

"Bravo, Sire!" said the queen. "In your place, I'd want to know who's written to this young lady, and what it says."

"But I'm desperate! The king mustn't know," said Mademoiselle de Hautefort. She rose.

"We'll see about that," said the king. And he rose as well.

Mademoiselle de Hautefort backed quickly away. The king made a move to grab her. The door to the queen's boudoir was behind her, and she ran for it. Louis XIII chased her through it, the queen right behind, calling "Watch your pockets, Hautefort!"

The king cornered her and raised his hands, clearly intending to search the girl. But she, knowing the king's prudery, pulled the letter from her pocket and thrust it into her bosom. "Take it from there, Sire," she said.

And with the shamelessness of innocence, she presented her chest to the king. The king hesitated, and dropped his arms.

"Take it, Sire, take it!" cried the queen, laughing aloud, to the great embarrassment of her husband. To remove the young woman's last defense, she grabbed Mademoiselle de Hautefort's hands and pinned them behind her back. "Now, Sire—take it!"

Louis looked around, caught like a sugar cube in silver tongs . . . and then chastely, without touching her skin, drew the letter from its warm sanctuary.

The queen, who hadn't really expected this, released Mademoiselle de Hautefort's hands and murmured to herself, "I may have no choice but to adopt Fargis's proposal."

The letter was from Mademoiselle de Hautefort's mother. The king read it and, ashamed, returned it. Then all three went back into the salon, each with different emotions.

Madame de Fargis was chatting with an officer who'd just arrived from the army, bringing, he said, important news for the king.

"The Comte de Moret!" murmured the queen, recognizing the young man she'd seen only two or three times before, though it was always Madame de Fargis who'd spoken to him. In truth, he was quite handsome.

Then she said, even lower: "He does look a bit like the Duke of Buckingham." Was she just noticing it now, or did she suddenly wish for a reason to find a resemblance between Richelieu's messenger and the former ambassador of the King of England?

HERE ENDS
the manuscript of *The Red Sphinx* ~
the story of the Comte de Moret
and Isabelle de Lautrec continues in
THE DOVE

PART II
The Dove

I

May 5, 1637

Beautiful dove with your silver plumage, your black collar and pink feet, since your prison seems so cruel that you threaten to batter yourself to death on its bars, I give you your freedom.

But, as you doubtless want to leave me to rejoin a person you love more, I must justify your week's absence.

I need payment for the service I render you in setting you free from eternal captivity—for the heart is selfish, and does nothing without asking payment in return, often at double value.

Go then, gentle messenger, go and, by your return, tender these regrets to the person who calls you despite the distance. This note, which I attach to your leg, is the proof of your loyalty.

So goodbye—the window opens, and heaven awaits. . . . Farewell!

II

May 6, 1637

Thank you, whoever you are, for returning my sole companion. But that blessed act must be its own reward. If only the charming messenger who brought me your letter could have known how to thank you, or tell me where you live, for I'd hate you to think me cold and uncaring.

But the same restlessness that took her to your home brought her back to mine. Yesterday Iris was full of the joy of her return to me. However, this morning—how changeable we are!—this morning, I wasn't enough for her. She beat with her wings and her beak, not at the bars of her cage, for she never had a cage, but at the panes of my window. She is no longer mine alone—she belongs to both of us.

Now, my opinion may not be shared by many, but I think that by sharing we double what we have. From now on, our Iris is not single, but double—and notice how prescient I was in naming her Iris, as if I knew she would become our messenger! Your Iris will bring you my letters, and my Iris will bring me yours—because I hope you will kindly reply to tell me how she came into your hands.

It may surprise you that I'm so quick to be familiar with a stranger, an unknown—but I know you must be a good man or woman, since your returned me my dove. Furthermore, the tone of your letter bespeaks a person of distinction and heart; all such noble spirits are sisters, all such refined minds are brothers. So treat me as a brother—or a sister, if you will—because I need to find the brother or sister I never had.

Iris, my dear friend, go back to where you came from, to that person I refer to as him or her—and add that I'd rather be thought of as her than as him.

Go, Iris—and remember that I'm waiting for you.

III

The same day, as the *Angelus* tolls

My sister,

For the delay, blame neither Iris nor myself. I wasn't in my room when your messenger arrived, but I'd left the window open to catch the first breath of the evening breeze. Iris landed on the window sill, and as if the charming little creature understood that she had a letter to deliver and a reply to bear away, she patiently awaited my return, and when I came in, she flew to my shoulder. . . .

Hélas! In my uneven descent from the heights of human eminence, I've experienced along the way both the heights of joy and depths of sorrow. And I've never felt more sad than when I first sent away your dove, whose name I didn't even know, consigning her to some unknown destination—and then, believing her gone forever, I was never happier than when I found her in my room and felt her cool wing caress my cheek as she alighted on my shoulder.

Dear God! For man, the eternal slave of his surroundings, how little it takes to trigger joy and sorrow! The tears of one who has lost a kingdom, who trembled at the wind of the ax as it took the heads of those around him, he cries just the same watching a bird escape into the heavens, and trembles feeling the wind from the wings of a dove! This is one of your great mysteries, dear God! And only you, with your divine mysteries, know if you have a more humble and devout worshiper than this one, who prays at the foot of the cross of your holy Son to bless your glory and greatness!

So I thought upon seeing the dear dove I'd thought I'd lost, even before I read the letter she carried.

Then, having read the letter, I fell into a deep reverie.

What good, I wondered, poor castaway that I am, who have gambled with death and tried to hoodwink the hurricane, *what good is it, lost in the immensity of the ocean, to grasp at this drifting plank, the last remnant of my broken ship of life, when Providence is within reach of my hand? Is that temptation worse than the temptation of hope? Aren't I just catching my coat on the edge of the doorway out of this world, just when I thought I was completely done with the vanities and illusions of earthly life?*

You see, my sister, how much I had to consider: God above my head, the abyss beneath my feet, and around me the world I could no longer see because I'd shut my eyes, no longer hear because I'd stopped my ears—if I listened to the wind, I'd hear the hurricane once more, and carelessly open both eyes and ears.

But maybe, with imagination, I'll see beyond my reality; maybe, if I don't try too hard, I can look beyond the horizon of events.

You asked, my sister, for a simple story. I'll tell you one.

About a week ago I was sitting in the garden, reading. Would you like to know what I was reading, my sister? It was that treasure of love, religion, and poetry called *The Confessions of Saint Augustine*. As I read it, my thoughts merged with those of that blessed bishop, who had a saint for a mother before he was a saint himself.

Suddenly I heard a fluttering over my head and, looking up, saw a plummeting dove, pursued by a hawk who already had some of its prey's feathers in its beak.

God, who in his majesty regards the fall of a sparrow the same as the crash of an empire, God had told this poor bird, in mortal menace from the hawk, to seek succor with me.

In any event, I took hold of the poor thing, trembling and bloodstained, and clutched it to my chest, where it nestled, eyes closed, heart hammering. And I, seeing the hawk watching from the top of a poplar, took it inside to my cell.

For five or six days, the hawk didn't leave its observation post for a moment, and day and night I saw him sitting motionless on his dry branch, watching for his prey.

The dove, for its part, doubtless sensed the hawk's presence, for that entire time she sat, sad but resigned, on my windowsill.

Finally, the day before yesterday, the hawk disappeared, and the instinct of the prisoner must have told her that her enemy was gone, because almost immediately she began beating herself against the window pane, so roughly that I feared she'd break it.

Suddenly I was no longer a protector, but a jailer; my room no longer a refuge, but a prison. For a whole day I tried to reconcile her with me, for a whole day I held her while she struggled. Yesterday I finally gave in to pity; I wrote the brief letter you received, and then, with tears in my eyes, opened the window through which I expected her to disappear forever.

Since then, I often thought about that hawk sitting still and watchful on the highest branch of the tree—and in it I saw a symbol of the enemy of mankind, always there though we see him not, watching for his prey, *quærens quem devoret*, so he can devour it.

And now, since at your desire I've related how your dove came to me, and then brought you my letter, I have a request: tell me, my sister, how Iris came to leave you, as I've told you how she came to me.

Tomorrow, at the first light of dawn, I'll open my window, and your messenger will ride that light back to you, carrying my answer.

Meanwhile, may the cherubim we call dreams flit quietly 'round your bed, cooling your brow with the waft of their wings!

IV

May 10, after *Matins*

I waited three days before responding, as you can see by my letter's date. Your letter gave me pause: I had hoped to be calling you sister, but I must either call you brother or renounce writing you altogether.

You fear, you say, that you're catching your coat on the edge of the doorway out of this world. So you pass through this world in solitude?

You also say you descended from the heights of human eminence. Were you thus at the apex of society, so that your fall should take you so far?

You lost a kingdom, and passed under the ax that took the heads of those around you. So you lived among the great? You took part in the struggles of princes?

How am I to believe that, with all you've been through, you are yet young—and humble, too, claiming to speak from your knees?

On the other hand, what point would there be in deceiving me? You don't know me—don't know if I'm a noble or peasant, young or old, ugly or pretty.

Besides, it hardly matters whether I know who you are or you know who I am. We are two forlorn creatures, apart from one another, unknown to each other, and powerless to physically meet.

But, aside from physical meeting, there is the meeting of minds; beyond touch and sight of the body, there is the brotherhood of souls, that mysterious agape in which we drink the Lord's words from the same cup, and bathe in the same glowing aura of the Holy Spirit.

That's all I want from you. That's all you want from me.

That said, if we find sympathy between our minds, affinity between our souls, what harm can there be in the eyes of God if our minds and souls communicate through space, like the light of two friendly stars crossing the lonely ether of the firmament?

Now, this is how poor Iris left my room:

The evening before you saved her life, I was kneeling in prayer, my lamp placed near the curtains of my bed. Around midnight, while praying, I fell asleep. Perhaps ten minutes later, my door, left ajar, was pushed open by the breeze; the wind ruffled my curtains, the lamp flared, and the curtains caught fire. In an instant, my small room was filled with flame. I awoke already half-suffocated. My poor dove fluttered against the ceiling, struggling amid the smoke. I ran to the window and opened it. It was scarcely open before she rushed through it, and I heard her dart into the branches of her favorite tree, in which she always spends part of the day.

Hoping she would return at daybreak, I left my window open—but the day came and went, and she never came back. Terrified by the fire, she had probably taken to her wings. That day was doubtless the one she was pursued by the hawk and came to you for aid. You gathered her in and guarded her, and then long after I'd believed her lost, I heard her beating her wings against the panes. I opened the window and admitted the runaway, who, though she carried her own excuse, was already forgiven in advance.

That's the story of poor Iris. Was that all you wanted to know, or did you have anything more to ask? If not, our messenger will return without a letter. I'll know what that means, and if that's the case, I'll just say now: *Farewell, my brother. May the Lord be with you!*

May 11, at daybreak

Iris returned, without a letter. The poor little thing seemed sad to lose the office of messenger; she raised her empty leg and looked at me, as if to ask what it meant.

It means, dear Iris, that you are mine alone; that today the sky will be dark, for the brother was no kin, and the friend was indifferent.

And this, little one, I write for myself. This grievance from a soul who laments her isolation. And I say, I suffer; and I say, I weep; and I say, I am unhappy.

Alas! Your justice, my God, is sometimes unfair, the blows you intend for the guilty are diverted, perhaps by some evil, invisible spirit, to fall on the innocent. The pains of this life prepare us for the happiness of the next, we are told, but why should pain strike one who did nothing worse than make a mistake—that's no crime for which to atone! Didn't Jesus forgive the Magdalene? Didn't Christ bless the adulterous woman? Why this discipline for me, my God?

I have loved, it's true; but I responded with love to love from another. I was born for the life of the world, not the life of the cloister. I followed the law of love imposed by you on all creatures, persons, and plants. All must love in this world, all seek to join and merge into a single life, brooks into streams, streams into rivers,

rivers into the ocean. The stars that, at night, rise from one horizon and cross the sky to the other, are swallowed in the glowing aura of a greater star rising; our souls themselves, these emanations of your divine breath, seek other souls here on earth for companions to love, and when our souls leave our bodies, they seek again to merge with you, who are the soul universal and the love endless.

Well, my God, for a moment I rejoiced in the hope, toward the end of my horizon, that I'd found not just another soul, but a sister in suffering; in those first laments, I thought I heard the words of a suffering heart. Why, poor suffering soul, do you not wish to share in my pain, as I share in yours? It's a law that shared burdens are lighter, and a weight that would crush two who are alone could be borne by two united.

I hear the bell toll; you call me, my God, and I come to you! I go to you in confidence of my purity of heart, a heart open for you to read. If I have, by any act or omission, offended you, my God, please let me know by sign, vision, or revelation, and I will prostrate myself at your altar, forehead in the dust and hands outstretched until you have forgiven me.

You, dear dove, be the faithful guardian of these feelings of my weak heart, these thoughts of my poor soul! Fold your wings over this paper that I fold to hide it from all eyes, as I await the next and final half-cup of bitterness.

V

May 11, at noon

Indeed, you guessed right, my poor suffering soul; I'd resolved not to write to you, because what good, when lying in the grave, comes of raising one's hands from the tomb, if not to raise them to God? But a sort of miracle has changed my resolution.

That letter you wrote to yourself, that letter in which you poured out your soul at God's feet, that letter, intimate memento of your mind, half-full of the bitterness that was to fill to overflowing with your tears—that letter, the dove, disloyal to you for once, brought to me, not tied to its leg, but in its beak, like the dove of the Ark with the green twig that showed the flood ebbing from the surface of the world, just as tears dry on the face of a forgiven sinner.

Be it so! I accept the task you assign me to bear part of your pain, because I see I belong not just to myself, so long as, with the strength God has left to me, I can make of myself a lever to lift others in their misfortune.

My soul, from this moment, is empty of its own misfortunes; pour in yours, as a stream seeks a river, as a lonely meteor seeks a star.

You ask why you suffer, having done nothing wrong. Take care! When you question God, you draw near to blasphemy, a short step to a long fall.

Down here, pride is our greatest enemy. It's said that a recent philosopher has redefined all of nature as a series of whirlpools. In this philosopher's view, every fixed star is a sun, surrounded by worlds like ours, and all these worlds, subject to the laws of gravity, revolve through space, each around its center of weight, without collision or confusion.

Quite a system, isn't it? God grows to infinite greatness, but man shrinks to nothing.

So can our own world be divided into millions of worlds. Our pride makes each of us believe himself a sun around which all revolves, when we are at most a mere atom, one grain of dust that the Lord's breath moves among the stars, greater and lesser, and those called kings, emperors, princes, are champions of earthly power whom God has given, as a sign of their power, a scepter or a crosier, a tiara or a sword.

Well, who told you that immaterial things matter less than the material? Who told you the woes of this world don't contribute to the happiness of the next? Who told you that, by the moral laws of nature, one-half the heart should not weep while the other half knows joy, just as one-half the Earth is in darkness when the other half is in light?

Tell me your troubles, poor suffering soul—because, whatever your misfortunes, they can't compare, I think, to mine. Tell me, and I'll have, I hope, a consolation for each of your complaints, a balm for each of your injuries.

But on your side, I beg you, drink from my stream of words without seeking the fountain from which they flow, drink as the black Ethiopians and pale children of Egypt drink from the Nile, while they think it sacrilege to try to follow the river to its source.

Based on a few of my stray words, you thought to read into my past life, to see me as one of the lofty of this world who has plunged from the heights, thrown down from heaven to earth like a fallen angel.

Do not deceive yourself: I'm just a humble monk with a humble name. My past, dark or bright, modest or proud, is lost to my memory, and, unlike the ancient philosopher who remembered the siege of Troy from another life, in my death I remember no yesterday, and tomorrow I'll know not today.

This is how I wish to walk into eternity, erasing every vestige I leave behind me, to arrive before my Lord as I came out of my mother's womb: *solus, pauper et nudus*; poor, naked, and alone.

Farewell, my sister; I will give you everything I can, but do not ask for more than I can give you.

VI

May 12

Yes, you've understood everything. Yes, I was prostrate at God's feet, asking him to account for my suffering, rather than asking forgiveness for my doubts. Yes, by a kind of miracle, God has restored this consolation I thought I'd lost, and our messenger, through disloyal devotion, carried you what had spilled from my mind—or rather, my heart—onto the paper.

If you wish to remain unknown, then do so! What matter if the sun is hidden by clouds, or a fire is veiled by smoke, if the sun still shines its light, and the flames still warm? God is also invisible and unknown, but we still feel God's hand extend over the world.

I will not tell you I'm a modest and humble woman. I was a noble, I was rich, I was happy—I'm none of those now. I loved a man with all my heart, a man who loved me with all his soul; that man is dead. The cold hand of sorrow has stripped me of my worldly finery; now I wear religious robes, the habit of limbo, the funeral attire of those who no longer live but are not yet dead.

So these are my injuries. I entered a convent to forget the one who died and remember only God; though sometimes I forget God and remember only he who is dead.

That's why I complain, and lament, and cry to the Lord, "God, have mercy on me!"

Oh, tell me what you've done to empty your soul of the pain that once filled it! Have you put pressure on it, as one pinches a wound? I do all right while I'm praying—yet afterward, I find my soul filled again with worldly love, as if the liquor of bitterness had been drained, only to be refilled by ardent spirits from a lake of fire. How do you do it?

Your answer will be quite simple, and I know it in advance: "I have never loved."

But if you have never loved, what right have you to boast that you've suffered?

What will we have to say if you say to me "I have never loved"?

This: though first I asked for your help and consolation, and then had to accept your distance and silence, I had really just passed you by as one passes a marble statue a sculptor has given human form, but in whose chest no heart has ever beat.

If you've never loved, then this time I'm the one to say to you: do not reply, we're not of the same world, we haven't lived the same life. I was fooled by appearances; what reason is there to exchange useless words? You won't understand what I say; I won't understand what you say. For we don't speak the same language.

Oh, but if you have loved! If you have, tell me where, tell me who, tell me how—or, if you don't want to tell me any of that, talk to me about something else, whatever you like. Anything. Tell me about your room, if it faces the east or west, the south or north; if you greet the sun when it appears, if you say goodbye to him as he leaves, or if, eyes dazzled by the blazing southern rays of afternoon, you try to distinguish the face of God in that shimmering radiance.

Tell me all this, then tell me more: what you see from your window, plains or mountains, peaks or valleys, streams or rivers, lake or ocean. Tell me all, and it will distract my thoughts from the troubles that plague my mind—and then perhaps my heart, distracted by my thoughts, will manage to forget, if only for a moment. . . .

No, no, no, tell me nothing. I will never forget!

VII

May 13

The one you loved is dead: that's why you still have tears. The one I love betrayed me. That's why I have none!

Tell me about your love all you want, but don't ask me to speak of mine.

For four years I've lived in a monastery—and yet I'm not a monk!

Why, you may ask, is that?

I'll tell you.

When my love, which was my last link to life, failed me, I fell into such despair that I gave myself to God—not from virtue, but from pain.

I've waited for this despair to subside so the Lord wouldn't have to receive me as the abyss receives the blind, but as a generous host receives a weary pilgrim who, after toilsome travels, seeks a night's rest at the end of a long day.

I wanted to bring him a strong spirit, not a broken heart, a whole body and not a cadaver.

But now, four years after seeking such solitude, though daily purifying myself with prayer, I've not yet dared to trade the habit of a novice for the robes of a monk. My former self still lives in me, and it would be sacrilege to offer so worldly a creature to our heavenly Creator.

Now you know as much of my past and private life as I can tell you. As to my present life and situation, here is what I can say:

I live, not really in a monastery, but rather in a hermitage built halfway up a hill, in a room with whitewashed walls, lacking all ornament but the portrait of a king for whom I have a special reverence, and an ivory crucifix, a masterpiece of the sixteenth century, which was given to me by my mother.

My window is surrounded by a luxuriant jasmine whose branches are laden with flowers; they scent my room as they open with the rising sun, on the horizon which is probably toward where you are: for from there I see our dove approaching from afar, and when she leaves I see her start in the same direction and fly for a mile or so until, dwindling, she merges into the azure sky or gray clouds.

Given the lay of the land, dawn has a particular charm for me. It's a view I adore and will try to describe.

My horizon is bounded to the south by the high Pyrenees, with their purple slopes and snowy peaks; to the east by a hilly ridge that rises toward the main range; while to the north there stretches as far as the eye can see a country of plains, dotted with olive orchards, lined with small streams among which, like a sovereign receiving the tribute of its subjects, one of the greatest rivers of France majestically winds.

The plateau beneath me slopes down from south to north, from the mountains to the plains.

It has three very different aspects: in the morning, noon, and evening.

In the morning, the sun rises behind the ridge of hills to the east. Ten minutes before it appears, I see a ray of rosy light stream slowly up until it fans across the sky, darkening the hills to black silhouettes. Through this fan spike the spearheads of early sunlight, all the colors from brightest pink to fiery yellow. As the sun rises behind the hills, it begins to gild their contours with its rays, the highest hill all aglow until, like a moving fire, ever expanding, the day star itself appears, splendid, gleaming, streaming flames, as if from the crater of some inextinguishable divine volcano. As it rises into the heavens, the life of the earth below is reborn; the tops of the Pyrenees shimmer white and silver; their dark sides slowly lighten from black to purple, and from purple to light blue. As light floods down from over the ridge, day spreads across the plain. The streams glisten like silver strands, the river twists and undulates like a shining ribbon; the birds sing in the oleander bushes, among the pomegranates, in the clumps of myrtle, and an eagle, the king of the sky, soars through the ether, banking around a circuit of a league or more, disappearing and reappearing.

At noon, the entire basin I just described becomes a fiery furnace. Lit from top to bottom, the mountains cannot conceal their naked flanks, stony limbs that extend into the granite bones of the earth. Broken sunlight rebounds from shiny rock surfaces, streams and rivers seem torrents of molten metal, the flowers fade, the leaves bow down, the birds grow silent; invisible cicadas sing from the branches of creaking pine trees, and the only living movement that animates this baking desert is a green lizard that sometimes climbs my window trellis, or a mottled snake that, coiled in a spiral, pants with its mouth half open, ignoring the midges that pass within range of its fangs.

In the evening, life is reborn for a while, like the last flare of a lamp before it goes out. One after another, the cicadas fall silent, their buzzing succeeded by the plaintive but monotonous cries of the crickets. The lizards flee, the snakes disappear, the bushes are agitated by the anxious fluttering of birds seeking lodging for the night. The sun goes down toward the horizon behind me, and as it descends, I see the Pyrenean snows change from soft pink to purple, while the shadows elongate across the plains, filling the spaces between them until, according to natural law, the whole world belongs to darkness. Then all noise ceases, the earthly glow is extinguished, the stars emerge silently from the sky—and in the middle of the night's silence, a single melody unfolds into space: the song of the nightingale, star-lover, dark-singer.

You asked me what I could see from my window, and I've told you. Fix this triple vision in your mind, and allow your mind to distract your heart, for your salvation in this world is in nothing but this word:

Forget!

VIII

May 13

Forget! You tell me to forget!

Listen to what is happening to me. You must understand: when darkness comes, it brings with it something frightening, something incredible and unnatural. When I sleep, death is no longer death, and the dead return to life! He is next to me, with his long dark hair, his pale face, his manly features imbued with all the nobility of his heritage. He is there—I speak to him—I extend my hand, I cry out "Are you still alive? And do you still love me?"

And he replies that yes, he still lives, and yes, he still loves me. This same vision, undeniable, unrelenting, almost palpable, is repeated every night, only to disappear with the first light of dawn.

My God, what must I do to get this nightmare, this vision from the angel of darkness, to stop tormenting me?

I've prayed at the sacred altar, wrapped holy rosaries around my neck and wrists, laid a crucifix on my chest and fallen asleep with my hands crossed on the feet of the divine martyr—but all was vain, futile, useless; the day brings me back to God, but the darkness returns me to him. I'm like the queen described by the poet Homer, whose work every day was undone every night.

If there were no night, there would be no sleep, and if no sleep, then no dreams—and then maybe I could forget.

Can you get God to grant me that?

IX

May 14

All that can be obtained from God through prayer, I'll obtain for you; for you are sorely wounded, and the wound is grievous and deep.

Let us pray.

X

May 15

I don't know, but somehow, through writing to you, I gain some peace and a certain relief.

This is indeed a new turn to my life; I was alone in the world, without family, isolated from all, half in the grave, weeping and desperate—and now suddenly I've found a brother.

Because it seems to me you're like a brother . . . a brother I never knew, one who left France before I was born, but whom I've been waiting and searching for. And now, you come at last: revealed, though not present, revealed by voice alone. I cannot see you, but I hear you. I cannot touch, but I listen.

You have no idea how the landscape so brilliantly conjured by your pen occupies my thoughts. Let no one deny to me the reality of shared vision, for shared vision exists. By the constant force of my will, your landscape is now reflected in my mind as in a mirror. I see everything, from the rosy morning rays rising behind the hills to the creeping gray shadows of evening; I hear everything, from the sound of the flower as it opens its petals to the morning dew, to the song of the nightingale trilling out into the solitude and silence of the night.

And I see it all so clearly that, if I ever found myself within the circle of your vision, I could say, "There are the flaming hills, there the snow-capped mountains, there the silver streams, there the gleaming river, here the pomegranates, here the oleander, here the myrtle—all here!"

So clearly do I see your hermitage rising above the walls of the garden, with its window veiled by jasmine and vines. Then I see you in your whitewashed cell, kneeling in front of our brother Christ, praying for yourself and, especially, for me.

Tell me who is the king whose portrait hangs in your cell, this king for whom you have a special reverence, so I, too, can envision this king's portrait, and my reverence can echo yours.

But you, as well, I would like to see you . . . oh, only in my thoughts, rest assured of that!

You said that the *you* of the past no longer existed, and I should ask only about the person of the present and the future. Let the past fade, then—tell me how old you are now, and those traits that will help me imagine you clearly. Tell me how and when you came to this hermitage, and what accounts for your bidding farewell to the world.

I would also like to know how far you are from me. Is it possible to calculate that distance?

You seem so good, I have no fear of tiring you; you seem so learned, I'm not afraid to ask the impossible.

I shall think about how you might answer; and when you do, I shall think about how you replied.

Go, dear dove—fly, and come back soon!

XI

May 15, 3 o'clock in the afternoon

There, you see: by occupying your mind, I was able, for a moment, to distract your heart.

The soul is not like the body; if one who is soul-sick can forget why he suffers, he suffers no more.

You want me to tell you about me, to see if you can find something to like in this man, physical or moral, alive or dead? Well, listen.

I was born at Fontainebleau on May 1, 1607, so my age is thirty years and fourteen days.

I'm sturdy of frame, brown-haired, blue-eyed, with a pale complexion and high forehead.

I retired from the world on January 17, 1633, when I took a vow that, unless something occurred to change my destiny, I would devote myself to God for the next five years—which would be my last.

I withdrew from the world in the aftermath of a great political disaster that swallowed up my dearest friends—and after a deep personal injury that broke my heart.

The portrait of the king that hangs in my cell, for whom I have a special reverence, is of King Henri IV.

Now, you wanted to know the distance between us. It's now just short of three o'clock. I'll date this letter at three o'clock exactly, the time I shall release our messenger. Pigeons fly at fifteen or sixteen miles per hour, as I learned when I was in a circumstance to employ them. Note the time you receive this letter, and calculate.

Don't reply for two or three days; take those days to imagine me, poor recluse, and then put your ideas, whether illusion or reality, on paper. Then send me a summary of your research, the distillation of your dreams.

God be with you!

XII

May 15, two hours after receiving your letter

Listen! Hear me! It's not in two or three days I must answer you, but now!

My God! What mad idea grips my mind, my heart, my soul! What if . . . the one I love is not dead! What if *you* are the one I love, the one I call, the one I seek, the one who appears to me every night!

You were born on May 1, 1607—so was he! You're strong—like him! You are brown-haired, blue-eyed, with a pale complexion and high forehead—like him!

Then remember the words you told me in another letter, which remain alive in my memory: you fell from the heights of human eminence, you trembled at the wind of the ax as it took the heads of those around you, and in your fall you lost a kingdom.

I don't know how all these things can apply to you, but if they do—my God! My God! It must really be you.

You have in your cell a portrait of a king whom you love and revere, a portrait of King Henri IV. And he, he, he was the *son* of King Henri IV!

If you are not Antoine de Bourbon, Comte de Moret, said to have been killed at the Battle of Castelnaudary, then *who are you*?

Answer me! In the name of heaven, answer me!

XIII

May 16, at daybreak

If you are not Isabelle de Lautrec, whom I believed unfaithful, then who are you?

I am Antoine de Bourbon, Comte de Moret, whom all think died at the Battle of Castelnaudary—but who lives, not by the mercy, but by the vengeance of the Lord.

Oh! If things are as I fear they are, then woe to us both!

The dove must have gotten lost in the night, or perhaps she got tired and was forced to rest. She didn't arrive until the first light of dawn.

XIV

May 16th, seven in the morning

Yes, yes, yes, O sufferer! Yes, I'm Isabelle de Lautrec!

You believed me unfaithful? Me? How? Why? For what reason? To defend myself, I must know.

Did you know the dove takes only two hours to go from you to me or me to you? Did you know there must be only thirty miles between us?

Tell me, tell me, how have I deceived you? How have I betrayed you? Speak, speak!

Fly, dove: you carry my life!

XV

May 16, eleven o'clock

The eyes, the heart, the soul—can all be deceived at once?

Are you or are you not the Isabelle de Lautrec I saw enter Valence Cathedral on January 5, 1633?

Are you not she who was dressed as a bride, and who walked behind Emmanuel, Vicomte de Pontis, dressed as a groom?

Or was it all an illusion of the Archfiend?

No quibbles, no hesitation, no half-answers.

Proof, or silence.

XVI

May 16, 3 o'clock in the afternoon

Proof? You shall have it! It's easy enough to provide.

Everything you saw had the appearance of truth, yet everything you saw was false.

But I have a long story to tell you, and alas! Our poor dove is exhausted and needs rest. Instead of the usual two hours, it took her nearly four hours to fly back to me.

I'll write part of the story tonight.

Dear Lord God, give me some peace—my hand trembles so, I can barely hold the pen.

But first, my God, I must give thanks to you for letting him see.

. . . There. I spent three hours on my knees, praying, pressing my burning forehead against the chilly flagstones, and now I'm calmer.

To return to you.

Let me tell you all, tell you everything, from the moment I left you in Valence, to that woeful moment when I pronounced my vows.

The night you left, do you remember it as well as I do? It was August 14, 1632, when we parted; you said goodbye to me without telling me where you were going.

I was full of foreboding; I couldn't let go of the edge of your cloak. It seemed to me it wasn't to be a parting for a few days, as you'd promised, but a parting forever.

Eleven o'clock was tolling from the church in the town; wearing a dark cloak, you mounted a white horse; you rode slowly at first, and three times you turned back to say goodbye. The third time, you made me go inside, because you said if I stayed in the doorway, you might never leave.

Why didn't I stay? Why did you go?

I went in, but only to run up to my balcony. You looked back, and saw me waving a handkerchief wet with my tears. You lifted your hat, plumes fluttering, and I heard your farewell waft on the wind, diminished by distance to no more than a sigh.

A great cloud drifted across the sky and obscured the Moon; I raised my hands as if to stop it before it could cut off the silver radiance by which I could still see you. Finally, like a dark aerial monster, it opened its mouth and swallowed the pale goddess, who disappeared within it. When I lowered my eyes to the horizon, I sought for you in vain. I could still hear the sound of hooves ringing on the road in the direction of Orange, but I could see you no more.

Suddenly a flash tore open the cloud, and by the lightning's gleam I glimpsed your white horse. But you, in your dark cloak, had already merged with the night. Your mount rode away quickly, but seemingly without a rider. Twice more the lightning flashed to reveal your horse, fading like a ghost. Then even the sound of the hooves was lost. A fourth flash came with a roar of thunder, but the horse was gone.

All that night, the thunder growled, while the wind and rain beat against my windows. The next day, nature, distraught, disheveled, and drained, seemed to grieve like my heart.

I knew what was happening in the direction toward which you'd disappeared—that is to say, in Languedoc. It was said your friend the Duc de Montmorency, who was governor there, had joined the party of Monsieur and the exiled queen mother. Prince Gaston had crossed France to meet the Duc de Montmorency, raise the province in revolt and muster troops to march against the king and Monsieur de Richelieu.

So you went, to join one of your brothers to fight against the other—and far more dangerous, to draw your sword and risk your head against terrible Cardinal Richelieu, who had already broken so many swords and taken so many heads!

As you know, my father was in Paris with the king. So I followed you south with two of my ladies under the pretext of a visit to my aunt, who was Abbess of Saint-Pons—but really to get closer to the theater of events in which you were to play a role.

It took me eight days to travel from Valence to Saint-Pons. I arrived at the convent on August 23. The holy women there were unused to affairs of the world, but the events occurring nearby were so grave, they were the subject of all conversations, and every inhabitant of the convent was discussing the news.

And what had they heard? They said the king's brother, Monseigneur Gaston d'Orléans, had met up with the Maréchal-Duc de Montmorency, bringing two thousand men he'd raised in the Principality of Trier; and these, added to the four thousand already with Montmorency, brought their total troops to six thousand.

With these six thousand soldiers, he held Lodève, Albi, Uzès, Lunel, and Saint-Pons, where I was. Nîmes, Toulouse, Carcassonne, and Beziers, though populated by Protestants, had refused to join him.

It was also said that two armies were on the march against the Duc de Montmorency. One of them, commanded by Marshal Schomberg, was coming by way of Pont-Saint-Esprit. The other, led by the king, as the cardinal had decided Louis XIII himself was needed in the theater of war, was said to have arrived at Lyon. A letter that caught up to me from Valence not only confirmed this news, but informed me that my father, the Baron de Lautrec, was with His Majesty.

This letter came from my father, and also announced that he and his old friend the Comte de Pontis had decided to strengthen the ties between our two houses by a marriage between me and the count's son, the Vicomte de Pontis. As you'll remember, I'd already spoken to you of this proposed marriage, and you'd said to me, "Just give me three months. In three months, things will be different for everyone. Give me three more months, and I'll ask the Baron de Lautrec for your hand."

Imagine my torment at knowing you were allied with those my father called rebels, as fear and hatred grew between your house and that of my father, a loyal and faithful servant of the king. In his mind the king and the cardinal were one, and almost daily he announced, "He who is enemy to the cardinal, is enemy to the king."

On August 23, a royal decree declared the Duc de Montmorency attainted, forfeiting all honors and dignities, property and domains, and ordering him to appear before the Parliament of Toulouse for trial.

The next day, the rumor spread of a similar declaration against you, son of a king though you were, and against Monsieur de Rieux.

Imagine the feelings these rumors inflicted on my poor heart!

On the 24th, an emissary of the cardinal passed through Saint-Pons, going, they said, to offer peace terms to Monsieur de Montmorency. I persuaded my aunt to offer him refreshments, and he accepted, stopping in her parlor. I spoke with him there, and what they said of his mission was true. It gave me hope.

My hope increased when I heard that the Archbishop of Narbonne, a close friend of Monsieur de Montmorency, had passed through Carcassonne for the same purpose, to ask the marshal-duke to lay down his arms. The proposals he was carrying to the Governor of Languedoc were, they said, fair, reasonable, and conducive to his fortune and honor.

The rumor soon followed that Montmorency had refused.

As to you—because, you understand, you were the subject of much talk, which was a cause of both consolation and dread for me—as to you, it was said that a letter had been written to you by the cardinal himself, but you had replied that your word had long been promised to Monsieur, and that Monsieur alone could release you.

And alas! That selfish coward refused to let you go.

On August 29, word came that the armies of Marshal Schomberg and the Duc de Montmorency were face to face. But the wily old marshal knew that Richelieu was a minister who could fall, and the king was a man who could die—and that Monsieur, against whom he was pitted, was heir to the throne, and would then become King of France. So he sent Monsieur de Cavoie to parley and open one last negotiation.

We heard all the reports. My soul rose at each bit of hopeful news. I anxiously awaited Monsieur de Montmorency's final answer.

You know his response. Whether from despair or conceit, fear or courage, he said, "First we'll fight; after the battle, we'll talk."

Thereafter, since all hope of accord was lost, and a victory by the Duc de Montmorency was your only salvation, I forgot my duty as a daughter, I forgot my duty as a subject, and, prostrate at the altar, I prayed to God Almighty to look with favor on the hero of Vellano and the son of the victor of Ivry.

From that moment, I lived only to wait upon news of the battle.

Alas! On September 1, at five in the evening, came the terrible, fatal, heartbreaking news.

The battle was lost. The marshal-duke was a prisoner, and you were either mortally wounded or . . . dead!

I didn't wait to hear any more. I went to fetch the gardener, whom I'd spoken to in advance. I told him to prepare two horses and meet me at nightfall at the garden gate.

The night came, I met him, and we mounted and rode for the battlefield. We skirted the base of the mountains, crossed two or three streams, passed on the left the little village of Livinière, and reached Caunes at eight o'clock, where we stopped.

My horse was lamed and limping; I determined to trade him for a fresh horse and discover what news I could. They said Montmorency and de Rieux were both dead. As to you, reports were conflicting: some said you were dead, others mortally wounded.

If you were dying, I wanted to close your eyes; if dead, I wanted to wrap you in your shroud.

We left Caunes at half past eight, crossing the fields and avoiding the roads; the gardener was from Saissac—he knew the country, and took us straight to Montolieu.

The weather resembled that of the night we parted: dark clouds rolled across heaven, gusts roared through the trees, and a warm, suffocating wet wind spat large drops of rain, while thunder rumbled behind Castelnaudary.

We rode straight through Montolieu without stopping. Beyond that small town, we met the first outpost of Monsieur de Schomberg's troops.

I repeated my questions. The battle had begun around eleven in the morning and lasted an hour or less; barely a hundred people had been killed.

I asked if you were among the dead. They weren't sure, but had heard a soldier of the vanguard say he'd seen you fall. We found him; he had indeed seen one of the leaders go down, but wasn't sure it was you. I wanted to take him with me, but he was on duty and couldn't come. But he told the gardener it was definitely the Comte de Moret who'd led the charge, and if he'd been killed, it was by an officer of fusiliers named Bitéran.

As I listened to these details, a chill came over me, my chest froze so I couldn't speak, and beads of sweat rolled down my face to mingle with my tears.

We resumed our journey. We'd come twelve or thirteen leagues in five hours, but as I'd changed horses in Caunes, I knew I could make it to Castelnaudary. If the gardener fell behind, he promised to keep up by linking his reins with mine.

Leaving Montolieu, we passed patrols in the woods. We recognized our location, and found our way to a ford over the Bernassonne. After crossing two more streams, we were well on our way again.

Between Ferrals and Villespy, the gardener's horse fell and couldn't get up again, but fortunately we were almost there: we could see the bivouacs of the royal army, and saw lights moving about the field where the battle had taken place.

My companion told me the lights were probably those of soldiers out to bury the dead. I asked him to make one last effort to follow me; I dug my spurs into my horse, itself ready to fall, and rode past the first campfire.

I was just passing the village of Saint-Papoul on my right when my horse reared. I bent down to see a shapeless mass: a dead soldier. I had found the first corpse.

I jumped from my horse and left it to its own devices. We had arrived. The gardener ran toward the nearest group of torches. I sat on a grassy hillock and waited.

The sky was still strewn with dark clouds, and thunder continued to rumble in the west, the occasional flash lighting the battlefield.

The gardener returned, carrying a torch and followed by some soldiers. He had found them digging a large pit, and looked to check for bodies, but none had yet been thrown in.

Finally, I began to get some positive news. Monsieur de Montmorency, though wounded twelve times over, was not yet dead, but he was definitely a prisoner; he had been captured and then carried to a farm a quarter of a mile from the battlefield, where he'd made his confession to Monsieur de Schomberg's chaplain. Then his wounds had been dressed by the surgeon of the light horse, and he'd been brought to Castelnaudary on a litter.

Monsieur de Rieux had been killed, and his body positively identified.

As for you, you'd been seen falling from your horse, but after that no one could say what had become of you. I asked where you'd been seen to fall, and was told it was at the ambuscade.

The soldiers wanted to know who I was. "Look at me," I said to them, "and guess." Sobs choked my voice, and tears streamed down my face.

"Poor woman," one of them said, "she loves him!"

I seized the man's hand—I could have kissed him. "Come with me," I said, "and help me find him, dead or alive."

"We'll help you," said two or three soldiers. "Follow us," one of them said. The one I'd chosen to be our guide took the torch and lit the way. I came after.

One of them offered to let me lean on him. "Thank you," I said, "but I'm strong enough."

In fact, I felt no fatigue, and it seemed to me I could go to the end of the world if I had to.

We walked three hundred paces. Every ten steps there was a body, and I wanted to check to see if it was you, but the soldiers drew me forward, saying "It wasn't here, Madame."

Finally we came to a little ravine beneath some olive trees, where a path ran along a stream. "Here," the soldiers said.

I passed my hand over my forehead and staggered, feeling faint for a moment. Then we began the search, starting down from the crest. I took the torch from the guide and bent low to the earth. One after another, I checked every body. Two were face-down, one dressed as an officer, with dark hair like yours. I turned him on his back and parted his hair: it wasn't you.

Suddenly I cried out—I'd spotted your hat! I stooped and picked it up. There were the plumes I'd put on it myself—there was no mistaking it.

This was where you had fallen. But had you fallen dead, or only wounded? That was the question.

The soldiers who'd come with me were speaking in low voices. I saw one of them gesture toward the stream. "What are you saying?" I asked.

"We were saying, Madame," replied the one who'd gestured, "that a wounded man, especially one who's shot, is always thirsty. If the Comte de Moret was only wounded, perhaps he crawled to the stream at the bottom of the ravine to drink."

"Oh! It's a hope!" I cried. "Come!" I darted through the olive trees.

The slope was steep, but I barely noticed. Ceres, torch in hand, seeking for lost Persephone, could have gone no quicker, goddess though she was. In an instant, I was beside the stream.

In fact, two or three of the wounded had tried to reach it. One had died on the way; the second had gotten his hand into the stream, but no more; the third had his head in the water, and had died while drinking.

One of the three sighed; it was the man who had reached the edge of the stream and then passed out. The coolness of the night air, or some miracle, had brought him around.

I knelt beside him, lit his face with the torch—and uttered a cry. It was Armand, your squire.

At the sound, he opened his eyes and looked at me, confused.

His eyes focused on my face. "Water," he croaked.

I fetched water in your hat and brought it to him. One of the soldiers stopped me. "Don't let him drink," he said in my ear. "Sometimes they die while drinking."

"Water!" the dying man repeated.

"Yes," I said, "I'll let you drink, but first tell me what happened to the Comte de Moret."

He looked more closely at my face, and recognized me. "Mademoiselle de Lautrec!" he murmured.

"Yes, Armand, it's me," I said. "I'm looking for your master. Where is he? Where is he?"

"Water!" he demanded, voice fading.

I remembered I had a vial of smelling salts in my pocket. I held it to his lips, and he seemed to revive a little.

"Where is he, in heaven's name?" I asked.

"I don't know," he replied.

"Did you see him fall?"

"Yes."

"Dead or wounded?"

"Wounded."

"Where did this happen?"

"On the banks."

"Which side?"

"The side toward Fendeille."

"Among the king's troops, or Montmorency's?"

"Montmorency's men."

"And then?"

"That's all I can remember. I was wounded myself, my horse was killed, I fell. Night came, and I crawled, because I was so thirsty. I nearly reached the stream, but I fainted. Water! Water!"

"Let him drink now," the soldier said. "He's told us all he knows."

I cupped water from your hat. The soldiers raised the wounded man's head, and I brought the water to his lips. He drank three or four sips, greedily, and then leaned back, sighed, and stiffened.

He was dead.

"You see, you had to make him talk before letting him drink," said the soldier. He released poor Armand's head, and it fell heavily to the ground.

I stood for a moment, wringing my hands anxiously.

"What do we do now, Madame?" asked the gardener.

"Do you know which way is Fendeille?" I asked him.

"Yes."

"Then we go toward Fendeille." I turned to the soldiers and asked, "Who will come with me?"

"All of us!" they said.

"Then let's go."

We followed the path up out of the ravine, then over into a meadow, where we saw an officer at the head of a dozen soldiers. My companions spoke softly to each other. "What are you saying?" I asked.

"We say that officer might be able to give you some information."

"Which one?"

"That one." They pointed at the captain leading the patrol.

"Why do you think he could give me information?"

"Well, because he fought here."

"Let's go to him, then." And I walked quickly toward the officer. One of my soldiers stopped me. "Pardon," he said, "but you see . . ."

"Why do you stop me?"

"Are you sure you want to know what he has to say?" the soldier asked.

"At all costs!"

"No matter what he tells you?"

"No matter what."

"Then I'll call him over." He stepped forward. "Captain Bitéran?"

The officer paused, peering toward him through the darkness. "Who calls?" he asked.

"We'd like to speak with you, *mon officier.*"

"Who is that?"

"A lady."

"A lady! On the battlefield, at this hour?"

"Why not, Monsieur—if that lady comes to the battlefield seeking one she loves, to treat him if he's wounded, or bury him if he's dead?"

The officer approached; he was a man of about thirty. Seeing me, he removed his hat, to reveal a noble and distinguished face framed by blond hair. "Whom do you seek, Madame?" he asked me.

"Antoine de Bourbon, the Comte de Moret," I replied.

The officer looked at me more closely. Then, paling slightly, voice altered, he repeated, "The Comte de Moret? You seek the Comte de Moret?"

"Yes, the Comte de Moret. These good men tell me that you, better than anyone, should be able to tell me what happened to him."

He looked at my soldiers, grimaced and frowned. "*Mon Capitaine!*" one of them said. "It seems this lady is his fiancée, and she wants to know what's become of him."

"Monsieur, in heaven's name!" I cried. "You saw the Comte de Moret, you know something about him. Tell me what you know."

"Madame, here's what I know: I was sent with my company of fusiliers to hide in ambush there in the ravine. We fired a volley, then pulled back to draw the enemy in. The Comte de Moret, who never refused a fight and was quick to show his courage, charged recklessly at us, and fired his pistol at . . . well, Madame, I won't lie . . . at me. His bullet cut the feather from my hat. I shot back, but more accurately, I'm sorry to say."

I uttered a cry of terror. "It was you?" I said, drawing back.

"Madame," the captain said, "it was a fair fight. I thought I was dealing with just another officer of the marshal-duke's army. If I'd known that he who charged me was a prince, and moreover the son of Henri IV, I'd certainly have forfeited my own life before taking his. But it was only when I heard him shout 'To me! For the Bourbons!' that I realized what a catastrophe I'd caused."

"Oh, yes!" I cried. "A terrible catastrophe! But, tell me, was he killed?"

"I don't know, Madame—just then, their musketeers opened fire. My fusiliers replied in good order. We withdrew, and I saw them standing over the body of the count, bloody and hatless."

"Oh! His hat, it's here!" I crushed it passionately to my lips.

"Madame," the captain said, with genuine pain, "give me your orders. After causing such a calamity, how can I . . . I won't say atone, but at least help you in your search? Tell me, and I'll do everything in my power to help."

"Thank you, Monsieur," I said, trying to get hold of myself, "but the only thing you can do is tell me in which direction the count was carried away."

"Toward Fendeille, Madame," he replied; "but for safety's sake, follow the path that starts a hundred paces to your right. After a mile, you'll come to a house where they should know something."

"Very well," I said, and then, to the gardener, "You understand, don't you?"

"Yes, Madame."

"Let's go."

"I could offer the lady my horse," the officer said timidly.

"Thank you, Monsieur," I replied. "I asked you for all I needed, and you gave me all I asked."

I passed a handful of crowns to my three soldiers. Two went off, but the third insisted on escorting me to the house of which we'd been told. However, I couldn't resist the desire to take one last look at the ground consecrated by your blood; I turned, and saw the captain standing where I'd left him, staring at me like a man stunned by misfortune.

On the way to the house, we found corpses all along the path, but I was used to them by then and walked with a firm step through bloodstained grass that rose to my knees.

We reached the house, which was overflowing with wounded from both sides, some lying outside on ground strewn with straw. I came into this asylum of pain to question the dying with my voice, and the dead with my eyes. At my questions, one dying man raised himself on his elbow. "The Comte de Moret?" he said. "I saw him go past in the carriage of Monsieur."

"Dead or wounded?" I asked.

"Wounded," said the dying man, "but he was like me, more dead than alive."

"My God!" I cried. "Where were they taking him?"

"I don't know—but I did hear them mention a name as the carriage turned at the crossroad."

"Whose?"

"That of Madame de Ventadour."

"Yes, that makes sense—Madame de Ventadour is nearby, at the Abbey of Prouille. That's it! Thank you, my friend."

And, leaving a few crowns beside him, I went out and told the gardener, "He's at the Abbey of Prouille."

Prouille Abbey was about two miles from there. The gardener's horse was exhausted, and I'd left mine in the meadow of the battlefield. It was impossible to find a carriage, or even a farmer's cart, and to search for one would have wasted valuable time. I felt no fatigue, so we set out on foot.

We'd gone barely a mile when the threatened storm finally broke and it began to rain. But all I could think of was you—I didn't feel the rain, I couldn't hear the storm, I marched through torrents of water on a path intermittently lit as bright as day. We came to a large oak; the gardener begged me to shelter there a while and wait until the storm had passed, but I shook my head and continued on my way without answering. A minute later, lightning struck the oak and shattered it to splinters.

I paused long enough to point out what had happened. "Yes, Madame," the gardener said, "you're protected from the sky, so, for as long as God gives you strength, let's go on."

We went on for another hour or so, until the lightning showed us the abbey where we were bound. I doubled our pace; and soon after, we arrived.

In the abbey, all were asleep, or pretending to sleep. I made enough noise to awaken them from the deepest slumber: gatekeeper, sisters, and the abbess herself.

After a thousand precautions, they finally opened up. They'd clearly heard me knocking, but seemed to fear the assault of some rapacious horde. I hastened to identify myself, and immediately asked for news of you.

The sister gatekeeper knew who I meant, but claimed not to have seen you, or even to know you'd been wounded. I asked to speak to Madame de Ventadour, and they took me to her.

I found her in full habit—having heard the noise I'd made, she'd arisen and dressed. I thought she looked pale, and seemed to tremble. She dismissed this as signs of the fear she'd felt when she heard me knocking, afraid it was rogue soldiers at the gate.

I reassured her, and told her I'd come from Saint-Pons, how I'd gone to the battlefield, and found the place where you'd fallen. I showed her your hat, still clenched in my hand; I told her what I'd learned from the dying soldier, and begged her, in the name of heaven, to tell me what she knew about you.

She replied that he must have been mistaken, or that the coach, after turning on the path to the abbey, must have gone another way, either right or left, and taken another route. In any event, she hadn't seen you, and had no news of you.

I dropped my pleading hands and slumped onto a nearby settee—my strength had left me, along with my hope.

The abbess summoned her women, who stripped me of my soaking clothes, still stuck to me from the drenching rain. I'd lost my shoes somewhere in the muddy road, and had walked at least a mile in bare feet. They brought a bath and placed me into it, where I lapsed into a stupor, almost unconscious.

As I slowly came around, I heard them talking about someone having seen a carriage take the road to Mazères. I questioned them: the information came from a peasant who had brought the convent their evening milk.

The abbess offered me her own carriage and horses, if I wanted to continue my search. I accepted.

They brought me my clothes, for, seeing the first light of day streaming in, I didn't want to lose a moment before taking up the trail. It was quite possible they'd taken you to Mazères, as Mazères was a château that had stood on the side of Montmorency.

Madame de Ventadour lent me her personal driver, and we departed.

At Villeneuve-le-Comtat, at Payra, at Sainte-Camette, we sought information, but not only had nobody seen anything, but in those villages they didn't even know the Battle of Castelnaudary had taken place.

We continued on the road to Mazères. There, somebody would have to know something: the gates would be guarded by sentries loyal to Monsieur de Montmorency, who would have no reason to conceal the presence of the Comte de Moret.

We arrived at the gates: they hadn't seen a carriage, didn't know the Comte de Moret was wounded, and their first news of the Battle of Castelnaudary came from us.

We soon had proof that this was the truth, as an officer galloped up at full speed, announcing that Monsieur de Montmorency was a prisoner, Monsieur de Rieux was dead, all was lost, and it was every man for himself.

After that, everyone was too busy to answer more questions.

I had completely lost track of you! We began to search at random, casting around the theater of events in a great circle, as hunters do when tracking game. We visited Belpech, Cahuzac, Fanjeaux, Alzonne, Conques, Peyriac; in none of these places was there any hint of your passage. Somewhere between Fendeille and the abbey, your carriage had disappeared like a mirage.

At Peyriac, I found the steward of our house in Valence. My father had sent word that he would spend two or three months at our château there. They implored me to come home, and that put an end to my search.

After three weeks of looking, I'd lost all hope of finding you. I went to the château.

My father arrived the next day. He found me despondent. After a word from the steward, everyone in the château was very considerate, and no one mentioned my journey.

My father came and sat by my bedside. He was a very serious, even severe man, as you know. I'd told him of my love for you, and your promise to be my husband. The honor of such an alliance was so great that he'd given up his favorite project, that of my marriage to the Vicomte de Pontis, the son of his oldest friend. But with your death, that project once again was his foremost desire.

Besides, Louis XIII had had words with him about his daughter's love for a rebel. As you were his brother, the king was particularly angry with you. Your property and domains were all confiscated, and if you hadn't been presumed dead, you would have been tried and treated just as Montmorency had been, king's son though you were.

So it was a blessing that you were dead, and had died on the battlefield. That captain I'd seen and interrogated, that killer whom I'd cursed and whose pale face haunted me in my dreams, that murderer had saved you from the scaffold.

I listened, sadly and somberly, to my father. His mind was made up: the Comte de Pontis, who had fought in the army of Marshal Schomberg, was in the royal favor. It was my father and him against me and the cardinal.

On my side, I did what I could. I asked my father for three months: if, after that time, I'd had no news of you, or your death was confirmed, I would go to the church with the Vicomte de Pontis.

On October 30, Monsieur de Montmorency was executed. Then I almost blessed your murderer, for I knew that if you'd had to suffer like the poor duke, it would have killed me.

There was no doubt about your fate—everyone said you'd been killed. I was a widow who'd never been married!

Three months passed. On the last day of the third month, my father came to the château with the Vicomte de Pontis.

I knew how punctual my father was, and didn't want to keep him waiting. When he arrived, he found me already in my bridal gown.

The clock struck eleven. The priest awaited us at the church. I rose and rested my arm on my father's. The Comte de Pontis walked behind with his son. They were followed by five or six mutual friends, a few dozen relatives, and the servants.

We made our way toward the church.

My father didn't speak, only looked at me. He seemed surprised to find me so quiet.

Like a martyr marching to her death, my face lit up as I approached the place of execution.

As we entered the church, I was pale but smiling, like a castaway fighting a storm who sees the safety of port.

The priest was waiting at the altar; we approached, and all went down on their knees. I'd been afraid that when I arrived at this point, my strength would fail me. But I was still strong, and I thanked the Lord for it with all my heart.

The priest asked the Vicomte de Pontis if he took me for his wife. "Yes," he replied.

He gave me the same question, asking if I took Monsieur de Pontis as my husband. "My husband in this world and the next," I replied, "is my divine savior Jesus, and I shall never have another."

I made this response in a tone so calm and firm that no one in the church missed a word.

Monsieur de Pontis looked at me with a frightened air, as if I'd gone mad. My father took a step forward.

But I, I passed through the gate that separated me from the altar, raised my arms to heaven, and cried in a loud voice, "From this moment, I belong to God, and only God has a right to claim me!"

"Isabelle!" my father shouted. "Would you defy my authority?"

"There is an authority higher and holier than yours, my father," I replied respectfully. "It's the authority of the one who sustained my faith while on the road to misfortune. Father, I am no longer of this earthly world—pray for me. As I will pray for all of you."

My father moved to pass the gate and snatch me from the altar, but the priest held his arms out to block him. "Woe!" said he. "Woe to he who would impede this call to vocation, or try to prevent it! This girl has given herself to God, and I receive her in his name. The house of God is a holy sanctuary where no one, not even her father, has a right to take her against her will."

My father might not have been stopped by this warning, but the Comte de Pontis dragged him away. The viscount and the rest of the entourage followed the old man out, and the door closed behind them.

The priest asked me where I wished to retire. I had myself driven to the Ursuline convent.

My father went to Paris at once, to appeal to the cardinal. But all he got from the cardinal was an order that I was not to take my vows for the term of a year.

That year passed. After a year and a day, I took the veil.

That was four years ago. For four years, not a day has passed without my praying for you, kissing the feathers of the hat I'd picked up on the battlefield at Castelnaudary, the only relic of you I had.

Now, you know everything.

And now, in your turn, tell me all, in detail; tell me by what miracle you live; tell me where you are; tell me how I can see you. And tell it all quickly, before I go mad!

—17 May, four in the morning

XVII

Six in the morning, immediately after your letter

For a moment, God turned his eyes away from us—and in that moment, the angel of evil passed over us and touched our heads.

Listen in your turn.

You know what pledges I'd made to my brother Gaston. I'd hoped that, by making good on one, I'd account for them all.

The king's prime minister seemed to think only of the king, not of the rest of us. Such tyranny was intolerable to the Sons of France; every time the cardinal employed the king's name, and used his seal, without consulting him, was a mark against his minister. Daily he gave orders in the house of Henri IV without regard for his sons, including the one who was on the throne.

And meanwhile, as he gathered a fortune of two hundred million, barely a third of France's people could get decent bread; another third lived on coarse oat bread, while the final third, like filthy farmyard animals, sustained themselves on acorns and mash.

Across the realm he'd been granted control of numerous royal fortresses and domains. He had Brouage, Oléron, Ré, La Rochelle, Saumur, Angers, Brest, Amboise, Le Havre, Pont-de-l'Arche, and Pointoise, at the very gates of Paris. He was master of the province and citadel of Verdun. In addition to the garrisons of all these towns, forts, and citadels, he was Admiral of the Navy. He had his own personal company of guards. He held in his hands all the keys to France.

The rest of France, gathered against him, wasn't enough to raise an army to oppose his own. The prisons had become graves to bury the true servants of the king, and the crime of *lèse-majesté* no longer applied to those who rebelled against the king or the State, but to anyone who lacked the zeal and blind obedience to follow the will and purposes of his prime minister.

I had to say all this, first and foremost, because it's my excuse for leaving you and taking the side of one who, later, would deny us all, alive or dead.

It was the trial and execution of the old Maréchal de Marillac that decided everything for me. I had been in correspondence with my brother Gaston and with Queen Marie de Médicis, who had always been perfectly friendly to me. I determined to join my fortune to theirs.

Do you remember how melancholy I was at that time? Do you remember my emotion, my voice breaking into sobs when I told you that my future was less certain than that of the new leaves on the tree under which we sat? Do you remember how I asked you for three more months before making you my wife, while saying that my happiest day would be the day I became your husband?

In fact, from that moment, I was privy to all the affairs of my brother Gaston and acted as intermediary between him and poor Montmorency.

You ask me not to leave out any details. And I won't forget or omit anything, if only to justify myself to you—and to me.

We had to have the Spanish and Neapolitans on our side. And in fact, when Montmorency declared for us, the Neapolitans did indeed appear off the coast of Narbonne, but they didn't dare to land. As for the Spaniards, they mustered at Urgel on their side of the border, but never crossed to ours.

You saw the insurrection rise all around you. You heard the cries of revolt in Bagnols, in Lunel, in Beaucaire, and in Alais. One morning I received—with a heavy heart, because I knew it betokened our separation—one morning there came the manifesto in which my brother Gaston declared himself Lieutenant General of France.

Shortly thereafter, as you learned in a letter from the king to your father, ordering him to Paris, Gaston returned to France with eighteen hundred horse, who burned the outlying suburb of Saint-Nicolas and the houses of the members of parliament who'd tried and condemned Marillac.

A day later, in my turn, I too received a letter. My brother wrote to me from Albi and summoned me to keep my oath to him.

That was the day I took leave of you, August 14, 1632—a fatal date, burned as deeply into my heart as yours.

Oh, all your details of my departure are true! Your depiction of that night is perfect, except I could see you for longer than you could see me. You were on the balcony of your room, lit from behind, while I plunged into deepening darkness. But eventually the road reached a turn, beyond which I'd see you no more.

At that point, I halted my horse, wondering if it wouldn't be better to forget all my oaths and commitments, sacrificing honor to love to return to you.

But your window closed, your light went out, and I thought it a warning from God to continue on my path. So I dug my spurs into my horse, wrapped my head in my cloak, and rushed forward into the darkness drowning the horizon, while urging myself "Forward! Forward!"

Two days later, I was in Albi, where I nearly caught up to my brother, who'd left five hundred Polish horse as my command and marched on to Béziers. On August 29, I received orders from the marshal-duke to join him. I went with my five hundred, and reached him on the night of August 30.

On the 31st, we met to consider our position. We believed Monsieur de Schomberg was marching on Castelnaudary, and marched there in our turn. But Schomberg got there first and occupied a house only ten minutes from the field, where he formed up a corps of Guards.

It was then September 1, at eight in the morning. The marshal-duke was apprised of the situation; he took five hundred men to scout Schomberg's army in force; and when he reached the house, he charged it.

Those within soon abandoned their posts. Monsieur de Montmorency left a hundred and fifty men to guard the house, and returned to us quite pleased with this initial success.

He found us gathered in the largest house in town: my brother Gaston, Monsieur de Rieux, Monsieur de Chaudebonne, and me. Approaching my brother, Montmorency announced, "Monsieur, today you will triumph over all your enemies, today the son will be reunited with his mother. But," he added, gesturing with his bloody sword, "only if by tonight your sword is like mine, that is to say, red to the hilt."

My brother doesn't care for swords, especially when they're bloody, and he turned away. "Eh, Marshal!" he said, "Do you never tire of boasting? Always you promise me great victories, but these hopes are never fulfilled."

"In any case," said the marshal, "assuming you're still with me and I, as you say, have given you hope, today that's more than anyone's done for your brother the king—for there's not just hope at stake here, there's life itself."

"Why, Marshal!" Gaston said with a shrug. "Do you really suppose the life of the heir apparent is in play? No matter what happens, I'm sure to make my peace, as I did the last three times."

The marshal smiled sourly and, turning from the prince, approached the rest of us. "Well, now we come to the bout," he said, "and our man already has a nosebleed. He says he, at least, will get away clean. But I think if he does, neither I, nor you, Monsieur de Moret, nor you, Monsieur de Rieux, will be part of his escort."

We said we certainly would not.

"Very well," the marshal-duke continued, "then come with me— because we swore that when this day came, we'd meet it sword in hand."

Just then, the report came that Schomberg's army had left the woods and was marching toward us. "Come, gentlemen," the marshal-duke said, "the time has come—every man to his post."

We had to pass over a river on a small bridge where they might have disputed our crossing, but no one did. On the contrary, Monsieur de Schomberg's plan was to draw us forward into an ambush on that sunken road where you found my poor squire.

The bridge crossed, I took my position on the left wing, which was under my command. It was, as you know, my first battle. I was eager to show that, though of the same blood as Monsieur, my blood ran hotter than his.

Ahead, I saw a troop of fusiliers detached as forward skirmishers: I charged them. I particularly noted the officer you met on the night after the battle. He was a brave gentleman, as calm under fire as if he were on parade. I spurred straight at him and discharged my pistol which, as you said, trimmed the feather from his hat. He returned fire. I felt a blow to my left side; I put my hand to it without knowing what I'd find, and drew it away covered with blood.

I didn't feel much pain at the time, but something like a red cloud passed before my eyes, and the earth spun beneath me. My horse shied, a movement I didn't have enough strength to control. I felt myself slipping from the saddle. I cried, "To me! For the Bourbons!" And I saw a vision of you.

As my eyes closed, I seemed to hear a volley of musketry, and a curtain of flame unrolled before me.

Doubtless my Poles bore me away, because from that moment until I recovered my senses, a mile or two from there, I was unaware of what happened to me.

I was in terrible pain when I came to. I opened my eyes, to see a curious crowd peering in from around the carriage. I tried to figure out where they were taking me.

I remembered the sister of my friend Monsieur de Ventadour was the abbess of a nearby convent. With an effort, I put my head out the door, and gave orders to take me to Madame de Ventadour.

You see, your dedicated pursuit put you on the right trail, and it isn't your fault you didn't catch up with me.

The pain that had awakened me then plunged me back into unconsciousness. I don't know quite how I was brought before Madame de Ventadour, but when I awoke I found myself lying on an excellent bed. However, I was in some sort of underground vault. The doctor of the convent was near at hand, but someone beside me, seeing my eyes open, whispered to me, "Don't say who you are."

You'd been my final memory, and you were my first thought. I looked for you, but you weren't there. I saw only unknown faces, and a man with rolled-up sleeves and bloody hands. It was the doctor who'd tended to me.

I closed my eyes.

Later that night you came to the abbey but, due to their fear of the cardinal, they told you they hadn't seen me. So you didn't know I was there, and I didn't know you'd come. We came so close, but missed each other.

I have little sense of what happened during the two weeks after I was wounded. It was less a recovery than a pause at the door of the tomb.

Finally, my youth and strength of will prevailed; I felt life return to my feverish and languid limbs, and from that moment, the doctor declared I had turned the corner.

But I was forbidden to leave my bed, or be taken outdoors. I was still at risk of my life for another four to six weeks.

It was during this time that they tried and executed the marshal-duke. That execution only reinforced the terror of the poor sisters who were tending me. They had no doubt that even a prince of the blood would be treated like Monsieur de Montmorency. For hadn't Montmorency allied with the traitorous Marie de Médicis?

Outside, everyone decided I must be dead, and as it was in everyone's interest to believe it, the news of my death soon spread.

After two months, I could get up. Though I'd remained hidden in the vaults beneath the convent until then, now my recovery required fresh air. It was November, but Languedoc's mild winter didn't prevent night-time walks. I was allowed to take the night air in the convent garden.

Along with thought and feeling—though not yet strength, because I was so feeble, I couldn't go up or down stairs—my love for you, numbed till then by the nearness of death, returned with full force. I spoke only of you, longed only for you.

As soon as I could hold a pen, I asked to be able to write to you. They gave me what I asked for, and a messenger took my letter away—but as a message would reveal that I still lived, and as Madame de Ventadour was terrified that such news would result in their persecution, imprisonment, perhaps even death, the messenger just stayed in the area for two weeks, then returned to say that your father had taken you to Paris, and he'd delivered my letter to those of your women who seemed most devoted to you.

That reassured me. I was certain my appeal to your love would bring a prompt reply.

A month passed; every day that went by was another blow to my confidence, a wound to my hope.

It was three months since the Battle of Castelnaudary. I ached to know the current news. Wounded at the outset of the fight, I knew nothing of the result.

They hesitated to tell me the news until I threatened to go find out for myself. Finally they told me everything: the loss of the battle, Gaston's flight and reconciliation—his fourth, as he'd said—the trial and death of Montmorency, the confiscation of my property, the loss of my rank and my dignity.

I took this news better than they expected. Certainly the death of the poor marshal was a heavy blow. But after the execution of Monsieur de Marillac, we'd foreseen that death was a possibility for both Monsieur de Montmorency and myself, and had discussed it more than once.

As for the loss of my rank, my dignity, and my fortune, I met that with a contemptuous smile. Men had taken from me everything that could be given by men—but they'd left me with what God had given me: your love.

From that moment, your love for me was the one hope I had left in life. It was the only star shining in the sky of the future, which had become as dark as that of the past had been radiant.

The messenger hadn't found you—so I resolved to be my own messenger. Your response had never come, so I decided to seek an answer for myself.

But leaving the convent wasn't going to be easy. They kept a close watch on me, afraid I might be seen and recognized. I therefore told them I proposed to leave, not just the convent, but France itself.

For the abbess, this was the best proposal I could possibly make. It was agreed that I would disguise myself as a fisherman and travel among others as far as Narbonne, where I would leave them. At Narbonne Abbey, I would dress in ecclesiastical garb and continue in the abbess's carriage. I'd never been to that area, and besides, everyone thought I was dead, so it was unlikely that I'd be recognized.

The good abbess put her coffers at my disposal. I thanked her, but when wounded I'd had on me two hundred crowns or so, which was still in my purse, plus diamond rings and brooches worth ten thousand crowns at least.

And you were rich, so what use had I for money?

I left the abbey in early January, full of gratitude for the hospitality they'd given me. Alas! I had no idea how dearly that hospitality had cost me.

It was twenty-eight leagues to Narbonne, and I was still so weak that I could walk for only short distances—though perhaps I exaggerated my weakness a bit, so they'd underestimate me.

The first night, we lodged in Villepinte; the second, in Barbaira; the third, in Narbonne. The next day, they made arrangements to sail me to Marseilles. I was to be a sick prelate with ailing lungs ordered to take the air at Hyères or Nice.

I rested for a day at Narbonne and departed the next. With a good wind behind me, forty-eight hours later I was in Marseilles. There, I paid my boatmen, said farewell to the two servants of the abbess who'd come with me, and was once again perfectly free.

In the market I hired a coach to take me to Avignon, and from Avignon up the Rhône to Valence.

My cavalier airs might betray me, so I made myself an officer's uniform of the Cardinal's Guard. Wearing that uniform, I was sure I wouldn't be bothered.

I left Marseilles and reached Avignon in three days. In Avignon, the wind was blowing up from the sea, ensuring good navigation, so I entrusted myself to the Rhône. When the wind died, we roped the boat to horses and were drawn along by a cable.

Early one day, I saw your château in the distance. It was there that you would be waiting for me—or, if what I'd been told was true and your father had taken you to Paris, it was there that I'd find news of you.

I wanted to be put ashore, the boat got on so slowly, but unfortunately I was still too weak. Oh, if only I'd arrived just one hour sooner! If only I'd seen you first! But it was not to be—we were doomed. . . .

I could only stand in the prow and await our arrival. Even so, half a league short of Valence, I disembarked. I could walk only slowly, but that was faster than the boat.

Moreover, the hope of seeing you revived my strength. From far off I saw your balcony, the one from which you'd waved goodbye as I turned the corner of the road—but the balcony was empty and the blinds were shut. There was something about the château, which I'd yearned to see for so long, something bleak and empty that chilled me.

Suddenly, I saw the main gate open. A procession marched out, turned toward the city, and disappeared.

I was still a quarter-league away, but without knowing why, I felt my heart sink and my strength fail me.

I leaned against a tree beside the road, sweat beading my forehead; I wiped it away and resumed my trek.

I came upon a servant. "My friend," I asked, hesitating, "does Mademoiselle Isabelle de Lautrec still live in that château?"

"That's right, *mon officier*," he said, "Mademoiselle Isabelle de Lautrec. But half an hour from now, she'll be called something else."

"Something else! What will she be called?"

"Madame la Vicomtesse de Pontis."

"Why the Vicomtesse de Pontis?"

"Because in half an hour she'll be the wife of my master, the Vicomte de Pontis."

I felt myself go pale and mopped my face with my handkerchief. "So," I said, "the procession I saw leaving the château . . . ?"

"Was that of the betrothed."

"And at this moment . . . ?"

"At this moment, they're in the church."

"No! It's impossible!"

"Impossible!" said the servant. "Well, if you want to see it with your own eyes, Officer, there's still time. Take this shortcut, and you'll be at the church soon enough."

I couldn't believe the man's story—I wanted him to be wrong, I wanted to see with my own eyes that there was no such terrible reality. For some reason he must be telling me a lie, a bald-faced lie.

I knew Valence, having lived there for three months. I quickly crossed the bridge, entered the town, and followed the streets that would take me most directly to the church. Besides, I was guided by the jubilant sound of the bells.

The cathedral square was crowded with people. Despite the pealing bells, despite the crowd of celebrants, I still couldn't believe—I told myself the man had misled me, that someone else was walking to the altar.

But though I passed through a teeming crowd, I didn't dare to ask anyone. If I hadn't been dressed as one of the Cardinal's Guard, I certainly couldn't have pushed through to the front ranks, but the crowd parted at the sight of my uniform.

And then . . . oh, it takes all my strength to recount these terrible details—until yesterday I didn't know for sure it was you who was writing to me, I hadn't yet reopened this lethal wound. . . . You suffered through my death, but oh, I suffered through your betrayal.

Your betrayal . . . forgive me, Isabelle, forgive me, I know now it was only the appearance, but oh! For me, unhappy wretch, it was reality.

When I saw you, a cloud rose before my eyes like the one when I was shot from my horse by that officer. It was the same feeling, but more painful—because while the bullet struck my side, this pierced my heart.

I saw you appear: you were pale, but almost smiling. You walked with a firm stride across the square, seemingly in a hurry to get to the church.

I passed a hand over my eyes, stumbled, panting, muttering in a low voice that surprised those around me, "My God, my God, this can't be true . . . my God, my eyes, my ears, all my senses must be deceiving me . . . ! But she's alone, alone—she couldn't wrong me, she couldn't wrong me so."

You passed no more than ten feet from me, but I was struck dumb, hoping you wouldn't enter the church, that you would turn away, you would cry out that this was a violation of your love—and then I, I would rush forward, and though it cost my life I'd cry, "Yes, I love her! Yes, she loves me! Yes, I am the Comte de Moret, dead to everyone but her, Isabelle de Lautrec, my bride in this world and the next! Let me be with my fiancée!"

And I would have carried you away in the face of all of them, despite everything, because I felt I had the strength of a giant.

But Isabelle! O Isabelle! You didn't speak, you didn't stop, you went on into the church. A long cry, a heartbreaking wail rose from the depths of my breast as you disappeared through the doors . . . and then, before anyone could ask me why I moaned so, I turned, darted through the crowd, and disappeared.

I returned to the riverbank, I found my boat, I threw myself amid the boatmen, burying my hands in my hair and crying "Isabelle! Isabelle!"

They left me a while in my despair. Then they asked me where I wanted to go.

I pointed downriver. They loosed the boat, and the Rhône carried us away.

What more can I say? I must have survived the next four years, since today you find me, still alive and still in love. But before today, I didn't exist.

I've been waiting to take my vows until the end of the term I'd imposed on myself. That term, you have brought to an end—thank you! Since I know you didn't betray me, since I know you still love me, entering my vocation will be easier for me, and now I can go calmly to God.

Pray for your brother . . . as your brother prays for you.

—Three o'clock in the afternoon

XVIII

Half past five, the same day

What's this you tell me? I don't quite understand. You have found me; you're sure I didn't betray you; you know I love you; and this, you say, ends the term of waiting to take your vows, makes your vocation easier, makes you calm enough to consecrate yourself to God!

Good Lord! Would you continue with your strange project of renouncing the world?

Just listen to me: God is not unjust. When I dedicated myself to him, it was in the belief that you were dead. But you live! God won't require me to keep a vow made in despair, if the cause of my despair doesn't exist. I'm free, despite my vows.

Yes, yes, it's as you say: we nearly touched each other at the abbey, but had no way of knowing we were so close to each other. Oh, but I'm wrong, I belie my own heart, for an inner voice cried to me, "Stand firm, argue, insist—he is here."

Yes, I understand, the poor abbess was terrified, afraid of what the hospitality she gave you would cost.

Oh, why couldn't I have found you! I'd been proud of the mission God have given me to save the son of Henri IV. I wanted the pride and glory to be able to say "When the whole world abandoned him, I alone endured, I alone rescued him."

Fool that I am! Saying that would have betrayed you, and you'd have been lost like the marshal-duke.

Better, then, for her to hide you from me so you should live—better that I should suffer, should despair, should die.

But why despair now? Why should I die? You've yet to take your vows, and I regard mine as invalid. Let's leave, let's go to Italy, to Spain, to the end of the world. I'm still rich—and besides, why do we need money? We love each other! Come! Let's go!

Oh, answer me. Yes, tell me where you are, tell me how to find you.

Consider this: you doubted me—me, your Isabelle! You thought me deceitful, and you owe me expiation.

I wait, I wait.

XIX

Five in the morning

Your letter stirs the most secret depths of my heart.

Ah, for what was to have been ours! You offer me the happiness I sought, expected, desired all my life—and I cannot accept that happiness.

Isabelle! Isabelle! You are a lady, as I am a gentleman. Neither of us would betray a promise made to men, let alone an oath made to God.

Don't try to deceive yourself: the vows you made are real, and God doesn't admit of equivocation.

For us there is only one future, the one to which misfortune has led us. You showed me the sacred path, and you were the first to take it. I follow you—and we shall arrive together, since we have the same goal. I will pray for you, as you pray for me. We pray as one, not for ourselves, but for the eternal life and eternal love that we shall receive from the Lord, in place of worldly love and mortal life.

And don't believe that, because I tell you this, I love you less than you love me. No, I can't love you less, I know—I love you with the heart of a man much stronger since he fell from his heights to the depths, and who, having touched death with his hand, returns pale from the tomb bearing revelations of another life beyond.

Believe me, Isabelle, the more I love you, the more certain I am on this point. Don't risk your eternal salvation on such sophistry. The life of this world is to eternity as a second is to a century. We live for a second on the earth, but we live forever with God.

And then, moreover, listen to this, my bride in this world and the next: though it was God who willed despair into your heart when it was deceived, that power to bind has the power to unbind. Urban VIII is pope, and your family has powerful allies in Italy. Use them to get a nullification of your vows. On that day, Isabelle, you truly can tell me, "I am free!" And then, then . . . oh, I dare not think of what blessed happiness, what bliss without remorse we would find!

XX

Two o'clock in the afternoon

Yes, you are right; there must be no shadow on our happiness. In our hearts shall be neither fear nor remorse, and our dark and stormy sky shall be followed by a firmament glittering with stars. Yes, I spoke to one who has listened to me; yes, she assures me she'll find mercy for me; yes! I ask you for three months to go free myself, and if in three months our dove hasn't borne you the ecclesiastical order that liberates me, then our only hope is in heaven.

Then you may give yourself to God as I did, bound by an unbreakable oath.

Oh, I couldn't bear to know that you were free, when I am forever chained!

Tomorrow, I'll be on my way.

XXI

Half past four in the afternoon

Go, and may God be with you!

June 1, 1638

It's just a month since I received your last letter; a month I've spent watching for the coming of our dove; a month with no words about you, except those from my heart.

How the time passes! Now, minutes become hours; hours become days; days become years. Can I live like this for two more months?

Yes, because I will hold out hope until the very last day.

I write this letter without knowing if you'll ever receive it—but I write for that day that shall separate us or bring us together. For you know, Isabelle, I think about you with every beat of my heart.

XXII

June 22, 1638

Fly, beloved dove, fly to my dear returned one, tell him it was his prayers that protected me—tell him I'm free, tell him we are happy!

Free! Free! Free!

Let me tell you, my beloved. . . .

I don't know where to start, I'm so mad with joy!

As you may know, the same day I wrote my last letter to you, the good news came, officially confirmed, that the queen was pregnant. To celebrate the occasion, there were to be great festivals throughout France, and pardons granted by the king and cardinal.

I resolved to go and throw myself at the feet of the cardinal, who has, in ecclesiastical matters, all the powers of Rome.

That's why I asked you for only three months.

The same day I wrote you, I departed, with the permission of our mother superior.

My neighbor in the next cell agreed to take care of our dove. I was so sure of myself, I left her without fear.

I departed—but despite my best efforts, I couldn't get to Paris in less than seventeen days.

The cardinal was at his country estate in Rueil. I left for there immediately.

At first he was ill and couldn't receive me. I took lodgings in the town and waited, after leaving my name with Father Joseph. On the third day, Father Joseph himself came to tell me that His Eminence was ready to receive me.

I rose at this news, but fell back in my chair, pale as death. My heart quivered, and my legs were too weak to hold me.

They say Father Joseph isn't tender of heart—and yet, when he saw me collapse at the mere idea of an audience with the cardinal, he did his best to encourage me, telling me that if I had something to ask of His Eminence, the time was right, as the cardinal was better than he'd been for quite some time.

Oh, my entire life, and yours, depended on what was to happen between that man and me!

I followed Father Joseph, blind to my surroundings, my eyes fixed only on him and matching my pace to his, as if his movements directed mine.

We passed through the town and entered the estate. We went up an avenue of tall trees. I saw everything at once, all blurred together, so the details escaped me.

Finally, I saw before us an arbor of honeysuckle and clematis, and under it a man half lying on a couch. He was dressed in a white robe and wearing a red cap, the biretta of a cardinal. I pointed toward the man, and Father Joseph understood. "Yes," he said, "that's him."

Just then I was passing a large tree; I paused and leaned against it, for I felt that if I took another step without support, I'd fall.

The cardinal saw my hesitation, the stagger that betrayed my weakness; he rose. "Approach without fear," he said. An indescribable tone softened his usually gruff voice, and it was that change in his voice that suddenly filled me with hope. I regained my strength and, almost running, I threw myself at his feet.

He waved Father Joseph away, who obeyed, retreating out of earshot but still within view.

I bowed and extended my hands before me. "What do you want of me, my daughter?" asked the cardinal-duke.

"Monseigneur, Monseigneur, a blessing upon which depends not just my life, but my salvation."

"Your name?"

"Isabelle de Lautrec."

"Ah! Your father was a loyal servant of the king—a rare thing in this time of rebellion. We had the misfortune to lose him."

"Yes, Monseigneur. Is it permitted to invoke his memory in your presence?"

"Were he alive, I would grant him whatever he asked, except for those things that are in the purview of the Lord, for whom I am but a simple vicar. Speak: what do you wish?"

"Monseigneur, I have taken vows."

"So I recall, because, at your father's request, I opposed these vows with all my power, and instead of granting your wish to take them, asked you to delay for a full year. So you took these vows despite the year's delay?"

"Alas, Monseigneur, I did!" I admired the prodigious memory of this great man of affairs who recalled so unimportant an event as a poor child he'd never seen taking the veil.

"Ah, and now you repent them."

I preferred to blame my repentance on inconstancy rather than desire. "Monseigneur," I said, "I was just eighteen years old, and the death of a man I loved had driven me mad."

He smiled. "I see. And now that you are twenty-four, you've become more reasonable."

I waited, hands clasped.

"So now," he said, "you would break those vows, as with time the woman has overcome the holy sister. The memories of the world have pursued you in your seclusion, and though you swore your body to God, your soul, I perceive, remains on earth. O human weakness!"

"Monseigneur! Monseigneur!" I cried. "I'm lost unless you have mercy on me!"

"It was, however, freely and voluntarily that you took your vows."

"Yes, freely and voluntarily. I repeat, Monseigneur—I was mad."

"And what excuse can you give God for this failure to keep your oath?"

My excuse—an excuse already well known to God, who had preserved your life, my beloved—that I couldn't tell him, or all would be lost. I remained silent, but for a tiny moan.

"So, you have no excuse," said the duke.

I wrung my hands in agony.

"Well, then, I must find one for you," he said, "however mundane."

"Oh, help me, Monseigneur, aid me, and I'll bless you till the last breath of my life!"

"H'mm! As minister to King Louis XIII, I don't wish a name as loyal and good as yours to perish. Your house is one of the true glories of France, and the true glories of France are dear to me."

Then, gazing at me, he asked, "You love someone?"

I bowed my head into the dust.

"Yes, that's it," the duke continued. "I guessed as much: you love someone. And the one you love is free?"

"Yes, Monseigneur."

"He knows of your request, and expects it?"

"He is waiting."

"Very well. You shall be free, and this man shall join his name, whatever it is, to that of Lautrec, so that the name of the victor of Ravenna and Brescia shall not perish."

"Oh, Monseigneur!" I cried, kissing his feet.

He lifted me, breathless with joy, and beckoned to Father Joseph, who approached. "Escort Mademoiselle Isabelle de Lautrec back where you found her," the cardinal said, "and in an hour you can bring her the order that releases her from her vows."

"Monseigneur, Monseigneur, how can I thank you?"

"That's easy enough: when you're asked your opinion of me, say that I know both how to punish and how to reward. Living, I punished the traitor Montmorency; dead, I reward the loyal Lautrec. Go, my daughter, go."

I kissed his hands ten times over, and then followed Father Joseph. An hour later, he brought me the order that nullified my vows.

I left at once, without losing a minute, the precious order next to my heart, which was even more devoted to God since God had released me from my words.

My return trip took only thirteen days, and here I am, writing to you, beloved—not telling all I have to say, because that would take a book, and it would be a week before you knew that I'm free, I love you, and we shall be happy!

I hasten to finish because I don't want to delay this wonderful news a single minute. I'm keeping the horses harnessed—at the return of the dove, I'm ready to go. Just tell me where you are, and wait there for me.

Go, my dove: I've never had such need for your wings. And then return!

Do you hear, my beloved: tell me nothing but where I need to go to find you. I don't want to delay our reunion by even so long as it takes to write—

I love you!

Ten minutes later

Oh, woe! Woe is upon us! That man is fatal to us, beloved—perhaps even more so the second time than the first.

Listen, listen, although you can't hear me. Listen, although you may never know what I must tell you.

Listen!

I attached my letter as usual to the leg of our dove, this letter in which I told you everything, this letter that bore our whole future happiness. I had released little Iris, and followed her with my eyes as she sprang into the sky—when suddenly, from the other side of the cloister walls, I heard a gunshot, and saw our dove stop in its flight, flutter, and fall.

I gave so agonized a shriek, I feared my soul would leave my body. Frantic, I immediately rushed from the convent. It was so obvious that I was in distress that no one tried to stop me.

I'd seen in which direction the dove had fallen, and ran that way.

Fifty paces beyond the walls of the cloister, I saw an officer dressed for the hunt. It was he who had shot the dove; he held it in his hands, gazing with astonishment and some regret at the letter attached to its leg.

I approached him with outstretched hands, unable to say anything but "Woe! Woe! Woe!"

Four steps away I stopped, faint, struck to the heart as if by lightning—this hunter, this officer, who had just shot our dove, was the same I'd seen that night on the Castelnaudary battlefield. It was that same Bitéran who shot you from your horse!

We recognized each other.

Oh, I tell you, his pallor was almost equal to mine; he saw me dressed as a nun, and realized who it was beneath the sister's habit. "Ah, Madame," he whispered, "I am truly desolate!"

And he handed me our poor dove, who struggled in his hand and fell to the ground. I picked it up—fortunately, it had only a broken wing.

But she holds the secret of your location, my beloved. And this secret she keeps to herself. How can I find you if she can't fly to you? Fly to tell you where to find me, that I'm free, that we should be happy!

Oh, beyond doubt, that poor little creature has a soul. If you'd only seen, my beloved, how she looked at me as I carried her into the convent.

Meanwhile, motionless and speechless, the assassin's eyes followed me, as they'd followed me when I'd walked away through the bloodstained meadow grass of that battlefield. I don't know if this man will ever be able to make good all the evil he's done, but if there's no redress for this, I'll curse him until my final hour!

I laid the dove in a basket, and placed the basket in my lap. Fortunately, the wound hadn't injured her body, just the end of her wing.

I detached the blood-spattered letter from her leg. My God! My God! If not for this sudden accident, by now it would almost have reached you.

Where are you? Where are you? Who will tell me where to find you?

Ah, I'd sent for the convent's doctor, and here he comes. . . .

Four hours later

The doctor is a fine man, a good man; he understands that existence is mysterious and strange, and sometimes the life of a dove is as precious as the life of a king.

He understood when he saw my despair, and when he saw the blood-spattered letter.

The injury, he said, was minor, and the dove would survive—once he took off her wing.

I snatched her back, and then fell to my knees, saying "If you take her wing, you take my life. She must fly! She must fly!"

"To save the wing is much harder," he said, "and I can't answer for its success—but I'll do everything I can. If all goes well, in only two or three weeks, she'll fly once more."

"So it will take up to three weeks—but she'll fly! She'll fly!"

You understand, my love: all my hope is in this.

He bound her wings against her body. She seems to understand, poor thing—she can't move, but she looks at me. I put grain and water within reach of her beak, but she will only take food from my hand.

What to do while I wait? How can I tell you what happened? What messenger can I send to find you? How should I know, like a castaway lost at sea, in which direction to send my distress signal?

Why wasn't it one of *my* arms that was broken, instead of her wing?

June

Yes, you were right, my beloved: if I hadn't gotten a release from my vows, there would always have been a shadow of remorse on our happiness—or, rather, we'd have had no happiness at all, for it would not have been sanctioned by God!

When I told you "I'm free, let's go off together, we'll be happy," I wanted that to be so, but deep in my soul was a voice of regret that, no matter how strong my love, could not be silenced.

Today I'm very sad, because I don't know how to find you or see you, but my conscience is clear; and when I say, when I repeat, "I love you, my husband," I no longer feel the hollow in my heart I'd felt when I said, "Don't worry, my beloved, we'll be happy."

I have cared for our poor dove as I would have watched over an ailing sister. She suffers, and sometimes I can see the pain in her eyes. Then I bathe her wing in ice water, and it seems to do her good. She strokes me with her pink beak, as if to thank me.

Poor dove! She has no idea how much selfishness there is in the care I give her.

But you, you! My God! What must you be thinking?

XXIII

July 1, 1638

Two months have passed, and still no news. My eyes are worn out from scanning the horizon, vainly seeking our beloved dove.

Each black dot I see in the sky, I think "This is it" . . . and then, after a moment, I realize my mistake, and my chest, which had heaved with hope, deflates with a sigh.

No matter: I still wait, I still hope. You live; you love me; why am I so desperate for happiness?

But . . . the time passes. It's now two months since you left. If I calculate correctly, it's eight or ten days since you should have returned.

O my God! My God! Would you deny me, and turn this heart to bronze? Even though she said she still loves me?

Lord my God, do not abandon us!

XXIV

July

Oh! If you knew, poor beloved of my heart, everything I've written to you in the last fortnight! In there, you'd see a whole world of thoughts, desires, hopes, regrets, and memories!

If we're ever reunited—God willing, as I ardently pray every day, and more so at night!—if we're ever reunited, you'll read all of it, and then, only then, I swear to you, will you understand how much you were loved!

If we never meet again . . . oh, all the tortures of hell are wrapped up in that fear . . . well, it is I who will reread these letters, it is I who will daily add another note more desperate than that of the day before, it is I who, until I die, will still write "I love you!"

Each day I think I've exhausted all the anguish and joy in my heart—and then I feel that ahead there are still depths of joy or pain I've not yet glimpsed!

Tomorrow! Why does my hand shake so when writing that word?

It's because tomorrow will be the day that decides my life; tomorrow, I'll see if our dove can fly. It's already three days since she left the basket; she moves about the room, she stretches her wings, she flits from the door to the window. She seems to understand, poor thing, how important it is for us that she finds the strength to fly.

Tomorrow! Tomorrow! Tomorrow!

I will write a short note for her to carry, so as not to load her with unnecessary weight. Just a few words, but enough to tell you everything. Tomorrow, my beloved! I'll spend the night in prayer. I won't even try to sleep, it would be useless.

What are you doing to us, God? Do you doubt how much I love, and how much I suffer?

July 6

It's dawn, beloved, and as I told you, I haven't slept for a moment. I spent the night in prayer; I hope God has heard me, and that today you'll know where I am, that I'm free and waiting for you.

The dove is even more anxious than I; it beats against the window with its beak and its wings.

We'll open that window, little one! God grant that your wing is strong enough for the trip you're about to take.

I interrupt this long letter to write the short note she will carry to you—or perhaps, alas, only try to carry to you!

Four in the morning, July 6

If our dove happens to reach you, my beloved, read this post and leave without losing a second—as I would do myself, if only I knew where to find you.

I'm free, I love you, and I await you at the convent of Montolieu, between Foix and Tarascon, on the banks of the Ariège.

You'll see why I don't write more, why this note is so short, and the paper so thin.

You'll know all this and a thousand things more, all our misfortunes, our fears, our hopes, if our beloved messenger reaches you—for if that happens, you'll set out at once, won't you?

I await you, my beloved, as the blind await the light, as the dying hope for life, and as the dead await resurrection.

Go, beloved dove, go!

July 6, five in the morning

We are accursed!

Oh, my beloved, what have we come to? There's nothing left for me but to die in tears and despair.

She cannot fly; after a hundred paces her wing faltered, and she landed in the topmost branches of a poplar she was trying to fly over—but she flew right into it and, branch by branch, fell to the ground.

I ran to her, arms outstretched, heart breaking—I ran with a moan that became a cry of pain. I picked her up, and she rested a moment, and again tried to fly—and again she fell!

And I fell beside her in despair, rolling on the ground, tearing at the grass with my hands and my teeth.

My God! My God! What will become of me? I was too proud, too happy, too certain of bliss, I had it all in my grasp, and then fate struck me down and my dearest treasure is gone. O my Lord! Send me an inspiration, a light, a hope!

Lord, Lord, help me! Pity me, O Lord! I'm going mad. . . .

Wait. Wait.

Divine goodness, you hear me! You answer me!

Listen, listen, beloved, hope has revived in my heart, hope that comes to me from on high.

Listen! From my window, I've often watched the flight of our dove, from when she departs to a distance of, if I'm not mistaken, two or three leagues. She passes over the sources of the broad stream that flows into the Ariège at Foix. She flies over the small wood of Amourtier, then above the Salat between Saint-Girons and Oust.

Well, here's what I'll do:

I'll don a pilgrim's cloak, and then begin looking for you, starting at the small village of Rieupregan. I always lose sight of the dove near that village; once I've passed it, I'll find which way to go from her. She can fly about a hundred paces at a time. So, I'll let her fly a hundred paces, rest for a while, and then fly another hundred. She'll be my guide, and I'll follow her like the Hebrews followed the column of flame by night and the column of smoke by day—because I, too, am in search of the Promised Land, and I'll find it, or die of pain or exhaustion along the way.

Alas, I know the road will be long! Poor dove, forgive me for how I'll make you suffer, a martyr to our love! The dear thing won't be able to go more than one or two leagues a day—but no matter, my beloved, for if it takes the rest of my life to find you . . . oh! Then I'll seek you for the rest of my life.

So I'm leaving—today, immediately.

I've told our mother superior everything—everything, except your name. She's a worthy woman, a holy woman, who's suffered along with my pain and cried along with my tears. She offered to send someone to accompany me, but I refused. I don't want anyone; what I must do I understand, instinctively, involves only heaven and myself. But I promised to write to her if I found you. If I don't write, she'll know I've died, or gone mad, or hidden myself away in the corner of some wood or along a back road on the bank of a lonely river.

I go, carrying with me all these letters I've written that you haven't received, that perhaps you'll never receive. Oh, if one day I can drop them all at your feet and tell you, "Read! Read, my beloved!" You will see, on that day, how I've suffered—but on that day, how happy I'll be!

I go now; it's three o'clock in the afternoon, and I hope to make it to Rieupregan before the end of the day.

July 7, at night

Before leaving, I passed through the chapel, in order to bring God, as it were, along with me. I prostrated myself before the altar, pressed my forehead on the carved stone where the sculptor had carved a cross, and I prayed.

Oh, it's true: there is a comfort in prayer. Prayer is the green knoll where one sits and rests after a tiring journey. Prayer is the cool stream where one finds refreshment in the middle of the desert.

I left the chapel full of strength and hope, feeling like God had attached angel's wings to my shoulders. It has always been prayer that lifted me from the earth and carried me to the Lord.

This is only a test, Lord, is it not? You haven't cursed me, have you, my Lord? That's not what I'll find, will I, Lord, at the end of this road I've only just begun?

Wait for me, beloved, wait for me, because I swear, one day soon I'll get there.

ॐ

I've paused for a moment to lean on the sill of a window that looks out toward the village of Boussenac. That village is along my road, and I'll reach it tomorrow, unless our dove takes me a different way. A dog is sadly howling, probably lost in the small wood I see to my right, a dark blot on the landscape.

I said to myself: "If the dog stops howling, it will be a good omen, a sign that I'll find him."

And the dog fell silent.

One is superstitious when suffering, don't you think, my heart's beloved? Are you suffering, too?

Dear God, what a beautiful night! I imagine you're at your window as I am at this one, looking toward me as I look toward you, thinking about me and God, as I think about God and you.

Did you see that lovely shooting star that carved a fiery furrow across the sky? How many miles did it cover in just a second?

Oh, if only I had the power to reach you in a second, even if, as I arrived, I sparked and burned out! I would embrace such a bright second of happiness, even if what followed was eternal night.

Tomorrow, my beloved—tomorrow, I hope, I will be nearer to you than ever.

July 9

I've stopped at a small village named Soulan. Dear God, what a storm! What had the Earth done for the Lord to menace it in such a terrible voice?

The water fell in torrents and swelled the Salat, making it impossible to ford. I'd have to go back to Saint-Girons to find a bridge, and that would cost me two days.

I've been told that tomorrow, once the river ebbs to its usual level, I should be able to resume my journey.

Oh! A day lost! A day during which you await me! A day in which, perhaps, you'll lose hope in me!

July 12, evening, in the village of Alos

A farmer agreed to be my guide, and I crossed the river on his mule. In the river there was a moment, only a third of the way across, when all was almost lost—the beast stumbled in its footing, and I looked up to heaven, crossed my hands on my chest, and said, "If I die, my God, you know I died for him."

But you see, all must be well, since I didn't die.

July 15

My marathon continues, guided as ever by our dove. On the 13th, we went from Alos to Castillon; that was a big day for our poor girl. I should have been more sorry for her—we must have gone three leagues.

The next day, the 14th, I was repaid for my cruelty of the day before, as we made barely a league. Now it's the 15th, and I've reached Saint-Lary, just across a small unnamed stream that flows into the Salat.

At least I'm sure I'm on the right road. The dove doesn't hesitate for a moment, doesn't deviate for a second. She goes straight ahead without pause.

Only, time is passing, while still you wait. Time is flying toward the day you take your vow.

Oh, that vow, be in no haste to take it, beloved! Believe in me, believe in your Isabelle.

If you doubt me for a moment, it could cost us everything.

July 18

For three days I've wandered almost at random, through woods and along streams. Alas, the air lacks the obstacles of the land, and the dove often goes where I can't!

I confess, O my beloved, that for once my courage and strength have failed me, and I've collapsed at the foot of a tree, desperate and dying.

It's already eleven days since I left, and I've covered only fifteen to eighteen leagues of what she flew in only an hour when she was our messenger of love, flying fast as an arrow above the miserable beings who call themselves kings of creation, but haven't the abilities of a bird, and must take eleven days to travel what a dove can do in an hour.

Tell me, how can it be that a wretched magnetic needle knows where north is, while I, a thinking being, made in the image of God, don't know where you are?

How is it a ship can sail from one point in the world, go to the far side of the Earth and find a particular island in the ocean, while I can't seem to find you, though you were close enough to speak to or reach out and touch?

Oh, I know well, dear God, that if I want to find him, it's not to him but to you that I must reach out.

My God, support me! My God, go with me! My God, guide me!

July 29

I return to my senses; to daylight; to life.

I nearly died, my beloved—and few would disbelieve that then, at last, I'd know where you are, for the dead know everything; few would disbelieve that the ghost of your Isabelle could enter your cell at night, in the hour when the spirits walk.

And that's why I wish to live. If you saw my shadow, you'd have known I was dead—whereas if you see neither my shadow nor my body, you may think I've only forgotten or betrayed you. Don't say, alas, that you no longer believe in me! For I haven't forgotten or betrayed you—I love you! I love you!

I nearly died—that's all.

Do you remember the dying soldier I saw that night, who'd dragged himself to the stream, leaking his last drops of blood, gasping his last breath, yearning for water, and then dying at his first swallow? Well, that was almost me.

After a long trek through a forest that I was told was called the

Mauleon, I arrived breathless at a spring. This spring came right out of the rock, and was icy cold. I drank, thinking it would restore my strength and I could continue my journey. I continued, but walked for only a hundred steps and then stopped, shivering. A chill overcame me, and I fainted beside the small path I was following.

I don't know what happened after I passed out. All I know is that yesterday, when I came to, the light was very dim. I looked around and found myself in a fairly clean room, on a bed, watched from its foot by an unknown woman. Beside me on the bed perched our dove, stroking my cheek with her poor wounded wing.

This woman had found me while returning with two men from the Mauleon market. They saw I was still breathing, took pity on me, and brought me where I am now.

Where I am is a small village near Nestier, or so I've been told. The room I'm in must be at some altitude, because from my bed, out the windows I can see only sky.

The sky! The sky is the only road to he who awaits me.

Yesterday I asked the date, and was told it was July 28. Alas! I've spent more than twenty days in my wandering. Where am I—near to you, or far?

I asked for paper, ink, and a pen, but after tracing just a few letters, my head was swimming and I couldn't continue.

Tonight I'm better, and can write almost without tiring—I've had to stop only three or four times so far while writing this letter.

I thanked the woman who was watching over me. I no longer need constant care, I'm better, I feel strong. Tonight I'll try to get up, and tomorrow resume my journey.

It would kill me to just lie here while you're waiting for me—as you'd expect, wouldn't you, my heart's beloved, who waits for me?

The dove is also well rested. I hope it will be capable of longer flights, and therefore guide me to you more quickly.

I'd planned to spend all night in writing to you, but I'd

overestimated my strength. I must stop, I must say goodnight to you—my ears are ringing, the room spins around me, and my pen seems to trace letters of fire.

Ah . . . !

Nine in the morning

I slept for two hours or so, a horrible, restless sleep more like delirium. Fortunately, upon opening my eyes, I saw the day was almost born.

O my beloved, what a beautiful thing daybreak would be, if we were near each other, and watched together as the stars disappeared—all those stars whose names you know, and that merge and disappear into the ether ahead of the sun, who chases them and appears in his turn!

I just opened my window to gaze out upon a huge expanse. Alas! The more land I see, the more lost I feel.

My God! The love story of Theseus and Ariadne, was it truly just a fable? My prayer, deep, ardent, and eternal, is that you'll send me some blessed angel who will bring me a thread that leads me to him.

Oh! I listen; I watch; I wait.

But there is nothing, dear God, nothing! Only the sun, that is to say, your image, which, still tinted pink, colors the atmosphere above and the mountain behind which it rises.

If only my heart were calm, this spectacle would be beautiful.

The hills emerge, their blue outlines silhouetted against the golden rays, showing their lovely and graceful forms. The ridge of mountains that girds the southern horizon is vast and beautiful, with snowy peaks that shimmer and sparkle like the flames of a divine star. A great river appears crossing the plain, broad and majestic, like . . .

Oh, my God!

My God, I can't be mistaken! The angel I begged for, pleaded for—he came, invisible but real! Those hills behind which the sun rises, the double crest he tops, these snowy mountains that seem like silver pillars supporting the vault of heaven, that great river flowing from north to south taking in tributaries as a sovereign receives his subjects . . . it's the hills, the mountains, the river he described to me, that he sees from his window. My horizon is his! My God—did I lose my way, only to find at last my road to him? Did you close my eyes, just to show me the light I'd see when they opened?

My God! Your mercy is infinite!

You are great, you are holy, you are good, and it is only on my knees that I should address you.

Kneel, therefore, faithless heart who doubted the goodness of the Lord! On your knees! On your knees!

Four in the morning

I have thanked God, and I depart. My strength came back to me with my faith. I was weak only because I was desperate.

But first, a final look.

Oh, it's your picture to the life, my beloved! Painter, I have seen your vision! Poet, it is as you described so well!

There are the peaks of the Pyrenees, changing from white to shining silver; their dark sides gradually lightening from black to purple, from purple to blue, as a flood of light flows down from the high peaks; there the daylight spreads across the plain, there are the streams that glisten like silver strands, there the river that twists and undulates like a ribbon of satin; here are the birds singing in the oleander bushes, the pomegranates and clumps of myrtle; and there flies the eagle, king of the sky, circling in the ether.

Oh, my beloved! We are joined in vision, and I see what you see. Only, from where do you see it?

Wait, wait, your letter is here. Oh, your letters, they don't leave my side for a moment; when I die, they'll be next to my heart, and those who lay me in the grave will be charged under pain of sacrilege to bury them with me.

From where do you see it?

Dear God, it's as if I just read it. Fortunately, I know them by heart—if I lose them, I could rewrite them without missing a word, I've read them so often.

"My window is surrounded by a luxuriant jasmine whose branches are laden with flowers; they scent my room as they open with the rising sun."

That's it! That's it! The sun has just risen to my left, so you are to my right.

"The plateau beneath me slopes down from south to north, from the mountains to the plains."

That's it, exactly. Yes, that's the very horizon. Thank you, Lord, for making the day so clear! Yonder are the highlands where I'll find your hermitage.

Oh, why are they still so far away, and why is the human eye so feeble? I see hundreds of white specks scattered among the green trees—which of all these white specks is your hermitage?

Oh, darling dove—beloved dove—dove, daughter of heaven—it's up to you to tell me that.

I go, my beloved, I go; each minute of delay is a minute stolen from our happiness; to delay is to tempt Providence.

For wasn't it only by the delay of a minute that you lost me?

Come, dove! Yes, tomorrow, perhaps even tonight, we'll see him again!

July 31

The night has interrupted my search, beloved—but I hope, I hope!

I questioned everyone I met, and was finally shown, on a distant ridge, a Camaldolese monastery, and near it a small house that looks to me like the one you described. I saw it shining through the rising mists of evening; perhaps it's yours, perhaps you looked out over your horizon without knowing that it hid, invisible to your eyes, a poor, anxious creature who lives only for you, and will die without you.

I was told that that small house is inhabited by a recluse, a sage and man of God, but one still young and handsome.

That man is you, my beloved, is it not? It's you. And if so, during the day sometimes you must visit the village of Camons, where I am now. You once visited a poor carpenter who broke his leg falling from a roof; you took care of him, and healed him. When the whole family kneeled before you as you were leaving, you said, "If you are consoled, pray for the consoler."

Oh, that's you—I recognize your sorrowful way of speaking. You wait for me, not knowing what's become of me, and you suffer.

You suffer, because you doubt. Oh, man must always doubt; if you didn't doubt, I'd think you were dead.

To think that if I'd arrived here only two hours earlier, I might perhaps have met you!

I say perhaps, for if I was sure it had been you, it would break me—I'd hire a guide, I'd even have them carry me. But what if I was wrong? Our dove's instinct is the best guide of all; she hasn't deviated for a moment. If by some fate I just missed you, I can still rely on her.

What are you doing at this moment, wherever you are, my beloved? Unless you are thinking of God, I hope you're thinking of me.

It's eleven o'clock. Tomorrow! Tomorrow! This great hope, too strong not to have come from heaven, says I'll see you—tomorrow.

XXV

July 31, eleven o'clock

I don't know if you're returning to me, heart's beloved, but hurry, hurry—midnight approaches, and the stroke of midnight will end the last day of my life as part of the world.

Tomorrow is the day on which I'm to take my vows. I waited religiously for the full three months, but I cannot forever postpone my promise to God. God speaks to me, since you are silent; God calls me, since you leave me alone.

Oh, it's not without deep sorrow that I renounce this hope. If only you had come, if but for a moment.

I have dwelled, body and soul, in the past, that is to say, in happiness; it will cost me more to set aside that happiness than it would cost me to set aside life.

The life of the cloister, no matter what people say, is neither death of the body nor death of the soul. I have often examined corpses, cast my eyes over their pale and livid faces, and it's only the material flesh that has broken down. No dream stirs in those sleeping brains, no pain, physical or moral, afflicts those flaccid fibers.

I have often examined, on the other hand, these living corpses called monks. Their faces are as pale or paler than those of the dead, but their visages are not those of the deceased: tears flow forever from their hearts, a deep and inexhaustible source that reddens their eyes, sinking them in their sockets, and plows bitter furrows down their cheeks. By this we recognize God's suffering elect, whom I hope, at least, derive some comfort from his love.

The nervous energy that drives the living animates them only with sadness. It's neither the composure of life nor the quiet of the grave; it's the agony, the fever of slow consumption, the withering from this world to the next, from life to death, from the cradle to the grave.

Well, Isabelle, I can fool myself no longer, and postpone the abyss by plumbing its depths; I, too, will embark on this agony, in hopes it will quickly carry me to death!

Goodbye. I shall spend the night in prayer. The monastery bells will sound at two o'clock to say that a soul, though not a body, is leaving the earth for heaven.

At nine in the morning, those who will be my brothers in God will come for me.

August 1, five in the morning

I just saw my life's last rising of the sun. He has never been brighter, more splendid, more magnificent. What matter to him the pains of this poor little world he illuminates? What matter the tears I shed that drown this paper? I've watched his dawn break for but ten short minutes, and already he drinks the dew that trembles at the tip of a blade of grass, or glistens like a diamond in the petaled chalice of a flower.

I shall never see his dawn again. The cell assigned to me looks into a high-walled courtyard; through an archway, I can just glimpse the corner of the cemetery. I'll try to have them put my grave in that corner—I want it to be as close as possible, so the journey will be short.

Now, pray!

Nine in the morning

The chanting approaches; they're coming for me.

I don't want those men coming in here. I don't want them to see your letters, or what I've been writing. I don't want them to see my tears.

I'll wait on the threshold. My soul remains with you: they bear away only my corpse.

Adieu!

The cry that rose from all of creation at the death of the Son of God was not deeper, more agonizing, or more lamentable than that which I utter at the death of our love.

Adieu! Adieu! Adieu!

XXVI

Ten o'clock

Your empty chamber! Your letter, wet with tears! Your final goodbye!

I arrived half an hour too late.

If only your vows have not yet been spoken!

My God! My God! Give me strength.

Oh, dove, my dove, if only I had your wings, broken though they are!

XXVII

(This fragment of a letter was found in the archives of the Ursuline Convent at Montolieu, but the first part is missing.)

. . . At daybreak I left the village of Camons, where I told you, dear Mother Superior, everything had led me to believe he sometimes spent the day.

I had questioned the entire family of the poor injured carpenter, and I would have known him from their descriptions, even if my heart hadn't already told me it was him.

Moreover, the words he'd spoken upon leaving them—"If you are consoled, pray for the consoler"—those could have come only from a suffering soul preparing to give himself to God.

My strength was restored by the hope of seeing him again. I set out on foot, for if I took a horse or a carriage, I'd have to make a wide detour to reach that white speck beside the vast, dark Camaldolese monastery, which, though almost three leagues off as the crow flies, sent me the sound of its bells on the wings of the wind.

Upon leaving the village, I let fly the dove. The poor dear made one of its longest flights, nearly two hundred paces toward the house my eyes devoured. There was no doubt—I was headed toward the goal she'd shown me with the last of her strength.

Unfortunately, there was no marked path; I had to follow the slope of the mountain, sometimes split by ravines, sometimes crossed by streams, sometimes cloaked with small woods which I dared not enter, for fear of losing myself.

I walked three hours without pause, but due to these detours, I covered only two leagues.

The house was often out of sight, and without my darling dove, I'd have been lost. I cast her in the air and followed wherever her flight led me.

Finally, it seemed to me my route became a bit easier. I heard the bells of a small village sounding eight o'clock; I don't know why, but the tone of the bells seemed so sad, I felt my heart clench. It seemed that every hour, as it passed me on wings of bronze, pealed out "Hurry! Hurry!"

So I hurried, and soon I could distinguish the details of the house. As I approached, I recognized it from the description he'd given me: the window through which he watched the sun rise, and the jasmine that shaded the window and seemed to me like a green palisade.

For a moment I thought I could see him in that window, and whether illusion or reality, I spread my arms and shouted. Alas! He was still over a mile away, and neither saw nor heard me.

The bells of the monastery were ringing. I remembered the continual peals of the bells the night before I took the veil, and a terrible suspicion crept into my mind and heart that these bells tolled for the same reason.

But I shook my head and told myself, "No, no, no!"

As I approached, I saw a long procession of monks make their way to the little white house and then, moments later, return toward the monastery.

Who did they seek in that house? Someone alive—or dead?

Soon I'd know, for I was barely a hundred steps from the house, when suddenly a deep mountain stream barred my way. It was a steep cascade, muddy and full of rocks, so deep I didn't dare try to cross it.

I climbed toward its source, despite my fatigue, but it felt like I'd never reach that house before my fleeting strength abandoned me.

After a quarter hour's walk, I found a tree that had fallen across the chasm. At any other time, I wouldn't have dared to venture upon so flimsy a bridge. But I leaped onto it, my feet sure, my eye fixed on the far side, and then I was across.

There I found, instead of obstacles, a sort of paved path, so I went ever faster as I approached.

I reached my desired goal; the door was open; I crossed the threshold; a stairway opened to my right, and I rushed up it without calling out. I hadn't dared breathe since passing the doorway—I was convinced I'd find an empty room.

The chamber was empty, the window open, and a letter was on the table, all wet with tears.

This letter, O my mother! It was less than half an hour old, and it was his final farewell.

I had arrived half an hour too late: he was at the church, taking his vows.

I felt the house shiver beneath my feet; everything seemed to spin around me. I began a shriek that would end as my last breath, when suddenly the thought came that maybe his sacrifice wasn't yet made, his vows were not yet pronounced.

I rushed out of the house, instinctively taking my dove, which had perched on a branch of the blessed jasmine.

The monastery was no more than a hundred paces away, but I felt my strength would fail me before I reached the church. My brain was empty of thought, my lungs gasped for air.

I heard the priests singing the *Magnificat*.

I heard the organ playing the *Veni Creator*.

My God! I had only seconds, no more.

And woe betide me! As luck would have it, I'd gone

around the wrong side of the apse—the door was on the other side.

The window to the nave was open—but how could I hope my voice would be heard above the organ and the chanting of the monks?

I tried to shout, but all my chest could produce was a dull rattle.

It was a moment in which it seemed all was lost, all was in vain.

My mind was confusion, my thoughts were a blur—and then, in the midst of this chaos came a light, and a fire lit my heart.

I cast my dove through the window, and fell in a swoon.

Heaven be praised! When I came to, I was in his arms.

He already wore the robe of a monk and had the tonsure of a priest—but he was mine! Mine! Mine!

Then, and forever.

The oath was upon his lips when the dove, like the Holy Spirit descending on a sunbeam, had interrupted it.

Beloved dove, your image will be carved on our tomb, asleep in our intertwined hands!

I promised I would write to you if I found him, Mother Superior. God, in his infinite mercy, has allowed me to find him—and so I write.

> Your respectful and ever grateful daughter,
> Isabelle de Lautrec, Comtesse de Moret
> Palermo, September 10, 1638

TRANSLATOR'S NOTES

Imagine it's the middle of the nineteenth century, you're a well-educated Englishman or American, and it's your job to translate popular French literature into English. You are fully conversant with then-contemporary standards of the English language, in which "proper" writing is formal, staid, and largely in the passive voice. Everyone agrees that elevated diction is the hallmark of cultured literacy.

Then your publisher assigns you to translate a new novel by Alexandre Dumas.

What on Earth is this? It isn't proper French, like Chateaubriand, or Alfred de Vigny, or even that young firebrand Victor Hugo, who at least writes solid, conventional prose. This fellow Dumas writes in a disturbingly dynamic style, propelling his story's action with vigorous language in sentences that are strangely short and direct. His theatrical dialogue is sharp, punchy, and concise, almost like the way real people talk. There's violence in the tale, sudden and brutal, and erotic thoughts and behavior are depicted in a frank and open manner quite unsuitable to a general audience.

In short, while the writing has an undeniable power of sorts, it's rather vulgar and must be corrected.

And correct it these translators did. To be fair, those gentlemen knew their business, and gave their English and American readers what they expected, which was historical adventure in the tone and manner of popular authors like Sir Walter Scott and James Fenimore Cooper—a style stiff and stuffy by our modern standards, but entirely in line with the expectations of the day. Their translations of Dumas, conventional and bowdlerized though they were, were immensely popular, and they made "Alexandre Dumas" a brand name that stood for historical adventure with vivid characters and engaging, fast-moving stories.

But these early translations, endlessly reprinted and, in many cases, still the only available English versions, haven't aged very well. For most twenty-first-century readers, they seem awkward, dense, and difficult—more trouble than they're worth, really. And that does Dumas a terrible disservice, because his writing was truly ahead of its time, a precursor to the more direct, earthy styles of Mark Twain, Bret Harte, and Robert Louis Stevenson. He was in many ways a very modern author who wrote in a theatrical, almost cinematic style. And this should come as no surprise when you consider that he started out as a playwright, whose early fame came from lurid melodramas that shocked and captivated Parisian theatregoers. Dumas wrote in *scenes,* vivid set-pieces conveyed by sharp action and even sharper dialogue, punchy lines meant to carry impact all the way to the cheap seats at the back of the hall.

For us here in the twenty-first century, after a hundred years of Hemingway, Hammett, and Hollywood, original, unvarnished Dumas delivers exactly the kind of storytelling we want. As a fan of contemporary adventure fiction, I'm here to tell you that translating Alexandre Dumas for the modern reader is a lot of fun. The man was the living embodiment of *joie de vivre,* and that love of life permeates every line of his tales. His vibrant characters, trembling with passion, practically leap off the page, their lines rapped out in snappy patter that might have been written by Ben Hecht or Lawrence Kasdan. In short, Dumas *rocks,* and his work deserves to be presented in a fashion contemporary readers can appreciate.

So much for Dumas in general; now let's turn to *The Red Sphinx* in specific. It's a work from late in the master's career, and while it's not quite in the class of his early masterworks like *The Three Musketeers* or *Monte Cristo,* it's definitely comparable, and when Dumas has the bit in his teeth, the story still races along like his best work. With *The Red Sphinx*, Dumas was making a deliberate attempt to recapture the glory of his early triumphs, and in the main he succeeded. The characters are as captivating and charming as any of their predecessors—especially Cardinal Richelieu, a figure Dumas clearly admired, and whose weaknesses are depicted as lovingly as his strengths. The action sequences are taut and exciting, the heroes are bold and clever, the period details ring true, and the king's jester always manages to get in a zinger as the last word.

If only it had an ending! Fortunately, that's where *The Dove* comes in. As mentioned in the Introduction, I think part of the reason Dumas couldn't wrap up this novel is that he'd already written an ending for his protagonists fifteen years earlier, and couldn't get easily from Moret as Richelieu's protégé in 1630 to Moret as his antagonist in 1632. And when his publishing vehicle, *Les Nouvelles*, went on the rocks, he just shrugged and gave it up.

Does *The Dove* really do the job of wrapping up the story of the Comte de Moret and Isabelle de Lautrec? I would argue that it does—and in spades. It was the only story Dumas ever wrote in epistolary, or exchange-of-letters, form, but he used that stylistic constraint to great effect. An unabashed romance, Dumas wrote it when still at the height of his powers, and the language is concise and emotionally compelling. Unlike the novel that precedes it, the pacing of *The Dove* is flawless, generating significant suspense even as we know, in our hearts, how it must turn out, finally culminating in a perfectly timed and entirely satisfying climax.

Some editorial notes: *The Red Sphinx* originally appeared in *Les Nouvelles* in four parts, or "volumes," with the chapter numbering restarting with each new volume; since these divisions seem nowadays confusing and arbitrary, for the sake of simplicity and streamlining I abandoned that structure and just numbered the chapters sequentially, from I (1) to LXXIV (74). Also, Dumas's spelling of character and place names was occasionally inconsistent from one part of the novel to the next; I have tried to remedy this by settling on one spelling in each case, usually the most historically recognizable.

Speaking of history, just how accurate in that regard are the events of *The Red Sphinx*? In the main, Dumas's account of King Louis's Court and Richelieu's transalpine campaigns of 1629 and 1630 is on the money, though the side adventures of the Comte de Moret and Étienne Latil are entirely invented. In fact, we don't know for sure exactly what the historical Comte de Moret was doing during the French invasion of Piedmont and Savoy—but no one can prove he *wasn't* involved in it, and that was good enough for Dumas.

As for *The Dove,* did Antoine de Bourbon really survive the Battle of Castelnaudary that ended Prince Gaston's fourth rebellion against his brother King Louis? According to history, almost certainly not, despite the persistent rumors and legends of the time that had him surviving in seclusion until late into the seventeenth century. But, as with the rumors about who was really behind the assassination of King Henri IV, Dumas always preferred to follow gossip and scandal, because they invariably make better stories.

The reader who wants to know more about the historical background of *The Red Sphinx* is invited to visit the translator's website, www.swashbucklingadventure.net, and click through to the *Red Sphinx* page. There are other articles and reviews on the site that may be of interest as well. Feel free to drop in and leave a comment.

PUBLICATION HISTORY

Dumas's final visit to the milieu of the Musketeers has an interesting publishing history. *The Red Sphinx*—or *Le Comte de Moret,* as it was then known—was first published as a serial in the Parisian weekly *Les Nouvelles,* from October 17, 1865, to March 23, 1866. Because it was unfinished, and because the author's brand of historical adventure was temporarily out of vogue in France, at the time it received no book publication in its author's native land—and wouldn't for the better part of a century.

However, Dumas's name still had considerable cachet in the United States, where all his works were in print, and publishers were even commissioning ghost writers to concoct sequels to his bestsellers that they then unashamedly published under his name. Even an unfinished novel by Dumas was considered worthy of publication, and late in 1866 *Le Comte de Moret* appeared in a French-language (and probably unauthorized) edition from the tiny New York publisher H. de Mareil, as part of their *Bibliothèque du Messager Franco-Américain* series. It was presumably this edition that the prolific hack writer Henry L. Williams, Jr., used as the basis of his English translation, which appeared as *The Count of Moret* from the likewise-tiny Philadelphia publisher Peterson Bros. in 1868. Though Williams wrote his own ending to the novel, in which Moret personally broke the Siege of Casale at the head of a troop of swashbucklers before dying in Latil's arms, it was an awful translation, and the book disappeared without a ripple. In fact, there may be no more than three copies still in existence. (For the curious, bits of this "lost" translation can be found in *The Works of Dumas,* a one-volume collection of novel excerpts published in 1927 by the Walter J. Black Co. of New York without editorial attribution.)

And that was the end of the story for *The Red Sphinx*—or would have been, if not for a dramatic event so unlikely that it could have come from the pen of the master himself. In 1945, Dumas's original handwritten manuscript of the novel, or at least the first three quarters of it, was unexpectedly discovered in near-perfect condition "in a Paris garret" (according to Dumas bibliographer Frank Wild Reed). After authentication by experts—the text was entirely in Dumas's well-known longhand—this manuscript version was published as *Le Comte de Moret* in 1946, in two volumes, by Paris publisher Édition Universelles. It was republished in 1964 by Éditions Galic, appearing for the first time under the title *Le Sphinx Rouge.*

In general, the 1946 manuscript version differed little from what had appeared in *Les Nouvelles* eighty years before—some spelling differences, such as *Lathil* instead of *Latil,* and *Pisani* instead of *Pisany*—with one notable exception: the manuscript contained an *entire chapter* omitted from the published serial version. Upon reading this missing chapter, titled *Les Habitués de l'Hotel de Rambouillet,* one quickly sees why it was omitted, as it is no more than 3,500 words about the amusing eccentricities of certain members of the Rambouillet household and social set. This series of anecdotes, mainly lifted from the *Historiettes* of Tallemant des Réaux, are just the kind of juicy historical gossip Dumas delighted in, but they add exactly nothing to the progress of the novel—in fact, they stop the book dead in its tracks. I think Dumas (or his editor, Jules Noriac) made the right decision in leaving this chapter out, and I've followed their example for this edition of *The Red Sphinx.*

As noted above, the original French version of the novel had first been published in book form in the United States as *Le Comte de Moret* in 1866, but as of the first years of our current century it still had yet to appear in the author's native France. To rectify this, prominent Romanian editor Radu Portocala painstakingly mined original copies of *Les Nouvelles* out of the depths of the French

Bibliothèque Nationale to compile a full serial version of Dumas's incomplete novel; and, thanks to his work, 2008 finally saw the first complete French book publication of *Le Sphinx Rouge* (Éditions Kryos, Paris). Portocala even included the lost *Habitués* chapter from the 1946 manuscript version—so if you want to read this novel in the original French, that's the edition this editor recommends.

The Dove (in French, *La Colombe*) was originally published in 1850 in Brussels by Alphonse Lebègue, and then the following year in Paris by Cadot. A novella, or short novel, it was an awkward length for book publication, and wasn't printed much again until publishers started compiling Dumas's "Complete Works" in the 1870s, after his death. The only known English version prior to the current edition was by the noted English translator Arthur Allinson, published by Methuen & Co. in London in 1906 in combination with another short Dumas novel, *Maître Adam*. It's a rather rare edition, and this editor hasn't actually seen it, but I've read other Allinson translations of Dumas, and they're pretty good. This volume's version of *The Dove* is the story's first appearance in English in the United States.

Dramatis Personae: Historical Character Notes

Ancre see CONCINI

ANGELY: *l'Angely, King's Fool to Louis XIII.* Not much is known about King Louis's *fou de titre*, other than that he was said to have been "of a noble family, but poor," and may have been an equerry to the Prince de Condé before entering the king's service.

ANNE: *"Anne d'Autriche," Anne of Austria, Queen of France* (1601–66). Eldest daughter of King Philip III of Spain and sister to King Philip IV, Anne was wed to King Louis XIII of France in a political marriage at the age of fourteen. A Spaniard among the French, unloved by the king, proud but intimidated, and vulnerable to manipulation by her friends, Dumas's depiction of Anne is, in the main, accurate. The eventual mother of Louis XIV, she will outlive her husband and reign as regent in her son's name, appearing as a major character in the next novel in the cycle, *Twenty Years After.*

BARADAS: *Chevalier François de Baradas, "Monsieur Baradas."* Royal equerry and king's favorite in 1628–29, the handsome but shallow Baradas fell from Louis's favor after engaging in an illegal duel.

BASSOMPIERRE: *François de Bassompierre, Marshal of France, Colonel-General of the Swiss Guard* (1579–1646). A gentleman of Lorraine, this suave and adaptable chevalier was successively a favorite of Henri IV, Queen-Regent Marie de Médicis, and Louis XIII, and one of the leading ornaments of their Courts—especially by his own estimation. As a general, a lover, a diplomat, and above all a courtier, he cut a swath, but delved too deep into intrigue and spent the last years of his life in the Bastille. His lively memoirs of the period are among Dumas's primary sources.

BAUTRU: *Guillaume Bautru, Comte de Serrant* (1588–1685). Courtier, wit, poet, and diplomat, Bautru was one of Richelieu's trusted envoys. A mediocre writer, he was nonetheless one of the founding members in 1634 of the Académie Française, mainly due to his association with its patron the cardinal.

BERINGHEN: *Henri, Comte de Beringhen, Premier Valet de Chambre, "Monsieur le Premier"* (1603–92). The king's loyal valet, his weakness was pride, and he would be banished in 1630 after falling for Madame de Fargis and conspiring with her and Vautier.

BÉRULLE: *Cardinal Pierre de Bérulle* (1575–1629). Though eventually outmaneuvered and sidelined by Richelieu, as a leader of the "Devout" party and ally of the Queen Mother, Bérulle was a big noise in the early years of the reign of Louis XIII. Though influential at the time, he wasn't a deep thinker, and was important mainly as a figurehead of the pro-Spanish faction opposed to Cardinal Richelieu.

BOIS-ROBERT: *François Le Métel de Boisrobert, "Le Bois"* (1592–1662). One of the cardinal's Five Poets, Boisrobert was a diligent aide in all Richelieu's literary pursuits, and the prime mover in the founding of the Académie Française. A priest before becoming a poet, his sharp-tongued irreverence frequently offended the devout, but he was nonetheless granted posts as a canon and abbot. After Richelieu's death he attempted to transfer his loyalty to Mazarin, but the Italian didn't care for him, so he turned his hand to writing plays, at which he prospered until well into the late 1650s.

BRANCAS: *Charles de Villar, Comte de Brancas, Marquis de Maubec et d'Anilly* (1618–81). Though well-known at the salons of the Hotel de Rambouillet at a later date, Brancas was too young in 1629 to be the crony of Voiture and Pisany depicted in *The Red Sphinx*, as Dumas was doubtless well aware. But the author had a weakness for likeable buffoons, so he added a decade or two to Brancas's age, which gave him an excuse to recount some amusing anecdotes. Brancas really came into his own during Anne's regency, when he was a knight-of-honor to the queen.

BUCKINGHAM: *George Villiers, the Duke of Buckingham* (1592–1628). Favorite and boy-toy of both King James I of England and his son, Charles I, Buckingham was handsome, brilliant, charming, manipulative, politically savvy, an inveterate womanizer, and, thanks to his royal patrons, the most powerful man in the English Court. A narcissist of epic proportions, from 1625 to 1628 he conducted a clandestine and illicit flirtation with Queen Anne of France that infuriated Louis XIII. Buckingham (and thus England) supported the Huguenots of La Rochelle when that city was besieged by Louis and Cardinal Richelieu, and he was on the verge of leading a relief expedition to raise the siege when he was assassinated in Portsmouth on August 23, 1628—an assassination, according to the plot of *The Three Musketeers*, engineered by an agent of Cardinal Richelieu. Contemporary accounts relate that Anne of Austria was shocked by his death, and genuinely mourned the passing of her chivalrous would-be lover.

Cardinal see RICHELIEU

CAVOIS, CAPTAIN: *François d'Ogier, Sieur de Cavois, Captain of the Cardinal's Guards* (?–1641). Cavois was the first Captain of the Cardinal's Guard, though that company wasn't actually formed until 1634. A gentleman of the petty nobility, the stolid Cavois's loyal service to Richelieu was the making of his fortune, so much so that one of his sons became a Marshal of France. Cavois died fighting the Spanish at the Siege of Bapaume in Flanders. Curiously, Dumas refers to him as "de Cavois" in *The Three Musketeers,* but denies him the nobiliary particle in *The Red Sphinx,* possibly to emphasize the cardinal's willingness to promote men of low rank if they showed talent and loyalty.

CAVOIS, MADAME: *Marie (not Mireille) de Lort, Madame de Cavois* (?–1665). Dumas got his anecdotes about Madame de Cavois from the *Historiettes* of Tallemant des Réaux, who said of the lady, "Never did any wife love her husband more." The two of them had ten children, and Tallemant says that it was in order to support them after her husband's death that Richelieu gave her one-half the Parisian monopoly on covered sedan chairs. The reality is less romantic: when the cardinal awarded one-half of the monopoly to Souscar-rières in 1639, he gave the other half to Capitaine de Cavois as a reward for his loyal service.

CHALAIS: *Henri de Talleyrand-Périgord, Comte de Chalais* (1599–1626). Chalais, one of Louis's handsome young favorites and the Master of the King's Wardrobe, came under the influence of the Duchesse de Chevreuse and joined one of Prince Gaston's early con-spiracies against Richelieu and the king. When the cabal was dis-covered and broken up, the high-ranking plotters mostly escaped punishment; Chalais, a mere tool, was made the scapegoat, and was executed in a spectacularly bungled beheading that took the amateur headsman hired for the job over thirty blows to complete.

Charles-Emmanuel see SAVOY

CHARPENTIER: *Denis Charpentier, First Secretary to Cardinal Richelieu* (?–1647). Richelieu's loyal, long-time secretary had come with him from Poitou and had been in the cardinal's service since at least 1608. He was entrusted with the keys to the cardinal's coffers, an important role at a time when governments did their business on a cash basis. Charpentier outlived his master, and was remembered in Richelieu's will.

CHEVREUSE: *Marie-Aimée de Rohan-Montbazon, Duchesse de Chevreuse* (1600–79). One of the most remarkable women in a century full of remarkable women, Marie de Rohan was a vector of chaos who challenged every social convention of her time with wit, cheer, charm, and unshakeable self-confidence. Throughout the reign of Louis XIII she was a steadfast friend and ally to Anne of Austria when the queen had few of either. Brilliant, beautiful, free-spirited, mischievous, adored and adorable, she had a long list of lovers on both sides of the English Channel, many of whom ended up dead or in prison thanks to her habit of involving them in plots and conspiracies against the French Crown. She first came to prominence in 1617 when she married Albert de Luynes, Louis's former falconer and first favorite, whom the king elevated to the rank of duke and Constable of the French Armies. When Luynes fell from favor in 1621 and died of a convenient bout of purple fever, Marie avoided obscurity by quickly marrying the Duc de Chevreuse, a wealthy Lorraine noble and perennial ornament of the French Court. Marie and her second husband had what nowadays would be called an "open marriage," leaving Madame de Chevreuse free to pursue her own interests, which were romance and treason in equal measure, mixing the two whenever possible. She was involved in every notable conspiracy of the reign of Louis XIII, and was an inveterate enemy of Cardinal Richelieu. La Chevreuse continued to intrigue after the death of both king and cardinal, and will play a prominent part in *Twenty Years After*, the next novel in Dumas's Musketeers cycle.

CHRISTINE: *Christine Marie de Bourbon, Princess of Piedmont* (1606–63). Like King Louis's other two sisters, Princess Christine was married off at a young age to a foreign monarch—but she must have drawn the short straw, because whereas Elisabeth got Spain and Henriette got England, Christine ended up in the relatively minor Duchy of Savoy. But of the three Daughters of France, she was probably the only one whose marriage could be called even remotely happy. In 1619 she was wed to Victor-Amadeus, Prince of Piedmont and heir to Charles-Emmanuel, the Duke of Savoy. Thereafter she was known as Princess of Piedmont until Victor-Amadeus assumed the throne upon the death of his father, after which she was Duchess of Savoy. After the death of Victor-Amadeus in 1637 she successfully ruled Savoy for another quarter-century as duchess and regent.

COËTMAN: *Jacqueline Le Voyer d'Escoman, or Coysman, or Cotman, "Dame de Coëtman"* (1585–1618?). A lady in the service of Henriette d'Entragues, the embittered former mistress of King Henri IV, Jacqueline le Voyer became acquainted with the regicide Ravaillac when he stayed at the Entragues estate, and was later implicated in the king's assassination. Despite evidence that she actually attempted to prevent the murder, she was tried and sentenced to prison *à perpétuité*. Conspiracy theories abound regarding King Henri's assassination, and the unfortunate Dame d'Escoman figures in many of them.

COMBALET: *Marie Madeleine de Vignerot du Pont de Courlay, Madame de Combalet* (1604–75). Marie de Vignerot was one of Cardinal Richelieu's several nieces, and of them certainly his favorite. In 1620 she was married to the Sieur de Combalet, a nephew of then-Constable de Luynes; it was a sad mismatch, and after he died in 1622 the Widow Combalet became a Carmelite nun and swore off marriage and men. But she'd developed a taste for high society, and thanks to her position as a lady-in-waiting to Queen Mother Marie de Médicis (due to Richelieu's influence), every door was opened to her. She became a habitué of the Rambouillet salons, a patron of the arts and artists, and very probably Richelieu's mistress. Her hand was sought by a series of great nobles seeking an alliance with the cardinal-minister, but nothing ever came of these courtships—and indeed, she didn't need a high-ranking husband, as she was made Duchesse d'Aiguillon in her own right in 1638 for her (ahem) services to the State. After the cardinal died, she withdrew from high society but continued her patronage of the arts and sciences, sponsoring mathematicians, poets, and writers, including Pierre Corneille, whose breakthrough play *The Cid* was dedicated to her.

CONCINI: *Concino Concini, Maréchal d'Ancre* (1575–1617). Concini was a handsome Italian courtier who was a favorite of Queen Marie de Médicis. During Marie's regency after her husband King Henri IV was assassinated, the arrogant Concini was showered with posts and preferment, including the Marquisate of Ancre, governorships of numerous provinces and cities, and the baton of a marshal, though he had no military experience. He lorded it over the French nobility, and they cordially hated him for it, no one more than young King Louis XIII, whose mother made him defer to Lord Concini. Luynes, the young king's favorite, engineered Louis's rise to power (and his own) when he orchestrated Concini's public assassination in 1617.

CONDÉ, PRINCE: *Henri II de Bourbon, Prince de Condé, "Monsieur le Prince"* (1588–1646). Head of the "cadet line" of the

Bourbon dynasty, Condé was second in line for the throne after Prince Gaston, and spent a life of power and privilege wallowing in royal entitlements, despite his negligible abilities and obnoxious personality.

CONDÉ, PRINCESS: *Charlotte Margeurite de Montmorency, Princesse de Condé, "Madame la Princesse"* (1594-1650). For many years the reigning beauty of the French Court, Charlotte de Montmorency's charms were first noticed by the roving eye of King Henri IV, who intended to make her the next in his series of royal mistresses by marrying her in 1609 to his cousin the Prince de Condé. This was intended to keep her near at hand, but Charlotte was having none of it: rather than submit to the aging Henri's advances, she fled with her new husband to the Low Countries. After Henri's assassination, the Condés returned to France, where they became leaders of the fractious nobles opposed to the queen mother's elevation of Concini—so much so that Marie had them both imprisoned, though they were freed after Louis XIII came to power. During Louis's reign, Charlotte gloried in her role as Madame la Princesse, and was loyal to her thoroughly unpleasant husband and the perquisites that came with being his wife. She was the mother of Anne Geneviève de Bourbon, later Duchesse de Longueville, and Louis de Condé, called "The Grand Condé"—both major historical figures who will play key roles later in the Musketeers cycle.

CORNEILLE: *Pierre Corneille* (1606–84). Son of a Norman lawyer, Corneille's talents as a poet and playwright brought him to the attention of Cardinal Richelieu, who made him one of the Five Poets who collaborated on his literary projects. But Corneille's literary ambitions and abilities exceeded those of his patron, and he broke with Richelieu over the innovations in his play *The Cid* (1637). Corneille's play is considered one of the greatest French tragedies of the 17th century, a precursor of the work of Racine and Molière, and was just the beginning of the poet's successes. Dumas revered him.

CRÉQUI: *Charles I de Blanchefort, Marquis de Créquy, Prince de Poix, Duc de Lesdiguières, Governor of Dauphiné and Marshal of France* (1578–1638). Maréchal de Créqui came of a noble and military family and thought he deserved to be Constable of France, but though a talented general he was a poor politician and often found himself on the wrong side of quarrels with the king and cardinal.

DELORME: *Marion Delorme, or de Lorme, or de l'Orme* (1613–50). A witty, irreverent, sophisticated, and beautiful French courtesan, Marion was renowned for her liaisons with the high and mighty—including, it was rumored, Cardinal Richelieu. She was too young in 1629 to play the part assigned to her in *The Red Sphinx*, but Dumas had few scruples about adjusting the historical record if it meant he could add a fascinating character to his cast. And though she did have a house in the Place Royale, it was sometime after Richelieu had his residence there.

ÉPERNON: *Jean Louis de Nogaret de La Valette, Duc d'Épernon* (1554–1642). One of King Henri III's notorious favorites the *mignons,* d'Épernon was elevated to the peerage at an early age, and acted thereafter as a monster of pride and entitlement who caused nothing but trouble throughout the reigns of Henri IV and Louis XIII. Though implicated by rumor in the assassination of King Henri, he was a key supporter of Queen Mother Marie de Médicis during her regency, so long as plenty of money flowed from the royal treasury into his pockets. Though by all accounts a capable politician, in every other way d'Épernon was a thoroughly nasty character.

Escoman see COËTMAN

FARGIS: *Madeleine de Silly, Madame de Fargis, "Marina"* (?–1639). Though he disliked and distrusted women, the reign of Louis XIII abounded with clever, brave, and free-spirited ladies—an irony that wasn't lost on Dumas, who wrote them in wherever possible. La Fargis was smart, talented, irreverent, and mischievous, and Dumas couldn't resist making her drop-dead gorgeous into the bargain, though she didn't need looks to enthrall her impressive roster of high-ranking lovers. As a young woman, her amorous adventures scandalized her father, who sent her to a Carmelite convent to straighten her out, but it didn't take. When he died, she rejoined the salons of Parisian society, and soon captivated Charles d'Angennes, Comte de Fargis, who promptly married her and carried her off to Madrid, where he'd been appointed as French Ambassador. After outraging the prim and prudish Court of Philip IV for four years, she returned with her husband to Paris—right about the time the king had banished the Duchesse de Chevreuse from Queen Anne's household, and Richelieu was looking for someone to replace her. Madame de Combalet admired La Fargis's brains and wit and recommended her to the cardinal, who sponsored her to the role—but once in Her Majesty's household she quickly gained Anne's trust and transferred her loyalty to the queen. To Richelieu's displeasure, Fargis soon became almost as troublesome as Madame de Chevreuse.

FERDINAND: *Ferdinand II, Emperor of the Holy Roman Empire* (1578–1637). Head of the House of Hapsburg, Catholic overlord of the Germanies and distant uncle to Anne of Austria, Ferdinand was the arch-enemy of Protestantism in Europe and as responsible for the bloodbath of the Thirty Years War as anyone.

GASTON: *Prince Gaston de Bourbon, Duc d'Orléans, "Monsieur"* (1608–1660). Younger brother to Louis XIII and first heir to the throne, favorite son of Marie de Médicis, Gaston seems to have had no redeeming characteristics whatsoever. Proud, greedy, ambitious for the throne but an arrant coward, he was the figurehead in one conspiracy after another against the king and cardinal. These plots failed every time, after which Gaston invariably betrayed his co-conspirators in return for immunity from consequences—because as the healthy heir to a chronically unhealthy king, he knew his life was sacrosanct. Despite his being a worm, the Great Nobles turned to him time and again in their long struggle to resist France's transition to absolute monarchy, and he was too weak to resist joining any plot that might put him on the throne.

GONZAGUE: *Princesse Marie Louise de Gonzague (Gonzaga)* (1611–67). Daughter of the Duc de Nevers, and a mere ingénue at the time of *The Red Sphinx,* her status as the probable heir to the Duchy of Mantua made her a handsome prize to whoever might win her hand. Prince Gaston made a play for her, and though it was almost certainly insincere, her marriage to Monsieur would have given him a power base outside the country; this was an outcome the king and cardinal dared not risk, so they placed Marie under virtual house arrest for a while to take her out of circulation. Though treated as a pawn in the Mantua affair, she had considerable brains and willpower behind her undoubted good looks, and she carved out an independent life for herself in Parisian high society throughout the 1630s. In 1639, Cardinal Mazarin finally strong-armed her into a political marriage with the King of Poland, where she surprised everybody by taking an active role in Polish politics, leading that country ably through difficult times.

GOURNAY: *Marie Le Jars, Demoiselle de Gournay* (1565–1645). A novelist, poet, and essayist, de Gournay was one of France's most important early female writers, and a far more capable person than Dumas's rather condescending depiction would indicate. A protégée and "adopted daughter" of Michel de Montaigne, she supported herself entirely through her writing, though late in life she did receive an honorary stipend from Cardinal Richelieu. She wrote forcefully and persistently on behalf of equality of the sexes. She never married.

GUISE: *Charles, Duc de Guise* (1571–1640). Though the House of Guise in Lorraine reached its height of power in France during the Wars of Religion in the late 16th century, when the Guises led the Catholic League, they retained considerable wealth and prestige well into the reign of Louis XIV. Charles, the fourth Duc de Guise, was past his prime by 1629, and was known mainly for his lechery and overweening self-importance.

GUSTAVUS ADOLPHUS: *Gustave II Adolf, King of Sweden* (1594–1632). Widely regarded as the greatest military commander of the 17th century, King Gustave led Sweden to victory in the Thirty Years War and established his country as a great power. A dynamic, larger-than-life figure who led his troops from the front, Dumas admired him without reservation, perhaps because Gustavus reminded him of his own father, the famous General Dumas who commanded an army for Napoleon.

HAUTEFORT: *Mademoiselle Marie de Hautefort, "Aurora"* (1616–91): First brought to Court in 1630 as a maid of honor to the queen mother, Marie soon joined the household of Queen Anne, where she pulled off the astounding trick of becoming close friend and confidante of both the king and the queen. Her relationship with King Louis was platonic, and she seems to have been a genuinely good person who had only the best interests of Louis and Anne at heart. This baffled everyone; nobody knew what to do about it.

HENRI: *Henri de Bourbon of Navarre, King Henri IV, "Henri the Great"* (1553–1610). A complex and towering figure, a warrior king and at the same time a beloved man of the people, Henri IV ended the Wars of Religion, united France, and made it one of the great powers of Europe. His life and death overshadow every aspect of *The Red Sphinx*, as his royal sons—Louis, Gaston, and Antoine, Comte de Moret—and his greatest political disciple, Cardinal Richelieu, all struggle with Henri's legacy and try to define their roles in light of it.

ISABELLE: *Mademoiselle Isabelle de Lautrec.* The lady-love of the Comte de Moret is an invention of Dumas. She first appeared in *The Dove,* in which she is arguably the protagonist, and Dumas liked her well enough to revive the character for *The Red Sphinx.*

JOSEPH: *François Leclerc du Tremblay, "Father Joseph," Richelieu's "Eminence Grise"* (1577–1638). Capuchin monk, Christian mystic, politician, diplomat, and spymaster, Père Joseph was one of the most fascinating men of his age. The phrase *eminence grise,* for a shadowy advisor, derives from his role: he was the Gray Eminence to the cardinal's Red Eminence. Though he was undeniably effective, in person many found the intensity of his presence disquieting, even repellent—in short, if you imagine him as Peter Lorre at his creepiest, you won't be far wrong. But smart, hellish smart. His brother Charles du Tremblay was Governor of the Bastille, which was convenient, given Joseph's role as Richelieu's spymaster.

King see LOUIS

L'Angely see ANGELY

Lautrec see ISABELLE

LONGUEVILLE: *Catherine de Gonzague, Duchesse de Longueville, "The Dowager Duchess"* (1568–1629). A fierce old relic tempered in the previous century's Wars of Religion, the Dowager Duchess was left in charge of young Princesse Marie de Gonzague when the rest of House Nevers went off to the Duchy of Mantua to stake the family claim to the throne.

LOPEZ: *Alphonse (not Ildefonse) Lopez* (1582–1649). Persecuted in Spain for his Moorish, or possibly Jewish, descent, Lopez came to Paris in 1604, where he became a fashionable jewel merchant (and possibly moneylender) to French high society.

LOUIS: *King Louis XIII, His Most Christian Majesty of France, "Louis the Just"* (1601–43). Dumas wrote a great deal about Louis XIII and his reign, most of it quite accurate, thanks to the research of his assistant Auguste Maquet. Dumas had a good grasp of the melancholy king's character and portrayed it well.

LUYNES: *Charles d'Albert, Duc de Luynes* (1578–1621). The young King Louis's falconer and first favorite, Luynes engineered the assassination of Concini which ended Queen Marie's regency and put Louis XIII on the throne. The king rewarded Luynes by making him first a duke, and then Constable of France. Luynes was the first husband of Marie de Rohan, later Duchesse de Chevreuse.

Marie see GONZAGUE *or* MÉDICIS *or* COMBALET *or* CHEVREUSE

MAZARIN: *Giulio Raimondo Mazzarino, "Captain Mazarino Mazarini," later Cardinal Mazarin* (1602–61). Mazarin was a protégé of Richelieu, and succeeded him as cardinal and prime minister during the regency of Anne of Austria. He did in fact first meet

Richelieu while acting as a papal envoy during the War of Mantuan Succession, and was instrumental in crafting the treaty that ended that conflict. You will find him described in ample detail in *Twenty Years After,* the next novel in Dumas's Musketeers cycle.

MÉDICIS: *Queen Mother Marie de Médicis* (1575–1642). Marie was the second queen to France's King Henri IV, who married her in 1600 in a desperate search for an heir after the infertile Queen Marguerite was set aside. A nasty piece of work, Marie inherited all the ambition, pride, greed, and ruthlessness of the Medici, but none of their brains or finesse. However, she did give King Henri the royal heirs he wanted, including Louis XIII, whom Marie dominated but never liked much, and the worthless Prince Gaston, on whom she doted. Whether she actually helped conspire in the assassination of her husband, nobody can say for sure, but she was certainly capable of it.

Marion see DELORME

Michel see SOUSCARRIÈRES

MIRABEL: *Don Antonio de Zuñiga y Davila, Third Marquis of Mirabel, Spanish Ambassador to France* (1580–1647). A scion of the House of Zuñiga, who served the Kings of Spain as diplomats for generations, the Marquis of Mirabel was a suave and accomplished envoy who acted as liaison between Anne of Austria and her brother, King Philip IV.

"Monsieur" see GASTON

MONTMORENCY: *Henri II, Duc de Montmorency, Governor of Languedoc, Marshal of France, "The Maréchal-Duc"* (1595–1632).

Head of the Montmorency family, one of the greatest noble houses of France, and heir to a grand military tradition, Henri's driving goal was to become Constable (i.e., chief general) of France like his father and grandfather before him, and in fact he was a capable military leader. Handsome, well-mannered, and personable, he was popular at Court, though the king didn't like him because he felt Montmorency was too warm in his attentions to Queen Anne. He hesitated to speak in public due to a slight stutter; when others around him were being witty, Montmorency would just bow and smile, which gave him a reputation for wisdom that was perhaps undeserved. Like many of the *grands seigneurs,* Montmorency's great sin was pride: he held to the old conviction that when the nobles' rights and privileges were trespassed upon, they had a right to revolt to restore them, as the king was really no more than the leading member of the nobility. After the Day of Dupes in late 1630 confirmed Richelieu as prime minister and Louis as absolute monarch, that time was over—but Montmorency failed to get the memo, and joined Prince Gaston in one last nobles' revolt in 1632. He paid with his head, and leadership of House Montmorency passed to his sister Charlotte, Princesse de Condé.

MORET: *Antoine de Bourbon, Comte de Moret, "Jacquelino"* (1607–32). Son of King Henri IV and half-brother to Louis XIII, Moret doesn't appear much in the historical record—which means at least there's little to *contradict* the adventures Dumas recounts in *The Red Sphinx,* and that's good enough for Dumas. Moret was trained for a career in the Church, and was nominal head of several abbacies, but he didn't have the temperament to be a priest, and by age sixteen he was in Paris pursuing beautiful women—following in the footsteps of his father, whom he closely resembled. (Moret was said to have had a teenage crush on Madame de Chevreuse, but it was a rare cavalier who crossed paths with Marie de Rohan who didn't fall for her.) He joined the circle of chivalrous nobles who congregated around the Duc de Montmorency, and might very well have gone along with the Maréchal-Duc on the French expeditions to Savoy in 1629–30, but we're not sure. What we do know is that he joined Montmorency's rebellion in support of Prince Gaston in 1632, and when that revolt was put down at the Battle of Castelnaudary he was killed. . . . Or was he? Rumors persisted throughout the 17th century that Moret was only wounded at Castelnaudary, and then went into hiding to avoid Montmorency's fate at the executioner's block, living under an assumed name as a monk or religious hermit. His supposed survival became the stuff of a number of romantic novels, and in *The Dove* Dumas was already treading a well-worn path.

NEVERS: *Charles de Gonzague, Duc de Nevers, Duke of Mantua and Montferrat* (1580–1637). Even among the dukes of France, who were the least humble of men, Nevers was known for his pride and vainglory. At one time or another, he offended nearly every prominent member of the French nobility. Tracing his descent back to the Emperors of Byzantium, Nevers claimed to be heir to the throne of Constantinople, at that time capital of the Ottoman Empire, and actually tried to raise support in Europe for a new crusade to recapture the Near East for Christendom and make him its ruler. (Father Joseph was one of his few supporters in this folly.) When Duke Vincenzo of Mantua died in 1627, Nevers was named his heir, and though nobody liked him much, Cardinal Richelieu endorsed his claim as a matter of State, and persuaded Louis XIII to commit to supporting it.

Orléans see GASTON

PHILIP: *Philip IV, His Most Catholic Majesty the King of Spain* (1605–65). The dour monarch who reigned over the decline of the

Spanish Empire, Philip's wife was King Louis's sister Elisabeth, as Louis's wife was Philip's sister Anne, the four of them wed in a double marriage arranged by Queen Mother Marie de Médicis. These marriages failed to fulfill Marie's dream of making the two monarchs friends and allies, as their policies were invariably opposed.

PISANY: *Louis-Pompeo d'Angennes, Marquis de Pisany* (1615–45). Pisany, second son of the celebrated Marquise de Rambouillet, was a little too young to be chasing women and stabbing sell-swords in 1629, but Dumas adjusted history a bit once again to enable him to write a juicy character into *The Red Sphinx*. An incurable romantic frustrated by his hunched back and ugly features, he was probably less obstreperous than Dumas makes out, though he was given to writing sarcastic verses about his contemporaries.

PONTIS: *Emmanuel, Vicomte de Pontis*. The "engineer-geographer" who is Moret's rival for the affections of Isabelle de Lautrec was probably based on Louis de Pontis (1583–1670), a career military man from Provence who spent fifty years in the French army, served under Richelieu, and left behind memoirs that are still in print.

Queen see ANNE

RAMBOUILLET: *Catherine de Vivonne, Marquise de Rambouillet* (1588–1665). The marquise's literary and society salons at the Hotel de Rambouillet are justly celebrated as the crucible of modern French art and manners. Her kindness and generosity were boundless, especially to penniless writers, and in a society in which character assassination was a spectator sport, no one ever had a bad word to say about her. It is not too much to say that, by respecting French artists, she made French art respectable.

RAVAILLAC: *François Ravaillac* (1578–1610): Ravaillac was the Catholic fanatic who, in Paris on May 14, 1610, leaped onto Henri IV's open carriage and stabbed the king to death. Political assassinations by Catholic fanatics were so common in Renaissance and Early Modern France that it was practically a tradition, and Ravaillac was part of a pattern: if you led a Catholic movement, you had a murderous zealot being stoked up somewhere in the background, ready to be unleashed on your opponent if the political situation grew desperate. Ravaillac was the last such holy regicide, in France at least, as he slew a king so broadly popular that the public backlash was terrifying. Who sponsored him, and was he acting on their command, or had he simply waited too long for orders that never came and decided to act on his own? We'll almost certainly never know, because after his execution all the evidence appears, even at this remove, to have been systematically destroyed. There are any number of conspiracy theories to explain what few facts we have; Dumas, as usual, seized on the theory that best suited the purposes of his story.

RICHELIEU: *Armand-Jean du Plessis, Cardinal de Richelieu, "Monsieur le Cardinal"* (1585–1642), Louis XIII's incomparable prime minister. One of the two most important Frenchmen of the 17th century, exceeded only by Louis XIV, Richelieu has been the subject of scores of biographies (including one by Dumas), and his life and works have been analyzed in excruciating detail, starting with his own *Memoirs*. His deeds were momentous, but it was his character and personality that interested Dumas, who loved historical figures who were great but also greatly flawed. After deploying Richelieu in *The Three Musketeers* as the worthy antagonist of his most enduring heroes, Dumas couldn't resist revisiting the cardinal by making him a protagonist in *The Red Sphinx*. He admired his "man of genius," but didn't shy away from portraying Richelieu's darker side: his vanity, ruthlessness, and bouts of near-crippling insecurity. It's important to note that during the events of 1629–30 portrayed in *The Red Sphinx*, the cardinal was not yet the all-powerful prime minister he would be in the final twelve years of Louis's reign—he was still vulnerable to domestic enemies great and small, and time and again came within a hair's-breadth of banishment or assassination. Though gone from Dumas's Musketeers cycle after *The Red Sphinx*, Richelieu nonetheless casts a long shadow over the rest of the series, from *Twenty Years After* all the way through *The Man in the Iron Mask*.

ROSSIGNOL: *Antoine Rossignol des Roches* (1600–82). Richelieu's brilliant cryptographer entered his service during the Siege of La Rochelle, after he broke the rebellious Huguenots' ciphers in record time. He stayed with the cardinal throughout his ministry, served Mazarin after Richelieu's death, and then Louis XIV once the Sun King came into his own. Rossignol's innovations and refinements made French cryptography the envy of Europe, and the Grand Cipher he invented continued to be used for two generations after his death by his son and grandson, who followed in his footsteps as royal code-masters. After the death of Antoine-Bonaventure, the last of the Rossignols, nobody was left alive who could figure out how to use the Grand Cipher, and its secrets weren't solved until the late 19th century.

ROTROU: *Jean Rotrou* (1609–50). One of the cardinal's Five Poets, Rotrou, like Corneille, was a bourgeois from Normandy who came to Paris to make it as a playwright. A talented but rather conservative writer, he avoided the innovations that made Corneille's work so controversial; Rotrou's plays were solid and successful, but he was no Corneille or Racine, let alone Molière.

SAINT-SIMON: *Claude de Rouvroy, Sieur de Saint-Simon* (1607–93). First Equerry to Louis XIII, and the page who followed Baradas as the king's favorite, Saint-Simon was sufficiently clever and deferential to stay in favor long enough to be made a duke. His son Louis, one of the Sun King's courtiers, would write one of the leading memoirs of the 17th century; he appears in a prominent role in *The Vicomte de Bragelonne* later in the Musketeers cycle.

SAVOY: *Charles-Emmanuel I, the Duke of Savoy, "Prince of Marmots"* (1562–1630). Charles-Emmanuel ruled the small interstitial state of Savoy for fifty years, and in pursuit of his lifetime goal of expanding his duchy into a kingdom, got his small realm into one conflict after another. He never succeeded in making Savoy a great power, but on the other hand he maintained its independence during his entire reign, which was no small feat given Savoy's strategic location and powerful neighbors. Though reckless in his youth, he grew cunning with age and experience, and was every bit as wily as Dumas portrays him.

SOUSCARRIÈRES: *Sieur Pierre de Bellegarde, Marquis de Montbrun, Seigneur de Souscarrières, "Monsieur Michel"* (1595?–1670). One of the cleverest rogues of his time, Souscarrières had an entire chapter devoted to him in the gossipy *Historiettes* of Tallemant des Réaux, and his exploits were the subject of one of Courtilz de Sandras's lurid pseudo-biographies. A man of low birth who connived his way into the nobility, managing to hobnob with the high and mighty like one of their own, the actual facts of his background are a matter of some dispute—but the remarkable story related by Richelieu in *The Red Sphinx* is close enough, even if some of the details are off. He was in fact responsible for popularizing in Paris the enclosed English version of the sedan chair, the monopoly for which was shared between him and Capitaine de Cavois.

SULLY: *Maximilien de Béthune, Baron de Rosny, Duc de Sully, Prime Minister to King Henri IV* (1560–1641). Sully was Prince Henri of Navarre's right-hand man during the Wars of Religion, and continued in that capacity after the prince became King Henri IV. Born a Huguenot, he advised his coreligionist Henri to adopt Catholicism in order to rule effectively, though he remained a Protestant himself all his life. But stubbornness was central to his character, and a large part of what made him successful as Henri's chief minister of state—that, and a tight fist on the royal funds. His sharp tongue made him a lot of enemies, and though he survived his master King Henri by thirty years, they were lonely ones. Richelieu was an admirer of Sully, and adopted some of his methods, where he thought them appropriate to the new century. The Hotel de Sully, near the Place Royale, is now a museum, and is still much as it's described by Dumas.

VAUTIER: *François Vautier, or Vauthier, or Vaultier, Confidential Physician to Marie de Médicis* (1580–1652). The queen mother's conspirator-in-chief, whom Richelieu called in his *Memoirs* "the principal and most dangerous agent in the entire faction," was in fact an actual medical doctor of some renown. Though his treasonous career led Richelieu to eventually throw him in the Bastille, after the death of Louis XIII he was released and restored to favor, and ended up as the respected physician to young King Louis XIV during the regency of Anne of Austria.

VICTOR-AMADEUS: *Victor-Amadeus I, Prince of Piedmont* (1587–1637). Victor-Amadeus was raised largely at the Spanish Court in Madrid, and then married a French princess, King Louis's sister Christine, all of which helped him to assist in Savoy's eternal dance between France and Spain—a dance he continued as Savoy's ruler after the death of his father, Duke Charles-Emmanuel. Handsome and personable, he was an effective diplomat, and fortunately did not inherit the consuming ambition that drove his father to drag Savoy into one war after another.

VOITURE: *Vincent Voiture* (1597–1648). The most popular poet among the habitués of the Hotel de Rambouillet, favorite of the ladies and an intimate crony of Prince Gaston, Voiture was arguably more successful as a courtier than he was as a versifier. Indeed, despite his association with the hated Gaston, his tact and deference enabled him to mend fences with Cardinal Richelieu and become one of the earliest members of the Académie Française. A master of sly innuendo and the poetic in-joke, he knew just how far he could go in lampooning his patrons among the Great Nobles, and was the witty and insolent upstart you most wanted to have as a guest at your high society soirée.

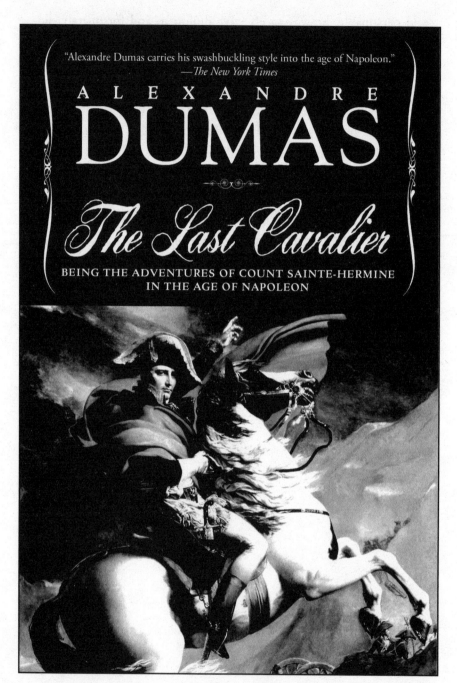

Also from Pegasus Books

THE FIRST-EVER PUBLICATION IN ENGLISH OF THE NEWLY DISCOVERED LAST NOVEL BY THE AUTHOR OF *THE THREE MUSKETEERS*.

R ousing, big, spirited, its action sweeping across oceans and continents, its hero gloriously indomitable, the last novel of Alexandre Dumas—lost for 125 years in the archives of the National Library in Paris—completes the oeuvre that Dumas imagined at the outset of his literary career.

Indeed, the story of France from the Renaissance to the nineteenth century, as Dumas vibrantly retold it in his enormously popular novels, has long been absent one vital, richly historical era: the Age of Napoleon. But no longer. Now, dynamically, in a tale of family honor and undying vengeance, of high adventure and heroic derring-do, *The Last Cavalier* represents Dumas's final literary achievement.

"Epic storytelling in the hands of a master. Pegasus Books has done a real service to world literature by giving us an English translation of this once-forgotten work." **—Nick Ochwar, *The Los Angeles Times***

"It's absolutely wonderful. I finished *The Last Cavalier* in a day. These 800 pages almost turn themselves. Alexandre Dumas remains, now as ever, the Napoleon of storytellers."

—Michael Dirda, *The Washington Post*

"Splendid. . . . *The Last Cavalier* is a lost treasure. The spirit of Monte-Cristo rides again." **—*The New York Review of Books***